Forever Mine

A Longing-for-Love Romance Collection

Alison Reid

Forever Mine - A Longing-for-Love Romance Collection

by Alison Reid

ISBN: 978-1-7644837-5-9

First edition

Independently published

Introduction to...

Forever Mine

A Longing-for-Love Romance Collection

Longing. Desire. True Love.

Welcome to **Forever Mine**—a collection of emotionally charged romances where hearts have waited years, and love refuses to be denied. From snowbound cabins to small-town heartbreak and rediscovered passion, these stories follow men and women whose longing for the one they love has never faded.

Each novel in this collection is a complete standalone romance, written in the spirit of classic Mills & Boon with a modern edge. You'll find slow-burning tension, protective heroes, second chances, and irresistible connections that can't be ignored.

Inside these pages, passion simmers, hearts are tested, and the love that has endured time proves impossible to resist. There is no cheating, and every story delivers a guaranteed happily-ever-after.

Whether you're revisiting favourite characters or discovering them for the first time, **Forever Mine** invites you to indulge in a binge-worthy collection where love finally finds its way home.

Enjoy the journey.

Table of Contents

Always You

Alison Reid

A complete standalone romance

Previously published individually

Chapter One

The clinic smelled faintly of eucalyptus oil and lemon disinfectant—the kind of scent that clung to scrubs and settled into the seams of long workdays. Jasmine Whitaker leaned over her patient, gently rotating the man's shoulder as he grimaced through the movement. Her touch was confident. Her tone, calm.

"You're doing well, Mr. Simmons," she said, her voice low and soothing. "Try to relax into it. We're halfway through."

He grunted something close to a compliment. Jasmine smiled, used to the grumbling. Most of her patients resisted her at first—until they realised she wasn't going to baby them. She was kind, yes. But she didn't deal in pity. She dealt in progress.

Her dark brown hair was tied in a low, effortless twist at the nape of her neck, though a few wavy strands had escaped to frame her face. She brushed them back absently, focused on her patient's range of motion. She wore her usual navy-blue scrubs and white sneakers—plain, practical. Yet there was no hiding her beauty: the long, graceful lines of her figure, the honey-brown skin that glowed in the morning light, and her almond-shaped eyes, the colour of warm tea.

But Jasmine had never cared much for the mirror. The only thing she truly noticed was whether she looked tired—and lately, she always did.

After finishing the session, she helped Mr. Simmons sit up and handed him a towel. "Take it easy on that shoulder, okay?"

He nodded, sweat beading along his brow. "You're tough, Miss Whitaker. You smile while you torture."

Jasmine laughed, the sound soft and genuine. "Occupational hazard."

She checked the time on the clock above the reception desk as she jotted her notes. Ten minutes until her next appointment. She exhaled slowly and made her way to the break room. Her body felt fine—it always did. Years of yoga and dance kept her strong. But her mind... well, that was another matter.

Her phone buzzed. A message from her brother, William.

Dinner at mine tonight. Mary's cooking, I'm not risking it. You better come. No excuses.

A smile tugged at her lips. William was always checking in—he couldn't help himself. Ever since their parents died in that crash on the coastal highway two years ago, he'd taken his role as big brother to a whole new level. Part protector, part nag, entirely hers. And she loved him for it, even when he overdid it.

She typed a quick reply:

Wouldn't miss it. As long as there's wine. And dessert.

Jasmine set the phone aside and stared absently out the window. Outside, the wind tossed gum tree branches against a bright winter sky. The light was gold and sharp—too pretty for how heavy she sometimes felt.

The truth was, no amount of time or therapy—ironically—had fully stitched up the hole her parents left behind. She still saw them in flash memories: her mother's laugh over breakfast, her father humming old jazz while fixing the tap that never stayed fixed. Some days, those memories made her smile. Other days, they hurt too much to hold.

Grief had changed her. Made her quieter. Stronger. Lonelier, too. She buried herself in work, pouring her energy into helping others move again, live again. It gave her purpose—even if it didn't always give her peace.

Her next patient arrived—an older woman with a knee replacement and a sunny disposition. Jasmine slipped back into professional mode with practiced ease. Her voice calm and steady. Her hands sure.

But deep beneath the routine, behind the smiles and the long hours, a quiet ache lingered. One she rarely acknowledged. One that came with green eyes she tried not to think about, and a name she almost never said aloud: _Robert Steele._

He wasn't part of today.

He wasn't part of her work.

He wasn't anything she could claim.

And yet… the heart rarely listened to reason. And Jasmine, for all her self-control, was only human.

By the time she pulled into her driveway, the sun had dipped below the line of trees edging her quiet suburban street. She stepped out of her car, grateful for the stillness, the way the early evening wrapped itself around her shoulders like a soft shawl.

Her townhouse sat in a tucked-away pocket of Bondi, not far from the beach where locals jogged at sunrise and tourists chased sunsets. It was modern and sleek—glass-panelled balconies, creamy sandstone walls, a view that caught just enough ocean breeze to make the curtains dance.

It was also worth a small fortune—the kind of home people her age only dreamed of owning.

But Jasmine hadn't dreamed it. She'd inherited it. Just like the cars, the investments, and the too-large bank account her parents left behind.

She had everything.

Except the only thing she truly wanted.

She would have traded every dollar, every property, every material comfort… just to hear her mother laugh again. Or see her father rolling his eyes as he grilled steaks too close to the flame.

But they were gone. Two years now. And some days, the grief still hit like a rogue wave—sudden, sharp, breath-stealing.

Inside, the townhouse was warm and quiet. Soft neutrals, timber floors, small touches of her: ceramic vases on the console, black-and-white family photos, a dog-eared romance novel on the arm of the sofa.

It was peaceful.

It was beautiful.

And sometimes, it felt completely hollow.

She set her keys down, slipped off her shoes, and padded to the bathroom.

The shower steamed quickly. Jasmine stood beneath the spray, letting it wash away the sweat and weight of the day. Eyes closed, she tilted her head back and allowed herself to feel… nothing.

Not grief.

Not longing.

Not even responsibility.

Just water. Just silence.

After, she pulled on a cream cashmere sweater and soft jeans. Her damp hair fell in dark, wavy strands past her shoulders. At the mirror, she paused.

The woman staring back was undeniably beautiful.

Even tired. Even barefaced.

But beauty meant little when your heart felt distant from your reflection. Her honey-brown eyes seemed older than twenty-four. Like they'd carried too much, too soon.

She applied a little lip balm, some mascara. Then reached for her phone.

It buzzed before she could unlock it. *Heidi.*

"Hey, troublemaker," Jasmine answered, settling on the bed.

"Hey yourself," came the cheerful reply. "You alive? You didn't text me after your last patient."

"I was elbow-deep in scar tissue and small talk. I survived."

"You do more rehab for other people than you do for yourself."

"Hazard of the job."

"Girls' night. Friday. No scrubs. No dates. No whining. Just wine."

"Sold."

"Lucía's. Seven-thirty. And yes, just us. No Sean."

Jasmine laughed. "You're relentless."

"I'm right, which is worse. You know you deserve better than casual, right?"

There was a pause. Jasmine fingered the edge of her blanket.

"I know."

But knowing and doing were two different things.

A knock at the door interrupted them.

"Probably Sean," Jasmine said flatly.

"Oh, goody," Heidi deadpanned. "Make him regret existing. Wear something hot. Talk Friday?"

"Talk Friday. Night, Heids."

"Night, babe."

Jasmine hung up and crossed to the door, smoothing a hand through her hair.

Beautiful. Tired. Guarded.

A woman standing at the edge of something she couldn't yet name.

She opened the door.

Sean stood there—navy shirt, dark jeans, a bottle of wine in one hand, and that smirk he wore like a habit.

"Wow," he said, eyes scanning her. "You look gorgeous."

Jasmine smiled politely. "Thanks."

He stepped in and wrapped an arm around her waist, pulling her close. His lips brushed hers, but she turned slightly—the kiss landing at the corner of her mouth.

He leaned back, brow furrowing. "What was that?"

"You caught me off guard," she said, smoothing her sweater.

"I wanted to see you before we deal with your brother's cooking—"

"It's Mary's cooking," she corrected.

"Even worse."

Jasmine paused. "You don't have to come if you don't want to."

He blinked. "Wait—you'd go without me?"

"Yes, William's my brother."

He hesitated. Then smiled. "Right. Of course. Whatever you want, Jaz."

She nodded, stepping past him to lock the door. But she could feel it—the irritation tucked behind his grin, the charm too easily applied.

He was saying the right things.

But none of them felt right.

As they walked to his car, Jasmine glanced up at the sky. Heavy clouds were rolling in. A cool breeze swept past her, brushing her cheek.

She wrapped her arms around herself—not from the cold, but from the feeling she was moving farther and farther away from something real…

…and toward something that only looked like love from the outside.

Chapter Two

The aroma of garlic, rosemary, and something slightly burnt floated through William's open-plan kitchen. Jasmine stood by the counter, sipping from a glass of red wine as Mary fussed over the stovetop, poking a pan of roasted vegetables with the seriousness of a surgeon.

"Do not touch the lamb," Mary warned, without looking up. "It needs exactly four more minutes."

Jasmine grinned. "I wasn't touching the lamb. I was breathing in its greatness."

Mary shot her a mock glare, then turned back to her self-appointed role as Domestic Goddess. Petite and dark-eyed, she wore her apron like it was haute couture, moving around the kitchen with the effortless confidence of someone who actually enjoyed hosting. Jasmine had liked her instantly when they first met, and even after a year of dating William—followed by their wedding two months ago—Mary's warmth and charm hadn't faded in the slightest.

Unlike Sean.

Jasmine's casual boyfriend sat on the opposite side of the room, scrolling through his phone with one hand and holding a whisky tumbler in the other. He'd barely said five words since they arrived. She hadn't expected anything different—he didn't love family dinners, didn't love small talk. Didn't really *love* much of anything, as far as she could tell.

"You know," William said, walking in from the hallway and ruffling Jasmine's hair like she was still twelve, "we could just order pizza and save Mary from the culinary Olympics."

"You say that *every* time," Mary replied, not looking away from the pan. "And every time, you end up going back for thirds."

William smirked, kissed her on the cheek, and reached for a bottle of wine. He was tall like their father had been, with the same easy smile and disarming charm. Even now, in his early thirties, he still carried that boyish glint in his eyes—especially when he was teasing Jasmine.

"Is this one of your better experiments?" he asked Mary, eyeing the oven like it might bite him.

"It's rosemary and garlic rack of lamb with honey-glazed carrots, roasted parsnips, and herbed potatoes."

"So, not pizza."

"No, Will. Not pizza."

"Shame," he muttered, pouring himself a glass of wine.

Sean cleared his throat, finally looking up. "I could've made reservations, you know. The club has a new chef. We could've had the night off."

Jasmine turned slightly toward him, forcing a polite smile. "Mary enjoys cooking. And we enjoy eating."

Sean shrugged. "Sure. Just saying—it's a lot of effort for a Tuesday."

Mary raised an eyebrow, her voice sugar-sweet. "Effort, Sean, is how love shows up. Tuesday or not."

Jasmine held back a laugh and sipped her wine.

Dinner was served ten minutes later.

The food was delicious—despite Mary's nerves—and the conversation flowed easily, mostly between William and Mary, with Jasmine adding the occasional comment. Sean answered questions like they were job interviews—short, polished, impersonal.

"So," William said after a lull, cutting into his lamb. "Robert got that Byron Bay property. The eco-resort is officially happening."

Jasmine froze for half a breath; her fork suspended in midair.

Sean made a noise. "Of course he did. Steele always gets what he wants."

William looked up, a flicker of something narrowing his eyes. "That's because he works for it."

Sean took a sip of his drink, unconcerned. "Some people are just born lucky."

"Some people are born focused," William replied, a little too evenly.

Jasmine cleared her throat. "Is it the beachfront site? The one with the old sugar mill ruins?"

William's face lit up. "Yeah, that one. He's planning to restore the ruins into the spa and wellness centre. Said it reminded him of something our mum would've loved. It's going to be amazing, Jaz."

She nodded, swallowing around the emotion that caught her off guard. *Something Mum would've loved.* Robert still remembered details like that.

Of course he did.

Mary caught the shift in her expression and gently changed the subject. "So, Sean, what do you do again? Real estate, right?"

Sean straightened a little. "Private residential sales. Mostly high-end. Developers and international clients."

"So, you and Robert are competitors, then?" Mary asked, sipping her wine.

Sean's jaw tightened slightly. "Hardly. I don't sell sanctuaries in the middle of nowhere to yoga influencers."

Jasmine's spine stiffened. William shot her a quick look—he'd heard it too.

Mary, unfazed, smiled. "I think it's romantic. Creating peaceful places that are beautiful *and* sustainable. I'd stay there."

"Exactly," William said. "That's why we're putting some of our inheritance into the project."

Sean raised an eyebrow. "You're investing with Robert now?"

"Been doing it for years," William replied easily. "He's family."

That word lingered. *Family.*

Jasmine felt Sean's eyes flick toward her, measuring. He didn't say anything, but she could feel his disapproval like a draft under a door.

After dessert—Mary's chocolate lava cake that melted all tension for a few sweet minutes—Jasmine helped her clear the table while the men talked quietly over drinks.

"You okay?" Mary asked softly.

Jasmine nodded. "Of course. Why?"

Mary gave her a knowing look. "Because Sean is watching Robert's name come out of your mouth like it means something."

Jasmine sighed. "It doesn't."

Mary smiled. "Liar."

They laughed, but the echo of the truth lingered—quiet, stubborn, and impossible to silence.

Mary wiped her hands on a tea towel and leaned against the kitchen bench, her voice softening just enough to draw Jasmine in. "Are you... serious about Sean?"

Jasmine blinked. "No. Definitely not."

"Good," Mary said quickly, her eyes sharp now. "Because William wouldn't be happy if you were."

Jasmine arched a brow. "He told you that?"

"Not in so many words," Mary replied, lowering her voice to a whisper. "But he tenses every time Sean opens his mouth. And let's be honest, the man's not exactly warm and fuzzy."

Jasmine exhaled slowly. "We're not even serious. We haven't slept together, and we barely see each other. He wasn't supposed to be here tonight—he just invited himself."

Mary nodded like she suspected as much. "So why not end it?"

Jasmine looked away for a moment, toward the hallway where the murmur of the men's voices drifted faintly. "Because it's easy. It's familiar. And he doesn't ask for more than I'm willing to give."

Mary crossed her arms. "But you don't *want* to give him more."

"No," Jasmine admitted. "I don't."

The words hung there like steam on a mirror—real, visible, undeniable.

"Then let it go," Mary said gently. "You've been through enough, Jaz. You don't owe him your time just because he's persistent."

"I know," Jasmine said softly, forcing a smile. "It's just easier not to deal with it. And... honestly, it keeps me distracted."

Mary studied her for a long second. "From Robert?"

Jasmine froze.

"I didn't say anything to William," Mary added quickly, "but I'm not blind."

Jasmine let out a breath, her voice barely above a whisper. "It doesn't matter. He's dating Clair. He's William's best friend. He's... off-limits."

Mary rolled her eyes. "Please. That woman is so stuck up I'm amazed she can tilt her chin any higher. I really don't like her."

Jasmine gave a half-smile. "Tell me how you really feel."

"I'm serious," Mary said, crossing her arms. "She talks to people like they're beneath her. And the way she looked at you at Will's birthday dinner? Like you were something stuck to her Louboutin."

"I noticed," Jasmine admitted.

"She's not right for him," Mary said. "Everyone sees it. Well—everyone but Robert."

Jasmine's smile faded. "Exactly. *He* doesn't see it. Which is why none of it matters."

Mary reached out and touched her arm. "Maybe not right now. But just because someone's off-limits doesn't mean your feelings disappear. They just get quieter."

Jasmine nodded slowly, swallowing past the truth that lodged in her throat. "Quieter. Yeah."

But silence didn't mean absence. And buried didn't mean gone.

Not when it came to Robert Steele.

Later that evening, as the moon rose over the quiet, tree-lined streets of Bellevue Hill, the air carried the scent of jasmine and ocean salt. Jasmine stood on the front porch of William and Mary's beautiful sandstone home, her arms folded lightly as she watched Sean stroll toward his car.

He didn't look back.

He tapped at his phone with one hand and unlocked the car with the other, calling over his shoulder, "I'll pull around."

But he didn't. Instead, he slid into the driver's seat and started the engine.

Jasmine stayed where she was, unmoving.

William stepped beside her, the porch light casting a golden halo over his face. He slipped one arm around her shoulders and pulled her close.

"I love you, you know that?" he said, his voice low and steady.

Jasmine smiled and leaned into him, letting herself soak in his warmth. "I love you too," she whispered, pressing a kiss to his cheek.

He squeezed her tighter for a moment, then whispered near her ear, "For the love of God... get rid of him."

Jasmine let out a soft laugh. "*Maybe.*"

She said it playfully, but inside, she already knew. Sean was a door she was ready to close. She just wasn't giving William the satisfaction of saying it outright—not yet.

Mary joined them with a knowing look, pulling her cardigan tight around her shoulders. "He's already in the car," she said, nodding toward the driveway. "Doesn't even open the door for you. Charming."

Jasmine rolled her eyes. "It's fine."

"It's not," Mary replied. "But I know you already know that."

Jasmine turned to her, arms open. "Thank you for dinner. It was amazing."

Mary hugged her tightly. "Love you. Text me when you get home, okay?"

"Will do."

Jasmine stepped off the porch, heels clicking gently on the stone path as she made her way to the idling car. The headlights cast long shadows behind her, but she didn't look back right away.

When she finally did, she saw William and Mary standing side by side on the front steps—her family. The ones who stayed. The ones who knew her heart, even when she didn't say a word.

She slipped into the passenger seat and closed the door herself.

Sean didn't say much as he pulled away from the curb.

And Jasmine didn't either.

Because something had shifted.

She didn't know where her heart would land—but she knew exactly where it didn't belong anymore.

The drive back to Bondi was mostly quiet. The hum of the engine and the distant sound of traffic filled the silence between them. Sean tapped idly on the steering wheel as he turned onto Jasmine's street, lined with sleek, modern homes that whispered of quiet wealth.

He pulled up outside her townhouse and shifted the car into park. "You want me to come in?" he asked casually, glancing at her with that familiar smirk. "I could stay the night."

Jasmine smiled politely but didn't look at him. "Thanks, but I've got an early start tomorrow. A full client list and barely time to breathe."

Sean leaned toward her, undeterred. "You sure? We could just hang out. No pressure."

"I'm sure," she said, turning to face him now, her tone kind but firm. "Another time, maybe."

He didn't seem convinced. "Alright, alright," he said, feigning a light chuckle. "Just thought I'd offer."

Before she could reach for the door handle, he leaned in suddenly and kissed her—his mouth insistent, his hand brushing her cheek as if trying to anchor her there.

Jasmine froze for half a heartbeat before she gently pulled back—*as quickly and gracefully as she could.*

"Goodnight, Sean," she said softly, avoiding his eyes as she opened the door and stepped out into the cool night air.

He let out a breath and leaned back in the driver's seat. "Night, Jaz."

She closed the door, waved lightly, and didn't look back as she walked up the stone path to her front door.

Inside, the townhouse was still and quiet, but her heart wasn't. She leaned against the closed door for a moment, exhaling deeply.

That kiss had felt… off. All of it did.

Sean didn't make her heart flutter.

Not like *him.*

And as much as she tried not to think about Robert Steele, his name drifted through her thoughts like a whisper.

A whisper that was getting harder to silence.

Chapter Three

The rest of the week blurred by in a flurry of appointments, rehab plans, and long hours at the clinic. Jasmine buried herself in her work, letting the rhythm of her patients' progress distract her from everything else—Sean's kiss, Mary's words, and the thoughts she still refused to name.

But by Friday afternoon, she needed a breather.

She stopped by William's office just after four, bringing him his favourite coffee and a pastry from their childhood bakery in Paddington—a quiet ritual they'd kept since their parents passed.

Whitaker & Steele Architecture occupied the upper floor of a sleek glass building in Surry Hills, the kind of place with polished concrete floors, oversized light fixtures, and abstract art in all the right corners. Jasmine always liked the atmosphere—modern, clean, purposeful.

William looked up from a drafting table when she walked into his office, grinning. "Is that a cinnamon scroll I see?"

"Baked fresh this morning," Jasmine said, holding up the white paper bag like a trophy. "And you're lucky. I nearly ate it on the drive over."

He came around the table to hug her, pulling her into a tight, familiar embrace. "You're the best," he murmured. "I mean it."

She smiled and kissed his cheek. "I know."

They sat near the windows, sipping coffee as the late afternoon light poured in, golden and lazy. Jasmine kicked off her shoes and tucked her feet beneath her, relaxing in a way she rarely allowed herself.

"Long week?" William asked.

"The usual," she replied with a shrug. "Bodies in pain, progress in inches, and a whole lot of emotional baggage that no one wants to talk about."

He laughed. "Sounds like architecture. Just with fewer lawsuits."

They were still chuckling when the glass door opened behind them.

Robert Steele stepped inside, his presence immediate and effortless.

He wore a tailored navy suit with the top button of his shirt undone, a touch of Friday casual that somehow made him even more dangerously attractive. His short black hair was artfully dishevelled, and those piercing green eyes swept across the room—first to William, then to Jasmine.

"Hey," he said, his voice smooth as silk. "Didn't know I was walking into a family meeting."

"Just Jasmine feeding my pastry addiction," William said, rising to shake his hand.

Robert grasped it firmly, then turned to Jasmine with a smile—warm, familiar.

"Hi, Jaz," he said, stepping close enough to kiss her cheek.

Her breath caught—just for a moment. It was supposed to be harmless. Just a greeting. But it lingered, far too familiar to be innocent.

The brush of his lips against her skin sent a ripple down her spine, and she hated how her heart responded—swift, sudden, uninvited.

He stepped back quickly, the contact over in seconds, but something lingered in the air. A subtle shift. A quiet pull.

Jasmine caught it. So did Robert.

But neither of them acknowledged it.

"How's the week been?" he asked, slipping one hand into his pocket, suddenly all charming distance.

"Busy," she said lightly. "You?"

He gave a quick nod. "Productive. Actually, I came by to tell Will something in person."

Jasmine tilted her head.

Robert turned to William, his voice calm, but there was weight behind the words. "Claire and I are getting engaged. I asked her last night."

Jasmine's heart gave a quiet, traitorous lurch. She barely let it show. Her expression held steady—cool, composed—but her fingers curled slightly where they rested at her side.

William blinked. "Seriously?"

The disbelief in his voice landed hard between them. He looked at Robert like he couldn't quite believe what he was hearing. Then his gaze shifted to Jasmine, and something darker flickered in his eyes—disgust, frustration, a silent *you've got to be kidding me.*

Jasmine didn't flinch. She'd gotten good at keeping things locked down.

Robert gave a small nod, not missing the shift in William's posture.

Jasmine managed a polite smile, her voice soft. "Congratulations, Robert. I hope you'll both be very happy."

Robert looked at her then—just for a second too long.

"Thanks, Jasmine," he said quietly. "That means a lot."

But William was still staring at him, arms crossed, jaw tight. "You're really doing this?"

"I am," Robert replied, holding his friend's gaze.

William exhaled, short and sharp. "Right."

Jasmine turned her eyes away, pretending to admire the artwork on the wall. Anything not to feel the weight of that moment pressing against her chest.

"Wow." William clapped him on the shoulder "That's… big news. Congrats, mate."

"Thanks," Robert said, but his smile didn't quite reach his eyes.

He cleared his throat and shifted slightly, then turned to face them both. "Actually, I meant to ask—Claire and I are throwing a small engagement party next Saturday. Nothing too over the top, just close friends, a few industry people, family. I hope you'll both come."

William grinned. "Wouldn't miss it."

Robert's eyes flicked to Jasmine. "You too?"

Jasmine hesitated—only for a breath. "Of course," she said, her tone smooth. "I'll be there."

"Good," Robert replied, nodding once, though something unreadable passed across his face. "It'll be good to have everyone together."

Jasmine simply nodded. But her stomach had tightened, her breath shallow beneath the polite smile.

Everyone together.

As Jasmine disappeared down the hallway, her heels tapping a slow, fading rhythm, Robert watched the doorway for a beat longer than necessary.

William noticed. "You alright?"

Robert blinked and glanced away, slipping his hands back into his pockets. "Yeah. She just… looks good."

William smiled softly. "She does. Better than she has in a while."

Robert's brow lifted slightly. "She's still recovering?"

William nodded, folding his arms across his chest. "Yeah. From all of it. Losing Mum and Dad... it wrecked us both, but Jasmine—" he exhaled quietly, "—she was only twenty-two. And instead of falling apart, she built something. Her clinic's thriving, but I swear she's burying herself in work just to keep from feeling anything."

Robert's expression shifted, growing more thoughtful. "I always forget how young she was when it happened."

"She didn't get time to grieve," William said softly. "Not properly. She went straight into survival mode. Took care of everything—the house, the estate, me... even when she was the one who lost the most."

Robert didn't reply. Because he'd known Jasmine for years—and somehow, he'd never really seen that part of her.

"Is she still seeing that guy?" Robert asked, voice low. "Sean?"

William's mouth twisted in a grimace. "Unfortunately."

Robert turned, surprise flickering across his features. "Seriously? I thought that fizzled out months ago."

"I wish it had," William muttered. "I've told her—he's a tosser. Arrogant. Disrespectful. And frankly, I don't like the way he talks to her. Or looks at her, for that matter. It's like he sees her as a trophy, not a person."

Robert's jaw tightened. "I'm not a fan either."

William glanced at him, brow arched. "Well, don't let Claire hear you say that. She already thinks Jasmine is trying to steal the spotlight every time she walks into a room."

Robert let out a dry, humourless laugh. "Claire thinks everyone is trying to steal the spotlight."

William didn't laugh.

He just looked at Robert, something harder in his expression now. "It's not a joke, mate. She belittles Jasmine. Subtly, constantly. And you standing quietly next to her while she does it? That makes it worse."

Robert went quiet, a muscle ticking in his jaw.

William shook his head. "Jasmine deserves better. Better than Sean. Better than being treated like a threat just for existing."

Robert didn't answer right away. But in the silence that followed, something in his eyes shifted—just for a second.

Something that looked a lot like guilt.

Robert looked away first.

"So, next Saturday," he said, changing the subject. "Be there around seven."

William clapped him on the back. "We will. Just try to keep it classy. Claire and open bars don't always mix."

Robert gave a small smile, but his mind wasn't on Claire.

Not anymore.

By the time Jasmine got home, the sky had deepened into a soft navy haze, the lights of Bondi glittering like scattered stars. She showered quickly, towel-dried her long, dark hair, and stood in front of her mirror, trying to decide what kind of version of herself she wanted to present tonight.

Something fun. Bold. Unbothered.

She chose a sleek black dress—simple, fitted, and effortless. It clung in all the right places and hinted at confidence she didn't fully feel tonight. She added gold hoops, a flick of eyeliner, and a spritz of her favourite scent. Her waves dried into soft curls that framed her honey-brown eyes, and as she stared at her reflection, she offered herself a half-hearted smile.

Beautiful. Tired. Resilient.

She could live with that.

The Uber pulled up just in time, and Jasmine climbed in, checking her phone once before tucking it into her clutch. No new messages. She didn't know if that made her feel relieved or disappointed.

Lucia's townhouse was already glowing with laughter and music when she arrived. Jasmine had barely stepped inside before Heidi's voice rang out.

"Holy hell, Jas!"

Lucia appeared from the kitchen holding a bottle of prosecco. "Look at you! Smokin' hot. Who even are you tonight?"

Jasmine grinned. "I figured I'd show up and remind Sydney what they've been missing."

The girls whooped and raised their glasses.

"Damn right," Heidi said, handing Jasmine a flute. "But seriously, you okay? You look… amazing, but there's something behind your eyes."

Jasmine hesitated, then gave a small shrug. "Robert is engaged."

The air shifted.

Heidi's mouth tightened. Lucia set down her glass.

"Shit," Heidi said quietly. "You okay?"

Jasmine gave a little laugh and waved her hand dismissively. "It is what it is. I mean, he's been with Claire for a while. Was bound to happen."

Lucia narrowed her eyes. "You don't have to pretend with us."

"I'm not pretending," Jasmine said, straightening. "I'm just… not going to let it ruin my night."

Heidi reached over and took her hand. "You've loved him for years, Jaz."

"I know," she said softly. "But it doesn't matter. It never did."

Then she lifted her glass. "Now—let's drink, dance, and forget the name Robert bloody Steele for a few hours, yeah?"

They cheered and clinked glasses.

Later, at the club, the music pulsed through her body, steady, loud, and liberating. Jasmine danced with abandon, letting the bass carry her, the beat anchoring her to the moment. Men came and went, offering compliments, flirtatious smiles, a hand to pull her into the rhythm—and for once, she let herself say yes.

Heidi and Lucia were nearby, dancing with a pair of charming tourists who clearly thought they'd landed in paradise. Laughter and spilled cocktails. Glittering lights. Heat and movement.

And somewhere across the crowded room, Robert saw her.

He hadn't planned on it. Claire had insisted they stop by this new place after dinner— *'everyone's going there'*, she'd said, with that clipped excitement she saved for social climbing. He'd barely registered the name of the club. Just another stop on the endless carousel of curated outings.

But then he saw her.

Jasmine.

She was laughing, swaying to the music, her dark hair tumbling in soft waves over her shoulders. The low lighting kissed her skin with gold, and that dress—*God, that dress*—moved with her like it had been sewn for no one else.

She looked… effortless.

Free.

Alive in a way he hadn't seen in her since before Rosa and Jeremy died.

His steps slowed without meaning to. Claire was mid-sentence beside him; her manicured hand looped through his arm. She followed his gaze, and her expression cooled instantly.

"Oh," she said, her voice tight. "*Her.*"

Robert blinked. "She's just William's sister," he said, too quickly.

Claire's brows lifted. "Right. William's sister," she echoed, each word laced with suspicion and something colder beneath it.

She slid her arm more firmly around Robert's waist, staking silent claim. "Well, now that we've spotted the help, can we please sit somewhere not near her?"

Robert didn't answer.

There it was—exactly what William had warned him about. The quiet jabs. The casual cruelty dressed up in designer labels and a perfect smile.

He should say something. He knew that. But if he did, Claire would twist it, turn it into some dramatic scene. And tonight wasn't the night for that. It never seemed to be.

So, he stayed quiet.

But his eyes—his eyes betrayed him.

Because Jasmine was still laughing. Still radiant. Still effortlessly drawing the light to her like she was made of it.

And no matter how tightly Claire held on, he couldn't seem to look away.

He let Claire tug him toward the VIP section, but part of him stayed right there on the dance floor.

Watching her.

Wishing—quietly, impossibly—that she hadn't looked so damn happy without him.

Later, in the back of the black car as it glided through the city, Claire was still talking. Something about the cocktails being flat and the DJ being *'tragically predictable'*. Robert murmured agreement, eyes on the blur of passing lights outside the window.

But his mind wasn't on the music. Or Claire.

It was on Jasmine.

She hadn't seen him, not that he knew of. And maybe that was for the best. Tonight, he hadn't looked at her like William's sister. He'd looked at her like a man looks at the one he let get away.

He'd looked at her like a man looks at a woman he can't stop wanting.

And he hated that.

He ran a hand over his jaw, the tension in his shoulders refusing to release. He told himself it was instinct. That he was just being protective. Watching out for Jasmine like William would want him to.

But it was a lie. And he knew it.

She'd looked beautiful. Too beautiful. And when some guy pulled her in, hand at her waist, spinning her close—Robert had felt something white-hot and irrational curl in his chest.

Jealousy.

Raw and territorial and completely out of place.

Because he was engaged. To Claire.

Claire—who checked her reflection in every mirror, who cared more about appearances than connection. Claire, who didn't make him laugh without trying or know when he needed silence instead of words. Claire, who never really saw him— not the way he sometimes wished she would.

But she was the woman he'd chosen.

Claire loved him. And he loved her. He wouldn't have asked her to marry him if he didn't... *right?*

Jasmine had never been an option. She was William's sister. The line he'd promised not to cross. The girl he'd told himself to ignore, long before she ever became someone impossible to forget.

And yet... tonight had shaken something loose inside him.

Something buried. Something dangerous.

He leaned his head back against the seat, eyes closed, jaw tight.

He needed to shut this down. Whatever this was. Because if he didn't, it wouldn't just be a passing thought or a flicker of doubt—it would turn into something real. Tangible. Irreversible.

Claire already hated Jasmine. And maybe she had good reason—maybe she saw what he was too stubborn to admit.

But he wasn't interested in Jasmine.

He couldn't be.

He was engaged. To Claire.

And he would marry her.

He had to.

Because the alternative… was a risk he didn't dare take.

Not now.

Not with Jasmine.

Not when it could undo everything.

Chapter Four

The sun dipped low over Sydney's skyline, casting a golden hue over the manicured gardens of the private estate where Robert's engagement party was in full swing. Elegant strings of lights crisscrossed the open-air terrace. Waiters in crisp black and white moved between guests with trays of champagne and canapés, and the quiet hum of polite conversation was occasionally interrupted by bursts of laughter.

It was a perfect evening—on paper.

Jasmine adjusted the thin strap of her emerald-green dress as she stepped out of the car, Sean at her side. She hadn't wanted him to come. She hadn't said yes. He'd just assumed, invited himself, and now here he was—her plus-one to an event she already wasn't sure she could face.

"You look incredible, by the way," Sean said, brushing a hand over her lower back. "Gonna have to keep an eye on you tonight."

Jasmine gave him a polite smile, stepping just out of reach. "Let's just go inside."

The estate was Robert's—his latest acquisition, bought just last year after turning thirty. A sweeping sandstone property perched above the water in Vaucluse; it once belonged to one of his family's oldest friends. Now, it was his alone.

Classic. Grand. Dripping with old money and quiet power.

Jasmine took in the sprawling verandas, the curved archways, the manicured gardens that spilled down toward the harbour. Everything about it was elegant, timeless… controlled.

Much like the man who owned it.

She focused on the symmetry of the archways, the warm light spilling over the sandstone columns, the distant hush of waves against the cliffs—anything to stop her thoughts from spiralling.

Anything not to think about the man she'd be forced to smile at all evening. The man whose engagement was supposed to be a celebration.

And yet… her chest already felt tight.

Too tight.

She spotted William and Mary near the entrance, laughing with a group of guests. William's smile softened the moment he saw her.

"There she is," he said, wrapping Jasmine in a warm hug. "You look amazing, Jaz."

"Thanks," she said, then leaned in close as Mary pulled Sean into conversation. "Is it too late to run?"

William chuckled. "Not unless you want to leave me alone with Robert's terrifying aunt Evelyn and a tray of shrimp skewers."

Jasmine smiled but there was tightness at the edges. William studied her for a moment before lowering his voice.

"Listen," he said, glancing toward the terrace where Robert was deep in conversation with an older couple. "Just… keep things cool, yeah?"

She blinked. "What's that supposed to mean?"

William gave her a look. "You know exactly what it means."

"I'm not the one who needs the warning," Jasmine muttered.

William's gaze sharpened, quiet but firm. "Maybe not. Still… just be careful. You know how she is with you."

Jasmine opened her mouth to argue—but didn't. Because she did know.

Clair hated her. She didn't hide it. In fact, she wore it like perfume—sharp, cloying, and impossible to ignore. Every cutting remark, every cold stare across a room, was laced with something possessive and territorial. As if Jasmine was a threat she couldn't quite define but still wanted to crush.

And Robert, God help her, never stepped in. Never defended her.

Which somehow made her feel worse.

Before Jasmine could say anything, Mary reappeared and looped an arm through hers.

"Come on," she said with a knowing smile. "There's champagne with your name on it. And if we're lucky, a waiter who doesn't run when I ask for seconds."

Jasmine let herself be pulled into the crowd, but William's warning echoed quietly in her mind.

Be careful.

She just wasn't sure which of them he was trying to protect—her… or Robert.

They made their way into the party, and almost instantly, Jasmine felt Robert before she saw him.

And then—there he was.

In a perfectly tailored charcoal suit, standing tall and collected beneath the glow of the terrace lights. He was listening to someone speak, nodding with polite interest, but the moment he looked up and saw her—he faltered. Just for a beat.

Then his eyes moved to Sean, and something shifted in his expression. Not jealousy. Not anger.

Disappointment.

As though she'd let him down without even meaning to.

Claire appeared, draping herself on Robert's arm like she'd rehearsed it. Her platinum bob was razor-sharp, her ice-blue gaze sweeping the room with thinly veiled disdain.

She caught sight of Jasmine and made no attempt to smile.

Jasmine nodded politely anyway, lifting her champagne flute to her lips.

Across the room, Robert excused himself and approached. He greeted William first— gripping his friend's hand in that firm, familiar way—then turned to Jasmine.

"You made it," he said quietly.

"We were invited," she replied, coolly. "Would've been rude not to come."

Robert's lips twitched. "Still. I'm glad."

Sean appeared beside her a moment later, his hand slipping possessively around her waist. "Robert," he said flatly. "Congratulations."

"Thanks… Sean." Robert nodded, then turned back to Jasmine. "You look…"

He trailed off, but the way his eyes swept over her said what he didn't.

Jasmine swallowed. "Congratulations again. You two make quite the couple."

Robert's jaw tensed, just barely.

"Thank you," he said finally.

But Jasmine wasn't looking at him anymore. She'd already turned back to William, smiling at something Mary had said, doing everything she could not to feel the weight of his gaze lingering as she walked away.

She'd worn the dress for herself. Not for him.

That's what she kept telling herself, anyway.

From across the patio, Claire watched with narrowed eyes as Robert's gaze followed Jasmine through the crowd. She saw the way his jaw shifted when Jasmine laughed at something William said, the way his posture subtly tilted toward her like gravity itself was to blame.

As Claire approached, she gripped on his arm tight.

"She's just William's sister," Robert said, too quickly, before she could comment.

Claire's lips curled into a smile that didn't reach her eyes. "Of course she is."

Not far away, Jasmine was feeling the weight of something else entirely. Sean had been acting extra clingy all night—hovering at her elbow, sliding his hand around her waist every time Robert was in view, whispering possessive things into her ear that made her skin crawl instead of shiver. He'd kissed her temple when Robert passed by, kissed her cheek while Robert was talking to a client, kissed her hand when Robert happened to glance her way.

It was getting under her skin.

Mary caught her eye across the bar; brows raised in quiet understanding. William, ever the big brother, just frowned.

"I need the bathroom," Jasmine said finally, slipping away before Sean could offer to follow.

Inside the grand house, the air was cooler, quieter. The opulent bathroom was tucked at the end of a long hallway, and when she stepped inside, Jasmine let out a breath she hadn't realised she'd been holding.

She checked her reflection in the mirror, smoothing a hand over her dress and brushing her long waves off her shoulders. She looked collected. Composed. Nothing like the storm stirring just beneath the surface.

But when she stepped out into the hallway, Robert was there.

Leaning casually against the wall, hands in his pockets, eyes steady on her.

She stopped.

"You need to get rid of him, Jaz," he said quietly.

She blinked, recovering fast. "Robert, Sean's no concern of yours."

"He's no good for you."

Jasmine folded her arms across her chest. "Oh? And how would you know?"

He took a step forward, his voice lower now. "Because I've known men like him my whole life. I can see what he's doing. You can too—you just don't want to admit it."

She shook her head. "This isn't your place."

"No," he agreed, his jaw tightening. "It isn't. But I care about you, Jasmine. And watching him cling to you like he's marking his territory? You deserve better than that."

Jasmine's heart twisted. The worst part wasn't his words—it was the look in his eyes. The way his voice softened when he said her name. The way it felt like he was saying something else entirely. Something he wasn't allowed to admit.

"I should get back," she said, more to herself than to him, barely above a whisper.

She turned to go, but Robert's hand reached out—gentle, instinctive—and his fingers wrapped around hers. A soft tug, nothing forceful, but it stopped her like a wall.

She turned back toward him, breath catching in her throat.

The contact was light, but it lit something in her. Sharp. Electric. Like a fuse catching fire. And from the way Robert's grip tightened—just for a second—she knew he'd felt it too. He seemed to remember himself, easing back just enough to still hold on.

"Seriously, Jaz," he said, voice low and rough around the edges. "He's not good for you."

Her lips parted, a hundred things rising to the surface—retorts, confessions, the truth she wasn't ready to say. "I…"

But the words dissolved.

And for a moment, there was nothing but silence—and that heavy, breathless space between them. His eyes locked with hers, green to gold, and something unspoken passed between them like sparks leaping across dry kindling.

She should've pulled away.

He should've let go.

But neither of them moved.

It was dangerous. Reckless. Wrong.

And yet, it felt like standing on the edge of something too real to deny.

Then—

"What's this?" Clair's voice sliced through the air like glass. She stood at the end of the hallway, her ice-blue eyes narrowed, her platinum bob shining under the hallway light. "Did I interrupt a little moment?"

Jasmine's spine straightened as Robert let go of her hand.

Clair crossed her arms, a cruel smirk tugging at her lips. "Should I be worried, darling? Or is your friend's little sister just confused about which men are not available?"

"Clair—" Robert started, his tone sharp.

But Jasmine raised a hand, stopping him.

"Leave it, Robert," she said calmly, not even looking at Clair. Her voice was steady, graceful—like armour.

Clair wasn't worth it. Not tonight.

Without another word, Jasmine turned and walked away—head high, heart thundering, heels clicking like punctuation marks to a conversation that hadn't quite ended.

The music thumped softly from the other side of the garden doors, but out here—beneath the low golden lights strung across the hedges—the air was cooler. Quieter. Tighter.

Robert had just come back from the hallway, jaw tight, hands shoved in his pockets, when William appeared at his side with two drinks in hand. He offered one without a word. Robert took it.

For a long moment, neither said anything. They just stood there, watching the party swirl around them. Claire was laughing too loudly with a group near the firepit. Jasmine was nowhere in sight.

Then William broke the silence.

"You need to be careful, Rob."

Robert didn't look at him. "I know that."

"Do you?"

Robert turned his head slowly, his expression even—but his eyes gave him away. A flicker. Just enough.

William took a measured sip of his drink. His voice was calm, but iron lay beneath it. "I saw Jasmine's face when she came back. And I saw Claire's. I'm not blind."

"I never said you were."

"She's been through hell," William said, quieter now. "Losing Mum and Dad… she's still carrying all of that. You know how much she's held together by sheer force of will. She's strong, yeah—but even strong people break."

Robert exhaled through his nose, tension crawling up his spine. "I'm not trying to hurt her."

"I know you're not," William said. "But Claire? She doesn't like the way you look out for Jasmine. And she doesn't hide it."

A pause.

"She's not just my sister," William added. "She's, my person. You get what I'm saying?"

Robert nodded once, jaw tight. "Yeah. I get it."

William turned toward him fully now, his gaze steady. "Then for the love of God, figure out a way to get Claire off her back."

Robert's voice was low, clipped. "You think I can control Claire?"

"No," William said, without hesitation. "But if you can't, then you need to stay away from Jasmine. Because you're engaged to a woman who'd gladly shove my sister off a cliff if no one was watching. And whether you mean to or not, you make it harder for her—just by looking at her the way you do."

Robert's breath hitched in his chest. But he didn't deny it.

"I'll stay away," he said after a beat, his voice quieter now, measured. "Only because you asked me to. Because I respect you."

"I appreciate that," William replied, but his tone was sharper now. "Just don't forget who you're marrying."

Chapter Five

The party was in full swing.

Laughter spilled across the manicured lawn of the Vaucluse estate like champagne—bubbly, relentless, and a little too loud. The air buzzed with polite conversation, clinking glasses, and curated background jazz. Fairy lights blinked overhead like stars trying too hard to be noticed.

Jasmine stood near the edge of the crowd, a flute of untouched champagne in her hand, her smile fixed and practiced. The scent of saltwater drifted up from the cliffs below, mingling with perfume and the faint aroma of grilled prawns from the outdoor caterers. It was all perfect. On the surface.

But beneath it?

She felt hollow.

She laughed in the right places, nodded through conversations, but her chest felt tight. Like she'd been holding her breath for hours and hadn't quite found the moment to exhale.

Claire was the centre of attention, draped in something skin-tight and shimmered, wearing Robert's arm like an accessory. She floated from group to group with a sharp laugh and a gleaming smile that never quite reached her eyes. Jasmine tried not to look, but her gaze kept drifting. And every time it did, it landed on him.

Robert.

He looked calm, composed—hands in his pockets, head bent politely when people spoke to him. But every now and then, his eyes would stray too. And Jasmine hated that she knew exactly when they were looking for her.

"You look like you need saving," Mary's voice cut in gently, appearing at her side with a smirk and two glasses of wine. "Or at the very least, better alcohol."

Jasmine smiled gratefully, taking one. "You're a goddess."

They found a quieter corner by the edge of the patio where William soon joined them, tugging at his collar like it was trying to strangle him. "Remind me why I agreed to this engagement thing?" he muttered.

"Because you're a loyal best man," Jasmine said with a dry smile. "And Robert asked."

William gave her a long look. "Yeah, and he might've regretted that the moment Claire decided the colour scheme needed to match her aura."

Jasmine laughed, and for a second, it felt easier.

"Jasmine! William!"

They both turned at the familiar voices behind them.

Terry and Kelly Steele approached with warm smiles—Robert's parents always had a way of making their presence known without fanfare. Terry looked sharp in a navy jacket, silver at his temples, while Kelly wore a soft dove-grey wrap dress and pearls, elegant as ever.

"Look at you two," Kelly said fondly, pulling Jasmine into a warm hug first, then turning to William. "It's so good to see you both. It's been far too long."

Before William could answer, Mary stepped up beside them, offering a polite smile.

"Oh, Mary!" Kelly said brightly, reaching to kiss her cheek. "You look lovely, as always. It's so wonderful to see you."

"Thank you," Mary replied with her easy grace. "I wouldn't miss a Steele party— especially not one hosted at a place like this."

Terry chuckled as he reached to shake William's hand. "Still managing to keep this lot in line, I see," he said, nodding toward the women with mock seriousness. "God help you."

William smirked. "Barely. They're a handful."

Jasmine rolled her eyes, playfully swatting her brother's arm.

Kelly's attention drifted back to Jasmine, her expression softening. "You look beautiful, Jasmine," she said warmly. "Truly glowing."

"Thank you." Jasmine glanced down, brushing a hand over the fabric of her dress. "I wasn't sure this was the right choice."

"It absolutely is," Kelly said firmly. "And if Robert has any sense at all, he'll notice."

That last part came with a pointed undertone—one Jasmine wasn't entirely sure how to interpret.

Terry shifted, his expression more neutral. "The place looks incredible, doesn't it?"

"It does," William said, glancing around. "Classic Steele taste."

"Well, Robert's anyway," Kelly said, a hint of something wry in her voice. "He bought the estate last year—turned thirty and suddenly decided he needed ocean views and sandstone columns. Very dramatic."

Jasmine smiled. "It suits him."

Kelly's expression softened again. She lowered her voice just enough for only Jasmine to catch it. "I was always hoping it would be you."

Jasmine blinked. "What?"

Kelly touched her arm lightly, the kind of maternal gesture that made Jasmine's chest ache. "You've always been steady. Genuine. Not all… glitter and performance."

Terry gave a noncommittal nod but didn't disagree.

Jasmine swallowed hard. "That's kind of you to say."

"I mean it," Kelly said.

Across the patio, Claire's laugh rang out—sharp, theatrical. She was surrounded by a circle of guests, basking in their admiration like a woman who knew how to play a room.

"She's… certainly made an impression," William muttered, his voice low enough that only Jasmine and the Steeles could hear.

Terry offered a diplomatic smile. Kelly didn't bother.

"She's made an impression," she agreed, her tone carefully restrained. "Just not the kind I'd hoped for."

Jasmine didn't know what to say. But as the conversation shifted to safer topics, she couldn't stop thinking about the weight of Kelly's words.

'I was always hoping it would be you.'

If only things were that simple.

The night stretched on—elegant conversation, delicate hors d'oeuvres, and endless champagne. But Jasmine's heels were beginning to pinch and the too-tight smile on her face was starting to slip.

"I need to regroup," she murmured to Mary, who stood beside her near the back terrace.

"Bathroom?" Mary offered knowingly.

Jasmine nodded, grateful. "Please."

The two women slipped through the French doors and into the dim hallway, heels clicking lightly against the polished floor. The estate's interior was just as grand as the exterior—opulent lighting, intricate moulding, thick carpets. The kind of place that whispered legacy and expectation.

They turned the corner toward the guest bathroom but stopped short just before reaching it.

Voices.

Low. Intimate.

Mary grabbed Jasmine's arm instinctively, motioning her to wait. Around the corner, just barely hidden in the alcove behind a large decorative plant, stood Claire—her arms draped around a man Jasmine didn't recognise. He was tall, lean, in a dark suit. Hands on her waist. His head bent close to hers, mouths too near. Laughing. Whispering. Smiling like no one else existed.

Then—he kissed her.

Not a friendly kiss. Not a greeting.

A slow, deliberate kiss that lingered.

Jasmine froze.

Mary's breath hitched beside her, hand tightening on Jasmine's arm.

Claire pulled back slightly, brushing a hand down the man's chest as if to say not here. But the way she looked at him, lips parted, eyes sultry and sure—that wasn't someone unsure of her feelings. That was someone entirely comfortable in the secrecy.

They didn't see Jasmine and Mary. Too wrapped up in each other. Too confident in their invisibility.

Jasmine quickly pulled Mary back down the hallway, her pulse thudding in her ears. They ducked into the powder room silently, the door clicking shut behind them.

Inside, Mary exhaled hard. "What the hell was that?"

Jasmine didn't answer right away. She stared at her reflection, hands braced on the marble sink, the blush on her cheeks fading fast.

"Did we really just see that?" Mary whispered, incredulous.

Jasmine nodded slowly. "We did."

A beat passed.

Mary straightened, her brows drawn tight. "Do you think Robert knows?"

Jasmine stared at the mirror, her lips pressed together. "If he didn't before…" Her voice was low, steady. "He should."

Mary hesitated, then quietly asked, "Should we tell William?"

Jasmine's pulse thundered in her ears. The weight of what they'd seen wasn't just scandal—it was betrayal. And not just of Robert. Of a future, a choice, a trust she wasn't even sure he'd built on solid ground.

She nodded slowly. "Yes. I think he should be the one to tell Robert."

Mary's eyes met hers in the mirror, clear and steady. "Then let's go find him."

The weight of the moment hung between them as they stepped out of the powder room. The music still pulsed faintly from the terrace, laughter drifting from the party like nothing had changed. But for Jasmine, everything had.

They found William near the edge of the pool area, chatting with one of Robert's uncles. As soon as he saw their faces, his smile faded.

He stepped toward them, eyes narrowing. "What's wrong?"

Mary moved in first, her voice low and urgent. "We just saw Claire."

William blinked. "Okay?"

"She was kissing another man," Mary whispered, just loud enough for Jasmine and William to hear. "Not a hello kiss. Intimate. *Very* intimate."

"What?" William's voice came out sharp and disbelieving. His eyes darted between them, searching their faces for any hint of exaggeration. He found none.

"She was tucked away in a corner near the guest hallway," Jasmine said softly. "We weren't meant to see it."

William's jaw clenched. "Bloody hell."

He looked away for a moment, running a hand through his hair, then fixed his eyes on Jasmine.

"You saw it too?"

Jasmine hesitated, surprised by the question. "Yeah. I'm... shocked."

He turned to Mary. "Did anyone else see?"

"No. Just us."

William nodded slowly, absorbing the weight of it. Then his gaze darkened, voice dropping into something colder.

"Rob needs to hear this. Tonight."

Jasmine and Mary exchanged a glance, the weight of the moment stretching between them like a drawn breath.

"Yes," Jasmine said quietly. "It would be better coming from you."

William gave a short nod, his jaw tightening as he turned away, the set of his shoulders stiff with purpose.

And just like that, the mood of the night shattered—replaced by something real, raw, and utterly unavoidable.

Jasmine exhaled slowly, trying to steady herself.

But she didn't get a chance to linger in it.

"Hey, gorgeous."

Sean's voice came from behind her, syrupy and smug. She turned to find him grinning, his hand already reaching out.

"Dance with me?" he asked but didn't wait for an answer—he was already pulling her toward the makeshift dance floor where couples swayed under the glow of fairy lights and soft jazz.

Jasmine hesitated, glancing back at William and Mary.

Mary met her eyes. There was concern there… but also something else. A quiet understanding. A slight nod. *Do what you have to do.*

So, she let Sean lead her away, her fingers resting lightly in his as her heels clicked across the stone terrace. But her steps were uncertain, her heart racing—though not from anticipation.

She didn't want to be held right now. Not by him.

The music washed over her as Sean spun her into his arms, pulling her a little closer than she liked. His hand slid around her waist. Too familiar. Too tight.

"You've been quiet tonight," he murmured into her ear, mistaking her silence for mystery.

Jasmine managed a smile that didn't quite reach her eyes. "Just a lot on my mind."

He chuckled, slow and low. "Well, lucky for you, I'm great at helping people forget their problems."

She didn't respond.

Instead, she focused on the rhythm, the sway of the music, the practiced way Sean moved—confident and polished. But her body wasn't relaxing into it. Her chest still felt tight. Her thoughts still looped back to the hallway. To Claire. To Robert's face when he found out.

And—*whether she liked it or not*—to the way his hand had felt in hers.

She closed her eyes, trying to will the ache away.

But it stayed.

Persistent.

And suddenly, the party didn't feel like a celebration at all. It felt like the start of something unravelling.

Chapter Six

William found Robert near the back patio, half-listening to an older guest talk about property taxes. His glass was half-full, his smile practiced.

But William saw it—that flicker of distraction, the unease underneath. Maybe Robert already felt it. Maybe he just didn't want to.

"Hey," William said quietly, stepping beside him.

Robert glanced over, his brows lifting. "You alright?"

"Can we talk?" William asked, voice low but firm.

Robert studied him for a beat, then nodded once. "Sure." He excused himself and followed William down the short stone path toward the garden, away from the music and laughter.

Once they were out of earshot, William turned to him.

"It's about Claire."

Robert's brows knit. "What about her?"

William hesitated—just for a second—but then he said it straight. "Mary and Jasmine saw her. In the hallway. With another guy."

Robert blinked, thrown. "What?"

"They said it wasn't just a hug, Rob. It was a kiss, and they looked close. Intimate."

A short pause. Then, "Who?"

William motioned subtly toward the terrace. "Tall guy. Dark suit. Slicked-back hair. Over there by the bar."

Robert followed the direction of his gaze, squinting until his eyes landed on the man. His mouth quirked, and he gave a short, incredulous laugh.

"Oh, that's her agent. He reps a bunch of high-profile models and influencers. He's probably just dramatic by nature. You know how those types are."

William didn't laugh.

"I don't think so."

Robert turned back to him, his tone edging toward defensive. "Come on, Will. It's Claire. She's always touchy with people she knows. You've seen it."

"I have," William said. "But not like that. And Jasmine isn't the type to stir up drama unless she's sure. Neither is Mary."

Robert looked away, jaw tightening. He took a long sip of his drink.

"People misinterpret things all the time," he said finally, tone lighter than it should've been. "Especially when emotions are running high."

William studied him. "You really don't want to believe it."

"No," Robert admitted. "I don't."

He looked back toward the bar where Claire now stood, laughing at something her agent had whispered.

William's voice dropped. "Just… don't ignore this because it's easier than facing it. You deserve to know the truth—even if it's not the version you want."

Robert didn't answer right away. Just stared into his glass, the weight of too many things pressing down on his shoulders.

Then, with a forced chuckle, Robert muttered, "Maybe I've had enough drama for one night."

He turned and walked back toward the party, drink in hand, smile faintly in place. But the ease in his step didn't return. Not really.

And William watched him go, knowing the words had landed—deep enough to unsettle, even if Robert wasn't ready to admit it yet.

At the bar, Claire stood with Brian, their heads close in conversation and laughter that felt a touch too intimate. Robert's jaw tightened for just a beat before he smoothed it out and crossed the patio toward them.

He recognised Brian—Claire's agent. He'd met him a few times. Friendly, polished, always in expensive shoes and a tailored jacket. Robert was fairly certain he was married. Or had been.

Brian spotted him first and grinned, lifting his glass. "Robert Steele," he said smoothly, offering his hand. "Congratulations, mate. You're making an honest woman out of our Claire."

Our Claire.

Robert took the offered hand, the words ringing louder in his head than he expected. "Thanks, Brian," he said, voice level, controlled.

Claire turned then, her smile bright, slipping her arm through Robert's like a silk ribbon winding around him. "We are going to be so happy," she cooed, then rose up to kiss his cheek. "Aren't we, darling?"

Robert gave a small nod, his smile practiced. "Of course."

But something lodged in his chest, heavy and unmoving. Brian clinked his glass and turned away to greet someone else, and Claire began to chatter about her upcoming photo shoot next week in New Zealand.

Robert listened.

Or at least pretended to.

But the echo of William's words, the shadow of Jasmine's expression when she'd walked back from the bathroom, and the lingering sound of *'our Claire'* clattered in his mind like loose change in a jar.

Something didn't feel right.

And for the first time, he wasn't sure if it ever had.

William returned to the edge of the patio where Mary stood waiting, her eyes scanning his face the moment he came into view.

"Well?" she asked, arms folded. "What did he say?"

"He doesn't believe it," William said, still a little stunned.

Mary blinked. "Seriously?"

"Yeah. Said the guy's her agent. Thought you misread the whole thing."

Mary exhaled through her nose. "Well… we did the right thing. It's up to him whether he wants to open his eyes or not."

Before William could reply, Jasmine appeared, walking toward them hand-in-hand with Sean.

Mary immediately locked eyes with her. Jasmine gave the smallest shake of her head— barely noticeable, but enough. Nothing had changed. Not yet.

"Hey," Jasmine said lightly, though there was tension around her smile. "Sean's taking me home."

Sean, all confidence and charm, wrapped an arm around Jasmine's waist. "Long night, right babe?"

Neither Mary nor William responded right away.

Sean gave a nod, a thin smile that didn't quite reach his eyes. "Night, guys."

And with that, he turned, leading Jasmine away without waiting for a response—his hand firm at the small of her back, like she was something to be claimed.

Mary watched them go, jaw tight.

William's gaze followed Jasmine as she disappeared into the night with Sean, tension tightening his jaw.

"She didn't look happy with him," Mary said quietly, watching too.

William gave a dry breath. "She hasn't looked happy with him in a long time."

Mary turned to him, her expression softening. "Well, you'll be happy to hear this—she told me earlier she's ending it tonight."

William's shoulders dropped slightly, relief flashing in his eyes. "Thank God. I don't think I could've handled that smug grin of his much longer."

Behind them, the party rolled on—music pulsing, laughter floating through the air, champagne bubbling in flutes. But the real stories were happening in the spaces between.

A moment later, Robert approached with Claire draped elegantly on his arm, her smile polished but unreadable.

"Where's Jasmine off to?" Robert asked, casually scanning the crowd.

William didn't miss the flicker of something in his voice.

"She's going to dump the cling-on," William said, sipping his drink.

Robert blinked. "Really?"

Mary gave him a knowing look. "Really. Took her long enough."

Robert nodded slowly, but his gaze lingered on the space Jasmine had just vacated, like he was still chasing the ghost of her presence—one last glimpse before it was too late.

Beside him, Claire gave a light, dismissive laugh and curled her arm tighter around his. "Honestly, I don't know why he hung around so long. Jasmine is hardly a prize."

Mary sucked in a quiet gasp, but it was William who snapped his head around, his eyes flashing.

"Yeah, well, no one asked for your opinion," he said coldly. "My sister was way too good for that creep."

Robert straightened slightly, caught between the flare of conflict and the pressure of Claire's hand on his arm.

William looked directly at him now. "We're leaving. Congrats again. I'll see you in the office Monday."

Claire blinked, visibly thrown. "What did I say?" she asked, feigning innocence as she turned to Robert. "I was just being honest."

But Robert didn't respond. His jaw tensed, a muscle feathering near his temple. He knew exactly why William was angry—because he'd let Claire get in another jab at Jasmine and said nothing. *Again.*

And that knowledge sat heavy on his shoulders.

He didn't agree with Claire. Not even close. But defending Jasmine always seemed to spark something uglier in Claire. So, like a coward, he stayed silent.

And just like that, the polished glow of the evening cracked a little more around the edges—leaving behind something raw, unspoken, and quietly unravelling beneath the surface.

The car ride home was quiet—too quiet. Jasmine stared out the window as the city blurred by in a haze of streetlights and fading music. Her body still buzzed from the party, but her mind was somewhere else entirely. Or rather, on someone else.

Sean's grip on the wheel was tight. He hadn't said much since they left, aside from the occasional complaint about the traffic or how long it had taken for the valet to bring the car around. Jasmine didn't respond. She couldn't. Her thoughts were too tangled.

When they pulled up in front of her townhouse, she unbuckled her seatbelt without a word. Sean rushed out of the car to open her door—something that once might've charmed her, but now just felt like a performance.

He walked her to the door, hands in his coat pockets, that overly confident smirk playing on his lips.

"Well," he said, rocking back on his heels, "tonight was… something."

Jasmine gave a tight smile and reached for her keys. "Yeah. It was."

Sean stepped closer. Too close. Before she could say anything, he leaned in to kiss her.

She turned her face away. "Sean, don't."

He froze, blinking at her. "Don't?"

She took a breath. "I don't think this is working out. Us."

His brows lifted. "What are you talking about?"

"I just… I don't feel it anymore. I think it's better if we don't see each other again."

He let out a bitter laugh, stepping back with a scoff. "Oh, come on. This again?"

She frowned. "This again?"

Sean shook his head, his expression twisting. "You know what this is really about, don't you? It's always been about him."

Jasmine blinked. "What?"

"Robert," Sean said, spitting the name like it tasted wrong. "I was hoping that now he's engaged, you'd finally let go of whatever pathetic infatuation you've been holding onto. But no. You're still stuck on him."

Her spine straightened. "You have no idea what you're talking about."

"Oh, don't I?" he snapped. "You think I haven't noticed the way you go quiet when he walks into a room? The way you light up when he so much as looks your way. You think I haven't seen it?"

Jasmine stared at him, stunned by the venom in his tone.

"I thought dating you would be easy," he said, pacing in front of her now. "Smart, beautiful, low drama. But you're still mooning over your brother's best mate like some schoolgirl. It's pathetic."

"That's enough," she said, her voice steady now. Cold. "I told you this wasn't working. And you've just confirmed I made the right call."

Sean's mouth opened, but no words came. Jasmine stepped past him and unlocked her front door.

"Goodnight, Sean."

And with that, she closed the door behind her, locking it with a quiet click.

For a moment, she just stood there in the dark entryway, hand on the doorknob, heart thudding in her chest.

Sean was wrong about a lot of things—but not about everything.

Because she had felt something when Robert looked at her.

Something deep. Unwelcome. Unshakable.

She leaned back against the door, eyes closed, the silence of her townhouse pressing in around her.

She needed to stop. Needed to bury whatever this thing was between her and Robert before it unravelled everything—for him, for her, for William.

But Sean had never been the one to help her forget.

He never even came close.

It was time to let go—really let go.

Robert was getting married.

Whatever this was—this ache in her chest, the way her mind kept looping back to glances and moments that never should've mattered—it had to end.

She deserved more than quiet longing for a man who belonged to someone else.

Even if her heart hadn't caught up yet.

It was time to stop chasing shadows.

To stop aching for someone who could never be hers.

Who never should have been.

Jasmine pushed off the door and walked deeper into the quiet of her home. No more fantasies. No more late-night thoughts about what if.

It was time to reclaim her life.

And leave Robert Steele where he belonged.

In the past.

Chapter Seven

Wednesday afternoons were usually Jasmine's favourite—slightly quieter, with a gentler rhythm to the day. But this week had been a welcome blur. Busy. Full. Exactly what she needed.

Her final client of the afternoon was Gwen Fletcher, a graceful woman in her early sixties with sharp wit and a kind smile. Jasmine adored her. Their sessions always ended with laughter and stories—usually about Gwen's garden, her grandchildren, or her children.

Especially her son.

Jasmine had heard about him for weeks. "You'd like him, Jasmine," Gwen would say with a twinkle in her eye. "He's smart, grounded, and far too handsome for his own good. A lawyer. Works too much. And single. Did I mention single?"

Jasmine would always laugh it off. Until now.

Gwen gathered her things slowly, smiling as she reached for her scarf. "James should be downstairs by now. He's punctual to a fault. Like his father."

"I'll walk you down," Jasmine offered.

They stepped into the lobby together, Gwen chatting easily beside her. When the doors opened, a tall man in a charcoal suit stood by the entrance, scrolling through his phone.

Jasmine blinked.

Wow. Gwen wasn't exaggerating.

James looked up and smiled when he saw them—an easy, disarming grin that lit up his entire face. He had striking features: dark hair with just a hint of silver at the temples, strong jawline, intelligent eyes.

"Hi Mum," he said, then turned to Jasmine. "You must be Jasmine."

She extended a hand. "That's me. You must be the mysterious son I've heard so much about."

He laughed as he shook her hand—firm, warm, confident. "I hope it was all good."

Gwen waved a dismissive hand. "I'll be in the ladies', dear. I want to freshen up before we leave. Don't let him bore you while I'm gone."

As she disappeared down the hall, James looked at Jasmine, suddenly more serious. "She wasn't exaggerating, by the way. You're... kind of exactly what I pictured."

Jasmine blinked, surprised. "Pictured?"

He smiled again, a touch of mischief in his eyes. "She's been trying to set us up for weeks. I just didn't think you'd actually exist."

That made her laugh, warmth blooming in her chest.

"Well, here I am."

"Here you are," he echoed, his eyes still on her—curious, intrigued.

There was a pause between them. Not awkward, not forced. Just a beat of quiet, charged with something light and promising.

Then James added, voice low and easy, "Would you like to get a drink with me? Friday afternoon, maybe? Nothing fancy. Just… a conversation without our matchmaker hovering nearby."

Jasmine's smile curled softly at the corners, warm and real. "I'd love to."

He returned the smile, clearly pleased. "Great, I'll call you. Let's not mention it to Mum, though. I'll never hear the end of it."

Jasmine laughed. "Mum's the word."

Just then, Gwen reappeared, adjusting her scarf with a satisfied sigh. "Now, are we ready to go?"

Jasmine and James exchanged a quick, secret smile.

"Ready when you are," James said.

And just like that, Friday afternoon had something to look forward to.

Friday morning, the clinic phone rang just as Jasmine was reviewing notes between appointments. She answered with her usual calm tone.

"Jasmine Whitaker speaking."

"Hi, Jasmine. It's James Fletcher."

A smile tugged at her lips before she could stop it. "Hi, James."

"I was wondering," he said, his voice smooth, warm, and just a little nervous, "is five o'clock okay for you? There's a wine bar on Harrington Street—quiet, good lighting, no matchmaker in sight."

She chuckled softly. "Five sounds perfect."

"Great," he said, and she could hear the smile in his voice. "I've been looking forward to it."

"Me too."

They said their goodbyes and hung up, and Jasmine found herself staring at the phone for a moment longer, her pulse lighter than it had been in days.

By late afternoon, just as she was packing up to leave, her mobile buzzed. Heidi's name lit up the screen.

"Hey," Jasmine said, tucking the phone between her ear and shoulder as she slipped on her coat.

"Drinks?" Heidi asked without preamble. "Please tell me you're free tonight. I've had the week from hell and need a cocktail or six."

Jasmine laughed. "I can't tonight."

"What? Why?"

"I have a date."

"Please tell me you're not giving Sean another shot."

"God, no."

There was a beat of silence. "Wait... so this is a date-date?"

"A real one," Jasmine said, her smile tugging at the corners of her mouth before she could stop it.

"Well, colour me intrigued," Heidi said, clearly thrilled. "You have to call me after. I want a full report—top to bottom."

"You'll be the first to know," Jasmine promised with a laugh.

As she ended the call and stepped out into the warm late-afternoon sun, Jasmine felt something unexpected—a spark of real excitement. Not nerves. Not second thoughts.

Just... anticipation.

And it felt good.

The wine bar was tucked into a quiet corner off the main street—stylish without trying too hard, with exposed brick walls, low golden lighting, and shelves of carefully chosen bottles that lined the walls like art.

Jasmine stepped inside, brushing a hand down the front of her soft navy blouse. She wore her favourite ankle boots and a pair of tailored jeans—casual but polished. Her hair was loose around her shoulders, and as she scanned the room, her eyes landed on him instantly.

James Fletcher was already seated at a table near the window, nursing a glass of something deep red. He stood the moment he saw her, his smile easy and warm, his dark blazer crisp over a simple white shirt. The man looked like he belonged in a courtroom… and maybe a Ralph Lauren ad.

"Jasmine," he said, his voice low and pleasantly surprised. "You're right on time."

"So are you," she replied, smiling as he pulled out her chair.

He waited until she was seated before taking his own. "I figured being early was safer than making a woman wait—especially one my mother adores."

Jasmine laughed. "Gwen's been laying it on thick for weeks. I had no idea she had matchmaking tendencies."

"She only does it when she really likes someone," James said, lifting his glass. "And apparently, you're her favourite person at the moment."

Jasmine flushed, accepting the wine menu. "That's sweet. She's lovely. And extremely persuasive."

They both laughed, and the moment settled into something relaxed and open. They ordered a shared bottle of red—recommended by the server—and with each sip, the conversation flowed more easily. They talked about their work—his long hours and courtroom chaos, her passion for helping people rebuild their strength and confidence. They found common ground in books, travel, and their mutual love of dry humour.

James was attentive without being overbearing, charming without trying too hard. He listened, asked thoughtful questions, and when Jasmine spoke, his eyes stayed on hers— really stayed—as if he wasn't in a hurry to be anywhere else.

At one point, she caught herself laughing at something he said—really laughing. It had been a while.

"Can I be honest?" he asked, swirling the last of his wine. "I wasn't sure what to expect tonight. My mother oversells everything."

"And I wasn't sure if this was going to be awkward or adorable," Jasmine added.

"And?"

"I'm leaning toward adorable," she said, her smile slow and genuine.

James leaned back, clearly pleased. "Good. I'm already glad I asked." He glanced out the window, then back at her. "What do you say we go next door and get something to eat? There's a little Italian place I've been meaning to try."

Jasmine tilted her head, amusement dancing in her eyes. "Are you bribing me with pasta?"

"Absolutely."

She laughed. "Then yes. How could I possibly say no to that?"

A few minutes later, they stepped out into the evening air, and James led her just a few doors down to a narrow, warmly lit restaurant tucked between a florist and an old bookstore. The sign above the door read La Sorella in curling gold script.

Inside, the space was cozy and intimate—only a dozen tables, each lit by a small candle in a glass holder. The walls were lined with shelves filled with cookbooks, wine bottles, and faded family photographs in mismatched frames. The smell of garlic, basil, and slow-simmered tomatoes wrapped around them the moment they stepped in.

A hostess greeted them with a smile and led them to a small corner table by the window. Red-checkered linens, rustic pottery plates, and the faint sound of an old Italian love song playing softly in the background—it all felt like a little world tucked away from everything else.

"This is perfect," Jasmine said, taking it all in.

James smiled as he opened his menu. "Told you. My courtroom instincts are rarely wrong."

They ordered fresh bread, a bottle of Chianti, and two steaming bowls of handmade pasta—hers, a rich tagliatelle with mushrooms and truffle oil, his, a spicy arrabbiata. The conversation picked up right where it left off, weaving between stories from their childhoods, favourite travel spots, and the unspoken comfort of two people genuinely enjoying each other's company.

At one point, Jasmine caught him watching her, just for a moment, as she laughed at her own story about learning to roller skate too late in life.

"What?" she asked, cheeks slightly flushed.

James gave a small shrug, his expression soft. "I'm just glad I came tonight."

Jasmine's heart did a quiet little flutter. "Me too."

As the plates emptied and the wine grew low, the night wrapped around them like a warm blanket. There was no pretence. No pressure. Just the gentle unfolding of something that felt... promising.

And Jasmine, for the first time in a long time, didn't feel like she was holding her breath.

They lingered over the last sips of wine until the restaurant began to thin out. James settled the bill without fanfare, then offered her his arm as they stepped into the cool night air.

The breeze off the bay was soft, rustling through the trees lining the street. Jasmine walked beside him, her heels clicking lightly on the pavement, still caught in the quiet bubble the evening had created.

When they reached her car, he turned to her, hands tucked casually in his pockets.

"Would it be too forward if I asked for your number?"

Jasmine smiled and pulled out her phone. "Only if you don't actually use it."

He chuckled and handed her his phone. She typed it in, saving it under Jasmine W.

He looked down at the screen for a moment, then back at her. "I'm really glad you said yes."

"Me too."

There was a pause—not awkward, but full of something charged and uncertain. Then he stepped in, just slightly closer, eyes searching hers.

"I'd like to kiss you," he said softly, like he meant every word.

For the briefest second, a shadow passed through her—another voice, another kiss, another man whose name still lived somewhere beneath her ribs.

But it was just a flicker.

And then she looked at James—steady, kind, fully present—and the shadow faded.

"I'd like that," she said.

His hand found her waist as he leaned in, and their lips met in a kiss that was warm and unhurried—curious, tentative, and then just a little deeper. It wasn't fireworks. It wasn't fire. It was something better. Steady. Safe. Real.

When they parted, James exhaled a little laugh under his breath, his forehead briefly resting against hers.

"Wow," he murmured, voice low and full of surprise.

Jasmine grinned, cheeks flushed. "Yeah. Wow."

He stepped back reluctantly. "I'll call you tomorrow."

She nodded, still smiling as she opened her car door. "I'll answer."

As she slid into the driver's seat and closed the door, Jasmine sat for a moment before starting the engine, her fingertips brushing her lips.

And for the first time in what felt like forever, she wasn't thinking about the past.

Not the man who left her aching.

Not the kiss that has never happened.

Just this.

Just him.

Just now.

Chapter Eight

Jasmine curled up on her couch with a cup of tea, the glow of the evening still lingering in her chest. The city lights twinkled beyond her balcony, and everything felt a little softer, a little lighter.

She tapped Heidi's name on her phone and pressed it to her ear.

"Finally!" Heidi answered. "I was about to send out a search party. So? Spill. How'd it go?"

Jasmine smiled, warmth rising in her cheeks just from thinking about it. "It was… really good."

"Good?" Heidi scoffed. "That's all I get?"

Jasmine laughed. "Okay, okay—it was better than good. He was kind. Charming. Funny in this really understated way. We had a glass of wine, then ended up at this tiny Italian place next door. He walked me to my car, we kissed, and… yeah. It felt real."

There was a pause on the other end of the line, then Heidi said, more carefully, "So… you think James could make you forget Robert?"

Jasmine went quiet. Her fingers tightened around her mug, and she stared out at the night for a beat, her thoughts tumbling.

And then, with quiet certainty, she said, "Yes. I think he could."

Heidi's exhale of relief was audible. "God, Jaz. I hope so. You deserve someone who sees you. All of you."

"I know," Jasmine whispered. "And maybe for the first time, I think I'm starting to believe it too."

They sat in the easy silence of friendship for a moment before Jasmine added, "And don't worry—I'll keep you updated."

"You'd better. I'm fully invested now," Heidi said with a mock-serious tone. "This is officially my new favourite romance."

Jasmine chuckled. "Let's hope it has a happy ending."

Jasmine was halfway through replying to an email when her phone lit up with a call from James. A smile tugged at her lips as she answered.

"Hi," she said, tucking the phone between her shoulder and cheek.

"Hi yourself," James replied, his voice warm and easy. "I was wondering if you're free for lunch today. There's a little place near the courthouse that does a dangerous grilled haloumi salad."

Jasmine laughed. "Tempting, but I've already got plans. I'm meeting my brother and his wife at the Cruising Yacht Club in Rushcutters Bay."

"Ooh, fancy," he teased.

"Only a little," she said with a grin. "But… if you're free, you could join us? It's not too formal, and William's actually bearable when he's had a glass of wine."

James chuckled. "Is this your way of throwing me into the deep end?"

"I figure if you can survive my brother, you can survive anything."

There was a pause, then he said, "In that case, I accept the challenge. Text me the details?"

"I will. Noon-ish, dress casual-but-charming."

"So… like last night?"

"Exactly like last night."

He laughed again, and she could almost picture his smile. "Then I'll see you there."

"Looking forward to it," she said, her voice a little softer now.

When the call ended, Jasmine felt that lightness again—effortless and unexpected. And as she grabbed her bag and headed out, she couldn't help thinking that maybe, just maybe, something good was finally beginning.

The sun glittered off the water at Rushcutters Bay, sailboats rocking gently in their berths as Jasmine stepped onto the open-air deck of the Cruising Yacht Club. A crisp breeze tugged at the hem of her sundress, and the scent of salt and citrus from nearby cocktails hung in the air.

William and Mary were already at a table near the railing, sipping iced drinks and laughing about something. Jasmine smiled as she approached.

"Well, if it isn't my loving brother," she said playfully.

William looked up. "You're late."

"I'm fashionably timed," she countered. "And I brought company."

She turned slightly as James arrived at her side, dressed in a button-down shirt with the sleeves casually rolled up, his sunglasses tucked into the front.

"William, Mary—this is James Fletcher. James, my brother William and his much better half, Mary."

James extended his hand without hesitation. "It's great to meet you both. Jasmine's told me good things."

William shook his hand firmly, eyes narrowing just slightly in that protective older brother way. "Only the good things? That doesn't sound like Jasmine."

James grinned. "She might've left out the part where I'm apparently being tested today."

Mary smiled, already charmed. "Don't worry. You're passing so far."

"Drink?" Jasmine asked, slipping into the seat across from her brother.

"Absolutely," James said, taking the seat next to her.

Over the next hour, the conversation flowed as easily as the wine. James held his own—quick-witted, thoughtful, never overstepping but never fading into the background either. He asked William about his work and actually listened. He laughed at Mary's dry humour and matched Jasmine's sarcasm with gentle teasing of his own.

By the time dessert arrived—a shared plate of lemon tart and espresso—the air around the table felt settled, warm. Comfortable.

William leaned back in his chair and looked across at James, his tone more relaxed than Jasmine had expected. "So, you're a lawyer. That explains the charm."

James smirked. "Or it's despite the law degree."

Mary tilted her head, giving Jasmine a look. "He's lovely."

Jasmine tried not to blush. "He is."

James looked between them. "Should I give you two a minute?"

William chuckled, then raised his glass. "To decent company."

"Finally," Mary added.

They all clinked their glasses together, the clink light but full of promise.

As the afternoon sun began to soften into gold, Jasmine felt something settle inside her. James fit. Not in a forced way, or in a way that made her question herself—but in a quiet, certain way. Like he'd always been meant to sit at her table.

And when he reached over under the table and gently linked his fingers with hers, her heart didn't race with uncertainty.

It settled.

As Mary and Jasmine stood to leave the table, Mary leaned over to kiss William's cheek. "Bathroom break. Try not to bore James while we're gone."

"Impossible," William replied, smirking. "I'm extremely entertaining."

Jasmine rolled her eyes fondly. "Don't let him rope you into one of his conspiracy theories about avocado pricing."

James laughed. "I'll brace myself."

As the women disappeared into the interior of the club, William leaned back in his chair and gave James a wry look.

"This is the part," he said dryly, "where they go to the bathroom together and talk about you."

James raised his brows. "Oh yeah?"

William nodded, mock-serious. "It's a sacred ritual. Happens every time. They'll compare notes, dissect your handshake, probably rate your shirt out of ten."

James chuckled. "Should I be nervous?"

William took a sip of his drink. "Probably. Mary likes you. That's good. But Jasmine?" He set the glass down and looked at him squarely. "She doesn't let people in easily. So, if you're not serious…"

James met his gaze evenly. "I'm serious."

William studied him a moment longer, then nodded slowly. "Good. Because she's not just my sister. She's been through some crap. She deserves someone solid."

James didn't flinch. "She does."

There was a beat of mutual understanding before William cracked a grin. "Still rating the shirt a nine though."

James grinned. "It's the lawyer uniform. We don't have a lot of room for creativity."

William lifted his glass in a half-toast, amusement gleaming in his eyes. "Keep saying the right things, Fletcher. You're doing well."

The women's bathroom at the yacht club was all sleek marble and gleaming mirrors, with the soft scent of citrus hand wash in the air. Jasmine checked her reflection, smoothing a stray curl at her temple, but her cheeks were already flushed with something that had nothing to do with the warm afternoon.

Mary leaned against the counter, arms crossed, watching her with a knowing smile.

"Well?" she said.

Jasmine tried to play innocent. "Well, what?"

Mary snorted. "Oh, please. You're glowing. Spill it."

Jasmine laughed, then sighed, her expression softening. "He's… really lovely."

Mary arched a brow. "Lovely. That's dangerously close to boring."

Jasmine grinned. "Not boring. Just… easy to talk to. Kind. Smart. And he listens."

"Listens?" Mary echoed dramatically. "Be still my heart."

Jasmine rolled her eyes, but she was still smiling. "You like him?"

"I do," Mary said without hesitation. "And Will likes him, too. You saw the way he was grilling him the moment we sat down—like a dad with a shotgun. But James handled it. Cool as anything."

Jasmine's smile faded just a touch, a flicker of uncertainty crossing her face. "It's early, I know. I'm not jumping ahead."

Mary's tone softened. "Hey. I'm not saying you have to plan the wedding. But you're allowed to enjoy yourself. And he clearly likes you."

"I know," Jasmine said, quieter now. She looked down at her hands, then back up at her reflection. "I'm just not used to this… healthy."

Mary reached over and gave her hand a gentle squeeze. "That's a good thing, Jaz. You deserve someone who doesn't come with emotional whiplash."

Jasmine took a breath and nodded. "I'm trying."

Mary smiled, pulling her into a quick hug. "You're doing great."

As they headed back toward the table, Jasmine felt lighter—like maybe, she was finally stepping into something good.

James chuckled at another one of William's dry remarks, the afternoon sun casting a golden sheen over the polished decking of the yacht club. Laughter drifted from nearby tables, but the easy rhythm of their conversation shifted the moment footsteps approached from behind—measured, deliberate.

"William," came a voice both familiar and cool. "Didn't expect to see you here."

They turned.

Robert was approaching, Claire draped on his arm like a designer accessory. She wore an ivory halter dress that clung a little too tightly and a smile that didn't quite reach her eyes.

William's expression cooled by a few degrees. "Robert."

Claire's smile widened. "What a surprise." Her gaze flicked to James, and for the briefest second, it sharpened with interest. "And who's this?"

"This is James Fletcher," William said, tone polite but firm. "A friend of Jasmine's. James, this is my business partner Robert Steele and his fiancée Claire."

"Pleasure," James said, standing to shake Robert's hand. "Nice to meet you."

Claire didn't wait her turn. She leaned in just a little too close, offering her hand with a sultry tilt of her head. "Claire Montgomery. But I suppose you already knew that."

James took her hand briefly—professionally—then let it go. "Nice to meet you, Claire."

She lingered, as if waiting for something more, before pouting just slightly. "Fletcher… are you by chance related to Peter Fletcher? The barrister?"

"He's my uncle," James replied.

Claire let out a low, impressed sound. "Small world."

"Smaller than you think," James said, tone cooling as he took a step back just as Jasmine and Mary returned from the bathroom.

"Hello, Robert. Claire," Jasmine said politely, offering a polite smile.

James stood and pulled Jasmine's chair out for her with effortless charm, waiting until she sat before taking his seat beside her. Without hesitation, he reached for her hand beneath the table, his thumb brushing gently across her knuckles—a quiet, confident gesture that didn't go unnoticed.

Robert's eyes dropped to their joined hands.

His jaw tightened.

Claire noticed it too. Her smile wavered for half a second before she pasted on something far more cutting. Her gaze slid to Jasmine, sharp and artificial. "Well, you moved on from Sean quickly, didn't you, Jasmine?"

Mary stiffened.

Jasmine blinked slowly, lips parting in surprise—but before she could speak, James leaned forward slightly, his tone calm but edged.

"Is there a problem with someone recognising a good thing when they see it?" He said it without looking at Claire, but the implication hung in the air.

Claire let out a soft, incredulous laugh. "Oh, not at all. Just… surprised, that's all. Jasmine doesn't usually move so fast."

Jasmine straightened, voice smooth and composed. "Maybe I just needed the right reason."

Claire's smile froze. Robert looked away.

Mary broke the tension with a sip of her drink. "Honestly, it's been a long time since I've seen her smile like this. It suits her."

James glanced at Jasmine with a soft, genuine look. "I'd agree with that."

Claire opened her mouth as if to retort—but Robert touched her elbow gently. "We should go check in with Dad."

It wasn't really a suggestion.

Claire hesitated, but let herself be led away, her expression unreadable as her heels clicked sharply against the wooden deck.

As soon as they were out of earshot, Mary muttered under her breath, "I swear, one day I'm going to claw that woman's eyes out."

"Mary," Jasmine said with a quiet laugh, shaking her head.

"I know, I know," Mary sighed, waving a hand. "But the way she talks to you gets on my nerves. Like she's auditioning for the role of Queen Petty."

"She always has something to prove," Jasmine said softly, her gaze lingering on Robert's retreating form. "I just wish I knew what."

William took a sip of his drink, his eyes narrowing slightly. "You're not the only one. I just hope Robert wakes up before it's too late."

Jasmine glanced at him but said nothing.

James, seated beside her, gently squeezed her hand under the table again. She turned toward him, grateful for the warmth in his touch—and even more for the lack of drama in his eyes.

"I don't think he sees her clearly," Jasmine murmured.

"Obviously," William said, voice grim.

Chapter Nine

They had just gotten back to the car when Robert closed the door a little harder than necessary. Claire glanced at him, puzzled, but said nothing—at first.

He slid into the driver's seat, hands gripping the wheel, jaw tight. The silence stretched a little too long before Claire finally broke it.

"What?" she asked, feigning innocence as she adjusted her sunglasses.

Robert exhaled, long and slow. "You need to stop."

She turned to him. "Stop what?"

"The comments. The jabs at Jasmine." He glanced over at her, his expression calm, but his tone left no room for confusion. "It's not funny. It's not subtle. And it's causing problems."

Claire blinked, then scoffed. "Oh please. She can't take a joke?"

"It's not a joke, Claire," Robert said firmly. "You talk down to her. You mock her. And William's not blind—he's pissed. Mary, too. And honestly… I don't blame them."

Claire folded her arms. "So now you're defending her?"

"I'm asking you not to make things worse," he said. "William's my friend and business partner. Has been since we were kids. And he's protective of her, especially after everything their family's been through."

Claire let out a short laugh. "Protective? He acts like she's some delicate little flower. Maybe he should be more concerned about her bouncing from guy to guy."

Robert turned to look at her fully, eyes sharp. "Enough. I mean it."

Claire stared back, eyes narrowing. "You're really this worked up over her?"

"I'm worked up because you're stirring up drama that doesn't need to be there. It's childish. And it reflects on both of us."

For a moment, neither of them spoke. The air in the car grew heavy.

Finally, Claire looked away, muttering, "Fine. I'll keep my mouth shut."

"Thank you," Robert said, though the words didn't come with relief. His hands stayed tight on the wheel, knuckles pale.

He wasn't sure if this was the end.

But he knew—without question—that he should've said something a long time ago.

Robert stared out the windshield, the weight of a dozen moments pressing down on him—Claire's sharp-edged remarks, the tension that followed them to dinners and gatherings, the way she moved people around their lives like chess pieces, calculating, strategic, never sincere.

The silence in the car thickened, taut and uncomfortable. Claire sat rigid beside him, arms crossed, her gaze fixed out the window. He didn't need to look at her to know— she was already rewriting the conversation in her head, casting herself as the misunderstood one, the maligned party. She always did.

But Robert wasn't thinking about her anymore.

He was thinking about the way James had taken Jasmine's hand.

The quiet certainty of it. The ease. The familiarity that hadn't been there just days ago.

And the way Jasmine had let him. How her fingers had curled around his like it was the most natural thing in the world. Like it meant something.

And maybe… it did.

Robert's jaw clenched as the image replayed in his mind—James pulling out her chair, the subtle lean toward her, the shared smiles. The kind of ease that couldn't be faked.

She looked happy.

And that did something to him. Something sharp. Something he didn't want to name.

Claire shifted in her seat, breaking the silence. "Are we going or what?"

Robert turned the key in the ignition. The engine rumbled to life, but his thoughts stayed locked on Jasmine.

Not just the way James had looked at her.

But the way she'd looked back.

As the conversation at the table picked up again, Jasmine reached for her glass of wine, trying to shake off the residue of Claire's barbed comment. But before she could take a sip, James leaned in just slightly, his voice low, just for her.

"You okay?"

She looked at him and gave a small, tight smile. "Yeah. Just… the usual."

He studied her face for a moment—calm on the surface, but he could see the flicker of something beneath.

"She gets under your skin."

Jasmine hesitated, then gave a small nod. "Always has. And Robert just… lets her. He's been part of our lives for over fifteen years. It's hard to pretend it doesn't matter."

James didn't rush to respond. He studied her for a moment, his expression thoughtful. Then he said quietly, "You don't owe me an explanation. I saw how she looked at you. And how she looked at him."

Jasmine let out a breath, a soft sigh laced with old disappointment. "It's always been complicated."

James reached over and gently tucked a strand of hair behind her ear, his touch light, steady. "It doesn't have to be. Not anymore."

Her gaze lifted to his—steady, searching. "You make it feel… uncomplicated."

"Good," he said, his voice sure but kind. "Because you deserve someone who sees you. Who chooses you—clearly, openly. No drama. No hesitation."

For the first time all day, Jasmine felt something shift inside her. A loosening. A quiet settling. She reached for his hand beneath the table and laced their fingers together, grateful for the calm his presence brought.

"I'm really glad you're here."

James smiled, brushing his thumb over the back of her hand. "So am I."

As they stepped out of the yacht club into the soft golden light of late afternoon, William shook James's hand with a firm grip.

"It was good to meet you," William said, tone genuine. "I might see you again."

James glanced at Jasmine, his smile easy but laced with something more. "I hope so."

Mary leaned in and kissed him lightly on the cheek. "You've passed the first test," she teased.

He chuckled. "That's a relief."

Jasmine walked with him across the quiet parking lot, heels clicking softly on the pavement. When they reached her car, she paused and leaned back against the door, her eyes lifted to meet his.

James stepped in close, resting his hands on either side of her, caging her gently without pressure. His smile curved slow and certain.

"When can I see you again?"

Jasmine's pulse fluttered at the nearness, but her voice was steady. "Soon. Maybe next weekend?"

He leaned in just enough for her breath to catch. "You sure that's not too long to wait?"

She tilted her head, smiling up at him. "What do you think?"

James's grin deepened. "I think I'm already counting the minutes."

Then, with deliberate care, he brushed his lips over hers—slow and sure. When he pulled back, her smile was softer, touched with something she hadn't felt in a long time.

Hope.

"I'll call you," she said, her voice barely above a whisper.

"I'll be waiting," he replied, pressing one last kiss to her forehead before stepping back.

And as she slid into her car and drove away, Jasmine realised she wasn't thinking about Robert anymore.

Not even a little.

The scent of fresh coffee and warm banana bread lingered in the air as Jasmine opened the front door to find Heidi already grinning, holding a bag of pastries and a bottle of sparkling water.

"I come bearing sugar and unsolicited opinions," Heidi said brightly, sweeping inside.

Jasmine laughed. "Both are welcome. Kitchen's this way."

They settled at the table, sunlight streaming in through the windows, the comfortable ease between them like a well-worn sweater.

"So?" Heidi prompted, folding her legs beneath her on the chair. "Tell me everything. And don't skimp on the good bits."

Jasmine smiled, stirring her coffee slowly. "It was easy. With James, I mean. No pressure. No guessing. Just... calm."

"Calm is sexy," Heidi said, grabbing a slice of bread. "And rare."

Jasmine nodded, her expression softening. "I know it's early, but... he might be the one who finally makes me forget Robert."

Heidi's eyebrows shot up. "Really?"

Jasmine's voice was quiet but certain. "Yeah. With James, I don't feel like I'm waiting for someone to choose me. He already has. And I didn't even have to ask."

Heidi reached across the table and squeezed her hand. "I love that for you. You've been stuck in limbo with Robert for so long, Jaz. You deserve someone who sees you now. All of you."

"I think James does."

"And Robert?" Heidi asked carefully.

Jasmine hesitated, then shrugged. "He's marrying someone who can't stand me. That says enough, doesn't it?"

"More than enough," Heidi said firmly. "Let him deal with Claire. You? You get to start fresh."

Jasmine let out a slow breath, the kind that carried a little more freedom than it had the day before. "I think I already have."

Heidi smiled, lifting her glass. "To starting fresh. And to James."

Jasmine clinked her glass against hers. "To James."

And for the first time in what felt like forever, Jasmine wasn't looking back.

They both sipped, a quiet moment settling over them—until Jasmine set her glass down with a soft clink and leaned back in her chair.

"There's something I didn't tell you," she said, eyes flicking toward the window before returning to Heidi. "Something that happened at Robert and Claire's engagement party."

Heidi's brow lifted, curiosity instantly piqued. "Oh? What?"

Jasmine hesitated, then exhaled. "Mary and I... we saw Claire. Kissing another man."

Heidi blinked. "Wait. What?"

"She was in the hallway near the bathrooms. Wrapped around him like they were alone in a hotel room, not in the middle of an engagement party." Jasmine's mouth pulled into a flat line. "It was intimate. Not a mistake. And definitely not the first time."

"Holy—Jasmine!" Heidi leaned forward. "Did Robert see it?"

"No. But we told William. And he told Robert."

Heidi stared at her. "And?"

Jasmine shook her head, a bitter smile forming. "He brushed it off. Said the guy was her agent. Claimed we must've misinterpreted what we saw."

Heidi snorted. "Please. That woman couldn't act sincere if her life depended on it."

"I don't think he really believed it," Jasmine added quietly. "But he didn't want to deal with it. Not in front of everyone. Not with her there, on his arm."

"God." Heidi leaned back in her chair. "He's not just blind. He's wilfully blind."

"I know," Jasmine said, her voice softening. "And maybe he's always been that way with her. But it's not my place to fix it. Not anymore."

Heidi studied her for a long moment. "No. It's not. And you shouldn't want to. You're not his saviour, Jasmine."

"I think part of me was waiting for Robert to come back around. To look at me the way I looked at him. But I don't want to wait for anyone anymore."

There was a beat of silence, then Heidi grinned. "Well… sounds like James showed up at just the right time."

Jasmine smiled, her heart a little steadier. "He really did."

Just then, her phone buzzed on the table. Jasmine glanced at the screen and smiled. "Speak of the devil."

She picked up, her voice instantly warm. "Hello."

"Hey," James said, his voice low and familiar.

"I thought I was meant to call you," she teased.

"I know. I got impatient."

Across the table, Heidi was already watching her like a hawk, mouthing *Is that him?* Jasmine nodded, holding up a finger—one sec.

"You busy tonight?" James asked.

"Not really," she said, then hesitated—just a second—before adding, "Do you want to come over? I was thinking I could cook," she said, trying to keep her tone light, though her heart beat faster makes me than it should have.

"You cook?" he said, surprised but pleased.

"I do," Jasmine said, grinning. "And I'm actually pretty good."

There was a pause. Then, in that dry, charming way of his, James said, "Marry me."

Jasmine burst out laughing, the kind of laugh she hadn't let out in weeks, maybe months.

Heidi leaned forward, eyebrows raised, trying to read her lips.

"Bit soon, don't you think?" Jasmine replied, still smiling.

"Not when the woman in question offers home-cooked food, makes me laugh and looks like you."

She shook her head, her heart ridiculously light. "Come over around six. I'll text you the address."

"I'll bring wine."

"Perfect."

When she ended the call, Heidi leaned in with wide eyes. "Did he just propose?"

"He was kidding," Jasmine said, still glowing.

"Maybe. But he sounds smitten."

Jasmine sipped her drink, her smile lingering. "Yeah… I think he is."

Chapter Ten

Robert sat alone in the quiet of his Vaucluse estate, a glass of untouched scotch in his hand and too many thoughts crowding his mind. The house was still—eerily so—but his head echoed with the sound of Claire's voice, that smug, dismissive tone she'd used when she'd thrown her latest barb at Jasmine.

Smirking. Superior. Cruel.

The image clung to him like smoke.

He'd told her to stop. And in return, Claire had sulked for the rest of the night, slamming doors and tossing out thinly veiled insults like confetti—pretty, but cutting.

She hadn't stayed over. He hadn't asked her to. He hadn't wanted her to.

And for the first time in a long time, he was relieved not to see her face across the pillow.

He didn't want to look at her.

Not when all he could see was Jasmine's—the way she'd sat there, holding another man's hand, silent but steady, refusing to let Claire's words break her. *Again.*

A low sigh escaped him. The scotch remained untouched.

Because he couldn't stomach the taste of it.

Not with regret already burning in his throat.

He raked a hand through his hair, jaw clenched. He didn't even realise he was dialling Jasmine's number until it was already ringing.

She picked up after two rings.

"Hello?"

There was that familiar voice. Calm, composed… warmer than he deserved.

"Jasmine."

A pause. "Robert. What can I do for you?"

He exhaled slowly, rubbed a hand down his face. "I… I called to apologise."

There was another pause. "For what?"

"For Claire."

Jasmine didn't answer right away. When she did, her voice was calm, but cool. "That's not really something you need to apologise for. Not unless you agree with what she said."

"I don't," Robert said quickly. "I didn't. I told her to stop."

Silence stretched between them.

"I just…" He exhaled. "You didn't deserve that. You never have. And I should've said something a long time ago."

"Maybe," Jasmine said softly. "But better late than never, I guess."

Robert closed his eyes, the weight of her quiet grace pressing down harder than any accusation would have.

After a beat, he added, "James seems… good for you."

"He is," Jasmine replied, her voice lighter now—but still guarded.

"I'm glad you're not with Sean anymore."

A pause. "Your fiancée thinks I move from guy to guy a little too quickly."

Robert sighed. "She never should've said that."

"No," Jasmine agreed. "But she's been making digs for months, Robert. Why apologise now?"

He hesitated. "Because yesterday… I saw it clearly for the first time. How mean it's gotten. How it affects you. And maybe because—" He stopped himself. "Maybe because I should've paid more attention a long time ago."

Jasmine didn't speak. And when she finally did, her voice was quiet.

"Well. Thanks, but you shouldn't be apologising, she should be."

"I know," Robert said, the words tasting bitter. "I just… I wanted to say it anyway."

Jasmine's voice softened, but it held no promise. "Goodnight, Robert."

"Goodnight, Jaz."

He stayed there with the phone in his hand long after she hung up, wondering when exactly he'd stopped being the man she could trust—and whether *too late* was just something he was going to have to live with.

Jasmine hung up the phone and stood still for a moment, letting the quiet settle. The apology had surprised her, but she didn't want to dwell on Robert—not tonight. James would be there soon.

She turned back to the stove, giving the pan a gentle stir. The aroma of garlic, white wine, and fresh herbs filled the kitchen as the creamy lemon butter sauce came together. She was making seared salmon on a bed of wild rice and asparagus—simple, elegant, and light. A bottle of chilled sauvignon blanc waited in the fridge.

Once everything was prepped and under control, she wiped her hands and walked to her bedroom.

She wanted to look nice. Not like she was trying too hard—but like she cared.

After a moment of consideration, she pulled out a soft navy wrap dress. It hugged her waist just enough, with a V neckline that was flattering but not revealing. The hem brushed just above her knee. She paired it with delicate gold hoops and nude heels, her curls falling in loose waves around her shoulders.

She checked her reflection. Sophisticated. Effortless. Just right.

The knock at the door came as she was putting on a hint of gloss. Her heart did a tiny skip.

She walked to the door and opened it.

James stood there, casual but handsome in dark jeans and a button-down shirt with the sleeves rolled up. He held a bottle of wine in one hand and wore that same easy smile that made her feel… seen.

"Wow," he said softly, giving her a once-over. "You look incredible."

Jasmine smiled, stepping aside to let him in. "Dinner's almost ready."

"Smells amazing," he said, handing her the wine. "But I might be distracted."

She arched a brow. "By what?"

"You," he said simply.

And just like that, the rest of the day faded behind her.

James followed Jasmine into the kitchen, the soft lighting casting a golden glow across the benchtops. A low instrumental playlist played in the background, subtle and smooth.

"Okay," she said, setting the wine on the counter. "Don't judge me—I'm a better cook than I am a sommelier."

James leaned against the counter, watching her with open admiration. "If it tastes half as good as it smells, you could serve it with water, and I'd still be impressed."

She laughed, opening the fridge to retrieve the wine. "White, chilled. Should go nicely with the salmon."

"Perfect," he said, taking the bottle and opening it for her.

A few minutes later, they were seated at the small dining table she'd set with casual elegance—linen napkins, tall candles, nothing fussy. Jasmine plated the food: pan-seared salmon with lemon butter sauce, roasted asparagus, and wild rice pilaf.

James took a bite and closed his eyes for a second, dramatically. "Okay… now I'm really in trouble."

She smirked. "Why?"

"Because now I want to see what you cook for the next date."

She sipped her wine, her smile widening. "You're assuming you're getting one."

He grinned, unbothered. "Confident, remember?"

They ate slowly, the conversation flowing as easily as the wine. They talked about their families—his mother's overenthusiastic matchmaking, her close bond with Mary and William, and the trials of managing demanding clients.

"Honestly," James said, leaning back slightly, "I wasn't expecting this tonight."

"This?" Jasmine asked.

"This… ease. It's been a long time since I've sat across from someone and felt like I could breathe."

Her expression softened. "Yeah… I know what you mean."

There was a pause, but it wasn't awkward. It felt like the quiet between beats of a song—natural, essential.

He reached across the table, brushing his fingertips lightly over hers. "You really are something, Jasmine Whitaker."

She felt the words settle deep in her chest.

"So are you, James Fletcher."

After dinner, James insisted on helping clear the table while Jasmine stacked the dishwasher.

"You really don't have to," she said, reaching for the wineglasses.

"I want to," he replied, brushing his hand lightly against hers as he took one from her grasp. "Besides, I like seeing you like this."

She raised a brow. "Like what?"

He gave her a crooked smile. "At home. Relaxed. Not in work mode. Still gorgeous, just… softer."

Her cheeks flushed slightly, but she didn't look away. "Flattery and dish-duty. Dangerous combination."

Once the last plate was in and the dishwasher quietly hummed to life, she wiped her hands and turned toward him. "Couch?"

"Lead the way," he said.

She dimmed the overhead lights as they moved into the living room; the room lit mostly by the soft glow of a side lamp and the flickering candle she'd forgotten to blow out on the coffee table.

Jasmine tucked her legs up under her as she sank into the plush cushions. James sat beside her—close but not crowding her—his body angled toward hers, elbow resting casually on the back of the couch.

"Tell me something you've never told anyone on a date," she said, turning to face him.

He smirked. "That's bold."

"I had wine," she said with a shrug. "I'm brave."

James leaned back, considering. Then: "Okay. I don't like corporate law."

Jasmine blinked. "Really?"

"I'm good at it. It pays well. But… I kind of wish I'd done something else."

"Like what?"

He smiled, looking a little sheepish. "Don't laugh."

"I won't."

"Landscape architecture. I used to sketch gardens as a kid. Still do, sometimes."

She blinked, touched. "That's… not what I expected. But I love that."

His expression softened. "Your turn."

She hesitated, then said, "I used to be in love with someone who didn't love me back. For a long time."

His face sobered, the playful edge fading. "That's heavy."

"It was. I thought I was over it. But lately I've started to believe I might actually be."

He didn't speak right away. Just reached out and brushed a strand of hair behind her ear, his thumb grazing her cheek as it lingered.

"I don't know what he couldn't see," James said quietly, "but I'm glad you're starting to leave that behind. Because you… you deserve to be really seen."

Her breath caught.

And then, slowly, deliberately, he leaned in.

Jasmine met him halfway.

The kiss was soft at first, unhurried. A quiet question. When she didn't pull away, his hand slid to her waist, anchoring her as the kiss deepened just slightly—still tender, but edged with the kind of promise that made her heart stutter.

When they parted, she rested her forehead gently against his.

"Okay," she whispered, smiling against his lips. "That other date might actually happen."

James chuckled low. "You think?"

"I do," she said, curling in closer, her voice warm. "But you still have to earn it."

He grinned. "Challenge accepted."

They stayed curled up on the couch, the soft hum of the dishwasher in the background and the flicker of candlelight casting a golden glow across the room.

James's thumb traced lazy circles over Jasmine's hand, their fingers still loosely laced.

"So," he said, breaking the comfortable silence, "on a scale of one to ten, how would you rate my date performance?"

She leaned her head back against the couch and gave a thoughtful hum. "Hmm… let's see. You were on time, charming, helped with dishes, and you didn't try to mansplain anything."

"Ouch," he said with mock offense. "That last one feels like a low bar."

"It is. But you'd be surprised how many still trip over it."

James chuckled, his eyes soft as he studied her. "Okay, fair. But you didn't answer. What's the number?"

Jasmine pretended to weigh it a moment longer. "Eight and a half."

"Eight and a half?" He pulled back, hand to his chest. "Tough crowd."

"Well," she said, turning toward him, eyes sparkling, "you could nudge it higher if you kiss me again."

He didn't need telling twice.

He leaned in, brushing his lips against hers—slow and deliberate this time, a kiss that lingered, unhurried and full of promise. It left them both a little breathless when they finally pulled away.

"That's at least a nine point five," she whispered.

He smiled against her cheek. "I'll take it."

They sat like that for a while, tangled in each other, the world outside her apartment forgotten. No rush. No expectations. Just a growing comfort that felt like it had roots—like it might actually go somewhere.

Eventually, James glanced at the clock and sighed. "I should go. I don't want to, but…"

Jasmine nodded, her voice soft. "I know."

He stood, and she walked him to the door, his hand lingering at the small of her back.

At the threshold, he kissed her again, one last time—sweet, a little slower, and full of affection. When he pulled back, he looked at her with something close to awe.

"Thank you for tonight," he said.

"Thank you for calling," she replied, leaning lightly against the doorframe.

He backed away down the hall with a reluctant grin. "Another date, soon."

"Earn that extra half point," she teased.

He winked. "Game on, Whitaker."

And with that, he was gone—leaving Jasmine standing there, heart a little lighter, a smile tugging at her lips.

Chapter Eleven

After hanging up the phone with Jasmine, Robert sat in silence, the stillness of his home pressing in like a weight.

He should've felt better for calling her—for apologising. But instead, he felt more unsettled than ever.

Two weeks. He had only been engaged for two weeks, and already, doubt was seeping in like water through hairline cracks in concrete—slow, but inevitable.

He ran a hand through his hair and let out a slow breath.

Claire.

He needed to see her. Not to fight, not to argue—but to look her in the eye and ask himself the question he hadn't dared to voice aloud:

Is this the woman I'm supposed to spend the rest of my life with?

Lately, Claire had been all edges and vanity, her sweetness fading into something brittle and sharp. And the way she spoke to Jasmine—the smirking, the jabs, the territorial little comments—had unsettled something deep in him. A part of him that used to defend Jasmine instinctively… now stayed quiet. And that silence was starting to feel like a betrayal.

Without overthinking it, Robert grabbed his jacket and helmet and walked into the garage.

His motorbike sat under a sheet like a memory he'd tried to forget. It hadn't seen the road in months. Maybe longer. But tonight, he needed the ride. The speed. The noise. Something to cut through the static in his head.

He pulled the cover off and stared at the machine for a moment. Then he swung a leg over, turned the key, and let the engine roar to life.

The cold air slapped against his face as he weaved through the streets of Sydney, the familiar weight of the bike beneath him grounding him in a way nothing else had in weeks. He wasn't sure what he'd say when he saw Claire. But he knew he needed to see her. To look at her and know—*really know*—if marrying her was the right thing.

Or if it was just the easy thing.

Twenty minutes later, he pulled up outside her apartment building. The lights were on. Her car was parked in the carpark. She was home.

Robert took off his helmet, ran a hand through his hair, and exhaled.

Time to stop pretending he didn't already know the answer.

Robert's boots echoed softly against the polished floor as he approached Claire's apartment, helmet still in hand. The hallway was quiet, lined with warm light and the faint hum of the city beyond the windows.

He was maybe ten paces away when her door opened.

Claire stepped out, laughing—light and polished, the sound familiar. Following her was Brian.

Robert slowed, confusion threading through him. Brian—the agent. The man William had pointed out at the party. The one Claire swore was just a friend, just business.

Robert's stomach dropped—something in Brian's posture felt too familiar. Too easy.

Then Brian reached for her.

With casual familiarity, he slid an arm around her waist, pulled her close, and kissed her.

Not on the cheek.

Not a polite goodnight.

It was intimate. Familiar. Their bodies pressed together like it wasn't the first time.

Claire responded with a slow, lingering smile, her hand curling against Brian's chest. "Text me when you get home," she murmured, her voice unmistakably flirtatious.

Brian grinned. "I always do."

Neither of them had seen Robert yet. He stood there frozen, hidden just out of their line of sight; his breath caught in his throat.

For a second, all he could hear was the pounding in his ears.

And then Claire turned slightly—laughing again as she stepped back inside—and caught sight of him.

Her face froze. Just for a moment.

Then came the practiced smile. "Robert. I didn't know you were coming over."

Brian stiffened beside her.

Robert didn't move. Didn't blink. He just stared at her, stunned into silence. All the things he came here to say vanished like smoke.

Claire tilted her head, too casual. "Is everything alright?"

Robert's voice came low and deliberate, a razor beneath velvet. "I was about to ask you the same thing."

Her smile wavered, then reappeared—tight and brittle. "Everything is fine."

He took a step closer; eyes locked on hers. "So how long has this been going on?"

Her expression flickered. "What are you talking about?"

He didn't answer right away. Just looked past her to the door she'd just stepped out of. Then to Brian, who stood frozen beside her, suddenly less confident than he'd been moments ago.

"Don't insult my intelligence, Claire."

Claire's voice lost its edge of composure. "Robert, you're overreacting. Brian and I— he was just saying goodnight."

"Like that?" Robert asked, his tone sharp now. "Because it didn't look like a goodnight. It looked like a relationship. Or at the very least, a habit."

Brian cleared his throat, clearly uncomfortable. "Maybe I should go—"

"Good idea," Robert said, never taking his eyes off Claire.

Brian hesitated, then walked past them, mumbling something neither of them caught.

Once they were alone, Robert exhaled slowly, his jaw tight. "I came here because I thought maybe I was wrong. About you. About everything. I wanted to look you in the eye and remind myself why I asked you to marry me."

Claire didn't speak.

"And now?" she finally asked, her voice barely above a whisper.

Robert's answer came without hesitation.

"Now I wish I hadn't."

Claire stepped back into her apartment, leaving the door open as if daring Robert to follow. He did—slowly, silently—his expression unreadable.

She turned to face him, arms folded. "You didn't make a mistake, Robert."

He arched a brow. "Didn't I?"

"You're angry. I get it," she said, voice softening, trying to find the register she knew usually worked on him. "But you saw one moment. You don't know the context."

"I saw you kissing another man."

"Brian and I go way back. It wasn't what it looked like."

"That's the oldest line in the book, Claire."

She stepped closer. "I didn't cheat on you."

"Then what would you call it?"

Claire's jaw flexed. "A lapse in judgment. A mistake. One kiss."

"One kiss," he repeated, the words heavy between them, a quiet storm brewing. "Two weeks after I put a ring on your finger."

Claire's hand found its way to his chest, soft but insistent, as if trying to reestablish some kind of closeness, some control. "You're the one I want, Robert. That hasn't changed."

Robert's eyes narrowed slightly, his anger simmering beneath the calm surface. "So, Jasmine and Mary didn't see you kissing Brian in the hallway at our engagement party?"

The blood drained from Claire's face, her breath faltering for a second. She quickly recovered, plastering a smile that didn't reach her eyes. "No, of course not."

A sharp exhale escaped Robert, a bitter laugh threading through his words. "Jasmine wouldn't lie."

Claire's expression shifted, a flicker of something—anger, frustration, maybe guilt—shifting behind her carefully constructed facade. "Really? *Her* again?"

"Don't try to make this about her," Robert snapped, his voice low but filled with the weight of his growing doubt. "This is about you. About us."

Her hand slid away from his chest, and for the first time, Robert noticed how she seemed to retreat into herself, trying to regain composure. She smirked, that familiar, practiced charm creeping back into her voice. "I don't know what Jasmine thinks she saw, but it's not what you think. We've been through this before, Robert. Don't let her make you second guess everything."

But Robert's expression hardened. "It's not just her, Claire. It's everything. I've been looking the other way for too long. But I'm starting to see things clearly."

She took a step forward, her voice growing tight, desperate. "Robert don't do this. We've got something good here. Don't throw it all away because of one mistake."

"I don't know if I can keep ignoring the mistakes, Claire," Robert said quietly, the words cutting through the air with finality. "Not anymore."

Claire's voice tightened, sharp with disbelief. "So what? You're just going to walk away?"

Robert didn't answer right away. His silence stretched between them, heavy and undeniable. Then, finally—quietly, but with a certainty that landed like a blow—he said, "Yes."

Claire blinked, stunned. Then her composure cracked.

"Unbelievable," she hissed, stepping back as anger surged into the space where charm had just stood. "All this time, I've put up with your moods, your silences, your precious friendship with that woman, and now she gets to be the reason you throw everything away?"

Robert's jaw clenched, but he said nothing.

Claire's voice rose, brittle and cutting. "You think she's so innocent? Jasmine Whitaker, little miss perfect with her quiet smile and her pathetic loyalty—always lingering, always waiting for you like some lovesick schoolgirl. Do you really think she's better for you? She's not. She's weak. She hides behind her tragic eyes and lets everyone fight her battles."

"Enough," Robert said, his voice low but firm, the tension in his frame barely held in check. "Don't talk about her like that."

Claire scoffed, laughing without humour. "Why not? Because you're in love with her? Because she's your shining alternative to a life that's actually real?"

"I said enough," Robert snapped, his voice sharp and final, slicing through the air between them. The edge in his tone halted Claire mid-breath.

"You don't get to blame Jasmine for this," he went on, quieter now, but no less firm. "You're the one who cheated. You made that choice. Not her."

Claire stared at him, her eyes wide, the colour draining from her face. Her mouth opened slightly, but no words came. For once, the performance was gone—no quick retort, no twist of charm. Just silence.

Robert exhaled slowly, the weight of disappointment settling deeper in his chest. Then, without another word, he turned and walked away.

He didn't look back. Not once.

And behind him, Claire stood frozen in the hallway, watching the man she was supposed to marry disappear down the corridor—taking with him the last chance she'd already traded away—and hadn't even noticed.

Robert left Claire's apartment with a strange, unexpected lightness in his chest—like someone had finally loosened the knot that had been tightening for weeks. For months, if he was honest. He took the stairs two at a time, the cold evening air hitting his face as he stepped outside.

The familiar shape of his motorbike waited at the curb, and as he swung his leg over it, he felt something like peace settle into his bones. Maybe not clarity, not yet—but something close. He pulled on his helmet, started the engine, and let the powerful rumble beneath him drown out the last of Claire's voice echoing in his head.

The streets were quiet as he rode, the sky fading into deep velvet blue above the city skyline. Wind rushed past his face, clearing out the fog in his thoughts. He didn't know exactly what came next—but for the first time in a long time, he wanted it to be something different.

He was halfway through an intersection in Surry Hills, the light green, the road ahead clear—

When a truck came barrelling through the red light from the cross street.

Robert barely registered the blur of headlights, the screech of tyres. There was a flash of metal, the sound of crumpling steel, and then everything fractured into a deafening, sickening silence.

The bike spun out from beneath him, skidding across the asphalt like a ragdoll, sparks flying. Robert was thrown, the world spinning violently before the pavement met him with a brutal, shuddering force.

And then—

Stillness.

The truck had stopped. People began to scream.

But Robert lay motionless on the road, limbs twisted, helmet cracked, the serenity he'd felt moments earlier shattered beneath blood and glass and the unrelenting weight of what had just happened.

Chapter Twelve

Mary and William were in bed, the room dim and quiet, when the phone rang—sharp and sudden.

Mary frowned, sleep still clinging to her voice. "Who would be calling at this hour?"

William grabbed the phone, already uneasy.

"Hello?"

"William."

It was Terry Steele—Robert's father—and his voice was raw, barely holding together.

"Terry?" William sat up straighter, instantly alert. "What's going on?"

"It's Robert," Terry said, breath hitching. "He's been in an accident."

William's heart dropped. "What kind of accident?"

"Motorbike. A truck ran a red light… they said he was thrown… He's in surgery at St. Vincent's. They don't know—" Terry's voice cracked. "They don't know if he'll make it."

Mary had already sat up, her eyes wide and fearful. "What is it?" she whispered.

"It's Robert," William said quietly, gripping the phone. "Bad crash. He's in surgery now."

Mary's hand flew to her mouth, but she pulled herself together quickly. "We need to go."

William nodded, already moving to get dressed.

Then Mary said, "You have to call Jasmine. She'd want to know."

William hesitated, halfway into his shirt.

"She has a right to know, Will," Mary insisted. "She might want to be there. She should be there."

He reached for his phone without another word and found Jasmine's number. His fingers hovered for a second before pressing the call button.

The line rang twice before she answered, voice soft and slightly sleepy. "William?"

He didn't ease into it. "Jasmine… it's Robert. He's been in a motorcycle accident. It's bad."

There was silence on the other end, then a breath. "What hospital?"

"St. Vincent's. He's in surgery now."

"I'll be there," she said, already moving.

And with that, the night lost its calm completely.

Jasmine got out of bed the moment she hung up, her pulse thudded in her ears. Robert. An accident. Surgery. Please, God—let him be okay.

She dressed quickly—jeans, a soft sweater, and sneakers—barely aware of what she was pulling on. Her hands trembled as she grabbed her bag and keys, locking the door behind her in a daze.

The drive to St. Vincent's was a blur. She barely remembered the roads, only the weight in her chest that grew heavier with each passing second.

When she arrived at the hospital, the lights felt too bright, the air too sterile. She hurried to the front desk. "Robert Steele," she said quickly. "Motorcycle accident."

The nurse gave a brief nod. "Surgical waiting room. Down the hall, turn right."

Jasmine followed the directions, heart pounding. As she rounded the corner, she saw William and Mary seated together, pale and quiet. Terry Steele stood stiffly by the window, arms folded, jaw clenched.

And beside him—Kelly Steele. Robert's mother. Her face was drawn, her eyes red-rimmed, hands twisting a tissue between her fingers.

Kelly looked up and let out a quiet breath when she saw Jasmine. "Oh, Jasmine…"

Jasmine didn't hesitate. She crossed the room and wrapped her arms around Kelly, holding her tightly. "He's strong," Jasmine whispered, her own voice thick with emotion. "He's going to get through this."

Kelly clung to her, pressing her forehead to Jasmine's shoulder. "My boy…" she murmured. "My beautiful boy…"

Mary rose and placed a gentle hand on Jasmine's back. William gave her a quiet nod of gratitude.

Jasmine kept holding Kelly, her own fear pushed down beneath the need to be strong— for her, for them. For Robert.

Still holding Kelly, Jasmine looked over her shoulder at William. Her voice was quiet but edged with disbelief. "Has anyone called Claire?"

William nodded, his expression unreadable. "Yeah. I did. Just after I called you."

Jasmine's brow furrowed. "That was nearly an hour ago. Where is she?"

"I don't know," he said simply, his voice low. "She didn't say much."

Jasmine glanced at the clock on the waiting room wall. An hour. An entire hour.

Kelly let out a shaky breath and pulled back slightly, offering Jasmine a grateful look. Jasmine gave her a gentle squeeze, but her mind was spinning.

Claire was his fiancée. She should've been here by now. Should've walked in before Jasmine ever did.

Instead, it was Jasmine sitting beside his mother, holding her, praying for him.

And Claire… Claire was nowhere.

It was another agonising hour before the doctor finally appeared, his scrubs wrinkled and his expression carefully neutral.

Everyone stood at once—Kelly clutching Jasmine's hand, William moving to stand beside them.

"I'm Dr. Sandhu," the man said gently. "Robert made it through surgery. He's stable for now."

A collective breath was released, but it was short-lived. The doctor's pause stretched just long enough to signal that good news was only part of the story.

"He didn't sustain any head trauma," Dr. Sandhu continued, "and there were no fractures to his arms or legs. But the impact caused a burst fracture in his lower spine. L3 and L4."

Kelly blinked, her face paling. "His spine?"

The doctor nodded slowly. "There was significant swelling, and some damage to the spinal cord. We've done everything we can surgically to stabilise it, but… we won't know the full extent of the damage until the swelling subsides."

William stepped forward, his voice hoarse. "Are you saying he might not walk again?"

"There's a chance," Dr. Sandhu said, not sugarcoating it. "We're hopeful, but realistic. The next seventy-two hours are critical."

Kelly let out a quiet sob. Jasmine tightened her grip on her hand and pulled her into her arms again.

"What happens now?" William asked, steadying himself.

"He'll be in recovery for a while. Once we move him to ICU, you'll be able to see him, but just briefly. He'll be heavily sedated."

The doctor offered a sympathetic look before he turned to leave. "A nurse will come get you as soon as he's settled."

As he disappeared down the corridor, silence fell over them again. Heavy. Raw.

And Jasmine, still holding Kelly, felt the weight of the words press deep into her chest. *He might not walk again.*

Everything had changed in an instant.

Finally, after what felt like an eternity, a nurse approached them. "He's in Recovery Room Two," she said gently. "He's stable. You can go in. He should start to wake up soon."

The nurse led them down the hall in a quiet group—Kelly and Terry first, followed closely by Jasmine, Mary, and William. The room was softly lit, the steady rhythm of monitors breaking the hush.

Robert lay motionless in the bed, his body supported by braces and padding, an IV line threading from his arm. His face was pale and bruised, his normally strong frame looking far too still beneath the hospital blankets.

Kelly moved to one side of the bed, Terry to the other. They each took one of their son's hands, their expressions tight with worry and grief.

Jasmine stood near the foot of the bed beside Mary, William just behind her. She tried to steady her breathing; eyes fixed on the rise and fall of Robert's chest.

The silence stretched, broken only by the steady beeping of the monitor.

Then—his fingers twitched.

Kelly gasped softly. Terry leaned in, eyes locked on his son. Slowly, Robert's eyelids fluttered, his face tightening with effort.

His lips moved—barely.

Jasmine held her breath.

Then came a sound—faint, hoarse, almost lost beneath the machines.

"…Jasmine."

Her breath hitched. For a second, she couldn't move.

Kelly looked up sharply, then silently stepped aside, giving her space.

Jasmine moved closer, heart pounding, every nerve on edge. She reached for his hand, her voice low and trembling.

"I'm here."

Robert's eyes struggled to focus, flickering toward the sound. "You're... here."

Tears welled in her eyes as she reached out and gently touched his hand. "I'm here. We all are."

Mary gave a soft exhale beside her, and William rested a hand lightly on her back.

But Robert's gaze—weak as it was—remained on Jasmine.

Robert's eyes fluttered shut again, his strength fading fast. But even as sleep reclaimed him, his lips moved, the words slipping out in a whisper:

"I'm glad you're here... I'm sorry... Jasmine."

Then he stilled, his breathing deepening into the quiet rhythm of sleep.

Jasmine froze, her hand still resting on his. Her throat tightened at the sound of her name on his lips—spoken not in pain, not in confusion, but with intent. Like it mattered.

The nurse stepped in quietly, her voice low but firm. "He needs rest now. I'm afraid we'll have to ask you all to step out for a while."

Terry gave Kelly a look, and she nodded. "We'll stay just a little longer."

Mary reached for Jasmine's hand as they followed the nurse out into the hallway. William waited until they were alone before he turned to her.

His voice wasn't accusing—just curious. "Why didn't he ask for Claire?"

Jasmine looked down at her hands, still tingling from where she'd touched his.

William tilted his head slightly. "Instead, he asked for you."

Jasmine let out a breath, quiet and unsure. "I don't know."

But she did. And so did William. Neither of them said it aloud.

Whatever had broken between Robert and Claire... whatever had lived quietly between him and Jasmine... it was rising to the surface now, whether they were ready for it or not.

They waited quietly in the corridor until Terry and Kelly finally emerged, the weight of exhaustion written across their faces. Kelly leaned into Terry's side, her arm looped through his, but both of them managed small, weary smiles.

"Thank you all for coming," Terry said, his voice rough with emotion. "It meant a lot to him. And to us."

Jasmine stepped forward and hugged him tightly. Terry held her for a moment longer than expected, then kissed her gently on the cheek.

Then Kelly opened her arms, and Jasmine moved into them. The older woman's embrace was warm, familiar, and filled with a kind of unspoken knowing.

"I always knew it was you," Kelly murmured, so soft that only Jasmine could hear.

Jasmine pulled back just slightly, her breath catching. Their eyes met—Kelly's kind and steady, Jasmine's wide and uncertain—and in that moment, Jasmine understood exactly what she meant.

She didn't respond. She didn't have to.

Kelly simply gave her hand a small squeeze before letting go, then turned with Terry and headed down the hallway.

Jasmine stood there in silence, the echo of Kelly's words lingering in her chest. Mary touched her arm gently. "Come on," she said. "We better get home and get some sleep."

But even as they walked towards the carpark, Jasmine knew—nothing about this felt like the end.

It felt like the beginning.

It was the early hours of Monday morning by the time Jasmine finally made it home. The city outside was quiet, hushed in that way it only ever was just before dawn.

She moved through her apartment like a ghost—dropping her bag by the door, slipping off her shoes, barely changing before collapsing into bed. The adrenaline had long worn off, leaving nothing but a bone-deep exhaustion in its place.

As she lay there, eyes fluttering closed, the day washed over her in waves—Robert's accident, the waiting, the cold sterility of the hospital… and then, that moment.

His voice, barely audible, rough and broken.

'I'm glad you're here… I'm sorry… Jasmine.'

Her name, spoken like something he needed.

And just like that, she fell asleep—finally, completely—still wrapped in the sound of it.

Chapter Thirteen

The week blurred into a haze of client sessions, endless phone calls, and late afternoon hospital visits.

Jasmine threw herself into work during the day, determined to keep everything running smoothly. Her clients still needed her; deadlines didn't stop just because her world had. No matter how busy the day, the moment the clock struck five, she packed up without hesitation and headed straight for St. Vincent's.

She hadn't missed a single day.

She couldn't—not with Robert lying in that hospital bed, silent and unmoving, surrounded by machines that beeped and whirred with mechanical indifference.

He hadn't woken again since that first night. His eyes had fluttered open only briefly—just long enough to say her name, to whisper an apology—before slipping back into unconsciousness. The doctors assured them it was normal. His body needed time. Rest. Healing.

But Jasmine didn't care about medical timelines.

She just wanted him to open his eyes and know she was there.

Every evening, she took the same seat beside his bed. Sometimes with Terry and Kelly, sometimes alone. She held his hand, spoke softly, told him about her day. She read from whatever novel she had in her bag. Talked about a new client who forgot his own email address. The time she argued—loudly and irrationally—with the coffee machine in the waiting room and lost.

He didn't respond. But she kept talking anyway.

On Thursday night, just as she was slipping her coat on to leave, Kelly stopped her in the corridor. The older woman looked exhausted—her hair slightly mussed, her eyes rimmed with fatigue—but her voice was steady.

"He keeps asking for you," she said quietly. "When he stirs when the sedation lightens. It's always your name. Jasmine."

Jasmine's breath caught. "Are you sure?"

Terry nodded from where he stood nearby, arms folded across his chest. "Every time. You're the one he wants close. We don't know why—not yet—but we're grateful you've been here."

The words hit Jasmine square in the chest, tenderness blooming beneath the ache she'd been holding back all week. She tried to speak, but no words came. Just a tight nod. A small, tearful smile. And then she turned, walking quickly down the corridor before the tears spilled over.

She didn't stop until she was alone in the car, hands gripping the wheel, her heart twisting with something she wasn't ready to name.

By Friday night, she was running on fumes.

Traffic crawled along Campbell Parade as she made her way back to her townhouse in Bondi, the early evening light casting a golden hue over the sea. Usually, she found comfort in the view. Not tonight.

She unlocked the front door, kicked off her shoes, and dropped her bag with a weary sigh. The silence inside her townhouse wrapped around her like a heavy blanket—familiar, but uninviting.

She hadn't eaten. She hadn't even thought about dinner.

Her keys clinked on the entry table as she wandered toward the kitchen, not really sure what she was looking for—food, maybe. Or just something to ground her.

Then her phone buzzed.

She glanced at the screen.

James.

For a second, she considered ignoring it—letting it roll to voicemail. But something made her thumb across the screen and lift the phone to her ear.

"Hey," she said quietly.

"Hi." His voice was warm, familiar, a balm she didn't realise she needed. "I know it's late, but… when I picked up Mum from your clinic on Wednesday, you didn't look okay. And you definitely didn't sound it."

She paused, then walked back to the living room and sank down onto the armrest of the couch. "It's just been a week. A long one."

"I'd love to see you," he said gently. "If that's okay."

She closed her eyes for a moment, then nodded, even though he couldn't see her. "Yeah. I could do with the company."

"I'll be there in fifteen."

She was still standing in the middle of the living room, mentally debating whether she had the energy to tidy up, when the doorbell rang.

When she opened it, James stood there—takeaway bag in one hand, a bouquet of pale pink lilies in the other. He smiled, not too broadly, just enough to soften the ache that had been pressing at the edges of her chest all day.

"I thought you could use a pick-me-up," he said simply, offering both gifts.

Jasmine let out a breath that felt like it had been sitting in her lungs for hours. She stepped aside to let him in. "You're a good man, James Fletcher."

He shot her a playful look as he walked past. "I've been trying to tell people that for years. Nice to finally get some recognition."

She managed a faint smile as he placed the lilies in a glass on the kitchen counter, then began unpacking Thai takeaway onto the coffee table like he belonged there.

"Chicken satay, pad see ew, and extra spring rolls," he said, lifting the lids. "Don't say I don't know you."

The familiar scent of peanut sauce and soy filled the room, comforting and nostalgic.

They settled onto the couch, shoulder to shoulder. Jasmine took a bite, chewing slowly, then set her fork down.

"There's something I should tell you," she said.

James looked over, attentive. "Okay."

"It's Robert," she said quietly. "You met him at the yacht club last weekend."

He nodded, still listening.

"He was in an accident. Saturday night. A truck ran a red light… hit him while he was on his motorbike."

James's expression tightened, the lightness in his eyes dimming. "Jesus. Is he—?"

"He's alive," Jasmine said quickly. "But… he's in hospital. Sedated. They had to operate. His spine…" She trailed off, trying to steady her voice. "They don't know if he'll walk again."

James sat back slightly, exhaling. "God. Jaz… I'm so sorry."

She nodded, swallowing hard. "I've been going to the hospital every night. His parents are there too. He looks… so fragile. It doesn't feel real."

James didn't speak right away. Instead, he reached across and took her hand, threading his fingers through hers.

"You're doing what you need to do," he said gently. "And I get it. Whatever you need from me—patience, distance, company—I'm here."

She blinked fast, the sudden sting of tears catching her off guard. "Thank you. He's part of my life, James. Always has been. I just… I hate seeing him like that."

He nodded and gave her hand a reassuring squeeze before leaning in to kiss her temple. "Then we'll deal with it. Together."

A shaky smile tugged at her lips. "You're really good at this, you know."

"I'm also good at getting you to finish your spring rolls," he added, nudging the container toward her. "Don't make me break out dessert bribery."

She laughed softly and picked up her fork again.

And for the first time all week, the weight in the room lifted—just enough to breathe.

They ate quietly, the conversation drifting to lighter topics—her new intern, a ridiculous client request, a story James told about his first attempt at baking bread during lockdown that ended in smoke and a fire alarm. Slowly, the tension in her shoulders began to ease.

After dinner, Jasmine pulled a throw blanket from the couch and turned on a movie—something easy, with low stakes and warm lighting. James didn't argue. He just settled in beside her, stretching his legs out and resting one arm along the back of the couch.

Jasmine curled up next to him, the comforting scent of him—clean soap, subtle cologne, something warm and familiar—easing into her senses. The steady hum of the TV filled the space, but her mind kept drifting.

Somewhere between the second and third scene, she shifted, resting her head on James's thigh, half curled beneath the blanket. "I just need a minute," she murmured.

James didn't move. He only glanced down at her and gave a small nod. "Take all the minutes you need."

She didn't reply.

Her breathing slowed. The exhaustion she'd been holding off for days—propped up by sheer will and coffee—finally caught up with her. Within minutes, she was asleep.

James stayed still, careful not to shift too much beneath her. One of his hands settled in her hair, fingers gently brushing through the strands. The motion was instinctive, soothing—something he didn't think about, just did.

He watched her sleep, taking in the faint crease between her brows that was finally beginning to smooth out. Even now, she looked like she was still fighting something—some worry, some ghost of a memory. He wished he could take it from her, even just for tonight.

Outside, Bondi was quiet. A late breeze stirred the trees. In the soft glow of the TV, James let his fingers drift through her hair again and leaned back, content to stay right where he was.

For the first time since she'd told him about Robert, James let himself hope that maybe—there was space for him in whatever storm her heart was weathering.

And if not now, then... perhaps soon.

The movie had long since ended, the screen gone dark. But James was still there, one hand gently brushing through Jasmine's hair, his touch light and steady.

She stirred, murmured something under her breath, then slowly sat up, blinking groggily. Her eyes landed on him and widened in embarrassment.

"Oh no... I'm so sorry, James."

He smiled, brushing a strand of hair from her cheek. "It's fine. You're obviously exhausted."

Jasmine hesitated, then moved closer—settling herself in his lap, wrapping her arms around his neck. "How did I get so lucky?"

His hands found her waist instinctively, holding her with quiet ease. "I think I'm the lucky one."

She let out a soft laugh and tucked her head into the curve of his shoulder. "Oh yeah? So lucky I fall asleep on you and drool on your shirt?"

He looked down at his shirt, then grinned. "No visible evidence. I'll count that as a win."

She chuckled, and for a moment, the heaviness of the week lifted. Wrapped in his arms, Jasmine didn't feel quite so overwhelmed. For tonight, she let herself rest there—just for a little while longer.

Jasmine pulled back just enough to meet his eyes. Her expression was soft, unreadable at first, then settled into something tender.

"Thanks for being here," she said quietly, the words sitting between them like a truth long overdue.

Then she leaned in and kissed him.

It wasn't rushed or uncertain—it was gentle, steady, a thank you and a maybe all at once.

James responded without hesitation. His arms wrapped around her, pulling her in, anchoring her against him as he kissed her back. It wasn't urgent, but there was depth in it—a quiet understanding that whatever this was between them, it mattered.

When they finally pulled apart, Jasmine rested her forehead against his.

"Sorry," she whispered. "I didn't mean to…"

James smiled, his voice low and reassuring. "You don't have to apologise."

And in the quiet that followed, neither of them moved to let go.

"Can I see you tomorrow?" James asked softly, his hand still resting at the small of her back.

Jasmine giggled, her forehead still against his. "It is tomorrow."

He smiled, eyes crinkling. "Then can I see you later today?"

She laughed again, the sound lighter than it had been in days. "Yes," she said, brushing her nose against his. "You can see me later today."

"Good," he murmured, pressing a kiss to her cheek. "Because I'm not quite ready to say goodnight."

He kissed her again—soft, lingering. Then once more, and again, their lips brushing with a slow, growing heat. Jasmine's fingers curled at the back of his neck, holding him close as his hand slipped to her waist, anchoring her to him.

James groaned, pulling back just enough to rest his forehead against hers. "I better go," he said huskily, "before I beg you to let me stay."

Jasmine smiled, her breath warm against his lips. "And what if I did?" she teased.

He chuckled, brushing her hair back from her face. "Then I'd stay. And I'm not sure either of us is ready for that tonight."

She nodded, and this time the kiss was brief, tender—like a promise. Then she rose, walking him to the door with fingers still loosely tangled in his.

"I'll see you later," he said, pausing on the step.

"I'll be looking forward to it," she whispered.

And she meant it.

He gave her one last look—one that lingered—before disappearing down the path. Jasmine closed the door slowly, her heart still beating in his rhythm.

Chapter Fourteen

Jasmine woke early, long before her alarm. The pale light of dawn spilled through the blinds, casting soft shadows across her bedroom. For a moment, she lay still, listening to the quiet hum of Bondi waking outside her window. Then she swung her legs out of bed and laced up her runners.

The run helped. The salty air, the rhythmic pounding of her feet on the pavement, the crashing of waves in the distance—it was the only thing that had kept her grounded this week. She didn't push herself hard. Just enough to feel her lungs stretch and her mind settle.

By seven-thirty, she was showered, dressed, and in her car, a travel mug of coffee balanced between her knees as she headed toward St. Vincent's. Her stomach was a tight knot of anticipation, as it was every morning now, but she'd stopped letting it slow her down.

Upstairs, the familiar hallway smelled faintly of antiseptic and stale coffee. But when Jasmine stepped into Robert's room, she was greeted by something warmer.

Terry stood by the window with a coffee in hand, chatting quietly with William. Kelly sat on the chair nearest Robert, her hand resting gently on the edge of the bed. Mary, surprisingly, was perched on the small loveseat near the door, flicking through a magazine.

Jasmine smiled, touched by the sight of them all there—steady, loyal, waiting.

"Morning," she said softly.

They all turned toward her, and Jasmine moved through the room, kissing Kelly on the cheek, then Terry, then Mary. She wrapped William in a quick but affectionate hug.

"You look fresh," he teased. "Went for a run?"

She nodded. "Trying to outrun the exhaustion."

Kelly chuckled. "You've been here more than any of us this week."

"She's always here," Terry added, the gratitude in his voice unmistakable.

Jasmine didn't answer. She just crossed to the far side of the bed, to the spot that had become hers. She reached out, her fingers slipping easily around Robert's hand. It was warm. Strong. His breathing was steady, the rise and fall of his chest familiar now. A comfort.

"Morning, Robert," she whispered.

The room buzzed with quiet conversation—Terry asking William about work, Mary commenting on the state of the hospital coffee. Jasmine listened, half-participating, her thumb slowly stroking the back of Robert's hand.

Then, suddenly—barely audible over the soft murmur of voices—came a low sound.

A moan.

Jasmine stilled. Her eyes shot to Robert's face.

"Jasmine…"

The voice was hoarse, rough from disuse, but unmistakable.

Everyone went silent.

Jasmine leaned forward instinctively. "Robert?"

His eyelids fluttered. His head shifted slightly against the pillow. His fingers twitched beneath hers.

She held her breath.

"I'm here," she whispered, her voice tight with emotion.

Robert's eyes opened slowly—unfocused at first, then narrowing as they searched the room. They landed on her.

And even through the haze of pain and medication, he smiled.

"Hi," he croaked.

Tears sprang to Jasmine's eyes, unbidden.

"Hi," she whispered back, her heart in her throat.

Behind her, Kelly's hand flew to her mouth. Terry let out a shaky exhale. William blinked hard. Even Mary looked quietly stunned.

But Jasmine only saw him.

In that moment, the room fell away—the soft beeping of machines, the quiet gasps behind her, the rustle of someone standing still. None of it mattered.

All she could see was him.

The man she wasn't supposed to love.

And the first word he spoke… was her name.

Then, as quickly as he had surfaced, Robert's eyes fluttered closed again. His hand slackened slightly in hers, and his breathing eased back into that slow, steady rhythm.

It was over in seconds, but it left Jasmine trembling.

William stepped closer, brow furrowed. "Why you?" he asked softly, more to himself than to her.

Before Jasmine could respond, Mary's gaze shifted toward William. She gave a small, almost imperceptible shake of her head—firm, knowing, gentle.

Not now.

Jasmine didn't speak. She couldn't. She just held Robert's hand a little tighter, her heart echoing with a name that had never sounded more like a promise.

She stayed for another hour, sitting quietly at his bedside, her fingers laced with his. The conversation drifted around the room—soft, easy, nothing particularly important. Stories, memories, the kind of gentle chatter that filled the space without demanding anything in return.

William and Mary left just before she did. Mary gave her a warm kiss on the cheek, and William hugged her with a lingering squeeze that said more than words. There was a question in his eyes, but he didn't ask it. Not yet.

As Jasmine gathered her things, Terry and Kelly both stood to see her out.

"Thank you again for coming," Terry said, his voice low with gratitude.

"You really don't need to thank me," Jasmine replied gently. "I care about him."

Kelly's eyes softened as she touched Jasmine's arm. "He clearly cares about you too. You're the only person he keeps asking for—every time the sedation lightens, it's your name."

Jasmine looked down for a moment, swallowing hard. "Has Claire been here yet?"

Terry exchanged a glance with his wife before shaking his head. "Not that we're aware of."

There was something unspoken in the silence that followed.

Jasmine gave a small nod, then looked back toward Robert's room—her heart caught somewhere between hope and dread.

"Okay," she said softly. "I'll be back tomorrow."

And she would be. No matter what waited on the other side of this.

William and Mary made their way home in silence at first, the hum of the engine the only sound between them. As they pulled onto the Harbour Bridge, the city lights glowing in the distance, William finally spoke—more to himself than to her.

"Why does he keep asking for Jaz?"

Mary glanced over at him. "I don't know why Robert keeps asking for her," she said carefully, "but I do know Jasmine's loved him for years."

William blinked, turning to her as they entered their driveway. "She what?!"

Mary gave him a look, almost amused. "Surely you must've known."

He parked in their spot and turned off the engine, staring ahead in disbelief. "No. I didn't. She's never said anything. I knew she cared about him."

"Well," Mary said with a shrug, "I suppose it's not exactly something you'd bring up with your brother—being in love with his best friend."

He looked at her, stunned. "How long?"

Mary hesitated only a second. "At least three years. Probably longer."

William's voice pitched higher. "What?!"

Mary nodded gently, watching his reaction. "I figured it out a couple of weeks after we started dating. She told me that she thought he felt the same just before she turned twenty-one, but she said he just disappeared. She's just always been quiet about it. Loyal, too. She's never wanted to cause trouble."

William sat back in his seat, trying to process. "I asked Robert not to date her when she turned twenty-one."

Mary gave him a long look. "And he listened. But that didn't change how she felt."

The weight of it settled in William's chest—regret, confusion, guilt—all folding in on themselves. He didn't know what to say. So, he said nothing.

Beside him, Mary reached across and quietly took his hand.

But his mind was already drifting—back to a different night, just over three years ago. Their parents were still alive, the house full of noise and laughter. Jasmine had just turned twenty-one. She'd been radiant that night—grinning, flushed from champagne and dancing, her hair tumbling down her back as she floated from one guest to the next. Everyone had noticed. Including Robert.

It was the next morning, when things were quieter, that Robert had shown up at William's apartment, unannounced. He'd looked out of place—rumpled, uncertain, his usual easy confidence nowhere in sight.

"I need to talk to you," he'd said, voice low.

They'd sat on the balcony, mugs of coffee growing cold between them. Robert hadn't wasted time.

"It's Jasmine," he said. "I have feelings for her. Strong ones. I think… I think I've felt them for a while."

William had stared at him, stunned. The words had landed like a punch.

"Robert—she's my sister."

"I know," Robert said quietly. "But that doesn't change how I feel. I wanted to come to you first, out of respect. I care about her, Will. Deeply."

The words had been sincere. But William had panicked.

"Please don't," he'd said, his voice barely above a whisper. "She's just turned twenty-one. She's been through enough. She doesn't need complicated, not now. And I know you. You're… you. Women fall at your feet. I can't watch you break her heart."

Robert had gone quiet, his expression tightening. "You think I'd hurt her?"

"I think you don't know what you want yet. Not really. And I can't take the risk that it's her you figure it out on."

The silence had stretched. Finally, Robert had nodded once, stiffly.

"Okay," he'd said. "If that's what you want."

William hadn't realised until now what he'd truly asked for—not just for Robert to back off, but for Jasmine to never know how close she'd come to being loved by the one man she'd never stopped loving.

Now, in the dim car park, with Mary's hand warm in his, the full weight of that moment came crashing down on him.

And he couldn't help but wonder what might've been different if he'd said nothing at all.

"I think I might have made a terrible mistake," William said quietly, staring through the windshield at the front of their home. "It's obvious that Robert must still have feelings for Jasmine."

Mary squeezed his hand. "Robert respected you."

"Yeah, but maybe he shouldn't have," William murmured, a bitter edge to his voice. "Maybe I should've let him tell her how he felt. Let her decide."

"You were trying to protect her."

"I know. But from what?" He turned to look at Mary, eyes shadowed with guilt. "From a man who's always been steady, loyal, and who's loved her—probably for just as long as she's loved him?"

Mary didn't answer right away. Instead, she held his gaze, her voice soft when she finally spoke.

"You made the best decision you could with what you knew at the time. But maybe now… it's time to let go of that old promise."

William nodded slowly, but the knot in his chest didn't ease. Because deep down, he knew what he'd done hadn't just altered the path of Robert and Jasmine's lives—it might have kept them from something true. Something lasting.

"She's dating James now," Mary said gently.

"I know." William exhaled, the weight of it pressing against his ribs. "I like him. Jasmine does too. He's good for her."

He paused, jaw tightening. "But maybe it's already too late to undo any of it."

Mary didn't speak right away. She just held his hand a little tighter.

Because they both knew some choices echo longer than you ever expect.

Jasmine stood by the kitchen window, cradling a cup of tea that had long since gone cold. The early afternoon light filtered through the sheer curtains, painting soft patterns across the floor. Outside, the world was slowly waking—birds chirping, the distant hum of a garbage truck, a jogger passing by with rhythmic footfalls. But inside, her thoughts were loud and unrelenting.

He'd asked for her again.

Robert.

Even now, the sound of her name on his lips echoed in her mind—faint, hoarse, but unmistakable. The way his fingers had weakly curled around hers. The flicker of recognition in his eyes before they drifted shut again.

Her heart twisted, but she forced herself to breathe through it. To be rational.

He was confused. Sedated. In pain. Of course he was reaching for something familiar. Someone safe. They had history. She'd been there the night of the accident. Maybe some part of him remembered that—remembered her voice, her hand in his. Maybe he remembered the last thing he'd said to her before the world spun out.

'I'm sorry.'

Jasmine exhaled slowly and set the mug down on the counter.

That had to be it. He'd had finally told Clair to stop humiliating her. Maybe that apology had nothing to do with… feelings. Maybe it was just guilt. Robert had always been fiercely loyal, even to people who didn't deserve it. Maybe he just felt responsible for not stopping Claire sooner. Maybe this—asking for her, saying her name—was his subconscious trying to make things right.

She nodded to herself, trying to make the logic settle.

It didn't.

Because despite everything, the memory of that one word—her name—still lingered like a spark she couldn't extinguish. And the look in his mother's eyes when she told Jasmine he kept asking for her… it hadn't felt like guilt. It had felt like longing.

Jasmine blinked, shaking her head. No. She couldn't go there. Not again.

She turned away from the window and walked slowly down the hall, her bare feet silent on the hardwood. She looked at her phone on the bedside table—she thought about James. He'd been so thoughtful, so present. Dinner last night. The flowers. The way he held her without asking questions. The warmth of his hands, the steadiness of his affection.

That was her future.

Not a half-healed man in a hospital bed who had given a ring to another woman.

James was grounded. Whole. Honest.

He made her laugh when she forgot how. He kissed her like she mattered. And maybe she didn't feel fireworks every second they were together, but maybe that wasn't what love needed to be. Maybe it was about showing up. Choosing someone. Letting the quiet kind of love take root and grow.

Her fingers hovered over her phone before she finally typed:

Hope your morning's off to a good start. Thank you again for last night. I really needed it.

She hit send, then set the phone down and closed her eyes.

Because her heart was pulling in two directions—and she didn't know which one would hurt more to follow.

Almost instantly, her phone buzzed.

Dinner?

A small smile tugged at her lips. She typed back:

Would love to.

Pick you up at 7.

Can't wait

Chapter Fifteen

Jasmine had just walked through the door, dropped her bag by the hall table, and kicked off her shoes. Her body ached with exhaustion, but her mind buzzed with everything Kelly had told her at the hospital. They were planning to reduce Robert's medication. He should start coming out of sedation soon.

She didn't know how to feel about that—hopeful, anxious, terrified.

Curled up on the couch in her pyjamas, a cooking show playing quietly in the background, she barely registered the montage of soufflés and flambés flickering across the screen. When her phone buzzed, she glanced down—and smiled.

Heidi.

She swiped to answer. "Hey."

"Hey yourself," Heidi said, her voice already laced with mischief. "I've been patient for one whole day, but I can't hold out any longer."

Jasmine laughed softly. "That sounds ominous."

"Oh, it is. I need an update. How's it going with Mr. Tall, Dark, and Lawyer-y?"

Jasmine shifted, tugging a throw blanket around her legs. "It's… going well."

"Well?" Heidi dragged the word out. "That's it? *Well?* Come on."

"We had dinner last night."

James had taken her to a little French place tucked into a side street in Surry Hills. She'd worn a deep green dress she hadn't touched in months—just to see if it still made her feel like herself. When she opened the door, his stunned *'wow'* had made her blush all the way to her fingertips.

"Uh-huh," Heidi said. "And did dessert come after dinner?"

"Heidi…" Jasmine groaned, laughing despite herself.

"What?" Heidi said innocently. "I'm just asking if you've done the deed yet."

Jasmine could practically hear the smirk through the line.

"No," she admitted, voice a mix of humour and hesitation. "Not yet."

A pause followed. Then Heidi, more softly, asked, "Okay… is it going to happen?"

Jasmine bit her bottom lip.

She wanted to say yes. She liked James. A lot. He was warm and grounded, always showed up when he said he would, and made her feel seen in ways she hadn't realised she missed.

But when his hands found hers, or when he kissed her like she was the only woman in the room… something inside her faltered. Like her heart was waiting for permission it hadn't granted.

"I think so," she said finally. "Just… not yet."

Heidi was quiet. Then, surprisingly gentle. "Is this about Robert?"

Jasmine closed her eyes and leaned back into the cushions.

"I don't know," she admitted. "James is… everything I should want. But every time we start to get close, it feels like I'm betraying something. Something I've never said out loud."

Another pause. Then Heidi's voice, soft but firm.

"Jaz… you don't owe anyone anything. Not Robert. Not James. Not even me. But you do owe yourself honesty."

Jasmine nodded slowly, her throat tight. "I know."

A beat, then Heidi's usual brightness returned—warmer this time, not teasing but comforting.

"Okay. Enough soul-searching. Just promise me—if you end up horizontal with this man, it's because you want to be there. Not because you're trying to outrun something else."

"I promise," Jasmine said, meaning it.

There was a brief silence before Heidi's voice softened again. "How's Robert?"

"They're starting to reduce his sedation this week," Jasmine said. "He should start waking up soon. He still doesn't know about the spinal injury."

"That's rough," Heidi murmured.

"Yeah… it is." Jasmine glanced toward the window, where the city lights blinked softly in the distance. "But maybe he'll defy the odds."

"I hope so," Heidi said. "For his sake… and yours."

Jasmine swallowed. "Thanks."

There was a pause, then Heidi lightened the mood. "Anyway—go put something sexy in your mind, or on Netflix. I recommend the shirtless fireman doco. Episode three is life changing."

Jasmine let out a laugh, the tension easing from her shoulders. "Goodnight, Heidi."

"Night, babe. Text me if anything scandalous happens."

"Oh, don't worry—you'll be the first to know."

It was late Thursday afternoon when Jasmine arrived at the hospital. The halls were quieter than usual, the sharp scent of antiseptic lingering in the air as she made her way toward Robert's room.

She pushed open the door gently. A nurse looked up from adjusting the IV.

"Hi," Jasmine said softly.

The nurse offered a warm smile. "Hey there. His parents just left about ten minutes ago. He's been resting."

Jasmine nodded her thanks and stepped inside, letting the door click softly shut behind her. The room was dim, lit only by the soft amber of a bedside lamp and the steady green pulse of monitors.

She slipped off her coat and settled into the chair beside him. Without thinking, her hand found his—just as it had every day this week. Cool fingers wrapped in hers. Stillness, but not silence. The beeping of the machines had become oddly comforting. Predictable.

"Hey, it's me," she said softly, brushing her thumb over the back of his hand. "They're starting to reduce your meds now. I don't know if you can hear me yet, but… you're doing okay. You're still here."

She glanced at his face—unshaven, pale, but still so unmistakably him.

"The nurses said you opened your eyes a little yesterday. I knew you'd come back stubborn," she said with a small smile. "But that's okay. We'll take stubborn."

She sat back in the chair and continued to talk, her voice a gentle rhythm in the quiet room. She told him about William losing a bet on the rugby, how her patient Mr. Wilson had finally mastered using his walking cane without tripping over his dog, and that Heidi had found a new obsession with a reality show full of "shirtless Scottish tradesmen who inexplicably also do pottery."

She was mid-sentence when she felt a shift in his fingers.

A slight twitch.

She froze. Her heart hammered.

Then—

"Jasmine…"

His voice was hoarse. Barely audible. But it was real.

She blinked, sat forward, her grip tightening around his hand. "Robert?"

His eyelids fluttered open, unfocused at first, then slowly found her. His gaze was heavy with sedation, but there—there was recognition. Confusion. Relief.

"Hey," she whispered, her throat tight. "You're awake."

His eyes found hers—bleary but sure. A flicker of recognition, a trace of something softer.

"Hello."

Just one word. Barely audible. But it landed like thunder in her chest.

She leaned closer, tears stinging her eyes, one hand brushing a lock of hair off his forehead. "You scared the hell out of us."

He blinked again, slower this time. His mouth moved, trying to form more words. But the effort pulled him under again, his eyelids slipping shut, his fingers loosening in hers.

Still, she didn't let go.

She sat there in the quiet, her thumb brushing against his hand, heart pounding with something that felt suspiciously like hope.

By Saturday morning, Jasmine was running on muscle memory. Her jog along the cliffs of Bondi had done little to shake the tight coil in her chest, and the warm shower after hadn't loosened it either. Still, she'd dressed quickly, tied her hair into a low ponytail, and headed for the hospital.

She'd barely stepped off the lift when she spotted Terry and Kelly standing just outside Robert's room, their posture unusually rigid.

They both turned as she approached, offering their usual warm smiles—but something in their expressions felt… off.

"Morning, sweetheart," Kelly said, leaning in for a kiss on the cheek.

"Morning," Jasmine replied, hugging Terry lightly. "Is everything okay?"

Kelly exchanged a glance with her husband before answering. "Clair is here. Robert woke up this morning—more lucid than before."

Jasmine's breath caught. "He's awake? Properly?"

Terry nodded. "Yes, for a while now."

She blinked, a mix of relief and something sharper threading through her chest. "Why did it take so long for her to show up?"

"She told Robert she hadn't heard the message until yesterday," Kelly said coolly.

"But that's not true," Terry added. "She was apparently on her way to a photo shoot in New Zealand when she got the call."

"She didn't tell William that," Jasmine murmured, her stomach turning.

Kelly's mouth tightened. "No. And frankly, we don't believe she was."

Jasmine stepped closer to the room and peered through the glass.

Robert was sitting up in bed, weak but conscious. Clair was perched on the edge, arms looped around his neck, her lips brushing his cheek. His arms loosely circled her waist in return.

Jasmine's stomach plummeted.

They're engaged, she reminded herself. This shouldn't hurt.

But it did.

Because somewhere between hospital visits and whispered hellos in quiet rooms, she'd started to hope. Foolishly. Selfishly.

She'd told herself that Claire's absence meant something—that maybe Robert had seen through the polished perfection and found it lacking. That maybe… he'd wanted her there instead.

Her throat tightened.

"We gave them a minute," Terry said, his voice strained.

Jasmine straightened and offered them both a tight smile. "Then I should go."

Kelly reached out quickly. "You don't have to. Please—"

"I think it's for the best," Jasmine said, forcing calm into her voice. "Clair's never liked me. I don't want to upset Robert."

"But you've been here every day," Kelly whispered. "He's asked for you."

Jasmine's smile faltered. "And I'm grateful I could be here. But this… this is his fiancée."

She leaned in and kissed them both on the cheek, her movements gentle.

"Tell him I'm glad he's awake."

Then she turned and walked down the corridor. Only when she reached the car did the mask slip.

She slid into the driver's seat and let her head fall back against the headrest, eyes burning.

She hadn't cried in weeks. She wasn't going to start now.

Still, her hands trembled slightly as she turned the key in the ignition.

Because no matter how much she tried to reason with herself…

it still felt like goodbye.

The beeping was soft, steady, insistent.

Robert blinked against the sterile brightness, every part of his body weighted and sore. His mouth was dry, his limbs heavy with something deeper than exhaustion. Pain thrummed in his spine, dull but unrelenting, echoing faintly down his legs like distant thunder.

"Robert?"

The voice came from his right—familiar, too sweet.

Claire.

She leaned in, her glossy smile too bright, too ready, as if she'd rehearsed it. "You're awake. Finally."

His gaze drifted, slow and unfocused, toward her. Even that small movement cost him.

"How long…?" he rasped, his throat like gravel.

"Over a week," she said, smoothing a hand down his arm. "You scared us all."

He nodded faintly, but her touch made his skin flinch beneath it. Something about it felt… off. Like a coat that no longer fit.

He looked toward the window, grounding himself in the slant of morning light. His memories were scattered, a shuffle of broken images. The last thing he could grab hold of was the yacht club—Jasmine's laugh floating in the air, the faint citrus of her perfume, the way that man—James? —had taken her hand.

Then nothing.

"What happened?"

"You were in an accident," Claire said, softer now. "A truck ran a red light. You were on your bike."

He frowned, struggling to piece it together. "Was anyone else hurt?"

"No. Just you."

Her hand still rested on his, but it felt like an intrusion. Like something he should welcome—but didn't.

The comfort he instinctively reached for wasn't here.

"I don't remember anything after the club," he murmured, his brow drawing faintly.

Claire stilled, just for a heartbeat.

Then her expression softened, a practiced look of concern falling into place—only this time, it was edged with something else. A flicker of relief passed through her eyes, too quick for most to catch, but not lost on him entirely. As if a weight had slid off her shoulders.

"That's normal," she said, her voice smoothing into quiet reassurance. "The doctors said memory loss like that is expected after trauma."

She gave his hand a squeeze, just a little too eager, too rehearsed.

Robert's gaze drifted back toward the window, the ache in his body paling against the unease settling in his chest.

He didn't know what he was supposed to remember.

But somewhere, buried beneath the haze, he had the sharpest sense that something wasn't right.

And whatever it was… Claire was glad he'd forgotten it.

He closed his eyes for a moment, the pressure behind them pulsing. There had been a dream—or maybe it was real. Someone holding his hand. Warmth. A voice he trusted.

Jasmine.

He didn't say her name out loud. He didn't have to.

Claire's presence was a spotlight. But he felt himself turning away from it, drawn instead to the quiet memory of something softer, steadier.

He opened his eyes again. "How long have you been here?"

"I came as soon as I could," she said quickly. "I was out of the country when William called."

He nodded but didn't press. He didn't have the energy, and her answers didn't feel like anchors. They floated.

"How are you feeling, really?" Claire asked.

The words sounded more obligatory than concerned—like something she was supposed to say.

"Like I was hit by a truck," he muttered, too drained to soften the edge in his voice.

She didn't flinch, but she didn't lean in, either.

Her face didn't feel like home. Her touch didn't soothe him. Nothing about this moment aligned with what he thought he should feel—not for his fiancée.

"I'm sorry," he added after a beat, dragging in a shallow breath. "I just… I don't feel like myself."

Claire hesitated, then reached up to brush a hand through his hair. The gesture was gentle, but impersonal. Like a nurse performing a routine task.

"It's the pain meds," she said lightly. "You just need time."

Maybe she was right.

Maybe the fog would lift, and everything would fall back into place.

But even in the fog, one name pierced through like sunlight.

Not spoken aloud. Not for Claire's ears.

Jasmine.

He didn't know why he remembered her so clearly—only that her presence lingered in the spaces Claire couldn't reach. Like he'd already woken once, just for a moment, and it had been Jasmine's hand in his. Her voice he'd heard. Her warmth that had anchored him.

And even now, broken, half-lucid, barely whole—he knew who his heart had reached for.

Not the woman sitting beside him.

But the one who'd always hovered just out of reach.

The one he'd never been able to let go of.

The door opened.

His parents stepped into the room.

Claire stood, smoothing her skirt as if she'd been interrupted. "I'll come back later," she said, brushing a quick kiss against his lips.

He didn't kiss her back.

She didn't wait for him to.

When the door closed behind her, Kelly moved to his side, her expression softening.

"Jasmine was here," she said gently.

Robert's eyes flicked toward the door, hope rising unbidden in his chest. "Where is she?"

Terry sighed. "She left."

"Why?"

"Because she didn't want to cause trouble," Kelly said, laying a comforting hand on his arm. "She thought her being here might upset Claire."

"She knows how Claire feels about her," Terry added, his voice quiet with regret.

Robert's gaze dropped to the blanket, his jaw tightening. "She's been here, though?"

"Every day," Kelly said softly. "Without fail."

He closed his eyes.

And for the first time since waking, something settled in his chest.

Not peace—not yet.

But certainty.

She had been here.

Of course she had.

Chapter Sixteen

Jasmine finally started the car, her hands trembling slightly on the steering wheel. The hospital loomed behind her in the rearview mirror, a place of too many mixed emotions—hope, heartbreak, and now, the sharp sting of reality.

She didn't cry. Not yet. She just drove.

Instead of heading straight home, she turned left at the lights and made her way toward Bellevue Hill, a quiet, leafy suburb just fifteen minutes from Bondi. The streets were wide and tree-lined, dotted with elegant sandstone homes and jacaranda trees that spilled their purple blossoms like confetti along the footpaths.

She needed something familiar. Grounding. And William and Mary's place had always felt like that—warm, steady, safe.

William's car was in the driveway when she pulled in. The late morning sun filtered through the trees, casting long shadows across the path as she climbed the steps. She'd barely raised her hand to knock when the front door swung open.

"Thought I heard a car," Mary said with a smile that turned instantly to concern. "It's good to see you. We weren't expecting you."

"I hope I'm not intruding."

"Not at all. You're welcome anytime, sweetheart." Mary stepped aside, waving her in. "I thought you'd be at the hospital."

"I was," Jasmine said, her voice quieter now. "Robert's awake."

Mary froze mid-step, her eyes lighting up with relief. "Oh, that's wonderful news. Did you get to talk to him?"

Jasmine followed her through the hallway and into the kitchen, the scent of freshly brewed coffee lingering in the air.

"No… Claire was there."

Mary's expression soured instantly. "Of course she was. Decided to show up now, did she?"

That was when William walked into the kitchen, barefoot and holding a mug, a surprised smile crossing his face. "Hey, sis. What brings you by?"

Before she could answer, William pulled her into a hug. Jasmine sank into it, her arms winding around him like she was trying to anchor herself.

She hadn't realised how much she needed it—how much she needed them—until that moment.

William pulled back just enough to look at her face. "Did I hear right—Claire finally decided to show up?"

"Yeah," Jasmine said, her voice tight. "Apparently she told Terry and Kelly she was out of the country when you called to tell her about the accident."

William's brows lifted. "Seriously? She didn't say anything like that to me."

"She told them she was on her way to a photo shoot in New Zealand," Jasmine added. "But… they don't believe her. Honestly, neither do I."

William shook his head slowly. "Unbelievable."

Mary handed Jasmine a mug of tea and gave her hand a gentle squeeze.

William asked, "Did you get a chance to talk to Robert?"

Jasmine shook her head, her gaze dropping to the floor. "No. As soon as I saw Claire with his arms around her, I left."

William's jaw clenched, but he stayed quiet.

"I just… I didn't want to make things worse," Jasmine continued. "She's already made it clear she hates me, and I didn't want Robert waking up to another round of her spite."

Mary touched her shoulder. "You didn't deserve that."

"I know. But I couldn't do it. Not with her in the room acting like nothing's ever changed."

William's voice was quiet now. "Jaz… you've been there every single day."

Jasmine nodded, her voice soft. "And it meant something. All those days sitting by his side… it really did. But today… it didn't feel like I belonged anymore."

William exchanged a quiet glance with Mary, neither of them needing to say aloud what they were both thinking.

Just then, Jasmine's phone buzzed on the bench. She glanced at the screen.

"Just a sec," she murmured, stepping away as she accepted the call. "Hey."

James's warm voice came through the line. "Hey, gorgeous. Can I see you tonight?"

She hesitated—just for a heartbeat—then told herself it was time to move forward. Time to stop reaching for someone who may never reach back.

Time to accept that Robert Steele belonged to a different chapter of her life.

"Yes," she said, more certain now. "I'd love to."

"Great," James said, a smile in his voice. "How about you come over to mine and I cook for you this time?"

She laughed softly. "You cook?"

"Of course," he replied, mock offended. "If I didn't, I'd be living off takeaway. Don't worry—I've got a signature pasta dish that might just win you over."

She smiled, and for the first time today, it didn't feel like pretending. "Okay. I'm looking forward to it."

"See you at seven? I'll text you my address."

"See you then."

As Jasmine ended the call, she slipped her phone back into her bag and looked up to find William watching her carefully.

"You sure you're okay?" he asked gently.

She offered a small smile. "Getting there."

Maybe dinner with James really was the first step toward moving forward.

Mary, who'd been quietly setting mugs on the kitchen bench, glanced over. "Was that the gorgeous James?"

Jasmine's smile widened. "Yes."

Mary chuckled. "He is gorgeous, isn't he? Honestly, that man looks like he belongs on the cover of GQ."

Jasmine laughed. "I know. And apparently, he cooks too."

Mary raised an eyebrow, clearly impressed. "Handsome and domestic? Careful, Jaz—you might have to fight the rest of Sydney off with a stick."

William smirked as he grabbed a biscuit from the tin. "Sounds like he's trying to charm his way into the family."

Jasmine leaned back in her chair, the warmth of their banter settling into her chest. "Well... he's definitely giving it a good shot."

Robert lay in the hospital bed, staring at the ceiling as late afternoon light filtered through the blinds. The room was quiet now—Claire had left hours ago, and his parents had stepped out to speak with a nurse. For the first time since waking, he was truly alone.

He welcomed the silence.

But his mind wasn't quiet.

He shifted slightly, wincing as a sharp ache flared low in his back and spread down his legs. It wasn't the pain that bothered him most—it was the restlessness. The gnawing sense that something was missing. Or someone.

He didn't remember much after the accident. But he remembered Jasmine.

Not in flashes or fragments—she'd been a steady thread in the fog. The soft pressure of her fingers laced through his, warm and certain. The scent of something floral—jasmine, maybe, or something close—lingering whenever she leaned in to check his monitors.

Her voice had been there too. Low, steady, sometimes coaxing a response from him when no one else could.

She'd felt like peace. Like coming up for air.

She'd been here. He was certain of it.

He'd asked for her. He remembered that too.

And yet today, it hadn't been her he woke to. It had been Claire. Too much perfume. Too wide a smile. Too… much.

She didn't feel like home. She felt like a script he no longer remembered how to read.

And Jasmine?

Jasmine had felt like calm. Like steadiness. Like truth.

He glanced toward the door, wishing it would open, and she'd walk through. But it remained closed.

A knock finally came—but it was a nurse with his medication.

"Any pain?" she asked gently.

He nodded once, his voice low. "Yeah. A bit."

The nurse adjusted his IV. "Your parents mentioned you're starting to remember things. That's good."

Robert didn't reply. Instead, he stared out the window again, trying to piece together the gaps. Trying to understand why Jasmine hadn't come back."

Maybe she didn't want to see him. Maybe too much had happened.

Maybe he didn't deserve her anymore.

But even now, even in the middle of this sterile hospital room filled with uncertainty, one thing had never been clearer.

He wanted her here.

And not just because she soothed the ache.

Because she mattered.

More than he'd ever let himself admit.

He should never have asked Claire to marry him. Not then. Maybe not ever.

He hadn't seen Jasmine in months—buried in the Byron Bay deal, consumed by work and distractions that felt important at the time. But the moment he walked into William's office to share his engagement news, and saw her…

Everything shifted.

One look at her—standing by the window, sunlight catching in her hair, that familiar spark in her eyes—and his carefully constructed certainty began to crumble.

He remembered thinking '*what have I done*?

And now, lying in a hospital bed with Claire's perfume still lingering in the sheets and Jasmine nowhere in sight, that question echoed louder than ever.

What had he done?

And more importantly…

Was it too late to undo it?

The door opened before the weight of the question could fully settle.

His parents stepped in.

Kelly smiled softly. "Sweetheart, the nurse just told us the doctor will be in to see you soon."

He nodded, but his eyes flicked past her—toward the hallway.

"Okay." A pause. Then, quieter, more tentative: "Do you think Jasmine will come back?"

Kelly and Terry exchanged a glance. It wasn't pity—it was something gentler. Knowing.

"I hope so," Kelly said, moving closer to his bedside. "She's been here every day, Robert."

Terry added, "She left this morning because she didn't want to upset Claire. She was trying to do the right thing."

Robert stared at the ceiling, his throat tightening.

"Tell her I want to see her," he said softly.

Kelly reached for his hand. "We will. I promise."

A soft knock at the door broke the quiet.

A man in blue scrubs stepped in, followed by a nurse holding a tablet. The name on his badge read Dr. Karim—a calm, composed presence, his expression neutral but not cold.

"Good morning, Robert," he said, moving to the foot of the bed. "I'm Dr. Karim, one of the specialists overseeing your care. How are you feeling?"

Robert shifted slightly, biting back a wince. "Like I got run over by a truck."

Dr. Karim gave a sympathetic nod. "That would be accurate. You sustained multiple injuries—broken ribs, a punctured lung, a fractured collarbone. But the most serious is damage to your spine."

Robert's gaze snapped to his.

"My spine?"

The doctor pulled up a chair. "You've suffered a thoracic spinal cord injury—around the mid-back. The good news is, the swelling has gone down significantly, and you've regained some sensation. But there's still concern about motor function."

Robert stared at him, trying to process the words.

Terry stood beside the bed, his jaw tight.

Kelly's hand gripped his.

"I don't understand," Robert said, voice thin. "Are you saying... I won't walk again?"

Dr. Karim's voice was gentle, but direct. "At this stage, we don't know. Some patients recover mobility with intensive rehab. Others don't. Your MRI shows incomplete damage, which is better than a full transection. That gives us hope."

"But no guarantees," Robert finished for him.

"No," the doctor agreed quietly. "No guarantees."

The air felt too thick to breathe.

Robert's hands fisted against the blanket, trying to feel something solid. Anything.

"You're still in the early days," Dr. Karim added. "We'll start reducing your pain medication further over the next few days so we can better assess your motor response. From there, we'll tailor a rehabilitation plan."

No one spoke.

Terry cleared his throat. "What can we do?"

"Just be here," the doctor said. "Encouragement and stability make a world of difference."

He gave Robert a reassuring nod. "We'll monitor your progress closely. And if you ever want to talk through the details—what to expect, next steps, support options—I'm always available."

Then he stood. "Rest. Try to stay calm. You've come through the worst of it. Now we work on the rest."

He and the nurse exited, leaving behind a silence that felt like something sacred had shifted.

Robert sank back against the pillows, staring at the ceiling.

He felt his mother's hand tremble in his.

He didn't speak. Not right away.

Because how do you find the words for a future that might never look like the one you imagined?

And yet, even through the fear and the unknown, only one name came to his mind again.

Jasmine.

Chapter Seventeen

Jasmine stood in front of James's apartment, smoothing down her dress before she rang the bell.

The door opened almost immediately. James greeted her with that easy, boyish grin and a bottle of red wine in hand.

"You're right on time," he said, stepping aside. "Which is suspiciously attractive."

She laughed as she stepped inside. "And you're holding wine. Also, attractive."

"Wait until you taste my pasta," he said, leading her through to the open-plan kitchen. "Then I'll really win you over."

The apartment was warm and tastefully furnished—books on the shelves, a cozy tan leather couch with a knitted throw over the armrest, jazz playing softly in the background. The scent of garlic, tomato, and basil filled the air, instantly comforting.

"Wow, you weren't kidding," Jasmine said, peeking into the kitchen. "You actually cook."

James offered a mock bow. "Lawyer by day, culinary genius by night."

"Modest, too."

He grinned. "Always."

They ate by candlelight at the small dining table tucked near the window. The city lights twinkled beyond the glass, but Jasmine barely noticed them. James was easy to talk to. He asked about her work, her family, her favourite books—never once pressing about Robert or the hospital, though she knew he must be wondering.

She appreciated that.

He refilled her glass halfway through the meal. "So… how did I do?"

Jasmine swirled a forkful of spaghetti thoughtfully before giving him a nod of approval. "Honestly? This is better than most restaurants."

"I'll take that as a win." He leaned back in his chair, watching her with a quiet fondness. "You look relaxed tonight."

"I think I am," she admitted, surprised to realise it was true. "It's been a while."

After dinner, they moved to the couch with their wine, the jazz still low in the background. Conversation faded into comfortable silence.

James shifted closer. "I've wanted to do this all night," he murmured, brushing a strand of hair from her face.

Then he kissed her—slowly, with confidence but no pressure. Jasmine responded before she even had time to second-guess it, leaning in, her hand curling around his neck. The kiss deepened, warm, familiar, and grounding. When it ended, they rested their foreheads together, breaths mingling.

"Stay," James whispered, his fingers still gently tracing the curve of her jaw. "Just tonight. No expectations. Just… stay."

Jasmine closed her eyes, exhaling slowly.

Something inside her shifted.

Not in conflict. Not with guilt. But with clarity.

She'd held on to Robert for so long—through uncertainty, through years of waiting, through feelings that never quite settled. But Robert hadn't chosen her. Not then. Not even now.

And maybe… maybe it was time to stop standing still.

She opened her eyes and looked into James's. Kind. Steady. Open.

"Yes," she whispered. "I want to stay."

His smile was soft, content. He wrapped an arm around her as she tucked herself into his side.

And for the first time in a long time, Jasmine felt like she was exactly where she was meant to be.

Later, in the hush of the evening, the wine forgotten and the jazz reduced to a faint hum, they moved together with quiet tenderness. There was no rush, no fireworks—just warmth. A steady rhythm of shared breath and soft touches, a kind of intimacy that felt safe. James was gentle, attuned to her in a way that made her feel seen, not just desired.

Afterward, they lay tangled in the sheets, the bedroom dark except for the faint glow of the city through the curtains. James stroked her hair as she rested her head on his chest, his heartbeat a slow, reassuring rhythm beneath her ear.

"You okay?" he murmured.

She nodded, the motion brushing her cheek against his skin. "Yeah. I'm good."

And she was. It had been nice. Sweet, even. The kind of night she knew she was supposed to want. A night of moving forward.

But as James drifted into sleep beside her, a small, quiet ache settled in her chest.

It wasn't regret. Not exactly.

It was something softer. Sadder.

Because a part of her—just a sliver—still wished it had been someone else holding her like this. Someone who once made her heart race with just a look. Someone who felt like unfinished sentences and untaken chances.

She closed her eyes and pushed the thought aside.

This was good. James was good.

She had to let herself believe that.

Because Robert Steele was part of the past.

And tonight, she had chosen her future.

The morning light spilled through the curtains in soft gold, warming the sheets as Jasmine stirred beside James. His arm tightened around her waist as she moved, and she smiled, eyes still closed.

"Good morning," he murmured, his voice husky with sleep.

She turned toward him, her fingers lightly tracing the stubble along his jaw. "Morning."

There was no rush. No awkwardness. Just a quiet, natural ease between them. And when he kissed her, slow and unhurried, it felt like the most natural continuation of the night before.

They made love again, unhurried and wrapped in the lazy hush of morning. There was laughter, soft sighs, the scent of coffee drifting in from the kitchen, and the comfort of shared space. When they finally lay still again, tangled in the sheets and the warmth of each other, James propped himself up on one elbow and studied her face.

"I was thinking," he said, brushing a strand of hair from her cheek, "how would you feel about spending the day together?"

Jasmine stretched, then nestled against him again. "That sounds lovely… but I was planning to stop by the hospital."

James nodded, unfazed. "Then I'll come with you."

She blinked, caught off guard. "To see Robert?"

He gave her a small, calm smile. "He's a part of your life. I get that. If I want to be part of your life, it only makes sense that I get to know him too."

She stared at him for a moment, the simplicity of his logic disarming. No jealousy. No posturing. Just quiet understanding.

"You really want to go?"

"I do," he said. "Besides, it sounds like you could use someone to keep Claire's claws off you."

That made her laugh—unexpected and genuine. "You know what?" she said, reaching for his hand. "That might be a good idea."

James squeezed her fingers. "Consider me your human shield."

Jasmine grinned. "I'll try not to let her draw blood."

As they got out of bed and began getting ready, a strange sense of lightness settled over her. She wasn't sure how the day would go. But for now, she wasn't facing it alone.

And for the first time in days, that felt like enough.

Robert woke with the first pale ray of sunlight filtering through the hospital blinds. The stillness of the early morning offered no comfort—only the slow, throbbing reminder of pain in his spine, and the dull ache of uncertainty that had taken up permanent residence in his chest.

He stared at the ceiling, trying to will the numb heaviness from his legs, but the only thing he felt was the tightness that came with waiting.

He didn't know what the day would bring.

The doctor had been honest—no guarantees. No promises. Only the slow, uphill battle of rehabilitation and possibility.

But in spite of the pain, in spite of the thousand questions looping through his mind, one thought rose above all the others.

He wanted to see Jasmine.

He hadn't dreamt her presence—he knew that now. Her voice, her hand in his, the way she'd sat beside him in those quiet days when he couldn't speak but could still feel. She'd been there. When he was lost in the dark, she'd been the one tethering him to the light.

And now… he just hoped she would come again today.

Which meant, if he was honest, he was also hoping Claire wouldn't.

He was still thinking about that when a soft knock tapped against the door, followed by the gentle creak of it opening.

His heart leapt as Jasmine stepped into the room, the morning light catching in her hair, her eyes warm and familiar.

Relief hit him in a wave so powerful it nearly knocked the breath from his lungs.

But then… he saw the man behind her.

James.

Tall. Confident. Steady. His hand briefly touched the small of Jasmine's back as they entered, and Robert felt it—sharp and unmistakable—something inside him dropped.

She was smiling. Not the forced, polite kind. The real one—the one that reached her eyes. And James? He looked like he belonged at her side.

Robert tried to school his expression, but it was too late. The flicker of surprise—and the sting—had already passed through his eyes.

"Hey," Jasmine said, stepping closer to the bed. "You're up early."

"Couldn't sleep," he replied, his voice lower than usual. "Morning pain's a good alarm clock."

Jasmine smiled softly, brushing a hand along the rail of his bed.

James offered a polite nod as he stepped forward. "Good to see you again, Robert. I was sorry to hear about your accident."

Robert met his gaze, forcing a small, polite smile that didn't quite reach his eyes. "Thanks. Not exactly the five-star resort I had in mind."

James didn't linger. After a few minutes of light conversation—mostly Jasmine filling in the silence—he turned to her and touched her arm.

"I'll wait outside. Take all the time you need."

Jasmine nodded, her fingers brushing his lightly. "Thank you."

As the door closed behind him, the room settled into a quiet stillness.

Robert turned his head slowly, taking in the sight of her—familiar, grounding, yet somehow just out of reach. "So," he said carefully, "you and James… still a thing?"

Jasmine hesitated, then gave a quiet nod. "Yeah. It's going okay."

He looked away, jaw tightening just slightly. Pain was one thing. This? This was something else entirely.

Regret. Sharp and unrelenting.

Because it wasn't just that James was here.

It was that Robert was too late.

She moved closer and reached for his hand. Her touch was gentle, steady. "I came yesterday," she said softly. "But I didn't want to interrupt your visit with Claire."

His fingers curled around hers, holding on a little tighter than he meant to. "Yeah. Mum and Dad told me." A pause. "Mum also said you've been here every day."

"I have," Jasmine said simply. "Of course I have. I care about you, Robert. You're family."

His eyes found hers—unguarded, full of questions he wasn't ready to ask aloud. And for a moment, everything else fell away. The sterile hospital room. The pain. Even James waiting outside. It was just her. Just them.

Time folded in on itself—suspended between what was, what could've been, and what still lingered in the space between.

"I was surprised to see Claire yesterday," Jasmine said quietly, her gaze dropping to their linked hands. "I didn't know you two were still together."

She hesitated, then added, her voice low and edged with a vulnerability she hadn't intended to reveal, "If you were mine... I wouldn't have taken two weeks to show up."

Robert's jaw tightened slightly. "She said she was in New Zealand. A photo shoot."

Jasmine gave a small nod. "Right."

A beat of silence stretched between them. Then he looked at her—really looked.

"I remember you," he said quietly. "You were here. Talking to me... holding my hand."

His fingers tightened gently around hers. "Thank you, Jasmine. For not giving up on me."

Her throat tightened. "I would never give up on you, Robert. Not then... not now."

And then—before she could second-guess it—she leaned down and pressed a soft kiss to his forehead. The gesture was tender, instinctive... and it surprised even her.

When Jasmine pulled back, Robert's eyes were still locked on hers—wide, vulnerable, searching. The space between them pulsed with something unspoken, fragile and real.

"Jasmine..." he began, his voice low, cracked with emotion.

He was just about to say the words—*that he'd made a mistake, that it should've been her*—when the door opened.

Claire walked in without knocking.

Her gaze landed on their linked hands, and her expression hardened instantly. Her mouth pressed into a thin, disapproving line.

Jasmine gently released Robert's hand, the warmth of their shared moment dissipating like mist under a sudden chill.

Claire's voice cut through the room, sharp and saccharine. "Well, isn't it little Miss Perfect."

Before Jasmine could respond, James stepped into the room behind her, his gaze sweeping over the scene—the tension, the shift in Jasmine's body, the edge in Claire's tone. Without hesitation, he crossed the space with quiet assurance and placed a steadying arm around Jasmine's waist.

"I think she is," he said smoothly, his voice calm but resolute.

Claire blinked, visibly thrown. Whatever clever insult she'd been poised to deliver seemed to catch in her throat.

For the first time since her dramatic entrance, Claire faltered—thrown off by James's quiet confidence and the unwavering certainty in his words. The jab she'd come armed with wilted on her tongue.

Jasmine looked up at James and gave him a soft smile, a silent thank you shining in her eyes. Then she turned back to Robert.

"I'll see you soon," she said gently, and leaned in to press a light kiss to his cheek.

Robert's voice was low, almost reverent. "Thanks for coming."

As she stepped back, his gaze followed her—not just with longing, but with something sharper now.

Regret.

Because in the space of a few seconds, James had done what Robert hadn't—stood beside Jasmine, spoken up for her, protected her without hesitation. And that simple act made something ache deep in Robert's chest.

He'd failed her in ways he hadn't fully understood until now.

Chapter Eighteen

As Jasmine drove from work to the hospital that Monday afternoon, her thoughts drifted to James. They had spent all of Sunday together—lunch at a sun-drenched café in Bondi, followed by ice cream along the boardwalk. The sea breeze had whipped through her hair as they laughed, strolled, and people-watched from a bench overlooking the sand. Later, back at her place, they'd curled up with takeaway and ended up in bed again, the comfort between them easy and familiar.

She smiled at the memory. James was lovely. Thoughtful. Grounded. He said all the right things, did all the right things. With him, she felt safe—wanted, even cherished.

But the flutter was still missing.

That breathless, inexplicable catch in her chest—the one she always felt around Robert. The tension. The pull. That maddening, electric current she could never quite explain.

She reasoned with herself as the traffic inched forward. That kind of spark wasn't everything. It would come. It had to. Real relationships were built on trust, kindness, stability… all of which James offered in abundance.

Still, a quiet part of her whispered: *What if it doesn't?*

She shook the thought off and focused on the road ahead. This wasn't about Robert anymore. That chapter was supposed to be closed. James was here now—solid and steady.

She just had to give herself time.

And hope that eventually, her heart would catch up.

Jasmine parked her car and grabbed her tote from the passenger seat, pausing for a moment before stepping out. The late afternoon sun was dipping low, casting golden light across the hospital car park. As she made her way inside, her thoughts wandered— mostly to James, partly to Robert, and entirely to whether Claire would be in that room again.

She hated that the possibility made her hesitate at the door.

Jasmine hesitated, then knocked softly, hoping—*really hoping*—that Claire wasn't inside.

When she eased the door open, she exhaled with quiet relief. Only Robert and his parents were there, the atmosphere calm and easy. No sharp words. No icy glares. No tension thick enough to cut.

"Hello," she said with a smile, stepping inside.

Robert was already grinning. "Hello."

Terry and Kelly stood up to greet her, each offering a warm hug and kiss on the cheek.

"Hello, love," Kelly said, her eyes kind. "How was your day?"

"Busy," Jasmine replied, slipping her bag off her shoulder. "But it keeps me out of trouble." She chuckled lightly, already feeling more at ease.

Kelly smiled, motioning for her to sit. "That's what I used to say when Robert was a toddler. Little hands, big messes."

Robert rolled his eyes affectionately. "I'm right here, Mum."

Jasmine laughed as she took the seat beside his bed. "Good to know some things never change."

And just like that, the room filled with easy warmth—the kind of warmth Jasmine had always found at the Steele estate, and especially in Robert's presence.

Jasmine stayed for nearly an hour, though it felt like far less. The conversation moved easily, full of shared memories and small updates. Robert's voice was stronger today, and his eyes had that familiar spark that always made her heart squeeze, even when she tried to ignore it.

"William and Mary were in earlier," he mentioned casually. "Will's taking over the Byron Bay project while I'm out of action."

"That's great," Jasmine said, genuinely pleased. "He'll keep things steady for you."

Robert nodded, then looked at her with a half-smile. "Yeah. But it's not the same as being there."

She glanced at the time and rose reluctantly. "I should go; let you get some rest."

The disappointment in his face was clear, though he tried to mask it. "Thanks for coming," he said softly.

She leaned in and took his hand, giving it a gentle squeeze. Then she kissed him lightly on the cheek. "It's good to see you smile."

Kelly stood as well. "I'll walk you out—I want to talk to you about something."

Jasmine turned, surprised but curious. "Okay."

Terry stood too, giving her another warm kiss on the cheek. "Bye, sweetheart. Hopefully, we'll see you again soon."

"You will," Jasmine promised with a smile, then followed Kelly into the corridor.

The hospital door clicked softly shut behind them, leaving Robert watching the space where she'd just been, already missing her presence.

Kelly glanced over at Jasmine as they walked down the corridor. "Robert's coming home to the estate on Wednesday."

Jasmine's face lit up. "Oh, that's wonderful. I think he'll much prefer being home."

"He will," Kelly agreed with a soft smile. "We've converted the downstairs study into a recovery space for him. It's private, close to everything he'll need. We've also hired a nurse to help out, even though Terry and I will be there most of the time."

"That's great, Kelly," Jasmine said warmly. "He'll heal better surrounded by family."

Kelly paused, then turned to face her fully. "I actually wanted to ask you something. You can absolutely say no—but I'm hoping you won't."

Jasmine tilted her head, curious. "What is it?"

Kelly hesitated for only a moment before speaking, her voice gentle but deliberate. "Would you consider being Robert's full-time physiotherapist? Just until he— *hopefully*—gets back on his feet."

Jasmine blinked, caught off guard. "Oh… I wasn't expecting that."

"I know it's a lot to ask," Kelly said, her tone warm. "But he trusts you. He responds to you in a way he doesn't with anyone else. And if he's going to get through this… I think having you there might make all the difference—not just physically, but emotionally too."

Jasmine's breath caught slightly, but she recovered with a soft smile. "Thank you, Kelly. That means more than you know."

She paused. "I'm not saying no."

Kelly's shoulders relaxed, a flicker of hope lighting her eyes.

"But I do need to look at my schedule and see what's possible. I'll probably be able to give you an answer tomorrow. Is that okay?"

"Absolutely," Kelly said. She touched Jasmine's arm lightly. "Just knowing you're thinking about it… that's enough for now."

After Jasmine got home, she had a quick shower and made herself a light meal. The day had left her thoughtful—too many moments lingering in her mind. She curled up on the couch, tucked her legs beneath her, and picked up her phone.

She typed:

Got time to talk?

Not a minute later, her phone lit up with James's name. She smiled as she answered.

"Hello."

"Hi, sweetheart." His voice was warm and familiar. "How was your day?"

"Busy," she said with a soft laugh. "But good, mostly. Yours?"

"Long meetings. A mountain of paperwork. And a sandwich that tried to pass as lunch."

She chuckled. "Poor you. Want me to file a formal complaint with your assistant?"

"Please do. And request better sandwich standards across the board." He paused, then added more gently, "You sound tired."

"I am," she admitted. "But in a good way. It was one of those days that just… makes you think."

There was a beat of comfortable silence before he said, "Tell me."

Jasmine shifted slightly on the couch. "I went to see Robert after work."

"Okay."

"His parents were there, and just before I left, Kelly walked me out. She told me he's being discharged on Wednesday and they're setting up a room for him at the estate."

"That's great," James said. "He'll be more comfortable at home."

"She asked me to be his full-time physiotherapist while he recovers."

James was quiet for a moment, not out of surprise, but as if considering the weight of it.

"Wow," he said finally. "That's a big ask."

"Yeah. It kind of threw me. I wasn't expecting it."

"What did you say?"

"I didn't say no," she said honestly. "But I told her I'd need to look at my schedule and think about it."

"Well," James said, his voice steady, "whatever you decide, I'm behind you. If anyone can help him, it's you."

"You're not… weird about it?" she asked, her voice tentative.

"I get it, Jasmine. You care about him. You've been part of his life for a long time. I'd be lying if I said it doesn't give me a little pause… but no, it doesn't scare me."

She exhaled, tension she hadn't realised she was holding softening. "Thank you."

James's tone warmed. "You don't need to thank me. I want you to do what feels right. And if helping Robert is what that looks like, then I'll support you every step of the way."

Jasmine smiled into the phone. "You're kind of amazing, you know that?"

"I've been told," he said with a light chuckle. "But I like hearing it from you."

After Jasmine hung up the phone, the silence in her apartment seemed louder than before. She set her phone down on the coffee table and reached for her tablet, opening her calendar. Her week was already tight—client consults, two hospital visits, a workshop on Thursday. Still, with a little shuffling, she could make room.

But that wasn't the real question, was it?

She leaned back against the cushions, the soft glow of the lamp casting long shadows across the room. Her eyes skimmed over the appointments, the colour-coded boxes, the tidy blocks of time. She could do it. She could make it work.

But should she?

Helping Robert day in and day out—being in his space, touching him, encouraging him, watching him struggle and, hopefully, slowly improve—it would blur every line she'd spent years trying to hold.

Because as much as she'd told herself she was just his friend—his best friend—there had always been something more humming beneath the surface. Unspoken. Unacted upon. But always there.

And now? He needed her. Not just anyone. *Her.* Kelly believed in her, trusted her. Robert would too. And Jasmine knew she could help him—maybe more than anyone else.

But what she wasn't sure of… was whether she could protect her heart.

She closed her eyes, letting her head fall back against the cushion. James's voice echoed in her mind— *"Whatever you decide, I've got your back."* He meant it. He always did. Sweet, grounded, stable James. He deserved someone fully in it with him. Someone who wasn't still wondering *what if.*

What if Robert had looked at her differently? What if he finally said the words she'd waited so long to hear? What if this time, she couldn't keep the fantasies at bay?

Her chest tightened.

She had James now. She was happy—mostly. And yet, some foolish part of her heart still skipped whenever Robert smiled at her like she was the only one in the room.

She opened her eyes and stared down at the calendar again. Her finger hovered over the time blocks she could clear. Rearranging was the easy part.

It was everything else that would be messy.

And still… she wasn't ready to say no.

Chapter Nineteen

Robert sat upright in his hospital bed, eyes flicking toward the clock. Jasmine was due any minute. His parents were still with him, filling the room with light chatter—bless them, they were doing their best to distract him from the monotony of the hospital walls.

He appreciated the effort, even more so when they told him about the study they'd converted at the estate.

"It's all ready," Kelly had said with a smile. "Private, accessible, quiet. You'll be comfortable there."

Robert had nodded, genuinely touched. But comfort wasn't exactly what he needed. He needed control back—his legs, his independence, his life. Still, the gesture mattered.

Then the door creaked open—and it wasn't Jasmine.

It was Claire.

She stepped inside, and immediately, the atmosphere shifted. The warmth evaporated. Robert could sense the tension ripple from both his parents. There was no bright smile on Claire's face, none of her usual performative sweetness. Her shoulders were stiff, her expression unreadable.

"Claire," Kelly said politely, standing. "We'll give you two a moment."

Robert immediately straightened. "Can you leave the door open? Just in case Jasmine arrives."

His voice was calm but firm. He didn't want to miss Jasmine's arrival.

Claire's mouth tightened, her jaw visibly clenching. "Of course," she muttered. "Wouldn't want to interrupt your fan club."

Terry and Kelly exchanged a glance but quietly stepped into the hallway, leaving the door ajar.

Claire moved closer but didn't sit. She crossed her arms instead, eyes scanning Robert like she didn't quite recognise him. "I thought I'd feel guilty coming here," she began, her voice low. "But after that little performance, I'm not so sure."

Robert frowned. "Performance?"

"You asking your parents to leave the door open—*for her.*" Claire nodded toward the hallway. "You're still pining after Jasmine like a lovesick schoolboy."

He didn't hesitate. "Don't talk about her like that."

Claire laughed under her breath, but there was no humour in it. "Oh, please. You think I haven't seen it? Even before the accident—you lit up whenever she walked into a room. Always some inside joke, some stolen glance."

Robert's gaze didn't waver. "She's been a good friend to me. One of the few who hasn't treated me like I'm broken."

Claire's face twisted slightly, as if that was exactly what she'd come to say.

She inhaled, then said with forced calm, "I've been thinking about this a lot. About us. And I've made a decision."

Robert felt a shift in the air, but it didn't come with dread—it came with quiet relief.

"I'm calling off the engagement," Claire said.

He blinked. "Are you sure?"

She gave a bitter laugh. "You don't even sound upset."

"I'm not," he said quietly.

Claire's eyes flashed. "Wow. Okay. That makes this easier."

He didn't respond. He had nothing left to fight for with her.

But she wasn't finished.

"I didn't sign up for this," she said, gesturing vaguely to the hospital bed, the wheelchair parked beside it. "I didn't imagine our future with me pushing you up ramps and planning dates around accessible toilets."

Robert flinched, the words landing like fists.

"And let's be honest," she continued, her voice growing cold, "I doubt any woman does. Do you really think Jasmine—or anyone, for that matter—wants this life? Living with a cripple? Having to nurse a man who can't even walk himself to the bathroom?"

"Claire," he said sharply, but his voice caught on the last word.

Her words hung in the air like smoke, sour and suffocating.

She looked at him for a beat longer, then reached for her bag. "I hope you get better. I really do. But I'm not the woman who's going to stick around and play carer for the rest of her life."

And with that, she turned and walked out—heels clicking against the linoleum like a gavel.

Robert stared at the door long after she was gone, heart pounding. For a moment, he felt nothing at all.

Then the doubt crept in.

Would Jasmine really want this life?

Was he worth the effort now?

Or had Claire just said what everyone else was too polite to admit?

His gaze dropped to the wheelchair by his side.

The flutter of hope he'd felt earlier—the anticipation of seeing Jasmine—dulled beneath the weight of uncertainty.

He didn't feel like the man he used to be.

And suddenly, he wasn't sure he ever would be again.

Jasmine stepped out of the lift, the familiar corridor leading to Robert's room bathed in soft afternoon light. Her heart gave its usual flutter at the thought of seeing him. She adjusted the strap of her tote on her shoulder and rounded the corner—

Kelly and Terry were standing just outside the room, the door slightly ajar behind them. Kelly's face lit up when she saw her.

"Oh, Jasmine, perfect timing," she said warmly, stepping forward. "Robert didn't want to miss you. He asked us to leave the door open, so he'd know the moment you arrived."

Jasmine smiled, touched. "That's sweet."

Kelly's hand found her arm gently, her expression shifting into something more urgent. "He could really use a friendly face right now. Please—stay. Even if it's just for a little while?"

Jasmine nodded, concern rising. "Of course."

She took a step closer to the door, intending to knock and announce herself.

That's when she heard it.

Claire's voice—sharp, cutting—sliced through the quiet air.

'And let's be honest, I doubt any woman does. Do you really think Jasmine—or anyone, for that matter—wants this life? Living with a cripple? Having to nurse a man who can't even walk himself to the bathroom?'

The words landed like a slap.

Jasmine froze, her breath catching in her throat.

It took her a second to register that she'd actually heard her own name. That she hadn't imagined the disdain in Claire's voice. The cruelty. The casual venom.

A wave of nausea rolled through her.

Her hand instinctively pressed to her chest as the weight of the words settled there—cold and heavy.

Kelly, still beside her, had gone rigid. She looked like she might march back into the room.

But Jasmine reached out, gently touching her arm. "No," she whispered, her voice trembling. "Let her finish."

She didn't know what stunned her more—that Claire had said it, or that Claire believed it.

That Robert might believe it.

Her heart ached at the thought.

She had to keep herself still, had to breathe through the storm swelling behind her ribs. Because if she walked in now, she'd say something she couldn't take back—and this wasn't about Claire.

It was about Robert.

And how, no matter what Claire said… he was not broken.

Jasmine turned slightly, just enough so Claire wouldn't see her if she left the room. She waited, jaw tight, heart pounding, willing herself to stay composed.

Claire had no idea what she was talking about.

But Robert… Robert might believe her.

And that thought shattered something deep inside Jasmine.

A moment later, the door swung open with a sharp jerk. Claire stormed out, her heels clicking furiously against the tiled floor. Her face was taut with frustration, but her expression darkened further when she caught sight of Jasmine standing just a few steps away.

Claire's mouth curled into something that wasn't quite a smile.

"Of course, you're here," she said, her tone bitter and loud enough to carry. "Well, he's all yours. Good luck."

Jasmine stared at her, momentarily speechless. The venom in Claire's voice hit like a slap. She blinked, not because she didn't expect hostility, but because she hadn't expected such cruelty.

Claire didn't wait for a reply. She tossed her hair back, turned on her heel, and marched toward the elevators without a second glance.

Jasmine watched her go, heart pounding, mouth slightly open. She looked over at Kelly and Terry, who both wore the same expression—equal parts mortified and heartbroken.

Jasmine shook her head slowly, as if trying to clear the sting of Claire's words from her ears.

She'd always known Claire could be cutting—she'd endured more than her share of subtle digs over the years—but never like this. Never so openly cruel. And never to Robert.

Not to the man Claire had once claimed to love.

She had never heard such coldness packed into so few syllables—weaponised words, designed not just to wound, but to leave lasting scars.

And it wasn't the insult to her that stung—it was what Claire had tried to do to him. The way she'd spoken to someone already hurting, already stripped bare.

Someone Jasmine cared about more than she was ready to admit.

She turned toward the open door, her pulse still racing, and walked into the room—because Claire might've left poison behind, but Jasmine wasn't going to let it linger.

Not for a second longer.

Jasmine drew a steadying breath, squared her shoulders, and stepped into the room, Kelly and Terry following quietly behind her.

Robert sat propped against the pillows, pale and drawn, tension etched along his jawline. But the moment his gaze found hers, something in him shifted—his features softened, the storm in his expression easing just slightly.

"Hey," he rasped, his voice low and rough around the edges.

She crossed the room slowly, her gaze scanning his features, searching for the damage Claire had left behind. It was there—in the slight tremble in his fingers, the way his shoulders didn't quite relax.

"Hi," she said gently, setting her bag down beside the chair. "Your mum said you didn't want to miss seeing me."

A faint smile touched his lips, but it didn't reach his eyes. "Yeah. I'm glad you came."

She sat beside him, watching him closely. "Do you want to talk about it?"

He hesitated, then shook his head. "Not really."

She nodded, letting the silence stretch. He needed space, not pressure. But after a beat, he spoke again, voice low.

"She said I wasn't the kind of man a woman could build a life with anymore."

Jasmine felt something sharp twist in her chest. "She's wrong."

He looked away. "Maybe. Maybe not."

"Robert." She leaned forward, resting her hand lightly over his. "You are still you. The man people trust. The man people love. You've been hurt—physically, emotionally—but that doesn't change your worth. Not one bit."

He swallowed hard, his jaw working. "It's not just about me. It's about what I can't give someone."

She squeezed his hand. "Then maybe let them decide what's enough. You don't get to write yourself off."

His eyes finally met hers—raw, vulnerable, searching.

And she didn't look away.

She stayed with him in that quiet, painful space. Not rushing to fill the silence. Not offering platitudes or pretending it didn't hurt.

Just… being there.

Exactly where he needed her most.

Then Jasmine turned to his parents and offered a small, steady smile.

"I have some good news," she said. "I've rearranged my schedule. I'll be your full-time physiotherapist."

Kelly gasped and jumped to her feet, pulling Jasmine into a warm, grateful hug.

"Oh, that's wonderful," she said, emotion thick in her voice.

Robert gave a faint smile, the tension in his shoulders easing slightly.

"That's great," Robert murmured, the corners of his mouth twitching into something close to a real smile.

"Thank you," Terry said, his voice quiet, but weighted with emotion.

Jasmine turned back to Robert, her expression softening into something more familiar—gentle but resolute.

"And just because we're friends," she said, arching a brow, "doesn't mean I'm going easy on you."

Robert let out a dry chuckle, some of the heaviness in his chest loosening.

"I'd be worried if you did."

Kelly laughed softly. "She's always had a no-nonsense streak."

"Perfect," Jasmine said, flashing Robert a teasing smile. "Because nonsense doesn't get people back on their feet."

Robert met her gaze again, something quiet and grateful settling in his eyes.

For the first time in days, hope didn't feel quite so far away.

The next morning, the quiet hum of early traffic filtered through the open hospital window as Robert waited for the medical transport to arrive. His overnight bag was packed, his discharge paperwork signed, and yet a strange weight sat in his chest—not dread exactly, but something heavier than relief.

He was going back to his parents' estate—a place he hadn't lived in for years. It wasn't where he would've chosen to recover; if it were up to him, he'd be in his own home, surrounded by the life he'd built. But he understood why the decision had been made.

The Steele estate meant comfort, care, security. Familiar walls. Familiar voices. But it also meant confronting just how much had changed.

What was once a symbol of strength and privilege now felt like a quiet echo of everything he'd lost.

Kelly hovered nearby, checking and double-checking the time. Terry stood by the window, arms folded, gaze flicking between his son and the street below. Neither spoke much—they didn't need to. The silence was filled with enough unsaid emotion to stretch across the room.

When the medical van finally pulled up, a uniformed paramedic appeared at the door with a calm, efficient smile. A nurse in light blue scrubs followed close behind—early thirties, tidy bun, clipboard in hand.

"Good morning, Mr. Steele," she said. "I'm Megan, the in-home nurse your parents arranged. I'll be helping with your care once you're settled."

Robert offered her a polite nod. "Thanks."

The transfer was careful, precise. The paramedics moved Robert into a wheelchair and then into the transport van, Terry assisting while Kelly fussed with blankets and pillows, making sure he'd be comfortable for the short ride. Robert bore it all quietly, the mechanical process of it a reminder of just how far from normal things still were.

The estate was only twenty minutes away, but the journey stretched—every corner of the city was familiar, yet everything looked different from the passenger seat of a medical van.

When they reached the estate, staff were waiting. The front gate was already open, and the path leading to the house had been cleared for the van to pull as close as possible.

The downstairs study had been transformed. Gone were the shelves of legal journals and antique maps. In their place stood a hospital-grade bed, adaptive equipment, a cushioned armchair, and a wide window that overlooked the gardens. It was tasteful, warm. Homely—but functional.

Megan helped Robert settle into the bed while Kelly directed the placement of things around the room. Terry made sure the ramp was stable, and the intercoms worked. There was a quiet efficiency to it all, but even so, Robert felt like a guest in his own life.

He didn't say much. Just observed. Absorbed.

Megan adjusted the pillows behind his back. "Comfortable?"

"As good as it gets," he murmured.

Kelly perched on the armrest of the nearby chair and reached for his hand. "Jasmine will be by this afternoon to start your program."

Something flickered in Robert's eyes—relief, apprehension, maybe both.

"Okay."

He glanced out the window, watching a pair of gardeners move about the edge of the lawn.

This was home now—at least for a while.

And yet, nothing about it felt like home.

Chapter Twenty

The sun hung low in the sky as Jasmine stepped out of her car, the quiet elegance of the Steele estate stretching before her like a memory she hadn't meant to keep.

She tugged her tote strap higher on her shoulder, inhaled deeply, and made her way to the front door.

Kelly opened it before she had a chance to knock. "Jasmine, darling—you're right on time."

Jasmine smiled. "Wouldn't miss it."

Inside, the house was quiet, filled with the faint scent of lemon polish and fresh flowers. Kelly led her through the wide hallway, her heels clicking softly against the hardwood floors.

"He's in the study," she said, her tone warm but edged with concern. "We've done everything we can to make it feel like home, but…" She trailed off with a sigh. "He's still adjusting."

Jasmine nodded. "I'll go gently."

They stepped into the converted study, now bathed in afternoon light. Robert sat in the adjustable bed, dressed in a charcoal T-shirt and sweatpants, his posture stiff and eyes distant as he looked out toward the garden. The sharp angles of his face were more pronounced today—his skin a little too pale, his jaw a little too tight.

Megan stood nearby, clipboard in hand. She turned as they entered and offered Jasmine a polite smile.

"You must be Jasmine," she said, extending a hand.

"That's me. Nice to meet you."

"I'm Megan—full-time nurse. I'll be coordinating with you on care. Just so we're on the same page, I've got you down for sessions every weekday at three, Saturday mornings at ten, and Sundays off. Does that work for you?"

"Perfect," Jasmine said, setting her tote bag beside the armchair near Robert's bed.

Kelly hovered behind her. "We'll give you some space," she said gently. "Terry's just upstairs. Call if you need anything."

Megan nodded. "I'll stay nearby unless you want total privacy."

Jasmine glanced at Robert, whose gaze hadn't left the window. "Let's play it by ear."

Kelly squeezed Jasmine's arm lightly before she and Megan left the room, the door clicking softly shut behind them.

Silence settled like a second skin.

Jasmine crossed to the bed, keeping her movements unhurried, non-threatening. "Hey," she said, her voice light.

Robert turned toward her. "Hey."

His voice was flat, but not unkind.

Jasmine studied him a moment, taking in the tension in his shoulders, the dullness behind his eyes. "Ready for our first session?"

He gave a half-hearted shrug. "As I'll ever be."

Jasmine perched on the edge of the armchair, resting her elbows on her knees. "Listen," she said gently, "we don't have to go hard today. It's just about getting started. Rebuilding the connection between your body and brain. That's all."

His jaw flexed, but he didn't respond.

She opened her bag and pulled out a tablet with his exercise schedule, followed by a resistance band and a folded towel. "We'll start small. Just some ankle and knee activation, then see how you're sitting balance is. No pressure. No expectations."

"Except to move again," he said bitterly.

Jasmine met his gaze evenly. "No. The goal is progress, not miracles. One day at a time."

He looked away again, lips pressed thin. "Hard to see the point sometimes."

She didn't flinch. "Because you're scared it might not work?"

"Because I'm not sure it matters if it does."

The words landed like stones.

Jasmine didn't rush to fill the silence. She sat with it, let it hang.

Then, quietly: "It matters to me."

His gaze snapped back to hers.

She didn't look away. "Not because I want you to be who you were before the accident. But because I know who you are now still matters. You're not less. You're just... in a harder chapter."

Something flickered across his face—guilt, maybe. Or the beginning of hope.

"I don't know how to do this," he murmured.

"You don't have to know," she said softly. "You just have to try."

She unfolded the towel and positioned it beneath his calf, her touch gentle but sure. "Let's start with something simple. Can you press your heel into the towel for five seconds? Just a light contraction."

He didn't move at first. Then—slowly—he did.

"Good," she said, her tone bright. "Hold... four... three... two... relax."

They repeated it. Again. And again. Quietly. Steadily.

After a few minutes, she glanced up. "You're doing better than you think."

Robert exhaled, the corners of his mouth twitching upward—not quite a smile, but close.

"I'm not going easy on you, you know," she added with mock sternness.

He let out a dry chuckle. "God help me."

She smiled. "Too late for that. You've got me instead."

And for the first time that day, something in him loosened.

He wasn't ready to believe in his future just yet.

But maybe... he could believe in her.

Five days later.

The morning sun filtered softly through the tall windows of the Steele estate study, casting warm shafts of light across the wooden floor. Jasmine arrived a little before ten, as promised, and Megan greeted her with a quick smile before slipping out of the room. The house was quiet—Terry had gone into the city for a meeting, and Kelly was in the garden.

Jasmine set her tote down near the bed, where Robert sat upright, already dressed in loose black track pants and a plain navy T-shirt. He looked more alert today, less guarded—though the vulnerability still lingered in the lines of his face.

"Morning," she said, cheerful but calm.

"Hey," Robert replied. He was still getting used to how things started now—no more casual chats on the phone, no texts from her just to check in. She was here, every day, but not in the way he had once hoped.

"How are you feeling?"

"Sore," he said honestly. "But less… discouraged. So, I guess that's progress."

She smiled. "That is progress."

The session unfolded steadily. Jasmine guided him through a mix of passive and active movements: assisted leg lifts, ankle pumps, and weight shifts while seated. She used a small balance board to test his trunk control, encouraging him to engage his core as he leaned slightly forward, side to side.

"You're stabilising faster than you were on Monday," she said, watching his form carefully. "That's a good sign."

Robert nodded, sweat beading lightly on his brow. He wasn't sure what made him more exhausted—the exercises or pretending he wasn't constantly distracted by her presence.

By the time they wrapped, it was close to eleven. Jasmine helped him reposition in his chair, set the resistance band aside, and wiped down the equipment. She was just reaching for her water bottle when her phone rang.

Robert glanced at the screen before she did.

James.

A pulse of something dark and unwelcome rippled through his chest.

Of course it was James. The man with no injuries and perfect timing.

Jasmine saw the name, hesitated for a second, then answered. "Hey you," she said, her voice warming.

Robert looked away.

"Mmm… I'm still here. Just finished the session." She gave a small laugh. "Yeah, he survived. Barely."

Robert managed a faint smirk at that, but the knot in his stomach tightened.

"Oh? Lunch sounds nice." A pause. "Yes, I'd love that. Give me twenty minutes?"

She ended the call and turned back to him, slipping the phone into her tote. "That was James," she said casually. "He asked me to lunch."

Robert nodded, but the motion was stiff. "Sounds nice. He's good at that kind of thing."

Jasmine tilted her head slightly, sensing the shift in his tone. "He is," she agreed, tying her hair back loosely. "Kind, steady… just easy to be around."

Robert didn't respond. His eyes had dropped to his lap, his hands idle in his lap.

She softened. "I'll see you on Monday."

"Right," he said. "Thanks for today."

She gave him a long look—curious, maybe even a little hesitant—but didn't push. "You're welcome."

Then she was gone, her footsteps light down the hall. Her scent still clung to the air— eucalyptus and something sweet. It made the silence feel louder.

And Robert sat in the quiet that followed—surrounded by the soft hum of machines, the sterile scent of antiseptic, and the ghost of her touch still lingering on his skin.

Progress and pain.

He looked around the room—the framed family photo someone had set on the sideboard, the tray Megan had just cleared, the half-folded blanket at the foot of the bed. It all felt like effort. Like motion without meaning.

He had waited too long.

And now she had someone. Someone strong and steady, who made her laugh and protected her out loud. Someone who had never looked at her and thought *not yet*.

Robert leaned back against the pillows, jaw tight, breath shallow. He didn't know if it was the pain in his spine or the ache in his chest that throbbed more.

A soft knock came a few minutes later, and then William stepped in, his suit jacket slung over his shoulder, hair wind-tossed from the afternoon air.

"Hey," William said easily. "Thought I'd drop in, see how things were going."

Robert glanced at him and didn't answer right away.

William pulled a chair closer to the bed. "Kelly said the morning session went well. You're making solid progress."

Robert scoffed under his breath, voice low. "Doesn't feel like progress."

"It is. You're doing great, mate."

There was silence for a beat, then Robert turned his head, his eyes flaring with something that had simmered far too long.

"You remember when Jasmine turned twenty-one?" Robert's voice was low—quiet but laced with a razor edge.

William blinked, caught off guard. "Of course. That was the year—"

"You told me not to say anything." Robert's voice cracked around the words. "You said she was too young. That she needed time. That if I really cared about her, I'd wait. That I'd hurt her."

William straightened slowly, sensing a shift he couldn't unfeel. "Rob—"

"No." The word cut sharp. Bitter. "You told me to hold back. To protect her. And I listened to you. I buried what I felt. I kept my distance. I watched her live her life thinking I didn't want her."

"Robert, I was trying to do the right thing," William said, voice tight. "You were older. She was just starting her adult life. You agreed—"

"I was in love with her!" The words rang out, raw and unfiltered. Pain cracked through the room like thunder. "Even then. And I would've told her if you hadn't made me question every instinct I had."

William sat stunned, the air between them brittle with things unsaid.

"I watched her walk away this morning," Robert said, quieter now—defeated. "She's with someone else. And he's good. I even like the guy." He let out a breath that was more exhale than sound. "And I'm stuck in this bed. Can't even stand on my own. I let her go when I had the chance… and now I'm just the man who waited too damn long."

Silence bloomed between them, thick with regret. William swallowed hard.

"I didn't know," he said softly. "I didn't know you felt it that deeply."

"Well," Robert muttered, bitterly, "now you do." His eyes stayed fixed on the window. "And even if I said something now, why would she care? She's moved on. She's happy. And I'm—" his voice broke, "—a broken man who can't even walk to the damn door."

He turned his face away; eyes shut against the weight of it all.

And for once, William didn't try to fix it. Didn't reach for words that wouldn't help. He just sat there—still and silent—with his best friend in the raw aftermath of a truth too long buried.

And he didn't say what he'd just found out—that Jasmine felt the same way all along.

Because if Robert knew that now… it would only break him further.

Jasmine arrived at the café just off Hall Street in Bondi twenty minutes after leaving the Steele estate. The morning sun had settled into a mild, golden warmth, and the hum of weekend life buzzed softly around them. James was already there, seated at a table under a wide umbrella, looking relaxed in a pale blue shirt and dark jeans. When he spotted her, he stood and pulled out her chair.

"There's my favourite physiotherapist," he said with a teasing smile.

Jasmine laughed, slipping into the seat. "You're biased."

"Maybe," he admitted. "But not wrong."

He reached for her hand across the table, brushing his thumb gently along her knuckles. "How'd it go this morning?"

She shrugged lightly. "Good, actually. Robert's starting to engage more. Slowly. It's a lot of physical work, but… the emotional stuff's heavier. He's trying to hide it, but I can tell he's still struggling with what this means for his future."

James nodded, his expression thoughtful. "I imagine he is. And it's lucky he has you there—someone who sees him, not just the injury."

She glanced down, touched by his words. "When Kelly asked me to be his full-time physiotherapist until he's back on his feet. I was shocked but I rearranged my schedule. It's a big commitment, but I couldn't say no."

"I didn't think you would," James said. "It's who you are, Jaz. You care so deeply… I admire that about you."

She blinked at him, moved. "You're not… upset?"

"Why would I be?" He tilted his head. "Because you're helping someone who's important to you? That's part of why I care about you. You're all in with people you love. You don't just walk away when things get messy."

Jasmine felt a swell of emotion rise in her chest. "You're kind."

"I'm realistic," he said. "I know Robert matters to you. You've never pretended otherwise. And maybe I'd be lying if I said there wasn't a flicker of… insecurity sometimes. But I trust you. And I'm proud of you."

She exhaled, slowly. "Thank you. That means more than you know."

James smiled and leaned across the table to kiss her, his lips brushing hers in a soft, assured way that made her feel safe. *Seen.*

They lingered at lunch, sharing a plate of grilled barramundi and lemony greens, followed by coffee and a shared slice of passionfruit cheesecake. The ease between them grew, laughter folding between bites and stolen glances.

Afterward, he walked her back to her apartment. They didn't talk much as they walked along the boardwalk, hands intertwined. The quiet between them was companionable, unforced.

That night, James stayed.

And the next day, too.

Sunday was slow and cozy—an unhurried rhythm of breakfast in bed, reading side by side on the couch, and takeout Thai for dinner. He made her laugh. He brought a sense of calm she hadn't realised she'd needed. And when they fell asleep, curled together in the softness of her sheets, Jasmine felt something like peace.

But as she drifted off, her mind wandered—just briefly—to Robert's eyes that morning. The ones that didn't quite meet hers when she said goodbye.

James was everything he should be. So why did one part of her still feel like she'd left something unfinished behind?

And the flicker in her chest reminded her that even peace could be complicated.

Chapter Twenty-One

The late morning light filtered through the tall windows, warming the hardwood floors of the Steele estate's study-turned-therapy room. Outside, birds trilled faintly, but inside, the only sounds were the quiet thump of a resistance band against the floor and the low, tense rhythm of breath.

They'd been at it for three weeks now. No real breakthroughs. Just sweat. Setbacks. Stubbornness.

"Again," Jasmine said firmly, holding the edge of the stability board in place with her foot. "Lean forward from the hips—don't collapse your core."

Robert grunted, his arms bracing against the chair handles. "I am."

"No, you're bracing. That's not control." She crouched beside him. "You've got more in you. I can see it."

"Funny," he snapped. "Because all I feel is failure."

Jasmine's jaw tightened, but she didn't flinch. "That's not true. You've come a long way—"

"You think sitting half-straight for ten seconds is a long way?" His voice was sharp, the frustration in it barely contained. "I can't walk. I can't stand. I can't even piss without assistance. So, forgive me if I don't clap for a bloody ten-second balance hold."

Jasmine stood slowly, her face unreadable. "You want to be angry? Fine. Be angry. But don't aim it at the one person in this room who actually believes you can get better."

He stared at her, his chest rising fast. She rarely snapped. And she rarely left space for his bitterness. Today she was doing both.

She turned toward the therapy bag but paused, her voice quieter now. "Do you want to stop for today?"

"No." The word came out low, hoarse. "I don't want to stop."

Jasmine turned back. Their eyes locked.

"Then stop fighting me," she said. "Fight for you instead."

A long silence stretched between them—thick with all the things they hadn't said. His resentment. Her worry. The wound between them that James couldn't quite close.

Finally, Robert nodded. A rough, reluctant gesture. "Alright. Let's try again."

Jasmine approached carefully, repositioning the balance board under his feet. "Okay," she said, her voice steadier now. "Shift forward. Engage your lower abs, not your arms. Think tall spine. You're not just tipping—you're initiating."

He gritted his teeth, tried again. The movement was awkward, hesitant—then suddenly, something fired.

"Wait," he said, breath catching. "I—"

Jasmine was already moving. "What do you feel?"

"Heat," he whispered. "In my thighs. Tingling. It's—" He blinked rapidly. "It's different."

She dropped to her knees beside him. "Robert—can you wiggle your left toes?"

He looked down. Concentrated.

Nothing.

Jasmine didn't flinch. "Okay. Try the right."

He stared, jaw set. Then, barely—*barely*—the tips of his toes shifted inside the sock.

She gasped. "That was movement. Robert, that was you."

He exhaled hard, a sound between disbelief and relief. "I felt it."

She smiled, radiant and proud. "Then we're getting somewhere."

His eyes flicked to hers. "You were right. I do still have something left."

"You have everything left," she said, her voice soft, intimate. "You're just learning how to find it again."

The air shifted—tighter, warmer. Charged.

Robert's gaze lingered on her face, tracing the curve of her cheek, the flicker of determination in her eyes. He swallowed, his throat suddenly dry.

"Jasmine?"

"Yeah?"

"I'm sorry I've been… a bastard."

She didn't look away. "You've been scared."

A pause.

"So have I."

Her voice barely above a whisper, and something in it made his breath catch.

They were close—closer than they needed to be. Her hand was still wrapped around his wrist from the last exercise, her fingers warm against his skin. She hadn't moved, and neither had he. The space between them pulsed, electric. Familiar, forbidden.

His eyes dropped to her lips for the briefest second.

Dangerous territory.

Jasmine drew in a slow breath, her lashes fluttering. She didn't pull away.

And Robert—*damn it*—wanted to lean in, wanted to close that sliver of distance and finally, *finally* taste what he'd been denying himself for years.

But she was with someone else.

And he was still in a chair.

So instead, he gave her hand the slightest squeeze and said, voice low, "Thank you. For staying."

Jasmine nodded, eyes locked on his, unreadable.

"I always will."

And though neither of them moved, the room felt smaller. Warmer. Heavier with everything unspoken.

It was a breezy Saturday afternoon, and the café in Paddington was just beginning to hum with its usual mix of professionals and creatives. Jasmine and James sat at a sidewalk table, sharing a late lunch. She was laughing—head tilted, eyes bright—while James leaned in, his hand lightly resting on hers.

That's when Sean appeared.

"Jasmine," he said coolly, sunglasses pushed into his thick hair, the smirk already forming. "Well. Don't you look radiant."

Jasmine's smile faltered slightly. "Sean. Hi."

He turned to James, his expression sharpening. "And you must be the new boyfriend."

James stood to offer his hand. "James Fletcher."

"Sean Lennox." He gripped James's hand just a little too firmly, then let it go with an easy grin that didn't reach his eyes. "Old friend of Jasmine's."

James gave a polite nod. "Nice to meet you."

Sean's gaze flicked between them, then lingered a beat too long on Jasmine. "Glad to see you're moving on."

"Moving on?" James asked, brow raised.

"Oh, come on," Sean said, laughing like it was all a harmless joke. "You do know she was hopelessly hung up on Robert Steele for, what—three years? Maybe four?"

Jasmine's back stiffened, but Sean didn't stop.

"Honestly, we all thought it was a bit tragic—her little crush. Unrequited, of course." He sipped his takeaway coffee, then smiled at James. "But I guess everyone needs a rebound."

James's expression didn't shift, but something flickered behind his eyes.

Jasmine spoke, her tone clipped. "That's enough, Sean."

Sean raised a hand in mock surrender. "Hey, no shade. Just making conversation."

With a final smirk, he turned and strolled off down the street, as if he hadn't just lobbed a grenade into the middle of their afternoon.

James sat slowly, gaze still fixed in the direction Sean had gone. Jasmine reached for his hand again, but he didn't take it immediately.

"I'm sorry," she said softly. "Sean's just—he likes getting under people's skin."

James finally looked at her, his smile polite but thinner now. "You don't owe me an apology. I'm not worried about the past."

But even as he said it, Jasmine could feel the shift. A crack. A seed.

And Sean, wherever he was, would be pleased to know it had landed.

James sat on the edge of Jasmine's bed, shirt half-buttoned, watching her move around the room as she got ready for bed. Her laughter from earlier still echoed faintly in his ears, but now it was dulled by the edges of something sharp and persistent.

Sean's words.

'You do know she was hopelessly hung up on Robert Steele... everyone needs a rebound.'

He hated that it bothered him. He wasn't that guy—the insecure one who needed to be the centre of someone's world or dig through her past like it owed him something.

But still.

He glanced over at her now—hair tied back, face fresh from the bathroom. She was humming to herself, oblivious, warm, comfortable in his space. In their space, for the night. And he loved that about her. Her calm. Her kindness. Her loyalty.

But maybe that was the part that worried him.

Because if she had loved Robert—and James could see how that might have happened—then maybe her loyalty wasn't fully his to claim.

"You're quiet," Jasmine said, slipping under the covers beside him.

He smiled, too easily. "Just tired."

"Long week?"

He nodded. "Yeah. Work's been full-on."

She rested her head on his shoulder and sighed. "Same here."

He wrapped his arm around her and kissed the top of her head, anchoring himself in the moment. In her. She was here. With him.

But still, in the quiet that followed, his mind circled back.

'Hopelessly hung up. For years.'

'Tragic, unrequited…'

James closed his eyes, breathing her in, telling himself it didn't matter. Telling himself what they had now was what counted.

But even so, a quiet question lodged somewhere deep in his chest.

If Robert had asked…, would she have said yes?

And for the first time, he wasn't sure he wanted to know the answer.

The morning sun spilled in through the half-open blinds, casting soft golden stripes across the bed. Jasmine stirred first, stretching with a quiet yawn before rolling onto her side. James was already awake, propped up on one elbow, watching her.

"Good morning," she murmured, reaching up to brush his chest lightly with her fingertips.

"Morning," he said, but there was something in his voice—measured, distant.

She stilled. "You okay?"

He hesitated a beat too long. "Yeah. Just… thinking."

Jasmine's brows drew together as she studied his face. "About work?"

"No." His gaze dropped for a moment, then lifted again, locking with hers. "About something you said once."

She blinked. "What did I say?"

"That first night you cooked for me. You told me… *I used to be in love with someone who didn't love me back. For a long time.*"

Jasmine's heart skipped, just once.

"And now I'm wondering," James continued quietly, "was it Robert?"

She could have deflected. Laughed it off. But something in his eyes—steady, vulnerable—held her there. Demanded honesty.

"Yes," she said softly. "It was Robert."

James nodded once, as if he'd already suspected it. "And are you still in love with him?"

"I'm with you, James," she said gently. "That's not nothing."

He held her gaze, looking for more. "But is it everything?"

She reached for his hand. "I cared about him for a long time. It was… messy. And one-sided. He never knew how I felt. I never told him."

"And now?" His voice was calm, but his knuckles were tense beneath her fingertips.

"I still care about him," she admitted. "He's my friend, and I want him to get better. But I don't lie to myself about what didn't happen. I'm not waiting for him anymore."

James exhaled slowly. "You promise me that?"

She leaned forward and kissed him—soft, certain. "I'm here, James. Not in the past."

His shoulders eased, just a little. But as she pulled him into an embrace, James kept his eyes open, staring past her at the ceiling.

She didn't say she didn't love him now.

And that—no matter how much he trusted her—settled like a pebble in his chest, small but impossible to ignore.

The kettle clicked off with a soft snap, and Jasmine poured hot water over a tea bag, steam curling around her fingers as she cradled the mug. Sunlight streaked across her kitchen counter. It was Sunday morning—quiet, for once. Robert had managed to lift both legs off the mat yesterday, unassisted. Not high, not for long, but enough to make her heart pound with something dangerously close to hope.

Her phone buzzed across the countertop.

Heidi.

She smiled and answered. "Hey, stranger."

"Don't *'stranger'* me," Heidi said, faux-offended. "You've been off the grid. I was starting to think you ran off to Paris with your mystery lawyer boyfriend."

"Not quite," Jasmine said, easing onto a bar stool. "Just busy. Robert's therapy is intense."

"Yeah, yeah. The patient from hell. How's he doing now?"

Jasmine's smile softened. "Better. Honestly. He stood with the parallel bars yesterday. I mean—I had to support most of his weight, but he held on, and he stayed up. He didn't collapse. That's a win."

"Damn. That is a win. Go, Rob." There was a pause. "Still snarky and broody?"

"Infuriating," Jasmine said fondly. "But he's trying. He's pushing himself harder. And… letting me push him."

Heidi let out a thoughtful hum. "Sounds like progress on more than one front."

Jasmine didn't answer that.

Heidi pressed on. "So. What about James? How's your actual boyfriend handling all this time you're spending with your former crush?"

Jasmine sighed. "That's… complicated."

"Oh boy."

"Sean happened."

Heidi groaned. "Of course he did. What'd that idiot say?"

"He showed up while James and I were having lunch. And casually dropped that I'd been *'hopelessly hung up'* on Robert for years."

"Seriously?" Heidi's voice sharpened. "I'm going to throw my coffee at that man the next time I see him."

"Yeah, well, the damage was done." Jasmine took a sip of tea. "James didn't say much at the time, but the next morning he brought it up. Asked me if it was true."

"And you told him?"

"I couldn't lie. I told him yes. That I used to love Robert. That he never knew, and it was one-sided, and I've moved on."

Heidi was quiet for a moment. "And James believed that?"

"I think he wants to," Jasmine said. "But Sean planted a seed. And James… he's watching now. Not saying anything, but I can feel it."

A beat of silence stretched across the line.

Then Heidi asked, gently, "Does he have anything to worry about?"

Jasmine set her mug down and stared out the window. The jacarandas were in bloom again—late, defiant bursts of purple against the pale sky. She thought of Robert yesterday, his hands gripping the bars, sweat dripping down his temple as he stood with trembling determination. The look in his eyes when she'd told him she was proud.

And then James, folding laundry on her couch, bringing her coffee without asking, always steady, always kind.

Her throat tightened.

"I don't know," she said finally, her voice barely above a whisper.

Heidi didn't speak right away.

But Jasmine knew she'd heard it. Every aching syllable.

Heidi was silent for a moment. Long enough that Jasmine thought the line might've dropped.

Then, softly, "That's not a small thing to say, Jaz."

Jasmine exhaled, pressing her fingers to her forehead. "I know."

"I mean… I get it. Feelings are messy. Robert's been part of your life forever, and now you're basically in his space every day. Seeing him fight, struggle, get stronger. It's going to stir stuff up."

Jasmine swallowed. "It already has."

"And James," Heidi continued gently, "is falling in love with you. He's been solid, supportive… but he's not stupid. He sees it. Feels it."

"I hate that," Jasmine whispered. "I don't want to hurt him."

"I know you don't." Heidi's voice softened further. "But not wanting to hurt someone isn't the same as not hurting them."

Jasmine stared down into her tea. It had gone cold.

"I thought I was past it," she said. "Robert. The what-ifs. I thought I'd let it go."

Heidi didn't try to fill the silence.

"I mean, he's never even… nothing ever happened between us. He didn't choose me."

"Yeah," Heidi said. "But that doesn't mean *you* didn't."

That landed like a stone in Jasmine's chest.

"I don't want to mess this up," she said finally. "James is—he's good for me."

"And maybe he's the right one," Heidi said gently. "But if you're still in love with someone else—especially someone you're seeing every day—it's not fair to either of you."

Jasmine blinked hard, her throat tightening.

"What do I do?"

Heidi sighed. "Figure out what you actually want. Then be honest. With him. With Robert. With yourself."

A pause.

"I'll still throw my coffee at Sean though," she added, and Jasmine let out a small, shaky laugh.

"Thanks," she murmured.

"For the coffee or the truth?"

"Both."

Chapter Twenty-Two

Megan gave a soft knock on the door before poking her head in.

"Robert? You've got a visitor."

He sat near the window in his wheelchair, a book open but forgotten on his lap.

"Who is it?"

"Claire. She said she just wants a few minutes. Your parents are out, but... she was pretty insistent."

Robert's jaw tightened. There was a beat of hesitation before he answered.

"Let her in."

Lately, fragments of memory had started coming back—stray flashes at first, then whole conversations that played in his mind like scenes from someone else's life. The first came two days ago. He and Claire had just left the yacht club; the car filled with brittle silence.

'What?'

'You need to stop.'

'Stop what?'

'The comments. The jabs at Jasmine. It's not funny. It's not subtle. And it's causing problems.'

'Oh please. She can't take a joke?'

'It's not a joke, Claire. You talk down to her. You mock her. And William's not blind—he's pissed. Mary too. And honestly... I don't blame them.'

'So now you're defending her?'

'I'm asking you not to make things worse.'

'William's my friend. Has been since we were kids. And he's protective of her, especially after everything their family's been through."

'Protective? He acts like she's some delicate little flower. Maybe he should be more concerned about her bouncing from guy to guy.'

'Enough. I mean it.'

'You're really this worked up over her?'

'I'm worked up because you're stirring up drama that doesn't need to be there. It's childish. And it reflects on both of us.'

'Fine. I'll keep my mouth shut.'

'Thank you.'

The next day, another memory surfaced—his voice on the phone with Jasmine.

'I… I called to apologise.'

'For what?'

'For Claire.'

'That's not really something you need to apologise for. Not unless you agree with what she said.'

'I don't. I didn't. I told her to stop. I just… You didn't deserve that. You never have. And I should've said something a long time ago.'

'Maybe. But better late than never, I guess.'

'James seems… good for you.'

'He is.'

'I'm glad you're not with Sean anymore.'

'Your fiancée thinks I move from guy to guy a little too quickly.'

'She never should've said that.'

'No. But she's been making digs for months, Robert. Why apologise now?'

'Because yesterday… I saw it clearly for the first time. How mean it's gotten. How it affects you. And maybe because—maybe because I should've paid more attention a long time ago.'

'Well. Thanks. But you shouldn't be apologising—she should be.'

'I know. I just… I wanted to say it anyway.'

He remembered staring at the phone after they hung up, the screen gone dark in his hand. A thought had formed, quiet but insistent.

He needed to see Claire. Not to argue. Not to rage. But to look her in the eye and answer a question he'd been circling for far too long:

'Is she really the one I want beside me for the rest of my life?'

He'd grabbed his jacket. His helmet. Walked into the garage and peeled the cover off the motorcycle he hadn't touched in months. He'd swung a leg over, turned the key, and let the engine growl awake beneath him.

And then—nothing.

That was where the memory ended. He didn't remember arriving at her apartment. Just the roar of the engine… and then silence.

The door opened.

Claire stepped into the room in stilettos that didn't belong anywhere near hardwood floors and a silk blouse the colour of regret. Her makeup was pristine—too pristine. Not a smudge out of place. A porcelain mask.

"Robert." She smiled, small and tentative, clutching her handbag like a shield.

He met her eyes, steady but unreadable.

"Claire."

She approached slowly, like she wasn't sure if he'd bite—or break. "You look better. Stronger."

"I'm working on it."

She sat on the edge of the chaise across from him, crossing her legs delicately. "I've been meaning to come by sooner. I just… I didn't know if I should."

He gave a slow, noncommittal shrug. "You're here now."

There was a silence. She looked around the room, as if trying to make sense of the space that had replaced the life she thought she'd inherit by his side.

"I've been thinking about things," she said. "A lot, actually."

Robert's fingers tightened slightly around the book's spine.

"I know I walked away. And maybe I shouldn't have. Maybe it scared me, what you were going through—what I was going through. But I never stopped caring about you."

He didn't answer. His gaze was steady but distant, eyes fixed on something just beyond her shoulder. Something inside himself.

Claire leaned forward slightly. "I think… I made a mistake. I think we both did."

That's when it started.

A flash.

Not just where he was going—but why.

He wasn't going to Claire's apartment to apologise.

He was going to end it.

The memory unfolded like film unspooling—vivid and inescapable.

He had arrived outside Claire's building, helmet in hand, the air sharp with tension. As he approached her door, a thought looped through his mind:

'Time to stop pretending you don't already know the answer.'

He was just steps away when the door opened. Claire stepped into the hallway— laughing softly—with a man beside her. Brian. Robert remembered his name now.

Brian reached for her and kissed her.

Not a polite goodnight.

Not a friend's goodbye.

It was slow. Familiar. Their bodies fitted together like this wasn't the first time. Like they'd done it a hundred times before.

'Text me when you get home.'

'I always do.'

Neither had seen Robert—until Claire looked up.

She froze.

'Robert. I didn't know you were coming over.'

Brian stiffened beside her.

Robert didn't move. Didn't blink. Just stared.

Is everything alright?' Claire asked.

'I was about to ask you the same thing.'

'Everything is fine.'

'So how long has this been going on?'

'What are you talking about?'

'Don't insult my intelligence, Claire.'

'Robert, you're overreacting. Brian and I—he was just saying goodnight.'

'Like that? Because it didn't look like a goodnight. It looked like a relationship. Or at the very least, a habit.'

Brian cleared his throat, clearly uncomfortable. 'Maybe I should go—'

Robert didn't look at him.

'Good idea.'

Then he turned to Claire. His voice was calm. Measured. Devastating.

'I came here because I thought maybe I was wrong. About you. About everything. I wanted to look you in the eye and remind myself why I asked you to marry me.'

She blinked.

'And now?'

'Now I wish I hadn't.'

'You didn't make a mistake, Robert.'

'Didn't I?'

'You're angry. I get it. But you saw one moment—you don't know the context.'

'I saw you kiss another man.'

'Brian and I go way back. It wasn't what it looked like.'

'That's the oldest excuse in the book.'

'I didn't cheat on you.'

'Then what would you call it?'

'A lapse in judgment. A mistake. One kiss.'

'One kiss. Two weeks after I put a ring on your finger.'

'You're the one I want, Robert. That hasn't changed.'

'So, Jasmine and Mary didn't see you kissing Brian at our engagement party?'

Her expression flickered.

'No, of course not.'

'Jasmine wouldn't lie.'

'Really? Her again?'

'Don't make this about her. This is about you. About us.'

'I don't know what Jasmine thinks she saw, but it's not what you think. We've been through this before, Robert. Don't let her make you question everything.'

'It's not just her. It's everything. I've been looking the other way for too long. But now I'm starting to see it all.'

'Robert don't do this. We've got something good. Don't throw it away over one mistake.'

'I don't think I can keep ignoring the mistakes, Claire. Not anymore.'

'So, what—you're just going to walk away?'

'Yes.'

Claire's voice sharpened. 'Unbelievable. All this time, I've put up with your moods, your silences, your precious friendship with that woman—and now she gets to be the reason you throw it all away? You think she's so innocent? Jasmine Whitaker, little miss perfect, always lingering with those sad eyes and martyr complex—do you really think she's better for you? She's weak, Robert. She hides behind her grief and lets everyone else fight her battles.'

'Enough. Don't talk about her like that.'

'Why not? Because you're in love with her? Is that it? You think she's your perfect alternative to a life that's actually real?'

'I said enough. You don't get to blame Jasmine for this. You're the one who cheated. You made that choice. Not her.'

He remembered turning away from Claire that night, leaving her standing in the hallway, her voice chasing him as he walked out the front door.

And then—nothing.

The road. The engine. The truck.

Darkness.

He blinked, dragged back into the present.

Across the room, Claire sat with her hands clasped in her lap, watching him carefully.

"I still want to be with you," she said softly. "I know I said awful things. But I was jealous. You always had this… connection with Jasmine."

His gaze shifted—sharp and unforgiving.

"You were cheating on me."

Claire's face paled.

"Robert—"

"I remember now," he said, voice iron. "That night. I was coming to end things. That's why I got on the bike."

She froze. "You don't know what you're saying—"

"I do." He leaned back in the chair, the air around him turning cold. "I might not remember everything. But I remember enough."

Claire opened her mouth—then closed it. Her chin lifted, defensive. "So that's it? You're rewriting everything? We had years, Robert."

"And you threw them away," he said evenly. "I didn't lose my memory of the man I was becoming. You lost sight of the man I already was."

She stood abruptly, grabbing her bag, her expression brittle. "You're angry. You're hurt. I get it. But don't pretend you were innocent either."

"I wasn't perfect," he agreed. "But I didn't lie. And I didn't cheat."

Silence cracked between them like ice.

Finally, Claire looked away. Her voice was small.

"I should go."

He didn't stop her.

The door closed behind her with a quiet click.

Robert stared at the space she'd left behind, the memory still ringing in his ears like thunder trailing lightning.

But something in him had settled.

Not peace, exactly—but clarity.

He hadn't lost everything.

For weeks, everything had been fog and fragments. But now, there was ground beneath him again—and it wasn't Claire standing on it with him.

There was a knock at the door.

He turned, expecting Megan or one of his parents, but instead, there she was—*Jasmine*. Ponytail tucked through the back of a baseball cap, leggings and an oversized hoodie, clipboard under one arm. The familiar sight of her hit him like sunlight through fog.

"Hey," she said with a small smile. "Ready for another round of torture?"

"Yes."

"Was that Claire I saw leave?"

"Yes." There was a beat of silence between them before he added, more quietly, "I remember everything now. Before the accident."

Her brows lifted, hopeful. "That's good."

"She was cheating on me," he said plainly. "I went to her apartment that night to end our engagement."

Jasmine stilled. Her fingers tightened slightly around the clipboard, but her expression didn't flinch.

She didn't rush to fill the silence. She just looked at him—*really looked*—like she always did. Like she was taking him in, measuring what to say and what not to.

Finally, her voice came soft, even. "I'm sorry, Robert."

He gave a short, humourless laugh. "I'm not."

Still, she didn't speak. Just watched him with those clear, steady eyes that never tried to rescue or justify or fix—just saw him.

"I think I knew," he admitted. "For a long time. I just didn't want to face it."

Jasmine exhaled slowly, stepping further into the room. "And now?"

"Now I'm facing it."

A beat.

"Well," she said, voice dry but warm, "good. Because I've got new exercises for you, and none of them involve self-pity."

His brow lifted. "Brutal."

"You love it."

He smiled—*actually smiled*—and for the first time since the accident, it felt real. Felt like him again.

As Jasmine moved to set up the session, he glanced at her—this woman who had stayed, not out of obligation, but choice.

She hadn't asked for anything. And yet—she'd stayed.

Chapter Twenty-Three

The late afternoon light slanted through the tall windows of the converted study, casting long golden streaks across the floorboards. Outside, a kookaburra laughed somewhere in the trees. Inside, the only sound was the steady, determined rhythm of breath and the subtle creak of metal.

"Alright," Jasmine said, crouched beside the parallel bars. "You've done it with support. Now try without me holding your weight."

Robert's jaw tightened. Sweat dotted his brow, his palms gripping the bars with a white-knuckled focus. Six weeks of gruelling sessions, setbacks and small wins—today felt different. He could feel it humming beneath his skin. Something shifting.

He nodded once, curt and silent. Jasmine stepped back, just enough to let him feel the space.

"You've got this," she said, her voice low, firm.

He drew in a breath. Pressed down through his hands. Engaged his core the way she'd drilled into him daily. And then—he lifted.

Just a fraction. Then more.

His right leg steadied first, the left a second behind it. Wobble, catch—he exhaled through his nose, teeth clenched, determined. His shoulders trembled with the effort, but he didn't falter.

One step.

Then another.

Then another.

He reached the midpoint of the bars before he stopped, panting, stunned.

Jasmine hadn't moved. She just watched him, her clipboard forgotten at her side, lips parted slightly in awe.

"You did it," she said, her voice catching somewhere between pride and disbelief. "Robert—you walked."

He stared down at his legs like they didn't belong to him. His heart thundered against his ribs.

"I walked."

A beat passed.

Then—he laughed. A short, breathless, stunned sound. The kind that only came when you surprised yourself.

Jasmine blinked, and suddenly her eyes shimmered. She pressed her hand to her mouth.

"God, I'm not going to cry," she muttered, mostly to herself.

He looked up. Really looked. "You've been waiting for this as long as I have."

She gave a soft laugh, still teary-eyed. "Longer, maybe."

He reached the end of the bars and turned, slowly, with effort, his grip still firm but more confident now. Jasmine stepped closer, hands ready but not touching.

"You could've given up on me," he said quietly.

"I never was going to," she replied, just as quiet.

Their eyes held.

The silence between them was thick with everything unsaid—his gratitude, her loyalty, the echo of old heartbreak and the shape of something not quite spoken into being yet.

He straightened, taller now than he'd been in weeks. Still unsteady, still aching—but standing.

Jasmine smiled—warm, wide, a little breathless. "We're not done. Not even close. But today?" She paused. "Today we celebrate."

He nodded. "Today… I walk."

Robert was still catching his breath, his arms resting along the parallel bars, when Jasmine turned toward the door.

"I'll be right back," she said, her smile still wide, eyes a little glassy. "Don't move."

"I just started," he quipped, but there was a flicker of nervous anticipation in his voice.

Jasmine didn't answer. She slipped out into the hallway, jogging lightly down toward the sitting room where Terry and Kelly Steele were having tea.

"Terry—Kelly," Jasmine said, not even trying to hide the excitement in her voice. "You both need to come. Now."

Terry frowned slightly, rising. "Is everything alright?"

"Yes. It's—it's good. Just come."

They followed her, a little perplexed but quickening their steps at the urgency in her tone. When they reached the therapy room, Jasmine paused just inside the doorway.

"Okay," she said gently, turning to Robert. "Ready?"

Robert gave a tight nod. His jaw was set again—focused, almost stern—but beneath it was something raw and gleaming. He adjusted his grip, squared his shoulders, and slowly began to walk.

One step. Then another.

Kelly gasped softly. Terry's eyes widened, then blinked, as if he thought he was imagining it.

"Robert…" Kelly whispered.

He didn't look at them—his focus was forward, fixed, each step deliberate. But Jasmine saw the flicker of emotion in his eyes, the breath that caught in his chest when his mother covered her mouth and his father muttered a stunned, "Bloody hell."

When Robert reached the end of the bars, he stopped. Turned slowly. Met their gaze.

"I walked," he said simply.

Kelly stepped forward, tears already spilling down her cheeks.

"You did, darling," she whispered. "You did."

Terry cleared his throat. Hard. Then walked over and gripped his son's shoulder with a strength that said everything he couldn't.

"I knew you'd get there," he said, voice thick. "Knew it."

Jasmine stepped back quietly, giving them the moment. But Robert's eyes flicked to her—just for a second—and the smallest smile tugged at his mouth.

She smiled back, her heart tight in her chest.

This was why she'd stayed.

Not just for recovery.

Not just for him.

But for this.

For the man she always knew was still in there, waiting to rise again.

Jasmine couldn't stop smiling. Not a polite smile or a distracted one—but a full, radiant beam that softened every feature and refused to fade.

She knocked lightly before letting herself in, the keys James had given her swinging from her fingers.

He greeted her at the door with a warm kiss, his hand finding the small of her back. "Hey, you," he murmured, grinning. "You look… lit up."

"I am." She practically bounced inside, tossing her bag down. "He walked today. On his own. Just a few steps, but—he walked."

James blinked. "Wait, really? That's incredible."

"It was," she said, her eyes shining. "You should've seen the look on his parents' faces— Kelly started crying. And Robert—he didn't say much, but I could tell. He's different now. He's hopeful again."

James offered a smile, but something in his eyes dimmed. He nodded toward the kitchen. "Come tell me everything. I opened a bottle of that pinot you like."

They settled on the couch, glasses in hand. Jasmine launched into the details—Robert's grip on the bars, the moment his foot moved forward, the way he looked at her after. She didn't notice at first how quiet James had become, or how his smile stopped reaching his eyes.

But eventually, it hit her.

He was listening—but he wasn't really there.

Her voice slowed. "Are you okay?"

James set down his glass. "Yeah. I mean, I'm happy for him. That's a huge milestone."

She watched him, waiting.

He hesitated—then exhaled. "I guess I've just been noticing how… in tune you are with him."

"What do you mean?"

"The way you describe him. How you know when he's in pain, even when he doesn't say it. How you can read him without needing words." He ran a hand through his hair, then gave her a tired smile. "Sometimes I feel like I'm watching the two of you speak a language I don't understand."

Jasmine looked down at her wine.

"It's not like that," she said quietly. "Robert and I... we've known each other a long time. I've just gotten used to him."

James nodded. "Yeah. That's what I figured. But I'm also not blind, Jasmine."

She looked up.

He was calm—but there was something vulnerable in the way he held her gaze. Something that made her chest ache.

"I didn't plan on this," he said. "You and me. It started out light. Easy. But then it wasn't. Not for me." A beat. "I'm falling for you."

She inhaled sharply.

"I want more than this," James continued. "Not just dinner and stolen weekends and pretending we're casual when we're clearly not. I want a future with you."

Silence hung between them like a held breath.

Jasmine's fingers tightened around her glass. "James..."

"I know," he said quickly. "I know things are complicated. I know you care about me."

She swallowed hard. "I do care about you. So much."

"But?"

She looked at him—really looked—and in his face, she saw everything she'd always wanted. Stability. Warmth. A man who showed up, who didn't run. Who believed in her.

But her heart...

Her heart lived somewhere else. Somewhere unfinished.

Finally, she whispered, "I don't know."

James blinked but didn't look away.

"I wish I could say something else," she added, voice cracking.

He nodded slowly, then stood and walked to the window. Hands in his pockets. Quiet. Processing.

After a long moment, he turned back. "I'm not asking for an answer right now. Just... don't lie to yourself to spare me. Okay?"

Jasmine's eyes shimmered. "I never wanted to hurt you."

"I know." He gave her a sad smile. "But sometimes that's the problem with good hearts. You end up breaking your own just trying to protect someone else's."

The kettle whistled as Jasmine sank into the corner of Heidi's worn-in couch, curling her legs beneath her. She was still in leggings and a soft hoodie, hair pulled into a loose ponytail, the edges of exhaustion just beginning to catch up to her.

Heidi breezed in from the kitchen with two mugs in hand, passing Jasmine one before flopping onto the opposite end of the couch.

"You look wiped," she said, tucking her legs under a throw blanket. "Long day?"

Jasmine gave a small, tired smile. "Seven weeks in. We're finally hitting real momentum. He's stronger. He's standing on his own for longer stretches. The balance is improving."

"Good," Heidi said, watching her carefully over the rim of her mug. "That's really good."

Jasmine nodded slowly, staring down into the tea.

Heidi leaned forward. "But?"

Jasmine let out a breath. "James said he's falling for me. That he wants a future."

Heidi's eyebrows lifted. "Whoa. That's a big step."

"I know," Jasmine said quietly. "He means it. He's serious. I think he's been holding it back for a while now. And I... I didn't really know what to say."

Heidi tilted her head. "Do you feel the same?"

Jasmine hesitated. "I care about him. I trust him. He's been kind, thoughtful, steady... everything I told myself I needed."

"But?" Heidi said again.

"I didn't say it back."

Heidi didn't push. Just sipped her tea and waited.

After a moment, Jasmine added, "I told him I was trying. That I wanted to be with someone who sees me like he does."

"But not that you love him."

Jasmine shook her head.

Heidi leaned against the arm of the couch. "So. Here's the question that matters—does Robert want a future with you?"

Jasmine blinked, caught off guard. "He hasn't said anything like that."

"Has he hinted?"

"No." She looked down again, rubbing her thumb along the rim of her mug. "He's been focused on therapy, on recovery. We joke, we talk, we've had a couple of… moments. But nothing clear. Nothing real. Not like that."

Heidi was quiet for a moment. Then she leaned forward, her voice soft but direct. "So, James is offering you the next chapter. Robert hasn't even told you if you're part of his."

Jasmine looked away, her throat tightening. "Exactly."

Heidi leaned closer, gentle but firm. "Then maybe the question isn't what James wants or even what Robert hasn't said. Maybe it's—what do you want, Jaz? And how long are you willing to wait for someone to figure out if they want you back?"

Jasmine didn't answer right away. Her eyes shimmered, fixed on the tea in her hands as steam curled up and vanished into the space between them.

When she finally spoke, her voice was quiet—but clear.

"I can't keep waiting for someone who hasn't even said he wants me."

Heidi sat still, watching her.

"I've spent so long hoping he'd see it. Hoping he'd say something. But he hasn't. And maybe he never will. I can't keep building my life around a possibility that only exists in my own head."

There was no bitterness in her voice—just exhaustion. And, beneath it, a quiet ache of acceptance.

"I care about James," she added. "And he's not asking me to guess. He's here. He's ready. Maybe it's time I stop chasing a future that was never promised."

Heidi reached over and gave her hand a gentle squeeze.

Jasmine blinked, but this time, no tears fell.

She'd made herself small for a man who never asked her to wait—and never offered a reason to stay.

And she was done waiting.

Chapter Twenty-Four

Early Saturday morning, Jasmine stood outside James's apartment door, her breath clouding faintly in the cool air, heart hammering with a rhythm that wasn't fear, exactly. Just the weight of what came next.

She didn't knock at first.

For a moment, she just stood there, letting the silence wrap around her like a question. Her hands curled into fists at her sides, then loosened. She inhaled once, then again, grounding herself.

This was the right thing. The kind thing. The honest thing.

She knocked.

James opened the door almost immediately, barefoot and tousled, a T-shirt hanging loose over his frame. His expression shifted when he saw her—surprise flickering into something more guarded.

"Hey," he said, voice still scratchy with sleep.

"Hey." Her voice was quiet but clear. "Can I come in?"

He stepped aside, giving her space. She walked in, noting the familiar scent of his aftershave, the quiet hum of jazz playing low from the speakers in the corner. The room felt the same. She didn't.

James lingered by the arm of the couch, not quite sitting. "You okay?"

"I am." She turned to face him fully. "And I need to talk. About last weekend."

He nodded once; arms folded across his chest. "I've been waiting to hear."

They hadn't spoken since he'd told her he was falling for her. That he wanted a future.

She stepped closer, her pulse steady now. "I've made a decision."

His brow lifted slightly. "Yeah?"

"I want to be with you," she said. No hesitations. "Fully. No more holding back."

He didn't move, but she felt something inside him still.

"I've spent too long holding space for someone who never asked me to. Someone who never once said he wanted me. And I kept waiting… thinking maybe he would."

She swallowed, then met his eyes. "But I'm done with maybe. I'm done with silence."

James's jaw flexed, but he said nothing. Just listened.

"You've never made me question if I mattered to you," she said. "You've always been here, steady. Honest. And I want to choose that. I am choosing it."

He took a slow breath, letting it out like he was afraid to believe her. "So… what now?"

"I've told Robert's mother I'm stepping back," she said. "I've already started the process to bring in another physiotherapist. It'll take a couple of weeks, but I'll make sure the transition's smooth."

His eyes widened slightly. "Really?"

"Yes. He's stronger now. Walking with support. His progress is steady. He doesn't need me the way he used to. And I need room to figure out us."

She stepped forward again, close enough to feel his warmth. "You said you wanted a future with me. So, let's stop waiting for one to begin."

James searched her face, like he was trying to find the catch—but there wasn't one. Slowly, he reached for her hand, brushing his thumb across her knuckles. "You still have a session with him today?"

She gave a small smile. "Not anymore."

The room stilled.

Then he said, quietly, "Come away with me this weekend."

"I was going to ask you the same thing," she replied.

His mouth curved into the softest smile. "Where?"

"Anywhere," she whispered. "Just… away."

He pulled her gently into his arms, holding her like something precious—not claimed, but chosen.

And for the first time in a very long time, Jasmine felt the ache of longing give way to something lighter.

She wasn't waiting anymore. She was moving forward.

Saturday morning arrived with the usual routine—sunlight cutting across the far wall of the converted study, the faint aroma of fresh coffee from the kitchen, the steady thrum of birdsong outside.

Robert sat by the window in the therapy room, one hand resting on the wheel of his chair, the other lightly squeezing a resistance ball Jasmine had given him last week. He checked the time again.

10:08.

She was never late.

His brows drew together as footsteps echoed down the hall. A moment later, the door opened—but it wasn't Jasmine.

It was his mother.

Kelly stepped in gently, her expression carefully composed, though something unreadable shimmered behind her eyes. She held a small folder in her hand—neutral in tone but deliberate in timing.

Robert sat up straighter, heart giving an uncomfortable thud. "Where's Jasmine?"

Kelly hesitated. "She's not coming today."

He blinked. "Is she okay?"

"She's fine," Kelly said gently, walking further into the room. "But she asked me to tell you—she's stepping away from your therapy sessions."

Silence stretched thin between them.

Robert's jaw clenched. "What?"

"She said she's found a few physiotherapists she trusts. She'll be meeting with them next week and wants to find the right fit to take over."

He stared at her like the words didn't quite compute. "She didn't say anything yesterday."

"She made the decision last night."

He looked away, his grip tightening on the ball until his knuckles whitened. "Why?"

Kelly came to sit on the padded bench across from him, setting the folder gently on her lap. "Because she said it's time she started prioritising her relationship with James."

His breath caught—sharp and quiet.

"She said she's given all of herself to your recovery," Kelly added, voice soft. "But she needs to shift focus now. To the man who's standing by her. The one who's choosing her."

Robert didn't speak.

Kelly watched him closely, her gaze steady but warm. "You're upset."

He didn't deny it.

A beat passed. Then Kelly leaned forward, her tone gentle but firm. "Robert. Isn't it time to tell her how you really feel about her?"

His throat worked. "It's not that simple."

"Of course it is," she said. "You either love her, or you don't. You either tell her, or you let her go."

He looked at her, eyes dark and stormy. "She's with someone else."

"And yet you're still waiting by the window for her," she said. "Still hoping it's her voice you'll hear."

He turned away, jaw clenched, fighting the tension in his chest.

Kelly stood, her hand brushing his shoulder as she passed. "She's not asking you to fight for her. But maybe she's waited long enough for you to choose her."

Robert sat in silence long after she left the room.

And for the first time in weeks, the quiet didn't feel peaceful.

It felt like regret.

The late Sunday sun slanted gold through the windscreen as James pulled into Jasmine's driveway. The hum of tyres over gravel slowed to stillness, but neither of them moved at first. The quiet inside the car felt suspended—warm with the echo of laughter, late-night talks, the hush of eucalyptus trees, and the slow unfolding of something real.

Jasmine looked out the window at her front door, the familiar frame of home somehow changed after two days away.

"Home," she said softly.

James glanced at her, a smile tugging at the corner of his mouth. "That sounded like a question."

She gave a small shrug, still turned toward the window. "Just feels… different coming back, that's all."

He didn't push. He'd learned not to.

"You're quiet," he said instead.

She turned to face him, her features softened by the amber light. "It was a beautiful weekend."

He nodded. "It was."

"The quiet," she said, "the trees, the slow morning… it felt like I could breathe again. No noise, no shoulds, no expectations."

"Except that lyrebird outside our cabin at six in the morning."

Jasmine laughed, the sound easy and genuine. "I forgot about that. It sounded like a smoke alarm having an identity crisis."

James smiled but didn't let the moment drift. "You seemed… lighter there."

"I was," she said, more quietly now. "You made it feel easy. Being there. Being with you."

His eyes softened, but his voice held a hint of caution. "And now?"

She looked down at her hands in her lap, then back up at him. "Now I go back to everything. But maybe with clearer lines. Better boundaries."

He studied her. "Are you sure you're ready for that?"

Jasmine didn't flinch. "I have to be."

James reached across and gently tucked a strand of hair behind her ear. "If you need time, Jasmine, I can give you that. But I won't pretend I don't want this to keep going. I meant what I said—I want a future with you."

She leaned into his hand for a moment, letting the warmth ground her. "I know. And I want that too."

He exhaled, relief visible in his shoulders.

She reached for the door handle. "I should go inside. I promised Mary I'd call her tonight."

James hesitated. "You want me to come in?"

Jasmine smiled, then kissed him—soft, lingering, certain. "Not tonight."

He nodded, accepting the boundary. "Okay."

"I'll see you tomorrow?"

"You better."

She opened the door and stepped out, the breeze catching the hem of her linen dress. As she turned back one last time, James was still watching her, that quiet intensity in his eyes that never quite asked her to stay—but always hoped she would.

She gave a small wave, then turned toward her front door, the key already in her hand.

Behind her, the engine started.

And the weekend—perfect and fragile—settled into memory.

The water was hot, almost too hot, but Jasmine let it pound over her shoulders anyway, the steady stream melting the last of the Blue Mountains chill from her limbs. She closed her eyes and tilted her face into the spray, letting the steam wrap around her like a blanket. The scent of eucalyptus from the resort still clung faintly to her skin, like a memory.

By the time she stepped out, wrapped in a towel and hair damp against her shoulders, the ache in her legs had eased. She pulled on a soft cotton T-shirt and a pair of shorts, padded barefoot into the living room, and curled onto the couch with her phone.

It was just past seven. She thumbed to Mary's name and hit call.

The phone barely rang once before Mary picked up. "Well, look who finally remembered her friends exist."

Jasmine smiled. "Hi to you too."

"Are you back?"

"Just got in a couple of hours ago."

"So? Tell me everything. Was it romantic? Was it sexy? Did you get a couples massage in a rainforest cave or something?"

Jasmine laughed, stretching out on the cushions. "It was… perfect. Quiet. Peaceful. We talked, we hiked, we ate way too much. He booked this eco lodge—it had these floor-to-ceiling windows that looked out over the valley. And no reception half the time."

"Sounds like heaven. You sound… different."

"I feel different."

There was a beat of silence on Mary's end, like she was deciding whether to say something. Then— "Well, I'm glad. Truly. But I should probably tell you something."

Jasmine sat up slightly. "Okay…"

"William and I stopped by the Steeles' today. To see Robert."

Her heart gave a quick, reflexive squeeze, but she said nothing.

"He told us you're stepping back from his therapy," Mary continued. "Said you were finding someone new to take over."

Jasmine nodded slowly. "I am."

"Well, he wasn't happy."

Jasmine's fingers tightened slightly around the phone. "Did he say that?"

"No," Mary said gently. "But he didn't have to. He said it was your decision, that you had your reasons—but he was… tense. Quiet. He kept clenching his jaw the way he does when he's holding back."

Jasmine leaned her head against the arm of the couch, eyes drifting closed. "I told James I wanted to be with him. Really be with him. And that meant stepping away."

Mary didn't speak right away. "Do you regret it?"

"No." Jasmine opened her eyes. "But I didn't expect it to hurt so much."

"Because you care about him."

"I do," she whispered. "But caring isn't the same as staying stuck."

"No," Mary said softly. "It's not."

There was another pause before Mary added, "You should know—Robert knows James is the reason you were stepping back. I think he's finally starting to realise what he's losing."

Jasmine closed her eyes again, this time not from weariness but from something sharper. "It doesn't matter. He never said anything when he had the chance."

"Maybe he didn't know how."

"Maybe I got tired of waiting for him to figure it out."

Mary didn't argue. Just said gently, "I hope James knows what a gift he's getting."

Jasmine smiled faintly, her voice quiet. "He does."

Mary ended the call with Jasmine and set her phone down gently on the coffee table.

William stepped into the room, drying his hands on a dish towel, his brow lifting slightly at her expression. "Everything alright?"

She looked up at him, eyes steady. "It's time."

He frowned. "Time for what?"

Mary hesitated, then stood, crossing to him. "To tell Jasmine the truth. About what you asked Robert. About what happened when she turned twenty-one."

William's jaw tightened, the guilt flashing through his eyes before he looked away. "I know."

"She deserves to know why he pulled away," Mary said gently. "Why she's spent years wondering if she was never enough."

"I thought I was protecting her," he muttered. "She was still so young—she hadn't even graduated yet and Robert just got back from Europe after breaking up with Clair the first time. I didn't want her getting caught up in that and get hurt."

"I know," Mary said. "But Jasmine's not a child anymore. And Robert's not the same man he was either."

William nodded slowly, his shoulders sinking under the weight of memory. "He told me I'd made the decision for him. That he didn't fight for her because I asked him not to. And he's right. I saw the way he looked at her back then, and I still told him to stay away."

Mary touched his arm, her voice low. "And now he's watching her walk away, thinking he never had a chance. Jasmine deserves the whole story, Will. She needs to understand what really happened. She may still choose James, but she needs to know all the facts before she decides."

He looked down at the floor for a long moment, then gave a small nod. "I'll tell her."

Mary's voice softened. "And maybe it's time Robert told her too."

William exhaled, pain and regret swirling behind his eyes. "It might be too late."

"But maybe it isn't," Mary said quietly. "Not if they both stop waiting."

Chapter Twenty-Five

Jasmine stepped onto the back deck of her brother's house, the early afternoon sun spilling warm gold across the timber railing. She'd stopped by to return a book Mary had lent her, but now she lingered, her fingers brushing the weathered wood as a soft breeze stirred through the gum trees. Maybe it was the quiet that held her there—or maybe it was the weight in her chest that hadn't eased since Mary's call the night before.

She still had time before she was due at the Steele estate for Robert's therapy session. But even that felt different now—like standing at the edge of something and not knowing which way the ground would tilt.

William stepped out behind her, a beer in hand, his sleeves rolled up against the heat. He leaned casually against the post beside her, their silence easy at first—until he cleared his throat.

"Mary said you called last night," he said.

Jasmine nodded. "Just catching up."

William took a sip, eyes drifting toward the yard. "Robert told us yesterday you're stepping back from his therapy."

Her breath caught, almost imperceptibly. "I am."

"Mary said you're choosing James."

Jasmine turned to look at him, one brow lifting. "Is that a problem?"

He shook his head. "No. It's just… I've been thinking. About some things I should've said a long time ago."

Her posture shifted—subtle, alert. "Like what?"

William hesitated. Then, with a quiet sigh, he set his bottle on the railing and met her gaze. "Do you remember your twenty-first birthday?"

She blinked. "Of course. That party at the estate. Robert gave me that old copy of Jane Eyre."

He nodded. "Do you remember what happened after?"

Her brow furrowed. "No… not really. I remember he left early. I didn't see him much after that."

William looked down, guilt tightening his features. "That's because of me."

Jasmine frowned. "What do you mean?"

"He came to see me the next day," William said slowly. "Told me he had feelings for you."

Her breath stilled.

"I told him to back off," he continued. "Said you were young, and he was my best mate, and I didn't want him messing with your heart when he hadn't figured his own out yet."

Silence fell—sharp, heavy.

Jasmine's voice was a whisper, stunned. "You what?"

"I didn't say it to be cruel," he rushed on. "I was trying to protect you. But I made it clear I didn't think it was a good idea. And Robert... he listened. Too well. He walked away because I asked him to."

She stepped back, her eyes searching his face as disbelief and hurt rose in equal measure. "So, all this time... all these years I thought he didn't feel the same. I thought it was just me."

William nodded, shame lining every word. "He was furious with me. Said I made the decision for both of you. And he was right. I thought I was doing the right thing. I didn't realise how much it cost him."

Jasmine's hands curled around the edge of the railing. "It cost me too, Will."

"I know," he said softly. "I see that now."

She turned away, jaw tight, her voice brittle. "And he never told me. He just... disappeared."

"He thought he was respecting what I asked. And then Claire came back... I think he figured it was too late. That maybe you'd moved on."

Jasmine stood still for a long time, her eyes distant.

Then she said, barely audible, "It didn't have to be."

William's voice cracked. "I'm sorry, Jaz. Truly. If I could take it back, I would."

She turned back to him, her eyes shimmering. "Why now? Why are you telling me this now?"

"Because I see you trying to move on," he said. "And I see how hard you're trying to choose something safe. But I also see the part of you that's still stuck in what could've been. Robert had a go at me a few weeks ago—told me I robbed him of the chance to choose you. Maybe I did. But maybe it's not too late. Not if one of you finally says what needs to be said."

Jasmine looked down, her voice quiet. "I don't know what to do with this."

"You don't have to decide anything today," William said gently. "I just thought you deserved the truth. After everything."

She nodded slowly, the pain raw but cleansing. "Yeah. I did."

He reached for her hand, squeezing it with quiet care. "Whatever happens, I've got your back."

Jasmine didn't reply. But as she looked out across the yard, the breeze catching her hair, something in her shifted. Something long shut away began to stir.

Jasmine gripped the steering wheel tighter than necessary as she turned onto the winding road that led to the Steele estate. The late afternoon sun filtered through the windshield, golden and soft, but the light did little to warm the unease in her chest.

Her mind kept circling back to William's voice on the deck, the quiet guilt in his eyes when he said, "He walked away because I asked him to."

It didn't make sense—not with everything she'd carried all these years. How many times had she told herself she was delusional? That she'd read too much into the way Robert looked at her. That if it had meant anything to him, he would've said something?

But now… everything was shifting. The ground beneath her felt less like regret and more like revelation. And she didn't know what to do with that.

She'd spent so long convincing herself it was unrequited, that Robert had chosen Claire because he simply hadn't loved her the same way. But now, it turned out he had. He'd just… let her go. Because someone else told him to.

Her heart twisted. *Was that love? Or weakness?*

And worse—what if she still loved him anyway?

She let out a breath, slow and unsteady.

All this time—*years*—she'd carried the weight of unspoken feelings, convinced she'd imagined the way Robert used to look at her. The almosts. The maybes. The silences stretched just a little too long. She'd buried it, convinced he'd never seen her the same way. Convinced Claire had been his choice.

But it wasn't Claire.

It had been her.

And he'd walked away because someone else told him to.

Her hands flexed on the wheel.

How different would her life have been if William hadn't interfered? If Robert had stayed? If he'd said what he felt before silence turned them into strangers wearing familiar faces?

She slowed at the turn-off and signalled, the gravel crunching beneath her tyres as she pulled through the estate gates.

She wasn't angry—at least, not in the way she thought she should be. Mostly, she just felt… hollow. Like someone had rearranged the truth inside her without warning.

And what now?

Robert still hadn't said anything—not after the accident, not after Claire, not even when she let his mother know she'd be stepping back from his therapy. This would be the first time she'd see him since.

He probably thinks I chose someone else.

The way he once chose someone else over me.

Jasmine parked by the side of the house and sat for a moment, the engine ticking in the silence. She stared through the windshield, past the manicured gardens and sandstone pillars, seeing none of it.

All this time, she'd been waiting for a sign. A word. Something that told her she wasn't the only one holding the pieces of something that had never really begun. And now she knew—it had begun. It just hadn't been given the chance to grow.

She closed her eyes for a beat, trying to find her centre.

Then she stepped out of the car, shoulders squared, chin lifted.

She didn't know what she was going to say to Robert.

But for the first time in a long while, she wasn't afraid to say something.

Robert stood by the window of the therapy room, his hands braced on the wide wooden sill, knuckles white from the effort. His legs—still weak, still unsteady—shook beneath the weight of his body, but he refused to sit. Not today.

He heard Jasmine's car pull up. Heard the crunch of gravel, the quiet close of the door, the familiar rhythm of her steps approaching. His heart pounded, his breath coming faster than he liked—but he held his position, jaw clenched, determination pulsing through every aching muscle.

This might be his last chance. And he knew it.

The door creaked open.

Jasmine stepped in and stopped short when she saw him upright, unsupported except for his hands gripping the windowsill.

"Robert," she breathed.

He didn't look at her right away. He swallowed hard, eyes fixed on the horizon beyond the glass. The wind stirred the gum trees, and somewhere a bird called out—ordinary sounds that suddenly felt profound.

"I didn't sit down," he said at last, voice quiet but raw. "I didn't want you to walk in here and see me like I was before."

She moved closer, slowly. "You're standing."

"I needed to." He finally turned toward her, the movement cautious but deliberate. "For this. For you."

Their eyes met, and for a beat, nothing else existed.

"This… is the last time I'll wait," he said, the words trembling but clear. "I can't keep standing here, hoping you'll come back like nothing changed."

She opened her mouth, but no words came.

"I know you're stepping back," he continued. "I know you've chosen someone else. Maybe you should. Maybe I don't get a say anymore. But I couldn't let you leave without telling you what I should've told you a long time ago."

He shifted slightly, the movement sending a ripple of pain through his legs, but he didn't flinch. "I care about you, Jasmine. Always have. But I listened to everyone else—*especially your brother*—when I should've been listening to my own damn heart."

Her breath caught. Her eyes shimmered, stunned into stillness.

"I don't expect anything from you," he said softly. "I just needed you to know. I needed you to see me standing here. Finally saying what I should have said years ago."

Jasmine stepped forward then, slowly, like she wasn't quite sure if what she was seeing was real. Her gaze dropped briefly to his legs, trembling but steady. Then back to his face.

As he swayed slightly, her hands shot out on instinct—gripping his arms, steadying him like she had a hundred times before. But this time felt different. This wasn't part of his treatment plan. This was something else.

"I've got you," she said, voice low.

His eyes never left hers. "I know."

Her fingers curled around his arms, and for a moment, she felt the warmth of his skin— solid, real, achingly familiar. Like memory brought to life.

"You idiot," she whispered, voice thick.

Robert blinked, startled.

"You waited all this time?" Her voice broke. "You let me think you didn't want me. That I imagined it all."

"I thought I was doing the right thing," he said. "Letting you go. I didn't want to hold you back."

She shook her head, tears sliding down her cheeks. "You didn't hold me back, Robert. You broke my heart."

His face crumpled, just a fraction. "I know."

They stood there, silence stretching between them like a bridge half-built—fragile, uncertain, but possible.

She looked at him again—*really looked*—and for the first time since the accident, since the party, since everything fell apart… she saw him. Not the patient. Not the man she had to be strong for. Just Robert.

"You're standing," she whispered again, stepping closer.

"I'm standing for you," he said simply. "I don't want to lose you without trying."

Jasmine's breath hitched.

She hadn't expected this—hadn't dared let herself hope for it, not after weeks of silence, not after years of waiting for words that never came. But now they had. And they undid her.

"Robert…" she whispered, stepping toward him until they were only a breath apart. Her eyes searched his, searching for doubt, for hesitation.

There was none.

Only him.

Only everything she'd tried so hard to bury.

"You don't get to do this now," she said softly, her voice trembling. "You don't get to finally say all the things I needed to hear—after I've tried to move on, after I've said goodbye."

"I know," he said, voice rough. "I know my timing's a mess. But it's the truth, Jasmine. It's always been the truth."

She shook her head, her heart aching. "You think standing there and saying you care is enough? You think it undoes the years I spent wondering if I meant anything to you at all?"

"No," he said. "I think it's late. But I hope it's not *too* late."

The honesty in his voice cut straight through her. She turned away, needing space to breathe, to think—but even a few steps apart, she could feel the pull of him. Like gravity.

"I told James I was choosing him," she said, more to herself than to him. "That I was done waiting for someone who never asked me to."

Robert didn't respond right away.

"I didn't ask," he said finally, "because I thought I didn't deserve to."

She looked at him then, eyes filled with tears she didn't bother hiding. "And now?"

"Now I'm asking," he said simply. "Not as a patient. Not as someone who needs you to fix him. But as the man who should've fought for you years ago."

Jasmine closed her eyes, her heart aching with every beat.

"You broke my heart, Robert," she whispered.

"I know," he said again, softer this time. "But I want the chance to put it back together."

A long, heavy silence stretched between them.

Then—slowly—Jasmine stepped forward again. Her hands, shaking, reached out and rested lightly on his arms, steadying him even as her world tilted.

"You're standing," she said, voice breaking.

"For you," he said again.

Her lips parted, but no words came—just a trembling breath and the truth rising inside her, messy and undeniable.

"I don't know what this means," she said.

Robert's voice was low. "It means I'm not letting you go without telling you I love you."

Jasmine let out a sound somewhere between a laugh and a sob. And then—after everything—they stood there, not as a physiotherapist and her patient, not as almosts or what-ifs.

Just Jasmine and Robert.

And maybe, finally, the beginning of something real.

Jasmine looked at him, eyes shining with tears, her breath caught somewhere between hope and heartbreak.

"I want to believe you," she said softly. "God, I've wanted to hear those words for so long I used to dream about them. I thought if you ever said them—*really said them*—I'd run straight into your arms."

She paused, voice trembling.

"But things aren't that simple anymore."

Robert's jaw tensed, but he didn't speak.

"I care about James," she went on. "He's been good to me. He's never made me guess or wait or doubt myself. And walking away from him… it's not something I can just do on a whim."

He nodded, silent.

"I'm not saying no," she added. "But I need time. To think. To figure out what's real and what's just old feelings stirred up by everything we've been through."

She took a step closer; eyes locked with his.

"But I need you to understand something, Robert. If I walk away from James, it won't be for a maybe. It won't be for words spoken too late. If I choose you—it has to be because you're all in. No fear. No second thoughts. No leaving this time."

Robert swallowed hard. "I'm all in."

She gave him a long look—one last beat of silence.

"Then prove it."

And with that, she turned and walked toward the door—her heart pounding, her head spinning—but her spine stayed straight, shoulders squared. At the threshold, she paused.

Just for a second.

Then she lifted her hand and touched the edge of the doorframe—once, lightly. A memory. A farewell. A beginning.

And she left without looking back.

For the first time, she wasn't chasing or waiting. She was choosing. Herself, first.

Alone now, Robert finally let himself sag against the window ledge, legs shaking with strain. His chest burned—not from the effort, but from the weight of everything unsaid until now.

But she'd heard him. She hadn't shut the door all the way. And that… that was enough. For now.

Chapter Twenty-Six

Jasmine's hands clenched the steering wheel tighter than necessary as she pulled into James's apartment carpark. Her pulse still hadn't found its rhythm since she left the Steele estate. Robert's words still echoed through her chest, reverberating with every heartbeat. Her fingers tingled with the lingering memory of his skin—warm, familiar, heartbreakingly alive beneath her touch.

She parked and sat still for a breath, two, then three. No more thinking. Thinking would only unravel her.

She stepped out of the car; legs unsteady beneath her certainty and walked to his door. When she reached it, her knuckles hovered mid-air for a moment, caught in hesitation.

Then she knocked—softly, but firmly. A decision made.

James opened it a moment later, a smile already forming—until he saw her face. The smile faded into something more careful. "Hey… what's wrong?"

"I need to talk to you," she said softly.

He stepped aside. She walked in, her legs feeling strangely disconnected from the rest of her body. The living room was warm, tidy. Familiar. But today it felt like something was shifting out of place.

She turned to face him. "I saw Robert. I went to the Steele estate for his afternoon session."

James nodded once, lips pressed into a thin line. "I figured."

There was a pause—thick, heavy.

"I confirmed to him I was stepping back," she said. "And I meant it. But… he said something. Something I wasn't expecting."

James waited, his expression unreadable.

"He told me he's in love with me," she said quietly, voice trembling. "And for the first time… I believe him."

The silence that followed felt like it cracked the air between them.

James looked away first, his jaw tightening slightly. "Okay."

"I'm not here to make excuses," she said, stepping closer. "You've been nothing but patient, honest, and good to me. I should've been honest with you sooner."

James rubbed a hand over the back of his neck. "So, what now?"

"I think…" She swallowed. "I think my heart was always somewhere else. I tried. I really tried to give us a real chance, and I care about you so much. But I can't keep pretending there's not something unfinished with him. Not now. Not after today."

He didn't speak right away. When he did, his voice was low, careful. "You told me once you didn't want to build your life around silence and maybes. But it sounds like you're walking right back into both."

Her throat caught. "Maybe I am. But this time, I need to know. I need to see it through. Or I'll always wonder."

James's eyes met hers. There was pain in them but not anger. Just the quiet hurt of someone who'd hoped a little too long. "I wish I could hate you for this."

She gave a broken laugh. "I wouldn't blame you if you did."

"But I don't," he said. "Because I meant it when I said I wanted you to be happy—even if that's not with me."

She blinked back sudden tears. "James…"

He stepped forward and gently touched her shoulder. "Don't apologise. Just… don't lie to yourself anymore, Jasmine. Whoever you choose, whatever happens—do it with your whole heart."

She nodded, the tears slipping free now. "Thank you. For everything."

He gave her a sad smile. "Just go, okay? Before I change my mind and ask you to stay."

Jasmine lingered a moment longer, then turned and walked out, the door closing softly behind her.

As she stepped into the fading light, something in her chest lightened—and something else cracked wide open.

She didn't know how it would end.

But at least now, she wasn't running from it.

The door clicked shut behind her, and James stood there, motionless, staring at the smooth grain of the timber like it might offer some kind of answer.

It didn't.

He scrubbed a hand down his face, exhaling slowly—like all the breath he'd been holding onto had just walked out with her.

He wasn't surprised. Not really. The signs had been there—the way her eyes flickered when Robert's name came up, the quiet spaces in conversations where her mind clearly wandered, the ache behind her smiles. James had tried to ignore it, to believe that time and consistency could win over history and longing.

But in the end, it hadn't been about winning.

It had been about truth.

And Jasmine had finally told the truth—not just to him, but to herself.

He walked to the kitchen, poured himself a glass of water, but didn't drink it. Just stood there with his hands wrapped around the cool glass, staring at the streak of fading afternoon sun across the floor.

He wasn't angry.

That surprised him.

Disappointed, yes. *God, yes.* He'd seen something with Jasmine—something easy, grounded, full of quiet promise. She made him laugh. She let him in. He would've built a life with her without thinking twice.

But she'd never fully been his to begin with.

And now that she'd admitted it, at least they could both stop pretending.

He took a sip of water, finally, and set the glass down with a soft thud.

Maybe this was what it meant to really care about someone—letting them go when you know they're already halfway gone. Not punishing them for it. Not making them feel smaller for being honest.

He just hoped Robert Steele understood what he'd been given—and didn't waste it.

James turned away from the window and grabbed his keys from the bowl by the door.

He needed to clear his head. Maybe a long drive. Or a beer with someone who didn't ask too many questions.

But even as he walked out the door, a small part of him still wished—just a little—that she might come back.

Not because she was confused.

But because she was sure.

Jasmine slid into the driver's seat and closed the door with more force than necessary. The sound echoed in the silence, but it didn't stop the tears from coming.

They spilled freely now, warm and blinding as they streaked down her cheeks, soaking into the collar of her blouse. She didn't bother wiping them away. What was the point?

James's expression—quiet, heartbroken, but composed—kept replaying in her mind. The way he'd looked at her just before she left: like he already knew, like he'd known all along.

She let her forehead fall to the steering wheel, fingers clenched tight around the leather as her shoulders shook.

He didn't yell. Didn't ask her to stay. He just let her go with grace.

And that somehow made it worse.

Jasmine hated this part—hated that doing what felt right for her meant hurting someone who didn't deserve it. James had shown up for her, again and again, and she'd walked out of his apartment with his heart quietly breaking behind her.

A sob escaped her lips. She bit down hard on the edge of her thumb to silence it.

Then, through a blur of tears, her hand reached blindly for her phone—like instinct.

Heidi.

Her fingers hovered for only a moment before she typed:

Can I come over? Really need to talk.

The message delivered, and a beat later, three dots appeared. Then Heidi's reply blinked onto the screen:

'Cause babe... always. Kettle's on. Door's open. 🖤

Jasmine stared at the screen, then sniffed, the corner of her mouth twitching with something close to a smile. Relief. Gratitude. Love.

She wiped her face with the sleeve of her cardigan, drew a long, shaky breath, and started the car.

Heidi's townhouse sat warm and inviting at the end of the quiet street, golden light spilling through the front windows like a beacon. Jasmine parked out front, cut the engine, and took a moment to breathe. Her face was tight from dried tears, her heart still heavy with guilt.

She didn't knock.

Just like Heidi promised, the door was unlocked.

The moment she stepped inside, the smell of peppermint tea and something sweet baking in the oven wrapped around her like a hug. Heidi appeared in the hallway, barefoot, wearing leggings and an oversized hoodie, her blonde curls twisted into a messy bun.

Her eyes took one look at Jasmine's face and softened.

"Oh, honey."

Jasmine didn't say a word. She dropped her bag by the door, walked straight into Heidi's arms, and let herself be held.

They stood like that for a minute—Jasmine clinging, Heidi grounding—until Heidi gently pulled back and tucked a strand of hair behind Jasmine's ear.

"Kettle's boiled. Come sit."

They moved to the kitchen, where two mugs waited on the bench, steam curling lazily above the rim. Jasmine slid into a chair at the counter while Heidi poured, setting one in front of her before taking the seat across.

Neither spoke right away.

Finally, Jasmine whispered, "I broke his heart."

Heidi nodded gently. "Yeah."

"I didn't mean to. I thought I could... I thought I should try to make it work with James. He's kind, and steady, and... safe. He deserves someone who doesn't flinch every time another man's name is mentioned."

"Robert."

Jasmine's voice cracked. "Yeah."

Heidi reached across the counter, her hand wrapping around Jasmine's, thumb brushing gently over her knuckles. "So, what happened? What changed?"

Jasmine's voice was quiet, but raw. "Earlier today, William told me that right after my twenty-first... Robert came to him. Told him how he felt about me."

Heidi's brows lifted slightly. "And?"

"William asked him not to tell me. Thought Robert wasn't in the right headspace. That he'd hurt me."

Heidi blinked. "And Robert listened?"

Jasmine nodded, shame and disbelief threading through her voice. "Yeah. He stepped back because William told him to."

Heidi didn't speak—just waited.

Jasmine swallowed, her fingers tightening slightly around the mug. "Then, this afternoon... I went to the Steele estate for what I thought was going to be my last session with him. And he was standing, Heidi. On his own."

Heidi's breath hitched, her voice cracking. "He was standing?"

Tears welled in Jasmine's eyes. "He did it for me. He... he remembered everything. He ended things with Claire the night of the accident. Because she'd been cheating on him."

Heidi sat back, her own eyes shining. "Oh, Jaz..."

"And then," Jasmine whispered, "he told me he loved me. That he has for years. That he's done wasting time."

Heidi sat in stunned silence for a moment, then finally asked, "So what now?"

"I don't know." Jasmine let out a long breath, her voice tight with emotion. "I went straight to James. Told him everything. That I care about him, but I can't give him what he wants. And he just... took it. Quiet. Kind. Said he wanted me to be happy."

Heidi closed her eyes for a beat. "He's a good man."

"I know." Jasmine looked down at her tea, the first tear falling with a soft plink against the ceramic rim. "That's what hurts the most."

Heidi leaned forward, watching her closely. "And Robert?"

Jasmine shut her eyes again. "I told him to prove it. And I walked away, but my whole body... wanted to stay."

Heidi squeezed her hand. "Then maybe it's time to stop running from what you already know. You don't owe anyone a version of yourself that leaves you empty."

"I don't know what the right choice is yet."

"That's okay," Heidi said softly. "But maybe you finally believe there is a choice. That's something."

James spotted him just as he took another sip of beer.

William Whitaker.

Of course. The universe had a wicked sense of humour.

He considered finishing his drink and slipping out unnoticed, but it was already too late. William's eyes had landed on him, and a shadow of recognition crossed his face.

He approached with a bottle of Peroni in hand and a guarded nod. "James. Didn't expect to see you here."

James forced a tight smile. "Rough day."

William gave a quiet grunt. "Yeah. Same."

They sat in silence for a few beats, the noise of the bar fading under the weight between them.

Then William spoke, low and quiet. "She told you?"

James stared straight ahead. "Yeah. She left a few hours ago."

William exhaled. "I owe you an apology."

James frowned, glancing sideways. "For what?"

"For all of it," William said without hesitation. "The whole mess. It started with me."

James turned his body slightly, more attentive now.

"When Jasmine turned twenty-one, Robert came to me. Told me he was falling for her. And I told him to stay away. That she was too young, and he wasn't ready, and I didn't want him screwing things up."

James stayed quiet, watching him.

"And he listened," William said, his voice tight. "He walked away. And Jasmine thought he didn't feel the same. She spent years thinking it was all in her head."

James's jaw flexed. "And Claire?"

"She came back. He let her. But it wasn't the same, and we all knew it. Then the accident happened."

James ran a hand through his hair. "Jesus."

"She only found out today. And I saw it—it cracked something wide open. So, if you're hurting—and I know you are—don't hate her. Please. It's my fault. I took that choice away from both of them."

James stared down at his drink. "I don't hate her."

William blinked. "You don't?"

"I'm gutted," James admitted. "But I saw it. Even when she was with me… part of her was always somewhere else. I just didn't want to admit it."

William's voice softened. "You're a better man than I was."

James shook his head slowly. "Doesn't feel like it."

"No," William said firmly. "You gave her something she hadn't had in a long time—stability, care, a chance to believe in herself. That mattered."

They sat in silence again, this time less strained.

Finally, James said, "He better not mess it up."

William smiled faintly. "He won't."

James raised his glass. "Let's hope not."

They clinked bottles quietly—two men bound by the same woman. One stepping back. One stepping up.

Chapter Twenty-Seven

The house was quiet when Jasmine let herself in. The house was too quiet—the kind that seeps into walls and presses at your chest.

She dropped her keys on the hall table and stood there a moment, listening—to nothing. No footsteps. No tea boiling. No voices. Just the faint hum of the refrigerator and the sound of her own breath, uneven and tired.

She moved through the house slowly, like she was walking underwater. Past the photos on the shelf. Past the living room where James once kissed her hand. Past the couch where she'd once cried over Robert, unsure if he'd ever walk again.

Now she knew.

Now she knew everything.

In her bedroom, the moonlight spilled through the blinds in narrow slats, casting soft lines across her bedspread. She kicked off her shoes and sat on the edge of the mattress, her hands resting in her lap, her back hunched.

For a long time, she didn't move.

Not because she didn't know what came next—

but because, for the first time in years, she was finally feeling all of it.

The ache of letting James go.

The weight of William's confession.

The still-lingering warmth of Robert's hand in hers.

She pressed her palms against her eyes until stars danced behind her lids. Her body was exhausted, but her mind refused to quiet.

She had done what she needed to do.

She had spoken the truth.

But truth didn't always come with relief. Sometimes, it just left space.

And in that space, every version of herself hovered—

The girl who once waited for Robert to see her.

The woman who tried to love someone kind, even if her heart was elsewhere.

The soul who now stood at a fork in the road, terrified of choosing wrong again.

She lay back on the bed, arms spread wide across the comforter, her hair fanned out around her like a halo of indecision. Tears didn't come this time. Only the tightness in her chest and the slow burn of clarity.

She didn't know what tomorrow would bring.

Didn't know how to face Robert again.

Didn't know how long James's absence would echo in the spaces he once filled.

But she knew this:

She wasn't running anymore.

Not from Robert.

Not from the past.

Not from herself.

And for now, that would have to be enough.

But she also knew she needed time.

Time to breathe without guilt.

Time to let the dust of heartbreak settle.

Time to grieve what could've been—and gather courage for what still might be.

Time to choose—not out of fear, or history, or obligation—but out of truth.

Because loving someone was one thing.

But choosing them, fully, without hesitation… that would take everything.

And this time, she wanted to get it right.

It was Saturday morning, nearly a week since Jasmine had seen either James or Robert.

She was giving herself time.

All week, she'd buried herself in work, in routine, in the silence of her apartment. She'd needed the space—away from everyone else's expectations, even her own.

Earlier in the week, she'd spoken briefly with the new physiotherapist working with Robert. His words still echoed in her mind:

"He's progressing well. Better than expected, honestly. He seems… very determined. Like he's obsessed with getting back to where he was."

The thought stayed with her longer than she liked to admit.

Now, she stood in her brother's kitchen, hands wrapped around a mug of chamomile tea, the scent curled into her nose—familiar and just a little sad.

Across the counter, Mary drizzled honey into her own tea, her expression concentrated, domestic, warm.

"I swear, chamomile only works if it's basically syrup," Mary said, giving her cup a brisk stir. "Otherwise, it just tastes like regret and hot water."

Jasmine huffed a quiet laugh, the sound surprising even herself. "You might be onto something."

Mary glanced up, studying her. "You sleeping okay?"

"Some nights," Jasmine admitted, eyes dropping to the swirling tea in her cup. "Mostly I just… think."

"Thinking's overrated," Mary said gently, then softened. "But I get it."

Jasmine nodded, a quiet moment stretching between them.

"I heard from the new physio," she said after a beat. "He said Robert's doing really well. Better than expected."

Mary raised a brow. "I'm not surprised. He's got something to fight for now."

Jasmine's fingers tightened slightly around the mug. "Yeah. He does."

"You don't have to talk about it," Mary said after a moment. "We can just sit here and critique herbal tea."

Jasmine shook her head. "No… I want to. I think I need to."

Mary waited.

"I thought I'd feel more… broken, after ending things with James. But mostly I feel still. Like I finally stopped running, and now I don't know what to do with all the silence."

Mary nodded. "Stillness can feel like a kind of grief too. Letting go of the version of life you thought might work."

Jasmine stared into her cup. "I didn't love him the way he deserved."

"You were honest," Mary said gently. "That's rare. And brave."

Silence settled for a moment. A breeze drifted in through the open door, fluttering the edge of a tea towel.

Then, without looking up, Mary said quietly, "Have you spoken to Robert?"

Jasmine stilled. "No. I meant what I said—I needed space."

"But you're thinking about him."

Jasmine's throat tightened. "It's like he's everywhere and nowhere at once. I walk past places we used to go, and I half expect him to be there. I keep turning to tell him things, like I used to. And then I remember…"

Mary didn't interrupt.

Jasmine swallowed. "It's not just missing him. It's more than that. It's like… I miss the part of me that only ever existed around him."

Mary reached over and gently touched her hand. "That part's still there, Jaz. She's just waiting for you to catch up."

Jasmine let out a slow breath. "I don't want to rush back to him just because I miss him. That wouldn't be fair. Not to me, or him."

Mary gave her hand a reassuring squeeze. "That's not what I'm seeing. What I see is a woman who's finally still enough to feel the truth. No shame in that."

The back door creaked open behind them, and Jasmine glanced up to see William step into the kitchen, his brow lifting slightly when he saw her sitting at the counter.

"Oh—hey," he said, voice careful.

"Hey," Jasmine replied, matching his tone. Her fingers curled tighter around her mug.

William gave Mary a look—half question, half apology.

Mary, ever intuitive, rose from her seat and grabbed her tea. "I'm going to check on the laundry," she said lightly. "Take your time." She pressed a gentle hand to Jasmine's shoulder as she passed, then disappeared down the hall.

An awkward quiet settled.

William moved to the other side of the counter and leaned against it, rubbing the back of his neck. "Didn't know you'd be here."

"Just needed some air," Jasmine said. "And tea."

He nodded. "Good tea. Mary's specialty."

She gave him a small smile, but it faded quickly.

William exhaled, bracing his palms against the edge of the counter. "I owe you more than one apology."

"You already said sorry," she murmured. "The other day."

"I know. I just…" He looked down, jaw working. "It doesn't feel like enough."

Jasmine watched him, her voice quieter now. "You thought you were protecting me."

"I thought I knew better," William corrected, eyes lifting to meet hers. "And I didn't. I saw how close you two were, and I panicked. I thought I could keep things simple if I stepped in. But I didn't protect anyone. I just made a mess."

Jasmine's throat felt tight, but she nodded. "He didn't tell me, Will. Not until now. I thought it was all in my head."

"I know," he said. "And I'll carry that guilt, Jaz. But… I also know you wouldn't be here—right here, right now—if you hadn't gone through all of it. James, Robert, everything."

She looked down at her tea. "I hurt someone good."

William was quiet for a beat. Then, softly: "You're good too. You were honest. That counts for something."

Jasmine blinked, then gave a soft exhale. "You're being weirdly wise today."

William grinned. "Don't get used to it."

They shared a small, tentative laugh, and something in the air between them loosened.

Then he added, more gently, "Whatever happens next with Robert… don't let what I did keep you from what you really want."

She met his gaze, surprised by the clarity in his voice.

"I won't," she said quietly. "But I still need time."

"Then take it," William replied. "He's not going anywhere. Not this time."

Robert gritted his teeth as he shifted his weight forward, gripping the edge of the custom-installed parallel bars in the study.

The morning light filtered through the sheer curtains, warming the polished timber floors. Outside, birds chattered in the trees. Inside, the only sounds were the creak of his braces and the faint scratch of Mark, his physio, jotting notes onto a clipboard.

He closed his eyes, inhaled slow and steady, then shifted his weight forward—left foot, then right. The ache in his calves burned, but it was manageable now. Familiar. He could almost welcome it.

"Nice," his physiotherapist, Mark, said from nearby. "That's your third unassisted lap today. You're ahead of where I expected you to be."

Robert managed a tight nod, his breath still shallow. "Guess I'm just impatient."

Mark chuckled. "Impatient works, as long as it doesn't become reckless. You've come a long way, Robert. You should feel proud."

But pride wasn't exactly what he felt. Not today. Not really.

He stepped down carefully and turned toward the mat table, bracing himself as he lowered to sit. His muscles trembled in protest, but he welcomed the sting—it meant he was rebuilding.

It meant he was still fighting.

Mark handed him a water bottle. "You're pushing hard every day. What's driving it?"

Robert took a sip, letting the coolness soothe his dry throat. He didn't answer right away. Just stared at the window across the room, at the way the light filtered in, warm and hazy.

He didn't want to lie.

"Someone I care about asked me to prove something," he said finally, voice low but steady.

Mark tilted his head. "And are you?"

"I'm trying," Robert said.

The therapist nodded thoughtfully and stepped back, giving him space to breathe, stretch, process.

As Robert leaned forward to work on his hamstrings, his mind wandered—like it always did—back to that afternoon.

Jasmine. Standing in front of him, eyes wide, voice trembling. Her hands on his arms, grounding him. The flicker of belief in her face before she turned and walked away.

He could still feel the ghost of her touch.

Nine weeks ago, he could barely lift his legs without assistance. Now he was walking— cautiously, stiffly, but walking. Because of her. Because of the second chance her presence cracked open, even if she hadn't said yes. Not yet.

She had given him something to aim for.

And he wasn't going to waste it.

Not this time.

Chapter Twenty-Eight

The sky had already begun its slow descent into dusk when Jasmine pulled into the circular drive at the Steele estate. The sandstone walls glowed gold in the late afternoon light, and the frangipanis lining the path swayed gently in the breeze. Everything looked still, untouched.

But she wasn't the same woman who'd last stood on this porch.

She wasn't here to make a decision.

She just needed to see him.

The front door opened almost immediately after she rang the bell. Kelly appeared, her expression flickering with surprise before settling into something closer to relief.

"Jasmine," she said warmly, cautiously. "It's lovely to see you."

"Hi." Jasmine brushed her hands down the front of her jeans. "I hope it's okay. I… just wanted to check in."

Kelly hesitated for only a beat, then nodded. "Of course. He's in the study. I was about to bring him some water. But…" She smiled gently. "Go ahead."

"Thank you," Jasmine murmured.

The house felt familiar—its scent, its quiet elegance—but her footsteps were heavier as she moved down the hall. Soft strains of music floated through the air. Classical piano. Low. Grounding.

She paused at the closed study door, her fingers hovering just above the handle.

Then she knocked.

The music stopped.

"Yeah?" came Robert's voice, slightly breathless.

She opened the door.

He stood near the far window, facing away, a towel draped around his neck, sweat clinging to the back of his shirt. The parallel bars stretched out beside him, gleaming under the overhead lights. The room smelled of effort—muscle rub, lemon water, the faint tang of metal and skin.

When he turned and saw her, everything stilled.

His hand dropped from the towel. His chest rose and fell with unsteady breath. "Jasmine."

She stepped inside, unsure whether to smile or apologise—or leave. "Hi."

A beat passed.

"You came," he said.

"I wasn't sure if I should," she admitted. "But I wanted to."

He swallowed. Nodded. "I'm glad you did."

She glanced around—foam rollers stacked neatly, resistance bands coiled by the mat, dumbbells lined up like soldiers. "This is quite the setup."

"My parents went overboard," he said with a wry smile. "I didn't argue."

She smiled. "No point resisting Kelly Steele."

He shrugged. "Not when she's on a mission."

The silence that followed was heavier.

"I spoke to your new physio," Jasmine said softly. "He said you're doing well. Better than expected."

Robert reached for the towel, wiped the back of his neck, then tossed it over the chair. "Yeah. I'm making progress."

"Obsessed, I think, were his exact words."

That pulled a faint smirk. "I've been called worse."

She tucked a strand of hair behind her ear. "What's driving you?"

He didn't answer right away.

Then he met her eyes. "You."

Her breath hitched.

He took one step.

Then another.

She didn't move.

No walker. No bars. No steadying hand on the wall.

Just Robert. Steady. Determined.

"I wanted you to see," he said, now standing before her. "That I'm still me. That I'm not giving up."

Her eyes burned.

"I never thought you would," she whispered.

They stood there—close enough to touch but not touching. The heat from his skin, the tremble in his muscles, the quiet thunder of vulnerability in his voice—undid her.

"I brought something," she said, breaking the silence. She reached into her bag and pulled out a small, folded paper. "Some of the exercises we used to do together. I wasn't sure if they'd be useful, but…"

She held it out.

His fingers brushed hers as he took it.

"Thank you," he said, and it wasn't just gratitude. It was reverence.

She didn't pull her hand away.

"Robert," she said quietly, "I don't know what this means. I don't even know what I want yet. I just… needed to see how you were."

He didn't flinch. "It means everything. That you're here."

She nodded, the breath she'd been holding slipping free. "I should go."

"I know."

But neither of them moved.

Finally, she stepped back. Gave him a small, aching smile. "Keep going. You're doing it."

He smiled, tired and real. "I'm not stopping."

She turned, her steps slow as she moved to the door.

Before she could open it, his voice stopped her.

"Jasmine."

She turned.

"I'm not asking you to choose," he said. "Not yet. Just… don't disappear."

Her voice caught. But she nodded. "I won't."

Then she left.

And for the first time in weeks, Robert didn't feel like he was chasing something just out of reach.

He felt like maybe—just maybe—he was finally walking toward it.

The door clicked shut behind her, soft and final.

Robert stood motionless for a long time, staring at the space she had just vacated. The room still held her scent—jasmine, faint and fleeting, like a memory.

He looked down at the folded paper in his hand. Didn't open it yet. Just held it like something precious.

He didn't try to mask the pressure behind his eyes. Or the ache deep in his chest. Or the tremble in his legs—from exertion, yes, but also from holding himself together while she was here.

He eased into the chair by the window, bracing a hand against the armrest, still gripping the paper with the other.

Outside, the sky had deepened to amber. Shadows stretched long across the lawn. He sat in silence, jaw tight.

She had come.

He hadn't dared to believe it until she was there—standing in the doorway with wide eyes and something deeper stirring beneath them.

She still cared.

Maybe not enough. Maybe not yet.

But she hadn't let go.

Robert let out a breath he didn't realise he'd been holding.

Then he unfolded the paper.

Her handwriting greeted him—neat, slanted, familiar.

Single leg raises – 3 x 15 each side

Heel slides

Ankle pumps

Bridges

Balance work – eyes closed (when you're ready)

At the bottom, one line in smaller writing:

You're stronger than you think. Keep proving it.

—J

His throat closed.

He hadn't cried when he'd lost feeling in his legs.

Not when Claire left.

Not when he woke up alone and realised the one person he needed most was gone.

But now—holding this scrap of paper and a sliver of hope—he felt the sting behind his eyes and didn't blink it away.

Because Jasmine had seen him.

Not the broken version.

Not the man who'd stayed silent too long.

But the man still fighting.

He folded the paper slowly and placed it beside his water bottle. Then he stood—no walker, no bars. Unsteady but upright. He reached for the foam roller near the cabinet, laid it on the mat, and lowered himself down.

The light was fading.

But he was still moving.

Still hoping.

The knock came just as he finished stretching. Not urgent—familiar.

He didn't call out.

A moment later, the door opened, and William stepped in, holding a paper bag and a six-pack of ginger beer.

"Hope you're still off the hard stuff," he said with a crooked smile.

Robert smirked. "Only when you're around."

William set everything down on the table. "Mary made sandwiches. I told her you probably wouldn't eat, but she threatened emotional harm if I showed up empty-handed."

Robert stretched his leg, easing tightness from his hamstring. "She's terrifying when she wants to be."

"She's a Whitaker. Comes with the territory."

They sat side by side, ginger beers in hand, the room filled with the soft fizz of carbonation and the distant rustle of trees outside.

William broke the quiet first.

"She told me she came."

Robert didn't look over. "Yeah."

"And?"

"She looked good," he said after a moment. "Tired. But good."

William waited.

When Robert didn't continue, he took a sip and said gently, "You're not going to lose her, you know."

"You don't know that."

"She came. That means something."

Robert exhaled hard through his nose. "I spent years convincing myself we missed our shot. That she was better off."

"She's not," William said simply.

Robert turned. "You sure?"

William nodded. "I used to be scared you'd hurt her. That you'd pull her into the mess with you."

Robert blinked. "And now?"

"Now I know you're the only one who never treated her like she was breakable. Even when she was. Even when you were."

Robert looked down at the bottle, the edge of the label curling under his thumb. "I didn't fight for her. Not when it counted."

"You're fighting now," William said. "That counts."

A long silence stretched between them.

Then Robert asked, quiet, "Do you think it's too late?"

William didn't answer right away. Instead, he grabbed a sandwich, unwrapped it, took a bite. Chewed.

Then, finally: "I think you two have been circling the same truth for years. Maybe you had to fall apart first to really find each other."

Robert snorted. "You sound like Mary."

"She's rubbing off on me. Makes me look at things I used to avoid."

He turned to Robert. "Like the fact that I got it wrong."

Robert frowned. "What do you mean?"

William's jaw tightened, then relaxed. "I asked you not to go there with her. When she turned twenty-one. Told you to keep your distance."

"I remember."

"I thought I was protecting her." William's voice lowered. "But I only made things harder. For both of you."

Robert looked at him—really looked—and saw the guilt etched in his face.

"You're not the only one who got it wrong," he said quietly.

They sat there, letting it all settle.

Eventually, William rose and stretched. "I should get back. But listen… she's taking her time. That doesn't mean she's walking away."

Robert nodded. "I know."

William gathered the bottles. At the door, he paused. "If you get the chance to say everything you never said—don't waste it."

Then he was gone.

Robert stayed where he was, the untouched sandwich beside him.

He closed his eyes.

Jasmine's voice whispered through his mind, steady and sure.

'You're stronger than you think.'

Yeah.

He just had to believe it.

Chapter Twenty-Nine

The living room at his parent home was quiet except for the rhythmic click of Kelly's knitting needles and the soft rustle of the newspaper as Terry turned the page. Robert sat in the armchair across from them, one leg stretched out on the ottoman, the other resting stiffly on the floor. The scent of eucalyptus oil still lingered faintly in the air from his afternoon physio session.

He waited a beat before speaking. "She came yesterday."

Terry looked up instantly. "Jasmine?"

Robert nodded. "Yeah."

Kelly lowered her knitting, eyes thoughtful. "How'd it go?"

Robert leaned back, letting his head rest against the cushion. "Better than I expected. She didn't come to talk about us. Not really. But she didn't pull away either. She just… wanted to see me."

Kelly's face softened. "Of course she did."

"She brought physio notes," Robert said, almost smiling. "Some of the old exercises we used to do. That meant something."

Terry grunted, folding the paper. "She always had a good head on her shoulders. And a soft spot for you."

Robert hesitated. "I don't want to assume anything. But I need to be honest. With both of you. I'm not just trying to get better to prove something to myself anymore."

Kelly stilled. "You mean…?"

"I mean Jasmine," Robert said plainly. "I've wasted a lot of time, and I've hurt people—even her—without ever meaning to. But I'm not going to make the same mistake again by standing still."

There was a pause. Kelly's eyes were full, watchful, but calm. "Are you saying you want to be with her?"

"I'm saying I'm going to try," Robert said, his voice steady. "I know she needs space. I'm not asking her for anything right now. But I want to show her she's not the only one still carrying all of it. I've been carrying it, too. I just buried it deeper."

Terry's jaw worked, then he nodded once. "If you're going to do this, do it right. Don't push her. Don't let pride get in the way."

"I won't," Robert said. "I'm done letting fear make my decisions."

Kelly reached over and placed her hand over his. "Then I think you're more than ready."

Robert looked down at their joined hands and gave a small smile. "I don't know where it'll lead. But I'm not afraid to find out."

For a while, the three of them sat in quiet understanding, the late sunlight filtering through the curtains, casting a warm gold across the room.

Robert stood just off the sidewalk, heart thudding harder than it should after such a short walk. The café Jasmine liked—he'd confirmed it with William—sat tucked into the corner of a leafy side street, a few blocks from the surf. Mornings like this always reminded him of her: bright, quietly alive, a little chaotic if the waves were up.

He adjusted his stance, willing his leg not to betray him. Eleven weeks of physio. Enough to make this possible. Barely. But it wasn't just about walking. It was about showing her—he meant it this time.

He spotted her the moment she stepped out of the florist across the road—her coat loose over a grey hoodie, a bunch of eucalyptus tucked under one arm. She looked like Bondi itself: relaxed, sunlit, quietly strong. And then she saw him.

Her steps faltered. Just for a second. But in her eyes, something stirred—recognition, surprise… and something else. Hope, maybe. Or the careful shadow of it.

"Robert?" she said, crossing toward him.

"Morning," he replied, a little breathless. From the short walk. From seeing her.

"What are you doing here?"

He held up a ceramic coffee cup—navy blue with clean white lettering.

Heel. Toe. Hope.

"I brought peace," he said.

She blinked, lips parting with a surprised laugh. "You remembered this?"

"You used to chant it every time you got nervous about a session. Thought it might work on me too."

Jasmine took the cup from his hand. Her fingers brushed his. She lingered a moment longer than necessary.

He nodded to the café tables behind them. "Can we sit? Just for a few minutes?"

She didn't answer right away. But after a pause, she nodded. "Okay."

They settled at a small table under the striped umbrella, the scent of the sea and eucalyptus between them.

"You walked here?" she asked.

"From the corner," he admitted.

She frowned softly. "Robert…"

"I wanted to. I needed to." His eyes held hers. "I needed to see you."

Jasmine glanced down at the cup in her hands; the words printed across it suddenly heavier than ceramic. "It's been a week. I've been trying to make space for my own thoughts."

"I didn't want to intrude."

"You didn't." She lifted her gaze again. "I needed that space. Not because I was running—but because I wanted to be sure. That whatever I decide, it's mine. Not because of guilt or timing or anyone else's expectations."

He nodded slowly, listening.

"And the truth is…" Her voice caught. She swallowed. "I missed you. Stupid things. Your sarcasm. Your way of asking questions I don't want to answer. That look you get when you're trying not to laugh but you do anyway."

Robert's chest tightened.

"But," she added gently, "I also hated hurting James. He didn't deserve that. I didn't want to be the person who did that to someone good."

"I know," Robert said quietly. "You've always tried to protect people, even when it costs you."

She smiled, but it didn't quite reach her eyes. "And I'm tired of making decisions based on fear or obligation."

"You don't owe me anything, Jasmine," he said. "I'm not here asking for guarantees. I just want to be part of whatever comes next. If you'll let me."

She looked at him fully now. "I'm not afraid of what I feel for you."

That stunned him.

"I think I have been, for years," she continued. "But not anymore."

Robert's heart stumbled. "So where does that leave us?"

She exhaled slowly, steadying herself. "It leaves us here. I'm not ready to dive in headfirst—not yet. But I'm not walking away either."

He nodded, something easing behind his ribs. "That's enough for me."

"For now," she added, a hint of warning—but her tone was warm, not defensive.

Robert smiled. "Fair."

She took another sip of her coffee. "Just promise me one thing."

"Anything."

"No grand gestures. No speeches. Just… be here. Mean it."

"I can do that."

Her fingers brushed the side of the cup again. "Then let's see where this goes."

The afternoon light was soft, filtering through the blinds of Heidi's sunlit apartment. Jasmine sank into the worn, navy-blue armchair by the window, her hands wrapped around a mug of chamomile tea. Heidi sat opposite her, feet curled under, eyes warm and waiting.

Jasmine hesitated, then let out a slow breath. "I saw him today. Robert."

Heidi's smile was gentle but eager. "How did it go?"

"Better than I thought it would." Jasmine's gaze dropped to the rim of her mug. "It was quiet. No fireworks. No big confessions. Just… real."

Heidi nodded slowly. "That sounds good. Real's always better than the alternative."

Jasmine smiled, but it was tinged with uncertainty. "I was scared I'd feel nothing, or that it would all come rushing back and overwhelm me."

"And?"

"It was somewhere in between. I still feel everything—his stubbornness, his laughter, the way he looks at me like I'm the only person in the room. But there's also space. Space I haven't allowed myself in a long time."

Heidi leaned forward. "Do you think that space means you're ready?"

Jasmine's fingers tightened around the mug. "I don't know if I'm ready for all of it yet. Not the past, not the future. But I'm ready to stop running from it."

"That sounds like a start."

Jasmine sighed, a small smile breaking through. "I didn't want to hurt James. That part's still hard."

Heidi reached across, squeezing her hand. "You didn't. You were honest. That's more than most people can manage."

Jasmine looked up, meeting Heidi's eyes. "I want to see where this goes—with Robert. But on my terms. Slowly. Carefully."

Heidi's grin was wide and sure. "And I'll be here for every step."

They sat together in the quiet warmth of the afternoon, a soft peace settling between them—a promise of healing, hope, and the long road ahead.

The sun was dipping low over Bondi when Jasmine stepped through the door of her apartment, the familiar scent of sea salt and eucalyptus greeting her like an old friend. She slipped off her heels and padded into the kitchen, filling a glass with water before leaning against the counter. The day had left her body drained and her mind overrun, but the silence of home offered a small, welcome reprieve.

Her phone buzzed on the bench.

She glanced down.

Robert Steele.

Her fingers hovered for a second too long before she picked it up.

"Hey," she said, her voice soft, careful.

"Hey." His voice on the other end was warm and a little breathless. "Hope I'm not catching you at a bad time."

She sank onto the couch with her glass and tucked one leg beneath her. "You're not. I just got in."

"How was your day?"

She let out a tired breath. "Busy. Clients all day. I think I forgot to blink between ten and three."

He chuckled, and the sound settled something restless inside her.

"At least, tell me you had coffee."

"Three," she said, smiling faintly. "Which is probably why I'm still vertical."

"Some things never change."

The silence that followed wasn't awkward. If anything, it felt like a space being held.

"I, uh…" He cleared his throat. "I wanted to tell you something. About physio."

She straightened slightly. "Okay."

"I made it up the stairs today. The full flight. No railing."

Her heart caught.

"Robert…" She pressed her palm against her chest. "That's amazing."

"It felt like Everest," he admitted, "but yeah. I made it."

She could hear the quiet pride in his voice. Earned. Hard-fought.

"Mark says I'm ahead of schedule. Twelve weeks in and I'm doing things they didn't expect me to manage for months." He paused. "I've been pushing. Hard."

"For you?" she asked gently.

"For me," he said. Then, after a breath: "But also… for you. For the part of me that's never really stopped hoping."

She closed her eyes, overwhelmed by the sudden, sharp ache in her chest.

"I'm proud of you," she said quietly.

"I was going to text," he continued, "but hearing your voice felt better."

She didn't respond right away. Her throat was too tight.

"I miss this," he said, voice softer now. "Talking to you. Just… being in your space."

She nodded even though he couldn't see it. "Me too."

A beat passed.

"Would it be okay if I called more often?"

Jasmine looked out at the dusky sky through her window, the last of the light catching on the rooftops across the street. Her grip on the glass loosened, something in her finally unclenching.

"Yeah," she said. "I think I'd like that."

There was a smile in his voice when he replied, "Good. I'll try not to abuse the privilege."

She laughed—an honest, unexpected laugh—and he chuckled in return, and just like that, the air between them shifted.

They talked for a while after that. About Mark nearly dropping a weight on his foot. About her new client who fell off a horse and broke her shoulder. About how weird the world felt sometimes, and how grounding it was to hear a familiar voice at the end of a long day.

When she finally hung up, Jasmine sat in the quiet, her phone still warm in her hand. Outside, the sky had deepened into lavender, and the sea breeze curled through the open window.

She didn't move.

Not because she didn't want to—but because something inside her was starting to settle.

And maybe, she wasn't afraid of it anymore.

Chapter Thirty

The late afternoon sun slanted across Jasmine's desk, casting long golden stripes over her open laptop and the half-eaten salad she'd mostly forgotten about. She was jotting notes from a client's last session when her phone buzzed. She glanced down, brow lifting at the name on the screen.

Mark Taylor.

She hadn't spoken to him in a couple of weeks—not since she'd stepped back from Robert's care. A flicker of apprehension passed through her as she answered.

"Hey, Mark."

"Jasmine," he said, his voice warm but strained. "Hope I'm not catching you at a bad time."

"Not at all. Everything okay?"

There was a pause—just long enough to make her sit up straighter.

"Actually," he said, "that's why I'm calling. I've been meaning to reach out sooner, but things have been a bit… hectic."

"What's going on?"

"My parents," he said with a heavy exhale. "Both of them are unwell. Nothing immediately critical, but serious enough that I need to head up north for a couple of weeks. Help with appointments, the house. It's just me, really."

"Oh, Mark. I'm so sorry."

"Thanks. I appreciate that. Listen—I hate to ask, but I'm a bit stuck. I was hoping you might recommend someone to step in while I'm away. Someone you trust. Robert's been making great progress, and I don't want to disrupt that momentum."

Jasmine felt the air still around her.

Robert.

He'd been quiet since their phone call last week. Not distant—just patient. Present, but without pressure. Every night, she received a gentle goodnight text. Every day, a simple message: *Hope your day's going well. Just thinking of you.*

And every time, something in her softened.

It wasn't grand. It wasn't overwhelming. But it was steady. Thoughtful. And undeniably him.

She felt it with each passing day—how easy it was to let him back in. How much she still wanted to. But underneath that warmth, something new had taken root.

Readiness.

A deep, quiet knowing that she was done watching from the sidelines of her own life.

She took a breath. "Actually… I might be able to cover it myself."

Mark paused. "You sure? I know things were complicated…"

"They were," she said, with a small, wry smile. "But they're not anymore. Not like that. And I've kept up with his file. I know his program. Honestly, it might be good for both of us."

"Are you absolutely certain? I can keep looking if it's a stretch."

"I'm certain."

Mark let out a breath of relief. "You're a lifesaver, Jaz. Really."

"When do you need to leave?"

"Friday morning. I've got two more sessions with him before then. I can brief you properly."

"Perfect. Send me his schedule and anything new in his notes. I'll take it from there."

"You're a gem."

Jasmine smiled, already pulling up her calendar. "Take care of your parents, Mark. I've got this."

As she hung up, she stared at her screen for a moment, the cursor blinking steadily at the bottom of her notes. The decision settled over her like calm water.

She wasn't stepping back into the past. She was stepping forward.

To help. To heal. And maybe—to begin again.

The late-morning sun cast long shadows across the drive as Jasmine pulled up outside the Steele estate. Her hands rested on the steering wheel for a moment after she turned off the ignition, fingers flexing once before going still. The eucalyptus she'd picked up on the way lay across the passenger seat, tied neatly with twine. She glanced at it, then exhaled and stepped out.

The front door was already ajar.

She knocked anyway.

Terry answered, dressed in a well-worn polo and a broad smile. "He's been pacing the living room for the last ten minutes. Which, for the record, is impressive considering he's not supposed to be pacing at all."

Jasmine laughed softly, nerves melting just a little. "I'll keep him in line."

"I'm counting on it." He stepped aside, letting her in. "He's waiting for you."

She moved through the house quietly, the smell of fresh coffee and lemon polish filling the familiar air. At the doorway to the converted study, she paused.

Robert was already there, seated at the edge of the treatment table, stretching his right leg slowly. He wore a dark grey T-shirt and navy shorts; hair slightly damp from a recent shower. When he looked up and saw her, his expression changed—open surprise, then something gentler. Something steadier.

"Hey," he said.

"Hey." She held up the eucalyptus. "I come bearing gifts."

He took it from her when she stepped in, brushing her fingers without meaning to— or maybe meaning to after all. "Smells like you," he murmured, half to himself.

She didn't answer. Just offered a small, almost-shy smile and set her bag down in the corner.

The room was bright, clean, and familiar. The equipment was neatly stacked, the foam rollers lined up, the resistance bands hanging in a tidy coil. But it felt different with him here—not as a patient she was managing, but as someone she was slowly, tentatively choosing again.

"Mark left me a full update," she said, pulling out a notebook and glancing at the list of exercises. "You're ahead on strength and stability, but we're still building endurance and control. How are the stairs?"

"Not my favourite," he admitted. "But I made it up the full flight this morning."

"That's huge."

"Feels like it."

She knelt beside him and gently guided his leg into position. Her hands were clinical, steady—but she couldn't ignore the heat that coiled in her chest when his breath hitched just slightly under her touch.

They worked mostly in silence, the kind that didn't feel empty. His muscles responded well—tight but strong, no longer fighting her guidance but meeting it with effort and trust. She asked him to shift, to balance, to push and hold. He did everything she asked, and more.

"You're stronger than the last time I saw you," she noted after a particularly difficult set.

"I've been trying," he said. "Not just for the progress chart. For me. And… maybe for us."

She looked up at him, something unreadable flickering in her eyes. "I didn't come back to confuse anything, Robert."

"I know." He met her gaze, steady. "I'm not confused. I just wanted you to know I haven't stopped trying. For the right reasons, this time."

There was a beat of silence. The kind that stretched, held.

Robert's voice was soft when it broke the stillness. "Would you be able to stay for a little while?" His eyes searched hers, careful but hopeful. "Just so we could… spend time together. Coffee, lunch, a movie? Anything you're willing to do."

Jasmine stood still, her hand resting on the strap of her bag, her breath caught between instinct and intention. The way he said it—not pleading, not pressing, just asking—made something shift quietly in her chest.

She looked at him for a long moment. She should go. She had things to do, errands waiting, a dozen reasons to keep space between them. But none of them mattered as much as the warmth in his eyes or the way her body had already started to relax in his presence.

She should spend time with him.

She wanted to.

"Coffee," she said at last, her voice soft. "Then… we'll see what happens."

Robert smiled, and it lit something up in his face she hadn't seen in a long time—hope without fear.

"I'll put the kettle on," he said, already easing off the table.

And for the first time since everything began to unravel, Jasmine let herself stay.

Not because she had to.

But because she wanted to.

Robert moved through the kitchen with more ease than Jasmine remembered—still careful, still favouring one leg, but with a confidence that hadn't been there before. He reached for the French press on the counter, scooped in the coffee grounds, and filled the kettle. She watched him quietly, the domesticity of it both familiar and entirely new.

"Still drink it black?" he asked over his shoulder.

"Still strong enough to take paint off the walls?" she returned, smiling.

He chuckled. "You wound me."

When the coffee was ready, he poured it into mismatched mugs—one navy with a faded Vaucluse Juniors Rugby logo, the other pale yellow with a chipped handle—and led her through the French doors that opened onto the garden. The scent of rosemary and wet stone drifted on the air. The winter sun had broken through the clouds, casting the yard in a soft golden haze.

They settled into the old wooden bench beneath the jacaranda tree, their mugs warm between their palms.

"This was always my favourite part of the house," Jasmine murmured, glancing up through the tangled branches. "Quiet. Green. Doesn't feel like Sydney."

Robert nodded. "It helped. Especially in the beginning. When I couldn't even sit out here without help." He took a slow sip of his coffee, then glanced sideways at her. "I've been thinking about getting back to my place. Soon."

She turned to him. "You're ready?"

"Not completely," he admitted. "But I'm getting there. Physio's going well. I've got a handle on most of the daily stuff. And I think I need to try. To start doing things on my own again. Cooking badly. Leaving wet towels on the floor. Listening to music too loud."

Jasmine laughed softly. "Sounds like a man on a mission."

"I am." His gaze was steady, thoughtful. "I want my life back, Jaz. Not just physically. All of it."

She nodded slowly. "You'll get there."

"And maybe," he added, "eventually back behind the wheel."

Jasmine raised an eyebrow, a teasing edge in her voice. "I hope that doesn't include getting back on a motorbike."

Robert grinned, unabashed. "What, you didn't miss the death machine?"

"I didn't miss the heart attacks it gave me."

His smile softened into something more wistful. "I think I'm done with that part. The noise. The speed. It all felt important once, but now…" He trailed off, shrugging. "Now I just want things to be steady. Real."

There was a silence—not awkward, just full of shared understanding.

Jasmine wrapped her hands tighter around her mug. "Real sounds good."

They sat together in the fading winter light, the garden quiet around them, letting the coffee and the conversation warm what still ached—what still hoped—between them.

Jasmine turned her face toward the sun, eyes half-closed. "I used to imagine this," she said softly. "Not the injury. Not everything that came before. But… this part. Sitting here. Just talking to you. No games. No waiting for someone else to leave the room."

Robert didn't speak for a long moment. Then, quietly, "Me too."

She looked over at him, surprised. "You did?"

He gave a small, self-conscious smile. "More times than I care to admit. But I never let myself believe it could actually happen. I figured… you'd move on. Fall for someone less complicated. Less me."

She didn't smile, not quite. Her expression was open, honest, a little raw. "I did try. But none of it ever really let you go."

The space between them felt impossibly full, like breath held too long.

Robert reached out slowly, fingertips brushing her wrist. "Jasmine."

Her name was an anchor and a question all at once.

She met his gaze, heart suddenly loud in her chest.

"I know we said no grand gestures," he murmured. "But… if I don't do this now, I'll regret it."

She didn't stop him.

He leaned in, careful, giving her every second to turn away—but she didn't. Their foreheads touched first, a soft press that stilled everything around them. And then, gently, his lips met hers.

It wasn't urgent. It wasn't perfect. It was tentative, reverent, full of everything they'd held back for too long. Her hand found his chest, resting over the steady beat of his heart. His hand cupped her cheek, thumb brushing just below her eye.

When they finally parted, her eyes stayed closed for a breath longer. Then she opened them, smiled—small, real, unguarded.

"I've waited a long time for that," she said.

Robert exhaled a quiet laugh. "Me too."

They didn't speak after that. They didn't need to.

They just sat in the garden, side by side, the last golden light casting long shadows across the grass, and for the first time in years, nothing felt uncertain anymore.

Jasmine leaned back just enough to study his face. His eyes were still on hers—steady, searching—but softer now. The tension he so often carried in his jaw had eased.

"You okay?" she asked quietly.

He nodded, thumb brushing the back of her hand where it rested in his. "Yeah. More than okay."

Her smile tilted, a little teasing now. "Even with the eucalyptus in my lip balm?"

He gave a quiet laugh, the sound vibrating low in his chest. "Could've been motor oil and I wouldn't have noticed."

She laughed too, the sound threading through the stillness. Then a thought caught her. "Are we... different now?"

He didn't answer right away. Just reached for his mug and took a slow sip, as if letting the question settle before answering. "I think we've always been this. Or maybe we were just waiting to get here."

Jasmine nodded slowly, wrapping her hands around her cup again. "Feels a little terrifying."

"Terrifying," he agreed, then glanced at her sideways. "And good."

She bumped her shoulder lightly against his. "Mostly good."

They sat like that for a while—close, quiet, warm. The kind of silence that didn't require explanation. Birds rustled in the hedges at the edge of the garden, and somewhere inside, the soft creak of a floorboard reminded them they weren't entirely alone.

Robert shifted slightly, stretching his healing leg, testing its limits. "I've been thinking about going back to work."

Jasmine looked over, brows raised. "Soon?"

"Soonish. Maybe a week or two. I want to try. It feels… important. Like a milestone."

She nodded, understanding. "You want to feel like yourself again."

"Exactly."

He hesitated, eyes thoughtful. "I just need to get back behind the wheel of my car."

Her lips curved. "So, you're trading in the wheelchair for a steering wheel."

"That's the plan." His voice dropped, turning serious. "But I feel like I'm starting over. Not from scratch—just… with purpose this time. Everything feels clearer."

Jasmine looked at him, really looked at him, and felt the truth of it echo inside her.

"I can see that," she said softly.

He reached out again, slower this time, and took her hand properly, interlacing their fingers.

"I'm not trying to rush anything. I just need you to know—this means everything to me. You mean everything."

She didn't pull away. Instead, she gave his hand the smallest squeeze. "Then we'll go slow. Together."

He smiled then—full, open, unguarded. And she realised it wasn't just the kiss or the handholding or even the admission of feeling. It was him. The version of him she'd loved all along, now brave enough to show up.

Chapter Thirty-One

Jasmine stood barefoot in her kitchen, the cool tiles grounding her as the kettle clicked off with a soft hiss. Outside, the soft hum of Bondi murmured through the cracked window—waves in the distance, early joggers on the footpath, someone walking a dog that yapped at every passing bird.

For once, she wasn't rushing. Not her steps. Not her thoughts.

Her mug was warm between her hands; fingers curled around ceramic like it might steady the whirl of her thoughts. She'd barely slept—not because of nerves or regret—but because her mind wouldn't stop playing the moment over and over again. The garden. The kiss. The way his hand had cradled her face like she was the most important thing in the world.

Jasmine leaned against the counter, eyes drifting out toward the slice of ocean she could just glimpse from her window. She touched her lips lightly with her fingertips. Still tender. Still remembering.

Her phone buzzed on the bench beside her.

Robert Steele.

She didn't hesitate. Her heart fluttered a little as she opened the message.

Thinking of you. No eucalyptus lip balm required this morning. 😊

Her laugh escaped before she could catch it—quiet, warm, involuntary. She pressed her phone to her chest for a second, then set it down again, smiling into her tea.

She typed back.

Good. You got a free pass yesterday. Next time, lip balm mandatory.

Three dots appeared immediately.

Next time? I like the sound of that.

She stared at the screen for a long moment, her heart doing something complicated and soft in her chest.

There would be a next time.

But it was early. They weren't who they were before—not yet. He was still healing. She was still choosing. But something had shifted. Something real. Something that made her want to lean in, not run.

Jasmine took a slow sip of tea, the steam curling around her cheeks.

She didn't know what the rest of the day would bring. But for now, in this quiet sliver of morning, she felt something she hadn't in a long time.

Hope.

And maybe—love within reach.

It had been a quiet, golden afternoon when Robert said goodbye and thank you to his parents.

"You've done so much for me," he told them, his voice low but steady. "And I love you for it."

Terry clasped his son's hand with one and pulled him into a one-armed hug with the other. "Proud of you, mate. You've come a long way."

Kelly didn't speak at first—just wrapped him in a tight embrace, her eyes glossy with tears. "We are so proud of you, sweetheart. And we're always here for you."

"I know. Thanks, Mum," Robert said, his voice thick.

Then Kelly turned to Jasmine and pulled her into a warm hug. "Look after him, Jasmine."

"I will," Jasmine said softly, offering a small smile.

She followed behind him in her car as Robert drove the short distance from his parents' home to his Vaucluse estate. He'd insisted on driving himself, and she hadn't argued. Some things were about more than transportation.

Julie, his longtime housekeeper, was waiting for them at the door. She'd kept the place spotless during his recovery, and her smile widened when she saw him.

"Welcome home, Mr. Steele," she said, her eyes misty as she stepped aside.

Together, Jasmine and Julie helped Robert carry the last of his belongings inside. Well—they carried most of it. Robert insisted on taking one bag, stubborn as ever, even if it was just a duffel with a spare pair of shoes. His steps were careful but confident, each one placed with quiet determination. When they reached the top floor and stepped into his bedroom, he paused and straightened.

"I'm home," he whispered, almost to himself.

Jasmine smiled and began hanging up his clothes while Julie moved efficiently, folding and placing things in drawers. The room smelled like him—clean linen and cedarwood—and the space still carried his presence—like it had been holding its breath, waiting for him to return.

Her eyes drifted to the nightstand. A framed photo rested there—one she hadn't seen in years. It was of the three of them: Robert, William, and Jasmine, taken the summer she turned twenty-one. Sun-kissed, smiling, and carefree.

She picked it up, running her finger lightly along the edge of the frame. "How long has this been here?"

Robert looked over from where he was setting his watch on the dresser. "Since the day I got the photo."

Something in Jasmine's chest fluttered. She set the frame back gently, the air between them quiet—but full.

Julie reappeared a few minutes later with a silver tray balanced gracefully in her hands. On it sat two delicate porcelain cups, a small teapot, and a plate of shortbread biscuits.

"I thought you two might like some tea before I head off," she said, setting it down on the small on the bedroom balcony.

"Thanks, Julie," Robert said, his voice warm with appreciation.

Jasmine helped her pour the tea, adding a splash of milk to Robert's cup before handing it to him without asking—like she always used to.

"You remembered," he murmured, taking the cup from her hands. Their fingers brushed, and for a moment, neither moved.

"I remember a lot of things," Jasmine said, settling into the chair across from him as Julie quietly excused herself, closing the bedroom door behind her.

Outside, beyond the balcony, the late afternoon light filtered through the gum trees, casting a golden glow across the room. It was peaceful here. Familiar. Intimate in a way that felt unspoken but understood.

Robert took a sip of tea, then leaned back slightly. "This place feels bigger than I remember."

"You've been away for a while."

He nodded. "Yeah. But it's more than that. I think I see it differently now. Like... I don't just want to be back—I want to live differently in it. More intentionally."

Jasmine's gaze softened. "You already are. You've fought so hard, Robert."

He gave her a small, quiet smile. "I had a reason to."

She looked away at that, down into her cup, her cheeks flushing. But she didn't deflect. Didn't change the subject. Instead, she said, "It's good to see you here. In your space. You look... lighter."

He laughed under his breath. "Well, I'm still half titanium, but I'll take it."

Jasmine smiled, and they sat in silence for a few moments, sipping tea while the world beyond glowed with the end of the day.

Then Robert glanced at her. "You staying for dinner?"

She hesitated. "You're not tired?"

"Not yet." He gave her that familiar, crooked grin. "And besides, I owe you. You carried the heavy bag."

She laughed, shaking her head. "One meal. And I get to pick the playlist."

He raised his cup in a toast. "Deal."

They ordered Chinese from Uber Eats and unpacked it together in the kitchen, fingers brushing, bodies moving in quiet sync. When they both reached for the same container, her hip bumped his gently, and his hand settled at the small of her back—lingering just a beat longer than necessary.

It was easy now, this rhythm between them. New, yes—but not fragile. Like something that had waited patiently, putting down roots beneath the surface, steady and sure.

Later, they curled up on his couch to watch a movie. Jasmine tucked her legs beneath her; a throw blanket draped loosely over them both. Robert had changed into a soft grey tee, and she could feel the warmth of him beside her—the quiet strength of his presence, the calm steadiness in his breathing.

"You've got that look," he murmured, voice low.

She kept her eyes on the screen. "What look?"

"The one that says you're pretending to watch this movie but actually thinking about everything else."

She smirked. "I'm multitasking."

A comfortable silence followed. Then his fingers found hers—slow, deliberate. No urgency. Just intention.

When she turned toward him, the kiss was already there—unspoken, then undeniable. He kissed her like he had time. Like he wanted to take his time. No rush. Just the gentle, certain press of his lips against hers. It was the kind of kiss that made her feel seen, steady, and wanted in all the right ways.

When they parted, her forehead rested against his, her smile soft and slightly shy.

His thumb brushed along her cheekbone. "Stay. Just for a while."

She nodded.

They didn't cross that final line—not yet. Not because they were afraid. Not because of doubt. But because—for the first time in a long time—neither of them felt the need to fill the quiet with anything more than presence.

They talked. They laughed. He led her into his study to show her a framed photo on his desk—him and William, grinning like idiots at a barbecue three summers ago. Jasmine laughed, her fingers lightly tracing the edge of the frame, and he watched her like he was memorising the moment.

As the sun began to dip, casting the garden in dusky light, she curled into his side again, her head on his chest, their breaths in sync. The silence held no tension. Just warmth.

Neither of them said the word love.

But it was there—in the way he held her without needing more. In the way she tucked the blanket around them both. In the quiet safety of their bodies leaning close, the kind of closeness that wasn't just skin, but soul.

When she finally left, his lips pressed gently to her temple.

"Goodnight, Jaz," he whispered.

And she knew, deep down, something had shifted again.

They were building something real.

Not rushed. Not forced.

Just theirs.

The next day, Robert walked into the office for the first time in months. The quiet hum of activity, the familiar rhythm of keyboards clacking and voices low in conversation—it all felt strangely grounding, like slipping back into a suit he'd forgotten still fit.

William looked up from his desk through the glass wall just outside his office, eyes widening in surprise before a grin tugged at his mouth. He pushed back his chair and went out to greet Robert.

"Well, would you look at that. It's good to see you back, Rob."

Robert clasped his hand and pulled him in for a brief hug. "It's good to be back."

William clapped him gently on the back. "You sure you're ready?"

"I need to be," Robert said simply. And he meant it. Physically, he was getting stronger every day. Mentally? There was still ground to cover—but coming here, reclaiming the parts of his life that mattered, felt like the right step.

He walked into his office—the one that had sat untouched since the accident. The blinds had been drawn, the room clean but still. The cleaners must've been in recently; everything was spotless, sunlight catching on the polished wood of his desk. He placed his laptop down and sat slowly in his chair. It felt solid beneath him.

His gaze drifted to the small photo frame on the bookshelf—a candid shot from two years ago: him, William, and Jasmine on a boat, all sun-kissed smiles and windblown hair. Jasmine was caught mid-laugh, her face turned toward Robert like she was about to say something.

His chest tightened. Last night still lingered in him—in the warmth of her kiss, in the quiet curve of her smile as she'd curled into his side, in the soft click of the door closing behind her. He could still feel her presence in the room if he closed his eyes. No eucalyptus lip balm this time—just Jasmine. Real, close, and unguarded.

He leaned back in his chair and exhaled.

This—being here, stepping back into his life—felt different now. Purposeful. Because he wasn't just trying to return to who he'd been before.

He wasn't just reclaiming the life he had. He was building the one he wanted—with her in it.

Chapter Thirty-Two

The week had been busy—but the good kind. The kind that left Robert mentally sharp and physically spent in the most satisfying way. He and William had spent hours in meetings catching up on the Byron Bay project, the eco-resort their firm was designing on the cliffs just outside town. It was ambitious and green and exactly the sort of thing Robert had once lived for. He found, to his surprise, that he still did.

His days had started early and ended late, but there was a rhythm again. A pulse.

Physio had been folded into the week like clockwork—Monday and Wednesday sessions on the way home, and by Friday, his muscles ached in all the right ways. Not from pain. From progress. Mark had even texted that morning:

New gait pattern's holding steady. Proud of you, mate.

He'd walked into the office that day with a subtle swagger. Not for show. For himself.

By mid-afternoon, Robert was finishing a call with one of the landscape architects when a familiar scent hit the air—coffee, good coffee, and something sweet.

He looked up.

Jasmine stood in the doorway, her silhouette framed by the late light slanting through the glass wall behind her. She held two takeaway cups and a paper bag from the bakery two streets over—the one that did those dangerous hazelnut croissants he pretended not to like as much as he did.

Her smile was soft but sure. "I come bearing caffeine and sugar."

Robert stood, slower than he used to but steady. "You're either an angel or a saboteur."

"Depends on how much you've had to eat today," she said, stepping inside and setting the bag on his desk. "William said you tend to forget meals when you're focused."

"He's exaggerating," he said, accepting the cup she handed him. "I had lunch."

"Protein bar and half a banana doesn't count."

He smiled, watching her move around his office like she'd always belonged there. "So, what's the occasion?"

"No occasion." She shrugged, taking the chair across from him. "Just thought you might like company. And croissants."

Robert leaned against the desk, sipping the coffee. It was perfect. She was perfect.

And he felt it again—that subtle hum in the space between them. Unspoken but unmistakable.

"Thanks, Jaz," he said quietly.

Her eyes met his, soft and steady. "Anytime."

And in that still, comfortable moment, surrounded by blueprints and half-eaten pastries, Robert realised something simple and significant.

She hadn't just brought him coffee.

She'd brought him home.

A knock on the door broke the quiet.

William leaned in with a grin, eyes flicking from Robert to Jasmine and then down to the pastries on the desk. "What's this? I used to get the coffee and pastries. Now I get budget updates and stress headaches."

Robert smirked. "Perks of being back in charge."

Jasmine chuckled. "I'll bring you something next time, William. Cross my heart."

William stepped farther into the room, lifting the paper bag and peeking inside. "Hazelnut croissants?" He raised an eyebrow at Robert. "She never used to share these."

Robert gave him a wry look. "That was before I got my priorities straight."

William sighed dramatically. "So, you get pastries and flirtation, and I get spreadsheets and sarcasm. Nice."

Jasmine grinned, leaning back in her chair. "Sounds like we all know our roles."

William glanced between them, something flickering in his eyes—not quite surprise, not quite approval, but something close to both. Then he cleared his throat. "Anyway— just came to say I'm heading out early. Dinner with Mary."

Robert nodded. "Tell her hi."

William paused at the door. "Good to have you back, Rob."

"Good to be back," Robert said, meaning it.

The door clicked shut behind him, and Jasmine looked at Robert, amused. "You two really are like brothers."

He shrugged, sipping his coffee. "We kind of are. He's been there for everything."

A beat passed.

"You were always there for me too," he added, quieter now. "Even when you didn't have to be."

Jasmine's smile softened. "Maybe I always wanted to be."

Something unspoken settled in the air again—quiet, warm, and deeply familiar.

Robert didn't push it. Not yet. But the way she looked at him then, croissant in hand and sunlight in her eyes, told him he wouldn't have to wait much longer.

Robert put his coffee down on his desk then turned back to Jasmine, still perched on the edge of the desk, her smile lingering like sunlight through a window.

He stepped closer, just enough that the space between them shifted—charged, familiar.

"Have dinner with me tonight."

Her eyes lifted to his, the answer there before the words left her lips. "I'd love to."

Something in him relaxed. Not relief exactly, but a quiet, grounded joy. Without another word, he leaned in and kissed her—slow at first, then deeper, more deliberate. It wasn't rushed, but there was nothing casual about it. His hands slid gently to her waist, anchoring her against him, and she responded in kind, fingers curling into the soft cotton of his shirt, lips parting beneath his with a tenderness that stirred everything he'd been holding back.

When they finally drew apart, her breath hitched slightly, her eyes still closed for a beat longer than necessary.

"I've got physio with Mark this afternoon," he murmured, voice low against her cheek. "But I'll pick you up at seven."

She nodded, still catching her breath. "I'll be ready."

He smiled. "I'll look forward to it."

Jasmine touched his chest once—light, familiar—then turned and walked out, the scent of her perfume lingering in the air. And long after the door clicked shut, Robert was still standing there, grinning like a man who finally knew exactly where he wanted to be.

Jasmine stood in front of her bedroom mirror, smoothing her hands down the sleek lines of her black dress. It hugged her curves in all the right places—simple, elegant, and just sexy enough to make a statement. She'd taken her time getting ready, letting the ritual ground her: the soft curl of her hair, the sweep of bronzer across her cheekbones, the slow glide of her favourite lipstick.

This wasn't just any dinner.

Her phone buzzed on the vanity.

Heidi.

She put her earring in and answered on speaker. "Hey."

"Well?" Heidi's voice crackled through with a mix of teasing and genuine curiosity. "Are you wearing something scandalous or emotionally responsible?"

Jasmine laughed, tossing a glance at her reflection. "Sexy. But tasteful. I'm not trying to give him a heart attack."

"Just heart palpitations. Got it."

Jasmine smiled, running a final coat of gloss across her lips. "I'm ready."

There was a pause on the line, softer now. "How do you feel?"

She looked at herself in the mirror—really looked. Not just at the dress or the makeup, but at her eyes. There was something steadier there now. Clearer.

"Good," she said. "Really good. Nervous… but not scared. I want this."

Heidi exhaled, a quiet sound of relief. "Then go get it. And text me if you need an emergency exit—or if you need someone to tell you you're fabulous halfway through dessert."

"I'll text you when I'm home."

"Only if it's your home," Heidi said slyly.

Jasmine rolled her eyes but couldn't stop the grin from pulling at her mouth. She ended the call and slipped into her heels just as the doorbell rang.

Seven on the dot.

She grabbed her clutch, checked her lipstick one last time, and walked to the door—heart light, hope blooming in her chest.

Tonight mattered.

And she was ready.

Robert stood on her doorstep, hands in his pockets, looking devastatingly good in a navy button-down and dark slacks. The late sun caught the edges of his profile, and when Jasmine opened the door, his breath caught.

"Wow," he said, eyes sweeping over her with something between admiration and awe.

Jasmine's lips curved into a soft smile. "You clean up pretty well yourself."

"Pretty well?" He leaned in a little. "I was going for devastating."

She laughed, locking the door behind her. "Let's see how the night goes."

He walked her to the car and opened the door for her; the small gesture not lost on her. It wasn't flashy. It was quiet and natural—thoughtful. Like everything about him lately.

The drive to the restaurant was filled with easy conversation—music playing low, the city lights starting to flicker awake around them. When they arrived, Robert handed the keys to the valet and guided her inside with his hand resting gently on her lower back.

The restaurant was intimate, tucked away in Potts Point, with warm lighting and the clink of cutlery softened by ambient jazz. Their table was near a window that overlooked the harbour—subtle, romantic, not overdone.

Once seated, Robert ordered a single malt, neat. Jasmine chose a glass of sauvignon blanc.

"To finally getting around to dinner," he said, raising his glass.

She clinked hers against it. "To finally."

They ordered slowly—shared plates, small courses. He let her choose most of them but insisted on the grilled prawns. She didn't argue. Between bites, they talked. About work, about Julie's obsession with ironing tea towels, about how much he hated missing surf season.

"Still no motorbikes," she said, sipping her wine with a raised brow.

He held up a hand. "No motorcycles. I'm a changed man."

She grinned. "We'll see."

When the mains arrived, the space between them had narrowed—not physically, but in that almost imperceptible emotional way. The tension wasn't sharp. It was warm, expectant. Something alive between them now.

Robert looked at her across the table, eyes softer than she'd ever seen them. "I'm really glad we're doing this."

"So am I," Jasmine said, and meant it.

Dinner stretched on comfortably, the hours slipping by unnoticed. Neither of them wanted to leave just yet.

And neither of them quite said the things sitting just beneath the surface.

Not yet.

But soon.

They were sharing dessert—a flourless chocolate cake with vanilla bean ice cream, rich, warm, and decadent. Jasmine's spoon hovered midair as she let out a soft laugh at something Robert said, her eyes bright, cheeks flushed from wine and happiness.

"Excuse me," came a familiar voice.

Jasmine turned, spoon still in hand, and blinked.

"James," she said, surprised but smiling. She stood, brushing her skirt smooth, and greeted him with a kiss on the cheek. "Hi."

Robert rose as well, his expression open but guarded as he extended a hand. "James."

James shook it firmly. "Robert. It's good to see you back on your feet."

"Thanks," Robert said, offering a slight nod. "Feels good."

James glanced between them, then gestured over his shoulder toward a nearby table. "I'm actually here on a date."

"That's wonderful," Jasmine said, genuine warmth in her voice.

He smiled, a little sheepish. "Yeah. Early days, but... it's going well."

He looked at Jasmine then, and something unspoken passed between them—not regret, not quite. More like quiet closure.

"I'm happy for you both," James said, eyes steady. "Really."

Jasmine's smile softened. "Thank you."

Robert didn't respond right away. He just nodded, the weight of the gesture quiet but sincere. "That means a lot."

James looked like he might add something more, a flicker of hesitation in his eyes, but instead he glanced back toward his table. "I should get back."

He gave Jasmine one last lingering nod, then offered Robert a small, respectful smile before turning and walking away.

They watched him go, the moment settling like a soft exhale between them.

Robert reached for his spoon again, his voice quiet. "Well… that was unexpected."

Jasmine exhaled slowly. "Yeah. But I'm glad it happened."

He looked at her across the table. "You okay?"

She nodded. "I am."

And she was. More than she expected to be.

She took another bite of cake, and when she smiled at him again, it was only for him.

They finished the last bites of dessert, sharing spoonfuls of the rich chocolate cake between quiet smiles and soft glances. Neither rushed. There was no need.

Robert flagged down the waiter and settled the bill with quiet ease, then stood and reached for Jasmine's hand. Fingers entwined, they walked out into the balmy night air, the soft buzz of the restaurant fading behind them.

At the car, Robert moved to open the door for her—but paused. His hand hovered on the handle, and then he turned to face her fully. His gaze searched hers for a long, breath-held moment before he stepped closer, wrapping her gently into his arms.

"I'll take you home if you want me to," he said, his voice low, steady, honest. "But I was hoping you'd want to come home with me."

Jasmine looked up at him, her hands finding their way around his neck. The closeness, the quiet, the safety of him—it all wrapped around her like warmth.

She pressed her lips to his, soft and lingering, then whispered against his mouth, "I want to come home with you."

Robert smiled—slow, certain—and opened the door for her.

Tonight, there was no hesitation.

Only forward.

Chapter Thirty-Three

Jasmine woke to stillness.

Soft morning light filtered through Robert's bedroom window, casting a muted gold across the white sheets and the curve of his shoulder beside her. The world outside was quiet—the kind of quiet that wrapped around you like a blanket and made you want to stay exactly where you were.

She lay still for a moment, just breathing. Just being.

Robert's arm was draped loosely around her waist, his hand resting at the small of her back—warm and steady. His breathing was slow, even. Still asleep. His chest rose and fell in rhythm with hers, the two of them tangled in a closeness that felt at once new and impossibly familiar.

Jasmine shifted slightly, careful not to wake him. The sheet rustled softly as she turned her head to look at him.

He looked younger like this. Peaceful. The tension that so often sat behind his eyes—pain, responsibility, the weight of too many unspoken things—was gone. In its place was something softer. Vulnerable, even. And beautiful in a way that made her heart ache.

Her gaze dropped to his lips—soft, parted slightly in sleep—and the memory of last night rose to meet her, warm and breathless. The flutter of his kiss still lingered, echoing in her chest. Slow. Certain. Real.

She didn't regret a thing.

Last night had been a revelation—one she hadn't seen coming. She hadn't realised how different it would be with Robert, how much more right it would feel. There was no comparison. No memory that came close. He had been both tender and unreserved, patient and utterly consuming. Every touch had felt deliberate, like he wasn't just learning her body but remembering it—as if he'd known it in another life. The way his hands moved over her, the way he looked at her like she was something sacred... she had never felt that before.

Robert stirred beside her, his brow twitching faintly before his eyes blinked open—hazy with sleep, then slowly finding focus.

A slow smile curved his mouth. "Morning."

"Morning," she whispered back, returning his smile as her fingers gently traced the edge of the sheet between them.

He reached up, brushing a strand of hair from her cheek, his knuckles grazing her skin. "Did you sleep okay?"

Jasmine nodded. "Better than I have in weeks."

"Good," he murmured, voice thick with sleep. "I was worried I'd snore."

"You didn't." She paused. "Much."

He let out a soft laugh, then shifted onto his side, pulling her a little closer. His hand settled at her hip, his thumb drawing slow, lazy circles on her skin.

They lay there in the hush, no rush, no pressure—just the low hum of something warm and right.

Eventually, she spoke. "You have a really comfortable bed."

"I had to upgrade after I stopped sleeping on hospital cots," he murmured. "Glad it meets your standards."

"It does." Her voice was light, teasing, but something deeper flickered inside her. Because it wasn't just the mattress or the sheets or the way the early light made everything feel softer.

It was him.

The comfort was him.

Robert leaned forward, brushing his lips against hers in a kiss that lingered—soft, unhurried, and full of quiet meaning. There was no urgency in it, no need to rush toward something more. Just the warmth of skin and breath and the kind of closeness that came from finally knowing—they were exactly where they were meant to be.

Jasmine closed her eyes and let herself feel it.

Not the thrill of something new.

Not the ache of uncertainty.

Just peace.

A quiet belonging that settled into her bones and made her feel safe in a way she hadn't realised she'd been craving.

Then something shifted.

The kiss deepened—slowly, naturally—as if their bodies had been waiting for permission to remember what their hearts already knew. His hand slid to her waist, fingertips brushing the curve of her hip with a tenderness that made her breath catch. Her arms wrapped around his shoulders, drawing him closer, anchoring herself to him.

There was no script. No hesitation. Only instinct and feeling.

The hush of morning wrapped around them as they moved together, heat curling gently through her like a rising tide. The soft rustle of sheets, the brush of skin on skin, the reverent way he looked at her—like she was something precious, not just desired, but known—made her heart ache in the most beautiful way.

They made love—unhurried and real.

Not driven by passion alone, but something deeper. Connection. Trust. Love. Unspoken, but unmistakable in every touch, every sigh, every quiet whisper between kisses.

He held her like he'd never let go.

And she gave herself to him like she never wanted to.

It wasn't about erasing the past or proving something. It was about this moment—two people finding their way back to something they'd always carried, even when they didn't have the words.

Afterward, they lay tangled in the golden hush of morning, hearts beating slow and steady in time with each other, the world outside falling away.

And for the first time in a long time, neither of them felt alone.

"You hungry?" he asked eventually, his voice quiet against her hair.

"Depends. Are you offering something edible or just more coffee?"

"Could be both," he said. "But full disclosure—I don't have any of those hazelnut croissants."

She sighed dramatically. "Tragic."

"I'll make it up to you," he said, pulling back just enough to meet her eyes. "Let me make breakfast."

Jasmine smiled, brushing her fingers through his sleep-mussed hair. "I'd like that."

He kissed her again—soft, slow—and then eased himself out of bed. Jasmine watched as he padded barefoot toward the kitchen, the scar on his back just barely visible in the shifting light.

And for a moment she didn't move.

Because this—*this*—wasn't a fantasy or a someday or a maybe.

This was real.

And she wasn't afraid of it.

The smell of bacon and freshly brewed coffee coaxed Jasmine awake before sunlight fully reached the bedroom.

She padded down the hallway, wrapped in the oversized shirt he'd given her after she had a shower, the wooden floors cool beneath her bare feet. When she reached the kitchen, she paused in the doorway.

Robert stood at the stove, barefoot and tousled, flipping pancakes with practiced ease. A dish towel hung over his shoulder, and a faint hum escaped him—something low and tuneless, but warm. The domesticity of it all hit her square in the chest.

"You cook now?" she asked, a teasing lilt in her voice.

He glanced over his shoulder with a crooked smile. "You think I got through physio just to sit around looking pretty?"

She chuckled and stepped into the room. "I always thought you had people for this."

"I do. But this morning, I wanted to do it myself." He nodded toward the coffee machine. "Mug's ready for you."

She poured herself a cup and leaned against the counter, watching him move. There was something quietly captivating about it—his ease, the care he took, the way he checked the eggs without rushing. Not performative. Not for show. Just him.

A few minutes later, he set two plates on the table—pancakes, scrambled eggs, toast, and a perfect side of crispy bacon. She raised an eyebrow. "Trying to impress me, Mr. Steele?"

"Is it working?"

She took a bite and groaned. "Unfortunately, yes."

They ate together in the soft hush of morning, the occasional clink of cutlery and sip of coffee the only sounds between them. Every now and then, his foot bumped hers under the table. Once, his fingers brushed a crumb from her cheek, then lingered for just a moment longer than necessary.

After breakfast, Jasmine gathered their plates, but Robert caught her hand. "Leave it. Just stay."

She did.

He brushed her hair back, tucking it behind her ear with that same reverence he'd shown last night. Then he pressed a gentle kiss to her forehead—slow and still and full of unspoken things.

"You're dangerous," she murmured, her smile soft.

"I know," he whispered back. "But only for you."

And in that quiet kitchen, with sunlight spilling through the windows and the scent of breakfast still hanging in the air, it felt like something real was unfolding—steady, grounded, and entirely theirs.

Later, after breakfast had been cleared and the dishes now in the dishwasher, Jasmine wandered out to the terrace. A soft breeze stirred her hair as she leaned against the railing, her coffee cradled in both hands. The garden stretched out in quiet shades of green, the sunlight filtering through the gum trees in gentle dapples. Birds called lazily from somewhere in the distance, and the world felt… still.

Behind her, she could hear Robert moving through the kitchen—opening a drawer, shutting a cupboard, the faint clink of a spoon in a mug. Normal, domestic sounds. Familiar. And somehow, deeply intimate.

She exhaled slowly, watching the steam curl from her cup.

She hadn't said it yet.

The words hovered on the edge of her heart like something warm, delicate, and brave. She loved him. She knew that now—not with the aching, uncertain longing she'd carried for so many years, but with something steadier. Something that had been forged in quiet mornings and steady hands and nights where he'd held her like she was something worth waiting for.

It wasn't just the kiss in the garden, or waking up in his arms, or the way he'd made her feel last night—safe, seen, cherished. It was everything. The way he looked at her when he thought she wasn't paying attention. The patience in his voice. The softness he gave only to her.

Jasmine's thumb absently traced the rim of her mug.

She didn't want to say it just because it felt like the right moment. She wanted to say it because she meant it. Completely. And for the first time, she didn't feel afraid. There was no pressure. No deadline. Just a quiet certainty blooming inside her.

She heard him just behind her, and then he was there, standing close, their arms brushing. He held his own mug, and for a while they stood in companionable silence, watching the breeze ripple through the trees.

His voice came low beside her. "You okay?"

She turned to him, eyes meeting his.

"I'm good," she said quietly. Then, after a pause, "Better than good, actually."

He smiled. "Yeah?"

She nodded, her heart lifting. Not because he asked. But because she meant it.

She looked at him—really looked—and her chest ached with how much she felt. It pressed against her ribs, full and ready, and she knew… it wouldn't be long now.

She was almost ready to say it.

Not because she needed to hear it back.

But because love wasn't something she was afraid to claim anymore.

It was already here. Quiet and solid. Waiting on her own terms.

And when she said it—*soon*—it would be because she was finally, absolutely sure.

Robert reached for her coffee cup without a word, his fingers brushing hers as he took it gently from her hands. He carried both mugs to the small table behind them, set them down with a soft clink, and turned back to her.

For a moment, he simply looked at her—like he was memorising her in this light, in this moment, like she was something he didn't want to blink and miss.

Then, slowly, he stepped closer and slipped his arms around her waist, drawing her gently into him. Her palms came to rest flat against his chest, steady over the beat of his heart.

His voice was quiet. Rough at the edges.

"I have to tell you," he said, "or I'll lose my mind."

Jasmine looked up, startled by the shift in his tone.

"I love you, Jasmine," he continued, his eyes locked on hers. "More than I've loved anyone. I've loved you for a long time. I was certain of it the night of your twenty-first. I just…" He exhaled, one hand brushing her back like muscle memory. "I just wish I'd had the sense—and the courage—to tell you then."

Her breath caught, heart suddenly racing, but he didn't rush her. He held her steady. Grounded.

"You don't have to say anything," he said gently. "I'm not asking you to match it. I just needed you to know. I'm willing to wait… as long as it takes. And if the day comes that you feel the same way—" His thumb traced a slow, reassuring circle at her waist. "Then I'll be here."

She didn't move. Not right away.

She just stood there in his arms, feeling the weight of his words settle around her—not heavy, but full. Real.

And the only thing louder than her heartbeat was the swell of something fierce and beautiful inside her.

He was willing to wait.

That mattered more than anything.

But she wasn't willing to wait—not anymore.

No more holding back.

No more second-guessing what she felt.

She knew.

Jasmine lifted her gaze to his, steady and sure. Her hands pressed a little firmer against his chest, grounding herself in him.

"I love you, Robert," she said softly. "I have… forever."

His breath caught—sharp and unguarded. His eyes searched hers like he couldn't quite believe it.

She went on, voice low but clear. "The lead-up to my twenty-first… I thought we had something. I felt it. The way you looked at me, the way we were around each other— it felt like something was changing between us. I was so sure."

She paused, emotion thick in her throat. "But then you disappeared. You pulled away, and it confused me. And then you were back with Claire, and I thought… maybe I'd imagined it all. Maybe it was just me."

Robert's jaw clenched, regret flashing across his face, but he didn't interrupt. He just held her, as if afraid she'd vanish if he let go.

Jasmine's voice softened. "I tried to move on. I told myself it didn't matter. That it wasn't real. But it never went away—not the hope, not the feeling. Not you."

Her fingers curled into the fabric of his shirt. "And now… it's here again. Real. And I'm not going to push it away this time."

His hands framed her face, reverent, and his voice was rough with emotion. "Jasmine—"

She leaned into his touch, eyes shining. "I love you," she said again. "And I'm not afraid anymore."

Then he kissed her—not slow this time, not hesitant—but full, open, and sure. And she kissed him back with everything she had, because this time there was nothing left to hold back.

When they finally parted, he didn't let her go. His arms stayed firm around her, as if anchoring himself to the moment, to her.

His breath was warm at her temple. "I went to William the day after your twenty-first," he murmured. "Told him I had real feelings for you. I did that because I wanted him to be okay with it… with us."

Jasmine stilled, heart thudding. She leaned back just enough to see his face—open, raw.

"But he said you were too young," Robert continued, "that you'd been through too much with losing your parents, that you were still studying. He said you needed space, stability—not… me."

A flicker of old pain crossed his face. "And it hurt. Because I was sure William knew what was best for you. And I loved him, he's my best friend, and I trusted him."

He exhaled slowly, eyes never leaving hers. "So, I listened. I pulled back when everything in me wanted to move forward. Then you started dating someone—I can't even remember his name, which says everything. That's when I thought I'd missed my chance."

His hands tightened gently at her waist. "And stupidly, I took Claire back. That should never have happened. Not ever."

Jasmine's brows drew together, emotion rising thick in her throat. She placed a hand on his cheek, the tenderness in her touch silencing the rest of his regrets.

"I wish you'd told me," she whispered. "But I understand why you didn't."

He pressed his forehead to hers. "I've wished for this moment more times than I can count. And I don't want to waste another second."

Her lips curved, soft and certain. "Then don't."

They stood like that for a moment—hearts laid bare, histories acknowledged, and the future suddenly, finally, theirs to shape.

They weren't waiting anymore.

They were choosing each other—*finally*.

Epilogue

One Year Later – The Steele Estate

The late afternoon sun spilled gold across the rolling lawn of the Steele estate, casting a warm glow over the arbour draped in soft white roses and eucalyptus. Jasmine stood inside the bridal suite, the French doors open to the breeze, her veil trailing behind her like a whisper of memory.

Heidi was fussing with her bouquet—white peonies and blush pink roses, soft and fragrant—rearranging a stubborn bloom that refused to sit quite right. Beside her, Mary stood behind Jasmine, carefully fastening the final button on the back of her gown, her fingers steady despite the emotion glistening in her eyes.

In the corner of the room, nestled quietly in her travel capsule, Mary's newborn daughter—Jasmine's tiny, perfect niece—slept peacefully, her soft breaths a rhythmic hush beneath the stillness. Only a month old, the first child of Mary and William, she was already so deeply loved. Jasmine had snuck a glance at her earlier, marvelling at her miniature hands and the way her nose crinkled—just like William's—when she dreamed.

Everything felt dreamlike.

The bridal suite was awash in golden late-afternoon light, casting long shadows and warm glows across the vintage furniture and gleaming floorboards. Outside, the sounds of music, clinking glasses, and laughter floated up from the garden where guests had begun to gather. But in this room, there was stillness. Reverence.

"Okay," Heidi said at last, stepping back with a proud, slightly misty smile. "You look like the cover of a bridal magazine. No—better."

Jasmine turned slowly to the mirror, her breath catching as her reflection came into view. The lace of her gown hugged her frame like it had been sewn by memory. Her earrings shimmered softly with each movement—delicate pearls nestled in gold— something new, and something borrowed from Kelly.

But it was her expression that surprised her most.

She didn't look nervous. She didn't even look overwhelmed.

She looked certain.

She felt ready.

A knock came at the door, and then it opened just wide enough for Terry's kind face to peek in. He stepped inside with care, dressed in a charcoal-grey suit and wearing a quiet smile.

"Is it time?" he asked.

Jasmine nodded, warmth blooming in her chest.

He had offered to walk her down the aisle without hesitation. And though her heart ached for the absence of her parents, she knew—without doubt—they would have been proud. Of her strength. Of her heart. Of the man waiting at the end of the aisle.

Kelly followed behind him, her own eyes misty as she approached with the bouquet. "Here you go, sweetheart." Her voice wobbled just a little. "Robert won't know what hit him."

Jasmine smiled and took the flowers. As her fingers wrapped around the stems, she caught a sliver of sunlight glinting through the open window. The breeze lifted the edge of her veil, and just like that, her thoughts drifted to Bondi Beach.

Three months earlier, the air had still been warm from the fading summer, the sky streaked in hues of apricot and rose. Robert had taken her hand and walked with her along the shore, the sand cool beneath their feet, his steps a little slower now—but strong. He'd kept glancing at the horizon, checking the light as if waiting for something.

She'd almost teased him—until he stopped suddenly, just where the waves kissed the sand.

He'd turned to her, eyes alight with something more than love, more than certainty.

And then he'd gone down on one knee.

"I've loved you for years, Jaz," he'd said, his voice low, steady, and sure. "I don't want to waste any more time pretending I can live without you. Will you marry me?"

Her tears had come instantly. Her answer, even faster.

Yes.

The sun had dipped into the sea behind them, as if giving them its blessing.

A month after that, fate had given them another quiet gift. They'd run into James outside a coffee shop in Paddington. He was with a tall, elegant brunette named Shelby, who had an easy laugh and a grounded presence. James introduced her as his fiancée, and the moment that followed—unexpected and unplanned—had been genuinely sweet.

When Jasmine told him she and Robert were engaged, he hadn't flinched. He'd just smiled and nodded.

"I'm really happy for you both," he'd said, with the calm of a man who'd found his own peace. "It all worked out, didn't it?"

And now, it truly had.

Jasmine blinked back the burn of tears and smoothed her hands down the front of her dress. The fabric was cool beneath her palms. Real. This was happening.

She turned to Heidi, then to Mary, and finally to Terry—her heart full.

"Let's go," she said softly, her voice sure.

And the doors opened to the light.

Robert stood beneath the arbour, the breeze gently tugging at the lapel of his suit jacket. William adjusted his tie beside him, more nervous than the groom.

"You good?" William asked.

"I've never been better."

Robert looked out over the rows of guests, over the flowers and fairy lights, then back down the aisle that would soon carry her to him. His cane was gone now—had been for months. His stride was strong again, his body healed. But none of it compared to the way his heart had repaired in her hands.

He glanced at William, emotion softening his features.

"I want you to know," he said quietly, "I will love her forever. Through everything. That's a promise."

William clapped a hand on his shoulder, his eyes suspiciously damp.

"I know."

And then, as the first chords of music swelled across the grounds, Robert lifted his head.

The golden sun bathed the garden in light and promise. Guests rose, their faces turning toward the top of the aisle, where the trellis bloomed with trailing jasmine and pale pink roses.

First came his mother—elegant and proud—dabbing discreetly at the corner of her eye as she moved down the aisle with grace. Robert's throat tightened. Kelly had always believed in this day, even when he hadn't. She winked at him as she passed, and his heart squeezed.

Then Heidi appeared, radiant in soft blush, bouquet high, grinning at him like she knew every chapter of his story. Her pace was slow, deliberate, meaningful. Jasmine's protector. Her fierce cheerleader. And in this moment, Robert's quiet ally. A promise that Jasmine was on her way.

But when his father came into view, everything else fell away.

Because on Terry's arm, holding her bouquet with trembling fingers and a quiet, steady smile, was Jasmine.

Time stopped.

She looked like a dream brought to life—her gown glowing like it had been spun from the light itself, her veil catching the breeze, and her eyes—those deep, beautiful eyes—locked on his, unwavering.

Robert's breath left him in one quiet exhale.

This was the moment.

This was the woman.

And she was walking toward him with all the certainty in the world.

He barely noticed the tears rising in his own eyes. All he could do was stand a little taller, his heart thudding in his chest, and whisper to himself as she drew nearer—

Mine.

The End

Before I Fell

Alison Reid

A complete standalone romance

Previously published individually

Chapter One

The rehearsal dinner was in full swing. The spacious dining room of Ian and Marissa Turner's family estate buzzed with warmth and celebration. Laughter mingled with the clinking of crystal glasses, soft conversations floating above the gentle strains of a string quartet nestled quietly in the corner. The long oak table, polished to a gleaming shine, was bathed in the warm glow of flickering candles and crowned with elegant arrangements of blush roses and creamy hydrangeas — a setting perfectly suited to the joyous wedding it foreshadowed.

This was no ordinary gathering. Tomorrow, Ian Turner would marry Shelby Johnson — not only his closest friend but Marissa's as well. The two women had been inseparable since their first day of primary school in Perth, when a shy, freckle-faced Shelby had been seated beside a tall, confident Marissa. From that moment on, they shared school lunches, teenage crushes, whispered secrets at sleepovers, and stood side by side through heartbreak and triumph alike.

Now, Shelby slipped effortlessly through the crowd, her smile as warm and steady as the candlelight flickering on the polished oak table. She paused beside Marissa and pressed a gentle kiss to her cheek. "Thank you for being such a wonderful maid of honour."

Marissa's blue eyes softened, the depth of their lifelong bond shining clear in the glance they exchanged. "I couldn't be anything else. I love you, Shelby. And tomorrow, you'll be my sister for real."

Shelby's eyes sparkled with mischievous delight as she leaned in closer, lowering her voice to a confidential whisper meant only for Marissa. "Speaking of which… I see James has been watching you all night."

Marissa rolled her eyes, an exasperated sound escaping before she could stop it. James Calder had a way of making her chest knot tight — part anger, part something she refused to name. Once a man called you a hussy to your face, the ghost of it never truly left. That night had carved itself into her memory: the thrum of the club's music, the burn of his gaze, and then those words, sharp and cold, striking harder than any slap.

Shelby's smile faltered. "He still thinks—?"

"Oh, absolutely," Marissa cut in, bitterness flickering behind her light tone. "In James Calder's world, if you accept a drink or a dance, you must be sleeping with the man who offered it. And he's known me since I was eight."

Shelby reached out as if to soften the words, but Marissa was already straightening, slipping her armour back into place. A slow, teasing smile curved her lips — the kind she knew would irritate him if he saw it. "Let him think what he wants." Her gaze drifted toward the bar, where the blond bartender caught her eye and returned a slow, appreciative smile.

"Besides…" she tipped her chin toward him, a glint of mischief in her eyes, "the barman is cute, isn't he?"

Shelby followed her glance, her breath catching for a moment. The man behind the bar wasn't just cute; he was striking, with sun-kissed blond hair, a sharp jawline, and the kind of confident smile that needed no introduction. "I take it you're going to introduce yourself?"

Marissa's pulse quickened. It wasn't just the handsome bartender's smile — it was the game she was about to play. A silent challenge. A dance of appearances and truth only she fully understood.

Her smile turned wicked. "I'm just going to get a drink."

"Sure you are," Shelby teased, eyes sparkling with amusement.

Marissa glided toward the bar, her full-length strapless navy gown shimmering with every step. Tall and poised, her long auburn hair tumbled in glossy waves down her back. She knew the effect she had — and so did the bartender. His gaze locked onto her as she approached, a slow, knowing smile playing on his lips, equal parts charm, and challenge.

"What can I get you?" he asked smoothly.

Marissa's attention flickered beyond him, catching James Calder standing close enough to overhear. With a playful tilt of her head, she murmured, "Your phone number."

The bartender didn't hesitate. He scribbled something on a folded serviette, his grin broadening as he slid it across the polished counter.

Out of the corner of her eye, Marissa caught the way James's jaw tightened, his dark gaze sharpening like a blade.

She tucked the serviette into the side of her gown with a satisfied smirk, then turned to meet James's glare head-on. But before she could speak, familiar arms slid around her waist from behind.

"Come dance with me," Mark — her current boyfriend — whispered against her ear.

Marissa stiffened. She hated being held too close. That kind of intimacy had never felt safe. When a man wanted more than she was ready to give, she ended it quickly. That was one reason she was still a virgin. She didn't trust closeness. Not like that.

Ever since the day, seven years ago, when her parents' helicopter had crashed in a sudden storm, ripping them from her life when she was just sixteen, she'd learned that love could vanish in an instant. That loss had carved a hollow place in her heart, and she'd built walls to keep anyone from getting close enough to hurt her again.

The warmth of Mark's hands against her waist only pushed her deeper into her own thoughts. She could still imagine the sirens from that day, see the haunted faces of family friends who had delivered the news, feel the cold emptiness that followed. That was when she learned the truth: love wasn't safe. It never would be.

So, she wore her teasing smile like armour. She baited James and every other man who thought they understood her. She let them think she was untouchable, a wild thing who belonged to no one — and in a way, she was.

Pulling gently away from Mark's hold, Marissa turned to him with a soft, teasing laugh that barely hid the calculated edge beneath. Her gaze swept the room until it found James again — still watching her with that unreadable mix of irritation and something sharper.

"I'd love to," she told Mark, slipping her hand into his and letting him lead her onto the dance floor.

As his arms circled her, she was already planning how soon she'd tell him it wasn't working out. But for now, she savoured the small thrill of victory at the flicker of annoyance crossing James's face.

Let him watch, she told herself, a slow, secret smile curling the corners of her lips — knowing he hated her, and she hated him right back.

At least, that's what she kept telling herself.

James Calder stood just off to the side of the bar, arms folded tight across his chest, his dark eyes locked on Marissa as she moved through the room like she owned it. She had just slipped the bartender a practiced, devastating smile and taken his number — only to be gathered into another man's arms moments later.

It twisted something deep inside him, a bitter knot of frustration and something far more dangerous — something he refused to name.

He told himself it was irritation. Disapproval. The same contempt he'd always felt for women who courted attention like oxygen. But the truth, the one he buried so far down it almost didn't have a voice, was that she lit up every space she entered... and he couldn't look away.

He hated women like that. Or at least, he hated what he thought she was.

To him, Marissa Turner was a reckless heartbreaker — scattering herself like confetti, never settling, never serious. It was infuriating. Not just because she was his best friend's sister, but because she stirred memories he'd sworn to keep buried: the woman who had almost been his wife, caught in his own home with one of his closest friends.

Since that day, James had built his walls high and his rules higher. Keep beautiful women at arm's length. Distrust the ones who smiled too easily. And yet... here he was, watching Marissa like she was the only person in the room worth noticing.

And that made her all the more dangerous.

Ian appeared at his side, smirking. "You're staring at my sister again. People are going to start thinking you're in love with her."

James scoffed, shaking his head. "Not a chance. Marissa and I would kill each other within a day."

Ian chuckled, eyes gleaming. "I think you protest a little too much, my friend."

"I'm not interested in competing with every man in the room, thanks."

"Be careful, James," Ian warned, his smile softening into something more protective. "That's my sister you're talking about."

James raised his hands in mock surrender, though his gaze drifted back to her despite himself. "Sorry, but it's true — every man in here is watching her."

"Do you blame them?" Ian asked. "She's a beautiful woman."

James's jaw tightened. "And she knows it."

"You haven't trusted another woman since Victoria," Ian said quietly.

His stomach tightened at the name. "I learned my lesson, didn't I?"

"Don't you think it's time to move on?" Ian pressed.

"I date women all the time."

Ian's voice was steady. "You take them to bed, then walk away before they can mean anything. That's not moving on, James — that's hiding. Believe me, it's no way to live." His eyes softened, sincere. "I'm honestly grateful Shelby finally saw me for who I am."

James gave a humourless smile, eyes dropping to his glass. "Guess you're lucky you found the last faithful woman around."

Ian's tone softened. "Whoever Marissa ends up with will be lucky. She's fiercely loyal."

James said nothing. He couldn't — not without giving away too much. Out loud, he let her reputation stand in the way. In his mind, though, she was something else entirely: a maddening, impossible woman who got under his skin without even trying. A woman who could dismantle every defence he had left… if he ever let her close enough.

And that was exactly why he never would.

Ian's grin tugged at his lips. "Well, I'll be a married man tomorrow, and I can't wait. But there's something I need to ask you."

James looked up, meeting Ian's steady gaze. "Anything, Ian. You know you can ask me anything."

Ian's smile softened, concern threading through his words. "I'll be away for two weeks on my honeymoon. The longest I've ever left Marissa alone. I'm going to worry about her. Would you keep an eye on her for me?"

James blinked, caught off guard. "Me?"

Ian's voice was firm, resolute. "Yes, you. I trust you the most. Who else would I ask? I know Julie will be here, but I need to know someone I truly trust is keeping an eye on her."

The weight of the request settled on James's shoulders. He couldn't refuse — not to his best friend, his business partner.

"Okay," James said finally, meeting Ian's eyes with quiet determination. "I'll keep an eye on her for you. You just have a great time with your new wife."

Ian clasped his hand in a firm shake. "Thanks, James. It means a lot."

Chapter Two

The morning of the wedding dawned bright and golden, sunlight spilling across the Turner estate like a warm blessing, promising a day full of hope and new beginnings. Marissa was already awake long before the rest of the house stirred. Her short silk robe tied loosely at the waist, she padded softly into the kitchen where the comforting scent of fresh coffee curled around her like a quiet invitation.

"Morning, Julie." She bent to press a kiss to the cheek of their long-time housekeeper, who stood at the counter whisking eggs. "Ready for the big day?"

Julie turned with a smile that reached deep into her eyes. She'd been with the Turners for over a decade—starting as their housekeeper but over time becoming something far more: family. She had stayed through everything, even after the tragedy seven years ago that shattered the Turner household. In the years since, she had done her best to hold the pieces together, especially for Marissa.

"Morning, love," Julie said warmly. "More to the point—are you ready?"

Marissa's lips curved into a soft smile, a flicker of excitement lighting her eyes. "I can't wait. Shelby and Ian belong together. It's… right." She poured herself a cup of coffee, then leaned against the bench, gazing out the wide kitchen window at the gardens where later guests would mingle before the ceremony. "Shelby's been my best friend for as long as I can remember. Today feels like… I'm getting a sister too."

Julie's expression softened as she studied the young woman she'd watched grow from a bright, mischievous little girl into the beautiful woman standing before her now. "Well, you're going to look every bit the part. And I don't mind saying," she added with a wink, "James Calder won't know where to look when he sees you in that dress."

Marissa rolled her eyes, though the corners of her mouth lifted. "James always knows exactly where to look—straight down his nose at me."

Julie chuckled, shaking her head. "If you ask me, that man notices a lot more than he lets on."

Marissa took a sip of her coffee, eyeing Julie over the rim of her mug. "Seriously, Julie, you need to give up this idea of me and James. It's never going to happen. I can't stand him, and he can't stand me."

Julie made a dismissive little sound, waving the spatula in the air. "Pfft… maybe if you stopped flirting with every male in his presence, he wouldn't be like that. I've seen you, missy. You turn it on like a spotlight the moment he's in the room."

Marissa arched a brow, a sly smile playing at her lips. "And?"

"And," Julie continued with mock sternness, "you know perfectly well you only do it to get under his skin. Which, I might add, you manage very successfully."

Marissa leaned back against the counter, her smile turning wicked. "Maybe he deserves it."

Julie planted one hand on her hip, studying her as though she could see straight through the teasing exterior. "Or maybe it's because you like the way he notices you."

Marissa laughed, a quick, light sound. "Oh, please. James Calder noticing me is nothing new—he's been judging me since the day I turned eighteen."

Julie shook her head, a knowing gleam in her eyes. "Judging… or watching? There's a difference, love."

Marissa opened her mouth to reply, but Julie was already turning back to the stove, humming softly, leaving Marissa to sip her coffee and ignore the flicker of heat she felt at the thought of James watching her.

Her mind drifted back to five years ago—a night she wished she could forget but never truly had.

James had just broken up with his girlfriend, and to eighteen-year-old Marissa, he might as well have hung the stars. She'd admired him from a distance for years, secretly hoping that one day he might actually see her—not just as Ian's little sister, but as a woman.

That night, Ian had taken her and Shelby out—a rare evening where she felt grown-up, sophisticated. She learned later that it was the very night Ian began to pursue her best friend, though at the time she was too busy feeling the rush of the city lights to notice.

The music thumped loudly through the packed club, the dance floor pulsing with energy. Marissa was in her element—laughing freely, spinning with abandon, lost in the rhythm. Men noticed her, as they always did, but she wasn't interested in any of them. She simply loved to dance, and if someone asked her, she said yes. It was just dancing.

But some of the men were too bold, their hands lingering where they shouldn't. She brushed them off with a polite smile and stepped back when needed. She hadn't encouraged any of it—but James, walking in partway through the night, saw something else entirely.

When she finally stepped off the dance floor, breathless and flushed, she spotted him sitting alone at the edge of the room, his dark expression as sharp as a blade. She smoothed her hair, nerves fluttering in her stomach, and crossed to him, determined to at least say hello.

"Hey," she greeted softly, sliding into the seat beside him.

He turned his head, his gaze hard, jaw clenched. "You're acting like a hussy," he said, the words low but biting.

For a second, she didn't even process it—the insult landing like a slap she hadn't expected. Then the sting hit, sharp and deep, stealing the air from her lungs.

Her smile faltered. "Excuse me?"

His eyes didn't soften. "You know exactly what I mean."

She stared at him, hurt blooming in her chest, the kind that lodged there and stayed. He hadn't seen her brushing hands away, stepping back, laughing off unwanted advances. He'd only seen what he wanted to see.

And in that moment, whatever pedestal she'd once put him on shattered.

From that day on, she never looked at James Calder the same way. Whatever soft, secret admiration she'd once held for him had been buried beneath the sting of his words.

If he wanted to think she was a flirt, then she'd give him exactly what he expected. Every chance she got, she played the part—laughing a little too brightly, letting her gaze linger on some man just long enough for James to notice, accepting a dance when she saw him watching. It was never about the men themselves. It was about him. About proving that he didn't know her at all.

But she never took it too far. She never let it become cruel, never toyed with a man's feelings just for sport. That wasn't who Marissa was. Beneath the teasing smiles and the perfectly timed glances, she was still kind—to everyone except, perhaps, James.

She loved fiercely in the quiet ways that mattered: remembering birthdays, sitting with friends through heartbreaks, showing up for people without being asked. But when it came to romance, to letting someone in deep enough to matter… that was where she faltered.

After her parents died in that helicopter crash, something inside her had splintered. Love had become dangerous—a thing that could be ripped away without warning, leaving only jagged pieces behind. So, she kept her heart locked away, safe behind walls built of banter and mischief.

And maybe, just maybe, she liked knowing that James Calder—the man who thought he could read her so easily—never really saw past the façade.

She was jolted back to the present by James himself.

"Do you have to walk around the house like that?"

Julie had just stepped out of the kitchen when James strode in, his tall frame filling the doorway like he owned it. Marissa turned from the counter with deliberate slowness, placing her coffee cup down as though she had all the time in the world before facing him.

She wore a silk chemise and matching robe in the colour of champagne, its delicate straps disappearing beneath the matching wrap loosely tied at her waist. Her auburn hair tumbled in glossy waves down her back, catching the morning light like fire. She knew exactly how she looked — tall, poised, the kind of beauty people whispered about. But beauty had never been armour enough. She'd built that herself, brick by brick, after her parents' death, and she wore it now like a second skin.

"Like what, James?" she asked, her tone feather-light but edged. "I'm covered."

His gaze dipped before he caught himself, flicking back to her face with a jaw set tight. "Barely. It's the kind of outfit that makes men… distracted."

Her lips curved in a slow, dangerous smile. "Distracted," she repeated, letting the word linger. "Is that a complaint… or an admission?"

"Neither," he said, but his voice had dropped just a shade lower — and she heard it.

Marissa took her time crossing the kitchen, every step a silent dare. The silk whispered against her legs, a feline glide that she knew would test his control. She stopped close enough to catch the faint scent of his aftershave, her head tilting as her hand came to rest lightly against his chest. His heart beat steady — but harder than he'd like her to know.

"I'll go change," she murmured, her voice velvet and deliberately slow. "Just for you. Any special requests?"

Something flashed in his eyes — not the usual irritation, but something warmer, hungrier. His mouth parted, the beginnings of an unguarded answer right there on his lips… and then, in the span of a breath, it was gone, smothered beneath the familiar coolness.

"Wear something that doesn't make you look like you're auditioning for trouble," he said evenly.

Before she could answer, Julie bustled back in, humming, oblivious to the taut air between them.

Marissa stepped back with infuriating grace, her smirk firmly in place, as though his jab had bounced harmlessly off her armour. "Noted," she said lightly, turning on her heel. The silk of her wrap swayed as she left, hips moving with the kind of confidence that made him grit his teeth.

Chapter Three

James watched her go, his hands curling into fists at his sides. She thought she'd rattled him. She had — but not in the way she believed. Every slow, swaying step pulled at something inside him he refused to name, something that made his pulse quicken and his temper flare in the same breath.

God, she was sexy—infuriatingly, maddeningly so.

Those endless legs were the kind a man could lose himself in, the kind he'd imagined tangled around him more times than he'd ever admit, even to himself.

But it wasn't just her body—though that alone could silence a room—it was the way she inhabited it. Every step, every glance, every subtle tilt of her head carried an effortless power. She didn't need to flaunt it; it was simply there, woven into her like a second skin. The quiet confidence, the unspoken challenge simmering in her eyes... it wasn't accidental. She knew exactly the effect she had on him, and she wielded it with the precision of a blade, cutting straight through his defences.

He told himself it was just her way of needling him, of getting under his skin. And maybe that was true. But when she swept past him, her perfume lingered—warm, elusive, curling through the air like a whispered promise he had no business wanting. It settled over him, into him, refusing to let go.

She was trouble. Beautiful, dangerous trouble. The kind that could burn a man down and leave him grateful for the ruin.

And God help him... he tried not to want her. He told himself every day that he didn't. But the truth was clawing closer to the surface—the fight was slipping, and soon he wouldn't be able to resist at all.

He didn't trust women like her — beautiful, magnetic, the kind who drew every gaze the moment they walked in. He'd been down that road before with Victoria, and it had ended in betrayal that still burned in his bones. Women like that never stayed faithful.

At least, that's what he told himself. It was safer to believe... even if, deep down, a stubborn, treacherous part of him wanted Marissa to prove him wrong.

But she wouldn't. She couldn't. He'd seen her with too many men — laughing, leaning in, letting them act like she was theirs. Ian swore his sister was loyal. James swore he knew better. He knew what he'd seen.

And he remembered the day that proved, once and for all, why he would never let himself trust a woman like that again.

He could picture it as if it were yesterday—coming home from work, the faint trace of Victoria's perfume curling through the air like an invitation. All day, he'd been thinking about her, turning over the question in his mind: was it time to ask her to marry him? But every time he imagined getting down on one knee, something intruded—a flicker of auburn hair, a pair of blue eyes glinting with defiance. *Marissa.*

He'd shoved the thought aside, told himself it was nothing, told himself she was nothing. By the time he slid his key into the lock that evening, he'd almost believed it. Almost.

But then he heard it—the breathless laughter, the low, male groan—coming from the living room.

He stepped inside, and the world stopped. Terry, his friend, was sprawled on James's couch, hands gripping Victoria's bare hips as she straddled him, head thrown back in pleasure. They hadn't even noticed him standing there.

James hadn't said a word. Not then. Not ever. He'd just turned around, walked out, and closed the door on both of them—and on the man he used to be.

He drove for hours, city lights blurring past like a restless storm raging inside his mind. He didn't know where to go or what to do. The betrayal was a weight in his chest, dragging him deeper into confusion and anger.

Then his phone buzzed. A message from Ian. They were at The Loft—a nightclub in Perth where the music pounded as loud as the tension in the air. Ian said he should come and join them. James thought it might take his mind off things for a while.

James pulled up outside, hands gripping the steering wheel tighter than necessary. He walked in, found a seat near the bar, waiting for Ian to finish on the dance floor.

But then he saw her.

Marissa.

She moved through the crowd like she owned it—laughing, spinning, dancing with every guy who asked. Her auburn hair caught the neon lights, her smile bright and teasing.

To everyone else, it was carefree fun. But to James, it was salt in an open wound. The sight of her, so wild and untouchable, only sharpened the ache of betrayal.

He swallowed hard, reminding himself it wasn't about her—but the knot in his stomach tightened anyway.

James's eyes never left Marissa as she danced, her laughter ringing through the thumping bass and flashing lights. She was untouchable—or so it seemed. Every move she made was deliberate, daring, as if she was challenging the world to look away.

But all James felt was a tightening in his chest, a mix of frustration and something darker—jealousy, maybe, though he hated to admit it. He told himself she was just like Victoria. Careless, fleeting, impossible to trust.

Ian slid into the seat beside him, wiping sweat from his brow with the back of his hand. The pulsing beat of the music seemed to fade around them—a sharp contrast to the turmoil James carried inside.

"You okay, mate?" Ian asked, voice low but steady, full of quiet concern.

James shook his head slowly, fingers running through his hair as if trying to physically shake off the weight pressing down on him. His jaw tightened, eyes darkening with pain he barely knew how to voice.

"Not really," he admitted, voice rough. "I… I just walked in on Victoria with Terry. In my own apartment."

The words hung heavy between them. Ian's face tightened, flickers of anger and sympathy clear in his eyes.

James swallowed hard, the memory vivid and raw—the laughter, the betrayal, the silence that followed as he turned and left without a word.

"I was thinking about asking her to marry me," James continued, voice dropping to a near whisper. "And then… that."

Ian put a hand on James's shoulder, grounding him. "I'm sorry, mate. That's brutal."

James nodded, the hurt settling deeper in his chest. "Yeah. It's changed everything."

Ian's expression softened. He placed a steady hand on James's shoulder. "I know, mate. I'm sorry. But I told you—Victoria wasn't right for you."

James looked away, swallowing hard. "I wanted to believe she was."

Ian nodded gently. "I know. Sometimes we want to see what's not really there. But you'll get through this. You're stronger than you think."

Ian sat with James for a while, talking quietly, trying to ease the tension that clung to him like a shadow. After a time, Ian excused himself and slipped back onto the dance floor, leaving James alone with his swirling thoughts.

That's when Marissa appeared, sliding into the seat beside him with a bright, easy smile. "Hey," she said softly, her calm presence oddly grounding amidst the nightclub's chaos.

James had always liked Marissa—her wild spirit, her fearless charm. But that night, he wasn't himself. The pain and betrayal twisted his tongue, and before he could stop himself, the words slipped out—sharper and colder than he intended.

"You're acting like a hussy," he said, low and biting.

Her face froze, as if he'd slapped her. "Excuse me?" she breathed, hurt and disbelief shining in her eyes.

Instead of softening, James only made it worse. "You know exactly what I mean."

The silence between them grew heavy—the damage done.

She stormed off, the sting of his words cutting deeper than he realised at the time. From that night on, their relationship was never the same.

James tried countless times to apologise, to explain, to make things right. But every attempt backfired—Marissa always kept him at arm's length, her sharp tongue and fiery spirit cutting through his defences just as much as his blunt comment unsettled her.

No matter how hard he tried, she continued to get under his skin, and the distance between them only grew wider.

The last time James tried to apologise ended in an all-out argument.

About six months after his harsh words, James found her sitting alone in a quiet café, hoping the calm surroundings might soften the blow he was about to deliver. His voice steady, words carefully chosen and sincere, he reached out, desperate to bridge the growing gulf between them.

But Marissa wasn't having it.

"You really think I can forget what you implied, James?" she snapped, eyes blazing with frustration and hurt. "You've known me for nearly ten years, and that's what you thought of me?"

James's patience finally snapped, the weight of months pressing down on him. "I'm trying to apologise, Marissa. Can't you see that?"

Her laugh was bitter, hollow. She shook her head, voice cold. "You're not trying to take it back—you're trying to take back something you obviously believed. Well, I don't accept your apology. And as far as I'm concerned, you can stay away from me."

Without another word, she stood and walked away, leaving him abandoned and shut out—and she hadn't given him the time of day since.

He did regret what he said—deeply. At the time, he didn't truly believe those words; they were born from raw pain and betrayal, the hurt Victoria had left behind clouding his judgment and fuelling his anger.

But in the years that followed, Marissa had only seemed to prove him right.

Her endless string of boyfriends, the way she danced through life without ever seeming to settle—it was like she wore her heart on her sleeve but refused to let anyone in. To James, it confirmed his worst fears: beneath her beauty and charm, she was just as wild and untamed as he'd accused her of being.

And that realisation cut deeper than any argument ever could.

Chapter Four

Once she was out of James's line of sight, Marissa's slow, graceful retreat became a storming march up the stairs. Heat burned in her cheeks, not from embarrassment but from sheer fury.

What the hell was wrong with what she was wearing? This was her home. If she wanted to walk around in a silk chemise and robe, she damn well could. She could walk around naked if she pleased — not that she ever would. No man had ever seen her that way. And James Calder sure as hell wouldn't be the first to change that.

In the bathroom, steam filled the air as she showered, letting the hot water beat against her skin until her heartbeat slowed — but only slightly. She replayed his words over and over, that cool, assessing tone that managed to be both infuriating and… something else she refused to examine too closely.

When she stepped out, she dressed deliberately — not just for comfort, but for war. The shortest denim shorts she owned, worn soft from years of wear, frayed just enough to bare a teasing length of thigh. A simple white tank top clung to her in all the right places, brushing her ribs and leaving her midriff bare. The morning light from her bedroom window caught the warm glow of her skin, turning the casual outfit into something far more dangerous.

The choice was deliberate. Confidence was armour, and she meant for James to see every inch of it.

Padding downstairs, she let her steps be unhurried, the cool air of the house brushing against her bare arms. The faint clink of cutlery and the low hum of male voices guided her toward the dining room.

Ian and James sat at the table, mugs in hand, plates half-finished.

James looked up first. For a heartbeat, he didn't move — just blinked, eyes sweeping from the bare strip of her stomach to the frayed edges of her shorts before he caught himself. Marissa saw it, the split-second flicker of something unguarded, before his expression slid back into that infuriating mask.

She lingered in the doorway, tilting her head, lips curving into a sweet smile that didn't quite touch her eyes. "Is this better?" she asked, voice light, teasing… but with steel woven through it.

James's gaze flicked between her and Ian, his jaw tight. *'Better'* wasn't the word that came to mind — not with that bare skin glowing in the soft morning light, not with the image of her in silk still fresh in his mind. He forced his eyes back to his coffee, but the air between them was already thick, electric.

Ian glanced between them, brows lifting just slightly, but said nothing. Marissa moved to the sideboard for coffee, every step unhurried, knowing damn well James was watching. She didn't look at him again — but she felt him, the way his attention clung like heat on the back of her neck.

And James, for all his practiced detachment, couldn't stop wondering whether her choice of outfit had been for comfort... or for him.

Ian either didn't notice the tension—or chose to ignore it. He flashed his usual easy smile as he greeted her. "Morning, sis. Did you sleep well?"

Marissa returned the smile, warmth easing into her eyes. "I did, thanks, Ian. How are you? Ready for the big day?" She leaned forward and pressed a quick kiss to his cheek before settling down directly across from James at the table.

"I sure am. Can't wait," Ian replied, his excitement clear in his voice.

Marissa reached for a piece of toast and a small serving of scrambled eggs, the familiar morning ritual grounding her.

"So, what time are you heading over to Shelby's?" Ian asked, breaking the comfortable silence.

"Soon," Marissa answered simply.

Ian leaned back, a teasing sparkle lighting his eyes. "Shelby tells me she's worried you're going to outshine her today. Apparently, the dress she chose for you looks spectacular on you—her words."

Marissa smiled, her tone sincere. "I told her I'd wear a sack if that's what she wanted. But honestly, she looks absolutely gorgeous in her dress. No one's going to outshine her. And if anyone tries, well... they'll have me to deal with."

Ian chuckled warmly, shaking his head. "You've always got her back."

"Always," Marissa said firmly, her eyes shining with quiet loyalty.

James, sitting just a few feet away, couldn't help but watch the exchange. There was something in the way Marissa spoke—so genuine, so sincere—that caught him off guard. Beneath all the teasing and defiance, she truly cared. She always put her friends first, no matter what. It was one of the few things about her he couldn't deny, no matter how much he tried.

Then Marissa's gaze shifted to James, her eyes cooling into a sharper edge. "You just make sure my brother is ready and waiting," she said, her tone carrying an unspoken warning.

James straightened, defensive. "I will."

Ian cleared his throat, breaking the tension. "Actually, before you go, Marissa, I need to talk to you."

She turned fully toward him, curiosity and a hint of apprehension threading her voice. "Yes?"

Ian's expression grew serious. "I've asked James to stay here for the two weeks I'm away."

Marissa's eyes widened, disbelief flashing across her face. "What? Why?!"

"Because if he doesn't, I'll worry about you the whole time I'm gone," Ian said quietly, genuine concern lacing his tone.

Marissa rolled her eyes, trying to hide the flicker of affection beneath her teasing words. "Don't be ridiculous, Ian. I'm twenty-three—I can look after myself. Besides, Julie will be here, and the gardeners too."

Ian's hand came to rest gently on hers, the rare softness in his eyes undeniable. "Please, Marissa. I just need to know you're being looked after by a someone I can trust."

She looked at her brother, the weight of years pressing between them. When their parents died, Ian had been just a college student studying computer science. He had sacrificed his education and his own plans to take care of her. They'd inherited a substantial fortune, and when Ian asked if it was alright to invest it in the IT company he was starting with James, she hadn't hesitated.

He'd warned her it was risky—no guarantees of success—but she'd made it clear she trusted his judgment. They'd both thrived. The business was now worth billions, making them wealthier than she'd ever imagined.

She did trust him—he had always been there for her, steady and dependable.

So, with a slow, reluctant sigh, Marissa met his eyes and said, "If it makes you feel better... okay."

Ian visibly relaxed, a grateful smile spreading across his face. "Thank you," he said softly, then leaned over and kissed her gently on the cheek. "Try not to kill each other while I'm gone."

Marissa glanced over at James, who had been watching their exchange with sharp interest. Her lips curled into a sly smile as she met his gaze.

"I'll try," Marissa said smoothly, a teasing glint in her eyes, "if he does."

James spoke quietly, gaze locked on hers, steady and unflinching. "We'll be fine, Ian. Don't you worry about a thing." There was a weight in his tone, a subtle challenge buried beneath the reassurance—and Marissa felt it as keenly as she saw the stubborn set of his jaw.

Marissa rose with effortless grace, smoothing an imaginary crease from her shorts. "I'd better be going. Shelby will be waiting." She leaned down to press another kiss to her brother's cheek, her voice softening. "I'll see you soon."

James's gaze followed her as she walked away, the curve of her bare midriff catching the light, the soft cotton of her shorts hugging every line of her hips and backside. His jaw tightened, a muscle ticking as he forced himself to look away. If she kept dressing like that for the next two weeks, he wasn't sure he'd have the strength—or the sanity— to keep his hands to himself.

The moment she stepped through the door, the crisp morning air swept over her skin, cool and clean, a sharp contrast to the simmering heat James's stare had branded into her.

Not long after she arrived at Shelby's house, the bridal suite was alive with soft laughter, clinking glasses, and the faint scent of roses and hairspray. Shelby stood by the mirror, her white gown a dream of lace and satin—the bodice delicately beaded, the skirt flowing like mist around her. Her blonde hair was swept into a loose chignon, tendrils framing her radiant face, and her blue eyes sparkled with both excitement and nerves.

Marissa slipped easily into her role—buttoning the last row of tiny pearl fastenings, straightening Shelby's veil, and fetching her bouquet.

When it was time for Marissa to change into her own gown, the room seemed to still. The maid of honour dress was a rich shade of deep emerald silk, cut to skim her tall, elegant frame. The fitted bodice highlighted her narrow waist, while the skirt fell in soft folds to the floor, swaying with every movement. The colour made her blue eyes shine like sapphires and brought out the fiery undertones in her long auburn hair, which tumbled in loose waves over one shoulder.

Shelby grinned at her reflection in the mirror, shaking her head. "You are going to cause trouble in that dress."

Marissa's lips curved into a slow, knowing smile. "Let them try."

The late afternoon sun drenched the Turner estate gardens in a soft, molten gold, gilding the edges of every rose petal until they seemed lit from within. The air hung heavy with the mingled perfume of blooms and freshly cut grass, warm and heady enough to make the world feel dreamlike. Guests sat in neat rows beneath a billowing canopy of white silk, their murmured conversations falling away as the first notes from the string quartet unfurled into the air.

James Calder stood at the front, tall and immaculately put together, the very image of composure. His dark hair caught the light in sleek, disciplined waves, and his tailored charcoal suit — perfectly cut, naturally — framed the breadth of his shoulders with precise elegance. He leaned slightly toward Ian, speaking in low tones, but his eyes kept sweeping the crowd with the alertness of a man who noticed everything.

Marissa felt a spark of anticipation flicker through her. Any moment now, those dark eyes would find her.

She stepped forward into the aisle, her movements deliberate, each stride perfectly in time with the music. The whisper of emerald silk brushed the grass with every step, the fitted bodice sculpting her figure before spilling into a fluid skirt that swayed like water. Shelby had chosen the deep, jewel-toned green to flatter her hair, but Marissa wore it like armour — silk, satin, and unshakable poise.

When James's gaze found her, it was like being touched from across the distance. His expression barely shifted, but she saw it — the slight tightening of his jaw, the flicker in his eyes that was too sharp to be indifference. Irritation? Surprise? Or something far more dangerous?

Whatever it was, it wasn't nothing.

The corner of her mouth lifted in the faintest suggestion of a smile — private, aimed at him alone — before she looked away, the picture of cool disinterest. Inside, though, she was already plotting how to keep that look in his eyes for the rest of the night.

James stood near the front, hands clasped behind his back, his posture the definition of controlled stillness. He had been. Until he looked up.

Marissa had just stepped into view.

For a heartbeat, the world went silent. The chatter, the music, even the warm breath of the late afternoon breeze seemed to fade, leaving only the vision of her moving toward him. The emerald silk of her gown shimmered in the sun, her auburn hair tumbling over bare shoulders in loose waves that caught the light like molten copper. She didn't glance at him, her gaze fixed ahead, but James felt the air shift, the almost imperceptible jolt he always got when she was near — that maddening, magnetic pull she seemed to summon without effort.

His jaw locked tight.

She was breathtaking. Infuriating. Dangerous.

And with every step she took toward him, James felt his control splinter just a little more. God help him, he wanted her—with a hunger that made no sense, a need that defied reason.

Each measured stride pulled her into sharper focus: the effortless sway of her hips, the elegance in the line of her shoulders, the quiet command in the tilt of her chin. She didn't just walk into the garden—she claimed it. Every guest, every flower, every delicate note of the quartet seemed to fall into orbit around her, as though the world itself conspired to frame her arrival.

He told himself it was irritation that quickened his pulse. She'd worn that gown, or at least carried herself in it, knowing exactly what it would do to him. That had to be it. But then the sunlight struck her hair, igniting it into a halo of burnished fire, and the image jarred him — too pure, too untouchable — at odds with every cynical assumption he'd made about her.

She passed by, close enough for the faint trace of her perfume — something warm and floral, intoxicating in its subtlety — to coil through his senses, leaving thoughts in its wake he had no business entertaining.

Beautiful. Sexy. Untouchable.

And exactly the sort of woman he didn't trust.

He fixed his gaze forward, forcing himself to breathe evenly. He was here for Ian, not for her. That was the vow he'd made the day Ian had asked him to be best man. But as the ceremony began and the officiant's voice rolled over the garden, James had the unwelcome certainty of one thing — vows were far easier to make than to keep.

Chapter Five

The ceremony went off without a hitch.

Sunlight spilled generously over the Turner estate gardens, gilding the white silk canopy and illuminating the blooms that lined the aisle. Shelby was radiant, Ian looked happier than Marissa had ever seen him, and for forty-five uninterrupted minutes, Marissa managed to focus on them instead of the man standing just a few feet away.

Almost.

She felt James beside her through every vow, every reading, every quiet breath between. He was composed, attentive, a model best man… yet she caught him watching her more than once from the corner of his eye.

When the officiant finally pronounced Ian and Shelby husband and wife, applause rippled through the crowd. Marissa clapped and smiled, her heart swelling with genuine happiness for her best friend. The newlyweds moved to a small table beneath the canopy to sign the marriage register, the calligraphed pages laid open like something sacred.

Once the ink dried and the pen was set down, the photographer—a wiry man with an irrepressible spark of energy—took control.

"Alright, let's get the bridal party together! Bride, groom, best man, maid of honour—right here in the centre."

Marissa stepped forward, only to realise James was moving toward her at the same time. They stopped within a breath of each other.

"Looks like we're up," she murmured, her tone light though her pulse wasn't.

He gave her a cool nod, expression unreadable, but the heat flickering in his eyes told her he hadn't forgotten the way she'd looked walking down that aisle—every step meant to torment him.

The photographer waved impatiently. "Closer! You're supposed to look like you like each other."

Marissa arched a brow at James, her lips curving in the faintest challenge. "You heard the man."

To her surprise, James closed the space between them, his arm brushing deliberately against hers as his hand settled at her waist. Not heavy, not demanding—just enough to brand her through the thin silk of her gown. The heat of his touch seeped into her skin, a slow, dangerous burn that made her breath hitch.

"Smile," he murmured, low and husky, meant for her ears alone.

So, she did—slowly, deliberately—her lips curving into a smile that to everyone else would look sweet, innocent. But James would know better. He'd feel the dare in it, the promise she wasn't afraid to wield against him.

The photographer clicked the shutter. "One more—tilt your head toward him, Marissa. That's it. Perfect."

She angled her face toward him, his mouth so close she could feel the warmth of his breath graze her cheek. James's hand lingered at her waist, fingers tightening almost imperceptibly, as if he was daring himself not to pull her closer.

The photographer waved them apart, breaking the spell.

Marissa stepped back, her composure flawless. "See?" she murmured, not looking at him. "We can behave."

James's gaze lingered on her lips before lifting to her eyes. His voice was a low warning. "For now."

The reception flowed seamlessly from the garden ceremony to the grand marquee set up on the lawn. Inside, golden light pooled from chandeliers strung high beneath the white-draped ceiling, the scent of fresh flowers mingling with the rich aroma of champagne and canapés.

Marissa had barely taken a sip of her drink before the photographer reappeared like a man on a mission.

"Marissa, James—over by the cake, please. I want to get some shots before the crowd blocks the view."

She arched a brow. "Isn't that for the bride and groom?"

"Yes, yes, of course—but I need filler shots for the album. Now, over you go." He was already herding them toward a towering confection of white fondant and sugar roses.

James fell into step beside her. "You think he's doing this on purpose?" he asked, voice low and faintly amused.

"If he is, I might start charging him."

"Charging?"

She glanced up at him, eyes glinting. "For my time. And the inconvenience."

James's mouth curved, but whether it was a smile or something more dangerous, she couldn't tell.

The photographer positioned them so close their shoulders touched. "Look at each other," he instructed. "Laugh like he just told you something hilarious."

Marissa tilted her head, giving James a lazy, assessing look. "Well? Make me laugh."

He leaned in slightly, breath warm against her ear. "If I told you what I was actually thinking, you wouldn't laugh."

Her pulse stumbled. She kept her expression smooth, but the photographer captured the subtle spark in her eyes all the same.

"Perfect! Now—out to the garden with the lanterns. The light is gorgeous."

It went on like that for the next hour. The photographer somehow found them no matter where they were—the champagne bar, the rose arch, the dance floor before the first dance even began—each time insisting they pose just one more time.

By the time Ian and Shelby finally made their entrance into the marquee, Marissa had lost count of how many times James's hand had rested at her back, how many times she'd tilted her face toward his, how many seconds she'd spent wrapped in his scent—clean, masculine, faintly spiced.

And worst of all, she couldn't decide if she hated it… or if part of her didn't want it to stop.

The speeches had ended. Champagne glasses clinked, laughter mingling with the soft murmur of guests settling into the warmth of the evening. Shelby and Ian glided onto the dance floor for their first dance as husband and wife, a slow, romantic ballad wrapping the marquee in its tender embrace. Golden light pooled across the polished floor, illuminating the smiles of friends and family gathered around, enchanted by the couple's effortless grace.

When the song tapered to a delicate finish, the MC's voice rang out, cutting through the hushed reverence. "And now, we'd like all the bridal party to join the bride and groom on the floor."

Marissa froze mid-sip of champagne, the cool bubbles lingering uncomfortably on her tongue. Her gaze snapped to James, who was already looking at her—calm, steady, as if this moment had been plotted in his mind for hours.

"Oh no," she murmured under her breath, a shiver running down her spine.

"Oh yes," he said quietly, almost a whisper, as though he'd been waiting for her to say it.

She set her glass down with deliberate, practiced grace. "Try not to step on my toes, Calder," she warned, voice lightly teasing.

"Try not to make me regret this," he countered, offering his hand with a confidence that made her pulse thrum against her chest.

Her hand hovered for a fraction of a second before she placed it in his. His fingers were warm, firm, certain. She hated—*hated*—that it made her aware of the rapid beat of her pulse.

The moment they stepped onto the dance floor, he drew her in, close enough to stir something beneath her carefully maintained composure. Close enough that propriety brushed against desire, and her breath caught. The music wrapped around them, slow and deliberate, soft, and dangerous in the way it blurred the edges of her defences.

"You clean up nice," she murmured, trying for lightness, but there was a tremor she couldn't quite hide.

"You've already told me that once today," he said evenly, a quiet challenge in his tone. "I'm starting to think you mean it."

She tilted her head, pretending to consider the words, masking the warmth that curled at her chest. "Don't get used to it."

They moved together in easy, measured steps. His hand at her waist was steady, almost possessive, and she felt a prickle beneath the thin silk of her gown. She told herself it was irritation, though the truth was far messier.

"You've been quiet tonight," she ventured, testing him.

"Trying not to say something I'll regret," he replied, voice low, deliberate.

"Wise of you," she said, a faint curve at the corner of her lips.

"Don't push your luck, Turner."

A beat passed. One beat too long. She realised then that James wasn't watching her with his usual sharp disapproval, but with a careful, almost unsettling focus that made her pulse skip and her thoughts falter.

When he turned her in his arms, he pulled her just a little closer than necessary. The movement was subtle, easy to excuse in the flow of the dance, but deliberate all the same. His hand was steady at her back, the pressure of his touch sending heat curling low in her belly. He liked the way she felt against him—she could see it in the flicker of his gaze, in the tension of his jaw.

The song drew to a close, the final notes stretching like the last breath of something forbidden. Applause swelled around them, breaking the fragile cocoon of their moment. James released her hand at last, his touch lingering a fraction longer than it should have.

Marissa stepped back, the movement small but decisive, as though putting space between them might sever what had just passed—the spell, the heat, the dangerous promise simmering just beneath the surface.

But even as she moved toward the edge of the floor, she could still feel the imprint of his palm at her waist, a ghost of contact that lingered in a place no one else could reach. She hated the way it made her heart twist. Hated the way she wanted more.

She stepped back, carefully, deliberately, putting space between them. And yet… he could still feel her. Not just the memory of her hand in his, not just the warmth of her waist pressed against him, but the way her body had fitted against his, even for a fleeting moment. The imprint of her—soft, slight, impossibly precise—clung to him, as if the dance itself had left a mark only he could feel.

He forced himself to breathe, slow and steady, but the memory made it impossible to settle completely. Her scent, faint but intoxicating, lingered in the air between them. He hated that he noticed, hated that it stirred something deep and uncomfortable in his chest, something he had always tried to keep under control around her.

She walked away with measured grace, head held high, but he knew better. Every step carried a tension that mirrored his own, every subtle shift of her shoulders a reminder of how close she'd been. She'd felt… right. Frighteningly right.

He clenched his jaw, forcing his fingers to loosen, to release the phantom contact that wasn't his to hold anymore. And yet, even as he watched her disappear toward the edge of the crowd, he knew he wasn't done thinking about it. Not tonight. Not ever.

The pull between them was raw and undeniable, a dangerous current he had to resist no matter how fiercely it tempted him.

Later, Marissa was sitting on a bench outside, the night's coolness settling around her like a soft blanket, when a voice broke through the quiet.

"Marissa? Can I have a moment?"

She turned to see a man approaching—tall, in his late thirties, dressed casually but with the unmistakable air of a worried father. It was Tom, the father of one of her kindergarten students, a little girl named Lily who had been struggling with anxiety lately.

"Of course, Tom," Marissa said with a warm smile, rising to her feet. "Is everything alright?"

He looked relieved but still hesitant. "It's Lily… she's been having some trouble settling in at school. I wasn't sure how to help her, and I thought maybe you could give me some advice."

Marissa nodded, her teacher's heart opening. "Absolutely. Sometimes kids just need a little extra reassurance, especially when there's something new or scary going on. Does she talk about anything specific at home?"

Tom sighed, running a hand through his hair. "She's afraid of the dark, and it's been hard getting her to sleep or even want to go to school some days."

"I see," Marissa said gently. "One thing that helps is creating a predictable routine—a favourite story at bedtime, maybe a little nightlight. And during the day, I make sure she has a safe space in the classroom where she can go if she feels overwhelmed."

Tom smiled gratefully, his tension easing. "Thank you, Marissa. I didn't realise how much just a few changes could help."

Moved by the moment, Tom reached out and took her hand in his, squeezing it softly. Then, almost impulsively, he leaned in and pressed a gentle kiss to her cheek.

"Thank you. For everything."

Marissa's eyes widened slightly but she smiled warmly, touched by the genuine gratitude. "You're very welcome."

James had just turned the corner when he saw it—a man, unmistakably married, leaning in and pressing his lips to Marissa's. From where James stood, it looked exactly like a kiss on the lips.

Rage snapped through him like a live wire, hot and unrelenting. *What the hell…?* His chest tightened, his jaw clenched, and for a moment the world narrowed to the sight of her there, so casual, so unbothered.

The man pulled back, smiling as if nothing had happened, leaving Marissa standing there—light-hearted, serene, entirely oblivious to the storm he was about to unleash.

James stepped forward, every word edged with cutting disbelief. "Seducing married men now, are we? Not enough single ones lying around?"

Marissa froze, genuinely startled, as if she hadn't expected him to appear—or perhaps hadn't expected him to react like this. She opened her mouth to explain, to protest, but the raw intensity in his gaze, the tight line of his jaw, silenced her.

Instead, she let a slow, sly smile curl at the corners of her lips, deliberate and infuriating. "A girl's gotta do what a girl's gotta do," she said, voice cool, smooth, and dripping with defiance.

She held his glare for a heartbeat longer, letting the words settle like stones between them, before pivoting on her heel and walking away. Each step was measured, confident, and infuriatingly calm, leaving James rooted in place—burning with frustration, disbelief, and something darker he refused to name.

He watched her go, the sway of her hips, the casual lift of her chin, and it made his blood boil in ways he couldn't entirely admit to himself. Goddamn it, he thought, jaw tight, fists clenched at his sides. She was infuriating, maddening, and utterly impossible—and somehow, that only made it worse.

Every nerve in him wanted to stride after her, grab her arm, and demand the truth. To shake her just enough to make her see the storm in his eyes. But another part of him— the part he hated—knew it would be exactly what she wanted: proof that she had the power to unnerve him.

He ground his teeth, forcing himself to inhale, to slow the thrum of his pulse, but it was useless. He could still feel the phantom heat of her in his arms from the dance, the imprint of her body haunting him, sharp and irritating, like a brand he couldn't shake.

And yet… that memory made his anger twist, sharpened it. Because she had been there. Close. Too close. And now she was walking away, teasing him with a confidence he didn't deserve—and he was powerless to stop it.

He clenched his fists again, shoulders taut, and muttered under his breath, barely coherent: "Damn it, Turner… you're impossible."

Impossible. And yet, impossibly, he didn't want her to be anyone else.

Chapter Six

The rest of the night, Marissa made a decision.

If James Calder wanted to think she was some shameless flirt, then fine—she would give him the full performance.

She wasn't reckless enough to actually cross any lines, but she was determined that every time he looked her way, he'd see her laughing a little too freely, leaning a little too close, keeping company with anyone willing to play along. She would make it impossible for him to ignore—and impossible for herself to resist the thrill of the game.

It began innocently enough with one of Shelby's cousins—tall, boyish, and clearly charmed by her attention. She laughed at his stories, the sound light and easy, touching his arm lightly at exactly the right moments. From the corner of her eye, she caught James standing near the bar, jaw tight, hand gripping his champagne flute as if he could crush it with sheer will. A small, mischievous thrill coursed through her.

Later, near the dance floor, Marissa found herself paired with one of James and Ian's friends—a sandy-haired charmer with a dimple that promised trouble. When he offered to spin her to a fast-tempo song, she didn't hesitate. She let him twirl her under his arm, skirt flaring high enough to reveal a teasing flash of leg. She didn't have to look to know James was watching—she felt it, the weight of his stare searing her skin long before her eyes found him along the edge of the crowd. Dark. Intense. Unforgiving.

By dessert, she had become the room's centre of gravity. Shelby's cousins gravitated toward her table, the wedding photographer lingered for extra shots, the DJ stopped by with a grin, even the maître d' paused with a compliment. And Marissa gave it all back in kind—bright laughter, a tilt of her head, a brush of fingertips along a forearm, a smile that lingered a second too long.

James didn't speak. He didn't need to. Every taut line of his shoulders, every restless drag of his finger around the rim of his glass screamed his disapproval.

"Is she seeing anyone?" a low voice asked at his shoulder. James turned to find his friend—the same sandy-haired charmer now flushed from the dance floor—grinning like a schoolboy. "She's hot as hell, James. If she's free, I might try my luck."

James's jaw tightened. He forced a neutral smile that didn't reach his eyes. "She's not interested," he said flatly.

His friend blinked, thrown by the sharp edge beneath the words, then gave a shrug and slipped back into the crowd. "We'll see."

But James's gaze never left her. And Marissa knew it. Each playful flick of her wrist, each careless smile, each low laugh was for him, whether he admitted it or not. It was a dangerous game, and she relished every delicious second—especially knowing she had him on a leash he refused to acknowledge, the tether between them pulled tauter with every breath.

By the time the band slowed into their final set and the newlyweds slipped away for their send-off, Marissa was thoroughly satisfied. She had played her role perfectly—carefree, charming, untouchable.

But stepping into the quiet night, laughter and music fading behind her, she realised she wasn't alone.

James was waiting.

He stood near the lantern-lit path back to the house, tall and sharp in the shadows, his hands buried in his pockets as if that alone kept him from reaching for her. His gaze found her instantly—piercing, unyielding—and her pulse stuttered at the weight of it.

"Have fun?" His tone was deceptively mild, edged with something dangerous.

Marissa lifted her chin, her voice light but threaded with steel. "Immensely. Why do you ask?"

"Because," he said, stepping toward her with slow, deliberate precision, "I've spent the entire night watching you hang off every man who so much as glanced your way."

Her brow arched, lips curling into a knowing, infuriating smile. "Hang off? That's a little dramatic—even for you."

"Dramatic?" His jaw tightened, the muscle ticking with restrained fury. "I lost count after the fifth man you touched tonight. Was that the point? Keep me counting?"

A soft, incredulous laugh slipped from her, tilting her head in mock innocence. "Why on earth would you be watching me, James? You've made it perfectly clear I'm not worth your time."

His eyes darkened, voice dropping low, thick with something he couldn't quite hide. "Ian asked me to keep an eye on you."

Her lashes lowered, her smile sharpened. "Well, one of his friends asked me out. Maybe I should get him to keep an eye on me instead. What do you think?"

He stepped in close, the heat of him swallowing the air between them. "I told him you weren't interested."

Her pulse spiked, her breath catching in her throat. Anger flared, colouring her cheeks. "Excuse me?"

Before she could move, he closed the distance, his hand sliding to the small of her back as he hauled her into him and crushed his mouth to hers.

She stiffened in shock—then melted, his lips shifting softer, coaxing instead of demanding. Her arms wound around his neck almost without thought, her body giving him the answer her words never would. A moan slipped from her lips, swallowed instantly by his groan as he pulled her tighter against him, devouring her like a man starved.

And then—abruptly, violently—he tore himself away, breathing hard, eyes blazing.

Marissa staggered back, stunned, lips tingling, chest heaving. But then the shock gave way to fury.

"I may have agreed to let you stay here so Ian wouldn't worry," she bit out, her voice sharp enough to cut, "but you can damn well stay out of my way."

She swept past him, then paused, her head tilting just enough to glance over her shoulder. Her smile was cool, deliberate, devastating.

"Have you ever thought that maybe," she murmured, her voice silken with mockery, "you just don't like it when I give my attention to anyone but you."

Before he could answer, she turned on her heel and strode toward the house, her perfume curling in the cool night air like a challenge left hanging.

James remained rooted, every muscle taut, his burning gaze locked on her retreating figure. Her words—sharp, taunting, intoxicating—lodged deep inside him, setting fire to every inch of restraint he had left.

He stood frozen on the lantern-lit path, fists clenching uselessly at his sides as Marissa's perfume lingered in the air, taunting him long after she vanished into the house.

Christ. What the hell had he done?

He hadn't meant to touch her, let alone kiss her like that. One second, she was standing there, lips curved in that infuriating smile, poking at him, daring him—and the next, he had her in his arms, her mouth opening beneath his, soft and sweet and God help him—better than every fantasy he'd sworn he didn't have.

And she kissed him back. She moaned into his mouth, pressed her body against his, wrapped herself around him like she belonged there. Like she'd been waiting for him just as much as he'd been waiting for her.

That sound—the one he dragged out of her—it was going to haunt him.

He dragged a hand over his jaw, trying to steady the riot in his chest. It was useless. His heart was still pounding, his body hard and aching from the way she'd fit against him.

He'd kissed women before—too many to count—but never, *never* had one undone him like this.

And now she hated him for it.

Her words replayed in his head, sharp and mocking, cutting deeper than he wanted to admit. *'You just don't like it when I give my attention to anyone but you.'*

She was right.

He despised watching her smile at other men, hated the way they leaned in, hungry for her attention. It burned through him, hot and corrosive, and he couldn't disguise it, not even behind the cool front he always wore. The truth was ugly, undeniable—he didn't want her looking at anyone else.

Hell, he didn't even want her looking at him like that. With defiance. With challenge. With the promise of a war, he wasn't sure he could win.

James exhaled hard, tilting his head back to the night sky, but the stars gave him no clarity. He was in trouble. Deep trouble.

Because one kiss had told him what he'd been fighting against all along: he wanted Marissa—recklessly, dangerously, completely.

And wanting her was the one thing he couldn't afford.

The next morning, sunlight spilled through the wide kitchen windows, warm and golden, catching the faint sheen of silk as Marissa padded in. Her robe hung loosely over a pale champagne chemise, the delicate fabric skimming the length of her legs with every step. She'd tied her auburn hair in a loose knot, a few stray strands brushing the nape of her neck, soft and tempting in the morning light.

James was already there, leaning against the counter with a mug of coffee in hand. He looked maddeningly composed—dark shirt sleeves rolled up, jaw freshly shaven, eyes shadowed from too little sleep, but still sharp and unreadable. The kind of casual perfection that made it impossible not to notice him.

At the sound of her bare feet on the tile, he glanced up. His gaze swept over her slowly, deliberately, tracing the curve of her shoulders, the fall of her robe, the subtle hint of skin beneath. Her pulse ticked up under the weight of it. His lips thinned slightly, and she could almost see the words forming on his tongue—the disapproval he was holding back, the lecture he seemed poised to deliver.

She lifted her chin before he could speak. "Don't."

One brow rose, but he said nothing, only took another slow sip of coffee, his dark eyes fixed on her like a predator measuring distance.

"If you don't like the way I dress," she said evenly, her tone cool as glass though her pulse thundered beneath it, "you could always leave… or close your eyes. Actually—" her lips curved, wicked and deliberate, "if you don't like what I'm wearing now, maybe I should wear my shorter nightgown tomorrow." She dropped her voice to a sultry whisper; every word aimed at him like a blade. "It barely covers me. Maybe you could come up to my room, and I'll model it for you."

Silence crackled, sharp and dangerous. The fridge hummed, the wall clock ticked, but James didn't move. Didn't blink. His hand tightened around the mug, knuckles white against the ceramic.

Her mouth went dry.

Because the look in his eyes wasn't just disapproval—it was hunger. The same raw, unguarded hunger she'd felt against her lips last night when he'd kissed her like he couldn't breathe without her. She'd dreamed about it after, the heat of his mouth, the way his hands had claimed her, the sound of his groan tangled with her own. She'd woken restless, aching in places she hadn't thought about in years—or maybe ever.

And now, standing in the morning light, robe brushing against bare thighs, she could feel the weight of his stare like a touch, scorching her skin, dragging her back into the memory of that kiss.

Marissa crossed to the coffeemaker, her steps measured, deliberate. The silk whispered along her legs, taunting both of them. She turned her back to him, refusing to give him the satisfaction of seeing her flustered. Refusing to show how badly she wanted him to close the distance, to pin her against the counter, to finish what he'd started last night.

But she wouldn't give him the power of knowing that.

Even as she poured her coffee, she sensed him there, a presence as tangible as the morning light, as impossible to ignore as the thrum of her own heartbeat. She could almost feel the tension in the air, the quiet promise that one misstep—or one careless word—would shatter the fragile calm between them. And secretly, she wouldn't have minded if it did.

Julie breezed in, breaking the charged silence. "Morning, you two. Did you sleep well?"

Marissa turned with an easy smile, leaning in to kiss Julie's cheek. "Good morning, Julie. I slept like a log. Yesterday was wonderful, wasn't it?"

"It was a beautiful wedding," Julie agreed warmly.

"It really was. Ian and Shelby looked so happy," Marissa said, and the smile was genuine.

"Morning, Julie," James added, voice smooth but clipped.

Marissa reached for a plate. "I'll just have a piece of toast this morning. I'm heading out for a jog."

Julie frowned. "You're not going on the road, are you?"

"No, I'll stick to the estate," Marissa assured her.

Julie hesitated. "Just remember—the grounds crew is out there cleaning up after the wedding this morning. Watch your step."

Marissa nodded, reaching for the bread, still aware of James's eyes on her. She didn't need to see him to know whatever he was thinking, it wasn't about toast.

Marissa slid the toast into the toaster, refusing to acknowledge the weight of his stare. The kitchen seemed smaller with him in it, the air thicker.

"You shouldn't go alone," James said suddenly, tone deceptively casual.

She glanced at him over her shoulder, one brow arched. "I think I can manage a jog without a chaperone."

"It's not about managing," he replied, taking a slow sip of coffee. "It's about not being stupid."

Her fingers tightened on the counter, but her voice stayed cool. "If you're trying to insult me before I've had caffeine, you might want to rethink your strategy."

He set his mug down and moved toward her, steps unhurried but deliberate. "Ian asked me to keep an eye on you while he's away. That means making sure you don't end up twisted in a ditch because you weren't paying attention."

Marissa's laugh was light, but her eyes sharp. "How lucky for me that the best man also moonlights as a bodyguard."

"I'm not joking, Marissa."

She took her toast from the toaster, buttering it with meticulous care. "Neither am I, James. If I wanted company, I'd ask for it."

He studied her a moment longer, something unreadable flickering in his dark eyes. "Fine. But don't expect me to come looking if you get yourself into trouble."

"I never do," she said sweetly, brushing past him as she left the kitchen, the faint scent of her perfume trailing after her.

James stood near the counter, mug in hand, silently telling himself he'd let her go this time. Let her have the space she demanded. But deep down, he already knew the truth—he wouldn't. Not now, not ever.

When Marissa came back downstairs after changing, the sight of him changed into jogging gear in the kitchen ignited a spark of irritation deep inside her.

Without a word, she bent down and pulled on her running shoes, jaw tightening as morning light filtered through the window, casting soft shadows across the room. But inside, all she felt was a cold, burning resentment—a stubborn flame of frustration that refused to be soothed.

She moved with deliberate silence, every action sharp with unspoken words. The tension between them hung thick in the air, heavy and unavoidable.

James lingered near the door, watching her with that stubborn, intense look she hated and couldn't quite stop noticing.

"You're really going to do this," he said quietly, "run off like I'm some kind of obstacle."

She didn't answer. Instead, she grabbed her water bottle and headed for the door.

"Marissa," James called after her, voice low but firm. "Wait."

She stopped but didn't turn. "What?"

"You can't keep pushing me away. Ian asked me to look out for you."

"That's your problem, not mine." Her voice sharpened, anger bubbling to the surface. "I'm not a child. I don't need a babysitter."

James stepped closer, closing the distance she was trying to create. "I'm not babysitting you."

She whirled to face him, eyes blazing. "Then get out of my way."

Before James could react, Marissa shoved past him and bolted down the gravel path. The sharp crunch of stones underfoot echoed loudly in the stillness of the early morning.

"Marissa, slow down!" James called, footsteps quickening as he chased after her.

"It's not my fault you can't keep up," she shot back over her shoulder, breath ragged but voice defiant.

But she didn't slow—not even as her legs burned—driven by the desperate need to create distance, to escape the suffocating weight of his presence pressing in on her.

Rounding a bend near the ancient oak tree, her eyes suddenly caught movement—a worker rounding the corner, carrying a box of fairy lights freshly taken down from the branches. Marissa barely had time to react. She twisted sharply to avoid colliding.

Her foot caught on an exposed tree root, and suddenly her world lurched. Arms flailing wildly, she pitched forward.

The impact was brutal—her head struck the rough ground with a sickening thud, a sharp, searing pain erupting at the base of her skull.

The world tilted wildly, colours blurring and swirling before everything faded into darkness.

James was on his knees beside her in an instant, panic flooding his voice. "Marissa! Can you hear me? Marissa!"

But she didn't move, didn't respond.

She was completely unconscious.

Chapter Seven

James's heart hammered so violently in his chest it felt as if it might burst through his ribs. Time slowed, each second stretching unbearably as he took in the sight of her—Marissa—lying still and unresponsive on the cold gravel. Every instinct screamed that something was horribly wrong, and yet his mind froze, struggling to process what he was seeing.

Panic clawed at his throat, jagged and wild, leaving him gasping as if the very air had thickened. He dropped to his knees beside her, every nerve alight with shock and dread, and a strange, disorienting surge of emotions he didn't fully understand flooded him: fear, anger, helplessness… and something deeper, a raw, almost suffocating ache at the thought of losing her even for a moment.

"Marissa! Please, wake up!" His voice cracked, brittle with desperation, the sound raw and unsteady. He shook her gently, once, twice, as if sheer force could rouse her from the eerie stillness.

Her eyelids remained sealed, and her body lay limp against the gravel, cold and fragile, and the world around him seemed to blur. Every rational thought vanished beneath the tidal wave of panic and dread. He wanted to scream, to shake the universe itself until it returned her to him, but all he could do was hold her, heart racing, prayers spilling silently between ragged breaths.

For the first time, James felt the full weight of what she meant to him—the depth of how much he needed her safe, the undeniable truth that seeing her vulnerable like this shattered the careful control he always maintained. Every second without a sign of movement was a knife twisting in his chest, leaving him raw, exposed, and frighteningly aware of how completely she had claimed him.

Logic screamed at him to call an ambulance immediately—the safest, most sensible choice. The nearest hospital was miles away, and with every second that ticked by, precious time slipped through his fingers. Panic gnawed at him, sharp and insistent, but he forced himself to act. He prayed they would get here soon.

James yanked his phone from his pocket with trembling fingers and dialled emergency services.

"There's been an accident—a woman is unconscious with a head injury," he said quickly, voice taut but precise. "Please send help immediately. I'm at the Turner estate."

His mind spun, a chaotic storm of thoughts, fears, and adrenaline. She needed help. Now. And he was the only one who could get her to safety fast enough.

"Come on," he muttered under his breath, swallowing hard against the lump of fear lodged deep in his throat. Sliding one arm beneath her shoulders, the other under her knees, he summoned a strength born purely of desperation, lifting her as though she weighed nothing at all.

Standing, he cradled Marissa close, her fragile body pressed against his chest. The faint scent of her perfume mingled with the cool morning air, grounding him even as his pulse thundered in his ears. Her hair brushed his jaw, her warmth against him sharp in its reality.

"Hang on, Marissa. We will get you to the hospital. You're going to be okay. I promise," he whispered, his voice rough with tension and something else—something he hadn't allowed himself to feel until now: raw, unfiltered fear.

His footsteps pounded along the gravel path, adrenaline dulling the ache in his limbs, every second a reminder of how fragile she was in his arms. The world around him blurred, narrowed to a singular, urgent focus: saving her.

Bursting through the front door, he laid Marissa gently on the polished hardwood floor, careful not to jostle her more than necessary. He crouched close, watching her chest rise and fall in slow, fragile rhythm. Relief washed over him like a fleeting tide, but her closed eyes and stillness kept the panic alive, sharp, and insistent.

The faint but growing wail of sirens cut through the morning calm like a lifeline. James pressed his palm to her forehead, willing her to come back—to open her eyes—to fight. Every second without movement was unbearable.

The crunch of gravel outside heralded the ambulance's arrival. Paramedics stormed in, moving with swift, practiced efficiency. James stepped back slightly, reluctant to release her but unable to stand in their way. His gaze lingered on her face, searching for any sign of consciousness, any flicker of life, while his chest still heaved with a mixture of fear, relief, and helplessness.

Even as the professionals took over, his mind refused to let go, his heart hammering at the thought that for even a single moment, she had been in his arms, utterly vulnerable—and it had shaken him in ways he wasn't ready to admit.

Just then, Julie appeared in the kitchen doorway, her face draining of colour as she took in the scene—Marissa lying motionless on the floor, James pale and tense beside her.

"Is she breathing?" Julie asked, kneeling without hesitation.

James nodded, voice tight with fear. "Yes. She tripped over a tree root and hit her head."

The paramedics moved quickly, checking Marissa's pulse, oxygen levels, and vitals. They worked with calm precision, their practiced movements gentle but thorough.

One carefully lifted Marissa onto a stretcher while another prepared medical equipment, all while communicating in clipped, professional tones.

"We're taking her to the hospital now," the lead paramedic said firmly. "She needs constant monitoring."

James followed closely, heart pounding so loudly it felt like it might burst free. Julie grabbed her coat with urgency and turned to him.

"I'm coming with you," she said, voice steady but full of deep concern.

He gave a grateful nod, relief mixing with the anxiety knotting his stomach.

The ambulance doors slid shut behind them. With a roar, the vehicle sprang to life, sirens screaming as it sped toward the hospital. Inside James's car, the tense silence was broken only by Julie's whispered prayers—each one a fragile hope hanging in the air.

James and Julie arrived at the emergency entrance of a busy Perth hospital, the morning sun casting sharp shadows across the sleek glass facade. The ambulance had roared through city streets, but now they were on foot, rushing through sliding doors into the sterile, white-walled lobby.

James's heart pounded as they approached the reception desk, where a young nurse looked up from her computer, her expression calm but professional.

"We're here for Marissa Turner," James said, voice tense. "She was brought in with a head injury."

The nurse paused, fingers resting lightly on the keyboard. "Marissa Turner… yes, she's here. The doctor is with her now in the emergency ward."

Julie glanced at James; eyes filled with concern. "Do you know how she is?"

The nurse gave a small, reassuring smile. "I don't have details, but the doctor said he'll come out and update you as soon as he can."

James swallowed hard, nodding. "Thank you."

They stepped aside, the sterile hospital noises pressing in—soft beeps, distant footsteps, murmured voices—each sound sharpening the tension as they waited.

James paced slowly near the waiting area, hands clenched into fists at his sides. The hum of the hospital felt suffocating, the buzz of fluorescent lights above adding to his growing unease.

Julie sat quietly beside him, eyes steady but soft, watching him struggle with the silence.

After a long breath, James finally broke the stillness. "This is all my fault," he said, voice low and heavy with guilt. "I shouldn't have insisted on watching her. If I'd just let her go on that jog alone… none of this would have happened."

He stopped pacing, shoulders slumping as he met Julie's gaze. "I thought I was protecting her. But maybe I was just being… controlling. And now she's hurt because of me."

Julie reached out, placing a steady hand on his arm. "James, blaming yourself won't change what happened. You did what you thought was best. Right now, all that matters is being here for her."

He closed his eyes briefly, drawing in a shaky breath. "I just want her to be okay."

Julie nodded. "We all do."

After what felt like an endless eternity, the heavy, imposing door at the far end of the sterile waiting area creaked open, shattering the tense silence. A man in a crisp white coat stepped forward, his demeanour calm yet underscored with a serious gravity that set the air on edge. James and Julie sprang to their feet in unison, their hearts thundering in their chests as they braced for news.

The doctor approached with measured steps, offering a small, measured nod that carried a hint of reassurance. "Mr. Calder, Ms. White—I'm Dr. Matthews," he introduced himself, his voice steady and professional.

James swallowed hard, his fingers tightening around the edge of a nearby chair, the cold metal grounding him as he awaited the verdict.

"She's conscious," Dr. Matthews began, his tone deliberate, "which is a remarkable stroke of fortune considering the severity of her fall. We're monitoring her closely, and so far, there are no indications of internal bleeding or fractures—encouraging news indeed."

Julie let out a shaky exhale, relief washing over her features, while James released a breath he hadn't realised he'd been holding, the tension in his shoulders easing momentarily.

"But," the doctor continued, his voice shifting to a more sombre note, "there's a significant issue we need to address. Marissa is currently experiencing retrograde amnesia. It appears she cannot recall events from the past five years."

James's face tightened, disbelief flickering in his wide eyes as the words sank in. "Five years?" he echoed, his voice barely above a whisper, laced with incredulity and growing alarm.

Dr. Matthews nodded solemnly. "Yes. The injury has impacted areas of her brain responsible for consolidating recent memories. We'll continue to monitor her condition closely. It's possible she may recover some of those memories over time, but it's far too early to predict how much she might regain or how long the process could take."

A cold, leaden weight settled deep within James's chest, the initial relief swiftly overtaken by a new, heavier fear that coiled around his heart. Julie squeezed his arm gently, her touch a lifeline as she sought to ground him, while Dr. Matthews continued to outline the next steps with clinical precision. The room fell into an oppressive quiet afterward, the world outside humming with its usual rhythm, oblivious to the seismic shift that had just upended James's reality.

Julie glanced at the doctor, her voice soft yet tinged with urgency. "Can we see her?"

The doctor nodded with a compassionate smile. "Yes, of course. She's resting in the recovery room, just down the hall. Please, follow me."

James exchanged a tense, wordless look with Julie before rising to follow, his legs feeling unsteady beneath him. As they traversed the quiet corridor, the soft hum of hospital machinery and the faint shuffle of footsteps filled the space, but James's mind raced with a torrent of questions. Finally, unable to contain the storm within, he broke the silence. "How do we handle this? Do we tell her everything right away? Or… should we wait until she's stronger?"

Dr. Matthews paused, his expression thoughtful as he considered the delicate situation. "It's a nuanced process. With retrograde amnesia, patients can become overwhelmed if confronted with too much information at once. It's often best to begin with simple, reassuring facts—her identity, her current location, the assurance that she's safe. As she adjusts and stabilises, more details can be introduced gradually, tailored to her emotional and cognitive responses to avoid confusion or distress."

Julie nodded thoughtfully, absorbing the advice. "So, gentle honesty, paced carefully and with sensitivity."

"Precisely," Dr. Matthews confirmed, his tone firm yet kind. "It will require time, an abundance of patience, and unwavering support from those closest to her."

James exhaled slowly, steeling himself against the emotional tide threatening to overwhelm him. "Alright. We'll do whatever it takes—whatever she needs," he vowed, his voice resolute despite the tremor beneath it.

Julie pushed open the recovery room door with a gentle creak, and James stepped inside behind her, his heart pounding with a volatile mix of hope and anxiety. The soft beeping of monitors greeted them, a stark reminder of the fragility of the moment as he prepared to face Marissa, uncertain of what lay ahead but determined to stand by her side.

Marissa lay propped up on the hospital bed, her eyes brightening the moment she saw them. A genuine smile spread across her face, lighting up the sterile room.

"James," she said softly, voice sweet and clear, reaching instinctively for his hand.

James blinked, caught off guard by the warmth in her tone and the natural way she sought his touch. Slowly, he took her hand, feeling a surprising surge of tenderness.

Julie smiled gently, watching the connection between them. "Hey, Marissa. We've missed you."

Marissa squeezed James's hand lightly, her eyes shining. "I'm so glad you're here." Her sweetness and openness felt both comforting and fragile—a delicate bridge between past and uncertain present.

Marissa's eyes searched the room, then settled on James with a flicker of confusion. "Where's Ian?" she asked softly, voice carrying a trace of genuine curiosity and a hint of vulnerability.

Julie exchanged a glance with James before stepping closer. "Ian? He and Shelby just got married yesterday," she explained gently. "They're both so happy. It was a beautiful wedding."

Marissa's expression softened, a wistful smile touching her lips. "They're married?" Her voice dropped to a whisper, as if trying to process the news. "I… I can't believe I don't remember any of it."

James watched her closely, noting the rare vulnerability threading through her words.

Julie reached out, brushing a loose strand of hair from Marissa's face. "It's okay, Marissa. You'll get there. Memories take time to come back, and we're all here to help."

Marissa nodded slowly, eyes shimmering with a fragile mix of hope and uncertainty. "I want to remember. I want to feel like I was really there."

James glanced at Julie, then back to Marissa, voice low but firm. "We should call Ian. He needs to know what happened."

Marissa shook her head gently, a small, careful smile playing on her lips. "No… please, don't disturb him. They just got married. They're on their honeymoon."

She paused, then added with quiet hope, "Besides, I might have my memory back before they even get back." Her tone was soft but confident, as if holding onto that possibility gave her strength.

James studied her for a long moment, weighing every subtle shift of her expression, every flicker in her eyes. Part of him ached to protect her—to pull her close, shield her from anything that could hurt her. But the urgency of the situation pressed down, demanding logic over desire. He swallowed hard, forcing his emotions to stay in check.

Finally, he nodded slowly, the motion deliberate and careful. "Alright. But if you need anything, or if anything changes, we call him immediately. No exceptions." His voice was steady, though the tension beneath it betrayed the depth of his concern.

Marissa reached out, her fingers brushing his before curling around his hand in a brief, light squeeze. "Thank you, James," she said softly, her voice warm, almost intimate in its simplicity.

The weight of that small gesture—the way she trusted him, the subtle gratitude in her eyes—hit him harder than he expected. Her smile, gentle but luminous, made his chest tighten and his heart flip in a way that was entirely unfair. For a moment, he forgot the world around them, the urgency of what had brought them here, and all he could focus on was her—the fragile strength she carried, the spark of mischief that lingered even in the smallest curve of her lips.

He forced himself to look away first, but the memory of that smile lingered, igniting something deep inside him. It was infuriating, distracting… and impossibly alluring.

Chapter Eight

The next morning, Marissa was finally being discharged from the hospital. Her fingers trembled as the nurse helped her ease out of the soft cotton gown, its fabric cool against her skin. The air carried that unmistakable hospital scent—a mix of antiseptic, fresh linen, and something faintly metallic—so clean it almost felt unnatural. Sunlight streamed through the narrow window, making the room look gentler than it had in the night, though the memory of flashing monitors and whispered urgency still clung to her.

Her head throbbed with a steady, muted ache, but beneath it, the doctor's words lingered like a balm: *You're going to be fine.*

Julie was already beside her, a steady presence in the pale room. "Here, let me help you with your coat," Julie said softly, pulling the lightweight jacket off the chair and offering it to Marissa.

Marissa accepted it gratefully, shivering slightly as the cool hospital air brushed her skin. Julie's fingers were gentle as she guided Marissa's arms into the sleeves, smoothing the fabric over her shoulders.

"You're looking better," Julie said with a warm smile. "Just take it slow. James will be here soon he is just parking the car."

Marissa gave a small nod, her voice still quiet. "Thank you… for everything."

"Ready?" Julie asked, smoothing Marissa's hair back from her face.

Marissa took a deep breath, trying to steady the fluttering in her chest. "Yeah. Let's go."

Before they could move, the door opened, and James stepped inside. His dark eyes immediately found hers, sharp and intense. He wore the same serious expression from last night, but there was something softer now—concern, maybe even relief.

He stepped forward, voice low. "You ready to go home?"

Marissa nodded, the words stirring something unexpected inside her. Slowly, deliberately, she reached out and took his hand.

James blinked in surprise, his fingers tightening around hers for a heartbeat before he recovered. The warmth of her touch was undeniable.

For a long moment, neither of them spoke. The silence between them held more weight than any argument or confession ever could.

Finally, Marissa gave a small, almost imperceptible smile. "Lead the way."

James nodded, his jaw relaxing just slightly as he turned toward the door, hand still holding hers—steady, grounding, and utterly unexpected.

James opened the car door and stepped aside, his strong hand steady and sure as he helped Marissa ease into the passenger seat. She settled in, the soft leather cool beneath her fingers. He adjusted the seatbelt carefully, his eyes lingering for a moment on her face.

Julie slipped quietly into the backseat, offering Marissa a warm, reassuring smile. The familiar presence made Marissa feel more grounded, less fragile than she had since the accident.

James slid into the driver's seat, the engine purring softly to life. He turned his head just enough to catch Marissa's gaze, and for the first time that day, a genuine smile curved his lips.

"Ready?" he asked, voice low but steady.

Marissa returned the smile, a spark of something like hope lighting her eyes.

"Ready," she replied.

James shifted the car into gear, and as they pulled away, the road stretched ahead— open, uncertain, but hers to face. And for now, she wasn't alone.

The car ride back was quiet for a while, the hum of the engine filling the space between them. Finally, Julie broke the silence with a gentle nudge.

"We need to let your work know," she said softly.

Marissa blinked, confusion flickering across her face. "Oh… what do I do?"

Julie smiled reassuringly. "You're a kindergarten teacher."

"Oh wow," Marissa said, her voice tinged with surprise and something like delight. "I always liked kids."

James noticed the genuine joy lighting up her face and felt something soften deep inside him.

"We'll drop by and let them know," he said quietly. "It might help with your memory."

As they pulled up to the small school building, the late morning sun cast a warm glow over the brick façade. Marissa's steps were slow but steady as they approached the front office. James held her hand the entire way, something he had to admit he rather liked.

Inside, Julie spoke quietly with the principal, Mr. Henderson. Soon he emerged, his brow creased with genuine concern as he approached Marissa and James.

"Marissa," he said warmly but seriously, "it's good to see you. I understand you're having some difficulties?"

She nodded, frustration shadowing her features. "I don't remember any of it… none of the kids, or the classes."

Mr. Henderson gave a slow, understanding nod. "That's entirely understandable. We'll take it one step at a time. For now, just focus on resting. We'll be here whenever you're ready."

As they turned to leave, a man appeared from down the hall.

"Hey, Marissa!"

James's head came up instantly, his gaze narrowing. The man moved toward them with an easy smile, and before James could speak, Julie stepped in.

"I'll take Marissa to the car—she's had a lot for one day."

James gave a short nod, watching as the two women headed toward the door.

"Hi, Robert Holden," the man said, offering a firm handshake. "I work with Marissa."

"James Calder."

James quickly explained the previous day's events, and Robert's expression softened. "Please look after her. She's one of the kindest people I know."

That drew a flicker of interest from James.

Robert hesitated, then lowered his voice. "She saved my marriage."

James stilled. "How?"

Robert's smile was faint, touched with memory. "My wife and I were barely speaking back then. Marissa noticed. She had a way of making us talk—about little things at first, then the harder things. She looked after our kids, but she was looking after us too. I don't think she even realised the difference she was making."

James said nothing for a moment, weighing those words.

"She notices people," Robert added simply. "And she doesn't give up on them."

James nodded once. "I'll better get her home."

Robert's expression turned serious. "Take good care of her."

"I will."

Robert gave a small nod, then turned away, leaving James with a lingering echo of that conversation.

The car hummed steadily beneath his hands, the road unspooling smooth and quiet in the late morning light. Beside him, Marissa gazed out the window, her fingers loosely intertwined with his on the centre console. Julie was silent in the backseat.

But James's mind wasn't on the drive. *'She saved my marriage. She's one of the kindest people I know.'* The phrases turned over and over, refusing to settle.

He glanced at Marissa's profile—calm, almost pensive. The edges he'd once thought so sharp weren't gone, but Robert's words had sketched in something else alongside them. A different kind of strength.

Robert had spoken about how she noticed people others overlooked, how she stepped in without making a show of it. That didn't erase the banter or the tension between them. But it added a layer James hadn't expected.

He tightened his grip on the wheel. *What did that mean for them?* For the lines they'd drawn.

The estate gates came into view, sunlight dappling the drive. James made a quiet promise to himself: to pay attention. To look beyond the quick smiles and sparring words. To see what was really there.

Before it was too late.

The thought had barely settled when another image shoved forward—sharp and uninvited. The moment she had fallen.

He saw it as clearly as if it had just happened: her body tipping, hair spilling, the jarring thud. For one breathless second, he'd been frozen. Then the panic had hit—raw and immediate—leaving no space for pride or distance.

James wasn't easily shaken, but that moment had cut straight through him.

Now, with sunlight catching in her hair and the faint curve of a smile on her lips, he realised that fear still sat in him, quiet but stubborn.

The driveway curved ahead, shaded, and familiar, but he barely noticed.

It wasn't duty that had made his throat tighten when she didn't open her eyes.

It was her.

Something about the way her wit lived alongside her compassion. The glimpses of vulnerability she guarded like a secret. They'd lodged under his skin and refused to leave.

The car rolled to a stop. James looked at her again—really looked—and for the first time since they'd had their falling out, he didn't see an opponent to outmanoeuvre or a wild card to contain.

He saw someone who mattered.

Cutting the engine, James got out and walked around to her side. She looked up at him as he opened the door, offering the faintest smile—hesitant, but real.

In that moment, his promise solidified into something more than intention.

Because somewhere along the way, Marissa Turner had stopped being just a puzzle.

She'd become someone he wasn't prepared to lose.

Chapter Nine

When they stepped inside, the cool air of the house felt like a relief after the morning sun. Marissa touched her temple lightly. "I still have a bit of a headache," she admitted.

Julie gave her a reassuring smile. "That's to be expected. James, why don't you take Marissa out on the terrace, and I'll bring you both something to eat and drink."

"Thank you, Julie," Marissa said, her voice soft but sincere. She let James rest a hand at her elbow as he guided her through the wide French doors and out onto the sun-washed terrace.

They sat opposite each other at the wrought-iron table, the faint scent of roses drifting in from the garden. For a while, neither spoke. The quiet wasn't uncomfortable—more like each of them was adjusting to being alone together again.

Finally, Marissa broke it, a small smile tugging at her lips. "I still can't believe Ian and Shelby are married. I can see how they'd suit, though."

James's mouth curved in a chuckle. "Shelby didn't think so at first."

Marissa tilted her head, amused. "Oh?"

"She avoided him for nearly two years," James said, leaning back in his chair. "I think she was worried about what you'd think."

"Really?" Marissa's brows lifted, her surprise genuine. "I'm shocked she'd feel that way. They're my two favourite people. Them together..." She shook her head lightly, her smile widening. "I couldn't be happier for them."

James studied her for a moment, the warmth in her voice catching him off guard. It was the kind of unguarded joy he didn't often see in her—the kind that made it harder to keep the lines between them so neatly drawn.

The French doors opened again, and Julie stepped out with a tray. "Here we are—sandwiches, fruit, and some iced tea. Doctor's orders to keep you hydrated," she said with a wink at Marissa.

"Thank you, Julie," Marissa said.

Julie set the tray between them. "I'll leave you two in peace," she added before disappearing back inside.

James poured the tea while Marissa took a small bite of a sandwich, watching him intently. The garden was quiet except for the rustle of leaves and the lazy hum of bees.

After a moment, she leaned back in her chair, her voice casual but edged with curiosity. "So… do you have anyone special in your life, James?"

His hand stilled on the jug. "Special?" he repeated, his tone even, though something flickered in his eyes.

"You know," she said lightly, "someone who worries if you're home late. Someone who gives you that look when you've done something reckless."

He gave a faint huff of amusement, sitting back. "No. No one like that."

Marissa arched a brow. "By choice?"

James's gaze met hers steadily. "Mostly. My life doesn't exactly leave much room for… complications."

"Complications?" she echoed, lips curving. "Is that what you think a relationship is?"

A corner of his mouth lifted. "Sometimes."

Something passed between them—quiet, unspoken, and heavier than either of them acknowledged.

Marissa's smile turned sly, the sparkle in her eyes unmistakable. "So that's why you're single—you're afraid of a little complication?"

James gave a low laugh, shaking his head. "Not afraid. I just prefer… simplicity."

She tilted her head, pretending to ponder. "Simplicity. Like early nights, quiet dinners, no arguments?"

"That doesn't sound terrible," he said dryly.

Marissa took a slow sip of her tea, watching him over the rim of her glass. "It sounds… safe. Predictable. Maybe even a little boring."

One dark brow arched. "And I suppose you're an expert on the alternative?"

"Oh, absolutely," she replied without hesitation. "The alternative is much more fun. Messy, unpredictable… sometimes infuriating. But worth it."

James leaned forward slightly, elbows braced on the table. "Messy and unpredictable is fine in small doses. But eventually, it wears you down."

Her lips curved in challenge. "Or maybe it wakes you up."

For a moment, they simply stared at each other, the air between them taut.

James finally leaned back, breaking the moment with a faint shake of his head. "You have an answer for everything, don't you?"

"Of course," she said lightly. "Even if it's not the one you want to hear."

His mouth curved faintly, but his eyes had taken on a sharper focus, as though he were quietly cataloguing every contradiction she revealed.

Marissa, sensing the subtle shift in his expression, only smiled and reached for another sandwich, as if she hadn't just unsettled him more in five minutes than most people managed in years.

"Do I have anyone special in my life?" she asked again, tilting her head, curiosity bright in her eyes.

His lips pressed into a thin line. "No. Not that I'm aware of."

He hesitated. Part of him wanted to add more—to mention the string of boyfriends she'd once paraded past him, each more different from the last, a pattern he'd judged harshly. Maybe too harshly. But something in her expression stopped him.

Instead, he leaned back, watching her. "Why do you ask?"

She shrugged lightly, though the faint pink in her cheeks betrayed her. "I suppose I'm just... trying to piece together the people in my life."

James studied her in silence for a moment, then shifted the subject. "What's the last thing you remember before... all this?"

Marissa set her glass down slowly, her gaze drifting toward the gardens. "My eighteenth birthday," she said after a pause. "I remember the party, the dress I wore. The music. And then... it's all a bit of a blur after that."

"Nothing else?" he asked quietly.

She shook her head, tucking a strand of hair behind her ear. "There are flashes. Faces I think I know, but I can't place them. Moments that feel important, but they vanish before I can catch hold of them."

James's brows drew together. "And you've told the doctor this?"

"Yes. He said it can happen sometimes—trauma, stress... whatever happened when I fell might have made it worse." She tried to shrug it off, but her eyes betrayed unease. "It's strange, though. I keep thinking if I just push hard enough, I'll remember everything."

He leaned forward, his voice low and steady. "Don't push. Let it come in its own time. Forcing it will only make it harder."

Her gaze flicked back to his. "That's what the doctor said too—just take one day at a time."

He hesitated, then gave a slow shake of his head. "That's probably for the best. It'll come back soon enough."

Marissa studied him, sensing there was more he wasn't saying, but she didn't press. Instead, she gave a faint smile. "I hope so. I'd hate to lose five years of my life permanently. In the meantime, I guess you're stuck with me."

A corner of his mouth curved, though his eyes stayed serious. "I think I can manage that."

She shifted slightly, curiosity brightening her expression. "The business you and Ian started—I remember it was doing well, but... how is it now?"

"Better than we could have hoped," he replied without hesitation.

Her face lit with genuine pleasure. "Oh, that's wonderful."

"You should know," he added, watching her reaction, "you're a very wealthy woman, Marissa."

She blinked. "Really?"

"Yes. You own a third of it—and it's worth billions now."

She had just lifted her glass when the words landed, and the sip went entirely the wrong way. She coughed, setting it down hastily. "Excuse me—billions?"

James's mouth quirked, though his eyes glinted. "Yes. Billions. With a 'b'."

She leaned back, wide-eyed. "That... that doesn't even feel real. I can't imagine having that much money."

"You've had it for a while," he said lightly. "You just didn't notice because you were too busy living your life."

She tilted her head, lips curving faintly. "And what exactly was I doing in this glamorous, wealthy life of mine?"

His gaze held hers a beat too long before sliding away. "That's something you'll remember in your own time."

Her brow furrowed. "You're not going to tell me?"

"Some things," he said carefully, "are better discovered than explained."

She studied him a moment longer before letting it go with a soft huff. "Alright. I suppose I'll just have to trust you."

"Probably wise."

A pause settled between them, filled only by the low hum of bees and the soft rustle of leaves drifting in from the garden.

From the corner of her eye, Marissa studied James, careful not to let him catch her staring. She didn't tell him she also remembered how, years ago, she'd wished—hoped—he would notice her. Back then, she'd been half in love with him. Clearly, he never had.

So why was he here now?

"James… why are you here?" she asked quietly.

He met her gaze without hesitation. "Ian asked me to stay while he's away. Said he'd worry less knowing you weren't alone."

Her lips curved faintly. "Lucky me," she said, the sincerity in her voice surprising even herself.

James smiled back, though he knew she hadn't been thrilled when Ian first suggested it. Still, for reasons he wasn't ready to examine too closely, he found himself glad she was smiling now.

"I think I should have a lie-down," she said, brushing a loose strand of auburn hair from her face.

"Do you want help up the stairs?"

"If you don't mind," she replied. "I still feel a little… wobbly."

He rose with her, his hand steady at her elbow as they crossed the hall. Her steps were slow but sure, her slight weight leaning into him just enough for him to notice.

When they reached her bedroom door, she turned to open it—then paused. Before he could step back, she rose on her toes and kissed him lightly on the cheek.

It was the briefest touch, soft and unexpected, but it jolted through him all the same.

"Thank you, James," she murmured.

For a moment, he could only look at her, the echo of her lips still warm against his skin. He cleared his throat. "You're welcome. Get some rest."

She smiled faintly before slipping inside and closing the door.

James stood there a moment longer, staring at the panel of painted wood as if it might open again. Then, with a quiet exhale, he turned away—though the faint imprint of that kiss lingered long after.

James took the stairs back down slowly, one hand trailing along the banister. The house was quiet, sunlight spilling in through the high windows, but his mind wasn't on the surroundings.

He could still feel it—that light press of her lips against his cheek. Such a small thing, nothing more than a polite *thank you*… yet it had unsettled him more than he cared to admit.

He'd been kissed before. By women far bolder. Women who knew exactly what they wanted from him. But this… this had been different. It wasn't calculated or coy. There'd been no performance in it. Just warmth.

And that, somehow, was far more dangerous.

Chapter Ten

James spent the rest of the afternoon in the study, the familiar space, quiet except for the muted tick of the mantel clock and the occasional rustle of papers. He and Ian had often worked here side by side, and the room still held the faint scent of leather and old books that James found oddly grounding.

A soft knock broke his concentration.

"Come in," he called, looking up from his laptop.

Julie stepped inside, her expression as brisk and capable as ever.

"James, I just checked on Marissa."

He straightened slightly. "Is she okay?"

"Yes, but she said she doesn't want to come down to dinner—feels a little too weak. So, I took up some soup for her." Julie hesitated. "Do you want me to bring some to you as well?"

James leaned back in his chair. "She's probably better off resting. And yes—some soup and bread would be appreciated. Thank you, Julie."

She returned a few minutes later with a tray, setting it on the corner of his desk. The steam curled upward, carrying the scent of herbs and fresh bread.

"Good night, James."

"Night, Julie."

When the door closed again, James sat in the quiet, the soup untouched for a moment. His mind, traitorously, had already wandered upstairs.

James picked up the spoon, but his mind was nowhere near the study. The warmth of the soup did little to chase away the restlessness that had crept in since Julie left.

He pictured Marissa upstairs—propped up against pillows, her hair spilling over the covers, perhaps asleep, perhaps staring out into the night. The image unsettled him more than he wanted to admit. He told himself it was concern, the same concern he'd feel for anyone recovering from a fall. But that didn't explain the way her light kiss on his cheek kept replaying in his head, as vivid as the moment it happened.

It had been nothing—at least, it should have been. Just a gesture of thanks. But James knew better. The press of her lips, the faint scent of her hair, had lingered far longer than it should have. And it had stirred something he had no business feeling.

He set the spoon down and leaned back in his chair, staring at the shadows pooling in the corners of the room. Ian had asked him to stay for her sake, to make sure she was looked after. It was a duty—plain and simple. But somewhere between duty and tonight, the lines had begun to blur.

And James Calder didn't like blurred lines.

With a muttered curse, he pushed the soup away and reached for his laptop again, forcing his mind back to work. But even as he read, the words on the screen refused to stick. Upstairs, a certain auburn-haired woman was resting. And James, no matter how much he fought it, was aware of her every moment.

It was close to midnight when James finally pushed back from the desk. The reports were still untouched in any meaningful way, but he'd stopped pretending to focus on them an hour ago.

He told himself it was just to make sure she was comfortable. That after a fall like hers, it wasn't unreasonable to check in once before turning in for the night. Nothing more.

The hallway was quiet, the only sound the faint creak of the old floorboards under his feet. Her door was closed, but a thin line of light slipped out from beneath it.

He hesitated, then knocked softly.

"Come in," came her voice—soft, but not groggy.

James stepped inside. Marissa was propped against a mound of pillows, the covers drawn up around her. She had a book in her lap, though it didn't look like she'd been reading. Her hair spilled in loose waves over her shoulder, catching the lamplight.

"Couldn't sleep?" he asked.

"Not really," she admitted, setting the book aside. "My head's not too bad now, but I feel... wired, I guess."

He nodded, crossing to the side of the bed. "Any dizziness?"

"A little. But I'm fine, James." Her lips curved faintly. "You didn't have to check on me."

He folded his arms. "I was passing by."

Her eyes warmed with amusement. "You were working in the study. That's not exactly *passing by*."

James's mouth twitched, but he didn't rise to the bait. "I'll take your word for it."

There was a brief silence. The lamp cast a soft glow between them, turning the moment oddly intimate.

"You should try to sleep," he said at last.

"I will." She paused. "Goodnight, James."

He hesitated, then gave a short nod. "Goodnight, Marissa."

He turned to leave, but as his hand touched the doorknob, her voice stopped him.

"James?"

He looked back.

Her expression had softened, stripped of her usual teasing. "Thank you. For staying."

Something in his chest tightened. He gave a small, almost reluctant smile, then slipped out before he could say something he'd regret.

James lay in bed, staring at the ceiling, the moonlight slicing in pale ribbons across the room. Sleep didn't come—not because of the work still waiting in the study, but because of her voice, soft and unguarded, replaying in his head.

'Thank you. For staying.'

It wasn't the words so much as the way she'd said them—like they meant more than just gratitude for company. Like they were a rare truth slipping past her defences.

He shifted onto his side, but that only made his mind drift back to the light brush of her lips on his cheek earlier. It had been nothing, really. A simple *thank you*. But it had shocked him, left an odd imprint that still lingered.

This wasn't like him. Marissa Turner was trouble—always had been. Too beautiful, too reckless, too quick to draw the attention of every man within reach. And yet… Robert Holden's words came back to him, quietly dismantling that image. *'She saved my marriage.'*

What else didn't he know about her?

James exhaled sharply, throwing an arm over his eyes. This wasn't the time to figure her out. Ian had asked him to keep her safe, not… whatever this was turning into.

But as he finally drifted toward sleep, the last image in his mind wasn't of the work he'd neglected, or the responsibilities waiting for him tomorrow.

It was Marissa—her eyes soft, her voice warm—thanking him in a way that felt far too dangerous to ignore.

The early morning sun cast a gentle glow over the estate as Marissa strolled slowly along the gravel path, the cool air clearing some of the fog in her mind. The garden was quiet except for the distant chirping of birds and the soft rustle of leaves in the breeze.

As she rounded a bend near the rose bushes, a figure stepped out from behind a hedge—Fred, one of the gardeners. His face broke into a warm smile the moment he saw her.

"Morning, Miss Marissa. I'm glad to see you out and about. We were all worried."

Marissa returned the smile, her fingers brushing a stray lock of hair behind her ear. "Thank you, Fred. I wish I could say I remember more, but... I can't recall anything after my eighteenth birthday. It's frustrating."

Fred nodded knowingly. "It will come back. Sometimes the mind just needs time."

His mobile phone suddenly rang. "Excuse me," he said, stepping a few paces away.

Marissa watched as his face lit up with excitement. When he finished the call, Fred couldn't contain himself—he walked back over, grinning ear to ear, and without hesitation, scooped Marissa up into a gentle spin, swinging her in a full circle.

"My wife... Heidi... she's pregnant!" he announced, eyes sparkling with pride.

Marissa laughed, warmth spreading through her chest as Fred carefully set her down. "That's wonderful news, Fred! I'm so happy for you both."

Unbeknownst to them, James stood a short distance away, arms crossed and jaw clenched. A frown crept over his face as he misread their easy camaraderie. His mind spun—how had she pulled the wool over his eyes so quickly? *Was she always this charming when she wanted something?*

He stepped forward quietly, closing the gap without being noticed. Then he caught Marissa's voice again, bright, and sincere: "That's wonderful news, Fred! I'm so happy for you both. So, you married Heidi?"

Fred's grin was wide and proud. "I sure did. Couldn't let her get away."

Marissa's smile never faltered. "I'm so happy for you."

James's steps slowed, a flush of shame warming his cheeks. He realised how harshly—and unfairly—he had judged her.

They both turned toward him, surprise flickering across their faces.

Marissa's smile remained steady, unshaken. "I was just congratulating Fred. He and Heidi are expecting."

Fred nodded, eyes bright as he glanced between the two of them. "That's right. And we're both over the moon."

James's expression softened, the tension easing from his shoulders as he took in their genuine happiness.

Marissa caught his gaze and offered a dazzling smile—so pure and radiant it caught him off guard, making his breath hitch unexpectedly.

Then, realising they were watching him, James stepped forward and held out his hand. "Congratulations, Fred. Please tell Heidi I'm happy for you both."

Fred grasped his hand warmly, shaking it firmly. "Thanks, Mr. Calder. I'd better get back to work."

Marissa smiled again, her eyes bright as she turned back to James. Without hesitation, she hooked her arm through his, as naturally as if it had always been that way, and they began to walk.

"Isn't that wonderful?" she said, her voice filled with genuine joy. "I didn't even know they were married. I guess there's a lot I'm going to have to catch up on."

James nodded in agreement, though his thoughts lingered stubbornly on the wrong conclusion he had drawn earlier, refusing to let go so easily.

As they strolled down the garden path, James's mind churned, replaying the scene over and over. The carefree laughter, Fred's excitement, Marissa's genuine happiness—it all should have put his doubts to rest. Yet, a stubborn knot of suspicion tightened in his chest.

How could someone who seemed so vulnerable one moment be so effortlessly charming the next? he wondered. *Had she really been honest with me yesterday? Or was that just another mask, like so many others?*

He glanced at Marissa, her eyes sparkling with warmth, her smile lighting up the morning. She seemed so real, so unguarded. But still, the memory of his earlier mistrust lingered, shadowing his thoughts.

Marissa squeezed his arm gently, sensing the shift. "James, you're quiet. What's on your mind?"

He hesitated, then forced a wry smile. "Nothing. Just… surprised. You've got a way of surprising people."

She laughed softly. "Well, I guess that's one thing that hasn't changed."

He studied her closely. Beneath that teasing exterior lay something deeper—fragile hope, or quiet strength. It was clear there was far more to Marissa than he'd ever realised.

For the first time, James wondered if he was the one who needed to rethink his assumptions.

Finally, she slid the pan into the oven and wiped her hands on her apron. Without missing a beat, she began washing and drying the utensils, her movements calm and methodical. James stood, stretching his shoulders, then moved over to the sink to fill a glass with water.

When he turned back, his eyes caught a small dollop of batter clinging playfully to the tip of Marissa's nose.

He couldn't help the smile that tugged at his lips.

"Hey," he said softly, stepping closer.

Marissa tilted her head, catching his gaze, and reached up to wipe the mix away, but he gently caught her hand, his fingers brushing hers.

Their eyes locked, breaths mingling, the world shrinking until it was just the two of them in the warm, sunlit kitchen.

James leaned in slowly, his heart hammering in his chest.

Marissa moved toward him, as if drawn by an invisible magnet.

But just before their lips could meet, he pulled back gently, his finger brushing the stray dab of batter from her nose. His voice was a soft murmur, barely above a whisper.

"There—that's better."

Marissa's smile flickered, a brief shadow of disappointment crossing her features, but she nodded, understanding.

"Thanks."

He let out a shaky laugh and stepped back, the moment slipping away like a sigh.

Then the oven timer chimed, breaking the spell. Marissa turned to retrieve the cake, and the warmth between them hung in the air, as lingering and sweet as the scent of vanilla.

James picked up his laptop from the kitchen table, clearing his throat. "I need to make a few calls," he said, his voice steady but distant.

He stepped toward the door, but really, he just needed to get away—away from the pull, the heat, the almost-kiss that still hung heavy between them.

He couldn't believe how close he'd come to crossing that line again. Him—James Calder—about to kiss Marissa Turner.

Just another name on her list, another conquest she'd charm and discard. *No way.*

With a last glance back at her, he left the room, determination tightening his jaw. Not this time. Not with her.

Marissa watched him go, a strange flutter twisting in her chest. The moment had hung there—so close, so electric—and then he pulled away. Just like that.

She touched her nose where his finger had brushed off the cake mix, the warmth of his breath still lingering. For a heartbeat, she'd thought—no, hoped—that he would kiss her.

But then he left, retreating like a man trying to hold himself back from crossing a line.

She swallowed the sudden ache of disappointment, forcing a small, understanding smile. Maybe he had his reasons. Maybe this was how it had to be.

Still, the question nagged at her—did he see her as a woman, or just Ian's little sister.

Marissa shook her head softly and turned back toward the oven's gentle warmth. The cake was cooling now, but deep inside, a quiet hope stirred—that one day, he might truly kiss her for real.

Marissa heard the front door close softly, followed by the familiar sound of footsteps padding down the hall. Julie was back from grocery shopping. She glanced up from the kitchen counter where she was arranging the bags.

"Welcome back, Julie," Marissa said, wiping her hands on her apron. The cake sat cooling on the counter, its smooth white icing almost perfect. She felt a small spark of pride. "I think it turned out pretty well."

Julie smiled warmly. "Looks delicious, Marissa. You've got a knack for this."

Marissa moved to help Julie unpack the groceries. They worked side by side in comfortable silence, stacking fresh fruit and vegetables into the pantry and fridge. After the last bag was emptied, Julie bustled about the kitchen, putting the kettle on.

"Tea?" she asked, pouring hot water into two waiting mugs and sliding one across to Marissa.

"Thanks," Marissa said, wrapping her hands around the warm cup.

They sat at the kitchen table, the gentle clink of spoons stirring in the quiet room. After a pause, Marissa's voice broke the stillness, hesitant but sincere.

"Julie… can I ask you something?"

Julie looked up, her eyes warm and patient.

"Why don't I have a boyfriend? I mean… is there something wrong with me?"

Julie blinked, caught off guard by the sudden question, then offered a gentle sigh. "No, Marissa. There's absolutely nothing wrong with you."

Marissa hesitated, searching for the right words, then exhaled slowly. "I guess… after Mum and Dad died, I got scared. Scared of getting close to anyone. Scared of losing them too."

Julie's gaze softened, full of quiet understanding. "That's completely natural. Losing the people we love shakes us to the very core."

Unbeknownst to them, James lingered just beyond the kitchen doorway, the kettle long since silenced. He listened silently, the weight of Marissa's words settling deep in his mind.

Her vulnerability—so rare, so genuine—stirred something unfamiliar inside him, a quiet ache he hadn't expected.

For the first time, he glimpsed the truth behind the bright smile and playful defiance.

Without a sound, he stepped back, giving them their space, but his thoughts churned relentlessly, racing in a way they never had before.

Julie smiled as she stacked the last of the dishes on the drying rack. "I'll be going to my brother's place for dinner tonight," she said casually.

Just then, James walked into the kitchen, catching the tail end of the conversation. He glanced between the two women, a hint of a smile tugging at his lips.

"How about we have a pizza night Marissa?" he suggested, his voice easy.

Marissa's eyes lit up. "Oh, that sounds like a good plan."

Julie grabbed her coat and bag by the door, smiling warmly at Marissa and James. "I'll be back later—enjoy your pizza night!"

James ordered the pizza on his phone and before long, the soft hum of the doorbell echoed through the house.

James got up from the couch and headed to the door. He opened it to reveal the delivery person holding a warm pizza box.

"Thanks," James said, taking the box and closing the door behind him.

He carried the pizza to the kitchen table where Marissa was waiting, the aroma of melted cheese and tomato sauce filling the air.

Marissa's eyes brightened. "This is exactly what I needed."

James grinned, setting the box down. "Perfect way to end the day."

They sat side by side at the kitchen table, the warm glow of the overhead light casting soft shadows around them. The pizza was almost gone—cheese-streaked plates and empty crusts scattered between them.

Marissa leaned back in her chair, patting her stomach. "I couldn't eat another bite," she said with a satisfied sigh.

Just then, a sharp crack of thunder rolled through the sky, sudden and loud. Marissa jumped, her eyes wide and searching the dim kitchen.

James noticed immediately. Without hesitation, he reached out and gently placed his hand over hers on the table.

He didn't say anything, just held her hand steady.

He knew. The storms stirred something deep in her—memories she didn't talk about much. Her parents' helicopter had gone down during a violent storm years ago, and since then, the thunder had been more than just noise; it was a reminder of that loss.

Marissa's breath caught, but she squeezed his hand back, finding comfort in his quiet presence.

After a moment, she gave a small, grateful smile. "Thanks, James. It helps… having you here."

A sudden flash of lightning lit the kitchen in stark white, followed almost instantly by a deafening crack of thunder, louder than before. The lights flickered violently, then went out completely.

Pitch black swallowed the room.

Chapter Twelve

Marissa's breath hitched, her heart pounding fiercely in the sudden darkness. The blackness around them felt like a heavy curtain, swallowing every familiar shape and sound—except the distant roar of the storm.

"It's okay, Marissa," James's calm voice whispered through the shadows. "I'm here."

She tightened her grip on his hand, the steady warmth grounding her trembling nerves amid the chaos of thunder and rain battering the windows. Her fingers curled around his as if holding on could somehow tether her to safety.

"I'm not alone," she murmured to herself, leaning closer, her cheek nearly resting against his arm. The steady rhythm of his breathing was a quiet anchor against the storm's wild crescendo.

Outside, thunder cracked again—closer, louder—and a sharp shiver ran through her. James felt it too, the subtle trembling beneath his arm, the fragile tension in her frame.

"How about we move to the lounge?" he suggested gently, voice soft but steady.

She whispered back, "Okay," her words fragile, like a leaf caught in the wind.

He eased her up, slipping his arm securely around her shoulders. The hallway stretched dark before them, but with James's steady presence, the shadows felt less threatening. His fingers brushed lightly at the small of her back, a silent shield against the unseen.

Once in the lounge, they sank onto the couch side by side. His arm curved protectively around her, a barrier against both the storm outside and the fear stirring within.

Marissa rested her head on his shoulder, her breath shaky but slowly steadying.

"Sorry, James," she whispered, voice trembling with vulnerability. Her body quivered, muscles taut and tense, every crack of thunder making her flinch as if the past was crashing into the present.

James tightened his hold, silently promising to be her anchor—here, now, and whenever she needed.

"Don't apologise, Marissa. I'm here. You're safe with me."

"Thank you." Her voice was fragile and honest, quivering on the edge of tears.

Trying to shift her mind from the storm's growing roar, James asked softly, "Have you remembered anything yet?"

"No, unfortunately," she sighed. "I've tried, but nothing seems to stick."

"It will happen," he assured her gently.

A pause, then she ventured, "There was one thing I remembered… you were with Victoria. Did you break up? I thought it was serious."

James stiffened, a shadow crossing his face. Only Ian truly knew what had happened with Victoria.

"Yes, we broke up. Not long after your eighteenth birthday."

"Oh, I'm sorry."

"It was a long time ago now… best forgotten."

"That bad, huh?"

James hesitated, unsure why he was opening up, but the words slipped out before he could stop them. "She cheated on me."

"Oh, James, that's terrible. I'm so sorry. I can't stand people who aren't loyal."

James looked at her, feeling the weight of her words. She couldn't see him, and he couldn't see her, but her sharp judgment cut deeper than he expected. The irony stung—Marissa was the least loyal person he knew.

Marissa's voice softened, yet her conviction remained steady. "I think cheating on your partner is the worst thing you can do to someone you're supposed to care about."

James blinked, surprise flickering across his face. Then his expression hardened, hesitation and something deeper surfacing. "Really? I'm honestly surprised to hear that from you." His voice lowered, almost uncertain. "You're not exactly the most faithful person I know."

Marissa's eyes narrowed, a sharp edge cutting through her usual warmth, though he couldn't see the hurt flashing there. She pulled back slightly. "What do you mean by that? Why would you say something like that?"

James's chest tightened at the unspoken pain in her tone. His voice caught as he scrambled to explain, shaking with regret. "No—wait, I didn't mean it like that. I'm sorry. It came out wrong."

Marissa pulled free from his arm. He reached to pull her back, but she slipped away— silent resistance. Suddenly, a clap of thunder cracked through the house, and she jumped.

He moved to hold her again, but she resisted. Grateful he couldn't see the tears blurring her vision, she tried to steady her voice, unwilling to betray her anguish. "I think I'll go upstairs."

"Marissa!" His voice was desperate.

"Good night, James." Her words were soft but distant.

Another roar of thunder shook the windows. He heard her sharp intake of breath and the quiet ache in her voice—and something inside him broke.

He listened as she left, the soft sound of her footsteps fading into the quiet house. Then, barely audible, he caught the faint sniff of tears. The ache in his chest grew, and he wanted to follow her, to say something that would make it right—but deep down, he knew she needed space.

Marissa felt her way along the dark hallway toward her bedroom. Even if the lights had been on, she wouldn't have been able to see clearly—her vision blurred and stung with tears. What James said cut deeper than she expected. She had never been unfaithful or disloyal to anyone—unless, somehow, there was something she had done and simply couldn't remember. The thought alone twisted like a knife in her heart, a betrayal she couldn't even explain.

Finally reaching her room, she slipped inside and curled up beneath the doona, pulling it close around her like a shield. The distant rumble of thunder rolled on outside, but she tried to drown it out with quiet sobs, her tears falling freely in the darkness.

James sat frozen on the couch, the echo of Marissa's footsteps lingering in the silence between the bursts of thunder. He stared into the darkness, her last words replaying in his mind, each one heavier than the last. The faint choked sniff he'd heard moments ago gnawed at him. He'd hurt her.

He raked a hand through his hair, frustration, and guilt tangling in his chest. He hadn't meant it the way it came out—God, he hadn't meant to wound her like that. The truth was, he didn't even know why he'd said it. Maybe it was the storm, the intimacy of the moment, the way she'd surprised him with her stance on loyalty. Or maybe… maybe it was the fear that he didn't know her as well as he thought.

But now, instead of talking it out, she was alone upstairs, likely thinking the worst of him.

James stood halfway, thinking about going after her. He could tell her he was wrong, explain that his words were careless and undeserved. But something in the way she'd said *good night, James*—soft, but final—told him she didn't want him to follow.

He sank back onto the couch, elbows on his knees, listening to the rain hammer the roof. Every crash of thunder made him wonder if she was lying there in the dark, still trembling. Still hurting. And knowing he was the reason for it made the storm outside seem almost gentle compared to the one he'd just unleashed inside her.

If he could, he'd take the words back. Every one of them. But now, all he could do was sit there in the darkness, replaying the moment over and over, and hope—pray— that when the morning came, she'd let him try again.

Marissa didn't sleep much.

She lay curled beneath the doona, listening to the storm's fading growl, but her mind refused to rest. James's words had cut deeper than she wanted to admit, and now they echoed in the quiet darkness, gnawing at her. *'Not exactly the most faithful person I know.'*

Was that it? Was that why she didn't have anyone special in her life?

The thought sank like a stone in her stomach. *Had she been disloyal? Had she cheated on someone she cared about?* She didn't even know if she'd been intimate with anyone—her memories offered no answers, only jagged pieces that refused to fit together.

She'd told Julie the truth when she said she was scared to get close to anyone after Mum and Dad died. Scared of being hurt. Scared of losing someone else she loved. But now… a darker thought crept in. *What if I hurt someone before they could hurt me?*

The idea twisted in her chest, making it hard to breathe. God, she wished she could remember. She wished the fog in her mind would lift and show her who she'd been before all this. But it was starting to feel like the memories were holding back on purpose—as if they were waiting for the perfect, most painful moment to return.

And when they did… would she like what she remembered?

Or would she be ashamed?

Later in the morning, Marissa padded into the kitchen, her hair pulled back in a loose knot, eyes still a little puffy from the night before. Julie was already there, standing by the counter with the coffee machine humming, the rich scent filling the air.

"Morning, Julie," Marissa said softly. "How was your visit last night?"

"It was good, thanks, love," Julie replied warmly, glancing over her shoulder. "But how were you with that storm? It was a wild one."

Marissa gave a small shrug, forcing a smile. "It was a bit of a rough night, but I survived." She let out a short, breathy laugh. "I wish I could forget that."

But the laugh didn't quite make it to her eyes, and her voice caught on the last word.

Julie turned fully then, mug in hand, her brows knitting together. "Are you okay, love?"

That was all it took. The tears came fast, blurring Marissa's vision before she could blink them away. "No," she whispered, shaking her head.

Julie didn't hesitate—she set the mug down and crossed the kitchen in two strides, wrapping her arms around Marissa and pulling her close.

"Oh, Marissa," she murmured into her hair, hugging her tightly. "What's bothering you?"

Marissa couldn't answer right away. The sobs hit hard, racking her shoulders, and she buried her face into Julie's shoulder. Between breaths, she kept whispering the same word, over and over.

"Sorry... sorry... sorry..."

Julie stroked her back, her own heart aching at the broken sound of it. "You've got nothing to be sorry for, sweetheart. Not to me."

Marissa clung tighter, as if Julie's embrace was the only solid thing left in a world that felt unsteady and uncertain.

Her voice came out in a shaky whisper between sobs. "Have I... have I turned into a terrible person?"

Julie pulled back just enough to look at her, eyes full of concern. "Of course not. Why would you even think that?"

Before Marissa could answer, the sound of footsteps entered the kitchen. James appeared in the doorway, his gaze immediately catching on the redness in Marissa's eyes.

Marissa stiffened at his presence, her grip on Julie loosening. She swiped quickly at her cheeks, as if she could erase the evidence of her tears.

"I'm just going for a walk," she said, stepping away.

"I'll come with you," James offered, his voice quiet but tentative.

"No, thank you," she replied quickly, too quickly, already moving past him toward the door.

James turned to watch her leave, the air between them thick with something unspoken, while Julie's worried eyes followed Marissa until she was gone.

James stood frozen in the kitchen doorway, the faint scent of perfume clinging to her as she brushed past him. Her quick refusal cut deeper than he wanted to admit—sharp, clean, and final.

He turned slowly toward Julie, who was watching him with that look—half knowing, half protective—that told him she had put the pieces together, at least enough to know he'd said something wrong.

"I didn't mean—" he began, but the words felt hollow even to him. No matter how he turned them over in his mind, they still rang with the same sharp edge. Cruel. Unforgivable.

Julie gave him a long, knowing look over the rim of her mug. "It's about time you two got your act together," she said, her tone matter-of-fact. "It's obvious to everyone but you two that you belong together." She gave a slow shake of her head before returning her attention to her coffee, as if she'd just dropped a truth he could do nothing about.

Her comment pressed in on him, settling heavily in his chest. He dragged a hand down his face, the rough scrape of stubble grounding him in the present but doing nothing to quiet the image burning in his mind—Marissa's hurt.

He'd seen it in the way she'd avoided his eyes, the way her shoulders had gone rigid the instant she heard his voice. That small, almost imperceptible flinch had hit harder than any argument they'd ever had. It told him more than words ever could—that he'd gone too far. And the worst part was, he couldn't shake the memory of it, no matter how badly he wanted to.

He wanted to go after her. To explain. To tell her that he knew—*he knew*—she wasn't the kind of person who would betray someone. But last night had proved one thing: whatever fragile trust they'd been building, he'd just driven a crack straight through it.

And for now, maybe she didn't want him anywhere near her.

Chapter Thirteen

The morning air was damp and cool, heavy with the scent of wet earth after the night's storm. Marissa pulled her cardigan tighter around herself and stepped off the front porch, her boots squelching in the soft ground.

She didn't have a destination—just needed to move, to put distance between herself and the kitchen, between herself and James.

The gravel crunched under her feet in a steady rhythm, but her thoughts were anything but steady. His words from last night echoed over and over, slicing into her like small, deliberate cuts. *'You're not exactly the most faithful person I know.'*

Her chest ached. She wasn't that person. She couldn't be. But then... how would she know?

The more she tried to dig through the fog in her mind, the thicker it seemed to get. No matter how hard she pushed, she couldn't find anything solid—just flashes of feelings, fragments of moments that didn't fit together.

Was that why she didn't have anyone special now? Had she ruined something before it could matter? Had she hurt someone the way she feared being hurt? The thought made her stomach twist.

She walked faster, arms wrapped around herself, wind tugging at her hair. It was easier to focus on the bite of the breeze than on the uncertainty gnawing at her.

Her pace slowed. That was the part that frightened her most—realising that when her memories returned, she might not like the person she found.

The path curved ahead, the trees still dripping from the storm. Marissa stopped and tilted her head back, closing her eyes against the pale morning light. She breathed in deep, but the tightness in her chest didn't ease.

Maybe walking wouldn't fix it. Maybe nothing would—at least not until she could remember who she really was.

She had never been this person before. Not the girl who wandered aimlessly, feeling untethered and sorry for herself. That wasn't her. Or at least... it hadn't been.

The truth was, she wouldn't know the whole story until her memory returned. And when it did—if it revealed something ugly, something she hated—then she would deal with it. She could change. She would change. Because whoever she had been before, whatever she had done, it didn't have to define the woman she could become.

The sky was heavy with low, grey clouds, the kind that promised more rain, but for now the world was still. She noticed how the damp grass clung to her shoes, how the sound of her footsteps seemed too loud in the silence.

A bird cried somewhere in the distance, a single, high note that made her stop mid-step. Her breath caught—why did that sound feel familiar? Not just familiar—important.

She shook her head and kept moving.

Passing the old fence at the edge of the property, her fingers brushed the weathered wood. The texture—splintered, rough beneath her fingertips—sparked a flash of something. A hand, not hers, gripping hers tightly. A voice murmuring close to her ear. She froze, straining to pull the memory into focus… but it slipped away, leaving only a hollow ache in her chest.

Marissa swallowed hard, forcing herself forward. She wouldn't get answers by standing still. But each step seemed heavier than the last, the weight of the unknown pressing in.

She had no idea if she'd like the woman she used to be. But maybe that didn't matter. Because she had the chance to decide who she was now—who she wanted to become.

James stood just inside the doorway, watching as Marissa disappeared down the gravel path. The morning chill had painted her cheeks pink, and the soft way her hair caught the light made his chest tighten.

He wanted to call after her, to tell her she didn't have to carry all this alone. But he knew better than to push. Not yet.

There was a fragile distance between them now—a gap carved out by his careless words last night—and he wasn't sure how long it would take to bridge it.

His gaze lingered on the way she hugged her cardigan tighter around herself, as if trying to hold herself together. The uncertainty in her step, the quiet weight she carried—James felt the ache of helplessness gnawing at him.

He hated seeing her like this—vulnerable, scared, uncertain. The Marissa he knew was strong, fiery, full of life and fierce independence. Not this shadow of a woman, haunted by doubt and fractured memories.

But maybe that was what made her real. Not the flawless image he'd built in his mind, but this raw, fragile version struggling to piece herself back together.

James drew in a slow, steady breath, the damp morning air cool in his lungs. He had once believed he could love Marissa—truly love her. But then she started parading man after man in front of him, as casually as if she didn't care. It reminded him painfully of Victoria—the betrayal, the hollow promises, the sting of being left behind.

Yet last night, when she said, *'I think cheating on your partner is the worst thing you can do to someone you're supposed to care about,'* there was something in her voice—so sure, so convincing. It struck him with an unexpected force.

But how could she say that when, with his own eyes, he had seen her loyalties waver? *When the woman in front of him seemed anything but faithful?*

The contradiction unsettled him, deepening the knot in his chest. He didn't know who this Marissa really was—or who she might become when her memories fully returned.

James found her on the winding path back to the house, the early morning light softening the edges of the damp earth and fallen leaves. She stood still, shoulders tense, eyes fixed on the distant trees.

"Marissa." His voice broke the quiet as he stepped closer. "I need to apologise."

She didn't move. "Don't." Her voice was quiet but firm. "I've made up my mind—not to think about what was, until my memory comes back."

He closed the gap swiftly, taking her hands gently in his. "Please. I didn't mean to upset you."

She sighed, her fingers tightening around his. "It's not just you. I'm just… feeling sorry for myself. Not knowing—it's eating me up."

James searched her face, seeing the worry that clouded her eyes, the crease that had formed between her brows. "It'll all come back soon enough," he said softly.

She looked up at him, her eyes raw and uncertain. "But… will I like what I find?"

He lifted his hand slowly, brushing a stray lock of hair from her face, then let his finger smooth down that crease on her forehead. "The past can't be changed, Marissa. But the future—that's still yours. You can make it whatever you want it to be."

For a long moment, they stood like that—two fragile souls holding on in the quiet dawn.

His hand gently cupped her face, warm and steady. Marissa closed her eyes, leaning into the touch as if it were a lifeline. Slowly, his other hand rose, knuckles brushing softly down her cheek, tender and careful.

"You're very beautiful, Marissa," he murmured, voice low and full of something raw.

"Thank you," she breathed, barely audible.

Then his lips met hers—soft, hesitant at first, like the gentle brush of a feather. The kiss deepened just slightly, a quiet promise rather than a blaze, filled with a sweetness that made her heart flutter and ache all at once.

Her hand lifted, resting lightly on his chest, feeling the steady beat beneath her palm. Time seemed to still around them, the world shrinking to that small, fragile moment of connection.

The kiss deepened, slow and deliberate, as James wrapped his arms securely around Marissa's waist, pulling her closer, their bodies almost melting into one another. The warmth of his embrace pressed into her, steady and reassuring.

Marissa's arms rose, slipping around his neck, fingers tangling in the dark strands of his hair. The tentative softness of their lips gave way to a growing heat, a hunger that sparked between them.

His tongue gently coaxed her mouth open, exploring with careful, teasing strokes. She responded instinctively, matching his rhythm, their breaths mingling as the kiss grew more urgent, more passionate—a tender surrender to the moment they both silently craved.

The kiss deepened, the softness giving way to a fiery intensity that sparked between them. James pulled her closer with a desperate urgency, as if she were the only thing keeping him tethered to the world. His hands gripped her waist firmly, holding her like she was his lifeline—his breath quickened, mingling with hers in a heated dance of need and longing.

Marissa's heart hammered against her ribs, matching the fierce rhythm of his touch. Every inch of space between them vanished as they pressed into each other, the world shrinking until only their shared fire remained.

His hands slid slowly down her back, finally settling to cup her bottom with a firm, possessive grip. He pulled her even closer, their bodies flush against each other. A soft, breathy moan escaped her lips, mingling with the low, guttural groan that rumbled deep in his throat, vibrating against her mouth.

The kiss deepened, raw and urgent. His tongue traced along hers, coaxing and exploring, demanding entrance as their breaths grew ragged and shallow. Every touch burned with an intense heat, their hands roaming freely, hungry to claim and hold. Time seemed to warp, the outside world dissolving until there was nothing but the fierce connection igniting between them.

She could feel the undeniable heat of his arousal pressing against her, sending a rush of warmth flooding through her own body. Desire bloomed fiercely between them, every nerve alive with need. Her breath hitched, and her heart pounded in wild anticipation.

But then, as if jolted awake, he pulled back abruptly, breaking the heated moment. Their eyes met, both of them panting, breaths uneven and hearts racing. The sudden distance left a sharp ache, the tension hanging heavy in the charged air between them.

She looked up at him, her eyes searching his face, still flushed and breathless from the kiss.

He met her gaze, a conflicted shadow crossing his features.

"That shouldn't have happened," he said quietly, voice thick with regret and frustration.

Chapter Fourteen

James stood frozen on the path, watching Marissa's retreating figure dissolve slowly into the pale morning mist. Every fibre of his being ached to close the distance—to reach out, pull her back, and lose himself again in that kiss, over and over. The memory of her lips, the warmth of her breath against his skin, haunted him like a flame he couldn't put out.

But no. He couldn't. Not now. Not like this.

If he chased her, begged for forgiveness, he'd be nothing more than another fleeting name, a temporary mark on her bedpost. A distraction. A game.

So instead, he swallowed the desperate urge and let the silence stretch between them— heavy, suffocating, a weight heavier than any storm he'd ever weathered.

Marissa walked on, her mind a maelstrom of tangled thoughts and raw confusion. She wasn't sure what to think or feel—everything inside her buzzed with a strange, unfamiliar ache. That kiss had been unlike anything she'd ever known. Or at least, unlike anything she could remember.

Every nerve ending ignited, sending shivers that raced down her spine and settled deep in her belly like wildfire. Her lips still tingled where his had pressed against hers—soft, warm, demanding, impossible to forget. It was thrilling and terrifying all at once, stirring a wild, aching hunger she hadn't dared to acknowledge before.

Her breath came faster, her heart pounding in wild rhythms, a fierce cocktail of excitement and fear. It was a first—at least, the first she could recall—a taste of something intimate and powerful, unlocking emotions she'd kept carefully buried.

She stopped mid-step, trembling fingers pressed lightly to her lips as the memory of his touch lingered—electric, insistent, impossible to shake. It was as if a door inside her had creaked open, revealing a part of herself she hadn't known existed, or had long forgotten.

She wasn't sure where this new, aching feeling would lead, but one thing was certain: nothing would ever feel the same again.

When Marissa stepped back into the house, still flushed from the cold air—and from James—the sight waiting for her made everything else blur and fade.

Julie stood by the kitchen bench, tears streaming down her cheeks, her hands trembling as she clutched her phone like a lifeline.

"Julie?" Marissa's voice cracked with alarm as she hurried forward. "What is it?"

Julie's voice broke, brittle with shock. "It's my brother… he's had a heart attack. He's in the hospital."

"Oh, Julie…" Marissa's chest clenched painfully. She reached out, grasping her friend's hands as if anchoring her to reality. "You have to go to him."

Julie shook her head, panic clouding her wide eyes. "But what about you? I can't just—"

Marissa cut her off, voice firm but gentle. "If it were my brother, nothing would keep me away. You need to go, Julie—right now."

Julie hesitated, torn, tears shining fresh.

At that moment, James stepped into the doorway, his gaze sharp as he took in the scene. "What's going on?" he asked, voice low but urgent.

Julie's words wavered. "My brother… he's in the hospital. Heart attack."

Marissa glanced briefly at James, then back to Julie, her expression steady, leaving no room for argument. "We'll handle things here. You just get to him."

Julie blinked rapidly, voice barely above a whisper. "If you're sure?"

"Positive," Marissa said softly, squeezing her hand reassuringly. "Go."

Minutes later, once Marissa had made sure Julie was steady enough to drive, she watched her housekeeper and friend leave, taillights blinking out into the distance.

She lingered in the driveway, the cool air brushing her skin, her body still humming with the aftershocks of what had passed—and from James.

Without even turning, she knew he was there.

His presence pressed against her senses—silent, heavy, unspoken.

The tension between them thrummed in the air, almost physical, electric in the space they shared.

Slowly, she turned.

He watched her, dark eyes unreadable, jaw clenched tight as though holding back a storm of words.

When he didn't speak, she drew a steadying breath, lifted her chin, and started walking toward the house. Each step was deliberate—each one a small rebellion against the turmoil roiling inside.

Then she passed him, head high, as if his silence meant nothing—though he knew it meant everything.

He felt the faintest brush of air as she moved past, carrying her scent, her warmth, something twisting hard inside him.

He wanted to reach for her, to take her hand, to erase the distance he'd built.

But his feet remained planted.

He stood rooted in the driveway, feeling the invisible current running between them—tense, charged, relentless.

When she glanced back briefly, their eyes met, and for a flicker of a moment, he thought she might speak… or that he might.

But the words lodged stubbornly in his throat, tangled between apology and desire.

All he could do was watch her vanish inside, knowing he was the one who'd made that space between them.

Swearing under his breath, he finally moved—long, desperate strides eating up the space she'd just crossed.

The door was still swinging shut when he caught it, stepping inside.

She was halfway down the hall, her back straight, auburn hair catching the pale light from the windows.

"Marissa," he called, voice low but firm.

She didn't stop, didn't even glance back.

Two strides closed the distance; his hand caught her wrist.

She froze.

For a heartbeat, the only sound was the soft hum of the refrigerator and the faint patter of rain beginning to fall outside.

"I'm not letting it end like this," he said quietly, his voice rough but steady.

She turned slowly, eyes locking with his. There was fire there—yes—but beneath it, something raw: hurt, confusion, maybe even a silent plea she refused to voice.

"End what, James?" Her voice was calm, but he heard the strain buried deep beneath it.

He stepped closer, still holding her wrist, his grip gentle now.

"This distance. This wall you keep building between us. I can't stand it."

Her chin lifted, defiance flashing in her eyes.

"You're the one who built it."

That cut deep. His jaw tightened.

"Maybe I did. But I'm not walking away without knowing where we stand."

She shook her head, disbelief, and pain flickering in her gaze.

"Where we stand? You kissed me like you couldn't breathe without me, then pulled away like I burned you. Which is it?"

He didn't answer with words.

Instead, he stepped forward, backing her gently against the wall.

His hands came up, bracing on either side of her—an unyielding cage.

"I don't know what this is, Marissa," he said, voice rough, raw, "but I know I want you. More than I should."

Her breath caught, and in that suspended moment, neither moved.

The air pulsed electric between them.

He knew if he leaned in even an inch, he'd lose himself completely.

His hands stayed braced, head bowed as if sheer willpower could hold him back.

"Don't," he whispered—maybe to her, maybe to himself.

Then she looked up—blue eyes wide, lips parted.

His resolve shattered.

With a low, rough curse, he closed the distance and crushed his mouth to hers.

This kiss wasn't tentative.

It was fierce, claiming, a wave of heat that drowned out every reason to stop.

Her gasp opened the floodgates.

His tongue swept past her lips in a slow, deliberate stroke, drawing a helpless moan from deep inside her.

He pressed closer, one hand tangled in her hair, the other sliding down her back to pull her flush against him.

She melted into him, arms wrapping around his neck, holding him like she couldn't bear to let go.

The kiss deepened—hot, unrestrained, urgent.

His fingers splayed over her hip, urging her closer still, until no space remained between them.

Every nerve in his body sparked alive, muscles straining toward her.

The world outside ceased to exist.

Her body was warm and soft, fitting against his like she'd always belonged.

He could feel her heartbeat racing, matching his own.

The taste of her—sweet, intoxicating—dragged him deeper.

His hands slid over her curves, one cupping the back of her thigh to pull her closer, the other resting on the small of her back.

She whimpered softly against his mouth, and the sound tore a low groan from his throat.

He was drowning in her—her scent, her touch, the way her fingers tangled in his hair.

The heat spiralled upward, burning away every thought but one: *more.*

Then reality slammed back.

With a sharp inhale, he tore his mouth from hers, both panting, foreheads nearly touching.

"This—" His voice was ragged, unsteady. "This shouldn't have happened."

Marissa ripped herself away, breath ragged, chest heaving.

"You arrogant, infuriating man," she spat, voice sharp with fury.

"You can't just take what you want and then decide it was a mistake two seconds later. Do you have any idea how that feels? Or is hurting me just a game to you?"

Her hands shook—part rage, part something she refused to name.

But she refused to let the tears fall.

"Stay the hell away from me, James."

She spun on her heel and stormed upstairs, leaving him standing in the silent house— breathless, undone, and utterly lost.

He stood frozen for a heartbeat, watching her silhouette vanish down the hall and up the stairs, every instinct screaming at him to let her go. But he couldn't. He knew she did this—used every man she met as a game, a distraction—and he was just another notch on her reckless path. Yet the ache inside him wouldn't ease; he couldn't stop wanting her.

He moved before he even realised it, closing the distance with desperate speed.

By the time she reached her bedroom door and pushed it open, he was already there. In one swift, fluid motion, he caught her wrist, spun her around, and pressed her hard against him.

"James—" Her protest died in her throat as his mouth crashed down on hers—fierce, demanding, all-consuming. His kiss swallowed her words whole, silencing her resistance.

His arms tightened around her, as if he could hold her still, keep her from slipping away again.

She fought back with equal fire, her kiss wild and passionate, the tension between them igniting into something fierce and dangerous.

Then he tore his mouth away, lips trailing down to her neck, his breath warm against her skin. He murmured, rough and raw, "I want you, Marissa. Tell me to stop."

Chapter Fifteen

Marissa's breath hitched, her voice trembling with a fierce mix of longing and defiance.

"I don't want you to stop."

The words barely left her lips before James groaned low in his throat—a raw, desperate sound that mirrored the hunger blazing in his eyes. Without hesitation, he crushed his mouth to hers again—deep, fierce, and all-consuming—pouring every ounce of need and restraint into that single, searing kiss.

She kissed him back with a fire that rivalled his own, her lips urgent and demanding, pressing fiercely against his as if trying to merge their very breaths. Her hands tangled in his hair, pulling him closer, while her body curved instinctively to his, moulding against him with heated intensity. The kiss sparked electricity through their veins—raw, breathless, every touch igniting a fierce, desperate hunger that left them trembling on the edge of surrender.

Her hands moved with restless urgency, sliding to the hem of his shirt and tugging it free from his pants, fingers trembling as they pulled. He caught the motion, yanking the shirt sharply over his head, revealing skin flushed with heat and longing. Without missing a beat, he gathered her back into his arms, holding her tightly as if to keep her from slipping away. Her hands pressed boldly against his bare chest, fingers splaying wide, feeling the rapid beat of his heart beneath her touch—a silent promise pulsing between them.

He groaned deep in his throat at the feather-light brush of her hands against his skin, the sound raw and filled with hunger. His lips traced a fiery path down the delicate curve of her neck, each kiss a searing brand that made her breath catch and her skin flush. She threw her head back, exposing more of herself, her pulse pounding beneath his touch.

"James, please," she breathed, voice trembling with need and desperation.

Her cardigan was first to go then his hands slid with deliberate slowness to the zipper of her dress, fingers brushing her skin as they traced the seam. With measured, tantalising motion, he began pulling the zipper down—each inch unveiling more of her, heightening the electric tension between them as the world around them faded to nothing but the heat and ache they shared.

The dress slipped slowly from her shoulders, cascading down her arms like liquid silk, leaving her skin exposed to the cool air and his burning gaze. As the fabric pooled at her feet, he pressed a lingering kiss to the bare curve of her shoulder, lips warm and feather-soft against her skin.

She shivered beneath his touch, breath catching in her throat.

His hands moved with reverent hunger, sliding over the smooth expanse of her back before coming to rest on her bare breasts. Fingers gentle but sure, he cupped her, feeling the softness and delicious hardness beneath his palms. He tweaked her nipples with teasing precision, eliciting a sharp intake of breath—a mixture of surprise and pleasure that sent a ripple of heat spiralling through them both.

The room seemed to hold its breath around them, every touch and gasp weaving them tighter into this charged, intoxicating moment.

He pulled back just enough to look into her eyes, his gaze dark and intense, filled with raw, aching need. His breath hitched as he whispered, "You're so beautiful. God, Marissa… tell me you want me."

Her hands moved boldly over his bare chest, fingertips tracing the hard planes beneath her touch, mapping the heat radiating from him. Slowly, deliberately, they slid down lower, reaching the button of his pants. With trembling urgency, she began undoing it, the subtle movements charged with promise.

Her eyes never left his as she breathed, voice husky and filled with desire, "I want you."

The simple confession hung between them like a spark ready to ignite a wildfire, electrifying the space they shared.

Her fingers trembled with fierce, deliberate urgency as she undid the button of his pants, the metal cool beneath her touch. She slid the zipper down slowly, savouring the tension building between them with every small movement. Then, with a bold push, she pushed his pants down, letting them fall away in a soft rustle to pool at his feet.

His underwear clung tightly, offering no disguise for the hard, undeniable evidence of his desire. Without hesitation, her hand slipped down, wrapping firmly yet tenderly around him through the thin fabric.

A breathless gasp escaped her lips— "God, Marissa."—a whispered prayer and an exclamation all at once, the raw heat of the moment settling deep between them like fire.

He backed her up slowly, every movement charged with intent, until the soft edge of her bed pressed against the back of her legs. The world seemed to narrow, the air thick with anticipation and desire.

Then, without breaking eye contact, he dropped to his knees before her, his hands gentle yet purposeful as they found the delicate lace waistband of her panties. Slowly, reverently, he slid them down her long, smooth legs, the soft fabric whispering against her skin as it slipped away.

His gaze flickered with hunger as he leaned in, mouth descending to cover the exposed skin, lips trailing a scorching path of kisses—soft, searing, utterly consuming. Every touch, every breath spoke a promise of what was to come, drawing her deeper into the electric heat between them.

He reached down, fingers brushing softly against her ankle as he slipped her shoes off one by one, his touch light and deliberate, as if savouring every moment. The bare skin of her feet against his hands sent a shiver up her spine.

With slow, purposeful confidence, he lifted one of her long legs, hooking it gently over his shoulder. His eyes met hers—dark, intense, and unwavering—before he lowered his head.

His lips found her most intimate place with reverence and fire, pressing delicate, heated kisses against her womanhood. The sensation was electric—tender yet charged with raw desire—as he worshiped her with every breath, every flick of his tongue, drawing a gasp from deep within her.

Time seemed to melt away as he explored her, each movement weaving them closer in an intimate dance of need and surrender.

He traced slow, tantalising circles with the tip of his tongue, each delicate flick sending waves of fire rippling through her. His movements were both skilled and patient, building a rhythm that teased endlessly, never rushing but never letting up. Every touch, every gentle suck, was a silent promise—an unspoken vow to unravel her completely.

Her breath hitched, chest rising and falling erratically as the sensations spiralled higher, igniting every nerve ending. The world narrowed to the heated press of his mouth, the slick glide of his tongue, and the mounting ache pulsing through her.

Then, with a crescendo that shattered all restraint, she arched into him, voice trembling as it broke free in a fierce, raw scream—his name escaping her lips like a prayer, a plea, a surrender.

"James!"

He stayed with her, his tongue and lips never faltering, until the trembling waves that shook her body slowly ebbed, dissolving into soft, shuddering sighs. Gently, almost reluctantly, he unhooked her leg from his shoulder, letting it fall back down but keeping her close, his hands steadying her with tender firmness.

Then, rising to his feet, he captured her mouth once more in a kiss that burned hotter, deeper, every stroke of his lips heavy with mounting passion. She tasted herself on his tongue—sweet, intoxicating—and the electric connection sparked anew.

His breath ghosted over her lips as he murmured, voice low and raw with desire, "Marissa… I want you now."

The words hung between them like a challenge and a promise, igniting the space around them with undeniable urgency.

With fierce need burning in his eyes, he lifted her effortlessly into his arms, her body fitting perfectly against his. The heat of her skin against his sent a jolt through him as he lifted her onto the bed. Gently, he laid her down, his hands lingering on her curves as he took in the sight of her—vulnerable, radiant, utterly captivating.

Without hesitation, he shed his underwear, freeing himself, and slid beside her. Pulling her close, he wrapped his arms around her, holding her as if he never wanted to let go. His voice thick with need, he whispered against her lips, "I can't wait. I need you."

His mouth found hers again, fierce and demanding, pouring every ounce of longing into the kiss. Slowly, he pressed her back onto the soft mattress, his hands steady but tender as he eased her down. He settled himself between her thighs, the warmth of their bodies melding as the world outside ceased to exist—leaving only the heat of their desire and the electric promise of what was to come.

He positioned himself carefully at her slick, trembling entrance, feeling the warmth and welcome beneath him. Their eyes locked in a moment charged with anticipation and vulnerability. Then, leaning down, he captured her lips in a tender, searing kiss—an unspoken promise to be gentle—as he entered her in one smooth, fluid thrust.

Her cry of pain shattered the charged silence, sharp and raw, echoing through the room. He froze immediately, heart pounding as he looked down at her, eyes wide with shock and concern.

"Marissa?" His voice was barely more than a whisper, thick with worry. He searched her face desperately, desperate to know she was alright, guilt and fear crashing through him like a tidal wave.

His eyes widened in disbelief, searching hers as the realisation settled like a sudden storm between them. His voice came low, almost breathless, tinged with a mix of surprise, awe, and something deeper—something tender.

"You're... a virgin?"

The question hung in the air between them—fragile, weighty, almost sacred—as if voicing it aloud had drawn a line in the shifting landscape of their emotions. The room seemed to hold its breath, silence thick with unspoken truths and raw vulnerability. His heart hammered in his chest, each beat echoing the gravity of the moment. He searched her eyes, desperate for a sign, knowing whatever she said next would change everything between them forever.

Marissa met his gaze steadily, a flicker of something undefinable in her blue eyes. Her voice was quiet but unwavering, carrying a mix of honesty and guarded strength.

"I must have been."

Those four words settled between them like a fragile bridge—both a confession and a challenge—opening a new chapter in their tangled story, where desire, trust, and fear collided in the space they now shared.

Chapter Sixteen

"God, Marissa. You should have told me," he growled, the sharp edge in his voice betraying a swirl of anger and frustration.

She flinched at the intensity, her feelings crashing forward like a tidal wave. "How could I? I didn't even know," she shot back, her voice trembling with a mix of hurt and defiance.

He ran a hand through his hair, muttering, "Bloody hell." The frustration softened just a fraction, but the tension still crackled between them like electricity.

"If it's such a problem, then get off me," she snapped, the sharpness matching the trembling in her heart as she pushed him away. But he didn't budge. His presence remained steady—an unyielding anchor amid the storm of her emotions.

"Marissa," he murmured softly, cupping her face with a gentle, reassuring touch. His lips brushed hers in a slow, tender kiss—soothing and delicate, a sharp contrast to the fierce fire they'd shared moments before.

"It's just a shock. That's all. I swear, I would have been more careful if I'd known."

She shifted beneath him, pressing closer, her body responding instinctively to the raw need in his voice. A low groan escaped him, thick with pleasure and longing.

"God, Marissa…" he breathed, desire spilling over as the intensity deepened.

He couldn't hold still any longer. Every fibre of his being screamed for release and connection. Slowly, he pulled back just enough to tease the exquisite tension between them, giving her a moment to catch her breath. Then, with a deep, guttural growl, he thrust forward again—steady and sure.

Marissa's eyes flew open, a soft moan slipping past her lips as sensation rolled through her—raw and overwhelming. He repeated the motion, each thrust measured and deliberate, pushing deeper with a relentless hunger.

Again and again, he moved—unwavering and patient—until the sharp edges of her tension melted away, her body relaxing, softening beneath him. The initial pain gave way to growing warmth, a shared rhythm pulling them closer into fragile harmony.

As she began to move with him, matching his rhythm tentatively at first, he felt the subtle shift—her body melting into his, opening, responding. Encouraged, he picked up the pace, each thrust more urgent, more insistent.

Her soft moans and breathy whimpers spilled from her lips like fragile music, fuelling the fire between them. His hands gripped her hips, steadying her as she leaned into the growing wave of pleasure. Their bodies moved in an intimate dance of give and take.

He drove deeper, faster, coaxing every sigh, every shudder—until the tension coiled tight within her finally broke free. With a gasp that echoed raw and beautiful, she shattered, trembling beneath him as waves of release crashed through her, binding them in a moment of fierce, breathtaking connection.

He couldn't hold back any longer. The mounting pressure inside reached a tipping point demanding release. His thrusts, once steady and controlled, grew erratic and desperate, driven by fierce hunger consuming every thought.

Muscles tightening, breath hitching, he plunged deeper with frantic urgency, the world narrowing to the raw sensation between them. Then, with a shudder rippling through his entire body, he stiffened, overwhelmed by the crescendo of pleasure building within.

A deep, guttural groan tore from his throat—a raw, primal sound thick with release, need, and the weight of all he'd held back. It was surrender to the fierce, all-consuming fire blazing between them from the first touch—the inevitable breaking point where desire overwhelmed restraint.

For a long moment, he remained locked to her, every nerve alight, every breath heavy and ragged. Then, slowly, he pulled back just enough to meet her eyes—searching, vulnerable, awash with emotions neither could fully name.

His lips brushed hers again, softer this time—a tender seal on the intensity they'd shared. Reluctantly, as if leaving her would tear at him, he shifted away and settled beside her.

He drew her close, wrapping an arm securely around her trembling form. With the gentlest kiss, he pressed his lips to the top of her head—a quiet, unspoken promise that he wasn't going anywhere.

In that tender embrace, the storm between them softened, replaced by fragile calm whispering of something more—something deeper than hunger or passion—something waiting to grow.

And then, as the heat slowly ebbed, a cold wave of realisation crashed over him. *What the hell had he done?* All these years, he'd misjudged her—written her off as a flirt, a reckless game to be won or lost. Hell, he'd even called her a hussy, convinced she was nothing but trouble wrapped in temptation.

But now, holding her like this—vulnerable, real, utterly unlike the woman he thought he knew—he felt the weight of his mistakes settle heavy on his chest. How blind he'd been. How wrong.

She had been a virgin.

The truth slammed into him like a punch to the gut, knocking the air from his lungs. It wasn't just surprising—it was shattering. Every smug assumption, every offhand insult, every time he'd seen only the teasing glint in her eyes or the curve of her smile... all wrong.

The image he'd built crumbled in an instant, leaving only raw, unvarnished truth. With it came something far more unsettling—a gnawing guilt twisting deep inside. He'd taken something from her today, something he never imagined she still had to give, and wasn't sure if she'd ever understand how much that realisation shook him.

It wasn't just desire burning in his chest now—it was regret, protectiveness, and a fierce, unfamiliar need to make things right.

How was he going to face her when she remembered everything? When the haze faded and her memories came back—when she realised not just what they'd done, but their history—how would she look at him then?

The thought hollowed him out. All this—every charged glance, every sharp word, every reckless step today—had begun with his own careless cruelty. An offhand comment tossed out in anger after Victoria's betrayal. He'd been so wrapped up in wounded pride he hadn't considered the damage he might inflict.

And then, just last night, he'd as good as accused her of being untrustworthy, implying she wasn't loyal—cutting her with words he couldn't take back. The memory burned, shame curling in his gut.

Now, lying here with her soft against him, the weight was almost unbearable. She had trusted him—completely—and he had no idea how to make up for the things he'd said and thought before he knew the truth.

He looked down at her peaceful face, breathing soft and even. For a moment, he just watched—the faint rise and fall of her chest, a stray lock of auburn hair curved across her cheek. So unguarded, untouched by the turmoil in his head.

He needed to think—needed space to sort the mess of guilt, desire, disbelief clawing at him.

Slowly, carefully, he eased himself from her arms, every movement cautious, unwilling to disturb the fragile peace of her sleep. Her warmth clung to his skin, seared into him, a living reminder of what they had just shared.

As he reached for his discarded clothes, his gaze faltered—catching on the undeniable evidence of her innocence staining him. The sight punched the air from his lungs. Guilt coiled through him, sharp and relentless, settling like lead in his chest.

He dressed quickly, almost mechanically, each motion deliberate, the soft whisper of fabric far too loud in the stillness of the room. When he finally allowed himself one last look, she was sleeping soundly, her face serene, lips faintly parted as though still remembering his kiss.

Something inside him twisted.

Then he slipped from the room, closing the door with painstaking care—because no matter how quietly it clicked shut, silence could not contain what they had just undone.

Marissa woke slowly, the lingering haze of sleep slipping away as the afternoon sun streamed golden light through the window. The sheets were warm where he had been, and the faint scent of him still clung to the pillow beside her.

But he was gone.

A sudden hollow settled deep in her chest as she blinked against the brightness. The silence pressed in, thick and unfamiliar, the empty space where James had lain seeming to grow heavier with each passing second. She didn't know what his absence meant— if he had left because of her, because of what had happened, or something far worse.

Memories flickered through her mind like shards of glass—sharp, confusing, laced with questions she wasn't ready to face. The weight of it all tightened her stomach in knots.

She sat up slowly, pushing tangled hair from her face, and listened. The house was quiet—too quiet. James was nowhere to be seen.

Determined to find answers she didn't know how to ask, Marissa slipped out of bed, dressed and made her way outside.

There, leaning against the weathered railing of the terrace, stood James. His dark hair caught the late afternoon light, but there was nothing warm in his expression. Instead, his gaze was fixed beyond the horizon—empty and distant.

Her heart thudded painfully as she hesitated in the doorway. "James," she said softly.

He turned just enough to acknowledge her, then looked away again. No smile, no teasing remark—just stillness.

She stepped closer, every step heavy with the weight of what hung between them. "You left," she said, voice tinged with accusation she hadn't meant to put there.

His jaw clenched. "I needed some air."

The terse reply hit her like a slap. She searched his face, desperate to read the truth behind those dark eyes, but he gave nothing. That silence—the careful distance—was more painful than any words.

Her chest tightened, the sting of hurt prickling at her skin. "Right. Air." A humourless laugh escaped her lips as she glanced away, refusing to let him see the tremble in her voice. "I suppose that's a polite way of saying you regret it."

His head snapped toward her, sharp and sudden, but he said nothing. And that—more than any denial—confirmed the fear she carried.

Swallowing hard, she forced herself to meet his eyes. "It's fine, James. You don't have to say it. I get it."

Turning away, her pulse thundered in her ears. Each step back into the house felt heavier than the last, dragging her further from him and from the fragile hope she hadn't dared to speak.

Behind her, his silence lingered—thick and suffocating.

James watched her retreating figure, each step a cruel blow. He wanted to call her back—beg her to stay—but the words caught in his throat, strangled by the storm raging inside him.

She thought he regretted it. God, if only it were that simple.

Regret wasn't the word. He wanted her still—with a hunger that hadn't dulled since he left her—but underneath that desire was something deeper: the crushing truth he couldn't escape.

He'd been wrong about her.

Completely. Unforgivably.

All these years, he'd judged her, labelled her, shoved her into a corner she'd never belonged in. This afternoon had shattered every assumption, ripped them all to pieces.

His knuckles whitened as he gripped the railing, trying to steady the chaos inside.

How the hell was he supposed to look her in the eye when she remembered everything? When the memories came flooding back and she saw exactly what he'd thought—what he'd said?

The temptation to run after her nearly broke him, but the thought of her seeing the turmoil inside—the doubt, guilt, raw need—stopped him cold.

Not yet.

Not when he didn't know how to untangle the mess himself.

So, he stayed there, silent, watching her disappear inside, feeling with every heartbeat like he was letting the one person who mattered most slip further away.

Hours passed, dragging with an unbearable weight.

He hadn't seen her again until the evening, when he finally walked into the kitchen and found her there.

She stiffened instantly, though she didn't turn to face him.

The distance between them felt like a canyon, though only a few feet separated their bodies.

He wanted to close it—wanted to pull her into his arms, beg forgiveness, explain that everything between them had changed for him.

But how could he? How could he ask for her trust when she hadn't yet remembered the way he'd treated her before? When she had no idea how wrong he'd been?

She turned, intending to leave without a word.

Instinct overrode hesitation.

His hand shot out, fingers curling gently but firmly around her arm.

"Marissa."

She froze but didn't look at him.

When she finally met his gaze, he felt the sting of her pain like a physical blow.

"I know how this goes, James," she said, voice breaking despite her fight to stay steady. "When men get what they want, they walk away. I get it."

Her words cut deeper than she knew.

"Marissa, no—" He tightened his grip just enough to keep her from stepping away, voice low and rough. "That's not... that's not what this is."

She gave a short, bitter laugh. "Really? Because it feels exactly like that."

He dragged in a breath, jaw clenched tight.

He wanted to tell her everything—how wrong he'd been, how the truth about her innocence had shattered him, how the last thing he wanted was to lose her now.

But the words tangled with shame he couldn't shake.

Without another word, she wrenched free and walked away—each step carrying her farther from him and from the fragile hope he was too afraid to voice.

Chapter Seventeen

Marissa hadn't eaten all day—not because she was busy or distracted, but because the thought of food churned uneasily in her stomach, knotting into something she couldn't ignore. It wasn't hunger she felt—it was heavier, raw, and aching deep in her chest.

Lovesick.

That was the only way to describe the hollow ache gnawing at her, the bittersweet longing that left her fragile and off balance. Every memory, every stolen moment replayed behind her eyes, pressing so heavily she couldn't bring herself to do the simplest thing—eat.

Her stomach clenched as she pushed away the untouched plate she'd made earlier. She tried to focus on anything else—the hum of the house, the softness of the sheets—but the emptiness wouldn't be filled. It was as if her whole body refused nourishment while her heart still ached, torn between desire and regret.

She sat quietly, hands folded in her lap, the faint salt of tears lingering on her lips. She wondered if this pain would ever soften—or if it was meant to linger like a shadow, a reminder of everything that had shifted between them.

A deep longing twisted inside her—a desperate wish for clarity. She wished her memory would fully return, to unlock the pieces hidden just beyond reach. There was something vital buried beneath the fog.

The way James had looked at her kept surfacing—the raw intensity in his eyes, more than desire, something that unsettled her to the bone. That look was etched in her heart, and she was convinced it held the key to everything she'd forgotten.

She lay down, covers pulled close, hoping sleep might soothe her restless mind. But the minutes dragged, sleep staying stubbornly out of reach. Her thoughts tangled in the quiet darkness, turning stillness into a slow, simmering ache.

Sleep finally came in the small hours, creeping in softly like a whispered promise. It wrapped around her like a tide, pulling her down from the edge of wakefulness, until at last she slipped away—deep, heavy, and dreamless—until the first light touched the sky.

Marissa's eyes snapped open, heart pounding as fragmented images rushed in—sharp, raw, unbearably clear. The dream had torn through the haze like a knife.

She lay still, breath uneven, but the memories came anyway. The biting words. The cold glances. The way he'd dismissed her—called her a flirt, a hussy—like she was nothing.

She remembered the sharp edge in his voice, the cruel smirks, the countless moments she'd tried to reach him only to be pushed away. How often she'd convinced herself she was overreacting, that she'd misunderstood.

But there was no mistaking the truth now.

Each insult reopened wounds she thought were healing. She saw the real James—the man who had judged her without knowing her, who had assumed she was reckless and unworthy.

Tears stung her eyes, blurring the room into a haze. *How could she have ever believed in him?*

Worse—how had she let herself fall for him?

But she had. She'd fallen for him long ago, long before last night, long before she'd been willing to admit it to herself.

With a shaky breath, she swung her legs over the side of the bed, swiping at the dampness on her cheeks. The memories were hers now—every word, every look, every touch. And with them came something she hadn't had before.

The choice.

The power to decide what came next—and whether he would ever have the chance to hurt her again.

James was in the kitchen when Marissa entered. Her eyes were dry now, her heartbreak carefully hidden beneath a quiet resolve. He turned toward her, immediately noticing the difference—something steely, something final.

"Marissa?" His voice was cautious.

She held her ground. "I understand now, James."

Confusion flickered. "What do you understand?"

"That it must have been a shock," she said, tone sharp but steady, "to find out I was a virgin all along—when you thought I was some unfaithful flirt or hussy."

The blood drained from his face. "Marissa—"

She raised a hand. "Stop. I'm not interested in what you have to say."

She turned to leave.

"Marissa, please," James called, grabbing her hand before she could go.

She stopped, looking down at their joined hands. The touch that once comforted now felt like a chain.

"Take your hand off me. Now."

He dropped it instantly, as though burned. Silence thickened between them.

"Please, Marissa, let me explain," he said, voice raw.

"Explain what? That you thought you could take me to bed and then walk away. Just another *'boyfriend of the week'*?"

Her words hit hard—the same insult he'd thrown at her, now returned with razor-edge precision.

"Ian asked you to stay to look after me," she said bitterly. "I don't think he had this in mind."

"Marissa, please. I care about you. I wouldn't have made love to you if I didn't."

She laughed—a harsh, hollow sound. "Really? You cared so much you bolted straight after. Didn't speak to me all day because you needed *'air'*. Well, you can have all the air you want—away from me."

"Please, Marissa," he whispered, knowing he had no defence.

"Stay out of my way, James. You might have to be here until Ian gets back, but I don't have to talk to you."

She walked away—straight to her room—where the tears came again.

James stood frozen, watching her disappear down the hallway. His instincts screamed to follow, to make her understand. But the truth was, he didn't know if he deserved that chance.

The sharp click of her door closing echoed down the hall, sealing her away. Silence pressed in until it felt like the air was gone.

He dragged a hand over his face, a low curse escaping. Yesterday, he'd wanted her with a hunger he couldn't deny—wanted her so much he'd finally admitted the truth: he was in love with Marissa Turner. Had been for years, though he'd buried it under disapproval and wrong assumptions.

Now she hated him. And maybe she had every right.

For the first time in years, James Calder wasn't sure there was a way back.

The house was quiet, but James couldn't sleep. Every time he closed his eyes, he saw her face—the disbelief, the hurt, the finality.

Now he sat in the dim lounge, elbows on his knees, a glass of whisky in his hand. The amber glow barely registered; his mind was elsewhere, replaying the last twenty-four hours.

It had never been just desire. It had been her all along. He'd told himself otherwise because the truth scared him. Yesterday had stripped away every excuse.

Now she knew exactly what he'd thought of her—and exactly how fast he'd run.

Leaning back, he stared at the ceiling, thinking only of how badly he'd hurt her. Somewhere upstairs, she was probably crying again because of him.

He wasn't ready to give up. Not yet.

Past midnight, he set the whisky aside and walked upstairs until he stood outside her door. Light spilled faintly from beneath it. He lifted a hand to knock—then froze.

What could he even say?

That he'd been wrong?

That she terrified him because she mattered too much?

His hand hovered, then fell. For a moment, he listened—half-hoping she'd come to the door. But the house stayed still.

With a frustrated curse, he turned away and shut himself in his own room, feeling the chance to fix things slipping through his fingers.

Marissa lay curled on her side, staring at the wall. Sleep wouldn't come; every time she closed her eyes, she saw him.

She was drifting when she heard it—a creak in the floorboards outside her door.

Her heart leapt. She knew that step.

For a few seconds, she held her breath. She could almost picture him there, hand raised, debating whether to knock.

The ache sharpened. If she opened the door now, she might let him in. And then she'd crumble.

No.

She stayed still, even when she heard the faint scrape of his hand dropping away, even when his footsteps retreated.

When silence returned, she realised her cheeks were wet. She wiped at them impatiently and turned into the pillow.

If James Calder wanted to fix this, he was going to have to do more than hover outside her door.

The next morning, Julie was back. Marissa stepped into the kitchen and broke into a smile.

"Julie, you're back! How's your brother?"

She leaned in and kissed Julie's cheek.

"He's on the mend," Julie said with a relieved smile. "Luckily, it was only a mild one, but he's going to have to change his lifestyle."

Her gaze swept over Marissa's outfit. "You look nice. Going somewhere?"

"Yes," Marissa said, reaching for her bag. "I'm going back to work."

Julie frowned. "But—"

"My memory came back yesterday."

Just then, James walked in, his eyes immediately locking onto Marissa.

"Morning," he said carefully, like testing the waters.

Marissa barely looked at him. "Morning," she murmured—polite but distant.

Julie smiled warmly. "Morning, James."

"I hope this means your brother's feeling better," James said.

"Yes, thanks, James. He was lucky—thank goodness," Julie replied.

Marissa slung her bag strap over her shoulder and headed for the door. "Have a nice day. I'll grab something on the way."

"Marissa…" James called after her, but she didn't break stride, didn't even glance back.

Julie raised an eyebrow as the door closed behind Marissa. "What was that about?"

James exhaled sharply and rubbed the back of his neck, grimacing. "I messed up, Julie… badly."

Julie's expression softened. "Oh dear."

She watched the door close, then turned her full attention to James, concern knitting her brow.

"You don't have to tell me if you don't want to," she said softly, reaching out as if to comfort him. "But I can tell something's wrong. What happened?"

James looked away, jaw tight, searching for the words. After a long pause, he sighed and met her eyes with raw honesty.

"I… hurt her, Julie. Not just today, but for years. I was harsh, distant—too quick to judge. I pushed her away when I should have pulled her close."

Julie's eyes softened. "You care about her, don't you?"

He nodded, the weight of regret heavy on his shoulders. "More than I ever admitted. And now… I'm not sure she'll forgive me."

Julie gave his arm a reassuring squeeze. "Sometimes the hardest thing is showing you want to make things right. But if anyone can, it's you. Just don't give up before you try."

James swallowed hard, the fight to make it right just beginning.

Julie squeezed his arm again. "I know Marissa's been protecting herself from how she feels about you for years."

James frowned, searching her face. "What do you mean?"

She looked at him steadily. "Surely you noticed how she pretended you didn't matter. She hid behind those so-called boyfriends—using them like shields to keep you at a distance."

"I didn't know she felt anything for me," James admitted quietly, the vulnerability surprising even himself.

Julie nodded knowingly. "Of course she did. But she tried so hard to hide it. Just like you did. You watched her like a hawk every time she was near, didn't you? Every glance, every little reaction—deep down, you both knew there was something there, even if neither of you wanted to admit it."

James ran a hand through his hair, feeling the weight of years of denial pressing down. "Maybe that's the cruellest part—that we were both guarding ourselves, too scared to take the risk."

Julie smiled gently. "Exactly. But now you have a chance to stop running from it. To be honest—with yourself, and with her."

Chapter Eighteen

James sat in Ian's study, the late afternoon light slanting through the tall windows, turning the dust motes into slow-drifting sparks. The laptop sat open in front of him, a spreadsheet half-finished, numbers blurring into nothing he could make sense of. He'd been trying to work for over an hour, but every time he typed more than a sentence, his mind betrayed him—slipping away to the image of Marissa.

Where was she now? Still at work, probably. He pictured her walking through the school corridors, that long auburn hair pulled back, her eyes focused but bright. He wondered if she was tired. If she'd eaten lunch. If she was still angry.

His fingers tapped restlessly against the desk. The truth was, he wasn't waiting for her to come home so he could make small talk—he needed to speak to her. Really speak to her. Not with the clipped, defensive words they'd been trading for years, but with the kind of honesty he'd been avoiding for ever.

The clock on the wall ticked far too loudly. He glanced at the doorway every few minutes, listening for the sound of her car in the drive, the click of her heels on the hallway tiles. His pulse was already picking up at the thought of her walking in. But when she did… would she even give him the chance to say what he needed to say?

The sound of a car pulling into the driveway made James's pulse quicken. He stood abruptly from Ian's desk and moved toward the door, anxiety knotting his stomach.

Marissa stepped inside, her posture cautious, eyes tired but alert. She had clearly fought back tears, but the weariness lingered in her expression.

"Marissa," James said softly, his voice steady though his heart pounded. "Can we talk? Please. Just for a few minutes."

She hesitated, then slowly nodded, her voice barely above a whisper. "Alright. But just for a few minutes."

James felt a flicker of hope as he gestured toward the living room. "Thank you. That's all I ask."

They moved inside, the air between them charged but no longer impenetrable. Marissa settled on the sofa, her posture guarded, while James remained standing for a moment, as if afraid sitting would weaken his resolve. The silence stretched—heavy, but with a sliver of possibility now threading through it.

Drawing in a slow, steadying breath, James met her gaze. "I know I'm the one who started all this—the back-and-forth between us. That terrible thing I said at the club… calling you a hussy—it wasn't just cruel. It was the worst mistake I've ever made."

His throat worked as he swallowed, the memory cutting deeper than he wanted to admit. "That night… I wasn't myself. I'd just walked into my apartment and found Victoria with my friend. They didn't even notice me standing there. I was stunned, furious, humiliated. And instead of dealing with it, I lashed out—at you. I dumped all my hurt and anger on you, and that was wrong. You didn't deserve any of it."

His voice softened, the raw edge of vulnerability breaking through. "I pushed you away because I was scared—scared of how much I cared, scared of how much power you had over me without even knowing it. But none of that excuses how I treated you."

Finally, he stepped forward, closing some of the distance between them. "I don't expect you to forgive me right away. But you deserve to know the truth. I care about you— more than I've ever admitted. More than I even wanted to admit to myself."

Marissa's eyes locked on his, her gaze flickering with a painful mix of hurt and something softer, a whisper of hope that hadn't quite died.

He took another step toward her. "Can we start over? Not pretending the past never happened, but with honesty—really being real with each other for once?"

She looked up at him, her voice steady but laced with old wounds. "James, what Victoria did to you was terrible… but I didn't deserve to be attacked for another woman's mistakes."

"I know," he said quietly, the words heavy with sincerity.

Her brow furrowed slightly. "We've been at odds for nearly five years. Why now? What's changed?"

He let out a breath, almost a laugh but without humour. "Honestly? I think it's because, for the first time in years, you were not trying to get under my skin. You were not playing the game. I saw… the you from before I put my big foot in it. And it hit me— hard—what I've been pushing away all this time."

Something unreadable passed through her eyes, and though she didn't speak right away, she didn't look away either. The door between them wasn't open wide yet… but it wasn't closed anymore.

Marissa stayed quiet for a long moment, her fingers twisting together in her lap. He could almost hear the thoughts racing through her mind, the battle between old wounds and something more dangerous—hope.

Finally, she spoke. "You hurt me, James. More than I think you realise. That night…
it stuck with me. Every time you looked at me with disapproval after that, it just
confirmed what I thought you believed about me." Her voice wavered, but she steadied
it quickly. "It made it easier to pretend you didn't matter."

His chest tightened, but he didn't speak, didn't dare interrupt.

"But you did matter." Her eyes lifted to his, clear and unflinching. "You still do. And
that's what makes this harder."

He took another step, close enough now that he could see the faint sheen of unshed
tears in her eyes. "Marissa—"

"I'm not ready to forgive you," she said, cutting him off gently. "And I'm not saying
we can just wipe the slate clean. But…" She hesitated, as if the words cost her
something. "…I'll hear you out. No games. No posturing. If you want to be honest,
then be honest. I'll decide what to do with it."

James felt something loosen in his chest—relief, fragile but real. He nodded slowly.
"That's all I could ask for."

Her lips curved in the faintest ghost of a smile. "Good. Because it's all you're getting…
for now."

James let out a slow breath, relief mingling with something warmer, deeper. He
extended his hand to her, palm open, an unspoken request hanging in the air.

She hesitated—just a fraction of a second—but it was enough for him to feel the weight
of her choice. Then her fingers slipped into his, tentative but sure. He curled his hand
around hers, the contact sending a jolt through him, and drew her gently to her feet.

For a heartbeat they just stood there, close enough that he could see the tiny flecks of
silver in her blue eyes. Then, with a carefulness that felt foreign to him, he eased her
into his arms. It wasn't the fierce, claiming embrace he'd imagined a hundred times—
it was gentler, almost reverent, as if he was afraid she might vanish if he held on too
tightly.

She tilted her face up to him, searching, questioning. He didn't speak; words felt too
clumsy for this moment. Instead, he lowered his head and brushed his lips over hers—
soft, tentative, a question rather than a demand.

She didn't pull away. Her breath caught, her lashes fluttered, and for one fragile
moment, it felt as if the years of bitterness and missteps between them might dissolve
into nothing but this—two people standing in the quiet, daring to hope.

Marissa's breath trembled as his lips lingered against hers. It would have been so easy—
too easy—to melt into him, to forget the years of hurt and mistrust. For a fleeting

second, she let herself feel it—the warmth of him, the steady thud of his heart under her palm, the safety she hated to admit she found in his arms.

But just as quickly, the old wounds pushed through. The echo of his cruel words that night, the sting of every barb since, the years spent building armour just to keep him out.

Her fingers tightened against his shirt, not to pull him closer, but to steady herself as she eased back just enough to break the kiss. She kept her gaze on his chest, afraid that if she looked into his eyes, she might see everything she'd sworn not to want again.

"Don't think one kiss fixes this," she said, her voice softer than she intended, betraying more than she liked.

James didn't argue. He just nodded, as if he understood the fragile balance she was trying to hold on to. Still, his hand stayed at the small of her back, warm and steady, as though he wasn't ready to let go completely—and maybe, just maybe, she wasn't either.

Dinner was an exercise in polite fiction. Julie had outdone herself, serving roast lamb with rosemary potatoes and a pear-and-feta salad. Conversation stayed firmly in neutral territory—the weather, the company's latest contract, a local festival coming up.

Marissa passed James the salt without their fingers brushing, but her eyes darted away a fraction too fast. He asked her about work in a tone so casual it was almost studied, and she replied with equal coolness. They might have fooled anyone else, but not Julie. She saw the way James's gaze lingered a beat too long when Marissa laughed at something he said. She caught the way Marissa's hand hesitated over her wineglass when James's deep voice rolled across the table.

Julie said nothing, but she didn't miss a thing.

When the plates were cleared, Marissa helped Julie in the kitchen. James excused himself for a business call, his phone already pressed to his ear as he stepped into the hallway.

Julie handed Marissa a stack of plates to dry, her tone light. "So… you two are doing that thing again."

Marissa blinked. "What thing?"

"That thing where you pretend you can't stand each other, but your eyes keep giving you away." Julie arched a brow. "You've been doing it for years."

Marissa gave a small, incredulous laugh. "You've been imagining things."

Julie slid her a knowing look. "Am I? You know, parading a different man in front of James every few weeks might have been fun for a while, but it wasn't just for fun, was it?"

Marissa stilled, the tea towel in her hands motionless. "Excuse me?"

Julie's voice softened, though her gaze stayed steady. "You were protecting yourself. Making sure he never forgot you had other options. Making sure he couldn't hurt you again."

Marissa opened her mouth to argue, but the words stuck. She hated how accurate that sounded.

Julie shrugged lightly, turning back to the dishwasher. "All I'm saying is—if you're going to keep protecting yourself, fine. Just make sure you're not also shutting out the thing you actually want."

Marissa didn't answer, but later, when she lay in bed staring at the ceiling, those words would echo louder than she wanted to admit.

Chapter Nineteen

It was Saturday morning, and Marissa dressed on autopilot, her mind tangled in the restless thoughts that had stolen her sleep. Julie's words echoed relentlessly: 'If you're going to keep protecting yourself, fine. Just make sure you're not shutting out the thing you actually want.'

The truth of it struck harder than she expected. Julie was right—deep down, she knew she had to stop running from her own feelings. She needed to make a choice, to decide what she really wanted before the chance slipped away. And if she was truly honest with herself—she wanted James.

She didn't regret sleeping with James—not for a second. It had been… different. Special. The kind of intimacy that went beyond physical. But wanting him in her personal life was a much bigger question. Could she let go of the years of snide remarks, sharp edges, and stubborn pride that had defined them for so long? Could she trust that what they'd shared wasn't just a lapse in old defences?

James would always be part of her world. The business with Ian was partly hers— avoiding him forever wasn't an option. But letting him all the way in? That was dangerous, in a way she wasn't sure she could handle.

Her stomach tightened as she walked to the kitchen, the rich scent of coffee drifting through the hall. Julie and James were already at the table, mugs in hand, heads bent together in quiet conversation. Julie laughed softly at something he'd said, and for a fleeting second, Marissa felt as if she had stepped into someone else's morning.

"Morning," she said lightly.

Both looked up.

"Morning, love," Julie replied warmly. "Did you sleep well?"

"Yes, thanks," Marissa lied smoothly, sliding into a chair. In truth, she hadn't slept much at all—her mind had been too busy replaying every moment with James from the past week.

"Morning, Marissa," James said, polite yet intense, his gaze holding hers a moment too long. There was something searching in his eyes, as if he were trying to read her thoughts before she'd even had her coffee.

She reached for the toast rack, breaking the charged silence. "Big day ahead?" she asked, buttering a slice deliberately.

"For me? Always," he said, a crooked smile tugging at the corner of his mouth. He didn't look away—didn't even blink—until she finally did.

The quiet that followed carried weight—neither awkward nor casual—but each glance, each small movement hummed with the memory of the night they'd shared. She took a slow bite of toast, as if chewing could keep her from saying something she'd regret.

Julie pushed her chair back, brushing crumbs from the table. "Right, I'd better get the laundry started before it piles up on me," she said, collecting her coffee cup and moving toward the sink. A quick rinse, a faint hum, and she disappeared toward the laundry room, leaving the scent of toast and coffee behind her.

The moment she was gone, the air shifted—quieter, sharper, like the room itself noticed the absence of a buffer.

James leaned back in his chair, one arm draped along the backrest, though his gaze was anything but lazy. "You look tired," he said softly.

Marissa arched an eyebrow. "Thanks. That's exactly what a girl wants to hear first thing in the morning."

His lips twitched. "I didn't mean it like that. Just… noticed."

She wrapped her hands around her coffee mug, seeking warmth. "Maybe I've just had a lot on my mind lately."

One corner of his mouth lifted—not quite a smile, more a quiet recognition. "Anything I'd know about?"

Her eyes met his, lingering longer than she intended. "Possibly."

A faint flicker of warmth passed between them—unspoken, yet undeniable.

James hesitated, then asked carefully, "Would you like to spend the day together? Maybe get out of the house for a bit."

Marissa blinked, surprised but intrigued. "What did you have in mind?"

He shrugged, a soft grin tugging at his lips. "We could walk by the lake, grab some lunch somewhere quiet. No pressure—just fresh air and good company."

Marissa hesitated, then a small, genuine smile tugged at her lips. "That sounds… nice. I'd like that."

James's eyes brightened, hope shining through. "Great. We'll leave around eleven?"

"Eleven it is," she said, feeling a flutter, she hadn't expected. For the first time in a long while, the weight pressing on her chest seemed lighter—like maybe, she was ready to stop protecting herself for a while.

He stood, brushing a stray lock of hair behind her ear, a gentle, almost tentative gesture. "I'll plan something simple. Maybe a relaxing walk, then lunch at that little café you like—the one with the garden patio."

Marissa nodded. "I remember. Their lemon tarts are worth the trip alone."

He chuckled softly. "I'll make sure we get one each. And maybe we can just… talk. No games, no defences."

She glanced down at her coffee, then back up. "I'd like that too."

For a moment, the years of hurt and distance felt like a distant shadow, pushed back by the promise of something new, fragile but real.

The morning slipped away as James and Marissa drove toward the lake, the city's noise fading behind them and replaced by the soft rustle of leaves and the distant call of birds. The air was crisp, fresh with a hint of spring, full of possibility.

They walked side by side along the winding path, the crunch of gravel underfoot punctuating the quiet. James stole glances at Marissa now and then—the way her hair caught the sunlight, the small, thoughtful expressions that flickered across her face. She was quieter than usual, but softer too, a subtle openness he hadn't seen in years.

At a small wooden bench overlooking the water, James stopped. "Sit with me?" he asked gently.

Marissa hesitated, then lowered herself beside him. The space between them felt charged, but not uncomfortable.

They watched as a pair of swans glided across the glassy surface of the lake. The moment stretched, peaceful and fragile, the world reduced to soft ripples and quiet breaths.

"I want to know what you've been thinking," James said finally. "Really."

Marissa took a deep breath, twisting the edge of her jacket. "Julie said something last night that's been hard to shake… about protecting myself by shutting out what I actually want."

He nodded, his gaze steady. "It's not easy, is it? Letting go of those shields."

"No," she admitted quietly. "But maybe… maybe it's time."

James turned toward her, hope flickering in his eyes. "Maybe it is."

Marissa noticed how he listened, truly listened, and it made her feel seen in a way she hadn't allowed herself in years. She caught herself laughing lightly at one of his dry, sarcastic remarks, unguarded and free.

By the time they reached the lakeside café, the sun had climbed higher, spilling warm golden light across the garden patio. The air was rich with the scent of blossoms and freshly brewed coffee, the soft murmur of conversation and clinking cups forming a comforting backdrop. Over lemon tarts and steaming mugs, the invisible gap between them shrank imperceptibly. Each shared smile, each fleeting brush of hands, narrowed the distance that had defined them for years.

Marissa found herself leaning in without thinking, drawn to him like a quiet gravity. She caught his gaze more than once, lingering a second too long, sending a shiver down her spine. The space between them hummed with unspoken possibilities.

By the time they stood to leave, the sun had begun its slow descent, painting the lake in soft pinks and golds. The warmth of the day lingered, but so did the thrill of something fragile and undeniable taking root between them.

James offered his arm. "Same time tomorrow?"

Marissa smiled, this time without hesitation. "Yes."

The drive home was quiet at first, the hum of the engine and occasional birdcall filling the spaces between them. Marissa's hand brushed his on the console as she reached for her seatbelt, and neither pulled away. It was a subtle spark, a reminder that the day had been about more than tarts and coffee—it had been about them, threading their way back into each other's orbit.

"You have been quiet," James said softly, eyes on the road. "Thinking?"

Marissa glanced at him, a small smile tilting the corners of her mouth. "Always. About… a lot of things."

He nodded, understanding more than she said. "Me too," he murmured.

For a while, they drove in companionable silence, each moment heavy with the unspoken. Marissa noticed his hand hovering near hers, the warmth of his presence pressing against the space she'd tried so hard to guard. Every subtle glance, every deliberate motion, carried meaning she wasn't ready to voice.

When they arrived, James moved with familiar patience, opening her door. The air between them was charged, electric, as he gently gathered her in his arms. She didn't resist, leaning into him, letting the moment anchor them both.

Their lips met softly at first, tentative, testing whether this closeness could survive the past—fights, misunderstandings, half-truths. Marissa felt his hands steady her, warm and certain, as if guiding her through the maze of her own hesitation. Every brush of lips, every whispered breath, drew her closer, dissolving the walls she had built around her heart.

James deepened the kiss, savouring her response, the subtle shiver that ran through her, the tremor in her hands pressed against his chest. "Marissa…" he murmured, voice low, rough with years of restrained longing. "I've been waiting for this—waiting for you. Waiting for us. I don't want to wait any longer."

She tilted her head, breathing in the scent of him, the certainty of his embrace. Her fingers traced his jawline, pressing gently into the small of his back. It was a fragile surrender, but enough. "James…" she whispered, the sound barely more than a breath, carrying longing, fear, and hope.

He held her a heartbeat longer, feeling her pulse against his. "I'm not letting you go," he promised quietly. "Not now. Not ever."

Marissa closed her eyes, letting herself feel it fully—the warmth, the desire, the quiet certainty that they were exactly where they belonged. When she opened them again, she found him gazing down at her, unwavering, the devotion in his dark eyes undeniable.

It wasn't just a kiss anymore; it was a beginning, fragile but real. For the first time in years, Marissa allowed herself to believe that maybe—they could find their way forward together.

Chapter Twenty

The rest of the afternoon passed in a quieter rhythm. James disappeared into the study, his voice a low murmur now and then as he took calls and tapped at his laptop.

Marissa stayed in the kitchen with Julie, helping chop vegetables for dinner and letting the conversation drift from light gossip to household chatter. Every now and then, her thoughts wandered down the hall to where James was, wondering if he was replaying their kiss as much as she was.

By the time they all sat down at the table that evening, the atmosphere felt noticeably lighter. Conversation flowed easily—Julie recounting a funny story about the local grocer, James adding a wry comment that made Marissa laugh without even meaning to.

When the plates were cleared, James set his napkin beside his plate and stood. "Excuse me," he said, glancing toward the hall. "I've just had an email—there's a problem with the Pilbara site. I need to look into it before it escalates."

Julie nodded knowingly. "Go on then. I'll see if I can keep this one from stealing all the dessert while you're gone," she teased with a wink.

James's gaze lingered on Marissa for a moment—something unreadable in his expression—before he turned and headed back to the study.

Sunday morning arrived with the soft patter of rain against the windows, turning the garden into a blur of silver and green. Over breakfast, James glanced at Marissa with a faint, almost boyish smile.

"The weather's supposed to clear by mid-morning," he said. "Want to take a drive into the hills? There's a lookout I think you'll like."

She hesitated just long enough to make it look like she was considering. "All right," she said lightly. "But only if we stop for coffee on the way back."

His smile deepened, warm and certain. "That can be arranged."

By the time they wound into the high country, the clouds had thinned to wisps, revealing stretches of bright blue. The air smelled of damp earth and eucalyptus, and the lookout offered endless rolling green hills, broken by patches of sunlight. James leaned against the railing beside her, their shoulders brushing.

Their conversation flowed naturally, and the silences between them no longer carried avoidance, but comfort.

Later, on the drive back, they stopped at a small café tucked into a bend in the road. The scent of freshly roasted coffee wrapped around them as they stepped inside. They found a table by the window, sunlight spilling across the worn timber surface. James sat opposite her, teasing her about her overly sweet coffee order. She rolled her eyes, but her smile lingered.

The bell over the door jingled, and Marissa glanced up—then froze.

Greg.

Tall, broad-shouldered, wearing that easy grin she remembered all too well. He didn't notice her at first, heading straight to the counter to order a takeaway coffee. He'd been hinting at dinner for months, but she had always been with someone.

As he turned to leave, his gaze caught hers.

"Marissa," he said warmly, striding over. "Didn't expect to see you here."

James's hand stilled around his coffee cup, his expression unreadable.

Greg's eyes flicked briefly to him, then back to her. "I heard you're not with Mark anymore," he said lightly, though the implication was heavy. "That true?"

Marissa met his gaze without flinching. "It is."

Greg's smile sharpened. "Well then, how about we catch up sometime? Dinner, maybe?"

It would have been so easy to fall into her old habit—flashing a coy look, letting James see just enough to rile him. But the impulse didn't even stir.

"Thanks, Greg," she said evenly, "but no."

His smile faltered. "No?"

She shook her head, voice calm but firm. "I'm not available at the moment."

Greg's eyes cut to James, then back to her. "Oh… right. Well, if it doesn't work out, you know where to find me."

"Thanks, Greg," she said, polite but final.

With a nod to James that felt more like a test than courtesy, Greg left, the bell above the door giving a short, sharp jingle.

James's gaze lingered on the closed door before returning to her, a glint of curiosity and heat lighting his eyes.

"At the moment?" he asked quietly.

She met his gaze over the rim of her cup, the warmth of the coffee doing nothing to calm the flutter in her chest.

"Yes," she said softly, deliberately.

His brows lifted slightly, weighing the meaning behind her words. "And how long do you think… this *'moment'* might last?"

"That," she replied, setting her cup down, "depends."

"On?" His voice lowered, coaxing but edged with something that made her pulse jump.

Her lips curved faintly, though her eyes remained guarded. "On whether I decide it's worth the risk."

The corner of his mouth pulled into a slow, dangerous smile—the kind that suggested he already knew her answer. "I hope I get the chance to prove that it is."

Her fingers tightened around her cup, the awareness between them impossible to ignore.

"I'm sure you would," she said, standing before the moment swallowed her whole. "We should get going before the rain comes back."

He rose without argument, but the glint in his eyes as he reached for her coat told her this conversation wasn't over—not by a long shot.

By the time they stepped back into the cool, eucalyptus-scented air, the space between them felt charged, alive with all the things neither had dared voice. The road wound ahead, wet in shaded bends, but Marissa was far more aware of the man beside her than the scenery.

James drove with one hand on the wheel, the other resting loosely on the console—close enough that she could feel the warmth radiating from him. It was an easy, unhurried silence, but not the kind born of indifference. Every breath, every glance, seemed threaded with an awareness neither of them wanted to name.

She caught him looking at her once—just a brief flick of his eyes when he thought she wouldn't notice—but it was enough to send a flutter through her stomach.

"You didn't have to turn Greg down," he said after a while, his tone deliberately casual.

"I know," she replied, watching the countryside blur past.

"Yet you did."

She glanced at him, meeting his gaze for a beat before looking away again. "Maybe I'm tired of saying yes to the wrong people."

His lips curved, but he didn't push. Instead, he slowed as they reached the main road, the hum of the engine filling the space between them.

The sky had shifted again, the clouds thickening, shadows stretching longer across the bitumen. By the time they pulled into the drive, the wind had picked up, tossing her hair as soon as she stepped out of the car.

James came around to her side, his hand brushing lightly against her arm as he closed the door. It was a small touch, barely there, but her skin tingled from it all the way inside.

When they crossed the threshold, he didn't follow her straight in. He paused by the door, watching her slip off her coat. "Marissa—"

She turned, pulse skipping, but he only gave a faint smile. "Thanks for today."

And then he was gone, striding toward the study, leaving her standing there with the distinct feeling that they'd both been standing on the edge of something—and neither had taken the step.

Marissa found Julie in the kitchen, pulling a tray of fresh scones from the oven. The warm, buttery scent filled the room, instantly chasing away the last of the cool air from outside.

"You two were gone a while," Julie said lightly, glancing over to catch the faint flush lingering on Marissa's cheeks. "Scones will be ready in five minutes. I'll take a plate to James—he's in the study again."

Marissa busied herself with pouring tea. "It was a nice drive. That's all."

Julie hummed knowingly and disappeared, leaving Marissa to replay the morning's events in silence, heart still racing.

Down the hall, James's low voice drifted from the study, sharp with concentration. "When?"

Marissa's curiosity tugged at her, but before she could move, Julie returned with an empty plate. "Work," she mouthed, slipping past her.

Moments later, James emerged, phone in hand. Ending the call, he slipped it into his pocket.

"Everything all right?" Marissa asked.

"Not exactly," he admitted, raking a hand through his hair. "Our Pilbara site—server outages, security concerns. I need to go in person."

Her stomach sank, though she told herself it was silly. "When?"

"Tomorrow morning. Shouldn't be more than a week, but the hours will be long." His gaze softened. "I'll call or text. Every day if I can."

She managed a small nod. "Right. Well… I hope it's sorted quickly."

"I'll try," he promised quietly. The space between them felt charged, like there was more he wanted to say—but couldn't, not yet.

The next morning dawned clear but cool, the faint tang of eucalyptus drifting through the open front door. James's duffel bag rested on the hall table, zipper half-open, files peeking out beside neatly folded clothes.

Marissa stood in the doorway with her coffee, forcing herself not to watch him too closely as he double-checked his laptop bag. It was only a week, she told herself, yet the ache in her chest was real. Habit, nothing more.

Julie bustled in with a travel mug. "Strong coffee for the road," she said, pressing it into James's hand.

"Thanks, Julie." He glanced toward Marissa. "You sure you'll be all right while I'm gone?"

She shrugged lightly. "I'll manage. I've been looking after myself a long time."

His mouth curved in a small smile, but his eyes stayed serious. "Yeah… I know." He hesitated, like he wanted to say more, but zipped the duffel closed instead.

Outside, the car engine hummed, the driver loading his bags into the boot. James stepped forward, closing the small distance between them. "I'll call tonight," he said quietly.

She nodded, her gaze locking with his for a fraction longer than she meant to. "Safe trip."

For a moment, neither of them moved. The air between them was thick, heavy with all the words they'd never spoken, the tension that had built and twisted between them for years.

Then James closed the distance in a single step, his hand sliding to her waist as he drew her into his arms. His lips crashed against hers — fierce, unyielding, full of longing and regret, and promises he didn't dare give voice to. The kiss was everything he denied himself, everything she'd taunted him for never wanting, everything both of them had pretended wasn't there.

Just as abruptly, he tore himself back, his breath unsteady, restraint flickering hard in his dark eyes. For a heartbeat he lingered, his hand brushing against hers as though he couldn't bear to sever the contact completely. And then, with visible effort, he stepped away.

The soft crunch of gravel under his shoes was deafening in the stillness as he crossed the drive. At the car, his hand paused on the door handle, and he looked back. Even from across the space, Marissa felt the weight of his gaze — silent, intense, carrying a promise that went deeper than words. A promise that this wasn't over. That it could never be over.

She stood rooted to the spot, her pulse wild, her lips tingling with the echo of his kiss.

When the car finally disappeared down the drive, the silence pressed in. The house seemed emptier, quieter — as though it, too, missed the presence he left behind. Yet the air still hummed faintly with him, with the memory of his arms around her, the heat of his mouth.

Marissa closed the front door softly, leaning her back against it for a moment. The week ahead would test both her patience and her resolve, and she knew it. But under the ache of absence, something else flickered to life — a dangerous thrill, an anticipation she couldn't smother.

Because when James Calder returned, everything between them could shift again. And she wasn't sure either of them would survive it unchanged.

Chapter Twenty-One

Marissa got ready for work, letting the familiar rhythm of her morning routine push thoughts of James to the back of her mind. Dressing, brushing her hair, and packing her bag became almost mechanical, each movement grounding her as she tried to focus on the day ahead. The kids in her kindergarten class would keep her busy—their boundless energy and endless questions leaving little room for daydreams. Still, every quiet moment that slipped in brought him back: the way he had pressed her into his arms that morning, the brush of his hand against hers, the intensity in his dark eyes. He had only left hours ago, yet the house already felt emptier without him. Even the lingering scent of coffee on the kitchen counter seemed to tease her senses, a faint reminder of him.

By mid-morning, she found herself glancing at her phone far more often than she should have, half-expecting a message to appear. When the screen finally lit up, her heart gave an involuntary leap.

Got here safe. I already miss you.

Her fingers hovered over the keyboard, caught between the urge to be playful and the pull of honesty. A mix of excitement and hesitation tightened her chest, making her pause for a heartbeat longer than necessary. Then she began to type, letting instinct guide her words:

I miss you too. Can't believe it's only been a few hours.

She hit send before she could overthink it, feeling a small thrill as the message disappeared into the ether. Almost immediately, her phone buzzed again, and she smiled at his reply, a warmth spreading through her that she couldn't hide even amidst the chaos of crayons, giggles, and tiny shoes.

Counting the minutes until I see you again.

Marissa typed back quickly, her heart lighter than it had been all morning:

You'd better hurry then. I'll be here waiting.

The rest of Monday passed in a blur of lesson plans, sticky fingers, and the constant hum of children's voices. She moved from group to group, helping with art projects, wiping down tables, and answering questions that ranged from "Why is the sky blue?" to "Do you have pets at home?" Each small interaction was a distraction from the hollow ache James's absence left behind, yet every laugh and every hug carried a quiet edge, a subtle reminder that part of her mind was somewhere far away with him. Even the sound of a chair scraping across the floor or the faint rustle of a coat on a hanger pulled her thoughts back to him, to the last moments before he left.

By lunchtime, her phone buzzed again. A short text from James:

Thinking about you. Hope your day's going okay.

Grateful for the connection, she replied immediately:

Surviving, mostly thanks to glue sticks and glitter. Thinking of you too.

Even the afternoon's chaos couldn't fully push him from her thoughts. Corralling reluctant toddlers for story time, cleaning up paint spills, coaxing shy voices into group songs—every task seemed both grounding and a reminder of his absence. She found herself daydreaming about him walking through the door, brushing off a coat, and giving her that slow, certain smile that made her chest ache and her pulse catch.

Tuesday sharpened the edge of longing. She caught herself glancing at the clock far too often, imagining him in some distant city, sorting through servers, troubleshooting problems she couldn't even picture. Each text from him became a tiny relief:

Coffee break, thought of you... dangerous for productivity.

She couldn't resist replying:

Wednesday brought the clash of routine and longing into sharper focus. Even simple tasks—the way a crayon rolled off a table, the scrape of a chair across the floor—reminded her of his touch. She lingered in the staffroom longer than necessary, imagining James leaning against the doorway, eyes crinkling as he smiled at her, brushing off the faint scent of rain from his coat.

Thursday heightened the ache. A delayed message made her chest tighten, and the thought of him managing the Pilbara site alone sent a small spike of worry through her. Her fingers itched for her phone, craving the familiar buzz that always brought relief. Each moment without a message felt stretched, and every incoming text became a small beacon of connection.

By Friday, she had developed a quiet rhythm of hope and worry, each little ping of her phone either making her heart leap or sink. Saturday offered the rare chance to breathe outside kindergarten walls. She ran errands, tidied her room, and even managed a few hours of reading, but every moment carried the subtle weight of longing. The memory of James's kiss, the brush of his hands, and the easy intimacy of their recent days pressed at the edges of her mind like a quiet, insistent ache.

That evening, a short text from him sparked a thrill that made her cheeks warm:

She reread his message over and over, letting the warmth of his words wash over her, feeling the small surge of excitement and nervous tension in her chest. Her thoughts danced between anticipation and worry: What if the trip had been exhausting? What if he was distracted by work? But the doubts dissolved as quickly as they came. A week had passed. Soon, he'd be home, and the empty spaces in the house—the quiet corners, the stillness of the mornings—would be filled again by him.

As she lay in bed, the soft patter of rain against the windows matched the restless flutter of her heart. The sound was gentle, lulling, yet every drop seemed to echo with his absence. She closed her eyes and let herself surrender to the memory of him: the curve of his mouth when he allowed himself to smile, the steady warmth of his hand closing around hers, the solid strength of his arms pulling her in as though he'd never let go. She hadn't wanted to admit it, but she missed him — more than she'd thought possible.

Sleep came in fragments, fractured and shallow, woven with dreams that blurred the line between memory and longing. She felt him in those dreams — his touch, his nearness — tender moments laced with the sharp ache of knowing he wasn't there.

In her mind, she pictured the morning to come: the quiet creak of the front door opening, the scent of rain, coffee, and eucalyptus clinging to him as he stepped inside. His gaze finding hers across the room. That slow, certain smile — the one she knew he saved only for her.

Her chest tightened with the thought, a sweet ache that spread through her like fire and silk. She held onto it, let herself savour it, let the anticipation bloom. Longing. Hope. It settled deep in her bones, a truth she could no longer deny — even to herself.

Meanwhile, far from her thoughts, James zipped up his laptop bag for the last time, double-checking the reports his chief engineer, Sean, had prepared. The Pilbara site situation was finally under control—server outages fixed, security protocols reinforced, and the few lingering issues patched. Relief tugged at his shoulders, though a low hum of exhaustion remained from the long days.

He glanced around the temporary office one last time. "All set?" he asked Sean, who gave him a tight nod, papers tucked neatly under one arm.

"Everything's squared away. You can head back without worry," Sean replied.

James allowed himself a small, private smile—the kind that comes from knowing the hard part was done. He reached for his phone, thumb hovering over the keyboard, and tapped out a quick message to Marissa:

Getting on the chopper to leave. I can't wait to see you. I've missed you.

He hit send, feeling a rush of warmth spread through his chest as he imagined her reading it, maybe smiling at her phone, maybe letting herself feel the same flutter he did.

Outside, the roar of the helicopter blades cut through the morning air. James lifted his bag and followed his engineer toward the waiting chopper, the sun glinting off the polished metal. The wind tugged at his coat, but he barely noticed. His thoughts were entirely on her—the curve of her smile, the way her eyes lit up when she laughed, the faint scent of coffee and eucalyptus permanently etched into his memory.

He stepped onto the helicopter, pausing for a fleeting moment to cast a final glance at the land he'd diligently managed over the past week. With a quick wave to Sean, he slid into his seat, the engine's hum intensifying as the ground began to slip away beneath them. Almost instantly, his phone buzzed—a reply from Marissa:

I've missed you too. Hurry home. Don't make me wait any longer than I have to.

A low chuckle escaped him, and he leaned back, eyes closing briefly. The weight of the week, the tension, the long hours—all of it seemed to melt away. Soon, very soon, he would be back with her, and the empty hours apart would finally end.

As the helicopter lifted higher, cutting through the crisp air, James felt a thrill of anticipation building. This wasn't just a return home. This was a return to her—to the warmth, the laughter, the undeniable pull that had him counting every single second until he could see her again.

Her fingers trembled slightly as she hit send, then sank onto the edge of the couch, letting the phone rest against her chest. A soft laugh escaped her, light and unrestrained, though tinged with nerves. The room smelled faintly of lemon from the cleaning spray Julie had used earlier, mingling with the lingering warmth of coffee left from breakfast— but even those comforting scents paled beside the rush of heat flooding through her at the thought of James returning.

Her mind spun with anticipation, her thoughts racing faster than her pulse. In just a few hours, he would be home. She imagined him walking through the door, dark eyes scanning the room for her, that slow, confident smile tugging at the corners of his lips, the faint curl of amusement and affection that made her heart lurch. Her chest tightened at the thought, and her pulse stuttered as she traced invisible patterns on the arm of the couch, caught in the dizzying mix of excitement, longing, and nerves that left her trembling just a little.

Finally, she allowed herself to fully acknowledge the truth—something she hadn't dared to admit before. She was head over heels in love with him. Not casually, not in passing, not in a whisper of attraction—but utterly, all-consuming love that made the hours apart ache like a physical weight in her chest. Every flutter of her heart, every tug of longing, every impatient glance at her phone was proof. Her heart didn't just want him; it insisted, demanded, needed him in a way she could no longer deny.

She rose, pacing lightly as if the movement could steady the racing rhythm in her chest. Fingers threading through her hair, she stopped at the window and peered out at the driveway. The world beyond looked ordinary—the trees swaying gently, a neighbour's dog barking faintly—but to her, it shimmered with possibility, every shadow and glint of sunlight a reminder that soon he would be here.

She busied herself with small, almost ceremonial tasks: straightening cushions, checking on Julie in the kitchen, making sure the house felt as perfect and welcoming as possible for when he arrived. Every little action was punctuated by the hum of anticipation, the steady, insistent beat of hope that thrummed deep in her chest.

Marissa picked up her phone again, scrolling absent-mindedly through the messages they had exchanged over the past week. Each one felt like a tether, a lifeline connecting her to him across the miles. She could almost feel him beside her—the warmth of his body, the teasing lilt of his voice that always made her chest flutter, the faint brush of a hand against hers.

A soft, breathless sigh escaped as she sank back onto the couch, fingers drumming nervously on the armrest. She closed her eyes, imagining the moment he would finally walk in, the subtle rustle of his coat, the faint aroma of coffee and leather that always clung to him, the slow, certain smile. Every imagined detail made her pulse jump, made her chest ache with longing, made her feel both fragile and entirely alive.

The anticipation was intoxicating, overwhelming in the best way. She let herself sink into it, let the fluttering nerves, the rising excitement, the undeniable joy of loving him wash over her. In just a few hours, the wait would be over, and everything—the ache, the longing, the quiet, trembling hope—would be replaced by the reality of him, right there, in her arms. Nothing would ever feel quite the same again, and for the first time in a long week, she allowed herself to believe that was exactly how it should be.

Chapter Twenty-Two

James lifted off from the Pilbara site as the early morning sun cast long, dramatic shadows across the rugged, rust-coloured earth, its golden rays slicing through the dawn haze. Below, the vast terrain stretched out endlessly—a wild tapestry of jagged rocky ridges and sparse, sun-scorched scrubland melting into the distant horizon, where the nearest town lingered as a mere speck hundreds of kilometres away. The helicopter hummed with a steady, reassuring rhythm beneath him, the pilot skilfully navigating the untamed wilderness with a practiced hand. James let his mind drift to Marissa, conjuring an image of her at home, patiently waiting, her presence igniting a subtle yet persistent flutter of anticipation in his chest.

The chopper blades sliced through the humid Pilbara air, the horizon transforming into a striking patchwork of swirling dust and deepening shadows. As the wind picked up, carrying a low, ominous rumble of thunder from afar, James tightened his grip on his weathered duffel bag, his knuckles whitening with tension. Leaning toward the pilot, he raised his voice over the relentless rotor noise. "Pilot, are you sure that storm front isn't moving faster than we anticipated?"

The pilot's eyes flicked upward, scanning the darkening sky with a furrowed brow. "Too late to turn back now," he replied, his tone steady but edged with resolve. "We'll just have to push through and hope for the best."

Before James could respond, a jagged streak of lightning cracked across the heavens, its brilliance both awe-inspiring and terrifyingly close. A shiver raced down his spine as the air crackled with electricity. Then it struck—the blinding flash followed by a deafening crack as a bolt arced toward them, slamming into the rotor assembly. The helicopter shuddered violently, a jarring jolt rocking the cabin. Warning lights flared to life, bathing the cockpit in a harsh red glow, while shrill alarms pierced the air, their urgency unrelenting.

"Emergency! Emergency! We're going down!" the pilot shouted, his voice taut but controlled as he wrestled with the controls, his gaze darting for a viable landing spot. James's stomach lurched as the helicopter dipped sharply, the ground rushing up to meet them with alarming speed. His heart pounded in his chest; each beat a reminder of the peril they faced.

After tense moments of manoeuvring, they spotted it: a rocky clearing nestled amid low scrub and jagged stones, a fragile sanctuary in the chaotic landscape. The pilot set the skids down with a hard thud, the chopper rattling and groaning with every impact as it settled unevenly on the uneven terrain. The engines emitted an ominous hum, struggling to maintain stability as the storm raged overhead, rain pelting the windows in relentless sheets.

"Dead zone," the pilot muttered, his voice heavy with frustration as he yanked out his radio. "No comms. Satellite is down too. We're on our own until this storm blows over."

James swallowed hard, the stark reality sinking in, they could be stranded for hours, perhaps longer, isolated in this desolate expanse with no means of communication. His thoughts raced back to Marissa, picturing her at home, her blue eyes widening with worry as the hours ticked by without word from him. The thought of her fear tightened his chest, a pang of guilt mingling with his own unease. Pulling his jacket tighter around his shoulders, he braced against the hammering rain and fought to steady his breathing, determined to keep calm despite the uncertainty stretching before them.

It had been hours—interminable hours that stretched on like a relentless tide, each passing minute delivering a sharp, hammering blow against Marissa's frayed nerves. Her phone lay abandoned on the couch beside her, its screen dark and eerily silent, offering no solace. No text had come, not when he should have landed, not when he'd boarded his flight—he always sent a quick message to reassure her, a ritual she clung to with certainty. But now, there was nothing.

Her hands trembled faintly as she reached for the device once more, her fingers brushing over the smooth surface before scrolling through their message history. She lingered on the last note he'd sent: *'Getting on the chopper to leave. I can't wait. I've missed you.'* Tracing the words with a shaky fingertip, she willed them to conjure some semblance of reassurance, a lifeline in the growing void of uncertainty.

Julie appeared silently in the doorway, a steaming mug of tea cradled in her hands, and paused when her gaze fell upon Marissa's face—pale, drawn tight with worry, a portrait of mounting dread. "Marissa..." she began softly, stepping forward to set the mug on the coffee table with a gentle clink. "He's fine. I'm sure he's fine."

Marissa forced a brittle nod, but the words rang hollow in her ears, echoing in the cavern of her anxiety. She wrapped her arms around herself, a futile shield against the fear, and began pacing the small space in front of the couch, her footsteps a restless rhythm. "He... he should've texted by now. It's been hours. What if..." Her voice fractured, the unspoken terror catching in her throat like a sob.

Julie moved closer, resting a comforting hand lightly on her shoulder, her touch a steady anchor amid the storm of emotions. "I know it's hard, love, but letting your mind spiral into the worst isn't going to help. Sometimes flights are delayed, or there's no signal— especially out in those remote areas. He's probably just waiting for a clear moment."

Marissa closed her eyes, drawing in a shaky breath as she tried to cling to Julie's optimism, to believe in the possibility. Yet the gnawing pit in her stomach refused to relent, a dark well of dread. Unbidden images flooded her mind—flashes of isolation, danger, and the jagged memory of her parents' death when she was just a girl. The helplessness, the raw, piercing fear of that loss surged back, sharp, and unyielding, intertwining with her current anguish.

Julie's hand squeezed her shoulder gently, pulling her back from the edge. "I'm right here. Focus on me, on this room, on something solid. He's coming back to you. I promise."

Marissa opened her eyes, forcing herself to meet Julie's steady gaze, to draw in a ragged breath through the rising panic. She nodded again, a fragile gesture, but her fingers itched to clutch the phone once more, and her eyes kept darting to the driveway, as if sheer will could summon his return. The quiet hum of the house pressed in around her, oppressive and unbearable, each tick of the clock a relentless reminder that James was out there—somewhere far away, alone, and maddeningly unreachable.

The hours dragged on, the sky outside darkening under the weight of late-afternoon clouds that gathered like a foreboding shroud. Every gust of wind rattled the windows with a mournful wail, and the distant rumble of thunder sent a shiver through her, each peal a jolt to her already frayed nerves. Her phone remained stubbornly mute, its silence a taunting void, while her thoughts spiralled out of control. She pictured James trapped in that helicopter, battling a storm, the radio crackling with static or worse, silent. Her chest tightened painfully, memories of her parents' sudden, tragic death—the helplessness, the soul-crushing despair—flaring vividly in her mind, amplifying her terror.

Julie hovered nearby, a constant presence trying to tether her to the present, but she could see the fear etched deeply into every tense line of Marissa's face, a mirror to her own growing concern. "Why doesn't he text?" Marissa whispered, her voice barely audible as she clung to the armrest of the couch, her knuckles whitening as if it could anchor her to reality. "He always... he always texts..."

Julie's heart ached for her friend, a pang of helplessness mingling with her resolve. She knelt to meet Marissa's anguished gaze, her voice calm and deliberate. "I know it's terrifying. I know you're worried sick. But in storms like this, especially in such remote places, there's often no signal, no way to get through. It doesn't mean something's happened—it's just the nature of where he is."

Marissa shook her head, tears prickling at the corners of her eyes as doubt overwhelmed her. "But it could... what if something has?" Her voice cracked, a fragile thread snapping as she sank onto the couch, burying her face in her hands, the weight of her fear pressing down like a physical burden.

Julie exhaled slowly, wishing she could offer more than words, the tension in the house thickening like a fog. She reached out, her hand hovering near Marissa's, when suddenly—the sharp, unexpected trill of Marissa's phone shattered the silence. Both women froze, time seeming to suspend as their eyes locked, the sound reverberating through the room like a lifeline in the darkness.

Marissa's fingers quivered as she fumbled to answer the phone, her breath catching in her throat as she whispered, "James?" Her voice trembled with a fragile blend of hope and dread, hanging in the air like a plea.

The response came, steady but unfamiliar. "Marissa, it's Ian."

Her heart stuttered, a sudden jolt of unease replacing the flicker of hope. "Ian… how's the honeymoon?" The words spilled out, hollow and automatic, a feeble attempt to fill the suffocating silence with something mundane.

"It's fine. But listen—the Pilbara site just called. They've lost contact with James' helicopter. A storm rolled in fast, caught them off guard." His tone was clipped, laced with concern.

The air seemed to vanish from her lungs, leaving her gasping. "Lost contact?" Her voice cracked, fracturing under the weight of panic. "Ian, what if—what if it's like…?" The unfinished question lingered, heavy with the unspoken terror of her past, the memory of loss clawing at her mind.

He paused, sensing the raw fear threading through her words. "Marissa, this isn't the same. All we know right now is they can't communicate—that's it. He's alive until we hear otherwise, you hear me. Don't let your mind run to the worst just yet."

"I can't… I can't lose him too," she whispered, her voice barely audible, a fragile confession of her deepest fear.

"I know," Ian replied softly, his voice a lifeline across the distance. "But don't get ahead of the facts. James is strong, meticulous, and careful. The moment it's safe, they'll dispatch a search team to find him. Hold onto that."

Her grip on the phone loosened slightly, his words offering a faint thread of solace amid the chaos. "Okay… I'll try," she managed, her voice steadier but still laced with uncertainty.

"Good. Just breathe. I'll call the second I hear anything more—count on it." His reassurance lingered as the call ended, and Marissa nodded mutely, though he couldn't see her, letting his words anchor her trembling heart as the storm outside mirrored the tempest raging within her.

When the line went silent, she sank back onto the couch, wrapping herself in a thick blanket as if it could shield her from the growing dread. The phone rested in her lap, a silent sentinel, every sense attuned to the possibility of its next ring. The clock ticked with an oppressive loudness, each second a relentless drumbeat against her nerves. Wind rattled the house, a mournful howl that seemed to echo her inner turmoil, while in her mind, vivid images played unbidden—the storm swallowing the helicopter whole, its blades faltering against the fury of the elements. Every moment stretched interminably, elongated by a potent mix of fear, longing, and the weight of her memories.

Julie's voice drifted softly from the doorway, a gentle intrusion into her spiralling thoughts. "Marissa… love… I know it's unbearable right now. But letting panic take over won't help him—or you. We need to stay strong together."

Marissa swallowed hard, shaking her head as tears threatened to spill. "It's just… I can't stop seeing it. Mum and Dad… the way they were taken so suddenly… and now him. I can't—" Her voice broke, the words dissolving into a choked silence, too painful to voice fully. Speaking them aloud felt like inviting the nightmare into reality.

Julie knelt beside her, taking Marissa's cold hands in her warm ones, her touch a steadying force. "He's not your parents, Marissa. He's not. James is resilient, resourceful. You have to hold onto that strength, for both your sakes."

Marissa nodded weakly, her resolve fragile, but the storm churning inside her chest refused to subside. She pulled the blanket tighter around her shoulders, huddling against the couch as her gaze fixed on the rain-streaked window. Each gust of wind outside felt like a cruel reminder of the helicopter she imagined battling the tempest, its fate uncertain. Every second dragged on, stretched thin by the relentless interplay of fear, the haunting echoes of past loss, and the aching void of missing him already.

Even in the oppressive quiet of the house, Marissa realised she was grappling with a powerlessness she had never known before—helpless against the relentless storm, against the vast unknown stretching beyond her reach, and against her own heart, which throbbed with a desperate, all-consuming love for James. The weight of that love, mingled with terror, pressed down on her, a silent prayer forming with every breath that he would return to her unharmed.

Four hours had crawled by; each minute stretching like an eternity. Marissa had worn a path into the living room carpet, pacing from window to door and back again. The storm outside had eased, but inside her chest, the pressure only built. Her tea sat cold on the coffee table, untouched.

When her phone finally rang, she nearly dropped it in her rush to answer. "Ian?"

"Yeah, it's me," he said, his voice carrying a note of urgency—and something else.

Marissa gripped the phone tighter. "Tell me."

"They found the helicopter," Ian said, slow and deliberate, as if he wanted every word to sink in. "They're safe. Both James and the pilot. He should call you as soon as they get to the airport."

For a heartbeat, her knees gave out and she sat heavily on the couch, a sound between a laugh and a sob escaping her. "Oh my God… they're safe?"

"They're safe," Ian repeated firmly, as though he knew she needed to hear it more than once.

Marissa pressed a hand over her mouth, tears blurring her vision. She could picture him—maybe wet, maybe shaken, but alive. The coil of dread in her chest began to unravel, replaced by a flood of relief so sharp it hurt.

Ian's voice softened. "I told you it wasn't the same as before. He'll be with you soon. Just… breathe now, okay?"

She nodded, swallowing hard. "Thank you for calling me, Ian."

When they hung up, she sat in the quiet, letting the words settle: They're safe. She clung to them like a lifeline, whispering them to herself until the shaking in her hands finally began to ease.

Fifteen minutes later, her phone buzzed again. The sound jolted through her like an electric shock. She snatched it up without even checking the screen.

"Marissa."

Her breath caught at the sound of his voice. "James." His name came out in a shaky whisper; a thousand emotions tangled in just those two syllables. "Are you—are you really okay?"

"I'm fine," he said quickly, firmly. She could hear the faint hum of airport announcements in the background. "We had to put the chopper down when the storm hit—lightning got too close. No comms, no way to let anyone know. But we're fine, Marissa. I'm fine."

She pressed her eyes shut, tears spilling over again. "You scared me. God, you have no idea—I thought—" Her voice broke, the unspoken memory of her parents' crash hanging heavy between them.

"I know," he said gently, reading the thought she couldn't finish. "But this isn't then. I'm coming home to you."

Her breath hitched again. "I don't care if you have to crawl. Just… get here."

He gave a soft laugh, the sound frayed at the edges but so achingly familiar it made her chest ache. "I'll be there before you know it."

When the call ended, she sat still, the phone pressed against her heart, a fresh wave of relief washing over her. He was alive.

He was coming home.

And she would be waiting at the door when he walked through it.

Chapter Twenty-Three

Julie had already retired to bed, while Marissa remained awake, eagerly awaiting James. The low rumble of a car reached her ears before its headlights pierced the rain-slicked driveway. Her heart surged into her throat, and before the vehicle came to a complete stop, she was out the front door, the misty rain brushing against her skin as her pulse pounded in her ears.

James stepped out, retrieving his bag from the boot as the driver pulled away down the long stretch of gravel drive. He looked like he'd been carved straight out of the storm—coat still damp, hair tousled by the wind, his dark gaze sharp even in the half-light.

For half a second, they simply stared—her eyes wide, his unreadable yet locked on hers—and then she was moving, running toward him.

He caught her mid-stride, his arms closing around her with such force it almost hurt, but she clung to him just as fiercely. Her fingers curled into the back of his coat as if letting go might mean losing him all over again.

"I thought I'd lost you," she whispered against his neck, her voice breaking, trembling with everything she hadn't let herself feel until now.

"You won't lose me," he murmured, his mouth pressing into her damp hair. "Not now. Not ever."

The storm clung to him—rain and cold air, the tang of travel—but beneath it was the grounding scent of him, warm and achingly familiar, the one she'd missed so much it made her eyes sting all over again. She leaned back, her hands framing his face, needing to see him, to touch him.

"You scared me half to death," she said, her voice a mixture of accusation and raw relief.

His jaw tightened. "I know. I'm sorry. The storm came in fast—the pilot had to put us down in the middle of nowhere. No comms, no way to get word to you. I hated knowing you'd be here, waiting, not hearing from me."

"You hated it?" she breathed, a disbelieving laugh catching on the sob rising in her throat. "James, I…" Her words fractured, breaking apart under the weight of everything she couldn't say, and instead she pulled him down into a kiss—desperate, messy, salt from her tears mingling with the heat of his mouth.

He kissed her back with equal urgency, one hand sliding into her hair, the other pressed firm against her back as though anchoring her to him, vowing without words never to let go again.

When they finally broke apart, foreheads resting together, his voice was low, rough, unsteady. "I'm here now. And I'm not going anywhere."

She nodded, the relief flooding through her so deep it was almost dizzying. "Good. Because I'm not letting you out of my sight again."

A slow smile curved his mouth—steady, certain, reserved only for her. "I wouldn't dream of it."

He stooped to grab his bags, but neither of them released the other entirely as they walked back toward the house, hands brushing, her shoulder close against his.

Inside, James shut the door with a soft click that seemed impossibly final after the chaos of the last few hours. The house felt warmer than he remembered, carrying the faint scent of lemon polish and tea, but mostly it was her—her presence filling the hall, the air, the space around him until he couldn't breathe without it.

Marissa slipped off her shoes silently but didn't move far from him. She just stood there in the hallway, watching as he shrugged out of his damp coat. When he turned to hang it, she caught his arm, her grip surprisingly firm despite the tremor in her voice.

"Leave it," she whispered, her gaze holding his with a raw, unguarded intensity.

He let it drop to the bench and turned back to her. In the softer light of the hallway, she could see the exhaustion in his face—the faint lines around his eyes, the damp hair clinging to his forehead—but more than that, she saw the way he was looking at her. Like she was the thing that had kept him grounded through every rough mile of that storm.

They moved together without thinking, her hands finding his shirtfront, his fingers skimming the curve of her back. The kiss this time was slower, but no less intense—a deep, aching reassurance that he was here, that they were both still breathing the same air.

When they finally broke apart, she pressed her cheek against his chest, listening to the steady beat of his heart. "I kept thinking about my parents," she whispered. "The storm. The helicopter. It felt like... like it was happening all over again."

His arms tightened around her. "I know," he said quietly. "But I'm here. And I swear to you, I will fight everything in my power to stay here—with you."

She nodded, swallowing against the lump in her throat. For a long moment, they simply stood there, holding on as if letting go might invite the world to take one of them away again.

James brushed his lips over her hair. "You should sit. You've been through enough tonight."

She shook her head. "Not yet. I just… need you close."

That drew the faintest smile from him. "Then close you'll get."

Without a word, Marissa slipped her hand into his, her palm warm against his but faintly trembling. She turned toward the stairs, the pull of her touch both steadying and urgent. James followed, his dark eyes locked on her as if he were afraid to look away, as though one blink might make her vanish.

Their steps were slow, unhurried, the only sounds the soft creak of the stairs and the distant patter of rain against the windows. At the landing, she paused and glanced back at him. Her gaze lingered for a moment, searching his face, as if she still needed proof that he was really there—whole, safe, alive.

Her fingers tightened around his, and she led him down the hallway, the warm glow from the lamps spilling across the floorboards. With each step, the air between them seemed to thicken, saturated with the relief of his return and the ache of the hours she'd spent not knowing if she'd ever see him again.

When they reached her bedroom, she pushed the door open. The familiar scent of her perfume wrapped around them, mingling with the faint freshness of rain drifting in from the slightly open window. She turned to face him, her voice barely above a whisper.

"You're here."

He reached up, brushing a damp strand of auburn hair from her cheek. "I'm here."

For a moment they just stood there, the charged stillness holding them in place. Then, without breaking his gaze, she stepped back into the room, drawing him with her, the door clicking softly shut behind them.

The quiet of the room seemed to press in around them, the world beyond its walls forgotten. James stood close enough that she could feel the faint heat radiating from him, the steady rhythm of his breathing grounding her in a way nothing else had all week.

He reached for her, pulling her gently into his arms. She went without hesitation, her cheek finding the familiar hollow of his shoulder. The scent of him—warm skin, leather, and a faint trace of the storm—wrapped around her. For a long moment, neither spoke.

Her fingers gripped the back of his shirt, clutching him like she might lose him again if she let go. She'd held herself together all afternoon, clinging to Julie's reassurances, to Ian's voice on the phone, but now the dam was cracking. She pulled back just enough to see his face, her hands sliding up to frame it.

"I was so worried," she whispered, her voice breaking. "When Ian called and said they'd lost contact... all I could think about was—" Her throat tightened. "—about was mum and dad."

His eyes darkened with something she couldn't quite name—pain, understanding, regret. He brushed his thumb gently along her jaw. "I'm sorry you had to go through that. But I'm here, Marissa. I'm not going anywhere."

She searched his face, tracing every familiar line as if to memorise him all over again. The fear that had been gnawing at her since the storm hit twisted into something deeper—something she could no longer deny.

"I can't... I can't pretend anymore," she whispered, her voice trembling with vulnerability. Her heart hammered so fiercely she feared he might sense its wild rhythm. "I want to be with you." The words teetered on the edge of confessing her love, but she held back, not yet ready to take that daring leap.

For a fleeting moment, his expression remained an enigma—then his hand slipped into her hair, fingers weaving gently through the rich auburn strands. He lowered his forehead to hers, his voice a low, rough whisper. "You have no idea how long I've been waiting to hear you say that."

Her lips curved into a shaky, hopeful smile, her eyes glistening with unshed tears. "So, it's mutual, then?"

"Very," he murmured, his breath warm against her skin, before he bridged the small gap between them. His kiss was slow, deliberate, as if he wished to etch the moment into eternity.

They stood there for a moment, just looking at each other, until he kissed her again, deeper now, with nothing held back. His hands slid over her hips, up her sides, memorising her shape. She answered his touch with her own, fingers threading through his hair, tracing the familiar planes of his shoulders.

James's hands moved with deliberate slowness, as if memorising the feel of her all over again. He brushed his lips over hers, feather-light, before his fingers slid to the hem of her top. His touch was warm, reverent, and her breath caught as he eased the fabric upward, baring her skin inch by inch.

She didn't just stand there and let him—her own hands went to the buttons of his shirt, fumbling slightly in her haste, needing to feel his skin beneath her palms. The slide of cotton away from his shoulders revealed the strong lines she'd only been able to imagine all week, and her fingers traced them greedily, as though to reassure herself he was whole, safe, here.

When her top hit the floor and his shirt joined it, he caught her face between his hands, searching her eyes. His own were dark, intense, the raw honesty in them stealing her breath.

"I love you," he said, the words low and rough, as if dragged from somewhere deep inside him. "I love you so much, Marissa… it scares the hell out of me."

Her heart gave a wild, unsteady thud, but she didn't look away. "Then we're even," she whispered, her voice shaking but sure. "Because I love you too and it terrifies me as well—in all the best ways."

His mouth found hers again, the kiss fierce, almost desperate, as if those words had stripped away the last of his restraint. Her fingers skimmed over his chest, down his stomach, tugging at his belt until it gave way under her touch.

Piece by piece, they shed the last barriers between them, the patter of rain outside weaving into the soft rustle of clothing and the deepening rhythm of their breaths. Every touch carried the raw edge of relief; each kiss threaded with the unspoken truth of how close they'd come to losing this—losing each other. The echo of that fear sharpened the need between them until it felt almost unbearable.

James's hands slid to her hips, steady and certain, before he lifted her effortlessly, cradling her against him as if she were something precious, he refused to let go of. He lowered her onto the bed with slow, deliberate care, his gaze never leaving hers.

He paused, drinking her in, his chest rising and falling with uneven breaths. The shadows from the rain-swept window shifted across her skin, but his focus was absolute, reverent.

"God, you're beautiful," he murmured, his voice rough with something more than desire—something deeper, more permanent.

The way he said it made her feel like he wasn't just talking about her body, but about all of her—the messy, complicated, impossible parts too.

Marissa's breath caught at the look in his eyes—intense, hungry, and threaded with something deeper than desire. She reached for him, her hands sliding over the solid planes of his shoulders, down the ridges of his back, the muscles tight and warm under her touch. She wanted to hold every part of him, to anchor him to her.

He bent to kiss her, at first so tenderly it almost undid her. The brush of his lips was like an apology, a promise, and a claim all at once. Then the kiss deepened, his mouth moving over hers with a slow, deliberate hunger that made her toes curl.

When he pulled back just enough to meet her gaze, his voice was unsteady. "I love you."

Her heart stuttered, his words sinking straight into the deepest part of her. The fear she'd felt earlier—the clawing panic that he might not come back, the echo of her parents' loss—tightened in her chest before dissolving under the weight of this moment.

"I love you too," she whispered, her voice trembling but certain.

Something in him shifted, as if those words freed him. He cupped her face, kissed her deeply, and then his hands were everywhere—skimming her sides, sliding down her thighs, pulling her closer until there was no space left between them. She arched into him, her body moving instinctively to meet his.

His mouth left hers to trail along her jaw, down her neck, his breath warm against her skin. She shivered, clutching at his shoulders as his lips found the delicate hollow at the base of her throat.

The urgency between them built like the storm outside—swift, relentless. His hands smoothed over her hips, holding her steady as his body pressed into hers. She wrapped her legs around him, drawing him even closer, needing the solid weight of him against her.

"Marissa…" he breathed her name like a prayer and a curse, as if he'd been holding it back all week.

She answered with a soft moan, tilting her head back as he kissed her again, devouring her lips, her sighs, every sound she made. Every touch felt like rediscovery, every movement sharpened by the hours they'd been apart and the terrifying possibility of never seeing each other again.

When he finally moved into her, it was slow at first—measured, deep—his forehead pressed to hers, his eyes locked on hers as though he needed to see every flicker of feeling cross her face. She clung to him, their breaths mingling, their heartbeats pounding in unison.

Then the pace shifted, the tempo rising with each movement, the quiet broken by the soft sounds of their bodies, the storm outside, and the whispered words neither of them could hold back.

She felt herself shatter around him, her voice catching as his name fell from her lips. A heartbeat later, he followed, holding her tightly as if he could fuse them together.

For a long time, they stayed that way—breathless, tangled in each other, the rain falling in steady sheets beyond the glass. The world outside was chaos, but here, in the quiet cocoon of his arms, there was only peace. James's hand moved slowly up her spine, strong but gentle, smoothing away the last of her trembling. When he pressed his lips to her temple, it wasn't passion but reverence, the kiss of a man who knew exactly what he had almost lost.

"I'm not letting you go," he murmured against her skin, voice low and rough with the weight of it.

Marissa's lips curved faintly, though her chest still rose and fell too fast. "Good. Because I wasn't planning on letting you go either."

The storm would pass. Morning would come. But for now, time had narrowed to this—the warmth of his body around hers, the steady cadence of two hearts finally beating in the same rhythm, the unspoken truth neither of them could deny anymore.

Chapter Twenty-Four

When morning broke, soft, and pale against the curtains, they were still wrapped together. Marissa stirred first, blinking up at him through lashes heavy with sleep. James tightened his arm around her, a slow smile ghosting his lips as if he couldn't quite believe she was still there.

After a moment, he eased out of bed, the shift pulling a sleepy protest from her. But before she could reach for him, he bent and scooped her easily into his arms, sheets tumbling around them.

Her eyes widened, her voice husky with sleep. "What are you doing?"

His smile deepened, wicked and tender all at once. "I want a shower," he said simply, his dark gaze holding hers. "And I need you close."

Steam curled into the air as James turned on the water, the sound of it rushing against the tiles filling the small space. He set Marissa down gently, though his hands lingered at her waist as if reluctant to let her go.

She tilted her head up, auburn hair tumbling around her shoulders, her lips curving in a teasing smile despite the rapid flutter of her heart. "You really couldn't survive ten minutes without me?"

His gaze darkened, sweeping over her in a way that sent heat pooling low in her stomach. "Not anymore," he said simply, truth threaded through every syllable.

For a moment neither moved, suspended in the intimacy of the words. His fingers brushed her bare shoulders, reverent, almost hesitant, as though he couldn't quite believe she was real.

"Marissa," he breathed, her name a confession.

She closed the last inch between them, pressing her palms to his chest. "No more running," she whispered back.

The water was hot, cascading over them as he drew her beneath the spray. It slicked her hair down her back, glistened across his skin, turning every line of muscle to shadow and light. His mouth found hers with unrestrained hunger but threaded through the urgency was tenderness — the gentleness of a man who had almost lost the chance to love and knew it.

Her hands slid up, fingers tangling in his damp hair as she kissed him back with equal fervour, the steam wrapping around them like a cocoon. His hands roamed her back, steady, anchoring, pulling her closer until there was no space left between them.

When his lips finally left hers, they traced along her jaw, her cheek, the hollow of her throat, each kiss softer than the last, until she was trembling for an entirely different reason.

She leaned her forehead against his, breathless. "This feel—right."

James's eyes searched hers, raw and unguarded. "It is," he admitted, voice low, husky. "Because now, we are not pretending we don't love each other."

Her heart stuttered, then steadied, swelling so full she thought it might burst. She cupped his face in her hands, rainwater and tears and shower spray all mingling as she whispered, "Please don't ever stop."

And when his mouth captured hers again, it wasn't just a kiss. It was a vow.

The heat of the shower only heightened the urgency between them, steam curling like smoke around their entwined bodies. James pressed her gently against the tiled wall, his mouth claiming hers with a hunger that stole her breath. His hands skimmed her damp skin, reverent and aching, as if memorising every inch he'd denied himself for far too long.

Marissa arched into him, her nails grazing his shoulders, needing him closer, needing him completely. The water beat down around them, but all she felt was the solid strength of his body and the burning tenderness of his touch.

When he lifted her effortlessly, she wrapped herself around him, their kiss deepening into something desperate, unstoppable. Time blurred, every shiver, every sigh, every whispered word binding them tighter.

It wasn't just heat—it was release. It was years of denial and longing shattering in one fierce, beautiful moment. And as the water cascaded over them, it was more than passion that held them together; it was trust, it was surrender, it was the unspoken truth neither could keep buried anymore.

When at last the urgency gave way to quiet stillness, James cradled her face in his hands, pressing his forehead to hers. Their breathing slowed in unison, the sound of the shower soft around them like a lullaby. He brushed his lips across hers again, softer now, reverent.

"I love you," he whispered, the words rough, raw, utterly real.

Her heart tightened, and tears mingled with the shower spray as she smiled through them. "I love you too."

Later, the world intruded again. The storm had passed; pale morning light filtered weakly through the curtains as they moved around the bedroom, dressing slowly, almost reluctantly.

Marissa stood by the mirror, tugging the soft fabric of a pale sweater over her head, brushing her damp auburn hair back from her face. James came up behind her, still buttoning his shirt, and slid his arms briefly around her waist. Their reflections met in the glass—her smile shy, his gaze steady and full of something she'd never seen in him before.

"You look beautiful," he said simply, as though it were the most obvious fact in the world.

She turned in his arms, pressing a lingering kiss to his mouth before tugging the collar of his shirt into place. Her lips curved in a sly smile. "And you look like a very satisfied man."

His answering smirk was slow, deliberate, his dark eyes gleaming. "That's because I am."

Marissa rolled her eyes but couldn't quite suppress her own smile. Their fingers brushed as they moved toward the door, and without discussion, his hand found hers—warm, steady, grounding. Side by side, they descended the staircase, their steps in quiet sync as though they'd been walking together like this all along.

The kitchen was filled with the bright scent of fresh coffee and the sound of clinking china. Julie was already at the counter, robe wrapped snugly around her as she poured steaming liquid into mugs. She turned at the sound of their entrance, and her eyes immediately dropped to their joined hands.

One brow arched, a knowing smile curving her lips. "Well, good morning, you two. Looks like you both finally woke up—" her gaze lingered meaningfully, amusement glinting in her eyes, "—in more ways than one."

Marissa felt heat rush to her cheeks, but she lifted her chin, refusing to give her housekeeper the satisfaction of looking flustered. James only gave a short, low chuckle, the kind that said he was perfectly fine letting Julie assume whatever she liked.

Julie, unfazed, handed them each a cup of coffee, her grin widening as she added, "About time, if you ask me."

Julie slid the mugs across the counter, her eyes dancing between the two of them like a cat who'd cornered a pair of canaries. "So," she said lightly, "should I even bother asking how you slept, or is it written all over your faces?"

Marissa lifted her cup, forcing her voice into something breezy. "Perfectly fine, thank you."

"Mm-hm." Julie took a slow sip of her own coffee, her smile far too smug. "Of course you did. Nothing like a good… night's rest to take the edge off."

Marissa shot her a look over the rim of her cup. "Careful, Julie. Coffee has been known to scald."

Julie only laughed, leaning a hip against the counter. "You can glare all you want, sweetheart. But you should know—your smile kind of gives you away. I haven't seen you this happy in years."

That made Marissa falter, just for a second. She busied herself with the sugar bowl, spooning a little too much into her cup just to avoid Julie's knowing gaze.

James, however, seemed entirely unruffled. He took a long sip of his coffee, then said dryly, "You've always been too observant for your own good, Julie."

"Oh, don't start pretending you mind." Julie waved him off, grinning. "If anything, I think you're enjoying the fact you've finally stopped glaring at each other like you wanted to draw blood."

Marissa huffed. "We were never that bad."

Julie arched a brow. "Darling, please. Everyone avoided being in the same room with you two because of the tension. Honestly, it was exhausting to watch."

James's lips quirked, the smallest flicker of amusement breaking through his usual restraint. "I wouldn't say exhausting." His gaze slid to Marissa, dark and pointed. "Challenging, maybe."

Her pulse skipped. Heat pooled low in her stomach, though she forced herself to meet his stare with a cool arch of her brow. "You'll find I've always been up to a challenge."

Julie groaned dramatically. "Oh, God. Don't start with the sparring again or we'll never get through breakfast." But her grin said otherwise—if anything, she was enjoying herself far too much.

Marissa sipped her coffee, hiding her smile behind the rim. James set his cup down; eyes still locked on hers. And though neither said a word, the kitchen seemed to hum with the silent promise of everything that had changed between them.

They lingered over breakfast longer than usual; the air threaded with easy conversation and little sparks of unspoken glances. Marissa found herself laughing more than she expected, though every time James's knee brushed hers beneath the table, her pulse jumped.

Julie set her fork down with a satisfied little sigh. "Well, isn't this cozy? Almost like a family breakfast. Who knew all it would take was a storm and a sleepless night."

Marissa shot her a warning look, but before she could reply, the distant crunch of tyres on gravel reached them. All three heads turned toward the front windows.

A sleek black car was easing its way up the long drive, headlights catching in the wet sheen of the morning rain.

Julie's brows shot up. "Oh, this should be interesting."

Marissa's stomach dipped. Ian.

Sure enough, the passenger door opened, and Shelby stepped out first—radiant even after hours of travel, her smile bright as she pushed a loose strand of blonde hair behind her ear. Ian emerged from the driver's side a moment later, casual in a white shirt and dark jeans, his arm sliding naturally around his new wife's shoulders as they started toward the house.

Marissa didn't wait. She was already at the door, flinging it open and hurrying down the steps. "Hey, sis!" Ian's grin was wide as she threw her arms around him.

"Welcome home," she said warmly, squeezing him tight. "I hope you had a wonderful time."

"We did." Shelby's eyes sparkled as Marissa pulled her into an embrace next. "It was magical." She tilted her head toward her new husband, her expression soft with a kind of happiness that made Marissa's chest ache in the best way.

By then James had stepped forward, his tall frame straight and steady. He clasped Ian's hand firmly, the two men sharing a look that spoke of quiet respect.

"I'm glad you made it back safe," Ian said, his tone weighted with something more than casual brotherly concern.

James nodded once. "Yeah—it got a little hairy for a minute there. But I'm here now."

Almost without thinking, his arm slid around Marissa's waist, anchoring her to his side. She stiffened for only half a breath before leaning subtly into him, as if the gesture was the most natural thing in the world.

It was Shelby who noticed first. Her lips curved in a knowing smile as her gaze flicked from James's arm to Marissa's face. Then she looked at Ian, her voice light but edged with meaning. "Looks like our plan worked after all."

Marissa blinked, caught off guard. "Wait—what plan?"

Shelby only exchanged a look with Ian, her smile widening as they all made their way into the living room.

Julie greeted Ian and Shelby warmly as they all settled into the living room. Ian and Shelby sank onto the couch, while Julie took her usual armchair. James eased into the opposite chair, tugging Marissa onto his lap. She moved willingly, curling against him.

Julie spoke first, breaking the quiet. "I have to admit, I thought it was going to fail at first," she said, glancing at Ian and Shelby. "Marissa… she had an accident on the very first day and lost her memory."

Ian and Shelby exchanged shocked, worried glances. Ian leaned forward, concern etched on his face. "Are you okay, Marissa?" he asked gently.

Marissa tilted her head, a mix of disbelief and amusement lighting her face. "Yes, I'm fine… but what exactly is this 'plan' you're talking about?"

Ian shrugged, trying to look casual but failing to hide his exasperation. "Shelby and I were getting sick of watching you two circle each other like a couple of boxers in a ring. So, I asked James to stay, hoping that having both of you under the same roof would finally make you come to your senses."

Marissa's jaw dropped. She blinked at Ian and Shelby, then spun to Julie. "And you… you were in on this too?"

Julie grinned, practically sparkling with mischief. "Of course."

James chuckled low in his throat, tightening his hold on Marissa as she squirmed slightly against him. "Well," he said, his voice husky, "in that case… thank you."

Ian chuckled. "You're welcome. I'm just glad to see you both smiling. Shelby told me months ago that she was sure Marissa was in love with James."

Marissa turned to Shelby, wide-eyed and shocked.

Shelby's smile was teasing, full of warmth. "You told me after your eighteenth birthday that you wished James would actually notice you."

Marissa felt her cheeks heat instantly, a deep blush creeping across her face.

James grinned, his dark eyes sparkling with amusement. "Oh really? Well… you certainly made me do that—with all the boyfriends, I mean."

Marissa shot him a sharp glare, half embarrassed, half exasperated, while a small, reluctant smile tugged at her lips.

Ian laughed, shaking his head. "You weren't much better, James. You watched her like a hawk anytime she was around. We all saw it. Honestly, it was frustrating."

James smirked, his dark eyes locking on Marissa. "Yeah… well, it's hard not to look at her."

Marissa felt heat rise to her cheeks, quickly glancing away to hide the blush that threatened to betray her. But she couldn't stop the small, reluctant smile that tugged at her lips, and James noticed it—grinning wider as he tightened his hold on her just a little.

Julie smiled, her eyes warm as she said, "I'm just glad it worked out. You two belong together." Then, her gaze shifted to James, sharp and teasing. "Don't stuff it up."

James's dark eyes met hers steadily. "I don't plan to. I've waited long enough for her— I'm not letting her go ever again."

A satisfied grin spread across Ian's face. "I'm glad to hear it."

A teasing smile curved Marissa's lips as she glanced at Ian and Shelby, her eyes sparkling with mischief. "Well, enough of your treachery... how was the honeymoon?"

Shelby laughed, giving Ian a playful nudge with her elbow. "Absolutely perfect."

They spent the next few minutes sharing stories from their honeymoon, laughter and smiles filling the room. Marissa wrapped her arms around James's neck, resting her head on his shoulder, letting herself sink into the comfort of him. The group listened intently, caught up in their joy and the easy, happy chatter.

Shelby raised an eyebrow. "Aren't you supposed to be at work?"

Marissa shrugged, a playful smile tugging at her lips. "I'm taking a few days off. I have... other things on my mind."

Shelby laughed knowingly. "I bet."

Later, Marissa strolled hand in hand with James around the estate. The rain had stopped, leaving the grounds glistening in the sunlight, and a warm breeze carried the fresh scent of wet grass. They walked close together, sharing quiet smiles, the world around them peaceful and bright.

James stopped and pulled her flush against him, his hands firm on her waist. "So... what now?" he murmured, his voice low and urgent.

Marissa's fingers tangled in his shirt, her breath quickening. "I'm not sure. What do you want to happen?"

His dark eyes burned into hers. "I want you to come home with me. For good."

"Really?" she whispered, her pulse thundering.

"Really," he said, tilting her chin up, his lips brushing hers in a teasing, feather-light touch before pulling back just enough to speak. "I want us to make a real go of this, Marissa. I wasn't kidding when I said I'm never letting you go."

Her chest tightened, uncertainty mingling with desire. "Are you sure? That's… a big step."

He pressed his forehead to hers, voice rough with longing. "A step we both need to take." Then, with a soft, irresistible tease, he kissed the tip of her nose. "Please… say yes."

Marissa's lips curved into a smile, her heart melting as the warmth of him surrounded her.

Marissa's lips curved into a soft, radiant smile, her heart melting in the warmth of his embrace.

"Yes," she whispered, simple and certain.

James's face lit up with a triumphant grin before he swept her into a deep, passionate kiss. Marissa felt a rush of heat and exhilaration as his arms tightened around her, pulling her impossibly close. She kissed him back with equal fervour, her thoughts swirling—fear and excitement, longing, and relief—all tangled together. Every heartbeat, every brush of lips and fingers, confirmed that this was exactly where she was meant to be.

Epilogue

Six months later…

Marissa was getting ready for dinner, brushing a strand of her auburn hair behind her ear as she glanced at her reflection. Since moving in with James, their relationship had grown stronger with every passing day. He had a way of showing his love that left no doubt—small gestures, thoughtful surprises, quiet moments that made her heart ache with happiness.

A month ago, they had made a big decision: buying a new apartment together. A stunning penthouse of glass and marble, with sweeping city views and sunlight pouring through floor-to-ceiling windows. It was more than just a home; it was a statement of their life together.

Marissa had spent the past week there almost constantly, overseeing deliveries, arranging furniture, and adding little touches that made the space truly theirs. Every corner of the penthouse bore her mark—soft throws on the sofa, delicate vases filled with fresh flowers, framed photographs capturing their happiest memories.

As Marissa slipped into her blue silk dress, the fabric flowing over her curves, she paused and took a deep breath, feeling a swell of contentment. This was their life—built hand in hand, filled with love, laughter, and the promise of countless moments yet to come.

In just a few days, they would be moving into their new penthouse. The final piece—the bed—had just arrived, waiting to complete the home they had been creating together. Marissa's mind lingered on the idea of their life unfolding there, and a small, happy shiver ran through her.

She studied her reflection in the mirror, turning slowly. She looked good—radiant, confident, alive. Just as she was about to turn away, the sound of footsteps made her glance over her shoulder.

James appeared in the doorway, looking magnificent in his dark blue suit. His tall, muscular frame filled the space, and his dark eyes softened when they landed on her. Without a word, he crossed the room and slipped his arms around her waist from behind, his lips brushing her temple in a tender kiss.

"You get more and more beautiful every day," he murmured, his voice low and warm. "You know that?"

Marissa laughed, her head tilting slightly back against his shoulder. "I think you're a little biased," she teased, though her heart fluttered at the compliment.

James tightened his hold, resting his chin on her shoulder, his presence enveloping her in a comforting, thrilling warmth. "Maybe," he admitted with a grin. "But I don't care—I'll always think you're perfect."

Marissa melted into him, her smile softening, the room around them fading as they shared a quiet, intimate moment before the evening ahead.

James reluctantly pulled his arms away, though his hands lingered just a moment longer than necessary and offered his arm. "We better go, or we'll be late."

Marissa slipped her arm through his, then picked up her purse as they stepped out of the bedroom. "Lead the way," she said with a playful smile.

Downstairs in the carpark, James gently helped her into his sleek black BMW. The leather smelled faintly of newness mixed with his subtle cologne, a scent that made her heart skip. Sliding into the driver's seat, he started the car, and they drove through the city lights before pulling into the penthouse's private parking area.

Marissa tilted her head, confused. "Wait… I thought we were going out to dinner?"

James grinned, brushing a stray lock of hair from her face. "I just want you to see the final masterpiece," he said, taking her hand and helping her out of the car.

They rode the elevator in comfortable silence, fingers intertwined. When the doors opened, Marissa stopped short, her eyes widening in surprise. The rich aroma of roasted rosemary chicken, garlic, and simmering herbs filled the air, mingling with the delicate scent of fresh flowers. Every surface in the living room was covered with vases of blooms—white lilies, blush roses, and soft peonies creating a sea of colour and fragrance.

Marissa turned to him, bewildered. "What's all this?"

James's dark eyes softened. "It's for you. To say thank you… for all your hard work."

She shook her head, a laugh escaping her. "You don't need to thank me."

"I know," he said, gently tucking a strand of her hair behind her ear, "but I want to."

James guided her to the dining table, where a waiter in crisp black attire stood ready to serve. The table was a vision of elegance—soft candlelight flickered across delicate china and crystal glasses, casting a warm golden glow that danced across the room. Every detail had been arranged to perfection, from the folded napkins to the subtle floral centrepiece, and the quiet hum of the city beyond the windows added a soothing backdrop.

They shared a romantic dinner, laughter flowing easily alongside quiet conversation. James kept sneaking glances at her, his fingers brushing hers whenever they reached for the same dish, each touch sending tiny sparks of electricity through her. The hours seemed to stretch, intimate and unhurried, until dessert arrived—a decadent chocolate soufflé paired with a delicate raspberry coulis. The waiter quietly excused himself, leaving them alone in the golden candlelight.

James leaned forward across the table, his gaze dark and warm. "You know," he murmured, his voice low and intimate, "I could get used to this—just the two of us, like this, surrounded by beauty… and you."

Marissa's heart fluttered. She reached out, resting her hand atop his, her fingers lacing with his. "I think I already have," she whispered, her eyes shimmering in the soft glow of the candles.

James rose from his seat, a playful gleam in his eye, and walked to the stereo. He pressed a button, and soft music began to drift through the penthouse, the gentle melody wrapping around them like a private world. He walked back to her extended his hand toward her. "Dance with me," he murmured, his dark eyes locking onto hers.

Marissa's lips curved into a smile, her heart quickening. She placed her hand in his, letting him lift her gracefully from the chair. They swayed together, slow, and effortless, their bodies moving as if they had been made for this moment. The world outside seemed to vanish—only the soft music, the warmth of each other, and the quiet intimacy of the night remained.

After a heartbeat, James pulled back just slightly, his face radiant but tinged with nervous excitement. From his pocket, he produced a small velvet box. Marissa's eyes widened as he opened it, revealing a stunning baguette-cut sapphire ring, flanked by two sparkling diamonds.

Her breath caught. "James…"

He dropped to one knee, taking her hand in his. "Marissa Turner… you've made my life brighter, fuller, and happier than I ever imagined. Will you marry me?"

Tears welled in her eyes, a heady mix of surprise, love, and overwhelming joy. She nodded, unable to speak at first, then finally whispered, "Yes… yes, of course I will!"

A triumphant smile spread across James's face as he slid the ring onto her finger, his touch reverent. He lifted her hand to his lips, pressing a tender kiss to the sapphire before claiming her mouth in a deep, passionate kiss. Marissa melted against him, her hands threading into his hair, her entire body trembling as joy, relief, and desire collided in one perfect, electric moment.

When he finally drew back, his voice was rough with emotion. "I love you, Marissa."

Her eyes shimmered with tears, her smile radiant. "I love you, James."

For a heartbeat, they simply stared at each other, the weight of the promise between them settling deep into their souls. Then, without another word, James swept her effortlessly into his arms. Marissa laughed breathlessly, her arms wrapping around his neck as he held her impossibly close.

The soft music still played, drifting through the penthouse, and the candlelight flickered across the walls, painting the moment in gold. James carried her toward the bedroom, every step certain, every heartbeat full of promise. As the door closed behind them, the rest of the world faded away—leaving only the two of them, lost in love, and at the beginning of their forever.

The End

Before the Thaw

Alison Reid

A complete standalone romance

Previously published individually

Chapter One

Jade Bell jogged past rows of sleepy terraced houses as the first blush of morning painted the sky over Manchester. The chill bit at her cheeks, but she welcomed it—it kept her focused. Steady breaths. The pounding rhythm of trainers on pavement. The blur of familiar streets as she wound her way through the city she'd called home since university.

Her body moved like clockwork, but her mind was elsewhere dragging behind her like a shadow. Heavy with things she couldn't outrun.

She didn't jog to burn calories or chase any vanity. It was for this: the solitude, the clarity. This was the only part of her day that was truly hers.

A woman jogged by in the opposite direction, nodding a silent good morning. Jade barely registered her.

She slowed at the corner near the park, breath pluming in the cold air, and bent to stretch. Her long, golden hair was pulled back in a loose ponytail, wavy strands curling under her running cap. Most people called her beautiful—striking, even—but Jade rarely saw herself that way. She saw the muscle tone she worked hard to keep, skin a little too pale from hospital lighting, and eyes that had looked a little sad for longer than she liked to admit.

Striking blue, those eyes. The kind people remembered. The kind that had once made Dean stop in the middle of a crowded student bar and stare like he'd seen a ghost.

She glanced at her watch—she'd have just enough time to shower and change before her shift. Another day in the Acute Medical Unit. Another twelve hours of holding hands, steadying voices, and absorbing other people's pain. Dodging emotions that weren't hers but often felt just as heavy.

Jade Bell was twenty-seven, a nurse practitioner, and damned good at what she did. She'd worked hard for her role—pushed through years of study, overnight shifts, and moments where the exhaustion nearly broke her. But the work had purpose. It made sense.

Unlike her relationship.

Dean Clarke, her boyfriend of nearly three years, was a financial planner in one of the sleek glass towers near St. Peter's Square. Smart. Charming when he wanted to be. Good-looking in that sharply groomed, expensive-shoe sort of way. On paper, they worked.

But paper was thin. And lately, so was his attention.

None of her friends liked Dean. They'd stopped bothering to hide it. Her best friend Leanne had once called him "a Prada briefcase full of hot air and ego." Jade had laughed then. Now it just stung.

She hadn't told anyone what had happened two weeks ago.

Not Leanne. Not her mum. Not even herself, really. She'd locked it all in a box and shoved it down to the bottom of her chest where no one could see.

She saw herself again—barefoot in the bathroom at six in the morning, holding the pregnancy test with trembling hands. Her knees had nearly buckled, the shock like ice water and fire all at once. She'd sat on the edge of the tub, staring at the second pink line. A life. A future. Unplanned, yes. Unexpected.

But not unwanted.

She'd felt something warm begin to bloom in her chest even as her fingers shook. Something fierce and terrifying. The idea that her life could change—not just her schedule or her sleep, but her entire sense of purpose. She hadn't pictured a nursery or nappies or tiny socks. Not yet. But she'd pictured holding something that was hers. A heartbeat tethered to her own.

And then… Dean.

He'd blinked when she told him. Just blinked.

"Wow… okay," he'd said, like she'd told him they'd won a free weekend at a hotel. He'd smiled too quickly. Looked away too fast.

She'd waited for him to come around, to say something real. He hadn't.

And then, four days later, she woke with a cramp so sharp it doubled her over. The bleeding started minutes after that.

By the time she was in A&E, she already knew.

She sat alone in the waiting room at 3 a.m., arms wrapped around her stomach, scarf pulled up to her chin to hide the tears on her cheeks. Her name was called by a nurse with soft eyes and latex gloves. She'd nodded numbly, followed her in, answered the clinical questions like she was filing an insurance claim. Her legs had been cold on the exam table. Her body already empty.

Dean hadn't even offered to come with her.

When she'd told him, still pale from the blood loss, still sore, he'd glanced up from his phone and said, "It's probably for the best."

And that had been the moment.

Not the blood. Not the pain.

Not the heartbeat she never heard.

It was that—the indifference in his voice, the flick of his thumb across a touchscreen—that broke something in her she hadn't known was fragile.

That night, she'd curled on the edge of the bed with her back to him, too tired to cry. Too numb to move. He'd snored softly behind her like it was any other night. As if nothing had changed.

But everything had.

The tears had dried up somewhere between the sterile exam room and the Uber ride home. But the ache? That never stopped.

And that was when she knew: something had to change.

She was carrying too much alone.

She blinked back to the present, vision swimming.

Back at her flat, Jade peeled off her running clothes, tossed them into the hamper, and padded barefoot to the wardrobe. She pulled out the thick knit jumper she'd bought for the trip. Oatmeal-coloured, soft as a cloud. The kind of thing you wore by a fire, glass of wine in hand, pretending things weren't broken.

The cabin in Glenridding had looked perfect in the photos—stone walls, a wood-burning stove, miles from anything. She'd booked it before the miscarriage, before Dean's detachment turned into silence, before she started wondering whether she was the only one still trying.

She should have cancelled. There'd been a moment—sitting on the edge of her bed with a hot water bottle against her stomach, Dean already snoring beside her—where she'd opened the booking app and stared at the "Cancel Reservation" button.

But she didn't.

Maybe it was habit. Maybe hope. Or maybe it was her way of drawing a line in the sand.

She dragged her suitcase from under the bed and began laying out clothes: thick socks, jeans, her favourite scarf. A pair of silk pyjamas still with the tags on.

Dean didn't even know what colour they were. Hadn't asked. Had barely mentioned the trip, except to confirm the dates.

She reached into the drawer for her travel-sized toiletries, then froze. Her fingers brushed something unexpected—an envelope, small and white, tucked in the back like a secret. She eased it out, already knowing what it was. The ultrasound scan. Six weeks along. She'd asked a colleague to squeeze her in the morning after the test turned positive. It had been too soon to see anything clearly—no hands, no feet, just a tiny, bean-shaped blur. But even then, it had felt real. Undeniably real.

It still did.

She left the envelope where it was and zipped up the bag.

This weekend was her line in the sand—the point beyond which she couldn't keep pretending. If nothing changed, if Dean remained as emotionally checked out as he'd been for months, then she'd have her answer. They hadn't even had sex in over five weeks, not since that half-hearted attempt that left her feeling lonelier than before.

She was done pleading to be noticed.

Because the truth was, she was seen—by friends, by strangers, by everyone except the one person who was supposed to know her best.

The male orderlies at the hospital always found a reason to linger near her. Doctors grinned when she passed them in the corridor. Nurses complimented her charting, her bedside manner, her patience. Even patients—groggy on morphine—called her "an angel," or "the pretty one."

She never let it go to her head.

But she noticed.

They saw her.

Dean didn't.

She could wear a new dress, curl her hair, put effort into a night out, and he'd barely glance up from his laptop. She could tell him about a patient who died holding her hand, or about a child whose mother never came back—and Dean would nod vaguely and say, "That's tough, babe."

Three years together. And he'd never asked her to move in.

Not once.

She always packed the overnight bag. She always drove across town. She remembered standing in his kitchen once, stirring pasta while he scrolled through his phone at the breakfast bar, and thinking, when did this become so one-sided?

Still, she stayed. Still, she tried.

Because in the beginning, it had been a chase. And she'd been the prize.

At university, she'd been too busy to date—laser-focused on her degree, juggling shifts, sleep-deprived and running on coffee. Dean had been relentless. Energy drinks left at her locker. Flowers on her birthday. Coincidental run-ins at every café and study group.

Just before she finished uni, she gave in—finally stopped resisting what had always felt inevitable. And for a while, it was good. He made her laugh. He made her feel like she mattered, like she was chosen.

Now, she just felt tired. Bone-deep tired.

She sat on the edge of the bed and smoothed her hand over the folded scarf in her case.

Why am I still doing this?

She didn't cheat. She never would. No matter how many colleagues "accidentally" brushed her hand, no matter how many looks she got walking down the corridor at work—she was loyal. It was a principle.

But she wasn't blind.

And lately, the ache to feel seen again was growing louder than the guilt that kept her in place.

She stood up and zipped the suitcase closed with a sharp pull.

They were driving separately—Dean's idea, of course. Said it was easier that way since he had to work late and she was already off.

Typical. He couldn't leave an hour earlier. Make a gesture?

Apparently not.

"You go ahead, babe," he'd said. "I'll be up after I finish the quarterly review. Shouldn't be too late."

She'd nodded like it didn't matter. But now, as she looked around her flat—keys in hand, bag packed, the silence closing in—she felt the sting of it all.

It wasn't about the drive.

It was about the effort. Or the lack of it.

One weekend.

One chance to fix what was broken.

If he didn't show up emotionally... she'd walk.

For good.

The thought made her stomach twist—not because she didn't mean it, but because she did.

And because deep down, she already knew how this weekend would go.

Dean would arrive late. He'd be distracted. He'd say the right things but mean none of them. And she would try—like always—to fill the silence.

But not this time.

This time, if he didn't meet her halfway, she'd stop pretending.

She grabbed her coat, slipped her arms through the sleeves, and stood for a moment in the quiet of her flat. The home she'd built on her own. The life she'd carried while he kept his at arm's length.

She opened the door.

Paused.

She closed it behind her. This time, she wanted the sound to echo.

Chapter Two

Duncan Armstrong leaned back in the café chair; hands wrapped around a paper cup that had long gone cold. The London rain had followed him north, spitting against the windows in restless bursts that matched the churn in his chest.

He hadn't planned on stopping in Manchester for long—just a brief catch-up with Dean before heading on to his parents' place in the Lakes. But even sitting here now, ten minutes from the apartment building where Dean lived, he still wasn't sure why he'd agreed to meet up.

Old habits, maybe.

Loyalty. Or what was left of it.

They used to be best friends. Once. Before everything shifted.

Duncan was twenty-nine now, a successful trauma surgeon at a London hospital, with a well-cut coat, tailored shirts, and a string of relationships that had never made it past three months. On the surface, he had everything: career, money, respect, looks that turned heads. He was tall, broad-shouldered, his dark brown hair always slightly tousled in a way that made it look effortless, and hazel eyes that had once convinced a woman to miss her flight home from Rome.

But none of it mattered.

Because none of them were her.

He'd left Manchester not because he wanted to, but because he couldn't stand to stay.

Not after Dean had started dating Jade Bell—the one woman Duncan had spent years quietly falling for. The one he thought maybe—just maybe—had started to feel something back.

They'd all met at uni—Duncan, Dean, Jade, and Leanne. Leanne and Jade were a couple of years younger, but that hadn't mattered. Duncan had noticed Jade almost immediately, not long after she and Leanne started their medical degrees.

The four of them had been inseparable in the beginning—cramming for exams during late-night library sessions, spilling drinks at house parties, sharing greasy takeaway dinners on mismatched cushions in cluttered living rooms.

Dean had always been the loud one, the natural extrovert, sailing through his economics degree with charm to spare. He could walk into any room and own it in two seconds flat. Duncan, by contrast, was the quiet one—steadier, more grounded. The fixer. The one who noticed what others missed, who listened when no one else did.

And Jade—God, Jade.

The blue-eyed, golden-haired, too-brilliant-for-this-world woman who walked into Duncan's anatomy lecture wearing scrubs too big for her frame and a messy bun that still looked beautiful.

He hadn't stood a chance.

He'd watched her start dating Dean just before she finished uni. Watched her fall— slowly, inevitably—in love with him. Or maybe it only seemed slow because every second of it carved a little deeper into Duncan's chest.

The truth was, Dean hadn't even liked her at first. Not really.

Duncan had seen it clearly—clearer than Jade ever could. To Dean, it had been a game. A challenge. A chance to win something Duncan wanted before Duncan had the courage to reach for it himself.

And Dean played to win.

He'd known Duncan was going to ask her out. Duncan had told him as much—one quiet night at the pub, heart in his throat, fingers damp against a sweating pint glass. He'd finally gathered the courage, finally let himself believe it wasn't just one-sided.

He hadn't asked earlier for two reasons. The first—and biggest—was fear. He was terrified she'd reject him, and it would ruin everything. The second was respect: Jade had said she wanted to finish her degree before getting involved with anyone, and he'd taken her at her word.

But then, three days later, Dean asked her first.

And she said yes.

Dean had won.

Duncan had told himself to let it go. To be happy for them. To move on.

He tried.

But he backed away. Kept his distance. Tried to avoid them as much as possible.

He dated, of course. Flashed practiced smiles at beautiful women. Laughed at their jokes. Brushed fingertips across candlelit tables and nodded at the right moments, saying all the right things.

But no matter how many names he remembered, how many lips he kissed, none of it ever meant anything.

Because none of them were *her.*

None of them had Jade's eyes—bright and blazing when she was passionate about something. None of them had her laugh—the one that curled at the end like she couldn't quite contain it. None of them saw the world the way she did or made him feel like he mattered just by listening.

No one else came close.

And the worst part?

She'd never known.

Even now, all these years later, her name still made something tighten in his chest.

He'd finally left Manchester because he couldn't keep watching them together—even if it was only now and then, even if they were careful about it. But the real catalyst came when Dean pulled him aside and said, "You make Jade uncomfortable. She's noticed the way you look at her."

That was the moment.

He decided he'd had enough. Two weeks later, he packed his things and moved to London. No goodbyes. No explanations. Just distance.

He hadn't seen her in months. Dean rarely mentioned her anymore, and Duncan never asked. He couldn't. It was easier not to know.

But he couldn't help the flicker of hope when Dean texted him the night before.

Passing through this weekend? Grab a drink at my place? I'm around Friday afternoon.

It was casual. Brief. Typical Dean.

Still, Duncan said yes.

If he was being honest, part of him wanted to see Jade. Maybe he needed to know if time had softened the old resentment, or if it was still sitting there, sharp-edged and waiting. Maybe he just wanted to look Dean in the eye and remind himself why they weren't really friends anymore.

Or maybe—just maybe—some stubborn, hidden part of him was still hoping to hear that Jade was finally done with Dean.

That maybe, somehow, it wasn't too late.

He stood, tossed the untouched coffee into the bin, and pulled his coat tighter as he stepped back out into the Manchester chill. The air was damp, heavy with the kind of grey that settled in your bones.

He hadn't planned for the weekend to bring anything unexpected.

The idea was simple: have a drink with Dean, then drive on to his parents' place near Keswick. He hadn't told them he was coming—hadn't told anyone, really—but they'd be happy to see him. His mum would fuss, his dad would act like it was no big deal, and there'd be tea, stew, and a quiet room to sleep off the London static.

But if he was being honest with himself—really honest—he was hoping he'd see Jade too.

Just the thought of it made his pulse tick faster, an uninvited thrill humming under his ribs.

He didn't know why he tortured himself this way. Didn't know why the idea of maybe seeing her still rattled him after all this time.

He just couldn't help it.

Even now, years later, her name alone could crack him wide open. He'd tried to forget her. Tried to move on. But Jade Bell had never left him. Not really. She lived somewhere just beneath the surface of his every quiet moment.

He slid into his Audi and started the engine, the low hum grounding him as he pulled out into the afternoon traffic. Manchester hadn't changed much. Still grey, still humming with that strange blend of industry and nostalgia. Every corner was a memory—some easier than others.

Dean's apartment wasn't far. Sleek new build, glass, and steel and exactly the kind of place Dean liked to be seen in. Jade didn't live with him. That had always struck Duncan as… surprising.

If she were his, Duncan wouldn't let her out of his sight.

Not out of possessiveness—he wasn't that guy—but because being near her had always felt like oxygen. If she still looked anything like she had the last time he saw her—all long limbs, golden hair, and those impossibly blue eyes—she could have anyone she so much as cocked an eyebrow at.

But Jade wasn't like that.

She had principles.

Painfully so.

He knew that better than anyone.

She'd stayed loyal to Dean, even when Dean didn't deserve her. Even when Duncan had been right there, saying everything she needed to hear, silently, in the spaces Dean left empty.

Duncan pulled into the visitor lot outside the building and killed the engine.

He sat for a moment, jaw tight, eyes on the mirrored doors. Steeling himself.

Then he got out, locked the car with a beep, and headed inside.

The lift smelled faintly of citrus cleaner. The hallway was too quiet. When he reached Dean's flat, he hesitated for half a second—just long enough to hear the faint beat of music on the other side—then knocked.

Three firm raps. Confident. Controlled.

A heartbeat passed. Then two.

He wasn't sure what he expected to find behind that door.

But whatever it was, it wasn't the easy, careless grin that greeted him when the door swung open.

"Duncan, you made it."

Dean's tone was warm, as if nothing had ever come between them. As if they were still twenty-one, downing pints at the student union and plotting summer holidays they'd never take.

Duncan offered a tight smile and shook the outstretched hand. "Yeah. Figured I'd stop in before heading to the Lakes."

"Come in." Dean stepped aside, motioning him in with a casual wave.

The flat was pristine in that sterile, bachelor-pad way—everything chrome, leather, and glass, not a single cushion out of place. The faint thump of a playlist played from the speakers in the corner, something electronic and forgettable.

"Whiskey?" Dean asked, already moving toward the sleek bar cart without waiting for an answer.

"Sure," Duncan said, glancing around. "Place looks the same."

Dean chuckled as he poured two fingers of scotch into each glass. "Haven't had time to redecorate. Work's been insane. Portfolio expansions, high net worth clients, tax-year rollovers... you know the drill."

Duncan didn't. He didn't care to, either. But he nodded. "Sounds like fun."

Dean handed him the glass. "To surviving another week."

They clinked. Duncan took a sip. Smooth. Peaty. Overpriced.

He let the silence stretch just long enough for it to feel deliberate.

Dean sat on the edge of the couch, legs stretched out in front of him. "So, how's London? Still saving lives?"

Duncan gave a one-shouldered shrug. "Trying not to lose too many. Trauma's... busy. Keeps me sharp."

"Always knew you'd end up cutting people open," Dean smirked. "No offence."

"None taken." Duncan swirled the amber liquid in his glass, eyes flicking to the hallway just past the kitchen. "So... is Jade here?"

Dean's smirk faltered—only slightly, but Duncan caught it.

"Nah," Dean said, waving a dismissive hand. "She's up at Glenridding. She planned a weekend away for us."

Duncan's grip on his glass tightened.

"Oh?"

Dean leaned back, stretching like a man who didn't have a single weight on his conscience. "Yeah. She nearly gave me a bloody heart attack two weeks ago."

Duncan's brows drew together. "Why?"

Dean snorted into his drink, like it was a joke. "She got herself pregnant."

There was a pause. The kind of silence that buzzes under the skin.

Duncan's jaw clenched. "She didn't do it on her own, Dean."

Dean dismissed it with a lazy shrug. "Well, it doesn't matter now. She miscarried a week later. Thank God, honestly."

The words landed like a punch to Duncan's gut.

He stared at Dean, stunned, the air thick between them.

"Is she okay?" he asked, voice low and sharp.

Dean raised an eyebrow, surprised by the question. "She's... I don't know. Quiet, I guess. Mopey. I told her it was probably for the best. We're not exactly in a place to be raising kids."

Duncan set his glass down—slowly, deliberately—because he didn't trust his grip not to shatter it.

"You told her it was for the best?"

Dean blinked at him, unbothered. "Well, yeah. What was I supposed to say? I'm not gonna pretend I was excited. She's been all over the place lately. Emotional. Overreacting."

Duncan stood.

He didn't remember deciding to. His body just moved, charged with heat.

"She lost a baby, Dean. Your baby. And you couldn't even be decent to her."

Dean's face tightened just a little. "Don't do that. Don't turn this into one of your 'white knight' speeches."

"No," Duncan said quietly, "this has nothing to do with playing the hero. This is about being a decent human being. You were supposed to care. At the very least, you were supposed to give a damn."

"I'm moving on anyway."

Duncan blinked. "What?"

"I got a better offer this afternoon," Dean said, a self-satisfied smirk playing on his lips. "Spending the weekend with my secretary."

Silence stretched between them.

When Duncan finally spoke, his voice was lower, heavier.

"But Jade's waiting for you. In Glenridding."

Dean shrugged, completely unbothered. "She'll work it out."

Duncan stared at him in disbelief. His blood turned cold, then hot.

"You're cheating on her? How long?" He already knew the answer. But hearing it aloud made it real—and so much worse.

Dean took another slow sip of his drink, utterly unfazed. "Couple of weeks. It's no big deal. She'll get over it."

"Bloody hell, Dean." Duncan's voice was louder now, sharper. "You're unbelievable."

Dean scoffed. "Mate, not everyone's built like you. You fall in love with every doe-eyed woman who brings you coffee. I'm not wired that way."

Duncan's hands curled into fists at his sides.

"I loved her," he said, each word sharp, controlled, seething. "I loved her, and you knew it. And you went after her anyway."

Dean stood too now, still holding his drink, still smug. "Oh, come off it. She wasn't yours. She never was."

Duncan's jaw clenched. "You didn't even want her until you saw I did."

Dean's eyes darkened, his smirk sliding toward cruelty. "So what? You're still carrying a torch? You want me to step aside now and give you a shot? Is that what this is?"

Duncan shook his head slowly, the disgust plain on his face. "This isn't about me. It's about her. She deserves better than this."

Dean let out a bitter laugh. "Then go tell her."

He looked Duncan square in the eye, voice laced with contempt. "You think she'll fall into your arms after three years with me? Be my guest." He leaned back. "She's up at the cabin on Greystones Lane. Waiting."

A beat passed. Then, with a cruel twist of his mouth, he added,

"You can both cry about the miscarriage together."

Something inside Duncan snapped.

He took a step back, his jaw set, rage trembling just beneath the surface. Not just anger at Dean—but regret. Guilt. And all the words he should have said to Jade but never did.

His voice came out low, shaking.

"You don't just *not* deserve her," Duncan said, turning toward the door. "You never did."

Dean straightened, the smugness fading from his face. His voice tightened.

"Where are you going?"

Duncan didn't hesitate. "We're done, Dean. You're selfish, cruel and a complete ass."

Then he turned, walked to the door, and left the flat without another word.

The cold hit him like a slap as he stepped out into the grey Manchester evening.

But it did nothing to cool the fire burning in his chest.

Chapter Three

The motorway stretched ahead, grey, and endless, cutting through the damp sweep of countryside as Jade Bell pressed further north.

She'd left Manchester just after ten, hoping to get ahead of the weekend traffic. The clouds hung low, bloated with moisture, casting everything in muted tones. The kind of day that couldn't decide between rain or snow. The heater in her little hatchback blew warm air over her legs, the radio murmured quietly in the background, but her thoughts were anything but still.

She tapped the steering wheel lightly, thumb to the beat of a song she wasn't really listening to.

The roads thinned the further she got from the city—buildings giving way to wide fields and dense patches of trees that blurred past her window like smudged charcoal. Sheep dotted the hills in the distance, unmoved by the slow approach of winter.

This was supposed to be romantic.

A remote cabin tucked into the Lake District, a fire crackling in the hearth, the two of them finally talking—really talking. She'd imagined red wine and shared laughter, maybe even some closure if nothing else. But now, with each mile, the silence in the car felt heavier.

She glanced at her phone in the cupholder. No messages.

Of course not.

Dean hadn't even texted to say he'd finished work or ask how the drive was going. He wouldn't. That would require thought. Interest. Effort.

Jade exhaled through her nose, fighting the familiar sting behind her eyes. She wouldn't cry. Not on this road. Not over him.

Focus.

She turned onto the narrower country lane that led toward Glenridding. The trees pressed in closer now, branches arching overhead, their limbs bare and reaching like bony fingers. Patches of frost clung to the roadside, the first signs of winter tightening its grip.

Her GPS chimed, telling her she was ten minutes out.

As she climbed higher into the hills, the landscape opened up—valleys spilling out below, mist curled low over the lakes in the distance. It was beautiful. Wild and quiet in a way the city never was.

She'd chosen this place for a reason.

It was far enough away to feel like another world. A reset. A chance.

But even now, nestled in the beauty of it all, that ache in her chest wouldn't leave. Not quite.

She kept thinking of the scan photo she'd left in the drawer. Of the look on Dean's face when she told him she'd lost the baby—blank, like someone reporting a cancelled train. She remembered lying awake for hours afterward, wondering if she'd imagined it all—the moment of joy, the flicker of hope, the idea that something between them might still matter.

Now she wasn't sure what hurt more—losing the pregnancy or realising she'd already lost him.

The final turn appeared at last, a narrow track barely wide enough for her car. She drove slowly now, gravel crunching beneath her tyres, tree limbs brushing the windows as she navigated the winding path.

Then, finally, the cabin came into view.

Nestled at the base of a wooded slope, the cabin was all stone, timber, and ivy. Smoke curled from the chimney—lit, no doubt, by the property manager before her arrival. The lake glittered in the distance, just visible through the trees. The place looked exactly like the photos—and nothing like what her life felt like.

She pulled up to the edge of the gravel drive and turned off the ignition. The sudden silence was deafening.

For a moment, she just sat there, both hands still on the wheel, staring out at the cabin. Her reflection blinked back at her in the windshield—tired eyes, windblown hair, and a look she couldn't quite name.

She was early. Dean wouldn't be here for hours.

With a quiet sigh, she unbuckled her seatbelt and stepped out into the cold.

It wrapped around her like a warning.

Or maybe a welcome.

A snowflake landed on her nose, delicate and cold. More drifted down around her— soft, slow—hinting that snow was on the way.

She popped the boot and hauled out her suitcase, its wheels slipping slightly on the loose gravel. As she neared the cabin door, a robin fluttered down onto the branch above the porch. It hopped once, then again, tilting its head as if watching her—before darting off into the trees.

"Wish I could do that," she murmured.

Inside, the cabin was warm and softly lit. Wood panelling. Exposed beams. A fire crackling in the stone hearth, just like she'd pictured. There was a bottle of wine and two glasses on the kitchen counter, left as part of the welcome package.

It should have felt romantic.

It didn't.

She remembered researching the place late one night while Dean snored beside her— picturing them curled up on that sofa, wine in hand, maybe even talking about what came next.

Jade set her suitcase down and looked around the space. It was beautiful, peaceful. The kind of place people came to heal or fall in love again.

She took a slow breath in and let it out.

Now all she had to do… was wait.

Jade slipped off her boots and left them by the front door, her socks immediately sinking into the thick, sheepskin rug. The warmth of the fire hugged her skin like a blanket she hadn't known she needed. The room smelled of pine and woodsmoke and something faintly sweet—vanilla, maybe, from the scented candle flickering on the coffee table.

She walked through the open-plan cabin slowly, taking it in. The kitchen was compact but modern—polished oak cupboards, a stone countertop, cast iron pans hanging above the stove. She opened the small fridge and placed the welcome bottle of wine inside to chill, even though a voice in her head whispered that Dean probably wouldn't drink it with her. He wasn't a wine guy unless it was expensive and served to him by someone in a pressed apron.

The suitcase sat unopened near the fireplace. She left it for now, curling up on the wide armchair beside the hearth, letting the warmth sink into her bones. Her fingers hovered above the knit throw draped over the arm, smoothing it absently. Everything in this place was soft, quiet, calm—everything her life hadn't been lately.

She rested her head against the back of the chair and closed her eyes. A strange shiver ghosted down her spine—gone before she could place it.

Alone felt… easier. But something in her chest refused to settle.

Still, a part of her waited for the sound of tyres crunching up the gravel drive. Waited for Dean to arrive and finally show her something—anything—that said he still wanted to be here, with her.

But hours stretched long. And the only sound was the crackle of the fire.

Duncan stood at the curb, breath pluming in the cold, staring blindly at the rain-slicked windscreen of his car. His hands were shaking. He shoved them into his coat pockets, not out of chill—but to stop himself from going back inside and breaking Dean's face.

The man he used to call brother.

The man who had everything—and never appreciated a damn bit of it.

He forced himself to breathe. In through the nose, out through the mouth. A trauma response. It worked in surgery. It had to work now.

But this wasn't a surgical crisis.

This was Jade.

And she was alone.

Grieving.

And he hadn't even known.

A lump rose in his throat, thick and painful. It wasn't just anger now—it was grief. For what she'd been through. For the version of himself that once trusted Dean. For all the years lost to silence and cowardice and keeping his distance.

She'd deserved so much more than indifference.

And Dean had given her nothing but cold comfort and betrayal.

She got herself pregnant.

The words echoed, acid-sharp and unshakable.

As if it had been a mistake on her part. As if the loss hadn't ripped her open.

Duncan knew what that kind of pain did to people. He'd held women's hands as they wept into their hospital gowns, offered what comfort he could as they bled quietly on sterile sheets, their grief swallowed by clinical lighting and time constraints. But Jade… Jade was different.

She would've carried the weight with grace and silence. And he hadn't been there to soften a single second of it.

A rush of guilt punched him square in the chest.

He was done standing on the sidelines.

No more silence. No more distance.

She was in Glenridding—alone. Dean wasn't going. He'd made that perfectly clear between swigs of overpriced scotch and dismissive laughter.

She'll work it out.

The arrogance.

The cruelty.

Duncan climbed into his car, slammed the door shut, and pulled out his phone with trembling fingers. He opened Jade's contact but didn't hit call. Not yet. He couldn't say this over the phone. Not after everything.

She needed more than words right now.

She needed him.

And this time, he wasn't going to run from it.

He shifted the car into gear and pulled out of the lot, tyres hissing against wet asphalt. The rain had picked up—Manchester's familiar curtain of drizzle turning to something heavier, colder.

Fitting.

The city blurred behind him as he drove north, every kilometre peeling away another layer of hesitation. The further he got from Dean's apartment, the easier it was to breathe. The more certain he became.

He thought about their last real conversation—him and Jade, nearly a year ago now. They'd crossed paths at a hospital conference, both attending the same surgical ethics seminar. He'd seen her across the room, blonde hair tucked behind one ear, pen poised mid-note like she was still the overachiever he remembered.

They'd had coffee after. Talked about nothing and everything. She'd smiled, even laughed a little, but there'd been a shadow in her eyes. He hadn't known what it meant then.

Now he did.

He gripped the steering wheel tighter, jaw clenched. The road signs blurred by. He barely registered them.

The storm was coming in harder now, sheets of rain slamming against the windscreen as the wipers strained to keep up. The mountains in the distance disappeared into mist.

Still, he didn't slow.

She's alone. She's hurting. And I wasn't there when it counted.

But maybe—just maybe—he could still show up now.

For her.

For them.

Because even after all these years, all the silence, all the should-haves and almosts… there was still something between them. Something that never left.

And he was done pretending it didn't matter.

The sky had started to bruise with dusk by the time he hit the open stretch of road. Rain slashed at the windscreen in diagonal sheets, the wipers struggling to keep up. He turned on the headlights and pressed harder on the accelerator.

Every mile was a beat of resentment.

At Dean. At himself.

At the sick twist in his gut that was half-rage, half-grief—for the girl he could never stop loving, and the version of her that Dean had broken piece by piece.

He didn't know exactly what he'd say when he got there. But she needed to know the truth.

Not next week.

Not later.

Now.

Duncan tightened his grip on the wheel and kept driving, unaware that the weather was turning fast—and that the mountain roads ahead didn't forgive distraction.

Chapter Four

The rain had turned to sleet somewhere past Penrith, and Duncan could feel it in his bones. The temperature was dropping fast. His fingers were stiff on the wheel, the cold creeping in even with the heat blasting. Every gust of wind rocked the car like a warning, as he took the winding B-road toward Glenridding, headlights slicing through the thickening mist that curled over the moors like smoke.

He leaned forward slightly, both hands gripping the wheel, eyes narrowed. The road had narrowed, too—twisting now, hugging the shoulder of the hill as it rose toward the mountains. There were no other cars. Just him, the storm, and the knowledge that Jade was up there waiting for a man who didn't deserve her.

He should've told her years ago. Should've said it when she was still at university— before Dean ever got the chance to worm his way in and poison everything. But Duncan hadn't been that guy.

Hadn't wanted to risk their friendship. Hadn't wanted to make her choose.

So, he'd stepped back.

Coward.

He remembered the exact moment it happened. The moment he realised he loved her.

They were in the study room at the library. His final year. Late. Too late.

Duncan rubbed his eyes and glanced at the clock: 12:42 a.m. The fluorescent lights buzzed faintly overhead, and his anatomy notes had blurred into one long Latin nightmare.

Across the table, Jade was curled in one of the unforgiving plastic chairs like she'd been born there—bare feet tucked beneath her, hoodie sleeves pulled over her hands, her lower lip caught between her teeth as she typed like she was running out of time.

She looked exhausted. Pale, rumpled, drained.

And somehow—still radiant.

God, she always did that. Wore stress like a second skin, like if she carried enough of it for everyone else, she might outrun her own. She hadn't eaten properly all day. Hadn't taken a real break in hours.

And still—when she caught him watching her—she smiled. That lopsided, tired, perfect smile.

"Another hour?" she asked, voice hopeful. "I think I've almost cracked this section."

And that was the moment.

It didn't hit him like lightning. Didn't knock the wind from his lungs.

It just... settled. Quiet. Inevitable. Like something that had been there all along and only now made sense.

He loved her.

Not a crush. Not passing affection. Not the kind of fondness you laugh off in the pub.

The real thing. The terrifying, soul-deep kind that lived in his chest like a permanent ache. The kind that sat in your throat for weeks and never let you breathe properly again.

He loved her.

And he couldn't say it.

Not then.

Not when she looked at him like he was the one place she didn't have to pretend. Not when she leaned so fully into what they were—close, easy, safe.

Not when Dean had just started circling. Watching. Measuring.

Dean didn't love her. Not really. He loved the idea of her—the challenge, the status, the fact that Duncan had loved her first.

Duncan had seen it coming. And still, he'd said nothing.

He swallowed the truth, shoved it down like everything else, and gave her a crooked smile instead.

"Another hour," he said, pretending his chest wasn't splitting in two.

Bloody coward.

A fresh wave of sleet slapped the windscreen, snapping him back to the present. He swore under his breath and flicked the wipers to full. The trees blurred past—bare branches clawing at the sky like they were trying to hold him back.

The tyres slipped over a patch of slush, the car fishtailing just slightly before he righted it with a sharp jerk of the wheel. His heart kicked.

Steady. Stay steady. He had to get to her.

Now. Before it was too late again.

Just a few more miles.

Through the sleet, he caught a flicker of warm light—far ahead, tucked against the hillside. The cabin. Her.

The headlights caught a frozen patch too late. For a second, the car floated—weightless, unmoored—then gravity snapped the illusion.

Then the road dipped suddenly, sloped into a sharp curve hugging the edge of a steep drop into the valley below.

He braked.

Too late.

The tyres lost traction. The car fishtailed with a violent jerk, sliding sideways across the icy surface. Duncan fought the wheel, heart thundering in his chest, but the back end swung out and the entire car spun.

"Shit—!"

He barely had time to brace before the front right wheel hit the soft shoulder and dropped—off the road completely. Gravity yanked the vehicle down, and it careened into the ditch below with a bone-rattling crunch.

Airbags exploded in a deafening pop. Metal shrieked. His skull slammed into the headrest. Then—stillness."

Silence, except for the ticking of the engine and the distant hiss of sleet on the windscreen.

Duncan blinked.

His head throbbed. His shoulder screamed. The airbag deflated slowly against his chest as he sucked in a breath and winced.

He was alive.

Barely.

The car sat tilted awkwardly in the ditch, front end crumpled against a tree, steam rising in ghostly plumes from the engine. The headlights flickered, one of them gone entirely.

He tried the door.

It wouldn't budge.

He shoved again with his uninjured arm, gritting his teeth, and finally forced it open with a loud pop. Cold air rushed in like a slap. He staggered out of the car, boots crunching in the sleet and gravel, legs shaky.

The road was somewhere above him. But the cabin was—if he remembered correctly—less than a mile away.

He looked up through the trees toward the barely visible ridgeline.

No signal. No cars. No help coming.

"Of course. No bloody service." His voice sounded strange in the quiet. Like it didn't belong to him.

His jaw clenched.

He wasn't turning back.

Not now.

Duncan hauled his coat tighter around his shoulders and started walking, one unsteady step at a time, toward the faint promise of light through the storm.

Toward Jade.

The wind tore through the trees like something alive, shrieking through the bare branches with a voice full of warning. It lashed at Duncan's face, sharp as glass, cold enough to sear. Ice and snow stung his cheeks, blurred his vision, soaked through his coat, and settled into the creases of his gloves. The storm hadn't let up—it had deepened, grown teeth. He could feel it in the way the gusts battered him sideways, how the trees groaned above like they might give way at any second.

He climbed, boots slipping on the steep incline, body hunched forward to brace against the wind. Each step sent a fresh bolt of pain through his shoulder—the same shoulder that had slammed into the car door during the crash. His ribs ached with every breath, his thighs burned with effort, and his fingers had long since gone numb.

But he didn't stop.

He couldn't.

His thoughts raced louder than the wind. Every flinch, every slip, every breath that burned in his lungs was underscored by one truth: He was too late once before. He wouldn't be again.

The trees were thinning now, their skeletal limbs swaying and bending under the weight of snow. Flakes mixed with sleet, wet and heavy, clinging to his eyelashes, blurring the already-dim outline of the trail ahead. His coat hung heavy with moisture, plastered to his back. His jeans were stiff with ice from the knees down. He was soaked to the skin, every inch of him aching and trembling.

One foot. Then the other. Then the other.

The forest floor had turned treacherous—slick with wet leaves and hidden debris. He tripped once on a half-buried root, went down hard on both knees with a grunt of pain. He stayed there for a second, breathing through clenched teeth, his head bowed. The temptation to stop—to just stay there, let the storm take him—pressed hard against his spine like a weight.

But then he saw her face.

Not in front of him. In memory.

Jade, smiling with that soft kind of hope that used to undo him. Jade, turning away after he said nothing. Jade, hollow-eyed when she would eventually tell him she'd lost a baby—her baby—while Dean stood by with barely a flicker of emotion.

Rage surged up through the exhaustion, and he forced himself to his feet with a growl.

He'd been so goddamn quiet. So careful. So cowardly.

Letting her believe Dean was the safe choice. Letting her think Duncan had never wanted more.

Another gust of wind slammed into him like a fist. The storm screamed through the branches overhead, and the snow came faster now, thick and blinding. He staggered sideways, half-falling into a thicket of brambles, felt them tear at his coat and scrape his skin. He didn't care.

Somewhere in the blur ahead, light flickered.

His heart stumbled in his chest.

The cabin.

The faint glow of golden warmth barely visible through the wall of white. It didn't look real—looked like something conjured by a frost-bitten brain, a trick of his need. But it was there. He blinked hard, squinted through the swirling snow. Yes—light in the windows. Smoke curling from the chimney.

He was close.

Relief nearly undid him. His knees buckled, but he caught himself against a tree trunk and kept going. His steps were more a stagger now, the snow dragging at his legs like wet concrete. His jaw was clenched so tightly his teeth ached.

He'd made it this far. He wasn't giving up now. Not with her just steps away.

The porch appeared first—dim and hazy through the curtain of snow. Then the windows, glowing with firelight, golden and steady. The cabin looked exactly like he'd imagined—rustic, peaceful, tucked away from the world.

He reached the steps, boots dragging, his vision tunnelling. Every muscle in his body was screaming. His lungs were ragged. He was freezing to death, and he knew it.

But none of that mattered.

She was in there.

He lifted a hand toward the door.

The motion cost him everything.

His legs gave out. His shoulder hit the door with a sickening thud, and he crumpled to the porch like a puppet with its strings cut. His breath came in shallow gasps. He tried to push up on one elbow, tried to call her name—

"Jade…"

But his voice was hoarse, barely more than a breath. A whisper swallowed by the storm.

"Jade…"

His head dropped. The snow fell faster now, soft, and merciless, dusting his hair, settling on his lashes.

The last thing he heard was the muffled sound of the fire inside.

The warmth—just on the other side.

And then everything went black.

Hours had passed.

The fire crackled softly in the hearth, casting flickering gold light across the worn floorboards and knotty pine walls. The storm outside had gathered strength, turning from sleet to thick snow that now blanketed the trees and the gravel drive. Wind moaned around the eaves like a restless ghost, occasionally rattling the windowpanes with a hollow thud.

Jade sat curled in the armchair, her legs tucked beneath her, a half-empty glass of wine resting on the side table beside her. The bottle, still mostly full, had been returned to the fridge an hour ago. She hadn't even tasted the last sip. Her stomach was too tight, too sour.

It was snowing hard now.

It wasn't supposed to.

The forecast had said sleet—intermittent at best. Not this thick, relentless fall that blurred the trees and swallowed the sky. It clung to the windows in thick, melting streaks and buried the front steps in silence. The kind of storm that swallowed sound. And hours. Her phone rested silently on the armrest, dark and unbothered. No buzz. No light. No signal.

Probably the storm.

Possibly fate.

Either way, it mocked her with its stillness.

And still—no Dean.

She'd tried not to let it bother her at first. Told herself he'd show up. Told herself he was just late—caught at work, stuck in traffic, maybe even trying to surprise her by arriving after she'd fallen asleep. That would be just like him. Dramatic re-entries. Convenient timing. The illusion of effort.

But with every passing hour, the fantasy unravelled—thread by delicate thread. And the weather, relentless and uncaring, seemed to mock her for believing in it at all.

She glanced at the door again, as if her stare might will him into existence. But there was nothing. Just wind and shadows—and the slow, heavy ache of being forgotten.

She wasn't new to disappointment. Not with Dean. But this one cut deeper.

He knew what this weekend meant.

She'd told him—quietly, plainly. No fights. No ultimatums. Just truth. The kind that came from exhaustion more than anger. That weary kind of pleading that didn't sound like pleading anymore.

We need time. Space. Just us.

She needed this.

And still… he hadn't come.

The cabin, once peaceful, now felt claustrophobic. Heavy with unspoken things. The silence wasn't comforting anymore—it amplified everything. The creak of the old floorboards. The wind sighing beneath the eaves. The ticking clock in the kitchen, mocking every minute that passed without headlights on the drive.

What if he didn't come?

What if the roads were worse than expected? What if he'd turned around? Gotten stuck? Had an accident?

Her eyes flicked to the window, where the snow now blurred the glass like a veil. She wrapped her arms around herself, rubbed warmth into her elbows.

He'd call if he could but there was no service.

Or maybe he just hadn't tried.

Maybe this was easier for him—easier to let the weather be the excuse. Easier to avoid facing her. Avoid hearing what she really needed to say.

The fire cracked behind her, the flames dancing low and slow. She leaned forward and added another log. Watched it catch. Watched the light shift again, golden, and ghostlike on the pine walls.

It was getting dark now.

Still no car.

Still no Dean.

She rose and crossed to the window, peering out. Her reflection stared back—faint and pale against the glass. Snow swirled just beyond, thick as fog, blanketing the trees and driveway in a slow, relentless hush.

She couldn't even tell where the road ended anymore.

What if he tried to come and didn't make it?

A flicker of guilt twisted in her gut, sharp and cold. She didn't want him hurt. She didn't want him lost out there.

But God help her—she didn't want him to show up now either. Not like this. Not late and smug and full of excuses. Not with that same forced grin and "Sorry, babe" as if her time—her feelings—were an afterthought.

She set her wine glass down and rubbed her hands together again, more from nerves than cold.

Her chest was tight. Her eyes burned.

The silence deepened.

Then—

A sudden, heavy thump against the front door.

Jade's heart lurched so violently she nearly spilled the wine.

She froze.

The fire crackled behind her, but her ears strained toward the front of the cabin, listening. Nothing else came. No knock. No voice. Just that single, unmistakable sound.

Her pulse thundered in her ears. Slowly, she uncurled from the chair, setting both feet on the ground. The room seemed to hold its breath around her. She stood, muscles tight, and moved toward the door.

Her boots were still by the threshold. She stepped into them without thinking, her fingers trembling as they hovered near the latch.

It could be Dean. Lost. Cold. Regretful. It should be Dean.

But something felt... wrong.

She hesitated, then unbolted the lock and cracked the door open.

The freezing air rushed in like a slap.

And there—slumped across the threshold, half-buried in snow and barely conscious—was Duncan.

His face was pale, lips tinged blue, dark lashes rimmed with frost. His coat was soaked, dusted white with snow, and his arm was curled protectively across his ribs. One shoulder rested against the doorframe where he must have fallen. His eyes fluttered open just a fraction, barely tracking her face.

"Jade..." he rasped, voice raw and cracked. "Thank... god..."

Then he collapsed forward into her arms.

"Duncan!" she gasped, catching his weight, staggering back against the door as he crumpled fully into her.

Her brain snapped into clinical focus. He was freezing—soaked through, shivering violently, lips fading toward cyanotic. His body was too heavy, too limp.

"Oh my God," she breathed, "you idiot, what did you do..."

She wrestled him inside, half-dragging him over the threshold and onto the thick rug. The door slammed shut behind them, wind howling once more before it cut off like a scream.

The sudden silence was deafening.

She dropped to her knees beside him, already reaching for his pulse, checking his breathing, fingers moving with a nurse's precision.

"Duncan... stay with me."

But inside, under the focus and the instinct, her heart was still racing for a very different reason.

Duncan was here.

And Dean wasn't.

Chapter Five

Jade's hands trembled as she hooked her arms beneath Duncan's shoulders and dragged him fully inside, each step backward a struggle against his weight and her own disbelief. He was so much heavier than she remembered—dense, solid, unfamiliar in a way that reached deeper than muscle and bone. The heat from the fire barely touched her as she eased him over to the fire.

She hadn't touched him in years. Not like this. Not skin-to-skin through soaked clothes and half-buried memories. And certainly not with this urgency pounding in her veins, each heartbeat louder than the wind still screaming outside.

All she could hear was her breath—fast, ragged—and the uneven crackle of the fire. Her heartbeat thundered in her chest, wild and unsteady, as if some part of her already understood that this moment would change things.

Duncan lay crumpled on the sheepskin rug, melting snow pooling beneath him, his lips edged in a frightening shade of grey-blue. His dark lashes were dusted with frost; his cheeks flushed with the angry red from the cold. His chest rose and fell with a shallow, uneven rhythm.

"Shit," she whispered, knees hitting the floor. "Okay. Okay, come on."

Her fingers scrambled to his neck, seeking a pulse—silent prayer surging beneath the skin of her thoughts.

There. Thready. Fast. Too fast.

She gave him a small shake. "Duncan. Can you hear me?" Her voice cracked. "Duncan, say something."

Nothing.

His skin was ice beneath her touch. Her stomach knotted.

Adrenaline surged, shoving the panic aside. The nurse in her took over—trained, composed, methodical. She could panic later. He needed her now.

Get him dry. Get him warm. Keep his core temperature up.

She started with his gloves—leather frozen stiff, fingers limp inside. She tugged them off and cradled his hands between hers, rubbing briskly. His fingers twitched faintly.

Still a fight left in him.

Good.

She worked faster, eyes scanning him as she moved. His coat was a sodden weight, the zipper stuck halfway. She grunted, yanked harder, finally freeing him from it. The jumper beneath clung to him like second skin, soaked through, dark with melted snow and blood—no, not blood. Just bruises.

She peeled it back—then froze.

Bruising. Angry, spreading across his ribs like spilled ink.

Her breath caught, horror pressing sharp beneath her ribs.

"God, Duncan… What did you do?" Her voice was fierce now, trembling with something more than fear. "What were you thinking?"

She knew what he'd done. He'd walked. In a storm. Alone.

For her.

Tears threatened, but she blinked them back and kept moving.

Her hands hesitated at the hem of his shirt. Just for a second. Then she pushed through it.

No time for modesty. No space for memories of hope.

Still, when his skin came into view—cold, pale, familiar—her chest tightened. He was thinner than he'd been at uni, leaner in the shoulders, but still unmistakably him. That scar on his side was still there—the one from the motorbike accident during his third year. She'd patched it herself, half-drunk and terrified, pressing gauze and hope into torn skin while he'd gritted his teeth and made bad jokes.

Back when everything was simpler.

Before Dean. Before the truth of Duncan's sexuality.

Before things got complicated and hearts went quiet.

She swallowed and forced herself to focus.

"Sorry," she muttered, fumbling with the button of his jeans. "I promise this is medical, not personal."

The fabric was soaked stiff. She peeled them off, along with his socks, and wrapped him in the thickest throw from the couch. Then another. Then a third. Still, he didn't stir.

Her hands found his again, rubbing, coaxing. "Come on, Duncan," she whispered. "Stay with me. Please."

She rolled him gently toward the fire, careful of his ribs. He groaned—faint, but alive—and curled slightly toward the heat.

A sound.

A reaction.

Relief buckled through her so fast her breath hitched. Her fingers fluttered over his pulse again. Still fast. Still there.

She moved quickly now, gathering towels from the small linen cupboard—soft, clean, faintly scented with lavender and cedar. She knelt beside him and patted away the worst of the damp, smoothing the towel over his skin with quick, firm strokes. Her hands were steady, but her mind wasn't. It had splintered into past and present, tangled between what she knew and what she had hoped.

He looked older than she remembered.

Older, and tired—not just from the cold, but from something deeper. Grief maybe. Or guilt. Or both. But even now, half-frozen and unconscious, he was still undeniably Duncan. The same too-serious mouth. The same sharp jaw. That same… stillness.

Like gravity. Quiet. Certain.

She sat back on her heels and stared at him, her heart pounding hard against her ribs.

He'd come for her.

Through a storm. On foot. No warning. No explanation.

Her throat tightened.

Why? Why would he do that?

Her mind reached for the simplest answer. Dean must've asked him to check in. Maybe Duncan had been in the area. Maybe it wasn't personal.

But even as the excuses formed, she didn't believe them.

Dean hadn't mentioned anything. Hadn't texted. Hadn't called. And Duncan—he wasn't the kind of man to follow someone else's orders.

He'd made this choice.

Her eyes traced Duncan's face—pale, bruised, peaceful in a way that made her ache.

"What are you doing here?" she whispered.

Her voice cracked, thin and hoarse.

It wasn't angry.

It was confused. Raw. Worn out from waiting, from trying, from telling herself over and over that she mattered to someone who hadn't even shown up.

Because Duncan had come.

And Dean hadn't.

Her hand moved without thought, brushing Duncan's damp hair back from his forehead. Her fingers trembled as they passed over chilled skin, catching on a bruise above his brow. She paused there, her breath shivering from her lungs.

He came.

When no one else did.

And with that single truth, something inside her cracked open.

Her touch was slow now. Gentle. Careful, like he might slip away again if she wasn't.

"Rest," she whispered. "It's okay. I've got you."

But the past wasn't done with her yet.

It came back in fragments—old conversations, forgotten feelings, words she'd swallowed and truths she'd never questioned.

She remembered the day with painful clarity. Sitting with Dean in that tiny café just off campus, fingers curled around a chipped coffee mug, heart beating just a little too fast. She'd told him—nervously, quietly—that she was thinking of asking Duncan to be her plus-one to her brother's wedding.

She'd laughed when she said it, trying to sound casual. But the truth was, she liked Duncan. Had for a while. She'd liked the way he looked at her—intently, like she wasn't just background noise. She liked the way he listened, the way he laughed when she didn't expect it, the quiet confidence he carried like a second skin. It hadn't been a crush exactly. It had felt... *bigger*. Something that could've been real.

Until Dean had looked up from his coffee and said, in that calm, easy voice of his—the one he used when delivering bad news like it was a compliment:

"Jade... I didn't want to say anything, but Duncan's gay. He just hasn't told anyone yet."

The words hit her like ice water down her spine.

She blinked, caught completely off guard. "Are you sure?"

Dean nodded slowly, almost regretfully. "Yeah. He told me by accident one night. Slipped out after a few drinks." He leaned back in his chair, lifting his coffee cup to his lips. "I haven't told anyone—he's not ready for it to be public."

Her throat went dry. "But... I thought we were close. Why wouldn't he tell me?"

Dean exhaled, like it pained him to answer. "He trusts you. He does. But it's different. He just… he's not ready to talk about it. I only told you because I didn't want to put him in an awkward position. If you asked him outright, and he panicked—it'd be awful. For both of you."

Jade sat there, stunned. The café noise dimmed around her.

Stunned.

Embarrassed.

And worse—ashamed for ever thinking there might have been something between them.

Suddenly, it all made sense.

The lingering silences.

The way he'd looked at her—but never quite held her gaze.

The night she'd fallen asleep next to him on the couch, his arm draped loosely around her shoulders. She'd imagined the warmth between them meant something. That maybe he was just taking it slow. That maybe… he was nervous.

But now?

Now it felt foolish.

She'd packed those feelings away that night.

Neatly. Quietly.

Like an old box of love letters, she was never meant to send.

She told herself she'd misread everything. That she was lucky to have his friendship, and nothing more.

And when Dean asked her out a few weeks later—with that same easy charm—she said yes.

Because he wanted her. He made that clear.

And Duncan… couldn't.

Or so she believed.

And now?

Now Duncan was here.

In this place, in this moment.

And everything she'd buried was rising again—breath by breath, heartbeat by heartbeat.

Half-frozen. Bruised. Dragging himself through a snowstorm to reach her.

And the past—the version she'd clung to for so long—was unravelling at the edges.

Collapsed in her cabin, after walking through a storm.

For her.

She moved quietly, collecting the soaked clothes—boots, coat, jumper, jeans—and hung them near the fire. Steam rose. Heat licked the damp from the fabric. She adjusted the blankets again. Checked his pulse. Watched the colour creep slowly back into his cheeks.

Still unconscious.

Still breathing.

She changed into her sleep shirt and crawled under the duvet. The sheets were warm, but her body was cold in a way that had nothing to do with winter.

She stared at the ceiling. Listened to the wind. To the fire. To her own thoughts, circling like wolves.

Dean had to be coming tomorrow.

He must've sent Duncan ahead.

There was no other reason for this.

Right?

She rolled to her side. Clutched her pillow.

But still…

It was Duncan's name that echoed in her mind.

Over and over.

He came.

And he still hadn't woken up.

Chapter Six

Something warm touched his face.

Soft. Careful. A glancing pressure at his temple, then his cheek—fingertips dipped in light.

Duncan stirred beneath it, lashes fluttering as brightness leaked through the cracks of his closed eyes. The light was too sharp. His head throbbed with every heartbeat. His chest felt tight, each breath a scrape against bruised ribs. The cold still lingered inside him—coating his lungs, curled beneath his skin—like something that refused to let go. His muscles screamed at the idea of moving, like they'd been locked in place too long.

Then the warmth came again.

A hand. A voice.

Low, steady. Familiar.

Calling him.

"Duncan?"

He tried to speak, but his throat was raw, his mouth bone-dry. What came out wasn't a word so much as a rasp—fractured, barely audible.

"Shhh," the voice said again, urgent but gentle. "Don't move. You're okay. Just lie still."

Jade.

He knew her voice instantly, even in the haze. It hit him in the chest harder than the cold had. That name in his mind—a touchstone. A heartbeat.

Jade.

He opened his eyes, blinking against the firelight. Shapes formed slowly: the flicker of flame, the ceiling beams overhead, her silhouette leaning over him, strands of golden hair swinging loose near her cheek. Her face was upside down from where he lay, but still unmistakable—the worry etched into her brow, the exhaustion clouding her eyes.

"You're awake," she whispered, and there was something like awe in her voice. Or maybe disbelief.

He tried to smile, but his lips cracked with the effort.

"You...?"

She eased him upright, careful with every movement, then reached for the mug beside her. Holding it steady, she brought it to his lips.

The liquid was warm—overly sweet, but he didn't care. It anchored him, reminded him he was still here. He swallowed, coughed once, then winced as pain flared deep in his chest.

"You're in the cabin," she said gently, tilting the mug again. "You collapsed at the door last night. You've been unconscious for hours. Your temperature dropped dangerously low. I wasn't sure…"

She didn't finish the sentence.

He didn't ask.

Pain flared when he shifted slightly—through his shoulder, his ribs. He gritted his teeth against it.

"I think you cracked something," she said softly. "And your shoulder's bruised. But you're alive. That's what matters."

He nodded once, shallowly. "Thanks."

"What the hell happened?"

"Car went off the road," he rasped. "Walked the rest."

Her brow pulled tight. "In a storm?"

"There was no phone reception," he said, each word like glass in his throat. "Didn't want you here alone."

She froze. It was quick—just a flicker of something in her face—but he saw it.

"You came because of Dean?" she asked carefully.

He looked at her, jaw tightening. "Dean's not coming."

"I figured that part out," she murmured.

He turned his head to glance around the room. The flicker of the fire. His coat steaming near the hearth. The towel draped over a chair. The lingering scent of damp wool and tea and woodsmoke. All of it came together in slow, strange clarity.

"You looked half-dead," she said quietly. "I thought you were…"

She stopped herself.

She didn't need to finish.

He saw it in her face. In the way her hand hovered near his, like she wanted to reach for him but didn't quite know how.

"Did Dean send you?" she asked.

The words landed between them like something final.

Heavy. Hopeful. Already breaking apart.

Duncan closed his eyes. Drew one shallow breath. And gave the only answer he could.

"No."

Silence followed—long and brittle.

Then she stood, her movements careful and controlled. "You should rest. I'll make more tea."

He watched her retreat, mug in hand, spine too straight, shoulders too still.

She hadn't cried.

Not yet.

But the grief was there, tucked into the lines of her face, trembling just beneath the surface.

And he knew it wasn't just about Dean.

In the kitchen, Jade stared at the kettle as it began to steam again, her fingers clenched too tightly around the ceramic mug she hadn't even filled. The heat pressed against her knuckles, but it barely registered.

Dean wasn't coming.

She'd accepted it last night, even before Duncan's arrival. But now… now the truth had settled in her gut like stone.

He hadn't just forgotten. He hadn't been delayed. He'd made a choice.

He'd walked away without a word.

And that was the end of it.

Part of her—God, an embarrassingly large part—felt relieved. She wouldn't have to beg for scraps anymore. Wouldn't have to wrap her needs in soft language, pretending not to mind every time he didn't show up for her.

But another part burned.

Because he hadn't even had the decency to tell her it was over. He'd left her to wait in a storm for a message that never came. Left her to piece together his silence like a puzzle she should have seen coming.

Her stomach twisted with humiliation and fury.

Was I really that easy to walk away from?

The kettle screamed. She silenced it with a sharp movement; the clatter of the switch louder than it should've been.

She turned to glance at Duncan, still lying where she'd left him. He was awake, eyes half-closed, but alert. His chest rose and fell steadily now. The colour had come back into his face.

And she still didn't understand why he was here.

He lived in London now. They hadn't had a real conversation in years.

She'd seen him last year at a conference, but even then, over coffee, the talk had stayed safely on work and the weather. No questions, no warmth—just the surface.

These days, she only saw him when he visited Dean—and even then, he barely said more than a polite hello.

Reserved. Guarded. Almost cold.

He'd never once given her the impression he saw her as anything more than Dean's girlfriend.

And after Dean told her he was gay, she'd believed it. Why wouldn't she? Dean had said it like it was fact. Quiet. Casual. Said Duncan just wasn't out yet. Didn't want people to know.

So, she'd shelved her own feelings. Told herself she'd imagined the glances. The easy connection. The way Duncan sometimes seemed like he was on the edge of saying something and never did.

She'd stopped wondering.

And she'd dated Dean.

And now…

Now Duncan was here.

Collapsed at her door, frozen to the bone, cracked ribs and all—because he hadn't wanted her to be alone.

And suddenly she didn't know what to do with any of it.

Her grief rose unexpectedly—sharp and wild. Not just for Dean. Not just for the future she'd been trying so hard to salvage.

But for the baby she'd lost.

The baby she'd barely had time to dream about.

She'd never really grieved—not properly. Dean hadn't let her. Had brushed it off like a sad but manageable setback. Had told her not to "dwell," not to "be mopey," as if she was being dramatic for mourning the life they'd never gotten to meet.

So, she'd swallowed the sadness. Pushed it down. Went back to work. Told herself time would dull it.

But now it was all here—rising at once. Loss upon loss. The life that might've been. The love that never quite was. The truth she had been too afraid to admit, even to herself.

That she had been lonely for a long, long time.

Tears blurred her vision. She blinked them away quickly, one hand trembling as she poured the tea.

She wasn't sure if she wanted comfort or to be alone—only that something inside her had finally cracked, and all she could do was hold herself together long enough to not fall apart in front of him.

She wouldn't cry in front of Duncan. Not yet.

But later… maybe.

For now, she just breathed.

One steady breath after another.

And when she returned to his side, she sat cross-legged beside him and handed him the tea.

She didn't speak.

Neither did he.

But somehow, in the quiet between them—the soft crackle of the fire, the storm still murmuring against the windows—she felt more seen than she had in years. No performance. No forced smiles. Just… stillness. Presence. Him.

He took a slow sip, his hands still trembling slightly around the ceramic. She steadied it when it wobbled, watched him swallow, then gently took the mug back from his hands when his eyelids started to droop again.

Sleep tugged at him like a tide. And within moments, he gave in.

His breathing evened out. The tight furrow between his brows smoothed just a little. The blankets shifted slightly with the rise and fall of his chest, and something in her own body unclenched at last.

Chapter Seven

She watched him.

And for the first time in years, she really looked.

His face was leaner now—sharper at the edges, as if time had carved itself into the angles of his jaw and the hollows beneath his cheekbones. There were faint lines at the corners of his eyes that hadn't been there before. His stubble was darker, coarser, the kind that came from days without rest, not just fashion. He looked older. More tired. But not diminished.

Still—he was undeniably handsome.

That quiet kind of handsome that didn't shout but whispered.

The kind that made people turn their heads without quite knowing why. Especially when he wasn't trying.

Duncan stirred beside her, his breathing shallow but steady now.

Jade reached out, brushing a damp strand of hair from his brow, her fingers lingering a moment longer than necessary. His skin was warm again. Thank God.

But her thoughts wouldn't settle. Not even in the quiet. Not even with him here.

How many times had she nearly said something back then? Nearly crossed the line between friendship and more.

One moment stood out more than the rest…

They'd been in the cafeteria. Mid-afternoon. The sun had been streaming through the high windows, throwing soft gold across the worn tables and half-empty trays.

Jade stirred her iced coffee for the third time, her fingers tight around the cup.

Across from her, Duncan sat with a textbook open, a pencil tucked behind his ear, talking about something she barely followed—trauma protocols or some other med school madness. She didn't care. She was watching his hands, the way he gestured when he got excited, how his voice softened when he explained something.

She loved that about him. The quiet enthusiasm. The way he always made space for her to speak, even when she didn't know how.

She'd been meaning to ask him for days.

Her brother's wedding was at the end of June. The RSVP deadline was next week. And everyone kept asking if she was bringing someone.

She didn't want just anyone. She wanted Duncan.

As a friend, obviously. Technically. Probably.

"Hey," she said, interrupting gently. "My brother's getting married at the end of June."

He looked up, eyebrows raised. "June?"

"Yeah." She tried to sound casual. "I need to find a date."

She grinned to soften it, but her stomach fluttered.

Duncan hesitated. Just a flicker. But long enough that she noticed.

Then his eyes shifted away, drifting to the window.

"Jade..." he began, voice low, unreadable.

And that was when Dean appeared—sliding into the seat beside her like he'd been invited.

He slung an arm over the back of her chair, easy and possessive, and she stiffened.

"Oi, you two still living in here?" Dean joked, grinning. "I swear they're gonna start charging rent."

Jade managed a polite laugh. But Duncan didn't.

He closed his textbook without a word, stood, and walked out.

No explanation. No glance back.

She remembered sitting there, staring after him as he walked away, a hollow ache blooming in her chest that she didn't understand at the time.

She never brought it up again.

Because ten minutes later, Dean had leaned in with that casual smirk and told her Duncan was gay.

And back then, that had made sense.

It explained the hesitation. The silence. The retreat.

She'd told herself it was nothing. That she'd misread everything. That the moment hadn't meant what she thought it had.

So, she buried it.

Like so many other near misses.

All the little flickers that had lived between them—unspoken, unresolved—moments where Duncan had almost been hers.

And now here he was.

Not a memory. Not a daydream. Not a what-if.

He was here. Broken, bruised, real.

Her heart thudded unevenly in her chest.

What the hell was she supposed to do now?

She drew her knees up to her chest and wrapped her arms around them, the thick knit blanket pooling around her like armour.

The cabin was warm now, fire crackling in the grate—but the last twenty-four hours still lived in her bones. The cold. The fear. The not knowing.

And beneath it all, this steady ache that had never really left her.

And then, almost without realising it, she spoke. Her voice low, like she was afraid of waking him. Or maybe afraid of what might spill out if she didn't whisper.

"You know…" she murmured, "I thought we were friends."

It came out softer than she'd meant it. Sadder, too.

"I thought we were close. Back in uni." She exhaled shakily, her eyes never leaving his face. "You were… different from the others. You made it easy to talk. You were funny, but not loud. Thoughtful in a way most twenty-something-year-olds aren't. You stayed up with me before exams, even when you didn't need to. You walked me home after parties, carried my shoes more times than I could count."

Her lips curved at the memory, but it didn't quite become a smile.

"You listened," she whispered. "Really listened. Not just to what I said—but to what I didn't say. That mattered."

She shifted, pulling the blanket higher over her legs. Her gaze fell slightly, brows knitting in quiet frustration.

"And then one day… you just stopped talking to me."

The words hung in the air, brittle and unsteady.

"You started showing up less. Dean would say you were busy, that you had extra shifts, or new rotations. Said you were getting serious about your career. And I told myself that made sense. I tried not to read into it." She swallowed. "But when you did come around… it was like I wasn't even in the room anymore."

She shook her head, fingers tightening around the edge of the blanket.

"I didn't know what I did wrong."

Her voice cracked, just barely. But she didn't stop.

"I kept going over it in my head. Again, and again. Was I too clingy? Did I say something that pushed you away? Did Dean say something to you? I kept thinking… maybe I made it weird. Maybe I was the problem. Maybe you needed space."

She looked at him again, watched the soft rise and fall of his chest, the twitch of his lashes. He was still asleep. Still unaware of the confession unfolding beside him.

"I mean…" she said quietly, "when Dean told me you were gay…."

Her voice thinned with something unspoken.

"That wasn't what hurt," she said, quickly, like she had to clarify it to herself. "It didn't matter—not really. I just… I don't know. You used to tell me everything."

Her gaze dropped to her hands, where her fingers twisted the blanket into soft folds near his arm.

"I missed you," she said softly.

The words surprised her. Even now. They slipped out like a truth that had waited too long in the dark.

"I missed you so much I started dreaming you back into my life. In memories, in music, in the way I'd glance at the door and still half-expect you to walk through it."

Her voice was barely above a whisper now.

"I would've supported you. Always. Your life, your choices… they were never going to change how much I cared about you."

She paused, inhaling shakily, then exhaled like she was finally letting go of something that had been lodged inside her chest for years.

"So, I let it go. I packed up the weird little feelings I'd started having—those fluttery, foolish, completely inconvenient things—and rewrote the story in my head. You were my friend. That was it. And that was supposed to be enough."

She fell silent for a moment, her fingers stilling. The only sound was the soft hiss of wind against the windows, and the occasional crack from the fire.

"I just…" her voice faltered again, more fragile now, more human. "I didn't expect you to vanish like that. Not without a word. Not when you meant so much to me."

Her chest ached, suddenly too tight for the air she was pulling in.

"I pretended it didn't hurt." A pause. "But it did. God, it did."

She leaned back slightly, bracing herself on her palms, the wood floor cool beneath her fingers even through the blanket. Her eyes stayed on his face, searching for some hint of change, some flicker that he might have heard her.

"I know you probably didn't mean to hurt me," she said quietly. "Maybe you were going through something. Maybe Dean was right. Maybe it really had nothing to do with me."

She hesitated. Her brow furrowed, and her voice dropped to something smaller, more uncertain.

"He used to get annoyed when I brought you up. Said I was stuck in the past. Said you had your own life now, and I should stop trying to drag you back into mine."

A flash of guilt passed across her face.

"And I listened to him." Her voice cracked. "I let him convince me I was being silly. That I'd made it all up in my head. That I had to let you go."

She looked at Duncan again. Really looked. The warmth of the fire made his skin glow faintly, the shadows deepening the curve of his cheek, the line of his jaw. He looked both stronger and more vulnerable than she'd ever seen him.

"But you're here now," she whispered.

Her throat bobbed.

"And I don't know what to do with that."

The words hung heavy between them.

She drew in a long breath and let it out slowly, her shoulders sagging beneath the weight of everything she hadn't said until now.

"I don't know if this changes anything," she admitted. "Or if I even want it to. But I can't pretend it doesn't mean something."

She wrapped her arms around her knees again, tucking her chin lightly atop them. The silence stretched, but it didn't feel empty.

She didn't cry.

Not yet.

But something inside her had shifted.

And there was no going back now.

Jade had drifted into a light doze, her head tipped against the armchair, the blanket around her shoulders barely holding back the chill that still lingered in the room. The fire had burned down to glowing embers, casting soft shadows that danced across the floorboards.

A faint sound stirred her.

She blinked, sat up straighter.

Duncan shifted under the layers of blankets on the rug, his brow twitching, lips moving. At first it was incoherent—just a breathy murmur, broken by a low, painful exhale.

Then clearer, just enough to catch.

"Dean… doesn't… deserve you…"

She didn't move. Didn't breathe. Because in all the years she'd known him, Duncan had never said anything like that. Not even close. Not even in passing.

His voice was hoarse, barely more than a whisper, like it was pulled from somewhere deep in a dream.

"He never did…"

Her heart stilled. The air between them felt suddenly thinner, sharper, as if the words themselves had sliced through something silent and long-standing.

He stilled again, breath falling into shallow rhythm, his expression softening as sleep pulled him deeper.

Jade sat motionless, eyes fixed on him.

He didn't stir again.

But the words lingered—curling in her chest like smoke, impossible to ignore.

Dean didn't deserve you.

He never did.

And hearing it in Duncan's voice—so raw, so unguarded—shook something loose inside her.

She didn't know what it meant yet.

Why would he say that?

He was Dean's friend—had been since uni. The two of them were practically inseparable back then, thick as thieves in that easy, male way she'd always found slightly impenetrable. Duncan had never said a bad word about Dean. Never even hinted at disapproval. He was loyal. Quiet. Private.

So why now?

Why, after all this time, after the distance and the silence, would that be the thing to slip from his lips—even half-asleep, half-frozen?

Dean didn't deserve you.

The words echoed in her mind, louder than they should have, ringing through the quiet space like a dropped glass.

Her thoughts spun, grasping for something solid—some piece of the old story to hold onto. The one where Duncan was just Dean's friend. The one where he was gay, or uninterested, or incapable of wanting her in the way she'd secretly wanted him.

He'd never said anything. Not once.

Not when Dean began pulling away emotionally.

Not when the affection turned cold, the support turned sharp, and the love—if it had ever been real—started to feel like control.

Not when Dean began making subtle jabs about her ambition, her long shifts, her "intensity."

Not even when Jade stopped smiling as often. When she stopped laughing. When the version of herself she liked best began to fade.

And Duncan—

He hadn't crossed the distance between them, either.

So why now?

Why say it now, after all this time?

Had he always thought it? Had he watched her unravel and said nothing?

Because if he had…

If he had seen what was happening—had known, even a little—then why hadn't he told her the truth when it might've mattered?

Why hadn't he stopped her when she could still walk away without so much damage?

She would have listened. She knows she would have.

Jade looked at him now, stretched out under the soft light, his features finally at ease. Duncan looked… calm. Not entirely unburdened, but quieter inside. As if something that had haunted him for years had finally found breath.

But her own storm was only just beginning.

Because suddenly, she wasn't sure what she believed anymore.

Not about Dean—who had lied and blamed and gaslit her into silence.

Not about Duncan—who had stayed silent when she needed someone to speak.

And worst of all, not about herself.

Because maybe she'd ignored more than just the signs.

Maybe she'd ignored her own heart.

Duncan stirred slowly, his awareness returning in fragments—like pieces of a puzzle reassembling in the dark. The thick fog of sleep began to lift, retreating in sluggish waves, each one peeling back another layer of disorientation.

His body ached, but it was a quieter ache now—less sharp, less consuming. A dull throb pulsed along his ribs, and his throat still felt like it had been scraped with sandpaper, but the chill that had soaked into his bones was gone.

Replaced by warmth.

Real, solid warmth.

Not just the physical kind—the firelight, the blankets—but something deeper. A heaviness that wasn't discomfort so much as grounding. Like the moment his body had stopped fighting and finally started healing.

He blinked open his eyes, squinting against the flickering glow of firelight dancing across the ceiling beams. The storm had quieted to a low murmur in the distance, the wind outside reduced to the occasional brush against the windows, like a memory it hadn't quite finished letting go.

The rug beneath him was soft, the kind of thick, worn wool that had soaked up years of stories. He shifted slightly, trying to tug the blanket back over his shoulder, but the movement sent a sharp ribbon of pain flaring through his ribs.

He stifled a curse and held still.

And then—he saw her.

Jade.

Curled up on the floor just a few feet away, half-slumped against the armchair like she hadn't meant to fall asleep. One leg tucked beneath her, the other stretched toward the fire. Her head rested awkwardly against the worn fabric cushion, her golden hair loose and falling in soft waves across her cheek, catching the firelight in threads of honey and bronze.

One hand was tucked beneath her chin. The other still lay near the edge of the blanket he now realised had been wrapped around him.

She must've stayed with him. Through the night. Through the storm.

Through everything.

His throat tightened.

She looked… tired.

Not just physically—though the exhaustion was written in the curve of her spine, the faint smudge beneath her lashes—but deeper. In a way he recognised. A kind of quiet fatigue that came from holding too much for too long. From carrying pain without a name.

But still, somehow, she was beautiful.

Not in the bright, effortless way he remembered from university, when she lit up a room just by walking into it. This was different. She was stillness now. Strength. The kind of beautiful that had been earned, not inherited.

Worn in at the edges.

Carved by grief, maybe. But luminous all the same.

And for the first time in years—he let himself look.

Really look.

Not with restraint. Not through the lens of guilt or caution or the carefully constructed distance he'd kept between them for so long. But with the fullness of memory and longing and something that felt dangerously close to reverence.

His eyes traced the soft curve of her jaw, the subtle twitch of her fingers in sleep, the way her brows drew together slightly even in rest, like something deep inside her hadn't quite let go.

How had he managed to stay away so long?

How had he watched her from the sidelines for years—pretending indifference, forcing himself to be polite, distant, and casual—when every instinct in him had wanted to be near her?

To protect her. To hold her. To be hers.

He didn't know how long he'd been unconscious. Long enough for her to find him. Warm him. Stay up tending him through a winter storm in a remote cabin with no reception and God knows how much fear clawing at her chest.

Long enough for her to save his life.

Again.

Because that's what Jade did. She saved people.

Even when they didn't ask for it. Even when they didn't deserve it.

He swallowed hard, feeling the soreness ripple down his throat. He didn't speak. Couldn't. Not yet. The words were there—God, they were there—but they were knotted too tightly behind his ribs.

Instead, he just watched her. Listened to the subtle rhythm of her breathing. Took in the way the firelight curled across her face, softening every line, highlighting the shadows beneath her lashes.

Close.

So, close he could've reached out and touched her.

But still—so far away.

Because he didn't know what she thought of him anymore. He didn't know what she believed about the past. Or about him. He didn't know if she still saw him as Dean's friend. The quiet one. The background presence.

The one who'd walked away without a word.

He clenched his jaw at the thought, guilt blooming hot behind his eyes.

He'd let her go.

He'd watched her stay in a relationship that dimmed her light, all while saying nothing. Protecting some warped sense of loyalty. Preserving a fragile friendship that had already rotted at the core.

And for what?

For pride? For fear?

He didn't even know anymore.

But lying here now, in this flickering half-light, with her only inches away…

He knew one thing for certain.

He had never stopped thinking about her.

Not for a single day.

She was the thread that tugged at him in quiet moments, the ache that never quite faded. Every woman he'd dated since had been measured against her and come up short. Every time he imagined what could have been, her face filled the picture.

And now—somehow—they were here.

Together. Alone. The two of them still standing, despite everything.

Two ghosts. Two survivors.

Still circling the same fire.

And for the first time in years, Duncan let himself wonder what it might mean.

What this might mean.

If it wasn't too late to rewrite the story.

If maybe—just maybe—there was still a chance to tell the truth.

Chapter Eight

A small shift. A soft sigh. The kind that comes from dreams hovering close to waking. Her lashes fluttered, brows knitting slightly before her eyes opened—slowly, blearily, like her body hadn't yet caught up to her mind.

And then she saw him.

Awake.

Watching her.

Her breath hitched—just for a second.

"Hey," Duncan said softly, his voice still hoarse, but steadier than before.

Jade pushed herself up straighter, blinking the sleep from her eyes. The fire had burned lower behind her, casting a dim amber wash over everything.

"You're awake," she said, though they both already knew. Her voice sounded rough, the weight of her late-night confessions still thick in her chest.

"I am," he murmured, gaze steady on hers. "You were asleep."

She nodded. "Just…dozed off."

He didn't speak right away. Just watched her—his gaze steady, unflinching, as if seeing her for the first time in a long time. Really seeing her. And Jade felt it—not in a way that made her pull back, but in a way that invited honesty. Like the version of herself she used to be, before everything got messy. Before Dean. Before the distance.

"How are you feeling?" she asked softly, her eyes flicking to the firelight before returning to his. "You're lucky, you know. It could've been frostbite. Or hypothermia. Or worse."

His mouth lifted at the corner—a faint, tired almost-smile.

"Thanks to you."

She studied him for a moment, then spoke—quietly, but with an edge of disbelief.

"Why are you here, Duncan?"

Her voice was quiet, but the question landed hard between them. Her eyes searched his face—uncertain, a little wounded.

"I mean... it's strange, isn't it? You've barely spoken to me in three years. And now you're here—at a cabin you weren't even supposed to know about." She exhaled shakily. "You walked through a storm. Nearly killed yourself just getting here."

A pause. Her voice softened.

"Why?"

Duncan shifted slightly, bracing himself on one elbow with a wince. He didn't look away.

"Dean asked me over for a drink," he said finally. "Friday night. At his place."

Jade blinked. "What?"

"He just sent a message—told me to stop by. I figured you'd be with him."

She stared. "So... you were with him. Last night. When he was supposed to be coming here straight after work."

He nodded slowly. Guilt flickered across his features.

"And instead," she said, her voice rising, "he's at home having drinks?"

"It wasn't a party," Duncan said quickly. "Just the two of us. A glass of scotch. He was... smug. Like he already knew he wasn't coming."

Jade let out a bitter, disbelieving laugh.

"Unbelievable."

She stood abruptly, paced to the fireplace, then turned—both hands tangled in her hair.

"I sat here thinking the roads were bad. Maybe he'd lost signal. I kept telling myself not to panic. That he'd walk through that door at any second."

Duncan said nothing. He let her speak, let her anger burn through the silence.

"And he was just... sitting there?" she said. "Sipping scotch while I sat here wondering what I'd done wrong?"

He didn't answer. He didn't need to.

The truth sat thick in the air.

Jade's arms dropped to her sides, her breath shuddering. "God. I feel like such an idiot."

Duncan's voice was low but sure. "You're not an idiot, Jade. He is. Not you."

She looked at him—eyes glistening, hurt still raw beneath the surface—but she didn't argue.

Because deep down, she already knew he was right.

Duncan swallowed, then said softly, "He told me about the baby. I'm so sorry, Jade."

Her face froze.

Her breath caught.

"He told you?" she whispered, voice breaking, tears rising to the surface. "He actually told you?"

Duncan nodded, guilt flickering through his eyes. "He just… mentioned it, like it was nothing."

She shook her head slowly, as if trying to understand something that still didn't make sense. "He didn't even care about it," she said, barely audible. "He didn't care that I lost it. He wouldn't talk about it after. Not once. Like it didn't matter. Like it was just… something to forget."

"I know," Duncan said quietly. "He told me he said it was for the best."

Jade flinched like she'd been slapped.

"I told him he was selfish," Duncan went on, voice tightening. "And cruel. That it wasn't just his to decide. That it wasn't nothing."

She covered her mouth with her hand, a quiet sob escaping before she could stop it. Her shoulders trembled.

"I felt so alone," she whispered. "Like I wasn't allowed to grieve. Like I was being dramatic for caring."

"You weren't," Duncan said firmly. "You had every right to feel what you felt. Every damn right."

She looked at him again, this time like she was seeing him differently. Like maybe, for the first time in years, someone got it.

Someone saw her.

And it was Duncan.

Not Dean.

She sat down on the sofa slowly, as if her body was suddenly heavier, weighed down by everything she'd been holding in for too long.

"I wanted it, you know," she said quietly, staring at a spot on the floor as her fingers twisted in her lap. "The baby. I didn't care if Dean stuck around. I would've loved it."

Her voice cracked near the end, but she didn't stop. Didn't look up. Just kept going.

"I was scared, of course I was. But I wasn't ashamed. I was… ready. I could picture it. A tiny little person who was mine. Someone I could protect. Someone who'd never feel invisible."

Duncan moved closer—slowly, carefully—wincing a little as he shifted off the rug and onto the edge of the sofa beside her, the blankets still wrapped around him,

"I know," he said gently.

She looked up at him then, startled by how steady his voice was. How certain. There was no hesitation in his eyes. Just quiet empathy.

"I could see it in you," he said, softer now. "When Dean told me… Friday I was shocked at how relieved he sounded that you lost it."

Jade blinked fast, tears spilling before she could stop them.

"I hated how easily he brushed it off," Duncan said quietly, his voice rough with something raw. "Like it didn't matter. Like you didn't matter."

She turned her face away, wiping her cheek with the back of her hand. But Duncan reached out—slowly, cautiously—and laid his hand over hers.

Not forceful. Not asking for anything.

Just there.

Her shoulders lifted with a shaky breath.

"I still think about it," she whispered. "Not every day. But some days…" Her voice faltered. "A lot of them."

Duncan's fingers tightened gently around hers. "Of course you do. It's only been a little over a week, Jade. You don't have to rush through the grief just to make everyone else comfortable."

Her breath caught again—but this time, not from pain. From the quiet relief of being understood.

And for the first time since it happened, she didn't feel the need to apologise for that.

Or soften it.

Or explain it away.

Because someone finally saw her.

And it wasn't Dean.

It was Duncan.

He hesitated, fingers still wrapped gently around hers. His gaze didn't waver.

"There's something else I need to tell you, Jade."

She looked at him, her face streaked with tears, breath caught halfway to steady.

"What?" she whispered.

Duncan exhaled slowly. "Dean's cheating on you."

A beat.

Silence.

Then—

"With his secretary."

Jade stared at him.

The silence that followed felt like a cliff edge—sharp, breathless, disorienting.

Then her voice broke through it, fragile and stunned.

"Oh my God… are you serious?"

Duncan's jaw tightened. "I wouldn't say it if I wasn't."

She sat back, blinking hard, the words landing like a blow she hadn't seen coming—even if, deep down, some part of her had already suspected.

All the missed calls. The late nights. The vague explanations.

"I'm so sorry," Duncan added softly. "I didn't know how to tell you. I thought maybe it wasn't my place. But after everything… you deserve the truth."

Jade didn't speak right away.

She just sat there.

Tears drying on her cheeks.

Pain turning slowly—quietly—into something else.

Clarity.

And maybe, finally, the beginning of the end.

Duncan's voice was steady, but low. "He told me last night. That's when I decided to come here and tell you everything."

Jade blinked, as if the room had shifted under her. Her jaw tightened, breath catching on the sharp edge of realisation.

"So…" she said, voice raw, "he had no intention of coming here. None."

Her laugh was bitter, barely more than a breath. "He had every intention of being with his secretary instead."

She shook her head slowly; eyes glazed with something colder than shock.

"And then, just to top it off, he tells you—not me—but you, what a bloody fool I've been."

Duncan didn't interrupt. He let the words land because they needed to.

"He made me feel like I was asking too much," she whispered. "Like wanting one weekend—just one—to reconnect was selfish. Like losing the baby was something we could just… forget."

She stared at the fire, a flicker of something stronger rising behind her eyes now.

Anger.

Not wild. Not loud. But rooted. Righteous.

And maybe, finally, freeing.

Jade stared into the fire, its embers glowing soft and low, the only light in the room besides the weight of everything she now knew.

"I kept giving him the benefit of the doubt," she said quietly. "Kept making excuses—telling myself he was tired, or stressed, or just… bad at showing up."

Her fingers clenched in her lap, then slowly uncurled. "But he wasn't tired. Or lost. Or confused."

She turned to Duncan, her voice steady now. Low, but sure.

"He just didn't want me."

The words hung between them, solid and final.

"I thought maybe if I waited long enough, if I was patient enough, he'd come around." Her mouth twisted. "Turns out, he was already with someone else. All that time I was holding on, trying to fix things—he'd already moved on."

She looked down, brushing the corner of her sleeve over her cheek.

"I would've raised that baby alone," she said softly. "Gladly. I wanted to. And he made me feel like wanting it made me foolish. Weak. Needy."

A pause.

"I wasn't the fool, was I?" Her eyes lifted to Duncan's, searching, not for permission—just truth.

He shook his head. "No. You weren't."

And somehow, with Duncan's eyes on hers, Jade finally believed it.

She exhaled—slow and heavy—as if her whole body was finally releasing something it had held for far too long.

"I'm done," she said. "With him. With waiting. With wondering what I did wrong."

The pain was still there, yes—but it wasn't everything anymore. It was beginning to make room for something else.

Something clearer. Something steadier.

Space for herself.

She looked at Duncan, really looked, and something in her heart stirred. Quiet, uncertain, but alive.

"I don't know what happens next," she said. "But I know what doesn't."

And for now, that was enough.

Chapter Nine

Duncan watched her, the firelight catching in her hair, tracing soft shadows along her cheekbones. She looked… lighter somehow. Not unhurt—never that. But like she'd finally set something down. A grief. A question. A burden she'd carried far too long, and far too alone.

And she didn't even realise how beautiful she was in that moment.

Not because of how she looked—though God knew that had always undone him—but because of what was finally visible in her eyes. Truth. Stillness. No more shrinking. No more shaping herself around someone else's expectations.

She was Jade again. The one he remembered.

The one who used to stretch out on the library floor with colour-coded notes and caffeine-fuelled theories about love and anatomy. The one who cried during RSPCA ads and then pulled herself together with a laugh and a sniff. The one who used to find him in a room full of people and smile like it meant something.

And he'd walked away from her.

From all of that.

From everything he hadn't dared to want.

Duncan swallowed hard, guilt and regret sitting heavy in his chest. He cleared his throat, voice rough when it finally came.

"You were never the fool."

Jade looked over at him, her eyes still wet, cheeks flushed from heat and emotion. Her expression was guarded, but open—like she wasn't ready to fall, but maybe, just maybe, she'd stopped bracing for the impact.

There was something fragile in the way she held herself. Not broken. Just… delicate. Like someone who'd been strong for too long and didn't quite know how to stop.

But she didn't look away.

A flicker passed between them. Not quite resolution. Not yet. But something close. A recognition. A shared ache. The beginning of something they hadn't dared name in years.

She didn't argue. Didn't deflect with a joke. Didn't retreat behind the kind of shrug she used when her heart was bruised.

She just held his gaze.

And for a long, quiet moment, they simply breathed the same breath.

The fire crackled softly. Wind whispered against the windows, more memory than sound now. Between them stretched a kind of stillness—tentative, unguarded, threaded with everything they hadn't said but finally could.

Duncan didn't move. Didn't speak.

Neither did she.

Because somehow, even in silence, something was unfolding between them. Fragile. Honest. Real.

It felt, for a moment, like time had folded in on itself—like they were twenty again, sitting cross-legged in some echoing hallway, two coffee cups deep into a midnight conversation. Just them. Before things got hard. Before anything had to be explained.

His gaze drifted to her mouth. He caught himself, but not before she noticed.

And maybe it was nothing.

Or maybe it was everything.

Her expression shifted—barely—but enough. Not confusion. Not discomfort. Just a flicker of something unspoken.

Then she broke the silence, gently. "You must be hungry."

He let out a breath, something soft and grateful. "Starving."

A smile ghosted across her lips. Faint. Worn. But real.

"Let's fix that."

She rose slowly; the blanket still wrapped around her shoulders and padded toward the kitchen.

Duncan watched her go, his ribs aching—not just from the storm or the fall, but from everything he hadn't said. All the time they'd lost. All the ways she'd carried her grief alone.

But she wasn't alone now.

And if Duncan had anything to do with it—she never would be again.

Jade moved with quiet efficiency, ladling minestrone into two mismatched bowls. It wasn't much—just something from a tin she'd thrown herbs into—but it was warm and nourishing, and maybe that was enough.

She brought one bowl over, handed it to him with a small nod. "Here you are," she said softly. "It's not much, but… best to go easy at first."

"Thank you," he said, and his voice caught a little at the end. Because it meant more than soup. And she seemed to know that.

They sat side by side on the sofa, knees angled toward one another, firelight flickering in the spaces between. The soup steamed quietly in their hands. Outside, the wind had settled to a tired hush through the trees.

It wasn't the kind of silence that begged to be filled.

It was the kind that said: I see you.

After a few spoonfuls, Jade glanced sideways. "Are you still at St. George's?"

He nodded. "Yeah. Still there. Surgical rotation's endless."

Her brow lifted slightly. "You always said you'd outlast them."

"I think they just gave up trying to get rid of me," he said with a soft smile.

She smiled too, small, and tired. "I meant to ask before… before all this. Are you happy there?"

Duncan's spoon paused mid-air. He stared down into the bowl for a moment, like he might find the truth in the broth. "Some days," he said finally. "Other days… it feels like I'm just patching people up and sending them back into the same damage that brought them in."

Her eyes softened. "Sounds lonely."

"It is," he admitted, no hesitation. "But it was easier than thinking about everything I left behind."

Jade didn't reply straight away. She didn't need to. The silence between them was understanding enough.

After a moment, she said, "Anyone special in your life?"

The question was quiet, careful—but not careless. Not meaningless.

He hesitated. "No."

He didn't say: there's only ever been you.

But maybe she felt it.

She nodded, a faint shift in her posture. Not relief. Not disappointment. Just something closer to… knowing.

She glanced at him again. "Don't miss Manchester? Or is London everything you hoped it'd be?"

The words were light, but they weren't small. They carried history. And something bruised beneath them.

"I do miss it," he said.

A beat. Spoon to bowl.

Then he met her eyes. Held them.

"I didn't leave because of the city. I left because staying felt impossible."

Jade didn't speak.

Because she didn't need to.

Some part of her had always known.

They ate in silence after that—comfortable, full of the things that no longer had to be defended. Things that didn't need to be said tonight. Maybe not ever.

The space between them had changed. It wasn't empty now. It was shared.

And for the first time in a very long time, it felt like something might be beginning.

Not romance.

She knew that wasn't possible.

But Jade wanted her friend back.

And maybe—just maybe—he'd never really left.

The storm had passed, and the ground was beginning to thaw. If the weather held, tomorrow would be clear enough to leave.

But for now, all they could do was make the most of it.

They finished their soup in silence, not the awkward kind, but the kind that felt almost necessary. Sacred. A stillness that gave space for something new to breathe.

Jade stood first, gathered the empty bowls and carried them to the sink. The soft clink of ceramic, the rush of water—small domestic sounds that somehow felt more intimate than words. She washed them slowly, methodically, like she needed the task to anchor her. Then she put the kettle on, spooned tea leaves into a pot, and poured two mugs.

They drank that in silence, too.

No grand confessions. No tears. Just the quiet, steady hum of something repairing itself—thread by invisible thread.

After the mugs were rinsed and placed beside the bowls on the drying rack, Jade turned toward him, brushing damp hands on her jeans. Her voice was soft but sure.

"I think it's time for bed."

Duncan's head snapped up before he could hide it. His body went still; breath caught between confusion and instinct. "I'll sleep on the sofa," he said quickly, already feeling shifting forward like he meant to prove it.

Jade tilted her head. "Don't be silly," she said gently. "We're adults," she said with a small shrug. "And… it's not like there's anything between us."

Her tone was light. Dismissive. Matter of fact.

And it landed in him like a bruise.

Duncan managed a small nod, forcing his expression into something neutral. Casual. Like the words hadn't carved straight through his ribs. Like it hadn't taken everything in him not to flinch.

"Right," he said quietly. "Of course."

But inside, something folded in on itself.

Because she didn't know.

She didn't know the truth.

That everything was between them. At least for him.

But she still thought he only wanted to be her friend.

Not her lover.

Not her everything.

She still believed Duncan had never wanted her—never seen her the way he had, not in the quiet, aching way that had consumed him for years.

So, she offered him safety.

Friendship.

A shared bed with no threat of confusion or complication.

She meant it as kindness.

And it broke him a little anyway.

Jade turned without waiting for an answer and disappeared into the bathroom. A few minutes later, she emerged in silk pyjamas—light grey, soft against her skin, clinging in places Duncan forced himself not to linger on.

She crossed to the bed with practiced ease, brushing back the covers and sitting down with a sigh. He hadn't moved. Still rooted to the edge of the sofa, spine tight, heart heavier than it had any right to be.

She paused, then looked over her shoulder at him—something softer in her gaze now. Something like trust. And that, somehow, hurt even more.

"You'll be more comfortable in the bed," she said gently. "And honestly, I'd feel better knowing you weren't too far away… just in case. So, I can keep an eye on you."

There was no suggestion behind the words. No invitation. Just care. Pure. Uncomplicated. Platonic.

She nodded toward the bathroom. "There's a bathrobe hanging behind the door if you want to use it. Probably more comfortable than putting your clothes back on—they're not quite dry yet."

Duncan managed a nod, pushing himself to his feet. His limbs ached, stiff from the storm and the tension knotted through every muscle. But none of it compared to the weight behind his ribs—the truth he still hadn't spoken. The hope he hadn't quite let die.

"Okay," he said, voice quiet. "Thanks."

He walked toward the bathroom, one slow step at a time, his pulse loud in his ears. He closed the door behind him and leaned against it for a moment, letting his eyes fall shut.

He dropped the blankets and pulled on the bathrobe, only just realising she must have stripped him down to his underwear to get him warm. A flush of awareness passed through him, but he said nothing.

When he stepped out, the robe hung loosely on his frame, the fabric brushing against chilled skin. Jade was already in bed, curled onto her side beneath the covers. She looked up at the sound of his footsteps.

Her face, bathed in firelight, was soft and pale—calm, but tired.

She offered him a small, tired smile. "See? Not so weird."

Duncan nodded again, unable to speak. He moved to the opposite side of the bed and slid under the covers, careful to keep space between them, careful not to let himself want anything more than this.

Because she wanted her friend back.

And he wasn't sure he could ever be just that again.

But for tonight, he'd try.

Even if it cracked him open.

Quiet settled around them once more, broken only by the wind rattling softly at the windowpanes and the fire murmuring across the room.

Duncan lay still, staring at the ceiling, listening to the sound of her breathing.

And thinking, not for the first time, how much it hurt to be this close to someone you loved—and still feel so far away.

Chapter Ten

Duncan lay under the covers, mere inches from the only woman he'd ever truly loved, his breath shallow, every nerve attuned to her presence. He could feel her there—solid and soft beside him—though they hadn't touched. Not yet.

She was asleep, curled on her side facing him, her face partly obscured by a spill of golden hair that caught the faintest light from the hearth. Her breathing was steady. Peaceful. Untroubled, like the worst of the storm had passed and left her untouched.

But for him, the storm was still raging.

It surged beneath his ribs, coiled tight in his chest—the ache of everything he hadn't said, everything he hadn't done. The truth lived there now, unspoken, and bitter on his tongue. Close enough to burn.

He didn't dare move. Didn't dare reach out.

He lay perfectly still, counting the beats of his heart as if they might steady him. As if he could anchor himself to this moment before it slipped away.

The silence between them felt delicate. Sacred. A thread of understanding not yet spoken aloud but thrumming all the same.

And in that silence, Duncan let the ache take root.

He let himself feel the weight of every missed chance. Every moment he'd stood quietly in the background while Jade gave her light to someone who never deserved it. Every time he'd bitten back the truth because loyalty had demanded it.

God, he'd been such a coward.

And yet, here she was. Asleep beside him in a remote cabin in the middle of nowhere. After all the distance. All the silence. After the grief, the betrayal, and the storm that had nearly swallowed him whole.

She was here.

And that alone felt like a kind of miracle.

He didn't know what tomorrow would bring. Didn't know what she'd say when the morning came, and the fire had burned low and the spell between them was broken by daylight.

He just knew this: right now, she was safe. She was warm. And she was close enough to touch.

But he wouldn't.

He couldn't.

Instead, he closed his eyes and let her breathing guide him—slow and rhythmic, the sound of something deep, honest, and unguarded. He memorised it. Like he might never hear it again.

And slowly, gently, sleep began to pull him under.

Not the kind of sleep he was used to—not the fractured, restless half-rest that came in hospital break rooms or on long train rides home from the trauma ward—but something quieter. More vulnerable. Threaded with dreams he wouldn't remember and emotions he could no longer hold back.

But a few hours later, something shifted.

Something real.

The kind of shift that cut through sleep and landed deep in the body—warmth, weight, and the unmistakable presence of someone letting their guard down.

Jade.

She'd moved in her sleep, curled into him without even waking. Her head now rested in the crook of his shoulder, soft strands of her hair brushing against his jaw. One hand had slipped across his chest, splayed gently over the centre of his heart as if drawn there by instinct.

And his arm—God, his arm had moved too.

He didn't remember doing it. But it was there now, wrapped around her protectively, his fingers resting lightly against the curve of her back. Like this was where she belonged. Like his body had known before his mind did.

Duncan froze, afraid to breathe, afraid to wake her and lose this.

The heat of her against him was intoxicating—her body pressed to his like she trusted him, like she still trusted him, despite everything. Her breath was a whisper against his collarbone, warm and steady, and his own heart answered in kind, each beat heavy and wild beneath her palm.

She was still asleep. Completely unaware of the effect she was having on him. And that, somehow, made it worse. Or better. He wasn't sure.

Because this wasn't just desire.

This was longing.

Years of it.

Buried. Silenced. Deferred again and again.

He swallowed hard, blinking up at the ceiling, trying to hold the moment without breaking it. His chest rose in shallow breaths. His hand stayed exactly where it was, even as his fingertips itched to move, to trace the line of her spine, to tuck a strand of hair behind her ear and press a kiss to her forehead like he had the right.

He didn't.

Not yet.

But oh, how he wanted to.

For the first time in a long time, Duncan let himself imagine what it might be like— really be like—if she were his. If she had chosen him back then. If Dean hadn't gotten in the way. If he had been braver. If he had told her the truth when it still might have mattered.

Would they have ended up like this anyway? Curled together in the dark? Or would they have found each other under different circumstances—less broken, less hurt—but still this close?

He didn't know.

He only knew this felt right.

Painfully, beautifully right.

His arm tightened around her, just slightly. A silent promise. A breathless confession. He didn't know what morning would bring. But if there was even the faintest chance that she might feel something—anything—for him beyond friendship...

He would wait.

He would stay.

And maybe—just maybe—she'd look at him not as Dean's friend. Not as a shadow from her past.

But as someone who had always, always loved her.

And maybe one day, she'd choose him.

Not because she had to.

But because she wanted to.

Because, deep down, she always had.

Jade stirred just before dawn, the sky outside still cloaked in soft indigo, the fire downstairs long since burned to embers.

She didn't open her eyes at first. Just shifted slightly, her brow creasing, lips parting on a sleepy exhale as her body registered warmth and safety and something else—something unfamiliar but comforting.

Then she felt it.

An arm around her. A steady rise and fall beneath her cheek. Fingers resting lightly on her hip.

Her breath caught.

Her eyes blinked open slowly, adjusting to the low light. For a moment, she didn't move—didn't even breathe.

Her head was on Duncan's chest.

His chest.

And his arm was around her.

They'd moved in sleep—instinctive, unthinking—but now she was wrapped against him like it was the most natural thing in the world. Her hand was splayed over his heart, and God, she could feel it pounding.

Steady. Solid. Real.

Duncan was awake.

She felt the tension in him before she even looked up. The way his breath stalled. The way his body went still, like he wasn't sure if he was dreaming or terrified he might be.

She shifted, just enough to tilt her face up.

His eyes met hers.

And for a second—just one long, quiet second—neither of them moved.

The air between them was thick with something unspoken. Not fear. Not regret. Just something fragile. Unsteady. And entirely too honest.

Jade swallowed. Her voice, when it came, was a whisper.

"I'm sorry. I didn't mean to—"

"You don't need to apologise," Duncan said quickly, his voice low and rough with sleep. "It's okay."

A beat passed.

"You were cold," he added, softer this time. "You moved closer. I just… I didn't want to wake you."

She nodded faintly but didn't move away. Not yet. Her fingers were still resting on his chest, and she could feel the warmth of his skin beneath the robe, the steady thrum of his pulse under her palm.

"I must've been half-asleep," she murmured, cheeks colouring faintly. "Didn't even realise."

Another pause. His eyes never left hers.

"I didn't mind," he said. Quiet. Honest. Unapologetic.

Jade looked at him for a long moment, her heart beginning to thud in her chest in time with his.

There was something in his expression she hadn't let herself see in years.

Something she didn't quite know how to name.

Not yet.

But it didn't scare her.

Not anymore.

She swallowed again, then—slowly, gently—eased back just enough to settle onto her own pillow, her face still turned toward him, close but not touching.

She didn't say anything else. Neither did he.

But the space between them felt different now. Not empty.

Just full of everything that had begun to shift.

And even before the sun crested the horizon, Jade understood something she hadn't dared hope.

She might get her friend back after all.

And that meant something. More than she'd expected.

But as she lay there in the silence, with his warmth still lingering beside her, another thought crept in—uninvited but familiar.

She wished he wasn't gay.

She wished—selfishly, silently—that he could want her.

Not for a moment. Not for comfort. But in the way she'd sometimes imagined when she couldn't sleep.

What would it have been like… to be his?

Not just for a night.

But for a lifetime.

That thought had haunted her more times than she cared to admit.

And even now, lying inches from the man she'd once grieved like a heartbreak she wasn't allowed to claim, it returned—soft and aching.

It wasn't about lust. It wasn't even about loneliness.

It was about how he made her feel. Seen. Safe. Like she was enough, exactly as she was.

And if there had ever been a world where he could have looked at her and wanted her the way she'd once wanted him…

She would have chosen him.

Every time.

Every inch she moved away felt like another truth she didn't realise he was holding close.

He closed his eyes.

Pretended to go back to sleep.

Let her go.

Because she still believed he didn't want her.

Still believed that he wasn't capable of wanting her that way. That he only wanted friendship.

And the ache of that—of being this close and still so unseen—burned deep in his chest.

He heard the faint rustle of the blanket, the soft pad of her feet across the floor. The hush of the kettle in the kitchen, the clink of a mug.

She was moving on with the morning.

And he lay there, jaw tight, eyes shut, holding on to the ghost of her body next to his.

Trying not to break open with the weight of everything he hadn't told her.

Not yet.

But soon.

He couldn't stay silent forever.

Because loving her in the dark wasn't enough anymore.

Chapter Eleven

They ate breakfast in silence—just simple porridge, warm and filling. The oats were soft, slightly sweet, laced with cinnamon and the faintest hint of maple from a bottle she'd found at the back of the cupboard. It wasn't fancy. It wasn't even particularly good. But it was hot, and it anchored them. A small act of care in a world that had gone cold and uncertain.

Jade sat cross-legged on the sofa, bowl in her lap, her spoon moving slowly. She didn't rush. Neither did Duncan. Each bite gave them time to think. Time to sit with the things unsaid.

The quiet wasn't uncomfortable—not like it had been in the last months with Dean. It wasn't avoidance or tension. It was thoughtful. Careful. Each of them still navigating the fragile space between what had just been revealed and everything that hadn't yet been spoken aloud.

When they finished, Jade rose to take the bowls to the sink. The cabin was still dim, the fire little more than a cradle of glowing coals now, and the outside world remained hushed beneath a thick coat of snow.

When she moved back to the sofa, she glanced out the frost-edged window, her breath fogging the pane slightly before she turned to him.

"We should be able to leave later today," she said softly, pulling a blanket around her shoulders. "The roads should probably be clearer by then. Still no phone reception, though, so you'll have to wait a bit before you can call someone about your car."

She hesitated, then added gently, "I can drive you to your parents' place if you'd like. It's not too far from here."

Duncan nodded, slow and quiet. "Yeah. That would be good. Thanks."

There was a moment where neither spoke again, and Jade found herself studying him—not out of curiosity, but something deeper. Her eyes swept across his face, taking in the drawn lines beneath his eyes, the faint pallor that still lingered in his cheeks, the tired set of his mouth.

"You still look a little pale," she said, concerned. "Do you feel okay?"

He let out a breath, not quite a sigh. "My ribs are still sore, but the shoulder's not as bad as I thought. All things considered… I've been through worse."

"I'm glad," she murmured. Her voice softened, almost tentative. "You should probably take it easy for a few days. Let your body catch up."

Duncan nodded again, but his gaze had turned distant—somewhere else entirely. Somewhere older. He stared past her for a moment, then back, his eyes a little more shadowed now. Then, with surprising gentleness, he asked,

"What are you going to do about Dean?"

Jade didn't even flinch. Not anymore.

"Nothing," she said simply. "He hasn't made an effort in months. I'm just... done."

She exhaled, her shoulders lowering as if she'd been holding that breath for far too long.

"I'm going to act like he never existed. And eventually, I'll move on."

She paused, and something softer, almost stunned, passed across her face.

"Honestly?" she added, voice quieter, steadier. "I feel relieved."

Duncan didn't respond right away. He just looked at her.

A long, steady look—one that held more than gratitude. More than concern.

It held the weight of years. The ache of silence. And something else.

Something older.

Fierce and quiet.

A love that had waited too long to be spoken.

"I should've stayed your friend," he said at last. The words rasped low in his throat, rough from both the cold and regret. "I should've—" He stopped, dragging a hand across the stubble on his jaw, jaw clenched. "I should've been the one who showed up for you. Not him."

Jade didn't interrupt. She didn't rush to make him feel better or brush it away with the kind of casual forgiveness women so often felt pressured to offer. She just watched him. Steady. Silent. Present.

Duncan's gaze dropped to his hands. He flexed his fingers, then curled them into loose fists on his knees.

"He never deserved you," he said finally. The words weren't bitter. They weren't meant to wound. They were just... true.

And that kind of truth had its own sharp edge.

"I knew it," he said. "Even back then. But I didn't know how to say it without setting fire to everything."

Jade's expression shifted. Just barely. But he saw it. A flicker of confusion. Sadness. And something else that looked almost like… understanding.

Duncan looked back up at her, meeting her gaze. "He told me you were happy. That you were in love. That things were perfect between you. And I believed him. I thought you'd moved on. That you didn't need me anymore. Then he said…"

He swallowed hard. His throat worked around the words like they cost him something.

"He told me I made you uncomfortable. That you didn't like the way I looked at you, that seeing me made things harder for you. I didn't want to be the reason you pulled away."

Her brow furrowed. "What? Why would he say that?"

"You were my best friend, Duncan," she said, her voice trembling now. "I never felt uncomfortable with you. But then you just…" She shook her head slowly, disbelief on her face. "You disappeared. No texts. No calls. Nothing. You were just… gone."

"I never stopped caring," he said, voice thick with the weight of it. "I thought I was doing the right thing. I told myself I was giving you space. Letting you be happy. But the truth is—I was protecting myself. I couldn't watch you love someone else. Not when it was tearing me apart."

Jade blinked quickly, her jaw tight, eyes shining with unshed emotion.

"You were never the one who made me uncomfortable," she said, her voice a whisper. "You were the one I trusted."

Duncan closed his eyes for a beat, like the words physically hit him. Like they scraped something raw and long hidden inside his chest. When he opened them again, he leaned forward, elbows on his knees, hands clasped.

"I should've told you the truth," he said quietly.

A beat of silence passed.

Then Jade asked, softly, "Why didn't you just tell me… about being gay?"

His head jerked up. "What!?"

She hesitated. "Dean told me. Right before my brother's wedding. I was going to ask you to come with me—to be my plus one. I told him that I liked you. Really liked you."

Her voice dropped, thick with old hurt. "He said you didn't want anyone to know. That it was private. But that's why you pulled away."

Duncan stared at her, stunned. The room seemed to tilt.

"That's not true," he said. "God, Jade—that's not true at all. I'm not gay. I never told Dean that. Never even hinted at it."

Her mouth opened slightly. "But... he said..."

"He lied," Duncan said, voice flat and hollow. "He lied to both of us."

He shook his head, anger and heartbreak tightening his features.

"I told him I had feelings for you," he continued. "That I was going to ask you out. And then, out of nowhere, you and Dean were together. I thought I'd missed my chance. I thought maybe... maybe you'd never felt the same."

Silence dropped like a stone between them.

Jade stared at him, wide-eyed. "You liked me?"

"I still like you," Duncan said, and this time there was no hesitation. "I never stopped. Even when I walked away. Even when I thought I had no right."

His voice dipped lower, but steadier now. "I came here because I couldn't stay quiet anymore. Not after what he said. Not after everything."

Jade's breath caught. Her hands were clenched in her lap now, knuckles white.

"Why didn't you tell me sooner?" she asked, voice small, wounded.

Duncan's gaze softened, even as his heart cracked. "Because I thought I was too late. That you'd made your choice. That I had no right to ask you for anything."

He reached for her hand, didn't take it—just hovered close.

"But now?" he said. "Now I think maybe I should've fought harder. For you. For us. For the truth."

Jade looked down, shoulders rising with a shaky breath. "Dean took so much from me. From both of us."

"He did," Duncan said. "But he doesn't get to have the last word."

She looked back at him, eyes glassy but unflinching.

"And what now?" she asked. "What do I do now?"

Duncan met her gaze and held it.

"Whatever you want," he said. "But you don't have to do it alone."

She didn't answer right away. But she didn't look away either.

And for the first time in years... that felt like a beginning.

The words echoed inside her like a stone dropped in still water—rippling through disbelief, through ache, through the fragile thread of hope she didn't dare tug too hard.

She should have been angry.

Dean had lied. *Deliberately*. Rewritten her life to protect his own pride.

But what she felt now wasn't rage.

It was grief.

Grief for the time lost. For the love that could've been. For the version of her life, she'd never gotten to live.

"For years," she murmured. "Years, I thought I wasn't enough. That I imagined it all— that closeness, the way you used to look at me, the way I felt when you were near."

"You didn't imagine it," Duncan said softly. "Not a single second of it."

Her chest tightened. She looked at him like she was seeing him—truly seeing him— for the first time.

And for the first time… she let herself believe.

Not in the future. Not yet.

But in him.

"I don't know what I want," she said, honest and fragile. "But I know what I don't want. I don't want to feel small. Or afraid. Or unseen."

"You never have to feel that way with me," he said.

"I believe you."

The silence that followed was different this time.

Not full of uncertainty.

Full of possibility.

She leaned back into the sofa, her gaze drifting to the window. The storm had passed, the ice beginning to melt. Clouds were thinning. Light was slowly returning.

Not warmth—

not yet.

But the promise of it.

And maybe—if they were brave enough—something more.

Something that might, one day, be called love.

Chapter Twelve

They packed up slowly after sharing a light lunch—just soup and bread, simple and comforting. The earlier heaviness between them had softened into something more familiar, like an old rhythm slowly returning.

They talked about university days. About ridiculous pranks and midnight study sessions and that one time Duncan had tried to teach her how to cook pasta and nearly set off the fire alarm.

And they laughed.

Real, unguarded laughter. The kind Jade hadn't felt in months—maybe years. It loosened something tight in her chest. For a little while, it felt like time folded in on itself, bringing back the version of them that had once existed, untouched by all the hurt in between.

As the sky shifted toward a late-afternoon grey, Jade zipped her suitcase shut and hauled it out the door. Duncan followed, coat on, one hand tucked carefully into his pocket.

"I told you not to lift anything," she said, giving him a mock-stern look as she popped the boot of her car.

"I'm just supervising," he replied with a faint smile.

She rolled her eyes but couldn't help the grin tugging at her lips.

Duncan stood by the passenger side as she moved toward the driver's door, brushing stray strands of hair from her face, mentally preparing herself for the long drive back to the real world.

And then—a sound.

Gravel crunching.

An engine.

Jade looked up, blinking into the pale light as another car pulled up the long, icy drive.

Her breath caught.

The driver's door opened.

And out stepped Dean.

Jade froze in place. Her stomach dropped. The sound of his voice hit her like a splash of cold water.

She glanced instinctively at Duncan.

His jaw was tight, clenched so hard she half expected to hear his teeth crack. His hands were fists at his sides, unmoving—but his eyes never left Dean.

"Jade," Dean called, striding toward her like he hadn't practically ghosted her for months. "Thank God."

Before she could react, he wrapped his arms around her.

She didn't hug him back.

She stood stiff and stunned in his embrace, arms pinned at her sides, her heart thudding painfully against her ribs.

"What are you doing here?" she asked flatly, pulling away the moment her voice returned.

Dean's expression flickered—surprise, maybe even hurt—but he masked it quickly. "I'm here to say sorry."

Jade took a step back, just out of his reach. Her eyes stayed locked on his, steady and unreadable, but she could feel Duncan behind her now—quiet, grounded, solid. He'd come around the car, positioning himself close. Close enough to be there if she needed him.

"Sorry?" she echoed, her voice cool. "For what, exactly?"

Dean hesitated—just a beat—but it was enough to feel like a lifetime.

And suddenly, the air felt colder than the wind.

"For not getting here sooner," Dean said quickly. "The roads were blocked, and there was no service to call. I've been worried sick."

He stepped forward again, arms half-lifted like the hug he'd just forced hadn't landed like lead.

Jade took a sharp step back—straight into Duncan's chest.

"Don't, Dean," she said firmly, her voice like ice.

Dean froze mid-step, blinking. "What's wrong, Jade?"

She looked him directly in the face, lifting her chin. Her heart was racing, but her voice was steady.

"We're done, Dean."

His brows pulled together, confusion darkening his features. "What? Why? What are you talking about?"

She took a breath. "Duncan told me everything."

Dean's head snapped toward Duncan, his eyes narrowing. "Told you what?" His voice sharpened. "What lies have you been feeding my girlfriend?"

"She's not your girlfriend," Duncan said, tone low and even. "And I don't lie, Dean. That's your thing, not mine."

Dean opened his mouth, but whatever he was about to say stalled under the weight of Jade's stare.

Her silence said everything.

And for the first time since arriving, Dean looked uncertain.

His expression twisted, frustration bubbling beneath the shock. "Are you seriously going to believe Duncan over me? He hasn't even bothered with you for years, Jade."

Her eyes narrowed. Her voice was flat.

"That was your doing, Dean. All your lies."

Dean scoffed. "Lies? What lies? The only liar here is him. He disappeared, and now he waltzes back in and suddenly I'm the villain. You really can't see what he's doing?"

"I see everything very clearly now," Jade said calmly, though her hands were clenched at her sides. "You told me he was gay. You told him he made me uncomfortable. You told me he didn't care."

Dean's face paled. "Oh, come on. You're not seriously buying that. He's playing you. He always has."

"I know about your affair with your secretary," Jade said, her voice cold and cutting.

Dean blinked, stunned. "What? That's—no, that's not true. Who told you that?"

Jade tilted her head slightly, voice low but unwavering.

"You did, Dean. With every word you didn't say. With the way you've treated me for months. You haven't cared about me in a long time."

He opened his mouth. Closed it again.

"That's not true."

Jade let out a bitter laugh.

"No? Then what would you call it? You lied to me for years, Dean. About Duncan. About us. About everything."

Dean's eyes darted to Duncan, trying to find some angle, some control. His voice sharpened with accusation.

"He's manipulating you, Jade. He's always wanted you. That's what this is."

She took a step forward, fury rising, her eyes flashing.

"Good," she snapped. "At least one of you finally had the guts to say it out loud."

"Jade don't do this," he said quickly. "We belong together. You know that."

"Do I?" she spat. "Because from where I'm standing, I don't know a damn thing anymore—except that I've wasted years trying to love a man who made me feel small."

Dean's jaw tightened. "We can fix this. We can try for another baby."

Her breath caught like a blow to the chest. She stared at him, stunned.

Then her voice came, low and trembling with fury.

"Are you serious?" she whispered. "You don't even want kids, Dean. You didn't care about the one I lost. You wouldn't even talk about it. You went back to work the next damn day like nothing happened."

"Of course I cared!" he shouted. "I was grieving in my own way! Everyone grieves differently—"

"Bullshit!" Her voice cracked like a whip. "You weren't grieving. You were running. Hiding. Just like you always do."

Silence fell—thick and suffocating.

Duncan stood behind her, unmoving, a quiet fury etched into the tight line of his jaw. His eyes never left her.

And Jade—she didn't move either.

She didn't need to.

"You only came after me when you found out Duncan and I liked each other," she said, voice sharp. "Then you made sure we weren't even friends. Just in case. That's sick, Dean. Do you know that?"

Because for the first time in years, she wasn't confused. She wasn't second-guessing.

She was done.

And she knew exactly where she stood.

"You and I are over," she said, her voice cold and unwavering. "Never to be repeated. You weren't worth one minute of my time."

Dean's face twisted, rage and desperation colliding. He looked up at Duncan.

"This is your fault! You've been jealous of me for years—you couldn't stand that I had Jade!"

Duncan didn't flinch. His voice was low and dangerous.

"You only had her because you lied. Multiple times."

Dean laughed, but there was no humour in it—only venom.

"You think this means you win? She's not some prize you get to claim."

"No," Duncan said, stepping forward, his voice like steel. "She's not a prize. She's a woman you took for granted. And you lost her. That's on you."

Dean suddenly turned back to Jade, grabbed her hands, desperate now.

"Please, Jade. I love you. You love me too—I know you do."

She looked at him, tired, resolute.

"No, Dean. I don't." Her voice was quiet but firm. "And I don't think I have for a long time. You killed any love I had for you a long time ago."

Dean's eyes flicked between her and Duncan, his face flushing red. Then the bitterness twisted into a sneer.

"She'll leave you too, you know," he said, voice laced with venom. "Once she realises you're not the fantasy she's built in her head. You think she wants you? A bitter, lonely man who's been pining in silence for years? She'll get bored. Just like she did with me."

Jade turned slowly. Her expression didn't waver. Her voice—calm, steady—cut like glass.

"No, Dean. I didn't get bored. I got tired. Tired of being lied to. Tired of being alone in a relationship. Tired of you pretending to be someone you're not."

She drew a breath, her eyes narrowing.

"And the difference between you and Duncan? He doesn't need to lie to matter."

Dean opened his mouth, but there was nothing left to say. Nothing that wouldn't make it worse.

So, he turned, jaw clenched, stalked back to his car, slammed the door, and drove off—spinning the wheels in a spray of gravel.

And this time, Jade didn't stop him.

The silence that followed was heavy with finality.

Duncan stepped closer and gently placed his hands on her shoulders.

"Are you okay?"

Jade nodded—then shook her head.

"No. Not really." Her voice cracked, and she blinked hard. "But I will be."

She looked up at him then, truly looked—into eyes that hadn't left her once.

"I'm just… tired. Of everything. Of trying so hard for something that was already broken."

Duncan's jaw softened, the tension in his shoulders easing just enough.

"You don't have to try anymore. Not with him. Not with anyone."

A tear slipped down her cheek before she could stop it. She let out a breath, half-laugh, half-sob.

"God, I feel like I should be more of a mess."

"You're allowed to fall apart," he said gently.

"Maybe," she whispered. "But right now, I just want to breathe again."

Duncan nodded slowly, his hands still steady on her shoulders.

"Then start here. Just breathe, Jade. I've got you."

And for the first time in a long, long time, she believed someone meant it.

Chapter Thirteen

Jade drove them to Watermillock, a winding fifteen-minute trip from the cabin that hugged the shimmering edge of Ullswater. The storm had passed, but its shadow lingered—the sky a soft, bruised grey, the road slick and glistening beneath the tyres.

On the way there, she slowed as they approached the narrow bend where Duncan's car had gone off the road. The vehicle sat nose-first in a shallow ditch, the front bumper crumpled against a mossy embankment, one headlight shattered and dark. Mud streaked the sides, the tyres half-buried in soft earth, as if the car had tried to claw its way out before giving up.

Jade pulled over and cut the engine.

"I'll grab my bag," Duncan said quietly.

She watched him climb out—still stiff from his ordeal—and make his way to the boot. The back end of the car was tilted awkwardly, and he had to lean in carefully to retrieve the worn duffel he'd thrown in before leaving his flat in London.

Jade stayed behind the wheel, her fingers tightening on the steering wheel. The sight of the wreck—how close he'd come to serious harm—sent a shiver up her spine.

He closed the boot with a thud, slung the bag over his shoulder, and limped back toward the car.

"You okay?" she asked softly as he slid back into the passenger seat.

"I am now," he said, not quite meeting her eyes.

She turned the key in the ignition and eased them back onto the road. The Armstrong estate was just ahead, but her thoughts remained tangled in the wreckage they'd left behind.

Duncan sat beside her, quiet. Still healing. Still unreadable. But every so often, she felt his gaze shift toward her—watching. Steady. Saying things he wasn't ready to say aloud.

They turned down a gravel drive flanked by ancient oaks, and soon the Armstrong estate came into view—a grand stone house nestled into the hills, proud and timeless. It hadn't changed. Neither had the warmth it carried in Jade's memory.

As they stepped out of the car, the front door opened. Duncan's mother rushed out first—elegant as ever, her silver hair pinned up, arms already outstretched.

"Jade!" she cried. "Oh, love, look at you!"

And just like that—like no time had passed—Jade was swept into a familiar embrace that smelled of rosewater and lavender. Duncan's father followed behind her, slower but smiling warmly.

"Well, now," he said, stepping down. "There's our girl."

It was exactly how they'd greeted her the last time—three years ago. As if nothing had fractured. As if they'd simply been waiting.

Jade blinked fast, emotion catching her off guard.

They still saw her.

They hadn't stopped.

"It's good to see you both," Jade said, steadying her voice. "It's been a while."

Helen's eyes softened as she looped her arm through Jade's with practiced ease.

"Too long," she said, patting her hand. "We've missed you. Never understood why you stopped visiting."

Jade's smile faltered—just for a second—but she didn't answer. Not yet.

They stepped through the wide front doors into the high-ceilinged foyer, sunlight slanting through the tall windows. The house smelled the same—cedarwood, polished stone, something vaguely floral. Something safe.

Gary walked beside his son with quiet strength, nodding warmly at Jade. "Come in, come in. You're just in time for tea. Helen insists on baking when she's worried. You've arrived in the middle of a full-blown scone emergency."

That earned a faint chuckle from Duncan. But his eyes never strayed far from Jade.

Jade squeezed Helen's arm gently. "I've missed this house. Missed you both."

"And we've missed you," Helen said again, her voice more pointed this time. "You always belonged here, Jade."

Behind her, Duncan's steps slowed just slightly—those words landing deeper than maybe she'd intended.

In the warmth of the Armstrong kitchen, the air was thick with butter, citrus, and something sweet and rising. A tray of golden scones sat cooling on a wire rack while Maggie, the housekeeper, arranged cups and saucers on a silver tray.

"Let me help," Jade offered, already stepping beside Helen.

"Oh, nonsense," Helen waved a hand—but Jade was already reaching for the sugar bowl.

Maggie smiled over her shoulder. "It's nice having extra hands. Especially ones who know where everything is."

Jade smiled back, the ache of nostalgia blooming in her chest.

"Muscle memory," she said softly. "Hard to forget this kitchen."

Helen gave her a knowing glance as she poured the tea. "Good. Then maybe you'll stay a while this time."

Jade didn't answer right away. Her fingers skimmed the edge of a porcelain cup, the unspoken weight of Helen's words settling between them like a quiet dare.

Gary settled into the armchair, legs stretched out, hands loosely clasped. Duncan sat across from him on the sofa, elbows on his knees, the space between them heavy with unspoken things.

After a pause, Gary nodded toward the hallway. "So… Jade."

Duncan didn't move. "What about her?"

Gary shrugged, watching him carefully. "She's here. With you. Does that mean… something's happening?"

"She just broke up with Dean," Duncan said, voice flat.

Gary let out a grunt. "Never liked that Dean. Too smooth, too sure of himself. Always felt like he was performing."

Duncan's eyes met his father's. "He told Jade I was gay."

Gary blinked, thrown. "What?"

"That's why she chose him," Duncan said quietly. "He told her I wasn't into women— told her I was just being kind to her. Like I was… harmless."

Gary sat up straighter, his expression shifting from surprise to something closer to outrage. "Jesus, Duncan. Are you serious?"

Duncan nodded. "Dead serious."

For a moment, Gary said nothing. Then he exhaled sharply, shaking his head. "What a prick. And she believed him?"

"She didn't know what to believe. I didn't exactly fight for her."

Gary leaned forward, his voice softer now. "Well, maybe it's not too late to start."

"I'm hoping it's not," Duncan said quietly.

Gary studied him for a long moment. "So… you still care about her."

Duncan looked down, a faint, almost bitter smile tugging at his mouth. "I never stopped."

Gary nodded slowly, leaning back in the chair with a sigh. "Then don't waste the second chance."

Duncan glanced up.

"I've seen too many people live with regret, son. Your mother and I… we had our rough patches, and there were times I nearly walked away. But I didn't. Because I knew what mattered." He paused, then added, "And when something matters, you show up. You speak up. Even if it scares the hell out of you."

Duncan swallowed, the words landing heavier than he expected.

Gary softened his tone. "You've got a window here. Don't let pride or fear slam it shut again."

Duncan nodded slowly, his voice rough. "Yeah. I think I finally see that."

Jade followed Helen into the living room, carefully balancing the tea tray as the comforting scent of fresh scones drifted through the air. Duncan and Gary looked up from their conversation, the fire casting a soft amber glow over the room.

Jade set the tray on the coffee table and straightened a little too quickly. She offered a faint smile, then sat on the sofa beside Duncan—not too close, but not distant either. Close enough to share the space. Close enough to feel him there.

Duncan didn't move, but his eyes followed her every step.

Helen settled into the armchair beside Gary, smoothing her skirt with practiced elegance. She glanced from Duncan to Jade, warmth softening her expression.

"Oh, it warms my heart to see you two together again," she said, smiling gently.

Jade glanced down at her hands. Duncan shifted beside her, saying nothing, but she could feel his presence—solid, steady, quietly anchoring her.

"Just tea, Helen," Jade said lightly, trying to ease the weight of the moment. "And a few scones. Nothing dramatic."

"Still," Helen said, pouring with care, "there's something about seeing you both in this room again. It feels… right."

Jade let out a soft laugh, though her heartbeat pulsed in her throat. She reached for her cup, unsure how to respond—yet quietly aware she didn't entirely disagree.

Chapter Fourteen

Gary, sensing the weight in the room, cleared his throat and gently steered the conversation onto safer ground.

"So, what are you doing with yourself these days, Jade? Still at the hospital?"

She nodded, grateful for the shift. "Yes. I'm a nurse practitioner in the Acute Medical Unit."

Gary raised his eyebrows, impressed. "Busy job, I imagine."

Jade gave a small smile. "It is. A bit chaotic sometimes—but I like it. Keeps me out of trouble."

Helen chuckled as she passed a cup to Duncan. "You never were one for sitting still."

Jade shrugged playfully. "Still true."

Duncan glanced at her then—subtle, quiet—but the pride in his expression was unmistakable.

Helen looked over at her son, her brow creased with gentle concern.

"We didn't expect you. When we got your text this morning, it was a pleasant surprise. But are you feeling okay after your accident? What happened?"

Before Duncan could answer, Jade jumped in, turning slightly toward him with a look that was equal parts scolding and protective.

"Your ridiculous son," she said, voice edged with disbelief, "drove into a ditch in the middle of a storm—then walked a mile through it to get to me. He nearly killed himself."

Helen gasped, her hand flying to her chest. "Duncan!"

Gary let out a low whistle. "That's a bit dramatic, even for you."

Duncan held up his hands, the corners of his mouth twitching. "In my defence, I didn't mean to end up in a ditch. And I didn't know the storm was going to hit that hard."

Helen stared at him, clearly unimpressed. "You could've frozen out there."

"I know," he said quietly, glancing at Jade. "I wasn't exactly thinking clearly."

Jade crossed her arms, still glaring. "Clearly."

But her tone had softened, just a little—and Duncan noticed.

Helen shook her head, muttering, "Honestly. I'll never understand how the two of you managed to make it through university in one piece."

Gary reached for a scone. "Luck. And Jade, probably."

Duncan smiled faintly. "Definitely Jade."

They chatted a little longer, the conversation drifting through safe, familiar topics—hospital stories, Gary's ongoing war with the garden foxes, and Helen's passionate dislike for store-bought marmalade. The tension had thinned, replaced by a quiet comfort that felt almost like old times.

Jade finished the last of her tea and set her cup down carefully.

"I should probably get going."

Helen's head snapped up. "Oh, no you don't. You just got here!"

"I know," Jade said gently, "but—"

"She might have to get to work," Gary cut in, his voice mild but practical.

Jade offered a soft smile and shook her head. "I've got two more days off. I'm not due back until Wednesday."

That was all Helen needed to hear. Her eyes lit up instantly, already planning her next move.

"Perfect," she said brightly, already rising from her chair. "Then you're staying. At least for one night."

Jade blinked. "Helen—"

"No arguments. You're here, the room's made up, and I've already decided. We'll do something proper for dinner. You always liked my lamb stew."

Jade hesitated, her gaze sliding toward Duncan.

He was looking down at his cup, trying—failing—not to appear hopeful.

She exhaled quietly.

"Alright," she said, her voice soft. "One night."

Helen beamed. "Wonderful."

And from across the sofa, Duncan finally allowed himself to look at her.

Just then, Jade's phone buzzed on the coffee table.

"Sorry," she murmured, reaching for it. "Let me just check this—"

Her eyes scanned the screen, and her expression shifted—eyebrows lifting in mild surprise.

Duncan leaned slightly toward her; concern etched into his features.

"Everything okay?"

Jade nodded, though a small sigh slipped out. "It's Leanne. She wants to know if it's true about Dean and me."

Helen looked up from her tea, curious.

"Leanne—that's your nurse friend from university, isn't it?"

"Yeah," Jade said, her mouth tugging into a faint smile. "She says…" She paused, then read the message aloud.

"Babe. Just saw Dean. He told me you two are no longer together. Please tell me it's true."

Gary gave a quiet snort. "Didn't take him long to start talking, did it?"

Duncan's jaw tensed. "I'm surprised he told her. He doesn't even like Leanne."

Jade set the phone in her lap, her tone flat.

"Yeah. Well, the feeling's mutual."

She didn't look at anyone for a second, just stared at the message, thumb brushing the screen.

Helen gently set down her cup with a soft clink.

"Would you like some privacy, love?"

Jade shook her head, offering a small, grateful smile.

"No—it's fine. I'll call her later. I just wasn't expecting the fallout to start this fast."

She typed out a quick reply:

Yes, it's true. Long time coming. I'll call you later.

A second later, Leanne responded:

Thank God you saw the light. I'm here for you, babe. Always.

Jade couldn't help the small laugh that escaped her. She turned the screen toward Duncan so he could read it.

He leaned over, reading the words, and gave a quiet smile.

"She's got your back," he said softly.

Jade nodded. "She always has."

For a brief moment, the air shifted—lighter, safer, like maybe the worst really was behind her.

After everyone had finished their tea, Duncan excused himself to make arrangements for his car to be towed. Helen bustled back into the kitchen, already talking about preparing stew for dinner.

Gary rose from his chair, dusting off his trousers.

"Fancy a walk through the rose garden?" he asked Jade with a smile. "The glasshouse is still standing, believe it or not."

Jade returned the smile. "I'd love to."

They strolled out into the early evening air, the garden still damp from the earlier storm. A cool breeze stirred the petals as Gary led her along neat rows of rose bushes, pointing out new blooms with quiet pride.

Inside the glasshouse, the air was warmer, tinged with the delicate scent of roses in full flush. He stopped beside a cluster of soft pink blooms and leaned in slightly.

"These are new," he said. "Fragrant, aren't they?"

Jade bent forward and inhaled, closing her eyes for a moment. "They're beautiful. You always had a gift with these."

Gary smiled. "They've got good company."

There was a pause, and then, his voice softer, he added, "Duncan told me what Dean said—that business about him being gay."

Jade's expression tightened, but she nodded. "Yeah. Well… Dean told me a lot of lies, apparently."

Gary studied her face. "Why didn't you ask Duncan?"

She was quiet for a moment, considering. "I was going to. But Dean said it was private—that Duncan didn't want anyone to know." She let out a slow breath. "At first, I was hurt. I didn't understand why Duncan wouldn't trust me enough to tell me something like that. I thought we were close."

Gary waited, patient.

"Then I started thinking about it. He never went on dates with anyone. Never talked about girls. He was always just… around. Always with us."

Gary nodded slowly. "That's because you were the only one he was interested in."

Jade looked down at her hands. "Yeah," she said quietly. "I know that now. But I didn't then. And when Duncan pulled away—stopped calling, stopped showing up—I thought I'd done something wrong."

Gary let out a dry chuckle. "Well… in a way, you did."

Jade looked up sharply, and he gave her a pointed but gentle smile.

"You started dating that Dean fellow."

She huffed out a laugh, a little self-conscious. "Yeah. I suppose I did."

Gary gave her a warm pat on the shoulder.

"He's a good lad, our Duncan. Too proud for his own good sometimes—but his heart's always been in the right place. Especially when it comes to you."

Jade swallowed hard, her throat tightening with emotion.

"I know," she whispered. Then after a pause, she added quietly, "I just… need to get my head on straight before I decide what's next."

Gary nodded, thoughtful.

"Makes sense. No use rushing into anything. You need to be sure of what you want—and trying to figure that out while you're still recovering isn't the way."

"Exactly," she said, relieved to be understood. "I don't know how everything's going to pan out, but… I'll work it out."

Gary smiled. "I'm sure you will. You've always had a good head on your shoulders."

Jade let out a short laugh, shaking her head.

"Not recently. Not after everything with Dean. I've felt like a complete fool."

Gary raised an eyebrow. "You're not a fool, Jade. You trusted someone who didn't deserve it. That doesn't make you foolish. It makes you human."

Her smile faltered, but this time it was real.

“Thanks, Gary.”

He nodded once. “Anytime, love.”

Chapter Fifteen

After her quiet conversation with Gary and some time to herself, Jade slipped out to the back terrace with her phone. The afternoon air was cool, but not unkind, and the distant murmur of voices from inside gave her just enough privacy.

She tapped Leanne's name and lifted the phone to her ear.

"Babe; are you okay?" came the immediate, breathless response.

Jade smiled softly. "Surprisingly… yeah. I am."

A pause. "Where are you? I swung by your place to check in and you'd vanished."

"I'm at Duncan's parents' house. In the Lakes."

Silence. Then—

"Ohhh. So, you're at Dr. McDreamy's ancestral estate? Damn, that was fast." A beat. "Bit of a pity he's gay, though."

Jade rolled her eyes, but a helpless little laugh escaped anyway. "Turns out… he isn't."

Leanne's gasp was loud enough to make Jade wince. "What? But you told me—"

"No. Dean told me he was. Which, surprise, surprise—was a lie."

"You've got to be kidding me." Leanne's voice pitched upward. "What the actual hell is wrong with that man?"

Jade sighed. "Psycho."

"Utter psycho," Leanne echoed without missing a beat. "Wait—hang on. Have you kissed him yet?"

"No, Leanne!"

"Why the hell not?"

Jade groaned and pressed a hand to her forehead, pacing across the terrace. "I didn't call to be interrogated."

"No," Leanne said, smug and unrelenting. "But you did call me. Which means you do want to talk. So, talk. Spill. Everything."

Jade let out a long breath. The kind that felt like loosening something that had been wound too tight for too long.

So, she did.

She told Leanne everything—Dean's lies, Duncan showing up in the storm, the way the truth had come undone in layers she didn't see coming. The hurt, the confusion, the glimmers of something warm and familiar starting to take shape between them again.

And for once, Leanne didn't interrupt. She just listened.

When Jade finally stopped, the silence on the line felt thick with emotion.

Then Leanne spoke, her voice lower now. Fierce.

"I always knew Dean was a smug arsehole. But that? That's next-level manipulative."

"Yeah," Jade said quietly. "It really was."

"You okay?"

"I think so," Jade admitted. "I feel… raw. But also, like… something inside me finally clicked into place."

"Well," Leanne said, voice softening, "good. That click? That's you stepping back into your own damn power. And if Duncan walked through a storm to reach you? Babe, that man is not playing around."

Jade chuckled softly. "It's different with him. It always was."

"You deserve different. Better. Real."

"I'm trying," Jade murmured. "One piece at a time."

"I see you, babe. And I'm proud of you. Now—promise me one thing?"

"What?"

Leanne's tone turned sly. "If you do kiss him… I want every detail."

Jade laughed again, the tension finally breaking. "Of course you do."

"Damn right I do. And if he's got dimples, I want a separate report."

"I'm surprised Dean told you," Jade said.

"I was at a café," Leanne replied. "He walked in, looking like he'd swallowed a lemon. Came right up to me and said, 'You'll be happy now. Jade and I are no longer together'."

Jade blinked. "Seriously?"

"Oh, it gets better," Leanne said, smug. "I looked him dead in the eye and said, 'If that's true, then yes—I'm bloody ecstatic. You never deserved her'."

Jade burst out laughing, the sound full and real. "Leanne, really?"

"Yep. And I'm glad I did," she said without an ounce of regret. "Someone had to say it to his face."

Jade grinned, her chest feeling a little lighter. "Remind me never to get on your bad side."

Leanne snorted. "Please. You're stuck with me. Forever."

"I love you too," Jade said softly, smiling into the phone.

Just then, the terrace door creaked open behind her.

Duncan stepped outside with his parents, the soft clink of teacups in their hands. He paused mid-step, eyes flicking to her, a flicker of wariness crossing his face as he caught the tail end of her words.

Jade ended the call and turned to them, still smiling. "Leanne says hello."

Duncan visibly relaxed. "How is she?"

"She's in fine form," Jade said, settling back into her seat. "Apparently Dean copped the full Leanne treatment. She told him she was ecstatic that we were no longer together."

She giggled at the memory, and Duncan smiled at the sound—like he couldn't help it, like her laugh stirred something long dormant inside him.

They all took their seats again, the fire pit crackling gently at the centre of the terrace, casting warm, flickering light across their faces as dusk thickened around the garden.

"Did you get the car sorted?" Jade asked, shifting slightly to make space beside her.

Duncan nodded as he lowered himself onto one of the seats. "Yeah, finally. They said it's repairable. Shouldn't take too long."

Helen handed him a blanket. "And the tow?"

"They're sending someone tomorrow morning. I'll get a loaner while it's in the shop."

Jade arched an eyebrow. "You're just lucky you didn't hurt yourself more than you did."

Duncan offered a sheepish smile. "Yeah... I know."

Helen made a disapproving sound in the back of her throat but said nothing.

Helen passed him a mug of tea. "Still can't believe you drove out in that storm. Foolish thing to do."

"I know," Duncan said, glancing at Jade. "But I'd do it again."

Their eyes met for a second longer than necessary.

And the fire crackled on, warm and quiet, as the night drew in around them.

Before long, Maggie called them all inside for dinner. The table was already set, warm light spilling across roasted vegetables, bread still steaming in the basket, and a casserole dish in the centre that made Jade's stomach rumble.

As they ate, the conversation turned to family.

"So," Helen said with a fond smile, "how's your family doing, Jade? Is your mum still living in Wilmslow?"

Jade nodded, dabbing her mouth with a napkin. "She is. Still insists on tending that overgrown garden of hers like it's Kew."

Gary chuckled. "Sounds about right."

"And your brother?" Helen asked. "He was teaching somewhere, wasn't he?"

"He still is," Jade said. "At the same college in Stockport. And he and his wife are expecting again—second baby's due in a couple of months."

Everyone smiled, offering congratulations, but Jade glanced down at her plate as she said it, her fingers tightening slightly around her fork.

She didn't say anything else, but Duncan noticed. His eyes lingered on her, quiet and steady, reading what she didn't say aloud.

No one pressed.

And for a moment, only the gentle clinking of cutlery filled the silence.

Later that evening, after the dishes were cleared and the others had moved to the sitting room for tea, Duncan found Jade standing by the window, staring out into the darkened garden.

He approached quietly, not wanting to startle her.

"You okay?" he asked softly.

Jade didn't turn immediately. After a long pause, she finally looked back at him, her eyes shadowed.

"It's just… talking about my brother's baby," she said, her voice barely above a whisper. "It reminds me of what I lost."

Duncan nodded slowly, understanding the weight behind her words.

"I know," he said gently. "And I'm sorry. I wish things had been different."

She gave a small, sad smile. "Me too."

He reached out and took her hand, giving it a reassuring squeeze.

"It will take a while, you just need to take one step at a time," he promised. "No rush. Just whatever feels right."

Jade closed her eyes briefly, leaning into the warmth of his hand.

"Thank you, Duncan," she whispered. "For being here."

He smiled, a quiet hope blooming between them.

Helen and Gary turned in not long after dinner, leaving the house in a hush of clinking cups and soft footsteps on carpet. The fire in the sitting room had burned low, and the night pressed gently against the windows.

Duncan walked Jade down the hallway, the soft creak of the floorboards the only sound between them. He stopped outside the guest room—just next to his own—and turned to face her.

She smiled up at him, warm and a little shy. "Thanks for walking me to my door," she said lightly.

He didn't answer right away. Instead, he lifted his hand and, with the gentlest touch, brushed the backs of his fingers along her cheek.

"You know…" he said quietly, "you have the most beautiful eyes."

Jade's smile deepened, soft and wistful. "You've told me that before."

"It's still true," he murmured.

They stood there for a long moment, neither moving, caught in a current neither one of them fully dared to name.

Duncan wanted to kiss her—God, he wanted to—but something held him still. The fear of ruining the fragile trust between them. Of rushing her.

But then Jade leaned in.

Her lips brushed his—light, soft, hesitant. A question more than a statement.

It startled him—just for a second.

Her lips brushed his like a whisper, light and unsure. For a heartbeat, Duncan froze, hardly daring to believe what was happening.

Then she pulled back, just enough for their eyes to meet.

Her breath mingled with his, warm and uncertain in the stillness between them.

And then, without another word, they leaned in again—this time together.

The second kiss was deeper. Real. No longer tentative but tethered to something that had lived unspoken between them for years. Duncan's hands found her waist, drawing her gently closer, while her palms pressed to his chest like she needed to feel the thrum of his heartbeat to believe it was really him.

And it was him—completely.

For Duncan, it felt like breathing for the first time after holding his breath for far too long. Like everything he'd buried—wanting her, missing her, loving her—rose to the surface all at once. She was finally in his arms. No confusion, no secrets, no pretending they were only friends.

Just Jade. Soft and warm and heartbreakingly familiar.

The world outside that hallway didn't exist. Not the years they'd lost. Not Dean. Not the silence between them. In that moment, there was only the weight of her in his arms and the slow, aching realisation that he'd waited so long—for this. For her.

When they finally parted, breathless and still leaning into each other, Jade rested her forehead gently against his.

"I don't know what this is yet," she whispered, her voice a fragile thread of truth.

Duncan closed his eyes for a moment, steadying himself.

"I don't need it to be anything more than this," he murmured. "Not yet. Just you. Here. With me."

She let out a quiet breath, and he felt her nod ever so slightly.

Duncan nodded, his voice low. "That's okay. We don't have to name it. Not tonight."

She lingered for one more moment, then smiled softly, stepping back into the doorway.

"Goodnight, Duncan."

"Goodnight, Jade."

And as the door clicked softly shut, he stood there for a long while, heart racing, lips still tingling, soul quietly unravelling in the best possible way.

Chapter Sixteen

The scent of fresh coffee and baked apples lingered in the kitchen when Jade stepped inside, barefoot, and still wrapped in the soft cardigan Helen had left out for her. Morning light streamed through the tall windows, catching on the china teacups Helen was carefully laying out on a tray.

Helen looked up and smiled.

"Good morning, love. Sleep well?"

Jade nodded, tucking a strand of hair behind her ear. "Surprisingly well. That bed's like a cloud."

Helen gave a soft chuckle. "We keep it made up in case we get guests, but I always hoped you'd be the one in it again."

Jade paused, fingers brushing the edge of the counter. "I wasn't sure I'd ever be back."

Helen turned, her hands now idle, her eyes warm but sharp. "And yet, here you are."

Jade tried to smile, but something in her chest gave a quiet twist.

"I didn't expect any of this. Duncan showing up. Me being here."

Helen reached for the kettle, pouring hot water over a pair of tea bags. "Life has a funny way of pulling things back around when the timing's right."

Jade glanced toward the window. "Is the timing right, though?"

Helen didn't answer at first. She carried the mugs over and slid one in front of Jade.

"I won't pretend to know what's in your heart," she said gently. "But I know what I've seen. I know the way Duncan looks at you hasn't changed. And I know you didn't hesitate to help him when he showed up hurt."

Jade wrapped her hands around the warm mug. "It's complicated."

"Of course it is," Helen said, settling into the seat across from her. "The best things usually are."

Jade looked down at her tea. The steam curled softly upward.

"There's so much we never said back then. So much we both misunderstood."

Helen nodded. "Duncan's always been proud. Quiet when he's hurting. Never did know how to say the things that mattered most."

A pause.

"He nearly broke when you two grew apart. We didn't know why. He wouldn't tell us."

Jade's eyes met hers, heavy with the truth. "He didn't understand why I'd chosen Dean."

Helen reached across the table and placed her hand over Jade's. "Sweetheart, it's not about what happened three years ago. It's about what you want now."

Jade's voice caught as she said, "That's the part I'm still figuring out. It's all so fresh."

Helen gave her hand a gentle squeeze. "That's fair. But just remember—you don't have to figure it all out today. You just have to be honest with yourself."

Jade nodded, eyes glistening. "Thank you."

Helen smiled again, softer this time. "Just don't take too long, darling. Some hearts wait patiently. But even the strongest ones get tired."

From somewhere down the hall, a door creaked open—Duncan's steps, unmistakable and slow. Jade turned her head toward the sound, her heart picking up its pace.

Helen stood and picked up her tea. "I'll be in the garden."

She paused at the door, casting one last look over her shoulder.

"I always thought it would be you."

Then she was gone, leaving Jade alone with her tea, her thoughts, and the soft approach of footsteps just beyond the kitchen door.

The door creaked open, and Duncan stepped into the kitchen, hair damp from a quick shower, dressed in jeans and a soft charcoal jumper that clung just enough to hint at the strength beneath.

He paused when he saw Jade sitting at the table, her fingers curled around a half-finished mug of tea. Sunlight streamed in through the window behind her, catching the gold in her hair. She looked up, her expression unreadable—but softer than it had been the night before.

"Morning," he said quietly, as if testing the air.

"Hey," she replied, her voice warm but guarded. "Sleep okay?"

Duncan nodded, moving to the counter to pour himself a coffee. "Better than I deserved."

Jade let out a soft huff of breath—not quite a laugh, but close.

He turned to face her, leaning one hip against the counter, holding the mug in both hands.

"My mum corner you already?"

Jade lifted a brow. "Define 'corner.'"

Duncan gave a crooked grin. "Did she get all wise and poetic about fate and timing and what I idiotically threw away?"

"She was gentle," Jade said, a ghost of a smile touching her lips. "But yes. She definitely had… thoughts."

He looked at her carefully, eyes steady. "And?"

Jade shrugged, then looked down into her tea. "She made sense. Maybe more than I wanted her to."

Silence stretched between them—soft, not uncomfortable. Outside, a bird chirped, the sound cutting through the quiet.

Duncan set his coffee down and stepped forward slowly, his voice low and deliberate.

"I meant what I said last night. I don't need you to have answers right now. I just…" He hesitated, then added, "I'm not going anywhere this time."

Jade looked up at him, and for a moment, the air shifted—full of unsaid things.

"I don't know what I'm ready for," she said quietly.

He nodded, a thread of hope in his smile. "I know, just know I'm here."

She studied him for a long second, then finally reached out and took his hand.

"Thank you," she said softly.

He folded his fingers around hers, gently, as if afraid she'd vanish.

The kettle clicked off behind them, unnoticed.

And for the first time in years, they sat there, across from each other—not quite a couple, not quite the past—but maybe something beginning.

Something real.

"Come on," Duncan said, tugging Jade's hand out onto the back terrace into the sun-dappled garden. "You need some fresh air. And I need to show you what's become of Dad's tragic attempt at a putting green."

Jade narrowed her eyes, sceptical. "Last time you said that I ended up in a bush and had grass stains on my jeans for a week."

Duncan gave her a wounded look. "That was one time. And in my defence, you took the shot like a madwoman."

"You dared me," she shot back.

He grinned. "And you never could back down from a dare."

They rounded the corner of the garden where an old, slightly uneven patch of grass had been "professionally manicured" by Gary—or so he claimed. A lone flag marked the middle, fluttering lazily in the breeze. A sad excuse for a golf course but endearing all the same.

Jade burst out laughing. "It's even worse than I remember."

"Rude," Duncan said, pretending to be offended. "This is a championship-level disaster. We take it very seriously."

"Do you now?"

He handed her a small, worn putter with a flourish. "Ladies first."

Jade narrowed her eyes. "Do I get to warm up, or is this full gladiator mode?"

"You're stalling."

"You're provoking."

"Oh, we're doing this, are we?"

Jade grinned and stepped up to the ball, squinting with exaggerated focus. With one clean swing, she sent it rolling—

Right past the flag, over a molehill, and straight into a small dip.

Duncan clapped once. "And the crowd goes wild."

"Shut up," she said, laughing.

"My turn."

He lined up his shot like a pro, taking far too long, tongue peeking out in mock concentration.

"Are you seriously wagging your tongue? What are you, five?"

He stuck it out further and made his shot.

Straight into the flag.

"Oh, come on," Jade groaned. "You've been practicing."

"Years of training," he said proudly. "Hours of playing against Dad for who has to do the washing up."

She mock-bowed. "I concede to your genius."

"Finally."

Then, catching the glint in her eye, he added, "Wait—don't do it—"

Too late.

Jade took a running step and tackled him playfully, sending them both tumbling into the soft grass in a tangle of limbs and laughter.

Duncan landed hard on his back and winced, a sharp breath hissing through his teeth as pain flared in his ribs. Still, he managed a breathless laugh, eyes squeezing shut for a second before he looked over at her.

Jade was sprawled beside him, grinning like a kid, hair in her face.

"I can't believe you just did that," he said, half-laughing, half-groaning. "Pretty sure something shifted in my chest."

"I warned you," she said breathlessly. "Never provoke a Bell with a bruised ego."

They lay there for a moment, looking up at the blue stretch of sky, the laughter fading into a comfortable silence.

Jade turned her head toward him, her voice quieter now, threaded with something fragile and honest.

"It's easy... being around you."

Duncan propped himself up on one elbow, his gaze searching hers. There was a softness there—something reverent, something old and aching.

"Yeah," he said quietly. "It always was."

She reached up, her fingers brushing along his jaw before settling against his cheek. The warmth of his skin, the slight rasp of stubble beneath her palm—it all felt achingly familiar.

Duncan didn't move at first. He just looked at her, as if memorising every line of her face, every breath between them. Then, slowly, he leaned in.

She lifted her head as he lowered his, and their lips met—quiet, sure. A kiss that didn't rush, didn't reach—it simply landed where it always belonged.

It wasn't rushed. It wasn't fiery. It was steady. Sure. Like coming home after a long time away.

When they finally pulled back, their foreheads rested together, and neither one spoke.

They didn't need to.

And for a while, they stayed just like that—on the grass, beneath the sun, surrounded by half-forgotten hedges and the scent of damp earth—and somehow, it was perfect.

Chapter Seventeen

Later that day, Jade stood in the guest room, folding the soft cardigan Helen had lent her and placing it neatly on the bed. Her small suitcase sat zipped by the door. She took one last look around—the familiar room, the view of the hills beyond the window—and drew a quiet breath.

In the kitchen, Helen turned at the sound of footsteps, eyes widening slightly. "Oh, love… do you have to go now? You should stay another night."

Jade smiled apologetically as she adjusted the strap on her bag. "I wish I could. But I've got a few things to sort out before I'm back at work on Wednesday."

Helen's shoulders dropped slightly, her disappointment visible even behind her practiced grace. "Well, I suppose I can't argue with duty."

Gary stepped into the hallway, catching the tail end of the exchange. "You're always welcome here, Jade. Always."

"Thank you," she said, genuinely touched. She hugged them both—Helen's embrace lingering a second longer, Gary giving her a warm pat on the back.

"We mean it," Helen whispered as they pulled apart. "You don't need a reason to come back."

Jade nodded, swallowing past the sudden lump in her throat. "I know. And thank you. For everything."

Helen and Gary stood at the front step and watched as Jade walked to her car, Duncan following a pace behind.

The sun was lower in the sky now, casting a soft glow over the gravel drive. Jade opened the car door but didn't get in just yet. Duncan stood beside her, hands in his pockets, his expression quiet.

"So," he said, glancing down at the ground before meeting her eyes. "Back to the city."

She nodded. "Back to normal."

Duncan's brow furrowed slightly, as if the word sat wrong with him. "Does it feel… normal?"

Jade looked past him for a moment, toward the house, then back at him. "Not really. But I think that's okay."

He stepped a little closer. "You sure you want to go?"

"I have to," she said gently. "But that doesn't mean I want to."

Something flickered in his eyes—disappointment, maybe, or just the ache of letting her go again, even if only for now.

Jade reached out and touched his hand. "This weekend… it meant a lot."

Duncan turned his palm to meet hers, holding on just long enough to feel the warmth of her skin. "To me too."

Neither moved. The weight of what hadn't been said hovered between them, but neither tried to force it. It wasn't time.

Jade finally let go and opened the door. "I'll text when I get home."

Duncan nodded, stepping back. "Drive safe."

She slid into the car, started the engine, and rolled down the window. "Tell Helen I'll be back."

"I will," he said. "She'll hold you to it."

Jade gave a small smile. "Good."

Then she pulled away, the tyres crunching softly over the gravel as she disappeared down the drive.

The sound of her car faded into the distance, leaving only the hush of wind and the steady thud of his heart.

He stayed there long after she was gone—trying not to hope and failing.

The familiar hum of city traffic greeted Jade as she pulled into the parking space outside her flat. The late afternoon sun glinted off windshields and high-rise windows, and everything looked… the same.

Which only made how she felt even more disorienting.

She sat behind the wheel for a moment longer than necessary, fingers resting on the keys, the hum of the engine still vibrating under her skin. A deep breath. In, out.

Then she turned it off.

Inside her flat, the silence was immediate. It didn't hum like the Armstrong house. No scent of baking apples or wood smoke. Just the faint hint of jasmine from her diffuser and the unopened stack of mail on the console table.

She dropped her suitcase by the door and kicked off her shoes. The moment her feet touched the floorboards, a strange mix of comfort and sadness settled over her. She was home—but part of her still felt like she was somewhere else.

Or maybe someone else.

She'd barely curled up on the couch, blanket tucked over her lap, when a knock rattled the door.

Only one person knocked like that—three quick raps and a pause.

Jade opened it to find Leanne standing there in oversized sunglasses, a bottle of wine in one hand and a paper bag in the other.

"I bring offerings," she declared, sweeping inside without waiting for an invitation.

Jade blinked. "Did you apparate?"

"You texted me 'I'm home.' That's code for: 'I need wine and chocolate and to not think about men unless they're fictional and emotionally available.'"

She set the bag down on the counter and began unpacking it. "I've got salted caramel truffles, chocolate-covered almonds, and that ridiculous Pinot you love because it 'tastes like a forest in autumn.' Also…" She pulled out a DVD with a flourish. "About Time. Rachel McAdams. Time travel. Redheads. Sad British men. All the ingredients for a proper emotional cleanse."

Jade laughed in spite of herself. "God, I love you."

"I know," Leanne said smugly. "And I accept payment in gossip and gratitude. Sit."

Jade obeyed, curling back into the corner of the couch while Leanne poured two glasses of wine and slid one into her hand. The chocolate was already open between them.

"So," Leanne said, settling in and giving her a pointed look. "How's your emotional stability on a scale of one to 'I might text him at 2 a.m.'?"

Jade took a sip of wine, sighed. "Solid seven. Maybe a six and a half when I'm tired."

"Respectable." Leanne popped a truffle into her mouth. "Okay, now tell me —was it a soul-revealing weekend full of intense eye contact and unresolved longing?"

Jade smiled into her glass. "More than I was prepared for."

Leanne's brows shot up. "Details. Give me the good stuff."

And so, she told her—about Duncan's parents' home. She told her about Helen's quiet wisdom, the awkward moments that turned unexpectedly sweet, and the kisses.

That part—she kept soft. Like saying too much might make it feel less real.

Leanne listened in rare silence, her usual sass dialled down. When Jade finally stopped talking, there was a long pause.

"You really like him," Leanne said quietly.

Jade nodded. "I always did. I just… didn't realise how much until everything else fell apart."

Leanne topped up both their glasses and leaned back with a thoughtful hum. "Well, thank God it did. Dean was a spreadsheet with nice hair. Duncan sounds like the prologue, the epilogue—and the whole damn book in between."

Jade laughed, the sound lighter, freer. "That's very dramatic."

"So is life," Leanne said with a smirk, lifting her glass. "To new beginnings. Or second chances. Or whatever the hell this is."

Jade swirled the wine in her glass, then looked at her friend. "I just don't want him to be the rebound guy. I do like him. It's not just… timing."

Leanne tilted her head. "Sounds to me like Dean was the rebound. You liked Duncan before you even thought about Dean—didn't you?"

Jade hesitated, then nodded. "Yes."

"Then there you go." Leanne clinked her glass against Jade's with a soft smile. "I think you've finally found the right one."

Jade met her smile and returned the toast. "To not rushing. And to seeing where it goes."

Leanne grinned. "And to wine. Always to wine."

They both sipped, the warmth of friendship settling around them like a blanket—no pressure, no answers needed. Just two women, a bottle of red, and the fragile beginning of something new.

As the opening credits of About Time rolled across the screen and the city hummed on outside, Jade sank deeper into the couch, letting the warmth of friendship, possibility, and Pinot settle in around her.

For the first time in a long while, the future didn't feel like something to brace for.

It felt like something she might actually want.

Chapter Eighteen

Tuesday morning was bright—strangely, defiantly bright.

The kind of rare Manchester sunlight that made the windows gleam like they'd been freshly polished, the kind that tricked you into thinking the world was simpler than it really was. The kind that made promises it had no intention of keeping.

Jade woke late, cocooned in tangled sheets still faintly warm with the echo of laughter. Her cheeks ached from smiling, her limbs heavy in the most satisfying way. Leanne hadn't left until nearly one in the morning, armed with wine, chocolate, and a playlist of rom-coms they'd sworn off in theory but always returned to when life demanded soft endings.

She stretched, yawned, rubbed the sleep from her face, then padded barefoot into the kitchen, mentally cataloguing everything she needed to do before returning to work. Laundry. Groceries. A proper meal that didn't involve chopsticks or cardboard containers.

By midday, the washing machine was humming steadily, its gentle rhythm blending with the soft crackle of a podcast playing from her phone. The flat smelled faintly of lavender and citrus fabric softener. Sunlight slanted through the windows, catching on the dust motes in the air. She'd marched through the supermarket like a woman with purpose and returned with enough to feed a family, though it was just her. It always had been, in the end.

It was nearing three when she finally collapsed on the floor by the coffee table, folding clean towels into neat squares and humming under her breath. The world was calm, quiet. Settled.

Until the knock came.

A pause. Then another—soft, uncertain.

Jade froze; her hands still tangled in a half-folded jumper. Her frown deepened. No one dropped by unannounced. Not unless it was Leanne—and Leanne never knocked like that. She arrived with a bang and a bottle, not this hesitant... tapping.

She rose slowly, walked to the door.

And opened it.

Dean.

He looked like he hadn't slept—dark circles under his eyes, his hair messy in a way that was too careless to be styled. He wore a hoodie and jeans, not his usual polished work look. The sight of him hit her like a slap of cold air.

"Hi," he said, too softly. "Can I come in?"

She didn't move. "Why are you here?"

"I just…" He exhaled hard, like he'd rehearsed this, and it wasn't going the way he'd planned. "I wanted to talk. Please."

Against her better judgment, she stepped aside. He walked in, slowly, like the flat held memories he wasn't ready to face.

Jade closed the door behind him; arms folded tightly across her chest. "Well?"

Dean turned to face her, his eyes shiny with some self-pitying emotion that made her stomach twist. "I forgive you."

She blinked. "You… what?"

"You were with Duncan," he said, voice low and heavy. "Leanne saw me, and I figured it was only a matter of time before you told her. I get it. You were hurt. I pushed you away, and now you've… you've run back to him again."

Jade stared at him, stunned. "Dean—"

"I forgive you," he repeated, stepping closer. "I know it was emotional. You were vulnerable. But this doesn't have to be the end of us."

Her jaw dropped. "You forgive me?"

He nodded solemnly, like he was granting her some great mercy.

"*You* cheated on *me*," she said, her voice rising. "You lied to me for months. Slept with your secretary, gaslit me, and when I started to see through it—you made me feel like the problem."

Dean's mouth opened, but no words came out.

"I didn't do anything wrong with Duncan. Not while we were together. I didn't even know the truth about him because you lied about that too."

His expression shifted, defensiveness creeping in. "It wasn't like that."

"No?" Jade snapped. "Because from where I'm standing, it's exactly like that."

He took a step back, eyes narrowing. "You never stopped loving him. That's what this is about, isn't it?"

Jade's voice dropped, cold and deliberate. "Maybe I didn't. But I chose you, Dean. Again, and again. And you threw that away. You don't get to come back now and pretend you're the one doing me a favour."

A long silence stretched between them, the kind that made the air feel heavy.

Dean's jaw tensed. He looked around like he didn't recognise the place anymore. Like it had changed without him.

"We can work this out," he said tightly. "We were good together—before everything. You just need time. You're confused."

Jade took a step back, alarm prickling the edge of her nerves. "I'm not confused. I'm done."

His expression darkened. "You don't mean that."

"Dean," she warned, her voice sharp now, "you need to leave."

He moved toward her. "Don't do this. You owe me more than a door slammed in my face."

"I don't owe you anything," she snapped, backing up until her hip bumped the edge of the kitchen bench. "You cheated. You lied. And now you want to play the victim?"

"I made a mistake!" he shouted, the mask slipping. "But this thing with Duncan? It's nothing. You're not thinking straight."

He reached for her arm—not roughly at first, just firm, like if he could hold her still, she'd understand.

"Let go of me."

"You just need to listen—" His fingers tightened.

"I said let go!"

She tried to pull back, but he didn't release her. His grip turned rough, panic flaring in his eyes.

Then—

"Get your hands off her."

The voice cut through the tension like a blade. Deep. Controlled. Furious.

Dean froze.

Duncan was standing in the doorway—his chest rising and falling, jaw clenched so hard the muscle ticked. His eyes, locked on Dean's hand wrapped around Jade's arm, were cold enough to drop the room's temperature by ten degrees.

Dean let go like he'd been burned. "This isn't your business."

"It became my business the second you laid a finger on her," Duncan said, striding across the room in two quick steps.

He grabbed Dean by the front of his hoodie and shoved him back, hard, pinning him against the doorframe. "If you ever touch her again—ever—you'll deal with me."

"Alright! Alright!" Dean barked, trying to wriggle free. "I'm going!"

Duncan released him with a final shove. Dean stumbled, glared at them both, and without another word, wrenched the door open and stormed out.

The door slammed shut behind Dean with a crack like thunder.

Jade stood frozen, her chest heaving, back still pressed against the kitchen bench. Duncan turned to her immediately, eyes dark with concern, his hands raised in quiet reassurance.

"Hey—are you alright? Did he hurt you?"

She shook her head quickly, blinking hard. "No. I'm okay. Just… shaken."

He stepped closer, slow, and deliberate. "I'm sorry you had to deal with him alone."

"You didn't know he'd come," she said, her voice tight, still trying to steady itself. "I didn't either."

Duncan reached out, his fingers brushing her elbow. "You sure you're okay?"

She nodded, then exhaled a shaky breath. "Now I am."

Relief passed over his face as he pulled her gently into his arms. She collapsed against him, needing the strength in his hold more than she wanted to admit. His hand ran up and down her back, grounding her, anchoring them both.

After a long moment, she pulled back just far enough to meet his eyes. "Why are you here?"

He hesitated, then released her slowly. "I was on my way back to London. But I couldn't leave without seeing you. I hope that's okay."

A flicker of something raw moved across her face—surprise, gratitude, longing. "I'm glad you did."

She didn't think. She didn't pause to weigh the consequences or silence the ache inside her.

She reached up, cupped his face in her hands, and pulled him into a kiss—fierce and unrelenting. A kiss that demanded nothing and gave everything. Her hands gripped his face, like she needed him closer, like she never wanted to let go.

Duncan responded instantly, his mouth moving against hers with the same urgent intensity. One hand threaded through her hair, the other wrapped around her waist, drawing her flush against him. He kissed her like he'd been waiting years—because he had.

This kiss was nothing like the ones they'd shared over the weekend—those had been soft, tentative, exploratory.

This one was different.

It was fierce, hungry—charged with all the longing and desire they'd kept locked away for too long.

She gasped as his lips trailed from her mouth to her jaw, then lower, down the line of her throat. Her body arched instinctively, drawn to him, craving more.

"Jade," he murmured, his voice rough against her skin. "I don't want to stop. But if you tell me to, I will."

She didn't. She couldn't.

Instead, a soft moan escaped her lips as her fingers slid beneath his shirt, eager to touch the heat of his skin. He tensed under her hands, muscles tightening in response, then groaned low in his throat as he pulled his shirt off in one swift motion.

Jade's dress followed soon after, slipping to the floor without a word as they moved together, step by step, toward the couch. Their hearts pounded, breath mingling in the charged silence.

Only her lace panties remained—a final barrier that suddenly felt far too much between them.

His mouth found hers again—hot, hungry, possessive. Every kiss, every brush of skin against skin sent sparks racing through her.

He lifted her effortlessly, carried her down the hall, their lips never parting. When they reached her bedroom, he lowered her to the floor, hands lingering on her waist. His gaze raked over her, dark with reverence and need.

"You're so damn beautiful," he whispered, almost like a prayer, before he kissed her again—deeper this time, slower.

They undressed each other completely—no hesitation, no shame. Just quiet wonder. Every layer peeled away felt less like clothing and more like the unburdening of years. Of what-ifs and maybes. Every inch of newly exposed skin was met with reverent fingers, with kisses that lingered like promises long overdue.

Jade's breath hitched when Duncan gently lowered her to the bed, his body pressing her back into the soft warmth of the sheets. She shivered beneath him—not from cold, but from the gravity of it all. The closeness. The vulnerability. The way this moment seemed to fold time around them, pulling the past and the present into something whole.

The history between them no longer divided—but finally, beautifully—binding.

His hands explored her slowly, he was learning her for the first time, committing every curve and tremble to memory. His mouth followed, trailing kisses across her collarbone, down the slope of her breast, the dip of her stomach—each touch a wordless promise.

Jade's fingers threaded through his hair, her breath growing shallower, skin flushed beneath his mouth. He took his time, teasing, tasting, until her body arched beneath him, needy and open, a soft moan escaping her lips.

By the time he settled between her thighs, she was trembling—not from nerves, but from want. From the overwhelming feeling of being seen. Chosen.

When he finally entered her, she tensed—just for a heartbeat, her breath catching in her throat.

He noticed. Of course he did.

His movements stilled instantly, his hand cupping her cheek, thumb brushing gently across her skin. The other slid between her fingers, lacing them together with quiet strength.

"Look at me," he whispered, his voice low, tender.

She did.

And in that single gaze, something loosened inside her. The fear. The hurt. The walls.

Everything softened.

This wasn't about lust. It wasn't about escape. It was about them. About all they'd lost—and everything they were finally, finally reclaiming.

He moved slowly, reverently, like he was savouring her. Worshipping her. His eyes never left hers. She held on to him, legs wrapping around his waist, fingers digging into his back as he whispered her name between kisses—over and over, like a prayer. Like a homecoming.

He guided her through each wave of pleasure with aching tenderness.

Each thrust, a confession.

Each kiss, a vow.

And when she shattered beneath him, her cry swallowed by his mouth, Duncan followed—his release rough, unguarded, and absolute. He held her through it, arms wrapped tightly around her like she was the only thing keeping him tethered to this world.

Afterward, he didn't move away.

There was no rush. No retreat.

Only the quiet sound of their breathing, the warmth of shared skin, and the way his lips pressed soft, lingering kisses to her shoulder… her temple… the tips of her fingers.

As if to say, *I'm here. I'm not going anywhere.*

Chapter Nineteen

The room was quiet, save for the steady rhythm of their breathing. The afternoon sun filtered through the blinds, casting lazy golden stripes across the bed and the tangle of limbs beneath the sheets.

Jade lay on her side, facing Duncan, one hand tucked beneath her cheek, the other still loosely tangled with his fingers. Her skin was flushed, hair tousled, lips swollen from kisses neither of them wanted to end.

Duncan studied her in the hush, his gaze soft, thumb brushing small, idle strokes over the back of her hand.

"I wasn't sure if I should come," he murmured.

She blinked slowly, still coming down from the high of everything they'd just shared. "I'm glad you did."

A long pause stretched between them.

He shifted onto his side, propping himself up on one elbow. "Are you okay? Really okay?"

Jade turned her face to him. "Yes. Just… a little overwhelmed. Not in a bad way. Just…" She let out a quiet breath. "It's a lot."

He nodded, as if he understood completely. "I didn't come here expecting this. I didn't want to push you."

"You didn't," she said quickly. "It was me. I wanted it too. I just—" Her voice faltered. "I'm still trying to untangle everything in my head. What happened with Dean. What I want now."

"You don't owe me clarity," Duncan said gently. "Not today. Not even tomorrow."

Her brow furrowed slightly. "But you deserve honesty. You always have."

Duncan reached out and brushed a strand of hair from her cheek. "Then just be honest with yourself first. That's all I ask."

She held his gaze, her throat tightening. "I don't know what this is. I don't know where we go from here."

"We don't have to name it," he said, voice low. "We just… keep showing up. Keep choosing each other, one moment at a time."

Jade's heart clenched. It wasn't a promise wrapped in fantasy—it was real. Steady. Honest.

She reached up and touched his jaw, her thumb brushing the curve of his cheekbone. "You never stopped being the safest place I've ever known."

Duncan leaned in and kissed her—slow and deep, a kiss that spoke without words. When they parted, he rested his forehead against hers.

"I'm not perfect," he said quietly. "But I'll never lie to you. Not ever."

"I believe you," Jade whispered.

They stayed there like that for a while, wrapped in sheets and silence, the kind that felt full instead of empty. No grand declarations. No promises they weren't ready to make.

Just breath. And closeness. And the beginning of something new—built not on fairy tale illusions, but on truth, scars, and the fragile beauty of a second chance.

Duncan stayed the night.

They cooked dinner together—nothing fancy, just pasta and too much garlic—but it was easy and light, filled with soft laughter and the quiet rhythm of two people rediscovering something they hadn't realised they'd lost.

Afterward, they curled up on the couch, a movie playing in the background neither of them truly watched. His arm was slung around her shoulders, her head resting on his chest, and for the first time in a long time, the silence between them felt peaceful.

Later, in the soft hush of the night, they made love again—slower this time, unhurried. Less about urgency, more about connection. Their bodies spoke in whispers and touch, in soft gasps and shared breath, wrapped in the comfort of being known.

In the morning, sunlight crept in through the curtains. Jade stirred to the smell of fresh coffee and the sound of Duncan humming softly to himself in the kitchen.

He handed her a mug as she wandered in, still in her sleep shirt, eyes heavy with sleep but warm with something deeper.

"Morning," he said, his smile lopsided and tender.

"Morning," she murmured, taking the mug. "Thanks."

By eight, they were both dressed and ready to head out—Jade to work, Duncan back to London. He had a seven-day rotation starting that afternoon, and the hospital would demand everything of him.

Outside by her car, she paused, keys in hand. The air was cool and crisp, the kind that whispered the first hints of autumn.

Duncan stepped close and tucked a strand of hair behind her ear.

"I'll miss you," she said softly, eyes searching his.

He leaned down and kissed her—slow and sure. "I'll call when I can."

She nodded, her throat tight. "Be safe."

"You too."

He gave her one last look, then turned toward his loan car. She watched him go, heart full and aching all at once.

As she slid into the driver's seat and started her engine, Jade realised something quietly earth-shifting: she didn't know where this was going.

But for the first time, she wasn't afraid to find out.

The clinic was busy.

Wednesday mornings usually were, but today it felt like everything came at once— back-to-back patients, a late delivery of flu vaccines, and a printer that decided to stage a dramatic breakdown during the lunch hour.

Still, Jade moved through it all with surprising ease. Her body was tired, but her mind— her heart—felt steadier than it had in weeks. It was as if some internal knot had finally started to loosen.

She was halfway through reviewing a patient's chart when her phone buzzed in her pocket. A message from Leanne.

You alive? Or still dreaming about Dr. Tall and Tortured?

Jade huffed out a laugh and texted back:

Survived. Call you tonight? Too much to text.

By the time she got home that evening, she was already dialling.

Leanne answered on the first ring. "Alright, spill. Was there a man in your bed last night?"

Jade kicked off her shoes and flopped onto the couch, a smile tugging at her lips. "Yes."

A gasp. "And you made him leave this morning? Jade Bell, are you feeling well?"

"He had to go back to London. Rotation started this afternoon."

Leanne groaned dramatically. "Ugh. The NHS ruins everything."

Jade laughed softly, then let the smile slip. "It wasn't all rom-com perfect."

A pause. "What happened?"

Jade's voice sobered. "Dean showed up. Yesterday. Just after I'd done laundry, of all things. Like life doesn't give you a moment to breathe."

Leanne swore under her breath. "What the hell did he want?"

"To beg me to take him back." Jade's voice tightened. "He said he forgave me… for being with Duncan. Like I was the one who cheated. Like he was the one doing me a favour."

"You're joking."

"I wish I was. And when I said no, he got angry. Grabbed me. Tried to kiss me. I couldn't even get him out of the flat."

"What?!" Leanne's voice shot up. "You're alright though?"

"I'm fine. Duncan showed up just in time. Pulled him off me and threw him out."

There was a pause on the other end, followed by a sharp breath. "That bastard. I knew he had a dark streak, but that? You should've called the police."

"I almost did. But I just… wanted it over. Wanted him gone."

"Are you sure you're okay?"

"I am now," Jade said softly. "Duncan held me. Asked if I was alright before anything else. He didn't push. Then I kissed him and… you know…"

Leanne's voice gentled. "And then you let yourself feel what you've been holding back since uni?"

Jade nodded, more to herself than the phone. "Yeah. I don't know what it means yet, or where it's going. But I do know that last night felt… real. And safe."

"God, you sound different. Lighter."

"I feel lighter."

"Well," Leanne said, "for what it's worth? I'm glad you didn't waste another second on that lying, manipulative spreadsheet. Duncan sounds like the real deal."

Jade smiled into the phone. "He is."

There was a beat, then Leanne added, "I'm proud of you, you know. Not just for choosing better—but for finally choosing you."

Jade swallowed past the lump in her throat. "Thanks, Leanne. For always having my back."

"Always. Now, tell me—was it 'slow burn kiss in the rain' hot, or full-on 'BBC miniseries with a side of unresolved sexual tension' hot?"

Jade grinned. "Honestly? Both."

Leanne let out a whoop. "I knew it!"

And for the first time in a long while, Jade let herself laugh without hesitation.

It was nearly eight by the time Jade rinsed off her dinner plate and set it on the drying rack. The apartment was too quiet, the silence sharpening the ache she hadn't expected to feel so soon. The day had been long: back-to-back patients, paperwork she didn't remember starting, and that hollow feeling that had followed her since Duncan left.

She hadn't expected to miss him so soon.

But she did.

Deeply. Silently. More than she was ready to admit.

Her phone lit up on the counter, buzzing softly against the wood.

Duncan Armstrong

Her heart did a little flip.

She answered quickly. "Hey."

"Hey you." His voice was low, familiar, warm—like a balm to everything she didn't realise she'd been carrying. "You home?"

"Got in couple hours ago. Long day."

"Tell me about it. Only been back for four hours and it already feels like I never left."

Jade smiled, sinking onto the couch. "Busy?"

"Ridiculous. One emergency gallbladder, two urgent consults, and a junior doctor nearly fainted during a laparoscopic appendectomy."

She laughed. "Sounds like a glamorous return."

"Oh yeah. Totally living the dream." He paused, then his voice softened. "I've been thinking about you all day."

Jade tucked her knees under herself. "I've been thinking about you too."

There was a stretch of silence. Comfortable, but charged with the weight of what they'd shared.

"I didn't like leaving you this morning," he said. "Didn't like knowing Dean had been there. That I hadn't been there sooner."

"You got here in time," she said quietly. "And I'm okay. I really am."

"I know." A pause. "Still. It nearly broke me, seeing you like that. I don't ever want to see fear in your eyes again."

Jade closed her eyes, letting his words wrap around her like a blanket. "You didn't see fear. You saw someone who finally said no. And meant it."

He exhaled softly. "Yeah. You were incredible."

She smiled. "I still can't believe you turned up when you did."

"Honestly? I had to get back to London, I didn't know what I was going to say—I just knew I had to see you again."

"I'm glad you did."

There was a beat, and then he said, "Last night… I know we didn't talk much after, but it wasn't just about the moment. Or the heat."

"I know," she whispered. "It was more than that."

"It was you."

She swallowed, her throat tight. "And you."

Another pause. Then he added, quietly, "I don't know where this will go, Jade. But I want to find out. With you."

Her heart fluttered. "Me too."

He laughed softly, the sound like sunlight. "Good. That's really good."

There was a rustle on the line, like he'd shifted in his seat. "I'm just on my break, then I have to be in early tomorrow, but I'll call you when I can. Might be late."

"I'll keep my phone close."

"I'll miss you."

Jade smiled, eyes stinging just a little. "Miss you already."

"Sleep well, beautiful."

"You too, Doctor McDreamy."

He groaned. "I knew Leanne was still calling me that."

"Of course she is. It's her love language."

"Remind me to buy her silence."

"Too late."

He chuckled, and the sound stayed with her long after the call ended.

Chapter Twenty

It was nearly midnight when Duncan finally stepped out of theatre, shoulders tight and scrubs damp at the collar. Another emergency, another twelve-hour shift that blurred the edges of everything else.

But the moment his hands were washed and the surgical notes logged, his mind went straight to her.

Jade.

He hadn't seen her in three days, and somehow that felt longer than the years they'd spent apart. Maybe because now, he knew. Knew how her lips tasted. Knew how she looked in the morning light, barefaced and smiling into her coffee. Knew how it felt to hold her after almost losing her to someone who didn't deserve her.

His phone was already in his hand as he made his way to the on-call room. The hospital was quieter now, shadows lengthening across sterile corridors. A few nurses nodded tired hellos. Duncan nodded back, absently, his fingers already dialling her number.

She picked up on the second ring.

"Hey," her voice was soft, a little hoarse.

He smiled, instantly gentled by the sound. "Hey you. Did I wake you?"

"No," she said, but there was a yawn halfway through the word. "Just got into bed. Long day."

"Same," he said, sinking into the worn leather chair in the corner of the room. "Trauma case, full laparotomy. Almost forgot what daylight looked like."

"Sounds… brutal."

"It was," he admitted. "But I'm not thinking about that right now."

There was a pause on the line. A pause full of everything unspoken.

"I've been thinking about you," he added quietly. "Every damn minute I get."

She was quiet, and for a second, he thought the signal had dropped. But then he heard her exhale, long and shaky.

"I miss you," she whispered.

The words hit him low in the gut, simple and devastating.

"God, I miss you too."

"I didn't expect to, this much. It's only been three days."

"Feels like longer," he said. "Everything here's exactly the same, but without you… it all feels off."

"I made tea earlier," she said softly. "And reached for a second mug."

His heart pulled tight in his chest. "What kind?"

"Chamomile. The one you said smelled like wet flowers."

He huffed a tired laugh. "That's because it does."

"Still made it," she murmured.

He leaned his head back against the wall, eyes closed, picturing her curled in bed, hair messy, voice laced with exhaustion. Beautiful, even like that. Especially like that.

"I wish I could crawl through this phone," he said, half a groan. "Lie next to you. Just… be there."

"Me too," she whispered. "You made it feel safe again."

"You are safe," he said fiercely. "Always."

Another pause. Then, softer: "How many days left on your rotation?"

"Four. Then I've got three off."

"Come home?" she asked, the question fragile but full of hope.

His heart clenched. "If you'll have me."

"Always," she whispered.

He swallowed past the ache in his throat. "Sleep, Jade. I just needed to hear your voice. Make sure you were alright."

"I am now."

He smiled, the weight of the day easing just enough. "Sweet dreams, beautiful."

"You too, Doctor McDreamy."

He groaned. "You've been talking to Leanne again."

"Of course."

He could hear the smile in her voice now, and it wrapped around him like warmth. When the call ended, he sat in the quiet for a long time, phone still in his hand, heart full and hurting in the best way.

Four more days. He could make it through anything… if she was waiting at the end.

It was just past nine when Duncan finally dragged himself out of Recovery, his steps slow, muscles sore, and mind heavier than it had been in days.

The ache in his back was dull and persistent, but it paled in comparison to the growing hollowness in his chest—the kind that had crept in over the last seven days and refused to budge.

Seven long, restless days without Jade.

Seven days of sleep-deprived shifts that blurred into each other, of cold takeaway eaten standing up, of pretending not to hear her voice in every moment of silence. He hadn't told her—not properly—but this rotation had drained him. Not just physically, though the fatigue in his bones was proof enough. It was emotional. Mental. Soul-deep.

Because for the first time in years, he wanted to go home to someone. And she wasn't there.

His hand went instinctively to the back of his neck, rubbing the tight muscles there as he turned down the dim corridor toward the staff room. He told himself he just needed five minutes. Five minutes to sit down, to drink terrible coffee, to let his guard drop long enough to remember that he was human beneath the scrubs.

The hallway was mostly empty. Just the low hum of vending machines, the soft flicker of fluorescent lights, the occasional distant beep of a monitor.

He reached for the door.

Pushed it open.

And stopped.

She was there.

Jade.

She stood near the lockers, one hip leaned slightly back, arms loosely folded—but nothing about her posture was relaxed. Not really. There was tension in her shoulders, a subtle tightness in her jaw. She looked like she was holding herself still on purpose.

And she looked breathtaking.

Her dress was a deep, jewel-toned green that made her eyes glow under the harsh fluorescent lights. Her hair was styled into soft waves that curled just past her collarbone. Her makeup—subtle, refined—only enhanced what Duncan already knew by heart. She was stunning. Effortlessly so. Like someone who didn't need to try—but had, for him.

His heart gave a hard, unexpected thump.

But she wasn't alone.

Miles Carter—cardiology registrar and hospital-wide expert in flirting badly with anyone wearing scrubs—was standing far too close. Too relaxed. Smiling that smug, insufferable smile that always made Duncan want to punch something.

Jade wasn't smiling back. Her body was stiff, her posture poised but chilly. Her eyes didn't light up with amusement. Her lips were pressed into a faint, polite curve that said: I'm tolerating this, but only barely.

"Didn't realise the nurses had started recruiting models," Miles was saying, his head tilting with that lazy charm he thought worked on everyone. "You here looking for a lost patient, or just admiring the uniforms?"

Duncan's voice came out like a blade. Cold. Controlled.

"She's here for me."

Miles startled slightly, turning around too quickly to play it cool. "Duncan—hey. Didn't see you there."

Duncan didn't respond to him. His eyes were fixed on Jade.

"Jade."

At the sound of her name, her whole face changed. Like someone had flipped a switch and let the sun back in. The tension drained from her shoulders, her guarded stance softening as her eyes met his.

"Hi," she said, and it wasn't just a greeting. It was relief.

He crossed the room in two steps, close enough now to see the faint smudge of lipstick on her lower lip, the warmth in her gaze that undid something tight in his chest. His hand brushed her arm—a featherlight touch—but it felt like everything.

"Everything okay?" he asked, voice low, protective.

She nodded quickly. "Fine. He was just leaving."

There was a subtle shift in her voice—firm and dismissive. Miles picked up on it.

He chuckled awkwardly, holding up both hands like he wasn't completely rattled. "Didn't mean to step on anyone's toes."

Duncan gave him one look. A single, sharp glance.

Miles paled a shade, muttered something about needing to check a file, and edged out of the room like the air had turned toxic.

The door clicked shut behind him.

Jade exhaled, the breath coming out in a rush. "Well. That was gross."

Duncan didn't smile. Not yet. His heart was still thudding a little too hard.

"What are you doing here?" he asked, voice rougher than he intended.

She straightened slightly, brushing her hair back with one graceful sweep. "I wanted to see you," she said. "You've been working nonstop. I thought maybe… I'd bring you dinner. And maybe remind you to breathe."

His breath caught. Just for a second.

He reached for her hand, curling his fingers through hers like it was second nature. Her skin was soft, warm. Real.

"You're more than a reason," he said. "You're the only thing I've been thinking about since I left."

Her smile softened. No polish now—just real, radiant warmth. "Then I'm glad I came."

"You have no idea," he said.

His thumb brushed her cheek, skimming across the flawless makeup she'd worn for him. She'd done this for him. He didn't take that lightly.

"You look incredible."

"I wanted to look good for you."

His heart thudded hard enough that he was sure she could hear it. "You always do."

He pulled her into him, arms settling around her waist with a kind of ease that felt ancient. Familiar. His forehead rested against hers, their breath mingling in the hush of the staff room.

"I've missed you," he murmured. "So much."

"Same," she whispered.

He kissed her.

Slow. Deep. The kind of kiss that rewired his nervous system. His hand slid into her hair, anchoring her there, just long enough to taste the seven days of silence. Seven days of wondering what came next. Seven days of missing something he finally had the courage to want.

Her fingers slipped into his hair, tugged gently at the back of his neck, and he tightened his grip around her like she might vanish if he didn't.

And for the first time in a week, the noise in his head went quiet.

When they finally broke apart, breathless and flushed, he smiled against her lips. "This is the only kind of overtime I want."

She grinned up at him. "Good. Because I brought food, too."

"Food and you?" he said. "That's unfair. Now I'll never leave."

"You weren't supposed to," she said quietly. "Not really."

His eyes found hers again, locking in place. "I know that now."

She reached into her bag and pulled out a brown paper bag and a wrapped container. "You just need to warm it. Pasta, garlic bread, and something dangerously close to a chocolate tart."

Duncan laughed, the sound low and genuine. "You're spoiling me."

She raised an eyebrow. "I hope so."

He took the bag, set it on the nearby bench, then pulled her in again, more slowly this time. More deliberately. He held her like someone who finally knew what he wanted— and what he was never letting go of again.

As she rested her head lightly on his shoulder, he let his eyes drift shut.

And in that moment, with her in his arms and the faint scent of basil and red wine sauce in the air, he knew something with absolute certainty.

He didn't want her just in stolen hospital moments.

He wanted her in everything.

His break was nearly over, and the thought of leaving her again—even for a few more hours—felt like some small, quiet cruelty.

They'd sat on the staff room couch, their legs tangled as they ate the food she'd brought—microwave heated, homemade, like she'd poured comfort straight into

Tupperware and carried it across cities. She laughed when he groaned at the first bite. "It's just pasta."

"It's life-saving pasta," he'd said, mouth full.

Now she stood near the lockers again, her coat draped over her arm, her hair a little messier from his fingers, her lipstick slightly faded from kisses.

"I can go to a hotel, you know," she said, eyes flicking up to his. "I don't want to be in the way. You're tired, and—"

"Don't you dare," he interrupted, pressing his key into her palm and curling her fingers around it. "It's not even a question."

Jade looked down at the key, then back at him, brows lifting. "Are you sure?"

"I've never been more sure of anything." He pulled out his phone, typing quickly before sending it to her phone. "Address and door code. It's not fancy, but it's home. There are clean towels in the linen cupboard, and coffee. Real coffee."

She softened; fingers still wrapped around the key. "You're trusting me with your place?"

"I'm trusting you with a hell of a lot more than that."

Jade swallowed, her voice suddenly quiet. "I'll wait up."

His heart squeezed. "You don't have to."

"I want to."

He leaned in and kissed her again, slower this time. A promise pressed to her lips. Then he rested his forehead against hers, taking a steadying breath before stepping back.

"Text me when you get there," he said.

"I will."

He watched her leave, the key still clutched in her hand, and for the rest of his shift, every second ticked by too slowly—because for the first time ever, someone was waiting for him at home.

Chapter Twenty-One

When Jade stepped into Duncan's apartment, the words "not fancy" immediately became the understatement of the year.

It wasn't flashy, but it was beautiful—wooden floors that creaked softly beneath her feet, warm lighting, exposed brick on one wall, and floor-to-ceiling shelves stacked with books and journals in a way that was both chaotic and charming. A guitar leaned casually in one corner. A half-unpacked gym bag sat near the couch. There were mugs on the coffee table, a few shirts draped over the arm of a chair, and one of his scrub tops flung across the back of the dining stool.

She smiled as she took it all in—this was his space. Lived in. Real. Just like him.

And it smelled like him too—clean and masculine, with a hint of cedar and something deeper, something warm.

With a quiet hum, Jade moved through the apartment, tidying a little—not scrubbing or rearranging, just gently making the space feel ready. She stacked the books, folded the clothes, cleared the cups. It felt strangely intimate, more so than undressing in front of him. Like being allowed to see the parts of him he didn't show anyone else.

Afterward, she took a long, hot shower. The steam curled around her as she let the water work out the tension in her shoulders. When she stepped out, she towel-dried her hair and applied a light touch of makeup—not too much, just enough to feel fresh. She slipped into the silk negligee she'd packed at the last minute, not expecting to wear it tonight but suddenly grateful she'd brought it.

It was soft, pale champagne, the lace tracing delicately over her skin. She glanced at herself in the mirror, then wandered barefoot into his bedroom and curled up on top of the covers, switching on the lamp beside the bed.

She glanced at the time.

He wouldn't be long now.

Somewhere across the city, Duncan was finishing up—tired, no doubt, but maybe thinking about her too.

Meanwhile, Duncan stepped under the hospital shower, his body sagging with exhaustion, every muscle aching from a day that had taken more from him than he cared to admit. The hot water struck his back in heavy sheets, washing away sweat, tension, and the lingering residue of too many back-to-back cases. For a while, he just stood there—hands braced against the tiled wall, head bowed, steam curling around him like fog.

He let out a slow breath, eyes shut tight.

Jade.

Her name pulsed in his thoughts with every beat of his heart. Her smile. The curve of her neck when she tilted her head. The soft sound of her laugh when he said something dry and stupid just to make her roll her eyes. He could still feel the ghost of her hand in his, the warmth of her lips against his cheek, the gentle weight of her body pressed against his in the staff room hours earlier.

She'd been waiting for him.

And not just physically. Emotionally. Quietly. Unapologetically.

He'd never had that before.

The kind of presence that didn't demand anything—just offered something real. Something anchoring.

The memory made his throat tighten.

By the time he shut off the water and stepped out, towelling off quickly and tugging on jeans and a clean button-down, his exhaustion had taken a backseat to a different kind of need. A pull that started somewhere in his chest and sank all the way down to his gut. He needed to see her again. To hold her. To feel her beside him—not in a hospital hallway, but in his space. His world.

He was halfway home before he realised, he hadn't even checked his messages. His only thought was Jade. Just Jade.

The door clicked open just after one in the morning.

The flat was quiet, still. The soft hum of the fridge in the kitchen, the faint creak of floorboards under his tired steps. Duncan stepped inside, bag slung over one shoulder, hair still damp from his quick hospital shower. He dropped his keys in the dish by the door, toed off his shoes with a sigh, and padded toward the bedroom.

He expected the lights to be off. Expected her to be curled up beneath the duvet, half-asleep.

But when he stepped into the room, he froze.

The lights were dimmed low—just enough to cast a golden glow across the bed. The scent of lavender hung faintly in the air, layered with something warmer. Familiar. Her perfume.

His gaze found her instantly.

Jade.

She was curled up on top of the covers, one leg tucked beneath her, her hands resting lightly in her lap. Her negligee shimmered in the lamplight—champagne silk against the smooth, golden warmth of her skin. Her hair was down, soft waves spilling over her shoulders. Her makeup was still perfect, just a touch of sheen at the corners of her lips like she'd reapplied her gloss before he walked in.

She looked like a dream.

His dream.

"Hi," she said softly, almost shyly.

Duncan stood motionless in the doorway, his heart thudding against his ribs, the exhaustion of the day evaporating in one sharp exhale. "Jesus, Jade…"

Her lips curved. "I hope it's okay I tidied up a bit. Didn't touch much. Just… cleared the mugs. Your gym bag was threatening to conquer the living room."

He stared at her like he didn't quite believe what he was seeing. "You're here. You're actually here."

She nodded, her voice soft but steady. "You told me not to dare go to a hotel. So, I didn't."

That tugged a crooked, reverent smile from him. He stepped forward slowly, every movement deliberate, like he was afraid the moment might shatter. "You look…"

He stopped at a loss. Words didn't cut it. Not for this.

"You look like home."

Jade's breath caught visibly. Her shoulders relaxed a fraction.

He came to the side of the bed and knelt in front of her, resting his hands gently on her knees. He was still damp from the drive, still smelled faintly of hospital soap and cold night air.

"I missed you," he said, voice rough with honesty. "More than I expected. More than I knew how to say."

Her fingers threaded gently into his hair, tugging him close until their foreheads touched. "I missed you too."

He looked up at her, and for a moment, all the armour slipped. His eyes were wide open, unguarded, full of longing and something dangerously close to awe.

"I don't deserve this," he whispered. "But God, I want it."

"You do deserve this," she replied, her voice firm and tender all at once. "You deserve someone who sees you. Someone who doesn't walk away."

"I don't want you to walk away," he murmured, his lips brushing hers like a question.

"I'm not going anywhere."

He kissed her—slow and soft, like a man drinking from the only glass of water after days in the desert. Not rushed. Not greedy. Just full of reverence.

When they parted, she smiled gently and traced his jaw. "Go brush your teeth, Doctor. You're officially off duty."

He huffed a quiet laugh; forehead still pressed to hers. "Yes, Nurse Bell."

As he stood and disappeared into the ensuite, she watched him go—shirt wrinkled, hair damp and tousled, his gaze still lingering on her in the mirror as he brushed his teeth.

And Jade… had never felt more wanted. More seen. More cherished.

Duncan returned a few minutes later, barefoot, and clean, smelling faintly of mint and soap, his face scrubbed raw, the shadows beneath his eyes softened by something gentler now. He paused in the doorway again, taking her in.

Jade had risen from the bed, standing barefoot on the rug, her negligee catching the light with every breath she took. She looked like a question and an answer all at once.

Her hands were clasped lightly in front of her, and when she looked at him—really looked—her eyes shone.

He crossed to her in three quiet strides.

No words.

Just hands finding her waist.

Her arms slid up his chest, around his neck. And then their mouths met—deep and slow, full of the ache of missing and the sweetness of reunion.

There was no urgency. No frenzy. Just warmth. Familiarity. Craving dressed in softness.

When he lifted her, her legs wrapped around him instinctively, a soft gasp escaping her lips as he carried her to the bed, laying her down like she was something sacred.

"God, you're beautiful," he breathed, brushing a knuckle across her collarbone, the silk slipping gently from her shoulder.

Jade's smile was soft, eyes heavy-lidded. "I wanted to look nice for you."

"You always do," he murmured. "But this… this is going to ruin me."

Their clothes came off slowly this time—no urgency, no rush. Like an offering. A reverent exchange.

Each layer peeled away revealed something deeper, something older than memory and sharper than longing. Every inch of skin exposed was met with a kiss, a brush of fingertips, a whispered word meant only for her.

He rediscovered her with aching patience—mapping the curve of her hip, the slope of her collarbone, the softness behind her knee. Her breath hitched, her fingers threaded through his hair, and when she moaned, low and broken, he swallowed the sound like a prayer.

Jade's back arched as his mouth traced a path from her throat to the jut of her hipbone, his hands cradling her like she was something fragile and sacred.

And then she pushed him gently onto his back and climbed over him, her knees on either side of his waist.

"Do you want me?" she whispered, her voice shaky but sure.

He looked up at her, pupils blown wide, chest rising and falling in ragged bursts. "God, yes."

She guided him to her entrance, holding his gaze as she slowly sank down onto him, inch by aching inch.

"Jade…" he breathed, the word caught somewhere between reverence and desperation.

She started to move—slowly at first, deliberately—as his hands slid up her sides, cupping her breasts. His thumbs brushed over her nipples, coaxing soft gasps from her lips as her body responded to every touch, every shift, every pulse of pleasure.

His fingers grazed the peaks, teasing, then tweaking gently, and she moaned his name like it belonged to her.

And maybe it did.

In that moment—with her above him, claiming him, grounding him—he was hers. Entirely.

They moved together in a rhythm that was theirs alone, slow at first, then deeper, more urgent. Her hands braced on his chest, her head tilted back as pleasure built and curled through her like a tide she couldn't stop.

"Duncan…" she gasped, her voice breaking on a moan. "Yes—"

Her body clenched around him as she came, the sound of his name spilling from her lips like a prayer.

He caught her as she trembled, then shifted, flipping her gently onto her back without ever breaking their connection.

His pace quickened, the control he'd fought so hard to keep beginning to slip.

"God, Jade…" he groaned, voice rough with need, head bowed as his hips snapped forward, again and again, chasing the high of her release.

She arched into him, and then it happened again—another wave crashing over her, stealing her breath as she shattered beneath him a second time.

This time, he followed—his release a raw, broken sound pressed into the curve of her neck as he clutched her like he might come undone without her.

And maybe he would have.

Jade clung to him like he was the answer to a question she'd been too afraid to ask.

And Duncan held her like she was the only thing that had ever made sense.

He didn't roll away.

Didn't create distance.

Instead, he braced himself on one elbow, his body still pressed close, breath warm against her skin.

He stayed right there—tangled with her, anchored by the steady rise and fall of their chests. His hand drifted slowly across her hip, then up to the small of her back, stroking gently, like he was trying to memorise every inch of her through touch alone.

In the hush that followed—soft sighs, quiet breaths, heartbeats falling into rhythm—he whispered, "You feel like everything I didn't know I was missing."

Jade smiled, lips brushing the centre of his chest, where his heart beat loud and sure beneath her cheek.

Her fingers drew slow circles on his skin.

"You found me anyway," she murmured.

Later, he shifted just enough to gather her against him fully, their legs tangled, skin still warm and glowing from where they'd loved each other like it meant something. Because it had.

She rested her head on his chest again, letting the steady rhythm calm her, grounding her in a way nothing else had in years. His fingers combed lazily through her hair, the other arm wrapped tightly around her like he couldn't quite bear to let go.

"Jade?" he asked, voice quiet, like he was afraid of breaking something fragile between them.

"Mmm?"

"You didn't just come for the sex… right?"

She let out a soft laugh against his chest. "No. I didn't."

"Good." His voice was barely more than a breath. "Because I think I'm falling for you."

Her heart stuttered. She tilted her face up, eyes locking with his in the dim, golden light.

"I think I already have," she whispered. Then, with a slow, teasing smile:

"But… just to be clear—the sex was incredible."

He laughed, a deep, low sound that rumbled beneath her ear, warm and real and utterly him.

And in the quiet glow of his apartment, wrapped in sheets and shadows and everything unspoken, something between them shifted.

Not the end of anything.

Just the beginning—

Of something real.

Chapter Twenty-Two

They spent two more perfect days and nights wrapped in each other's company.

The world outside Duncan's apartment blurred into something distant and unimportant. They cooked side by side, laughed over burnt toast and mismatched mugs, shared memories, and secrets they hadn't realised they were still carrying. They wandered the city like old lovers finding their rhythm again—hands clasped, eyes lingering, ducking into bookshops and quiet cafés as if time had finally learned to wait for them.

At night, they tangled in bed—slow, sweet, certain. Their bodies spoke a language that required no translation. And in the quiet hours between dusk and dawn, they held each other like they were learning how not to let go.

But by the end of the second night, reality had crept back in. Soft at first, then undeniable.

Jade stood by the door, her weekend bag slung over one shoulder, coat folded neatly in the crook of her arm. Her makeup was minimal, her hair tied back—practical, understated. Still, Duncan couldn't look away.

He leaned against the kitchen bench, coffee cup in hand, watching her like he was trying to memorise every detail.

"You really have to go?" he asked, though he already knew the answer.

Jade nodded, a faint smile tugging at her lips. "Two back-to-back shifts starting tomorrow. The AMU would fall apart without me."

Duncan set his cup down and walked toward her slowly. "Still doesn't mean I have to like it."

She looked up at him, her gaze warm, a little sad. "I don't want to go either."

He exhaled, pulling her into his arms. "Feels like I just got you back. And now I have to let you go again."

She pressed close, her cheek against his chest. "It's not like before. I'm not vanishing. And neither are you."

"I could come with you," he murmured. "I've got a day before my next rotation starts."

She smiled into his shirt. "You'd spend most of it in traffic, and I'll be elbow-deep in-patient charts."

"I hate that I can't come with you," he whispered into her hair.

She leaned back, just enough to meet his eyes. "You'll come when you can. And I'll come back. We'll figure it out."

His hands cupped her face, thumbs brushing her jaw. "Just… don't forget about me up there."

"I couldn't if I tried."

He kissed her then—slow, deliberate, like he wanted her to carry it with her. When they parted, he rested his forehead against hers.

"Call me when you get home," he said softly. "I'll be waiting."

"I will," she whispered. "Promise."

One more kiss. One more tight embrace.

Then she stepped back, slipped on her coat, and opened the door.

Duncan watched her walk down the hallway, each step pulling something from him. She turned back once, just before the lift, and gave him a smile that nearly undid him.

He lifted his hand in a small wave; the words caught behind his teeth.

Then she was gone.

And the apartment—so recently filled with her laughter, her warmth, her light—suddenly felt just a little too quiet.

It went on like that for two months.

As soon as Duncan's hospital rotation ended, he'd drive to Manchester—often running on nothing but adrenaline and the sound of her voice on the phone. And when Jade's shift ended, she'd make the trip to London, tired but eager, craving the warmth of his arms more than sleep.

They made the most of every minute. Every shared meal, every quiet morning with coffee and bare feet on cold kitchen tiles. Every night tangled together, even if they both had to be up before dawn. It was beautiful. Messy. Intoxicating.

But it was wearing on them.

Duncan felt it first—the toll of constant driving, the scattered sleep, the ache that came with saying goodbye over and over again. It wasn't enough anymore.

He didn't want just weekends. He didn't want borrowed time or fleeting moments tucked between obligations.

He wanted her always.

Every night. Every morning.

The ordinary days, too—the ones where they both worked twelve-hour shifts, came home bone-tired, and still managed to fall asleep wrapped in each other's arms.

Jade felt it too, though she never said a word.

She missed him with a quiet, unrelenting ache—one that had rooted itself deep inside her, humming beneath her skin.

But she wanted him more than she wanted comfort. More than she wanted ease. And if this—these fractured weekends, these snatched hours, and too-short nights—was the only way to keep him, she would take it.

Without complaint.

Without pressure.

Without expectation.

Neither of them had said the words.

Duncan didn't—afraid that saying I love you out loud might push her away.

Jade didn't—afraid he didn't feel the same, and that the silence was safer than the risk.

So, they said nothing.

And slowly, silence began to stretch.

The calls that once lasted deep into the night grew shorter. The messages took longer to send. The goodbyes felt heavier, lingering like fog long after the door had closed. And the joy of reunion—once thrilling, once enough—came tinged with quiet dread.

The dread of another ending.

They were doing everything they could to hold on. Showing up in every way they knew how. But the distance—measured not just in miles, but in exhaustion and unanswered longing—was quietly, steadily wearing them down.

Not from lack of love.

But from the quiet, brutal truth that sometimes, love isn't the only thing you need.

Duncan hadn't told her he loved her. But he did. Fiercely. Fully. Without hesitation.

He wanted to say it every time they came back together. Every time he held her. Every time he watched her walk away.

But she hadn't said it either.

And he didn't know what that meant.

Was she not ready to hear it?

Or was she holding back because she didn't feel it at all?

Still, their effort never wavered.

When Jade had a rare weekend off, she'd drive to London—only for Duncan to leave for another rotation. And when his schedule opened up, he'd drive to Manchester—only to kiss her goodbye as she pulled on her scrubs at dawn.

They kept trying. Kept reaching. Kept hoping.

But it wasn't fair.

And it wasn't sustainable.

Something had to give.

So, when a job opened up at St George's Hospital in Manchester—a position in acute surgery, rare and competitive—Duncan didn't hesitate. He filled out the application the same night, long after a video call with Jade ended in shared yawns and reluctant goodnights. His flat in London was silent, his bed cold.

He didn't tell her.

Not because he didn't want to—but because he didn't want to get her hopes up. The last thing he wanted was to see that quiet light in her eyes and risk extinguishing it with a "maybe" that turned into a no. So, he kept it to himself. Just for now.

It wasn't about grand gestures. It was about showing up for the life he wanted. For the woman he couldn't bear to say goodbye to one more time.

So, he wrote the cover letter. Polished his CV. Hit send.

And every day after, he checked his inbox like a man waiting for the door to his future to swing open.

Two weeks later, the email came through mid-shift:

Interview Invitation – St George's Hospital, Manchester.

Duncan's heart kicked in his chest as he read the message twice, just to be sure. A video interview. Thursday at 7 p.m.

He cleared his evening, shaved, ironed a shirt he hadn't worn since his last registrar panel, and made sure his background was tidy—books, certificates, nothing distracting. When the screen flickered to life, three consultants appeared: the Head of Surgery, a senior HR manager, and the Clinical Director for Acute Medicine.

"Dr. Armstrong, thank you for making the time."

"Of course," he said, his voice calm, his palms slightly damp out of view.

The interview started with the usual questions—his clinical experience, surgical approach, management of high-pressure cases. But then came the curveballs.

"How do you manage emotional resilience over long rotations?"

"What makes you think Manchester is the right move at this stage in your career?"

He didn't flinch. "Because I want more than a career. I want a life," he said. "And that life is in Manchester."

They didn't press for details. They didn't have to.

The panel thanked him, signed off, and the screen went black. Duncan sat back, heart pounding, already replaying everything he wished he'd said better.

Then—two days later, mid-morning—a call came through. Unknown number. He answered on instinct.

"Dr. Armstrong? It's Dr. Patel from St George's. I hope you're sitting down."

He wasn't. He stood frozen by the window, the city behind him fading into silence.

"We'd like to offer you the position. Full-time surgical consultant. Start date negotiable."

For a full second, Duncan couldn't breathe.

Then he smiled—broad, stunned, entirely undone.

"Thank you," he said. "Thank you so much."

As soon as the call ended, he sat down. One hand still holding the phone. The other over his chest.

He was moving to Manchester.

And Jade didn't know yet.

Chapter Twenty-Three

Duncan wanted to tell her face to face. Not over the phone, not in some rushed, exhausted call between shifts—but properly. With eyes locked, hearts bare, and no distance between them.

So, when his rotation ended for the week, he packed a bag and hit the road—just him, the hum of the tyres, and the thoughts he couldn't outrun. Instead of heading straight to Jade's flat, he detoured to his parents' house first. She wouldn't be home from the hospital until late anyway, and he needed the calm before everything changed.

His mum hugged him at the door like she already knew, arms wrapped tight around her son, her cheek pressed briefly to his shoulder. His dad clapped a steady hand on Duncan's back, quiet pride shining in his eyes.

Over a cup of tea in the familiar warmth of the kitchen, his mum glanced at him with a knowing smile. "You going to see Jade?"

Duncan's lips curled into a smile—one edged with nerves and full of something deeper, something certain. The kind of smile that came from holding a secret close to the chest for too long.

"Yeah," he said. "I am." He paused, then added quietly, "I'm going to ask her to marry me."

His mother gasped softly, eyes instantly misting over. "Oh, Duncan."

Without another word, he reached into his bag and pulled out the small velvet box. He opened it slowly.

The ring caught the light—simple, stunning, quietly certain. A large deep blue sapphire—oval-cut—framed by two smaller diamonds, all set in platinum. The colour was almost exactly the shade of Jade's eyes. He'd noticed it the first day he met her. He'd never stopped noticing.

"Well done, son," his father said, voice low but full of emotion.

Duncan held the ring box in his palm for a long moment, his heartbeat pounding like it was trying to outrun time itself.

He was going to ask her to spend her life with him.

He didn't know exactly when—tonight, tomorrow, sometime soon—but he knew one thing with unwavering certainty: he wouldn't let another week, another visit, another goodbye go by without telling her what lived in his heart.

Tonight, he would tell her he loved her.

That he was done with fleeting weekends and long-distance calls.

That she wasn't just someone he couldn't stop thinking about—

She was it.

His person.

His beginning, his always.

His home.

He closed the box and tucked it carefully back into his bag, fingers lingering on the zipper before drawing it closed.

Tonight, he'd surprise her with more than just his arrival.

He'd give her the truth of everything:

The job.

The move.

And the words he'd been carrying in his chest for far too long—

That he loved her.

And he wanted to spend the rest of his life proving it.

He was still talking to his parents when his phone buzzed in his bag.

Duncan smiled faintly. "That's probably Jade."

He reached for it, expecting a quick message, maybe a teasing emoji or a "where are you?"

But it wasn't her.

Leanne. Calling.

His brow furrowed. Leanne didn't call—she texted, joked, sent voice notes at best. A call meant one thing: something was wrong.

He answered on the second ring. "Leanne?"

Her voice was breathless, panicked. "Duncan—where are you? Are you at work?"

"No, I'm at my parents'—what's going on?"

"Oh, thank God you're close. You need to come. Now."

His chest went tight. "What happened?"

"It's Jade," she gasped. "There's a Code Black at the hospital. Some guy stormed in—he's looking for his partner. They say he's armed. The AMU is in full lockdown."

The world shifted beneath him.

"What?"

"She was on shift. She's inside. She hasn't come out."

Duncan's grip on the phone tightened. His other hand was already grabbing his keys. "Is she hurt?"

"I don't know. No one knows. It's chaos. Phones are off, radios down. The police are on-site, but everything's sealed. I've tried her mobile—it goes straight to voicemail."

He was already shrugging into his coat, moving for the door. "How long ago?"

"Twenty minutes, maybe. Duncan—she was treating the woman he came in for. They think she refused to tell him where she was."

Of course she did, Duncan thought. Bloody brave. Bloody infuriating. So very Jade.

His voice came sharp, clipped. "I'm on my way."

"Just—" Leanne's voice cracked. "Just get here. Please."

He hung up without another word.

His parents looked up from the kitchen as he strode toward the door, the panic in his eyes unmistakable.

"What is it?" his mum asked, already rising.

"It's Jade," he said, grabbing his bag. "There's a Code Black at the hospital. A man with a weapon. She's inside. They think she's the only one left with him."

His mother gasped, a hand flying to her chest. His father swore quietly, standing frozen as Duncan threw open the front door.

"Oh, love," his mum whispered, following him out. "No…"

The silence that followed was thick with dread.

"She's brave," his mother said finally, voice trembling. "She'll get through this."

"She shouldn't have to," Duncan muttered, his jaw clenched as he threw his bag into the back seat.

His father stepped up beside him, quiet and steady. "Is there anything we can do?"

"Just… pray. Or something." Duncan's throat tightened as he blinked hard against the burn in his eyes. His voice dropped. "I can't lose her, Mum."

The words cracked something wide open in him—fear, truth, love.

"I can't," he said again, hoarse now. "I haven't even told her I love her…"

There was a pause. Not awkward. Just breathless. Still.

His mother pulled him into a tight hug, her voice close to his ear. "Then don't wait. Get to her. And when this is over—when she's safe—you tell her."

He nodded, eyes stinging. "I will."

Then he climbed into the car, started the engine, and tore down the road like his soul depended on it—because it did.

Leanne had said he was close. But "close" still meant two hours.

Two hours of silence.

Two hours of wondering.

Two hours of imagining every worst-case scenario his mind could conjure.

He'd never hated the distance between them more.

The motorway stretched ahead like a cruel test of patience, every signpost another reminder that he wasn't there yet. That she was still in danger. Still inside. Still out of reach.

His grip tightened on the wheel, jaw locked.

If this man hurt her—

If he laid a single hand on her—

God help him.

Because Duncan wouldn't be asking questions. He wouldn't be thinking like a doctor.

He'd be thinking like a man in love—who was too damn late.

And that was something he couldn't bear.

Chapter Twenty-Four

The morning had been chaotic—back-to-back patients, constant interruptions, the usual blur of pressure that came with working in the AMU. But one patient lingered, like a shadow in the back of her mind: the woman in Bay 3.

She'd arrived just after 8 a.m.—barely conscious, bloodied, in obvious pain. The paramedics had whispered the words domestic assault before wheeling her in. Jade had seen the signs too many times. She recognised them instantly.

Multiple deep bruises bloomed across her torso and arms, one eye nearly swollen shut. Her ribs were fractured—two, maybe three—and there was a split in her lip that bled no matter how gently Jade cleaned it. But it was the woman's eyes that stuck with her most.

Terrified. Hollow. Like she wasn't sure if she'd be believed.

Jade remembered that feeling.

Her mind flashed, unbidden, to the day Dean had grabbed her. The fury in his eyes, the way his hand had clamped around her arm like he had a right to her body, her choices. It hadn't left a mark, not one the world could see—but she'd felt it for days. And this poor woman… she'd been through so much worse.

Jade had held her hand while she arranged imaging, whispered reassurances, promised her she was safe now. And the woman—Cara, her name was—had finally nodded, tears slipping silently down her cheeks.

She'd just stepped out to update the attending team when she heard it. A voice raised in anger—harsh, male, unfamiliar.

Then a nurse's panicked shout:

"You can't go in there, sir!"

Jade turned sharply, heart lurching.

"Where is the bitch? I want to see her!"

The voice tore through the ward like a blade.

Chaos exploded in an instant. A crash. A startled scream. The sound of feet scrambling, radios crackling.

Jade's blood ran cold.

Her eyes met Mary's across the corridor.

And in that split-second, Jade knew.

It was him.

Cara's abuser had come for her.

And Jade was standing directly in his path.

There was no way in hell she was going to let him near her.

She drew in a breath that scraped like glass and stepped forward, heart hammering. Her voice, somehow, stayed calm.

"Sir, are you here to see Cara Jenkins?"

His head whipped toward her, wild eyes full of rage. "Yeah. Where is the bitch?"

Jade's stomach twisted, but she didn't flinch. She couldn't. She was the only thing between him and the woman cowering behind a curtain just metres away.

She nodded slowly, deliberately, keeping her tone neutral. "If you come with me, I'll take you to her."

She needed to get him away from the other patients. Away from Cara. Away from, Mary, the terrified young nurse still frozen behind him.

He started toward her, quick and angry.

That's when she saw it.

The glint.

A knife—large, filthy, clutched in his hand like an extension of his fury.

Oh God.

Jade's breath caught in her chest, but she didn't move. Didn't let her face betray the surge of fear flooding her limbs.

Instead, she took a step back—measured, careful—leading him toward the empty consultation room near the end of the hall.

"Right this way," she said, voice steady even as her heart pounded against her ribs.

She didn't know how long she could keep him calm. Or how far she could lead him before he caught on.

But she knew this much:

She wouldn't let him hurt anyone else.

Not Cara.

Not her team.

Not anyone.

Even if it meant standing alone.

Jade stiffened her spine and opened the door to the empty consultation room, forcing her hand to stay steady on the handle. Her heart was slamming against her ribs, but she kept her expression neutral, controlled.

"Go ahead," she said, praying he'd walk in first so she could slam the door shut behind him and lock him in.

But he stopped. His eyes narrowed, sharp with suspicion.

"You first," he growled.

Jade hesitated only a second. Just enough to know there was no other choice. Then she stepped inside, her breaths short and shallow, the air in the room suddenly too thin.

He followed—jittery, twitching—the knife still clutched in his hand. The door shut with a soft, chilling click.

And then his eyes took it in.

A small, windowless room.

A desk pushed against one wall with an old office chair tucked beneath it. A landline phone sat unused beside a stack of paperwork.

Cabinets along the back wall.

An exam bed stretched along the opposite wall, crisp paper rolled out over the vinyl.

No patient.

No Cara.

Just sterile walls, silence—

And Jade.

His face twisted. "You bitch."

He spun toward the door, but as he yanked it open, the distant sound of heavy boots pounding down the corridor reached them. The security team.

Jade moved instinctively, tried to move herself closer to the door, but he grabbed her arm—hard—and yanked her backward.

She cried out as he dragged her deeper into the room. The door slammed shut behind them with a hollow thud.

He locked it with a violent twist of the bolt. The sharp click of the lock sounded louder than a gunshot, then he shoved her roughly toward the wall.

Trapped.

Jade's back hit the cabinets, her breath catching in her throat.

Outside, she could hear shouting. The thud of fists against the door.

But inside—it was just her and him.

And the knife.

His phone buzzed again, lighting up the dashboard.

Leanne.

Duncan jabbed the answer button with a trembling finger.

"Leanne?"

She didn't waste a second. "I just spoke to someone from the hospital command centre. It's confirmed." Her voice was strained, like she was holding herself together by sheer will. "It's Jade, Duncan. She's the one he's holding."

His stomach dropped.

The breath left his lungs like a punch. "Confirmed?"

"Yes. The police say he asked for the nurse who treated his partner. Jade was the last one to see her. She was trying to protect the woman—of course she was."

He swallowed hard, his knuckles white on the steering wheel.

"What else do you know?"

Leanne hesitated. "The guy—his name's Daniel Stroud. Thirty-four. Known to police. He's got a record… domestic abuse, multiple assaults. And…" her voice faltered, "He's been accused of rape. Twice."

A cold wave passed through Duncan, replacing blood with ice.

"Jesus Christ," he muttered, voice low and full of fury.

"He's armed," Leanne added. "Police think it's a knife, but no one's gotten close enough to confirm. Tactical units are inside, but he's barricaded them in. It's been hours, Duncan."

"I'm thirty minutes out," he said tightly. "I'm on my way."

"Duncan—"

"Just keep me updated." His voice was clipped, shaking with the force of everything he wasn't saying.

He ended the call and pressed harder on the accelerator, the tyres humming beneath him as the city lights grew closer.

Thirty minutes.

She was inside with a violent man, and Duncan was still too far away.

Every second stretched like wire, pulled tight around his heart.

Just hold on, Jade, he begged silently.

Please. I'm coming.

Don't leave me before I get the chance to tell you everything.

Chapter Twenty-Five

Jade's heart pounded in her chest like a warning bell, but she kept her face calm—controlled.

She could feel the weight of his grip still on her arm, hot and bruising, even as he let go and spun around, realising what she'd done.

"You tricked me." His voice was low and deadly, the kind of quiet that came just before violence.

Jade took a careful step back, putting distance between them.

"There's no one here," she said evenly, her voice steadier than she felt. "Cara isn't in this room."

He laughed—a short, bitter sound. "You think I'm stupid?"

"No," she replied, gently, slowly, "I think you're angry. I think you're scared. But hurting me won't get you what you want."

His eyes narrowed. "Don't play games with me, nurse."

Jade kept her hands where he could see them, palms slightly raised.

Her eyes flicked to the desk phone behind him. Too far. Useless.

The walls felt like they were closing in, and the air grew thick with tension.

"You don't have to do this," she said softly. "We can walk out of here. I'll tell the officers you never touched me. No one has to get hurt."

His face twisted with rage, and he stepped toward her. "Don't lie to me!"

Jade didn't flinch. She wanted to. Every instinct begged her to. But she held the line.

"I'm not lying. But Cara's not here. And if you hurt me, that's all anyone's going to remember. Not her. Not your story. Just this."

He was breathing harder now, pacing the small space like a caged animal. The knife glinted in his hand, catching the overhead light.

Jade's eyes stayed on it, every nerve in her body screaming.

But she refused to back down.

Even if it meant standing alone.

She straightened her spine, voice calm but firm. "You don't want to be the monster everyone thinks you are."

His grip on the knife tightened until his knuckles went white.

"You don't know a damn thing about me," he growled, voice jagged with rage.

"No," Jade whispered, pulse pounding in her ears. "But I know what fear looks like. I've felt it."

His jaw clenched. Something fractured in his expression.

The kind of look that meant logic was gone. Nothing rational lived behind his eyes now—only fury, humiliation, and chaos.

"Let me help you," she tried, gently, desperately. "It needs to end here."

A moment passed. One second. Maybe two.

Then he lunged.

His hand shot out and wrapped around her throat, shoving her backward so violently that her spine hit the tall cabinet with a sickening crack.

Her head snapped back against the cupboard, stars flashing in her vision. His hand clamped around her neck—tight, then tighter—cutting off her air, cutting off thought.

And then she saw it.

The knife.

He raised it slowly, deliberately—just enough so she could see the serrated edge shimmer under the fluorescent light. His lips curled into a snarl, breath hot and sour.

"You set me up," he spat. "Maybe I should punish you for that."

Jade's body locked in instinctive terror, her fight-or-flight response screaming with no escape in sight.

Her heartbeat was a brutal drumbeat against his crushing fingers. Her lungs screamed for air. The blade gleamed inches from her cheek.

She didn't scream.

She couldn't.

Her mouth opened, but nothing came out but shallow gasps.

She had to think.

She had to survive.

Not like this.

Her eyes darted toward the door. No help. No movement. No sounds but the ragged wheeze of her own breath and the deranged rhythm of his fury.

She clawed at his wrist—not to fight, but to stay conscious. To stay present.

Because she needed to see a way out.

Because someone was coming.

They had to be.

His grip shifted, not loosening—just changing. Less choking now, more control. The knife stayed close, but his eyes moved.

Dark. Empty.

"You're a pretty thing, aren't you?" he said, his voice low and slick, as if he were commenting on the weather.

Jade was still gasping for breath, her throat raw from his grip. Her back throbbed from the impact with the cabinet. Her mind raced. Fast. Desperate.

"Maybe I should have some fun with you," he sneered. "Not like I'm getting out of here any time soon."

His gaze dragged down her body, slow and calculating.

Jade's stomach turned. A hot rush of nausea crawled up her throat. She fought it back—barely.

He leaned closer, the stench of sweat and blood and something fouler making her flinch.

"You look like you could please a man."

She didn't move. Didn't blink.

Every part of her wanted to scream, to run, to claw her way out. But the blade made rebellion a death sentence.

And he was already spiralling.

Instead, she made herself breathe. A little slower. Shallower. Careful.

No sudden moves.

Just stay alive.

Her voice came out hoarse, shaking. "You don't have to do this."

He grinned—something ugly and hungry. "Don't I?"

She kept her eyes on him, steady despite the horror screaming in her chest. "You want control. You've got it. You don't need to prove anything."

It was a gamble. Every word was a wire she walked barefoot.

His grin faded slightly. Confusion flickered. Not much—but enough.

Keep him talking. Keep him distracted.

Because help was coming.

It had to be.

Duncan barely threw the car into park before he was out and running.

The flashing blue of police lights cast eerie reflections on the glass façade of the hospital. Uniformed officers were everywhere—cordoning off entrances, speaking into radios, standing with tense shoulders and grim faces.

Inside the main doors of the AMU entrance, chaos buzzed beneath the hush. Nurses huddled in corners. Security stood rigid. A command post was being set up near reception.

And then—Leanne.

She was sitting beside a nurse Duncan didn't recognise, both pale and visibly shaken. As soon as she saw him, Leanne jumped to her feet and ran straight into his arms.

"Duncan—" Her voice cracked as she gripped him. "Thank God."

"What's happening?" he asked, breathless, scanning the hall. "Where is she?"

Leanne stepped back, her face tight with barely held-in fear. "The police are trying to make contact. He's not responding."

Duncan's heart lurched. "She's still in there?"

She nodded. "They've confirmed it's just her. Everyone else made it out."

He clenched his fists, jaw tight. "How long?"

"Over two hours."

A tremor rippled through him.

The nurse sitting beside Leanne wiped her eyes with the sleeve of her scrubs. "I—I was right next to her," she said softly.

Duncan knelt in front of her. "You were with Jade?"

Mary nodded shakily. "We were treating the woman… Cara. Domestic abuse case. She was in the cubicle next to us."

Duncan swallowed, his throat tight. "And Jade?"

Mary blinked fast, struggling to speak. "When he came in, shouting… demanding to know where Cara was—I froze. I couldn't move. But Jade… she didn't even flinch."

Duncan's heart stopped.

"She didn't even flinch," Mary whispered. "Just… stepped right between him and the curtains. Like it was instinct. Told him she'd take him to Cara, but she didn't. She led him away—out of the ward. She got him away from all of us."

Leanne clutched Duncan's arm. Her grip was tight, grounding.

"I don't think I could've done that," Mary whispered. "She didn't even hesitate."

Duncan's chest was a warzone of pride and fear.

That was Jade.

Brave. Selfless. Always putting others first.

But now she was in there. Alone.

He stood up, shoulders heaving with each breath. "They need to get her out. Now."

"They're trying," Leanne said, eyes red. "But he's not talking. Not yet."

Duncan turned toward the barricade, his mind racing, fists clenched so tightly his nails bit into his palms.

"Who's in charge here?" he asked, voice sharp.

"I'll take you," Leanne said quickly, already moving.

They weaved through the cluster of uniformed officers and staff until they reached a tall, broad-shouldered man in a tactical vest, speaking into a radio with clipped authority.

"Detective Inspector Mathers," Leanne said. "This is Duncan Armstrong—Jade Bell's partner."

Mathers gave a short nod, lowering his radio. "Mr. Armstrong."

Duncan didn't waste a second. "What are you doing to get her out?"

"We've been trying to establish contact," Mathers said evenly. "So far, no response. He has barricaded himself and Ms Bell inside an examination room. We're working with hostage negotiators now."

"She's been in there for over two hours," Duncan snapped. "With a violent offender holding a weapon."

"We're aware of his history—domestic abuse, prior rape charges. He's volatile," Mathers said grimly. "But so far, no screaming, no gunfire. That's something."

"That's not good enough," Duncan snapped, stepping forward. His voice shook with restraint. "That's Jade in there. She's not just some case file—she's the reason her entire team made it out alive."

Mathers didn't blink. "And that's exactly why we're taking this carefully. She's de-escalated him so far. Our job is to keep her alive long enough to get her out."

Duncan's jaw tightened until it ached. "Then do it. Whatever it takes. Just get her out."

"We've got a camera in the room," Mathers said after a beat.

Duncan's eyes snapped to him. "You can see her?"

"Yes. We've been monitoring the feed since we identified the room."

"I want to see her," Duncan said. His voice was low. Controlled. Desperate.

Mathers gestured to a side table where a small portable monitor sat. Duncan crossed the room in two strides.

There she was.

Jade. Sitting on the edge of the exam bed, her posture tense but upright. Her hands rested in her lap, steady. Across from her sat the man—rage in his body even as he stilled, the large knife glinting in his grip as he twitched restlessly in the office chair.

She looked calm.

Too calm.

Like someone walking a tightrope with a storm below.

Duncan's breath caught. "Jesus…"

"We're watching every second," Mathers said quietly behind him. "The moment we have a window—we go."

Duncan didn't take his eyes off the screen. His heart thundered in his chest.

"I'm holding you to that."

Mathers nodded. "Understood."

But to Duncan, even that promise felt like sand slipping through his fingers.

Everything wasn't enough—not until Jade was out of that room, safe in his arms, and breathing beside him again.

Chapter Twenty-Six

He eventually let go of her throat.

Jade stumbled back a step, coughing, her hand instinctively flying to her neck. It burned where his fingers had dug in. She could already feel the throb beneath her skin; knew it would bruise. Knew the ache would stay long after today.

"Sit," he barked, pointing sharply at the exam bed. "There."

She didn't move right away.

Every fibre of her screamed not to obey. Not to go near a bed. Not with him here.

But defiance could cost her everything.

So, she moved—slow, careful—and sat down on the edge of the bed. Her legs were stiff. Her hands curled into the paper sheet beneath her, grounding herself in the crackle of it. Her spine was straight; chin slightly lifted despite the tremble in her limbs.

He started to pace.

Back and forth across the small, windowless room, his boots scuffing the floor, the knife still clutched tightly in one hand. His other hand raked through his hair like he was trying to keep himself from coming apart at the seams.

Jade watched him carefully. Every movement. Every shift in breath. She knew this kind of man. Not personally—not until Dean had grabbed her in anger—but she knew the type. Furious. Fragile. Dangerous.

"Liars," he muttered under his breath. "All of you. Think you can hide her from me. Like I'm some monster."

He turned sharply and looked at her.

Jade didn't flinch.

She wanted to. But she didn't.

"I'm not the bad guy," he said, voice rising, cracking at the edges. "You know what she did? You think you know, but you don't. You don't know anything."

"I know she's hurt," Jade said softly. "I know she's terrified."

"So what? She deserved it." He stepped closer. "She ran. She lied. She said she loved me. But then she just... left."

Jade held his gaze. Her heart thundered in her ears. "That's not love. What you did to her—that's not love."

His face darkened. His grip on the knife tightened.

Wrong move.

God, Jade, think.

She looked away, dropped her gaze. Submissive. Not challenging.

"I'm sorry," she said quickly, breath shaky. "I didn't mean to make you angry."

He stared at her for a long moment, chest heaving.

"You married?" he asked, voice low and sharp.

Jade's throat was still raw, her voice thin. "No."

"Boyfriend?"

She hesitated, just for a heartbeat. "Yes."

His eyes narrowed. "You cheat on him?"

"No. Never."

He laughed then—a bitter, broken sound that scraped the air. "All you women lie."

She didn't respond.

What could she say? That not all men were like him. That love didn't mean control. That bruises didn't come from caring.

He wouldn't hear it.

He wouldn't believe it.

He resumed pacing, muttering under his breath. She couldn't catch every word, but the ones that landed chilled her to the bone—liar... whore... deserves it... can't trust them...

Paranoia. Rage. Regret. A storm circling in his mind, getting louder, tighter.

Jade sat perfectly still on the edge of the bed, hands tucked into her lap, body tense but composed. The paper crinkled beneath her. The sterile tang of disinfectant hung heavy in the air, mixing with sweat and something darker: fear.

She could feel it inside her. Cold. Heavy. Coiled around her spine.

But she wouldn't show it.

She wouldn't feed his fire.

She needed to stay calm.

She needed to survive.

And that meant saying what he needed to hear. Doing what she had to.

Staying small.

Staying still.

Just long enough.

Because someone had to be coming.

And she wasn't going to die in this room.

Not today.

Not like this.

Not before she told Duncan the truth.

That she loved him.

That the distance didn't matter anymore—only he did.

That she was done pretending their weekend visits were enough.

She would move to London. Change jobs. Uproot her life if she had to. Because nothing mattered more than being where he was.

If she got out of this alive, she would tell him everything.

No more waiting.

No more fear.

Just love. And the life they both deserved.

That's when the phone on the desk rang.

Once.

Twice.

Shrill. Jarring. A sound that sliced through the thick silence like a blade.

Jade's heart jolted.

But he didn't move.

The phone kept ringing.

She dared to speak, voice low. "Aren't you going to answer that?"

His eyes snapped to hers. Cold. Calculating.

"No."

His fingers flexed around the knife.

The ringing stopped.

And the silence that followed was somehow even worse.

Duncan and Leanne just sat and waited.

Minutes felt like hours. The tension in the air was thick enough to choke on.

"She'll be okay," Leanne said softly, though her voice wavered. "She has to be."

Duncan stared ahead, jaw clenched, his hands fisted in his lap. Then, without looking at her, he spoke—quiet but certain.

"I'm going to marry her."

Leanne turned to him slowly, eyes wide.

"You are?"

He finally looked at her, and in his expression, there was no hesitation—just fierce, aching truth.

"I bought the ring. I was going to ask her tonight. Tell her I'm moving back. That I'm done with the long-distance crap. I'm done waiting."

Leanne's eyes filled. She reached out and squeezed his arm gently.

"She loves you, Duncan. You know that, right?"

"I think so." He swallowed hard, voice thick. "I just need the chance to hear her say it back."

Leanne hesitated, then added softly, "She loved you in uni too."

Duncan's head snapped up. "She did?"

Leanne nodded, her expression tinged with quiet sadness. "Yeah. She was pretty wrecked when Dean told her you weren't into women. I remember her talking to me about it—asking if it was true if she'd misread everything. I remember her crying."

The words hit like a punch to the chest.

All those years… wasted on a lie.

And on his own silence.

His own damn cowardice.

He could've told her back then—should've. But he let her walk away with a broken heart while he buried his own.

Duncan looked away, his jaw clenched tight, shame and fury twisting in his chest.

A storm built behind his eyes—regret, love, desperation—all crashing together.

They sat in silence after that. Not peaceful—just heavy. Dense with truth. Weighted with everything unsaid.

Waiting. Hoping.

And praying that Jade Bell would walk out of that room alive… so she could finally hear everything he hadn't yet said.

They must have been in that room for hours.

Daniel sat slumped in the office chair, the knife still in his hand.

Jade remained where he told her to—on the edge of the exam bed, back straight, hands resting on her knees to stop them from shaking. Her throat still ached where his fingers had pressed too hard.

The phone rang again.

Every five minutes, like clockwork.

Then silence.

Then ringing again.

"They're just going to keep calling," she said softly, trying to sound calm.

Trying to keep him grounded.

Alive.

"I don't care," he muttered, not even glancing at the phone. His eyes were on her.

Always on her.

"You know we can't stay here forever."

That was when something in him snapped.

He stood suddenly and stalked toward her, his movements sharp and unhinged.

Before she could move, he shoved the knife close to her face, the point glinting inches from her skin.

"Stop talking," he hissed. "You women… you always twist things. Manipulate men. Especially the pretty ones."

His voice turned to venom. "You think being beautiful makes you powerful."

Then he pressed the cold, unforgiving edge of the blade against her cheek, and her skin prickled with the sick anticipation of pain.

Not hard—but close. Too close.

Jade froze. Her breath caught.

"Maybe I should change that," he sneered, his voice low and sick with menace. "Wouldn't be so pretty with a scar down your face, would you?"

She didn't flinch.

Not outwardly.

But inside, everything screamed.

She locked eyes with him. Forced herself to breathe.

To hold still.

To survive.

There was a sudden, sharp bang on the door.

Daniel jumped, eyes wild, knife jerking in his grip.

"Go away!" he roared.

A firm voice called through the door, muffled but calm.

"Daniel Stroud, you need to talk to us. We can't sort this out unless you do."

He started pacing again, muttering under his breath, each step more agitated than the last.

The phone rang.

Again.

And again.

And again.

The sound grated through the silence like a ticking time bomb.

"Make it stop!" he snapped at no one, spinning toward the desk.

Jade sat frozen, barely breathing.

Then, with a sudden snarl, Daniel snatched up the receiver.

"What!?" he barked into the phone, voice cracking with rage.

Jade's heart thundered in her chest as she watched him, the air around her charged with the static of danger.

Her fingers twitched against the paper. Every nerve screamed: *now*.

His back was to her. And that's when it happened.

Chapter Twenty-Seven

The door exploded open.

A deafening crash of splintering wood and steel filled the room as two fully armed officers stormed in, weapons raised, voices sharp.

"Drop the weapon! Now!"

Daniel spun, eyes wild, and lifted the knife—

A shot rang out.

Loud. Sudden. Final.

The knife clattered to the floor, skidding across the linoleum.

Daniel dropped to his knees, stunned, a small red welt blooming on his shoulder.

Rubber bullet.

He wasn't bleeding.

He screamed in rage, then fell forward, subdued instantly by one of the officers who tackled and cuffed him.

The second officer went straight to Jade.

"You're safe now. You're okay," he said, standing in front of her, blocking her from Daniel's view.

But Jade couldn't speak.

Her hands trembled. Her throat burned. Her eyes stayed fixed on the spot where Daniel had stood with a knife to her face.

Everything inside her was shaking.

But she was alive.

And it was over.

The officer forced Daniel to his feet, wrenching his arms behind his back and dragging him toward the door.

That's when Duncan appeared—storming down the corridor, eyes blazing, jaw clenched tight with fury.

"You bastard!" he roared.

Before anyone could stop him, Duncan threw a hard, brutal punch straight into Daniel's face.

Crack.

Daniel staggered sideways, dazed, blood dripping from his lip.

"You weak piece of shit," Duncan growled, shaking with rage. "You only go after women. Is that what makes you feel strong?"

He reared back for another hit—but an officer grabbed his arm from behind, pulling him back firmly.

"Sir—stand down!"

Duncan yanked free, chest heaving, teeth bared. He had never wanted to kill someone more. His fists were still curled tight when his eyes shifted past them—

And landed on her.

Jade.

Still sitting on the edge of the bed, pale and shaking, her eyes locked on his, the moment she saw him.

All the fight drained out of him in a rush.

He pushed past the officers and crossed the room in three strides.

"Thank God," he breathed, standing in front of her, cupping her face in his trembling hands.

"Thank God you're okay."

She didn't speak—just folded into him, arms clinging tight, body pressed close.

And for the first time since the nightmare began, she felt safe.

He had come for her.

He held her tight against him, like he'd never let go again. Her whole body was trembling now, the adrenaline finally giving way to shock. She clutched at his shirt; fists curled into the fabric like she was afraid he'd disappear.

"I've got you," he whispered, over and over, pressing kisses to her hair, her cheeks, her forehead.

"Nothing can touch you now. Not while I'm here."

Then he saw it.

The dark, mottled bruising blooming across her throat. Black and violet, angry and fresh.

He froze. His hands stiffened around her. His breath turned razor-sharp.

He pulled back slightly, just enough to get a better look, his thumb ghosting over the damage with unbearable gentleness.

She winced, just barely, and he stilled immediately, his touch feather-light after that.

"Jesus, Jade…" he whispered. "He did this to you?"

She didn't answer—she didn't have to.

His jaw locked. The fury returned, low and seething. It coursed through his veins like fire, barely contained beneath the surface of his skin.

"I should've killed him," he muttered, voice trembling with rage. "I swear to God, if they hadn't pulled me off—"

"Duncan."

Her voice, soft and raspy, cut through the storm inside him.

Her eyes met his. Still scared. Still raw. But steady.

"You're here. That's what matters."

He cupped her face again, brushing a tear from her cheek with his thumb.

"I should've been here sooner."

She shook her head, her voice barely a whisper.

"You came. You always come."

And that undid him.

Duncan wrapped his arms around her again, holding her like he could shield her from the whole damn world. His grip was firm but careful, like she might shatter in his hands.

"Thank God, Jade."

Leanne's voice broke as she came running into the room. She didn't hesitate—just threw her arms around both of them, a sob catching in her throat. Duncan didn't let go, didn't even loosen his hold, so Leanne hugged them both.

They stood like that—tangled in shock and relief until—

Footsteps. Fast. Heavy.

Then—

Dean.

He stormed into the room without so much as a glance at Leanne or Duncan. Shoved past them both like they weren't there and reached for Jade, pulling her into a hug she didn't ask for.

"Oh, thank God you're okay," he said, breathless. "I was so worried."

Jade froze, her hands pinned between them. Then she pressed both palms to his chest and shoved him back a step.

"What are you doing here?" she asked, her voice sharp and clear.

Dean blinked, stunned by the pushback. "Jade... I came because I love you."

Leanne's eyes narrowed, a warning sparking behind them. Duncan said nothing. His jaw tightened, fists flexing at his sides—but he didn't move.

This wasn't his fight.

Not anymore.

Jade had to choose.

And so, he held his breath.

Jade swallowed hard, her throat still burning, each breath scraping like sandpaper. But she sat taller. Her voice, when it came, was low and rough.

"Y-you didn't come for me," she rasped. "You came because you... hate losing."

Dean blinked. "That's not fair. I've loved you since uni—you know that."

Jade's lips pressed into a thin line. She took another slow, painful breath. "You loved... the idea of me," she said, barely louder than a whisper. "You loved knowing you won. You only saw me when Duncan did."

Dean flinched like she'd slapped him.

"Jade don't do this," he said. "Don't rewrite everything. What we had—it meant something."

She nodded once. "It did," she said quietly. "To me. For a long time." Her voice cracked. "But not anymore."

Dean's frustration flashed in his posture. "So that's it? You're with him now?"

Jade didn't hesitate. She glanced at Duncan, then back.

"Yes."

Dean scoffed, incredulous. "You're really going to throw away three years? Over one mistake?"

Jade's hands trembled slightly, but her voice stayed quiet—hoarse, but clear.

"No," she said. "You threw it away."

Her gaze didn't waver. "When you slept with your secretary. When you looked through me after the miscarriage. When you left me… in a hospital chair at 3 a.m. in pain and alone."

Dean took a step closer, but Duncan's body shifted—not aggressive, just present.

Dean hesitated.

"I messed up," he said, tone pleading now. "It was the biggest mistake of my life. I'll spend every day making it up to you. No one can replace you."

Jade's reply came slowly, pulled from somewhere deep and raw.

"I'm not asking… to be replaced." Her voice cracked. She placed a hand over her throat for a moment, steadying herself.

"I'm asking to be respected. To be seen."

A beat passed. Then, softly—

"With Duncan… I am."

Dean looked at her—really looked—and for the first time, something in his expression sagged. Collapsed.

He saw it now.

He'd lost her.

"You're making a mistake," he said tightly, bitter.

Jade gave a faint, tired smile. Her voice was just a whisper.

"No. I'm finally not."

Dean stared at her another second. Then without a word, he turned and stormed out, the door slamming behind him like the final punctuation on a story long overdue for an ending.

The silence that followed was brittle and still.

Leanne exhaled. "Well," she muttered, blinking back the emotion in her voice. "That was… overdue."

Jade didn't answer. Her throat hurt too much. Her heart ached more.

She turned her head to Duncan, still standing nearby. Still steady.

Their eyes met.

He didn't speak.

He just walked to her—where she sat perched on the edge of the bed like the last thread holding herself together—and stood in front of her. Carefully. Quietly.

Then he wrapped his arms around her.

Not tight. Not possessive.

Just sure.

Jade let herself sink into him, her head finding the curve of his shoulder like it had always known the way.

He didn't let go.

He didn't say a word.

And that was everything.

Eventually, hospital staff came to guide Jade to another exam room to reassess her injuries. Duncan moved when she did, his hand immediately reaching for hers.

She took it.

And he never let go.

Not through the corridor.

Not through the fluorescent buzz of the lights or the quiet murmurs of the nurses.

Not once.

Like a man who'd nearly lost her once and couldn't risk blinking again.

She sat quietly on the edge of the bed, her face pale and bruised, her throat already darkening with angry marks. Duncan stood at her side, his hand wrapped gently around hers.

When the police arrived, she tried to speak, but even a whisper scraped painfully down her throat.

Her voice rasped and cracked, but she insisted on talking. Duncan squeezed her hand, steadying her, grounding her.

She told them about Cara—how terrified the woman was, how she'd been hiding behind a curtain just meters away when her abuser stormed in. How Jade had stepped in, redirected him. Led him away.

And how he'd locked them in that room. The knife. The threats. The bruises.

The officer nodded grimly.

"We've reviewed the footage. We saw him raise the weapon to your face. Saw him grab you."

Duncan's hand clenched around hers, knuckles going white.

His other hand curled into a fist at his side.

"We're going to make sure he never touches another woman again," the officer added, voice low with conviction.

But Duncan didn't respond.

He was too busy watching Jade—her strength, her fragility, the way she still held herself upright even though she had every reason to collapse.

And as he looked at her, Duncan knew one thing with brutal, burning clarity:

She would never face anything like this alone again.

Duncan took Jade back to her apartment, treating her like she was made of glass—fragile, precious. Every step, every touch was careful, reverent. He kept his hand on the small of her back as they walked through the door, never letting her drift more than a breath away.

Once she was settled on the sofa, he called his parents to let them know she was safe, his voice low and steady, though the adrenaline hadn't quite left his system. Only after he hung up did he allow himself to breathe.

He ran her a bath—hot, soothing, laced with lavender and chamomile. While the tub filled, he helped her undress slowly, his hands gentle, pausing every time she winced or drew in a breath too sharply. She let him. Trusted him. When he eased her into the steaming water, she sighed—a soft, broken sound that made his chest ache.

"I'll give you some space," he said quietly, about to stand.

But her hand caught his.

"Stay," she whispered. Her eyes, still red-rimmed and heavy with exhaustion, held his with quiet pleading. "Please. I don't want to be alone."

He hesitated. "Are you sure?"

"Yes." The word was soft, but firm. She nodded once. "I need you."

He swallowed hard, nodded, and began to undress. His movements were unhurried, deliberate. When he finally slipped into the water behind her, she leaned back against his chest without hesitation.

Duncan wrapped his arms around her, his chin resting against the crown of her head, and held her there—close, warm, safe. The only sound was the gentle ripple of water and the soft, steady rhythm of their breathing as the storm outside finally began to fade.

The heat from the water soaked into their skin, but it was the closeness—his arms around her, her back pressed to his chest—that thawed something deeper. Jade closed her eyes and let her head rest against him, the weight of everything catching up all at once.

Her throat ached, her body trembled, and yet, with Duncan's arms around her, she felt steady for the first time since the world went sideways.

Slowly, her muscles slowly uncoiled, the last of the tension slipping from her shoulders, as the heat of the water and the warmth of his embrace seeped into her bones. Every breath she took became a little less shallow. A little less haunted.

Duncan felt the shift—her surrender to safety, to him—and held her tighter, one hand splayed over her heart like he could keep it beating steady with his own.

He wanted to tell her. God, the words burned on his tongue. But this wasn't the moment for confessions. She needed rest, not promises. Healing, not declarations. So, he stayed silent, offering her the only thing she needed: presence.

Just him. Just this.

She drifted off in his arms not long after, her breath softening, her body going loose and warm against him.

He waited, letting the stillness settle before gently shifting beneath her. Careful not to wake her, he eased out of the bath, dried himself quickly, then turned back to her.

She looked fragile in sleep, her lashes damp against bruised skin, her lips parted in shallow breaths. And still—utterly beautiful.

Duncan crouched beside her, whispering her name softly. "Jade… sweetheart."

She stirred, eyes fluttering open.

"I've got you," he said gently, lifting her with practiced ease. He wrapped her in a towel, pressing his cheek to her temple as he carried her from the bathroom. Every inch of him was full of reverence.

He dried her slowly, tenderly, as if she might shatter beneath his hands. Then he slipped one of his clean T-shirts over her head, the fabric swallowing her whole, and carried her to the bed.

She didn't protest—just leaned into him, eyes already drifting shut again.

He slipped in beside her and pulled the covers up around them, drawing her into his arms like she belonged there. Because she did.

And as her breathing deepened, her body finally succumbing to sleep, Duncan leaned in close and pressed his lips to her forehead.

"I love you, Jade," he whispered into the quiet. "More than life. I'll always be here for you."

And he meant it—with every breath, every heartbeat, every broken piece he'd finally found in her.

Chapter Twenty-Eight

Sunlight filtered through the blinds, soft and pale, casting golden streaks across the bed and warming the air with a gentle hush. The world outside Jade's window was still—too still. Like the city itself was holding its breath after the chaos of the day before. Like it, too, needed to pause, to reset, to remember how to begin again.

Jade stirred beneath the covers, her body aching in tired, deep places—her shoulders, her ribs, her throat. Every inch of her reminded her that she was still here. Still alive. But it wasn't the aches that grounded her—it was the warmth pressed to her back. The weight of an arm draped over her waist. The solid thrum of a heartbeat at her spine.

Duncan.

She didn't move. Not yet. Just lay still and let herself feel everything—his chest rising and falling with each slow breath, the splay of his fingers against her ribs, the softness of his lips where they'd come to rest against the back of her shoulder.

There was comfort in it. Safety. For the first time in days—maybe in years—Jade felt a quiet, unfamiliar peace settle through her bones.

Eventually, he shifted behind her, his arm tightening as if even in sleep, his instinct was to hold her closer. His lips brushed against her skin.

"Hey," he murmured, his voice thick with sleep, a low rasp that sent warmth spiralling through her chest.

She turned in his arms slowly, careful not to jostle the tenderness blooming across her throat. When her eyes met his hazel ones—full of something unspoken—it was like the world tilted back into alignment.

"Morning," she whispered. Her voice was barely there—rough, a whisper more than a word.

His brow furrowed. Concern flickered across his face. "Does it still hurt?"

She gave the faintest nod and lifted a hand to her throat, fingers ghosting over the bruises she hadn't seen yet but could feel like fingerprints from a nightmare she was still waking from.

Duncan reached out slowly, gently brushing her hand aside. His touch was feather light as he examined her neck, his expression darkening with every inch his eyes traced.

"I'm so sorry," he said, his voice tight.

"You didn't do this, Duncan," she said softly, reaching for his wrist.

"No," he admitted, jaw working. "But I wasn't there to stop it."

"You were," she said, her thumb stroking gently over the pulse in his wrist. "You came for me."

His eyes closed briefly, his throat bobbing with the weight of what he wasn't saying. "The wait nearly killed me. Three hours, and no updates. I kept thinking…" He broke off, breath shaking. "What if I never got to tell you?"

She stilled. "Tell me what?"

His eyes opened again, raw, and unguarded now, every wall between them lowered.

"That I love you," he said simply. "I always have."

Jade drew in a sharp breath, her chest tightening—not with fear, not even with surprise, but with something fiercer. Relief. Longing. Truth.

"Why didn't you tell me?" she whispered.

"I was protecting myself," he admitted. "Back then, I let Dean win. I let you believe I wasn't interested in you. Because I didn't know how to stay and watch you love him."

Tears prickled in her eyes.

"I should've fought harder. For you. For us."

She reached up, her hand cupping his cheek. "I loved you, Duncan. I still do."

He froze.

His hand, still resting lightly on her hip, tightened. "Say it again."

She smiled through the blur of tears, her voice steadier now. "I love you."

And just like that, the storm in him broke.

He kissed her—slow, reverent, like he was memorising the taste of her. When they broke apart, he rested his forehead against hers, breath mingling.

"You're it for me, Jade," he whispered, voice hoarse. "You always were. Even when I was too much of a coward to say it."

Tears slipped silently down her cheeks. "You're it for me too."

He exhaled, a tremor running through him like something uncoiled inside.

Then, without a word, he reached across her to the bedside table. Opened the drawer. Pulled out a small, square velvet box.

Jade gasped softly as he turned back to her. He held it in gently in his hand, like it was fragile.

He opened it.

Inside, a sapphire and diamond ring sparkled in the morning light—elegant, timeless, breathtaking.

He didn't look at the ring. He only looked at her.

"Marry me," he said, his voice barely more than a breath. "Be mine. Forever. I can't—I don't want to live another day without knowing you're mine."

Her heart felt like it might burst.

"Yes," she said, her voice cracking. "Yes, Duncan. Of course I will."

She threw her arms around him, burying her face in his shoulder as he held her tight. They clung to each other, trembling, laughing through their tears.

He slid the ring onto her finger with shaking hands, then kissed her again—slow, fierce, a promise sealed between them.

When he finally pulled back, a spark of something playful lit in his eyes. "I have one more surprise."

Jade blinked, dazed. "Another one?"

He nodded. "I got a job. At St George. Consultant position. Permanent."

Her lips parted in shock. "You're moving back?"

"In three weeks."

She laughed, breathless. "I was ready to move to London."

"You don't have to," he said. "I'm coming home. Because you're here."

"You already are home," she said softly, cupping his cheek. "Right here, with me."

After everything—the pain, the fear, the weight of what they'd nearly lost—making love felt like coming back to life.

It wasn't rushed. It wasn't frantic. It was slow, tender, and reverent. Duncan kissed every bruise with care, every inch of her with silent devotion, holding her like she was something precious that had been lost and finally found again. And Jade gave herself to him with quiet certainty, no hesitation, no fear—only love.

Later, sunlight spilled gently through the blinds, casting golden stripes across the bed as Duncan slipped out from under the covers. He pressed a kiss to her bare shoulder before tugging on his boxers and heading to the kitchen.

She lay there for a moment, eyes closed, hand resting over her heart—where everything felt full and whole for the first time in years.

The scent of fresh coffee and toast lured her out of bed. She padded into the kitchen, one of his shirts hanging off her frame, her engagement ring catching the morning light like a secret turned sacred.

They sat at the small table, knees brushing, hands touching between bites of eggs and buttered toast. He poured her another cup of coffee with a soft smile and leaned over to kiss her temple, just because he could.

That's when the knock came.

Three short taps, hesitant but familiar.

Jade stood, heart already racing—not with fear, but anticipation. She opened the door to find Leanne on the other side, still in her scrubs, hair pulled back into a tired bun, worry etched into every line of her face.

But the moment she saw Jade standing there—alive, safe, glowing—her eyes filled with tears.

And then she saw the ring.

Jade held up her hand wordlessly, a trembling smile playing on her lips.

"Oh my God," Leanne breathed, hands flying to her mouth. "You're engaged?"

Duncan stepped up behind Jade, wrapping an arm around her waist. "We are," he said, his voice soft but sure. "She said yes."

Leanne let out a laugh that was half-sob, half-squeal. "It's about bloody time."

Jade laughed too, leaning back into Duncan's chest as his arms tightened around her. And just like that, surrounded by the quiet aftermath of chaos, everything began to feel like the start of something new.

Something beautiful.

Something they'd both waited far too long to find.

Duncan pressed a kiss to Jade's temple. "I'll give you two some time," he murmured. "I need a shower anyway."

Jade turned her face to catch his lips for a soft kiss. "Don't be long."

"I won't." He brushed his knuckles down her cheek before disappearing down the hallway, the sound of the shower starting a moment later.

Leanne stepped inside, still stunned, still staring at Jade's hand. "He doesn't do things by halves," she said, her voice breathless. "That's not just a ring—that's a ring."

Jade looked down at it again, wonder flickering in her eyes. "He proposed this morning. Right after I woke up."

Leanne pulled her into a hug so tight it stole Jade's breath. "I've never been so relieved and so happy at the same time. After everything yesterday... I thought—" Her voice broke. "I thought we were going to lose you."

Jade held her tighter. "I thought that too. But the police got there just in time."

They sat down on the couch, the morning sunlight catching in their hair, warming the space that had once felt too quiet, too hollow.

"I still can't believe Duncan punched the guy," Leanne said, wiping under her eyes with the edge of her sleeve.

"I can," Jade said, a soft smile tugging at her lips. "He was pretty angry."

Leanne looked at her closely, her voice dropping into something quieter. "Yes he was. How are you, really?"

Jade was quiet for a moment, her fingers brushing over the tender bruise at her throat. "Shaken. Tired. But... safe. I think I'm still coming down from the adrenaline." She looked at Leanne, tears shimmering. "I was so scared. I've never felt like that before. But I just kept on thinking about Duncan."

Leanne smiled gently. "He loves you, so much."

Jade nodded slowly. "Yeah. I know. I've loved him forever. Even when we weren't speaking... even when I thought he didn't want me, he still lived in my heart like he belonged there."

Silence stretched between them, full of quiet understanding.

"I'm glad he found his way back to you," Leanne said finally. "You deserve that kind of love, Jade."

Jade blinked against the tears. "I almost lost my chance to have it."

"But you didn't." Leanne took her hand and squeezed. "You held on. You survived. And now, you get to live the rest of your life with someone who would burn the world down for you."

The sound of the shower stopped.

Jade smiled again, eyes distant and full of something fierce and gentle all at once. "I know."

Epilogue

18 months later....

Jade stood in the warm glow of the kitchen, putting the final touches on dinner. The scent of roasted garlic and herbs filled the air, blending with the soft flicker of candlelight. Their brand-new apartment—the one they'd chosen together, decorated with laughter and late-night dreams—felt especially cozy tonight.

It was their first wedding anniversary.

She checked the clock. He'd be home any minute.

As she smoothed the hem of her ruby-red dress and adjusted a candle, her gaze drifted to the framed photo on the sideboard—their wedding day. A soft smile tugged at her lips.

The ceremony had been everything they'd dreamed of. Duncan's parents had offered the family estate for the celebration, and the grounds had looked like something out of a storybook—white roses, fairy lights, and a stretch of blue sky that seemed to bless every vow. Her mother had cried through the whole thing. Her brother had walked her down the aisle, his hand trembling slightly against hers. His wife had beamed proudly from the front row; their two little ones dressed like tiny angels.

Leanne had been the perfect bridesmaid—calm, organised, and fiercely protective of Jade's happiness. Helen and Gary had cried too, telling them both through misty eyes, "We always knew you two belonged together."

But what Jade remembered most—what would live in her heart forever—was the look on Duncan's face as she stepped into view. That stunned, breathless expression. His dark suit. The nerves in his hands. And the way he looked at her like she was everything.

She blinked back a tear, shaking herself free from the memory as the front door clicked open.

Duncan.

He'd been thinking about her the whole drive home—about their year together, and how it still didn't feel real sometimes. He'd had good years before, even great ones. But this... this year with Jade had changed everything. He loved her to the point of distraction. And he knew, with absolute certainty, that she loved him just as fiercely.

The image of her walking down the aisle flashed through his mind again. God, she had looked stunning—hair swept up, veil trailing behind her like silk, but it wasn't the dress or the makeup that had undone him.

It was the way she looked at him. Like she already knew every part of him and loved him more because of it.

He stepped through the door and froze.

Candlelight danced across the room. Dinner was set on the table. And there she was—Jade—standing in a ruby-red dress that hugged her curves like it had been made for his eyes alone.

His breath caught. "Jade, you look—"

She crossed the room before he could finish, slipping into his arms and pressing her mouth to his in a kiss that said everything.

Welcome home.

I missed you.

I love you.

When they pulled apart, her eyes sparkled with that same love, still as fierce, still as certain as the day she became his wife.

"Happy anniversary," she whispered, her fingers grazing the back of his neck with a familiar tenderness that still made his breath catch.

Duncan smiled, heart full. "Best year of my life."

"And many more to come, I hope," she murmured against his lips, her breath warm and sweet between them.

"God, I hope so." He kissed her again—slow, sure, as if sealing a vow with his mouth.

She pulled back with a reluctant smile, brushing her hands down the front of his shirt. "Come on. I made dinner for my husband, and I really hope you like it."

"I love anything you do for me," he said honestly, threading his fingers through hers as she led him to the candlelit table.

They ate together in the flickering light, stealing bites from each other's plates, feeding each other with teasing smiles and playful kisses. Laughter filled the space between clinks of cutlery and soft music playing in the background. It wasn't just dinner—it was them, woven together in every glance, every touch.

After the last bite of dessert disappeared, Duncan reached for a small, wrapped box sitting beside his glass. "I have something for you."

Jade's eyes lit up as she took it, unwrapping it slowly. Inside nestled a slim, glittering eternity ring, its design delicate and elegant—crafted to match her engagement ring perfectly.

"Oh…" she breathed, eyes misting. "It's gorgeous."

"No," Duncan said, voice low and full of love. "You're gorgeous."

She leaned over and kissed him—deep, grateful, full of emotion.

Then she smiled and handed him a small, square box wrapped in silver paper. "Your turn."

He opened it to find a sleek, beautiful watch with a rich leather band and an engraving on the back that read: One year down. Forever to go. —J.

His throat tightened. "I love it," he said, voice thick with emotion.

Then he pulled her gently onto his lap, their bodies fitting together as naturally as breathing. He kissed her—slow, lingering, a promise wrapped in warmth and devotion. A kiss that said there would be a hundred more anniversaries… and a lifetime beyond that.

When they finally pulled apart, her smile turned shy, almost nervous. Her fingers played lightly at the collar of his shirt.

"I have one more gift for you," she said softly.

He raised an eyebrow, still catching his breath. "Oh? What is it?"

She met his gaze, eyes shining. "You're going to be a daddy."

For a heartbeat, he just stared at her—stunned, silent.

Then the words sank in.

His eyes widened, filling instantly with tears. "Are you serious?"

She nodded, barely able to speak. "I found out this morning."

Duncan's arms tightened around her as joy crashed through him like a wave. He kissed her again—this time with reverence, wonder, overwhelming love.

"I can't believe it," he whispered into her hair. "The best year of my life… and it's only just beginning."

"I'm a little nervous," she whispered, her voice barely audible. "I have to admit."

Duncan stilled. He didn't need to ask why—he already knew.

The memory of her quiet heartbreak, the pain she'd once carried alone, flashed through his mind. She had miscarried before. And though they'd never spoken of it often, the ache of that loss lingered just beneath the surface.

His arms tightened around her instinctively, protectively.

"Sweetheart," he murmured, pressing a kiss to her temple, "whatever happens—we get through it together. I'm not going anywhere. Not ever."

She nodded against his chest, and he felt the slight tremble in her shoulders.

"We're stronger now," he said softly, brushing her hair back. "You're not alone in this. You never will be again."

Her eyes filled, but this time it wasn't fear behind the tears. It was relief. Hope.

"Okay," she whispered. "Okay."

He rested his forehead against hers. "We'll take it one day at a time. And we'll love this baby—every single second we have them."

She smiled through her tears. "You're going to be an amazing dad."

"And you," he said, kissing her again, "are already the most incredible mum."

Seven months later, Duncan carried Simone Anne Armstrong through the front door for the very first time, tucked close to his chest in a soft pink blanket. She was barely a day old—tiny, perfect, and already the centre of his entire universe.

His incredible wife walked beside him, her arm linked through his, moving slowly but steadily. The birth had been long, and the pregnancy even longer—complicated at times, filled with worry after what she'd lost before. There had been restless nights, quiet hospital corridors, and more than one moment when fear had tightened around them like a vice.

But Jade had never wavered.

She'd carried their daughter with a quiet strength that left Duncan breathless. She endured every discomfort, every scare, every ache, with grit and grace. And now, standing in the doorway of their home, her eyes shining with exhaustion and something deeper, she looked up at him.

And he saw everything in her expression—love, pride, awe... and something fierce and unshakable.

She was still the strongest woman he'd ever known.

And now, she was the mother of their daughter.

"We're home," Duncan whispered to their daughter, voice thick with emotion.

Jade smiled softly. "Home," she echoed, brushing her fingers gently across Simone's downy cheek.

They stepped inside as a family—just the three of them—and for a long moment, everything was still. Peaceful. Whole.

Duncan looked at Jade, heart full. "I don't think I've ever been this happy."

She leaned her head on his shoulder. "Me neither."

And as Simone let out a soft sigh in her sleep, Duncan knew—without a doubt—that their greatest adventure had only just begun.

The End

Before You Go...

If you fell for these characters and want more love stories filled with emotion, passion, and second chances, my newsletter is where I share them first.

You'll receive:

💕 Early access to new releases

💕 Exclusive reader-only content and extras

👉 **Join my reader list here:** https://alisonreidauthor.com

I'd love to welcome you.

Alison Reid

Thank you for reading Forever Mine!

If you enjoyed this collection of irresistible love stories, keep an eye out for more upcoming romance collections by Alison Reid, including:

Alpha Kings - *A Billionaire Alpha Male Romance Collection*

Cautious Hearts - *A Trust-After-Heartbreak Romance Collection*

Dark & Dangerous - *Brooding Heroes Romance Collection*

Final Surrender - *Alpha Heroes Yielding to Love Collection*

Forbidden Hearts - *A Forbidden Love Romance Collection*

Guarded Hearts - *A Surrender to Love Romance Collection*

Hearts & Secrets - *Small Town Romance Collection*

Hearts in Peril - *A Suspenseful Romance Collection*

Hidden Truths - *A Secret Identity Romance Collection*

Lies & Hearts - *A Lies, Secrets & Betrayal Romance Collection*

Love After Regret - *A Second-Chance Redemption Romance Collection*

Misjudged Hearts - *A Love After Judgement Romance Collection*

Torn Between Hearts - *A Love Triangle Romance Collection*

All of Alison Reid's books feature standalone stories, swoon-worthy heroes, and guaranteed happily-ever-afters.

Books by Alison Reid

A Billionaire for Christmas

A Heart in Florence

After The Storm

Always You

Before I Fell

Before the Thaw

Beneath the Lies

Billionaire Bodyguard

Billionaire Rancher

Blueprints of the Heart

Branlow

Collide

Echoes of Deception

Falling for the Billionaire

Forever Yours

Heart of the Outback

Hearts on the Line

Hidden Gem

Kept Promises

Mended Hearts

Mistaken Hearts

New Year's Eve Kiss

Quiet Danger

Reckless Hearts

Find all my books on Amazon:

https://www.amazon.com/author/alisonreid1970

About the Author

Alison Reid writes contemporary and small-town romance filled with heart, passion, and second-chance love stories. Her novels often feature strong heroines, irresistible heroes, and the happily-ever-afters readers adore. When she's not writing, Alison enjoys reading, spending time with her family, and imagining new love stories. She hopes her books give readers a few hours of escape, joy, and swoon-worthy romance they won't forget.

www.ingramcontent.com/pod-product-compliance
Lightning Source LLC
Chambersburg PA
CBHW050953180726
48291CB00006B/1805